Cinderella in America

Cinderella in America

A Book of Folk and Fairy Tales

Compiled and edited by

William Bernard McCarthy

University Press of Mississippi / Jackson

www.upress.state.ms.us

The University Press of Mississippi is a member of the
Association of American University Presses.

First edition 2007
∞

Library of Congress Cataloging-in-Publication Data
Cinderella in America : a book of folk and fairy tales /
compiled and edited by William Bernard McCarthy. — 1st ed.
    p. cm.
 Includes bibliographical references and index.
 ISBN-13: 978-1-57806-958-3 (cloth : alk. paper)
 ISBN-10: 1-57806-958-0 (cloth : alk. paper)
 ISBN-13: 978-1-57806-959-0 (pbk. : alk. paper)
 ISBN-10: 1-57806-959-9 (pbk. : alk. paper) 1. Tales—
United States. 2. United States—Folklore. I. McCarthy,
William Bernard, 1939–
 GR105.C45 2007
 398.20973—dc22   2007003158

British Library Cataloging-in-Publication Data available

In any case, this interlinking of the New World

with all countries and ages, by the golden net-work

of oral tradition, may supply the moral of our collection.

—WILLIAM WELLS NEWELL

Games and Songs of American Children, 225

CONTENTS

Contents

Contents

Acknowledgments

Over the years in which this project has been in the works, I have incurred debts to many people and institutions. Let me begin by thanking Maryellen Green, my first research assistant, who found many of these stories in early folklore journals. Elena P. (Carmela) Morales read through dozens and dozens of Hispanic tales, taking notes and making recommendations. Debbie Gill answered some translation questions. Our local DuBois campus library staff was ever supportive. Anne Hummer, in particular, coordinated literally hundreds of interlibrary loans and article requests with unfailing good cheer. Karen Fuller helped with sticky research issues. Paul Fehrenbach transcribed the music. The Penn State English Department, the Commonwealth College, The Penn State Global Fund, and several DuBois Campus Directors of Academic Affairs provided travel funds. The Penn State Institute for the Arts and Humanistic Studies funded released time. The DuBois Education Foundation funded research assistants and travel. The DuBois Campus supported a sabbatical during which this book first took shape. Chris Klinger, the faculty staff assistant, was always ready to help. And other typists and research assistants contributed more than I can thank them for. Many folklore colleagues offered encouragement. Charles Perdue, in addition, sent a tale. Linda Dégh sent a valuable pair of tales. And Jim Leary sent a tale, photographs, and the analysis that now appears in chapter 18. The late George Reinecke translated a Cajun tale and Mary Beth Wesdock translated one of the Spanish tales. Brian Roberts read selected chapters in manuscript. Manuel da Luz Goncalves helped with transcribing Cape Verde Kriolu. The folks at the American Antiquarian Society were genial hosts for a week, as was my wife's aunt Dorothy Bourget, who provided meals and resting place during that week. The many copyright holders and other holders of rights are acknowledged elsewhere, but to them too I extend my thanks for their kindness and patience. And special thanks go to all the storytellers who shared their stories with me.

Finally, I want to thank my children, Will, Barbara, and Maura, who regularly reinvigorated my interest in folktales by asking for more. My wife, Eileen, and daughter Maura typed and helped with other chores. And all my family provided constant interest, support, and encouragement. To all of you and to all I have, alas, overlooked, many thanks.

CINDERELLA IN AMERICA

INTRODUCTION

Yarns Older than Uncle Sam

The rather hefty volume you are now holding would at one time have seemed an impossibility. American folktales? We knew what those were. They were the tall tales, the jokes, and the urban legends that Americans love so much. But tales of magic? Tales of clever heroes outwitting giants and ogres and oppressive masters? Tales of beautiful younger sisters wedding handsome princes? The kinds of things we call fairy tales? No, Americans never really told stories like that—except for a few that they got out of Grimm or Anderson and told to children until the children got too old for that kind of stuff. The great European tale tradition did not take root in America, we thought. The first settlers—and the later immigrants as well—were too practical-minded to enjoy such trifles, and besides there was no time in the busy workdays of our ancestors to tell those long stories. A quick joke in passing, an outrageous lie told around the stove, or a bit of gossip about some horrific coincidence that really happened to a friend of a friend—they had time for that, of course. But who had time for the long elaborate stories about kings and magicians and talking horses? About magical advice and magical countries beyond the beyond? Nobody. Certainly nobody in our hard-working democracy. Such was the conventional wisdom passed down in folklore courses and textbooks.[1]

American folklore, we thought, included ballads and dance tunes, arts and crafts, and traditions of cuisine, but not magical stories like those the

3

Grimm brothers edited in early nineteenth-century Germany, Asbjornsen and Moe collected in Norway, and Afanas'ev collected in Russia. But if that is true, if Americans did not tell those stories, then where did this heavy book come from? For here you will read about poor heroes and proud heroines, witches and giants, kings and wizards, magic whistles and talking horses—all the trappings of yarns older than Uncle Sam, older, indeed, than memory.

In point of fact, however, the land that we now call the United States has a five-hundred-year-old tradition of wonder tales. They came with wave after wave of settlers, beginning almost surely with the first Spanish settlers in Puerto Rico. They were entrenched well enough to be unambiguously documented by 1800.[2] And they have been collected by scholars, enthusiasts, and common folk for at least two hundred years.

What to Call These Stories

But before I can go on, there is a nagging problem that must be solved. What stories are we talking about, and what shall we call them? There is not any single term that unambiguously identifies the particular range of stories represented in this volume. Here are some of the choices.

1. We could call them *fairy tales*. In fact, I have used that term in the title of this book. In popular usage, *fairy tales* covers the ground fairly well. And it is the term used in English not only for the tales in Grimm but also for the tales in Asbjornsen and Moe's Norwegian collection, in Afanas'ev's Russian collection—both of them closer to oral tradition than the Grimm collection—and in Joseph Jacobs's rather mixed English collection. But of course most of the stories have nothing to do with fairies. Moreover, American scholars, wrestling with this terminology problem, now restrict the term *fairy tale* to writer-composed tales fashioned in imitation of traditional stories and story-forms—the tales of Hans Christian Andersen, for instance, or Carl Sandburg's *Rootabaga Stories*. So, now that we are past the title, we can't use that term further.

2. *Folktales* is a term much used in recent collections. The principal problem with it is that it is too broad. Jokes and legends, for example, are folktales. And many scholars would include personal experience narratives under this term. Moreover, the phrase *American folktales* almost always connotes *tall tales*. None of these genres figures prominently in the present collection or in the cognate European collections.

3. *Wonder tales* is also a term sometimes used, especially with reference to the cognate Irish repertoire. But it doesn't seem particularly apt for the animal tales or tales of clever tricksters that figure prominently in the American repertoire. And the term has not really achieved widespread acceptance and usage.

4. *Legends* is another troublesome term. Teens are fond of urban legends. Other types of belief legends are also found widely distributed in the United States. But these narratives are not the materials gathered in this volume. Moreover, for many people the term *American legends* means Paul Bunyan or Pecos Bill. These latter stories, insofar as they have any claim to being considered folktales, belong to the genre of tall tales. They are not what this book holds.

5. *Märchen*, a German term, covers much the same ground as *Wonder Tales*. But its use is sometimes restricted to stories of heroes (or heroines) and magic, such as "Jack and the Beanstalk," "Cinderella," or "Puss in Boots." This term will sometimes be used in the present collection when this particular type of tale is meant.

6. So we are left with *tales*. This term applies equally well to wonder tales or märchen, animal tales, jests, or humorous stories, to all the stories included in this volume, and it is the term that will usually be used. It is, of course, too broad. But all these terms are either too broad or too narrow, and this one at least has the virtue of simplicity.

The Old-World Roots of These Tales

The stories in this collection have their roots in the Old World, specifically in that part of it that extends from Ireland on the west to Russia and Armenia on the east, and from Scandinavia on the north to the Mediterranean countries on the south. This largely Indo-European world possesses as part of its traditional culture a single repertoire of tales and tale genres found throughout its length and breadth. This broad repertoire of tales is united by a European sensibility, worldview, aesthetic, and value system. And this sensibility, worldview, aesthetic, and value system distinguishes it even from closely related tale repertoires such as those of India or the Muslim Middle East, to say nothing of more distant repertoires such as those of the Far East, Sub-Saharan Africa, or Native America. Of course no single part of this region has possessed the entire repertoire as part of its traditional culture. But the traditional tale repertoires of the various subregions are representative of the whole repertoire at the same time that they are distinctive to the particular subregions.

Credit must go to the Grimm brothers, Jacob and Wilhelm, for recognizing the scope of this repertoire and its unity. Their famous collection of "fairy tales," the *Kinder- und Hausmärchen,* provided the model for many later national and regional collections. The Grimm collection includes a wide range of genres or types of tales. There are the magical wonder tales such as "Cinderella," "Godfather Death," and "The Singing Bone." There are novelle or romantic tales, much like wonder tales but without the magic element, such as "King Thrushbeard" and "The Robber Bridegroom." Animal tales include "The Wolf and Seven Kids," "The Mouse, the Bird, and the Sausage," and "The Bremen Town Musicians." Humorous tales include stupid ogre tales such as "The Young Giant," stories about human stupidity such as "Clever Hans" and "Clever Else," tales about human trickery such as "The Brave Little Tailor" and "Doctor Know-All," and tales about putting one over on the parson such as "Old Hildebrand." Several of the tales are formulaic, including "Clever Hans," "The Wedding of Mrs. Fox," and "The Louse and the Flea." These are the same categories of stories, and in many cases the same stories as were gathered in the earlier French and Italian collections and in the later national collections from all over the European world.

Obviously these are not the only folktales known in European culture. Jokes, tall tales, personal experience narratives, and legends also thrive. But tales from those genres are not a part of the tale repertoire identified by Grimm. And they are not usually found in the classic European collections modeled on the Grimm collection.

And indeed, this seemingly diverse range of tales does make up a unified repertoire. It is unified first by its distribution throughout the area under discussion. But it is further unified in that tales from any one of these distinct genres may feature the same central character, call him Jack or Hans or Ivan or Merrywise. He may be the bold hero who goes in search of a wonder-tale princess, or the fearless lad who overcomes a stupid ogre, or the clever trickster who outwits a mean employer or king, or even a human companion in an animal tale. Furthermore, storytellers who tell stories from one of these genres will usually tell stories from other genres without making any distinction. Zsuzsanna Palkó, for instance, the great Hungarian storyteller whose repertoire Linda Dégh published, includes numbskull stories, tales of stupidity, and tales of cleverness, as well as wonder tales and novelle in her repertoire. This repertoire is unified, too, with reference to traditional audience and occasion. The particular audience and occasion will vary as one moves across the continent and through time. But in any particular time and place there will be a sense that this repertoire of stories is suitable for particular people and circumstances—for adults at a wake, for men working at fishing or lumbering, for children at bedtime or when helping with work, for young women amusing themselves as they do handwork, or for family and guests whiling away the long hours of winter darkness between sundown and sleep. And in any such culture the occasion and audience for these tales is different from the occasion and audience for jokes, legends, tall tales, or personal experience narratives. When a group of adolescents is exchanging jokes, for example, no one would think of breaking into the conversation with a long wonder tale. And if a group of men is vying with tall tales in a lying contest, no one would try to slip in an animal tale. In short, in these European cultures the culturally established occasions for telling this kind of tale tend to be distinct from the culturally established occasions for jokes, tall tales, or legends. Finally, the point of these tales is different from the point of a joke, tall tale, or legend. Jokes exist to evoke a laugh, and tall tales are usually competitive, deliberately drawing attention to the performance of the teller, while legends seek to draw in the listener to respond with a *frisson* or a comment about belief. The tales we are here talking about, however, exist principally for the joy of narrative. They evoke delight in what happens. They exist for the sake of the story.

This repertoire of tales is principally an Indo-European repertoire. Indeed, the märchen itself may be a specifically Indo-European genre, though it is also shared by non-Indo-European peoples living in the region, such as the Finns and Hungarians.[3] Doubtless, parts of the repertoire originally came in from other regions of the world and from other peoples. And the process of colonization has in turn brought elements of this repertoire to other regions of the world, notably to Africa and to the New World (including the United States), where it has spread to the non-Indo-European populations, especially African American, and Native American.

SCOPE OF THIS COLLECTION

There are many collections presenting this repertoire of tales as it has flourished from Ireland to Russia and Armenia. The French and Italians were active in publishing these stories in the Renaissance and Enlightenment periods. And once the Grimm brothers began publishing their great collection, scholars and collectors from nearly every region of Europe fell into step behind them. Some of these collectors, such as Calvino in his relatively recent Italian collection, have retold and rewritten the stories, just as Jacob and Wilhelm Grimm did. Others, such as the various editors of European volumes in the series Folktales of the World, have sought to present the tales in the words of the traditional storytellers. The repertoire as it spread to Spanish America has also been collected and published. And in the United States scholars have published regional collections in both journals and books. But until now no collection has sought to present the larger U.S. picture, insofar as that can be done. That is the task of the present volume: to demonstrate the scope of the Old World tale repertoire as it settled into U.S. American culture, changing, developing, and acclimating in much the way the tales of this repertoire have always settled and acclimated, wherever they have found themselves.

The collection embraces wonder tales or märchen, novelle, animal tales, humorous tales, and formulaic tales. It limits itself to the tales derived directly or indirectly from the repertoire of European ancestors. (The Asian, African, Oceanic, and Native American repertoires are distinct, and a collection of such tales from the United States would demand a different approach.) Tales from the Iberian peninsula (Spain and Portugal), from France, and from the British Isles dominate, largely because the United States was first colonized from these three regions, but also because collectors sought such tales more aggressively. But this volume also includes tales from other European traditions. I have, moreover, included tales learned from Europeans by Native American peoples. Finally, I also include tales from the European repertoire as told by African Americans. In the latter case, as should be obvious, these tales often were learned in America from European Americans. But often too they had been learned in Africa from Europeans. Nor is it always easy to distinguish European tales brought to Africa by colonizers, travelers, or merchants from tales that may be quite as old in Africa as they are in the Indo-European world. Nevertheless, there can be no question of the importance of the African American contribution to the shaping of the European tale repertoire in the New World. We do not need to be afraid that recognizing how Africans have shaped tales from the European repertoire might detract from the recognition of how African Americans have preserved and shaped distinctly African elements of culture, any more than recognizing how African Americans have reshaped the European harmony system in jazz detracts from recognition of distinctly African elements in jazz. So this collection embraces such tales.

This collection, however, excludes jokes, tall tales, and legends as such. It also excludes composed stories in a folk idiom. Here you will not find Pecos Bill and Paul Bunyan. Here you will not find the tall tales of Davy Crockett and the Southwestern humorists. And here you will not find selections from Carl Sandburg's *Rootabaga Stories* (1922).

But excluding jokes and legends is not so simple as would at first appear. In U.S. oral tradition folktales from the repertoire in question frequently migrate into other repertoires and become transformed. Tales show up as jokes or legends: A numbskull story becomes a Cajun joke, while a particularly horrifying märchen becomes a legend about a maid who cooks the child and serves it to the parents. So I have included tales from the repertoire that have become jokes or legends, to show how the process works. Occasionally, too, the opposite process takes place. Legends *märchenize,* becoming wonder tales about wailing witches or monster snakes, and I have included examples.

This is the first time this range of American folktales has been gathered between the covers of one volume. Indeed, as I have already said, some have stated over and over that the old-world folktales did not gain any secure foothold in the United States. And yet I found many kinds of sources for folktales and a vast amount of material to choose from. The number of excellent regional collections, for example, is impressive. In addition, tales are lodged in journals, public archives, WPA files, archives of faculty collections and student papers at colleges and universities with folklore courses, proceedings of learned societies, and fugitive publications, as well as in my own field notes, in unpublished data generously shared by my fellow folklorists, and even on the internet. The earliest such tales to be collected in the United States were taken down not from a European American but from a Mahican-Miami chief by one John Dunne (Smith 1939). Dunne included the tales in his "Notices Relative to Some of the Native Tribes of North America" in the *Transactions of the Royal Irish Academy,* proceedings doubtless edited by Bishop Percy of ballad fame. The most recent tale here included was brought home from Girl Scout camp by my own daughter.

The range of traditional folktales available today in collections, archives, manuscripts, and fugitive publications is indeed impressive. Of course none of that material would be available if collectors, professional and amateur, had not busied themselves with gathering it. The converse is also true: what is now available in collections, archives, manuscripts, and fugitive publications is limited to what collectors have bothered to put there. And this anthology must perforce submit to those limits, at least in part. Thus the material here assembled reflects, more than I should like, the vagaries of folktale collecting in the United States since the earliest days of the Republic. A number of factors have affected what stories would enter the record. In the first place, the largest ethnic groups are, as might be expected, the best represented. What is now the United States was settled in the colonial period largely by migrants from Spain, France, the British Isles, and German-speaking parts of Europe, roughly in that order, and by enslaved peoples from Africa. These ethnic groups, along with Native Americans, have turned out to be the best represented in the folkloric record. Consequently, a large part of the present anthology consists of tales with European roots gathered from representatives of these six ethnicities.

But even within such limits the vagaries of collecting still operate. In the first three decades of the twentieth century, for example, it became very clear that the southern Appalachians housed a people with a rich musical tradition. One extended family, the Hickses and Harmons of western North Carolina, could boast of a seemingly limitless repertoire of songs to surprise avid collectors from Cecil Sharp to Frank and Anne Warner. But the equally rich folktale tradition was largely overlooked—despite significant publication in the *Journal of American Folklore*—until Marshall Ward, a cousin of the Hickses and the Harmons, confessed diffidently that he didn't sing but that he did tell stories about Tom, Will, and Jack. Collectors still visit this family, and the folktale material amassed from this one group of kinsmen is probably vaster than the traditional folktale collection from whole states elsewhere in the country.

Another decisive factor affecting what was collected was the early influence of Joel Chandler Harris's books. Harris's tales of Uncle Remus and Br'er Rabbit were a national sensation. In offering them to the reading public he inspired a whole cottage industry of gathering and setting down tales from the descendants of African slaves. Moreover, southern black servants, field hands, and tenant farmers conformed more closely to the definition of "folk" fashionable at the time of the founding of the American Folklore Society and the establishment of folklore as a field of enquiry. Consequently, many early folklorists devoted themselves to black tradition. Native Americans were the other U.S. group that seemed very "folk," as that word was understood a hundred years ago. For many years the *Journal of American Folklore* devoted one issue a year to American Indian material, including tales. And some of those tales were European in origin.

Fashion to some extent dictated not only which ethnic groups were suitable objects for folklore study but also which parts of the country were suitable regions for collecting folklore. Obviously, as we have already seen, the southern Appalachians seemed suitable. But indeed the whole South, from the Virginia tidewater to the Texas plains, featured picturesque rural populations from whom to gather tales. The Pennsylvania Germans were another such obvious choice for field collection. And the Schoharie Hills of New York, the Pine Barrens of New Jersey, and the rocky coasts of Maine offered good picking conveniently close to home—if home was one of the eastern colleges and universities where the study of folklore first took root. But whole sections of the country were relatively neglected, including the urban Northeast, much of the Midwest, and the Upper West and Northwest. This neglect has been corrected to some extent in the last forty years, but in the same period much of the nation has industrialized, and the collectible folklore in these regions as elsewhere in the country reflects this industrialized culture, often more than it reflects the old-world roots of the people.

Fashion of another sort was a negative factor affecting what got collected. The early New England collectors did not have much respect for French Canadians, though there were many in New England. Nor for the Irish. Nor, later, for the Polish. As a result, though all three of these groups are of significant size in the United States, the collected record of their folktale traditions is quite skimpy. We have already seen how the fashion of collecting music from the people of the southern Appalachians almost led to overlooking the tale tradition. Fashion in collecting had more serious effect in some other cases. I am convinced that the reason I was not able to find Scandinavian folktales, despite the fact that the Old World Scandinavian tradition was so strong, is that Swedes were the fashionable ethnicity to research, and foodways, crafts, and customs—especially Christmas customs—were the fashionable areas for research. As a result, Swedish folklife in the United States in the nineteenth and early twentieth century is well documented, but I have not found comparable data on a tale tradition, though some such tradition must have been there.

Sometimes, however, an ethnic group was simply too small or too isolated to call attention to itself. Some ethnicities, too, worked hard to assimilate, shedding their language and the tales that were a part of that language. And it is indeed true, as scholars have been claiming for a hundred years, that daily life in the United States often does not make room for telling long leisurely stories. So doubtless many tales died out because immigrants or their children could not find a place for taletelling in their daily life.

Carl Lindahl, in several publications, has indicated yet another reason why folktales go uncollected, calling them a "shy tradition." In one essay he says that storytellers felt that "these tales, which served principally to entertain children in intimate family settings, were completely out of place in the formal company of strangers" (2001: 9). He goes on to refer to storyteller Jim Couch's reluctance to share tales with outsiders: "We was all kindy skittish about strangers that way. We got the idea they wanted to know our family affairs, or make fun of us" (citing Roberts 1974: 7). Then he adds:

> In my own fieldwork, I have encountered several tellers who have shared Jim Couch's sense of privacy regarding the magic tale. The intimate, family-based, child-targeted nature of the Appalachian Märchen makes it difficult for most narrators to retell it to adult outsiders. Even willing tellers tend to render the tales only as plot abstracts unless or until children are present, and only then will they actually perform the tales. Ballads, on the other hand, generally are considered more appropriate as public and adult entertainment. (10)

Elsewhere Lindahl discusses the issue of a "clash between Märchen and mountain aesthetics" (and mores) characterized by "a strong tendency to call attention away from one's art." But the verbal art of the märchen, he asserts, calls attention to itself and cannot hide, so narrators tend to reshape the tale into a joke, legend, or tall story instead (2001: 89–90). This comment suggests a further reason why narrators who do tell märchen as märchen might wish to avoid performing them for strangers, lest they give the appearance of showing off. Although Lindahl is speaking specifically of the southern mountains, much of what he says may well apply more widely.

Finally, I suspect that one important strain of the märchen tradition in America is the one-story tradition. It is not uncommon for a significant person in a family to have one tale, and one tale only, that is "their story." On special occasions, or upon special demand, they will perform it for children in the family. Emma Neuland's story in chapter 14 and Jim Hickey's story in chapter 16 are just such stories, as is the story of "Peazy and Beanzy" in chapter 11. And I have heard others at times when I was not in a position to make a recording. I believe this family tradition is relatively widespread in the United States. But seldom does anybody outside the family know about such a tale. And more seldom is there a folklorist lurking about who can collect the tale, even if the storyteller should be willing to perform it for a recorder.

As a result of all these factors, the picture of the old-world folktale repertoire in America is uneven and incomplete, and must ever remain so.

AMERICAN TALES

It was once common to question whether one could even speak of a properly American folklore, apart from Native American tradition, because so many of us who make up the country derive from other parts of the world and our traditions too derive from traditions found in other parts of the world. But after five hundred years on the continent and two hundred years under the Constitution there is no longer any question that we *are* a distinct and distinctive people with a distinct and distinctive set of customs, traditions, mores, and folkways not shared by the visitor to our shores, and not yet wholly shared or even wholly understood by the new immigrant. The new immigrant may indeed come bearing some cultural element—a word, a custom, a fashion, or a food—that will eventually become as American as frankfurters, pizza, tacos, and fried-rice-to-go. Eventually, but not yet. The distinction is important. Not everybody in America is an American, nor is everything in America American. What is true of people and words and foods and customs is also true of tales. In the last fifty years American folklorists have gathered outstanding collections of folktales from immigrant narrators. One thinks of the Armenian tales Susie Hoogasian-Villa collected in Detroit (1966), or the Italian stories of Clementia Todescu (Mathias 1985). But these are Armenian and Italian stories, happily gathered from immigrants in Michigan or Arizona when they might not so easily have been gathered in the old homeland, but Italian and Armenian still. Though gathered in America, they are not American stories, except perhaps in some accidental sense.

The present collection, however, seeking to present tales that are distinctively American, focuses on storytellers whose families had already been on this continent for generations at the time each particular tale was collected. This focus meant the exclusion of beautiful immigrant tales, tales that I folded away in my files with many a wistful sigh. But it also meant the inclusion of tales that beautifully express the American experience just as surely as they reveal their old-world roots.

We all know, nevertheless, that there is more than one way to become American. Not every good citizen is born here. The same proved true of tales. Not every good American tale came from someone born here. Immigrants have not limited themselves to nostalgically retelling the tales of the homeland as faithfully as possible. They have also used tales to adapt to the new. And these adaptive tales, expressing the American experience of the immigrant whether ruefully, opportunistically, or enthusiastically, are also American tales. The anthology includes a representative sampling: tales turned into jokes on the immigrant's plight, tales used to enhance the livelihood available in lumber camps, and a tale that expresses wonder at the role of the businessman in our culture. For such tales could not have surfaced any place else but in America.

AMERICAN FOLKTALE SCHOLARSHIP

The study of folklore concerns itself with the informal, traditional, everyday, homemade aspects of life. It is not specifically concerned with what we study in school and the university or as part of our training in a profession. Nor is it really concerned with the media and the products and jobs of our technological society. It concerns itself, rather, with what we learn in immediate face-to-face contact with other people—parents, peers, friends—and with what we do in informal moments of our life, whether amusing ourselves and others or working at traditional trades or crafts. So folklorists are interested in handed-down skills, family recipes, home-grown beliefs, local language, homemade music and games, and the beliefs, recipes, language, music, and games of all sorts of groups, such as students, workers, teams, neighborhoods, and congregations. The stories that people tell as part of their family or other group are especially important to create group cohesion and preserve the group's traditions. And folklorists study these stories—these *folk* tales—too.

Though perceived as the Cinderella of American folklore studies, the folktale has in fact attracted distinguished scholarship in the United States. The 1880 publication of *Uncle Remus, His Songs and His Sayings* is as convenient a place as any to begin such a survey. Harris's book was a sensation and demonstrated to the world that the United States had a vital folktale tradition. When William Wells Newell undertook editorship of the *Journal of American Folklore* in 1888 for the newly organized American Folklore Society, he made discovery of American folktales one of his publication priorities. Beginning with the first issue, the early volumes were full of tales, especially from Native Americans, Louisiana French, and Americans of English ancestry. The first four decades of the twentieth century saw outstanding field collections formed from Puerto Rico (Mason and Espinosa 1922–1929), the Schoharie Hills of New York (Gardner 1937), the Cape Verdeans of Rhode Island (Parsons 1923a), the Sea Islands of South Carolina (Parsons 1923b), Florida (Hurston 1935), the Louisiana and Missouri French (Claudel 1941, 1942, 1944, and Carriere 1937), and the Southwest (Espinosa 1937 and Rael [1957]), among many others. In the 1930s, to combat the Great Depression, the Roosevelt administration organized employment for writers in the form of state writers' projects. These projects regularly made gathering folklore a part of their agenda. It was while working on such a project that Richard Chase discovered the Jack Tale repertoire of Marshall Ward and his Hicks and Harmon cousins in the Beech Mountain area of North Carolina (Chase 1943).

Meanwhile, folklorist Stith Thompson was analyzing American Indian repertoires to discover to what extent European folktales had infiltrated them. When Antti Aarne's great 1910 folktale index needed to be revised and translated into English, Thompson seemed the logical man for the job. He published a translation and modest revision in 1928, then undertook a major revision in 1935 that was not finally completed until 1960. (A further revision was published in 2004.) Thompson also completed a massive six-volume index of traditional motifs as found in European and world folk literature and literature with folk roots. These motifs are numbered according to a complex system, and prominent motifs are frequently referred to by number in discussing folktales. Thompson synthesized his vast knowledge in *The Folktale,* a 1946 handbook that is still a standard on the subject.

In the years after World War II the interest among American folklorists shifted from wonder tales and their kin to tall tales, jokes, and most recently legends. But collectors such as Vance Randolph in the Ozarks and Leonard Roberts in Appalachia resisted the trend. Richard Dorson collected significant numbers of tales in Michigan and Arkansas (1952, 1967). The time was ripe, too, for Francis Lee Utley to produce a magisterial article synthesizing New World folktale scholarship (1974). Subsequently, Herbert Halpert, who had begun by collecting tales on the East coast and annotating Randolph's Ozark collections, went on to do a monumental collection in Newfoundland with J. D. A. Widdowson (1996). This collection in its published form sets a high standard for all future folktale scholarship.

A revival of storytelling that came in on the crest of the folksong revival of the 1960s forced a reappraisal of the European folktale repertoire in the United States.[4] This reappraisal expressed itself in Margaret Read MacDonald's encyclopedic *Traditional Storytelling Today*. The long years of collecting in the United States are especially well represented in Carl Lindahl's *American Folktales from the Collections of the Library of Congress*. Other important collections are *Storytellers: Folktales and Legends from the South* by Burrison; *Swapping Stories*, a Louisiana collection by Lindahl, Owens, and Harvison; *Cajun and Creole Folktales* by Ancelet; and my own *Jack in Two Worlds*. Lindahl's volume, however, represents only one archive, while the last four collections tend to focus on the South, long perceived as the most folkloric part of the United States—a perception that even we folklorists are not entirely immune to. The present volume, by contrast, seeks to present the whole picture of folktale telling in the United States, insofar as that is possible (though the South still receives more attention than any other part of the country). By surveying the many collections made over the last two centuries, it provides an overview of scholarship as well as of tradition.

EDITORIAL PRINCIPLES

Many editors of folktale collections, from Jacob and Wilhelm Grimm to such recent authors as Virginia Hamilton and Richard Erdoes, have rewritten the tales so that they appear in the words of the author/editor, not in the words of the original storyteller. In such translation from one linguistic register to another something of the original storyteller must inevitably be lost along with his or her words, and something of the editor/author's world must inevitably creep in. To keep the tales as told, not as reimagined by the editor, this collection presents each narrative in the words of the original storyteller, as far as that can be determined. Not all storytellers are smooth and slick, of course, so some tales will seem more rough-hewn than we are used to. But the gain in immediacy surely compensates for any loss in fluidity.

Presenting the original storyteller's words faithfully is fairly straightforward in the case of a storyteller who created a recording on audio tape, or even better on video tape. In such a case the editor sets down the words as heard. Of course even then things are not entirely straightforward. Words can be ambiguous or hard to distinguish. And the division into sentences and larger units is still largely a matter of the editor's discretion, as is the decision about how many of the inevitable slips of the tongue, self-corrections, and *ers* and *uhs* to include. (I have included rather more than some editors would, but not everything.) In the case of publications based on oral recordings I went back when possible to the original recording and compared the published version to the recording, making corrections when I was able to catch something that eluded the original transcriber. It must be added that every transcriber misses things, as I was reminded every time I re-listened to a tape; for each time I caught further things that I had missed on previous passes through the material.

In the case of tales for which we do not have a recording but have the original field transcription, it is often possible to revise the printed version to accord more closely with the transcription. In the case of Richard Dorson's Upper Peninsula Michigan tales, for instance, he sometimes smoothed the narrative considerably if he was editing it for a more popular as opposed to a more scholarly publication (1952). Consulting his original field notebooks has enabled me to present tales more nearly in the storyteller's exact words insofar as Dorson set them down accurately.

For many tales, however, we have only the published version, and must rest content with that. The tale as published may have derived from an oral recording or from dictation more or less skillfully set down. In such cases we can be sure of being more or less close to the original words of the storyteller. But in the case of many earlier texts, the tale was set down from memory after the storyteller finished. Since early collectors often tended to focus on the plot rather than on the narrative style, such records may be only distant echoes. In some cases, too, the collector set down the tale long years afterward, making it even less likely that the text has captured the style and words of the earlier storyteller. If, however, the storyteller was a favorite family servant or favorite relative, the story was somewhat formulaic, and the child-that-was loved the storyteller and the way of the telling as well as the plot, in such a case there is hope that much of the original performance may be preserved, even in a record not made until many years after.

So, in the tales of our book we are never in direct contact with the speaking voice of the storyteller. There is always some level of mediation. But I have striven to present the record as faithfully as it has been preserved and never to falsify whatever echo of the original voice may yet be preserved.

But just as a photographer can enhance an old and faded photograph, enabling us to see without falsification what is there but formerly not clear, so the editor can enhance the presentation of the tale on the page, enabling us to hear it more clearly than before. The first and most obvious enhancement has already been mentioned, namely correction. When the printed text disagrees with the recording or the manuscript, I have accorded priority to the recording or manuscript. I have further sought to enhance the text by exercising editorial discretion on the matters that go beyond the determination of which words to print. Many of these tales were first published in journals that crammed everything into as small a space on the page as possible and did not use the ordinary conventions of paragraphing and quotation marking. The result is texts that are unnecessarily hard to read. Current publishing practice has rediscovered the virtues of white space for enhancing comprehension, and I have tried to follow those contemporary conventions as far as possible. Words of speakers stand in quotation marks. Paragraphing is frequent, marking the movement of the tale as well as indicating shifts in speaker. Indentations mark verse clearly. Abbreviations are spelled out. *Et ceteras* are expanded into full formulaic phrases or narrative units. Odd spellings are standardized. And when storytellers make slips of the tongue, or make references that were probably quite clear to a listener but are not so clear to the reader—a loose *he,* for instance, whose referent is not immediately clear—in such cases explanatory words in brackets clarify.

In the case of tales presented in Gullah or other African American dialects, the issue of spelling requires special care. When the transcription inspired confidence I did not tamper with the orthography. Nor did I try to regularize grammar in any case. But when the spelling seemed to be strictly eye-spelling, intended to indicate black dialect by calling on the conventions of the minstrel stage or comic strip, I did venture to regularize. I saw no reason to print *cawze,* for example, when *'cause* would do just as well and indicate just as clearly how the word was probably pronounced. In the case of other dialectical pronunciations I tried to retain essential nonstandard spellings, but only those. Often there seemed no particular reason to print *walkin'* or *talkin'* as if there were something extraordinary or idiosyncratic in such pronunciations: in point of fact most Americans truncate those words in casual conversation but feel no need to abbreviate the spelling to so indicate. When, however, a specialized spelling truly helps to capture specialized pronunciation or rhythm, it is entirely appropriate.

The range of language used in the United State is very broad. These editorial conventions help bridge the gap between ethnic or regional dialects and more widespread or standard practice. When the original language is French, Spanish, or a Creole, however, no amount of fancy editorial footwork will do the job. Translation becomes essential. (Indeed, translation was even essential for one Gullah tale.) Some of the translations are my own, some were done by colleagues at my request, and some were done by the original editors or collectors. In the case of previously published translations I have edited as I did English-language tales. This editing has on occasion extended to revision of a translation for accuracy or readability. So I must accept responsibility for any infelicities in the translations as they here appear.

There is a further editorial step that I chose not to take, although I took it in an earlier folktale book, *Jack in Two Worlds* (McCarthy, Oxford, and Sobol 1994). The present volume does not include any tales printed to represent an ethnopoetic analysis. In much oral tradition, including at least some folktale telling in the United States, the language falls into rhythmic or sense units that are clearly units of composition analogous to the lines, stanzas, and so on that occur in conventional poetry and song. We might call this use of language *ethnopoetry*. It is not a universal phenomenon. Of the tales included in *Jack in Two Worlds*, the six collected from southern mountain storytellers all exhibited the phenomenon: all were composed in ethnopoetry, no matter the education level of the storyteller (three were educators and one had a Ph.D.). The remaining two stories, however, one from a Pennsylvania educator and one from a Toronto performer, did not. They were clearly told in prose, the only discernible rhythmic or sense units corresponding to the grammatical units of the sentences.

Currently there are two main but mutually exclusive systems for ethnopoetic analysis. Each type of analysis is valuable. But each provides different information. Simplistically put, that developed by Dennis Tedlock looks at *rhythmic* units, identified by pause (sometimes emphasized by a rising inflection), and isolates the poetic beat of the piece (1983). That developed and used by Dell and Virginia Hymes looks at sense units organized into lines, stanzas, scenes, and acts, and articulates the overall structure of the piece (2003). Sense lines and rhythmic sound lines do not always correspond, however. Consequently there is a kind of Heisenberg indeterminacy at work here that makes it impossible to carry out the two types of analysis simultaneously: with rare exceptions, the more we determine the Tedlockian sound units, the less we can determine the Hymesian sense units, and vice versa. One can represent the rhythmic lines or the sense lines, but not both. Only a small percentage of the texts in the present collection, moreover, are suitable candidates for ethnopoetic analysis. To do a proper Hymesian analysis one must have an exact transcription of the story, just as the storyteller told it. But many of the tales in the present volume have been set down from memory, or written down by the storyteller rather than dictated, or in other ways distorted, as indicated above, so that we have lost the careful structure, phrase by phrase, of the master storyteller. To do a proper Tedlockian analysis one must have something even rarer, an audio recording. Without such a recording there is no way to know when the storyteller took rhythmic pauses. But the majority of the stories in the present book were set down without the benefit of audio recording. Finally, such analysis requires a great amount of space and time, more of each than I have at my disposal if this volume is ever to appear. So, while I am excited by the possibilities of these two complementary modes of analysis, the tales are here presented unanalyzed.

The reader will, however, find indentations and verse lines occasionally in the following tales. Sometimes a tale includes clear examples of verse, as in *cante fables* and riddle tales. Sometimes formulaic language and runs are easier to spot if printed as verse. And sometimes the language approaches verse in other ways. My aim is ever to make the tales more readable.

PRESENTATION OF TALES

Each tale appears with a title at the beginning and a note at the end. And each tale is cited in the index of tale types at the back of the volume. The titles are usually those that I found with the stories. Sometimes they were the titles given by the storyteller, and sometimes they were supplied by the original collector or editor. Occasionally, when the title was too misleading and there was no evidence that it came from the storyteller, I have substituted what I hope is a more appropriate title.

It is customary to put the notes at the head of the story. But I as a reader am usually impatient to get to the story, which certainly has primacy over anything a scholar might have to say about it. Halpert and Widdowson, in the Newfoundland collection referred to above, provide brief formulaic headnotes but reserve discussion for what might be called tailnotes. I have decided to go further and move all commentary to the tailnote of each story. These tailnotes contain the following information, in this order.

1. Source for the story. Usually this is simply a last name and a page number, referring to an item in the bibliography.

2. ATU number. This is the number assigned to stories of the type in question (i.e., stories that have that particular basic plot) in *The Types of International Folktales* (ATU, 2004), which uses a classification system first conceived by Antti Aarne, translated, revised, and expanded by Stith Thompson, and recently updated by a group of folktale scholars under the direction of Hans-Jörg Uther. Aarne, Thompson, and Uther are the A, the T, and the U of ATU. Most European folktales have been indexed in *The Types of International Folktales*. For example, Jack and the Beanstalk is ATU 328, and The House That Jack Built is ATU 2035. Many tales, however, are rather complex and have subtypes. For instance, the more familiar Cinderella story, with the two stepsisters, is ATU 510A, but the English Cinderella story that is called Rushen Coatie, which often includes the heroine's flight to escape incest, is ATU 510B. Similarly, the familiar Hansel and Gretel story is ATU 327A, but there are versions with other kinds of human flesh-eaters, other ways of escaping, and one or three children instead of two. And the popular tale of Beauty and the Beast is ATU 425C, while the classical tale of Cupid and Psyche is ATU 425B and the related Norwegian folktale East of the Sun and West of the Moon is ATU 425A.

Not every tale gets a simple ATU number, however. The ATU classification has been supplemented by special indexes for particular tale repertoires. For our purposes the Irish index by Ó Súilleabháin and Christiansen (1963), the Hispanic index by Hansen (1957), and the English and North American index by Baughman (1966) are most helpful, and, in a few cases, tales are identified by Ó Súilleabháin and Christiansen, Hansen, or Baughman tale type numbers, rather than by ATU numbers. In two cases, the older number from the Aarne-Thompson classification (AT) is given along with the new number from ATU. Finally, in a few cases, a whole tale has been built up around a single simple motif. In such cases the Thompson motif number is assigned to the tale. It is fairly common, moreover, for a particular tale to be a complex amalgam of tale types, sometimes with stray motifs added in. In such cases I have assigned what seem the most pertinent type and motif numbers. But I have not tried to identify all the motifs contained in the many tales here included—an endless task. Nor have I analyzed particular tales into their main motifs as Thompson and Uther did in *The Types of International Folktales*.

The Aarne-Thompson-Uther Classification gives each tale type a generic name. Sometimes this is the name of a familiar tale or related group of tales (e.g., *Cinderella and Peau d'Âne*). Sometimes it describes broadly the action of the story (e.g., *The Man on a Quest for His Lost Wife*, or *The Maiden in the Tower*). The Uther revision has considerably improved these titles. Like

Halpert and Widdowson, however, I have not employed them in the notes. They are not always appropriate as descriptors of the American versions of the tales in question. I have, however, included these Aarne-Thompson-Uther titles in the index of tale types at the end of the volume, where the curious reader can check them out.

This index of tale types, though it covers only tales included in this volume and not all the tales that have been current in American oral tradition, will help the reader appreciate the wide range of tales that Americans know and tell. It will also enable the reader to find alternate developments of tale types that may be of interest. For several very common tale types, such as ATU 313 (The Magic Flight; The Devil's Daughter), ATU 327 (The Children and the Ogre; Hansel and Gretel), ATU 480 (The Two Sisters), and ATU 720 (The Juniper Tree), I have included a number of versions from different traditions. By comparing these versions the reader can easily see the variation possible even within a single tale type as well as see how regional and ethnic traditions differ characteristically, even in their treatment of identical plot lines. For more on tale types, see the appendix, "Studying American Folktales," in this volume.

3. After supplying the source for the text and the appropriate tale type (or motif) number, the notes go on to identify the storyteller who provided this version of the tale. Ideally, there would be a great deal of information about storytellers, including how old they were, how many such tales they knew and told, whom they learned them from, how they understood the tale, and what value they put on it. But until sometime in the last half century or so most collectors did not think of asking for information of this sort. Prior to that, collectors tended to focus on the story itself and its affinities in the wider tale repertoire. So we often do not even know the storyteller or when they told the story.

4. Fortunately, information about the collector is usually available, even in the case of quite early texts. This information comes next in each note, followed by information about the circumstances of collection. Sometimes that information is quite detailed, in which case the note will be rather longer. The name of the translator, when required, is provided after the name of the collector or before the name of the storyteller, as is most convenient in each case.

5. The note may go on to comment upon unusual aspects of the story, the place of the story in the local or broader American repertoire, or other versions of the tale that are included in the present volume. The notes do not, however, provide exhaustive comparative and historical data or guidance to scholarship about the tale. Readers who are interested in learning more about

American or world folktale scholarship may turn to the appendix, "Studying American Folktales," at the end of this volume.

Each note tries to cover this ground as adequately as the surviving data allows. In most cases, however, the contextual data is inadequate. To compensate a little for this inadequacy I have included as a final chapter a story embellished with full discussion of the storyteller, the collector, the circumstances of the collection, salient points about the story, and photographs. This chapter will serve as a demonstration of what would be ideal if we were not constrained by issues of history, contingency, space, time, and economics. I am grateful to colleague Jim Leary of the University of Wisconsin, who collected the tale, took the pictures, and wrote the essay.

In compiling this anthology my aim has been three-fold. First I hoped to provide teachers, students, and families with a handy sampling of our rich folktale heritage. Then I hoped to equip scholars with a convenient book to consult and place on their shelves alongside the parallel collections from Norway, Russia, France, Spain, and all across the European world. And finally I wanted to present naysayers with irrefutable refutation of their argument that the wonder tale and its kin put down no lasting roots in America. I have nourished the collection and watched it develop and take shape for more than a decade. And like a healthy child, in that decade it has grown from a scrawny thing, little more than a gleam in my eye, to a stout and substantial parcel quite able, as I hope, to stand on its own two feet and fight its own battles in the schoolyard of the world. And I, ever the anxious father, pray as it goes forth that it will fulfill my fond hopes for it.

DuBois, Pennsylvania
Lincoln's Birthday, 2006

Further Reading

Readers who want to learn more about folktales might look at the following books:

Burrison, John A. 1991. *Storytellers: Folktales and Legends from the South.* Athens: University of Georgia Press.

Halpert, Herbert, and J. D. A. Widdowson. 1996. *Folktales of Newfoundland: The Resilience of the Oral Tradition.* Garland Reference Library of the Humanities, vol. 1856. World Folktale Library, vol. 3. Publications of the American Folklore Society, New Series. New York: Garland Publishing, Inc.

Lindahl, Carl. 2004. *American Folktales from the Collections of the Library of Congress.* Armonk, NY: M. E. Sharpe, in association with the Library of Congress, Washington, DC.

Lüthi, Max. 1970. *Once upon a Time: On the Nature of Fairy Tales.* New York: F. Ungar Publishing Company.

McCarthy, William Bernard, Cheryl Oxford, and Joseph Daniel Sobol. 1994. *Jack in Two Worlds: Contemporary North American Tales and Their Tellers.* Publications of the American Folklore Society, New Series. Chapel Hill: University of North Carolina Press.

Sobol, Joseph Daniel. 1999. *The Storyteller's Journey: An American Revival.* Urbana: University of Illinois Press.

Thompson, Stith. 1946. *The Folktale.* New York: Holt, Rinehart and Winston.

Zipes, Jack. 1994. *Fairy Tale as Myth / Myth as Fairy Tale.* Lexington: University Press of Kentucky. (Also see other titles by Zipes.)

Notes

1. "English-speaking readers customarily think of fairy tales as the main form of folk narratives, but they seldom are heard in the United States" (Dorson 1986: 287). "All of the European immigrant groups in the United States, to some extent, carried their *Märchen* here with them, but these were seldom translated by the folk into English and thus have not usually persisted as oral tales in the second generation" (Brunvand 1998: 235; Brunvand does go on to discuss the extensive Appalachian-Ozark tradition derived from English-speaking settlers). "[T]he oral American märchen is not particularly well known among Americans outside the Appalachians" (Lindahl 2004: liii).

2. See below and chapter 17.

3. One of the oldest wonder tales we have is an example of just that phenomenon. The Deuterocanonical (Apocryphal) Book of Tobit is a version of ATU 505–7, the Grateful Dead Man complex of tales. Indeed, it seems to be the oldest known example of a tale from that complex. The tale was probably adapted by a Jew or Jews living in the Indo-European Persian Empire. In the Book of Tobit it has been well Semitized. The Indo-European ghost has become a Semitic angel, for example, and the details of the burial reflect Jewish burial customs. Nevertheless, the Indo-European cultural background still shows through, most clearly in the pet dog of the young hero. Treating dogs as pets is a fundamental Indo-European cultural trait, but one not shared by ancient Semitic peoples.

4. For a rich account of the Storytelling Revival, see Sobel 1999.

Part I

THE EARLY RECORD

CHAPTER I

TALES FROM A NEW REPUBLIC

When the first settlers came to the eastern part of the New World from England, Scotland, Ireland, France, and the German-speaking states of Europe, we can be sure that they brought with them their wonder tales to soothe children and intrigue adults. These Americans of European extraction exchanged tales around the home fire, or in taverns, at markets, and wherever two or three gathered. But, so far as we know, there was no field collector in those early years going around the different communities to hunt out the great storytellers and persuade them to dictate their stories for posterity (though there were already people setting down Native American tales, including tales of European extraction; see chapter 17). So we must work indirectly to get some idea of American storytelling in those early years. To reach that goal there are really two routes we can follow. First, knowing that people tend to retell the good stories that they read, especially in an environment in which reading matter is at a premium, we can look at the folktales that surfaced in the popular press of the period, that is, in almanacs and chapbooks and on broadsides. Second, recognizing that people remember good stories for a very long time, we can look at certain tales set down in the waning years of the nineteenth century: Elderly people who heard tales in their pre–Civil War childhood from grandparents, aunts, and uncles who in turn had heard them in the waning years of the eighteenth century, did make some record of those tales. From these two sources we can partially reconstruct the content and even the context of storytelling on the East Coast, on the frontier, and in the Old Northwest Territory—north of the Ohio and west of the Alleghenies—in the first decades of the United States.

In those early years of the American Republic printers put out one-page broadsides and small chapbooks and almanacs that included tales of various kinds. Almanacs were the standard calendars of early America, and so in constant demand. In addition to providing a list of days, they indicated phases of the moon and other astrological information helpful to those who planted by the signs or otherwise directed their life by such considerations, as well as various other types of information such as commemorations, court days, tables of coinage, and bits of legal, economic, and medical wisdom. The layout of an almanac usually left room for filler, frequently historical or humorous. Brief folktales served the purpose, and printers reprinted stories from each other or from English (or German) sources (see Stitt and Dodge 1991). Many of the stories they reprinted were the sort that also passed easily back and forth when folk met at the crossroad, emporium, tavern, or hearth. This chapter begins with the sort of tales that provided humorous filler for almanacs. Like almanacs, chapbooks and broadsides also sold well in the early United States. Versions of Jack the Giant Killer were especially popular, as were two variants of the Cinderella story, Catskin and The Golden Bull (or Horse), both versified. This chapter includes a version of Catskin apparently copied out from a garland, as chapbooks of verse were sometimes called. This particular garland may have been printed in England or Scotland, but a copy was carried into Kentucky in the 1790s, where a young woman admired it and entered it by hand, word for word, into her commonplace book. Chapbook tales also circulated by word of mouth, thus entering oral tradition. In the early twentieth century, Catskins showed up in the repertoires of Jane Hicks Gentry of Hot Springs, North Carolina, and Sam Harmon, of Cades Cove, Tennessee, and The Golden Bull in the repertoire of Jane Buell of Schoharie County, New York. So, while we do not have any field-collected tales from the United States before 1800, we do have almanac and chapbook versions of popular tales. From these we can extrapolate to arrive at a view of tales and taletelling in the United States in those early years.

The memories of people who recorded their memories are the other main source for information about taletelling in the early days of the Republic. When the American Folklore Society was founded in 1888, William Wells Newell, the first editor of the *Journal of American Folklore*, considered it important to seek out and publish American versions of classic European tales. Most of the texts that came his way were "self-collected," that is, the people who remembered the stories wrote them down themselves just as they had heard them—as nearly as they could remember—and then communicated them to Newell for publication in the *Journal*. Although the resultant texts were in a sense literary, the contributors sometimes valued the oral qualities of the tales and made a successful effort to catch those qualities in their renditions. In some cases, too, they provided recollections of the storytellers, the style of narration, and the storytelling milieu. I have selected seven of these early tales as windows on American taletelling in New England and Ohio in the half century before the Civil War. Since six of them are in varying degrees formulaic, we can even hope that in these six at least we come correspondingly close to the very words of the early-nineteenth-century narrators. And all the tales except "The Forgetful Boy" have continued to be popular in one strand or another of American tradition.

These tales from almanacs, chapbooks, and broadsides, and from the memories of people who had heard storytellers tell stories learned in the eighteenth century can help us understand how important stories were to people in the first years of the Republic. When we think about that chapbook carried across the Cumberland Gap into Kentucky where Polly Webb then painstakingly copied it out, we can get some idea of the importance people there and in all parts of the new Republic attached to those frail and modest bits of printing. It is not hard to imagine a father, returned from Worcester or Boston or Philadelphia at the turn of the year, drawing forth the new almanac to read to his family the witty tales spread among the calendrical pages. It is not hard to imagine his children rereading the tales and sharing them with their friends, whose fathers would in turn perhaps have brought back different almanacs or chapbooks, with different tales. Nor is it hard to imagine the delight on the Kentucky or Ohio frontier when a newcomer had arrived who was a born storyteller or who had some few thin pieces of fresh reading matter. New tales could be shared and reworked and combined with other remembered stories to fit the circumstances of daily life. Reverend Joseph Doddridge writes in the 1820s about his boyhood on the Virginia frontier some fifty years earlier:

> Dramatic narrations, chiefly concerning Jack and the Giant, furnished our young people with another source of amusement during their leisure hours. Many of those tales were lengthy, and embraced a considerable range of incident. Jack, always the hero of the story, after encountering many difficulties, and performing many great achievements, came off conqueror of the Giant. Many of these stories were tales of knight-errantry, in which case some captive virgin was released from captivity and restored to her lover. . . . They certainly have been handed from generation to generation from time immemorial. (Cited in Purdue 1987: 97)

For the early settlers, tales filled the hunger of the imagination. Whether drawn from memory or from almanacs and chapbooks, they were precious commodities, shared and shared again from colony to colony, state to state, up and down the seaboard and across the mountains into the frontier.

1. Clever Crispin and the Calf: A True Story

A butcher who had purchased a calf sat out with it on a horse at a public house door, which a shoe-maker, remarkable for his drollery, observing, and knowing that the butcher had to pass through a wood, offered the landlord to steal the calf, provided he would treat him with sixpence worth of grog. The landlord agreed, and the shoe-maker set off and dropt one new shoe in the path near the middle of the wood and another near a quarter of a mile from it.

The butcher saw the shoe but did not think it worth getting down for. However, when he discovered the second he thought the pair an acquisition and accordingly dismounted, tied his horse to the hedge, and walked back to where he had seen the first shoe. The shoe-maker in the meantime unstrapped the calf and carried it across the fields to the landlord, who put it in his barn.

The butcher, missing his calf, went back to the inn and told his misfortune, at the same time observing that he must have another calf, cost what it would, as the veal was bespoke. The landlord told him he had a calf in the barn which he would sell him. The butcher looked at it and asked the price. The landlord replied, "Give me the same as you did for the calf you lost, as I think it is full as large." The butcher would by no means allow the calf to be as good, but agreed to give him within six shillings of what the other cost, and accordingly put the calf a second time on his horse.

Crispin, elated with his success, undertook to steal the calf again for another sixpenny worth; which being agreed on, he posted to the woods and hid himself; where, observing the butcher come along, he bellowed so like a calf that the butcher, conceiving it to be the one he had lost, cried out in joy, "Ah! are you there! Have I found you at last!" and immediately dismounted and ran into the woods. Crispin, taking the advantage of the butcher's absence, entrapped the calf and actually got back to the tavern before the butcher arrived to tell his mournful tale, who attributed the whole to witchcraft. The tavern keeper unraveled the mystery, and the butcher, after paying for and partaking of a crown's worth of punch, laughed heartily at the joke. And the shoe-maker got applauded for his ingenuity.

Evans 26569, *The Virginia Almanack for the Year of Our Lord 1795.* ATU 1525D. This particular "true story" was extremely popular with early almanac publishers, who often republished one another's stuff. Stitt and Dodge (1991), in their index of tales occurring in almanacs, list six occurrences in the eighteenth and early nineteenth century. The present version was placed immediately after a similar tale of a sharpster tricking three lawyers in succession out of substantial sums of money. The tale type is often called "The Master Thief," and the classification into subtypes is based on the initial situation and the particular tricks the clever hero plays in order to steal the seemingly unstealable. The present version is probably English in origin, but the story is also popular in French and Spanish traditions in this country. In fact, variations on this story have proved among the most popular in American tradition. In recognition of that popularity the editor has given variants of 1525 pride of place as the first and last stories in this collection.

As the title suggests, the incident was presented as having actually occurred. One almanac even includes the citation of the British newspaper whence the editor had obtained the tale, in a version verbally close to the present one. Folk tales that are presented as true or possibly true are called legends by folklorists. Legends frequently include ironic elements, as does the tale of Clever Crispin, and also assurances that the tale is verifiable, as does the alternate version that cites the English newspaper where the facts may be checked. The assurance that it is a true story moves this tale into the genre of legend, a fairly common move for märchen and märchen-like stories in North America. It is also worth noting that this clever shoemaker is named for St. Crispin, patron saint of cobblers and shoemakers.

The Evans number before the name of the almanac in which this tale appears, above, is the number that Charles Evans assigned to that publication in his *American Bibliography: A Chronological Dictionary of All Books, Pamphlets, and Periodical Publications Printed in the United States of America from the Genesis of Printing in 1639 Down to and Including the Year 1820.*

2. The Fortune Teller

There lived a schoolmaster in a certain village, who formed a particular satisfaction in the study of astrology or the art of telling by the position of the stars things to come. His prophesying of the weather proved to be more true, in general, than what was commonly put down in the almanac; for which reason the villagers reported him to be a fortune-teller.

The nobleman to whom the village belonged, hearing of the abilities of this schoolmaster, sent for him. The schoolmaster accordingly made his appearance one morning very early, before the nobleman was out of his bed.

"I have been told," said the nobleman, "that you pretend to be a fortune-teller."

The schoolmaster answered that he had never done the like, but as he was a lover of astrology, it so happened now and again that certain things came to pass as he, by the aspects, conjunctions, and influence of the heavenly bodies, had prognosticated. But the nobleman, who was an ignoramus, understood nothing of these words. "Hear me," said the nobleman in a passion: "If you do not answer me four questions which I am going to ask, you shall be treated as an imposture. First, you are to tell me where the center of the earth is. Secondly, how much I am worth. Thirdly, what I think. And, fourthly, what I believe."

The schoolmaster wanted to get clear of all this by telling the nobleman that it was God alone that was able to search the hearts of men and disclose their thoughts. But the nobleman insisted on having the above questions answered. The schoolmaster, seeing he could not disengage himself, requested the favour of having one day's time allowed him that he might consult his books. This being granted, the schoolmaster made his respects, and departed.

On his way home, he met a miller who lived in the same village. The miller, perceiving him to look much dejected, asked him what was the matter. The schoolmaster related all that had passed between the nobleman and himself. The miller laughed heartily at it, but at the same time promised that he would take the affair on himself. "For," said he to the schoolmaster, "as you made your appearance before the nobleman in a dark bedchamber so early in the morning, it was impossible for him to take a strict observation of your face. As for me, he don't know at all. It will therefore be very easy for me to represent your person after I have dressed myself in your clothes. As for his questions, I shall, no doubt, be able to answer them all completely." The schoolmaster very willingly consented, as he knew the artful miller was better able to satisfy the demands of the nobleman than himself.

Accordingly, the next morning the miller dressed himself in the schoolmaster's clothes, and, with a cane in his hand, repaired to the nobleman's house and let him know that the schoolmaster was come, in obedience to his orders, to answer his queries. The nobleman ordered him immediately before him, and asked him whether he really thought himself capable of answering his queries? The miller said he would stake his life for the performance.

"Well," said the nobleman, "where is the center of the earth?"

"I will not only tell you," said the miller, "but I will also show you the very spot, if you will follow me." They both went therefore into the adjoining field, and after the miller had measured the ground for a while with his cane, he stuck it in the earth. "Here, Sir, is the very spot," said the miller.

"How will you prove that?" says the nobleman.

"Have you it measured," replied the miller, "and if it fails one inch, I will forfeit my life!" The nobleman knew it was out of his power to have it done. He therefore dropped that query, and came to the second, that is, how much he was worth. The miller answered, "Our Saviour was valued at thirty pieces of silver, and, he was undoubtedly worth more than you. I hope you will not take it amiss if I value you at twenty-nine pieces of silver."

"You are right, my friend," says the nobleman. "But now let us hear if you can tell me what I think. I vow that will be somewhat heavier for you."

"Not at all," said the miller. "I would lay any wager that you think more on your own interest than on mine."

"That is very true," says the nobleman. "But what say you to my fourth query? Do you know what I believe?"

"O yes," said the miller, "you believe that I am the schoolmaster. Is it not so?"

"I certainly do," said the nobleman.

"But you are mistaken, Sir," replied the other, "for I am the miller in the village." So saying, he made a low bow to his honour, and departed.

Evans 23264, *The Columbian Almanac* for 1792, and Evans 23363, *Father Abraham's Almanac* for 1792. ATU 922. These two almanacs were both printed by the same Philadelphia printer, Peter Stewart. Though the first has thirty-six and the other forty pages, the central calendrical pages with their accompanying matter (such as this story) seem identical. Apparently the printer simply printed different sets of opening and closing pages for different clientele, while printing enough copies of the almanac proper to supply the two separate publications.

This tale is the subject of a classic early folktale study, *Kaiser und Abt*, by Walter Anderson. The present version, lifted, no doubt, from an English almanac, illustrates one way that colonial-period Americans would have heard the tale. They might also have heard the ballad King John and the Bishop (Child 45), which tells the same story though obviously with different personnel. In later American tradition the story becomes a reverse numbskull story or joke featuring a pair of brothers or Irishmen, in which the duller of the pair is rescued by the brighter. Usually there are three, not four questions. The first, second, and fourth questions and respective answers in this text are found in many other variants as well. The third question and its answer are more unusual.

3. The Three Wishes

A poor man was asked what three things he would have, could he have them for the wishing?

"Why, in the first place," says he, "I would have as much good strong ale as I could drink."

"Very well, what next?"

"Then I would have as much fat beef as I could eat."

"And what's your third wish?"

But now he was puzzled, for with him all happiness lay in fat beef and strong ale. At last, after much consideration, "Hang it," says he, "I'll have a little more ale still."

Evans 16167, *Bickerstaff's New-England Almanack* for 1779. ATU 1173A. It is fairly common in the U.S. tradition for a more formal tale to settle down as a simple joke. In the present version of ATU 1173A we can catch this process very early on, for this is a Colonial joke based on such a tale. In that more formal tale a peasant makes a bargain with the devil to sell his soul if the devil can grant him three wishes. His wishes: that the devil bring him all the grog in the world, all the tobacco, and then more grog. Since there can not be more than all, the man wins his bet, retaining the grog and tobacco. Ironically the same third wish that in the tale demonstrates the cleverness of the peasant serves in the joke to illustrate the poor man's simplicity and even his simple-mindedness.

4. Catskin

CATSKIN'S GARLAND, PART THE FIRST

Ye fathers and mothers, and children also,
Come draw near unto me, and soon you shall know
The sense of my ditty, for I dare to say,
The like han't been printed this many a day.

The subject which to you I am to relate,
It is of a Squire's son of a vast estate.
And the first dear infant his wife to him bear,
It was a young daughter of beauty most fair.

He said to his wife, "Had this child been a boy
'Twould have pleased me better and increased my joy.
If the next be of the same sort, I do declare
Of what I'm possessed she shall have no share."

In twelve months time after, this woman we hear
Had another daughter of beauty most clear,
And when that her husband knew 'twas a female,
Into a strong bitter passion he fell,

Saying, "Since this is of the same sort as the first,
In my habitation she shall not be nursed.
Pray let it be sent into the country.
For where I am, truly this child shall not be."

With tears his dear wife to him thus did say,
"Husband, be contented, I'll send her away."
Then unto the country with speed did it send
For to be brought up with one who was a friend.

Although that her father hated her so,
She good education on her did bestow.
And with a golden casket and robes of the best
This slighted young damsel was commonly dressed.

And when unto stature this damsel was grown,
And found by her father she had no love shown,
She cried, "Before that I lie under this frown,
I'm fully resolved to range the world round."

PART THE SECOND

But now, good people, the cream of the jest,
In what sort of manner this creature was dressed:
With cat skins she made for a robe I declare,
The which for her cov'ring she daily did wear.

Her new rich attire and jewels besides,
Then up in a bundle by her they were tied.
Now to seek her fortune, she wandered away.
And when she had traveled a whole winter's day,

In the evening tide she came to a town.
When at the knight's door she then set her down
For to rest herself, who was tired to be sure,
This noble knight's lady she came to the door.

And, seeing this creature in such sort of dress,
The lady unto her these words did express:
"From whence cam'st thou, girl, and what will you have?"
She cried, "A night's quarters in your stable I crave."

The lady said to her, "I'll grant thy desire.
Come into the kitchen, and stand by the fire."
Then she thanked the lady, and went in with haste
Where she was gazed on from biggest to least.

And being well warmed, her hunger being great,
They gave her a dish of good meat for to eat.

And then to an out-house this creature was led
Where she with fresh straw then made her a bed.

And when in the morning that daylight she saw,
Her rich robes and jewels she hid in the straw,
And being very cold, she then did retire
To go to the kitchen and stand by the fire.

The cook said, "My lady hath promised that thou
Shall be as a scullion to wait on me now.
What say'st thou, girl? Art thou willing to bide?"
"With all my heart, truly," to him she replied.

To work with her needle she could very well,
And for raising of paste few could her excel.
She, being very handy, the cook's heart did win.
And then she was called by the name of Catskin.

PART THE THIRD

This lady had a son both comely and tall
Who oftentimes used to be at a ball.
A mile out of town in an evening tide
To see the ball acted away he did ride.

Catskin said to his mother, "Madam, let me
Go after your son, this fine ball for to see."
With that, in a passion this lady she grew,
Struck her with a ladle, which she broke in two.

And being thus served, she then went away
And with a rich garment herself did array.
Then to see this ball with great speed did retire,
Where she danced so rarely all did her admire.

The sport being done, the young Squire did say,
"Young lady, where do you live, tell me I pray?"
Her answer was unto him: "That I will tell:
At the sign of the Broken Ladle I dwell."

She, being very nimble, got home first, 'tis said,
And with her catskin robes she soon was arrayed
And into the kitchen again she did go,
But where she had been none of them did know.

Next day the young Squire, himself to content,
To see the ball acted, away then he went.
She said, "Pray let me go this ball for to see."
And then struck her with a skimmer and broke it in three.

Then out of doors she ran with heaviness,
And with her rich garments herself then did dress,
And to see this ball she ran away with speed
And to see her dancing all wondered indeed.

The ball being ended, this young Squire then
Said, "Where is't you live?" She answered again,
"Sir, because you ask me, an account I will give:
At the sign of the Broken Skimmer I live."

Being dark, then she lost him, and homeward did hie,
And with her catskin robe was dressed presently,
And into the kitchen among them she went,
But where she had been they were all innocent.

When the Squire came home and found Catskin there
He was in amaze, and began for to swear:
"For two nights at this ball has been a lady,
The sweetest of beauties that ever I did see.

"She was the best dancer in all the whole place,
And very much like our Catskin in the face.
Had she not been dressed to that comely degree
I'd sworn it had been Catskin bodily."

Next night to this ball he did go once more
Then she asked his mother to go as before,
And having a basin of water in hand
She threw it at Catskin as I understand.

Shaking her wet ears, out of doors she did run,
And dressed herself, when this thing she had done.
To see this ball acted she then went her ways.
To see her fine dancing, all gave her the praise.

And having concluded, this young Squire he
Said, "From whence come you, pray, lady, tell me?"
Her answer was, "Sir, you shall soon know the same:
From the sign of the Basin of Water I came."

So homeward she hurried as fast as might be.
This young Squire he then was resolved to see
Where to she belonged; then, following Catskin,
Into an old straw house he saw her creep in.

He said, "O, brave Catskin, I find it is thee
These three nights together hath so charmed me.
Thou art the sweetest creature my eyes e'er beheld.
With joy and contentment my heart it is filled.

"Thou art the cook's scullion but, as I have life,
Grant me but thy love, I'll make thee my wife,
And you shall have maids to be at your call."
"Sir, that cannot be. I have no portion at all."

"Thy beauty, my joy and my dear,
I prize it fair better than thousands a year,
And to have my friends consent, I have got a trick.
I'll go to my bed and feign myself sick.

"There none shall attend me but thee, I protest.
So one day or other, when in thy rich dress
Thou shalt be dressed, if my parents come nigh,
I'll tell them 'tis for thee I'm sick and like to die."

PART THE FOURTH

Having thus consulted, this couple partéd.
Next day this Squire he took to his bed,

And when his dear parents this thing perceived,
For fear of his death they were heartily grieved.

To tend him they sent for a nurse presently.
He said, "None but Catskin my nurse now shall be."
His parents said, "No, Son." He said, "But she shall,
Or else I shall have no nurse at all."

His parents both wondered to hear him say thus,
That none but Catskin must needs be his nurse.
So then his dear parents, their son to content,
Up to the chamber poor Catskin they sent.

Sweet cordials and other rich things were prepared,
Which between this couple were equally shared.
And when they were alone in each other's arms
Enjoyed one another in love's pleasant charms.

At length on a time, poor Catskin, 'tis said,
In her rich attire she was arrayed.
And when that his mother the chamber drew near
Then much like a goddess Catskin did appear,

Which caused her to startle, and thus for to say:
"What young lady is this, Son, tell me I pray?"
He said, "Why, 'tis Catskin, for whom sick I lie
And without I have her, with speed I shall die."

His mother ran down then to tell the old knight,
Who ran up to see this amazing great sight.
He said, "Why, 'tis Catskin we hold in such scorn.
I never saw a finer dame since I was born."

The old knight said to her, "I pray thee, tell me,
From whence dost thou come, and of what family?"
Then who were her parents she gave him to know,
And what was the cause of her wandering so.

The Squire cried, "If you will save my life,
Pray grant this young creature she may be my wife."

His father replied, "Thy life for to save,
If you are agreed, my consent you shall have."

Next day with great triumph and joy as we hear
There was many coaches both far and near.
Then, much like a goddess dressed in rich array,
Catskin to the Squire was married that day.

For several days this great wedding did last.
There were many a topping and gallant rich guest,
And for joy the bells rang over the town,
And bottles of canary trolled merrily round.

When Catskin was married, her fame for to raise,
To see her modest carriage, all gave her the praise.
Thus her charming beauty the Squire did win,
And who loves so great as he and Catskin!

PART THE FIFTH

Now in the fifth part I'll endeavor to show
How things with her parents and sister did go.
Her mother and sister of life are bereft,
And now all alone the old Squire he is left.

And hearing his daughter was married so brave,
He said, "In my noodle a fancy I have:
Dressed like a poor man, a journey I'll make
And see if she on me some pity will take."

Then, dressed like a beggar, he went to her gate.
There stood his daughter who appeared very great.
He cried, "Noble lady, a poor man I be,
And I am now forced to crave your charity."

With a blush she asked him from whence he came.
With that he then told her, and gave her his hand.
She cried, "I'm your daughter that you slighted so;
Nevertheless, to you some kindness I'll show.

"'Tis through mercy the Lord hath provided for me.
Pray, Father, then come in and set down," said she.
Then the best provision the house could afford
For to make him welcome was set on the board.

She said, "You are welcome, feed heartily, I pray,
And if you are willing, with me you shall stay
So long as you live." Then he made this reply:
"I only am come, thy love for to try.

"Through mercy, my child, I'm rich and not poor.
I have gold and silver enough now in store,
And for the love which at thy hand I have found
For a portion I will give thee ten thousand pound."

So in a few days after, as I understand,
This man he went home and sold off all his land,
And ten thousand pounds to his daughter did give
And then all together in love they did live.

Webb 1797–1799. ATU 510B. From a manuscript commonplace book of Mary (Polly) Webb, Kentucky, 1797, in the possession of Duke University. ATU 510 is the broad number for the Cinderella family of stories, to which Catskin belongs. The word "garland" in the title probably indicates that Polly Webb copied the poem from a chapbook. In the original manuscript the words "Entered According to Order" are copied after the title. These words refer to the license required by British law, and indicate that the chapbook from which Webb copied was printed in England. According to dates in her commonplace book, Webb spread her copying over a little more than a week, completing her work on or about May 24, 1797. She filled out her commonplace book with other pieces in verse, mostly popular ballads. The tale is here presented as far as possible in modern spelling, including consistent spelling of the heroine's name, and with a very few silent emendations ("Her answer was unto [rather than under] him," for example), but metrical and syntactical irregularities that came from copying the verses out by hand have not been corrected.

Joseph Jacobs, in *More English Fairy Tales* (241), points out one particularly provocative detail in this story. When the mother throws a basin of water at Catskin, the girl runs outside "shaking her wet ears." One can't help wondering whether this detail remains in the story from an earlier version in which the heroine was under enchantment and transformed bodily into a cat, not simply dressed in cat skins. Such relic details, incomprehensible without reference to an earlier recension, are not uncommon in folktales.

Broadside and garland printings of Catskin were moderately popular in eighteenth-century America as well as in England, and ATU 510B seems to have secured a firm position in Appalachian oral tradition, with some ten versions identified from Kentucky, Virginia, Tennessee, and North Carolina (Lindahl 2004: 340). In the 1920s Jane Gentry, of Hot Springs, North Carolina, told Isabel Gordon Carter a version that included the motif of the incestuous father, a motif not found in this garland version (Carter 1925: 361–63; for more on Gentry, see chapter 13). Gentry's cousin Sam Harmon, aided by Harmon's granddaughter Alberta, also told a version for Herbert Halpert (Lindahl 2004: 40–42).

5. Lady Featherflight

A poor woman, living on the edge of a wood, came at last to where she found nothing in the cupboard of the next day's breakfast. She called her boy Jack and said, "You must now go into the wide world. If you stay here, there will be two of us to starve. I have nothing for you but this piece of black bread. On the other side of the forest lies the world. Find your way to it, and gain your living honestly." With that she bade him good-by and he started.

He knew the way some distance into the thickest of the forest, for he had often been there for fagots. But after walking all day, he saw no farm, path, or tree, and knew that he was lost. Still he traveled on and on, as long as the daylight lasted, and then lay down and slept. The next morning he ate the black bread, and wandered on all day. At night he saw lights before him, and was guided by them to a large palace, where he knocked for a long time in vain. At last the door was opened, and a lovely lady appeared, who said as she saw him, "Go away as quickly as you can. My father will soon come home, and he will surely eat you."

Jack said, "Can't you hide me, and give me something to eat, or I shall fall down dead at your door?"

At first she refused, but afterwards yielded to Jack's prayers, and told him to come in and hide behind the oven. Then she gave him food, and told him that her father was a giant, who ate men and women. Perhaps she could keep him overnight, as she had already supper prepared. After a while, the giant came banging at the door, shouting, "Featherflight, let me in, let me in!" As she opened the door he came in, saying, "Where have you stowed the man? I smelt him all the way through that wood."

Featherflight said, "Oh father, he is nothing but a poor little thin boy! He would make but half a mouthful, and his bones would stick in your throat; and beside he wants to work for you; perhaps you can make him useful. But sit down to supper now, and after supper I will show him to you."

So she set before him half of a fat heifer, a sheep, and a turkey, which he swallowed so fast that his hair stood on end. When he had finished, Featherflight beckoned to Jack, who came trembling from behind the oven. The giant looked at him scornfully and said, "Indeed, as you say, he is but half a mouthful. But there is room for flesh there and we must fatten him up for a few days; meanwhile he must earn his victuals. See here, my young snip, can you do a day's work in a day?"

And Jack answered bravely, "I can do a day's work in a day as well as another." So the giant said, "Well, go to bed now. I will tell you in the morning your work." So Jack went to bed, and Lady Featherflight showed him, while the giant lay down on the floor with his head in Featherflight's lap, and she combed his hair and brushed his head till he went fast asleep.

The next morning Jack was called bright and early, and was taken out to the farmyard, where stood a large barn, unroofed by a late tempest. Here the giant stopped and said, "Behind this barn you will find a hill of feathers. Thatch me this barn with them, and earn your supper, and, look you! if it be not done when I come back tonight, you shall be fried in meal and swallowed whole for supper." Then he left, laughing to himself as he went down the road.

Jack went bravely to work and found a ladder and basket; he filled the basket, and ran up the ladder, and then tried hard to make a beginning on the thatch. As soon as he placed a handful of feathers, half would fly away as he wove them in. He tried for hours with no success, until at last half of the hill was scattered to the four winds, and he had not finished a hand-breadth of the roof. Then he sat down at the foot of the ladder and began to cry, when out came Lady Featherflight, with the basket on her arm, which she set down at his feet, saying, "Eat now, and cry after. Meantime, I will try to think what I can do to help you." Jack felt cheered, and went to work, while Lady Featherflight walked round the barn, singing as she went:

> Birds of land and birds of sea,
> Come and thatch this roof for me.

As she walked round the second time, the sky grew dark, and a heavy cloud hid the sun and came nearer and nearer to the earth, separating at last into hundreds and thousands of birds. Each, as it flew, dropped a feather on the roof and tucked it neatly in. And when Jack's meal was finished the roof was finished, too.

Then Featherflight said, "Let us talk and enjoy ourselves till my father the giant comes home." So they wandered round the grounds and the stables, and Lady Featherflight told of the treasure in the strong room, till Jack wondered why he was born without a sixpence. Soon they went back to the house, and Jack helped, and Lady Featherflight prepared supper, which tonight was fourteen loaves of bread, two sheep, and a jack-pudding, by way of finish, which would almost have filled the little house where Jack was born. Soon the giant came home, thundered at the door again, and shouted,

"Let me in, let me in!" Featherflight served him with the supper already laid, and the giant ate it with great relish.

As soon as he had finished, he called to Jack, and asked him about his work. Jack said, "I told you I could do a day's work in a day as well as another. You'll have no fault to find." The giant said nothing, and Jack went to bed. Then, as before, the giant lay down on the floor with his head in Featherflight's lap. She combed his hair and brushed his head till he fell fast asleep.

The next morning the giant called Jack into the yard, and looked at his day's work. All he said was, "This is not your doing," and he proceeded to a heap of seed, nearly as high as the barn, saying, "Here is your day's work. Separate the seeds, each into its own pile. Let it be done when I come home tonight, or you shall be fried in meal, and I shall swallow you, bones and all." Then the giant went off down the road, laughing as he went.

Jack seated himself before the heap, took a handful of seeds, put corn in one pile, rye in another, oats in another, and had not begun to find an end of the different kinds when noon had come, and the sun was right over head. The heap was no smaller, and Jack was tired out, so he sat down, hugged his knees, and cried. Out came Featherflight, with a basket on her arm, which she put down before Jack, saying, "Eat now, and cry after." So Jack ate with a will, and Lady Featherflight walked round and round the heap, singing as she went:

> Birds of earth and birds of sea,
> Come and sort this seed for me.

As she walked round the heap for the second time, still singing, the ground about her looked as if it was moving. From behind each grain of sand, each daisy stem, each blade of grass, there came some little insect, gray, black, brown, or green, and began to work at the seeds. Each chose some one kind, and made a heap by itself. When Jack had finished a hearty meal, the great heap was divided into countless others; and Jack and Lady Featherflight walked and talked to their hearts' content for the rest of the day.

As the sun went down the giant came home, thundered at the door again, and shouted, "Let me in; let me in!" Featherflight greeted him with his supper, already laid, and he sat down and ate, with a great appetite, four fat pigs, three fat pullets, and an old gander. He finished off with a jack-pudding. Then he was so sleepy he could not keep his head up; all he said was, "Go to bed, youngster; I'll see your work to-morrow." Then, as before, the giant laid his head down on the floor with his head in Featherflight's lap. She combed his hair and brushed his head, and he fell fast asleep.

The next morning the giant called Jack into the farmyard earlier than before. "It is but fair to call you early, for I have work more than a strong man can well do." He showed him a heap of sand, saying, "Make me a rope to tether my herd of cows, that they may not leave the stalls before milking time." Then he turned on his heel, and went down the road laughing.

Jack took some sand in his hands, gave a twist, threw it down, went to the door, and called out, "Featherflight! Featherflight! This is beyond you. I feel myself already rolled in meal, and swallowed, bones and all."

Out came Featherflight, saying with good cheer, "Not so bad as that. Sit down, and we will plan what to do." They talked and planned all the day. Just before the giant came home, they went up to the top of the stairs to Jack's room; then Featherflight pricked Jack's finger and dropped a drop of blood on each of the three stairs. Then she came down and prepared the supper, which tonight was a brace of turkeys, three fat geese, five fat hens, six fat pigeons, seven fat woodcocks, and half a score of quail, with a jack-pudding.

When he had finished, the giant turned to Featherflight with a growl, "Why so sparing of food tonight? Is there no good meal in the larder? This boy whets my appetite. Well for you, young sir, if you have done your work. Is it done?"

"No, sir," said Jack boldly. "I said I could do a day's work in a day as well as another, but no better."

The giant said, "Featherflight, prick him for me with the larding needle, hang him in the chimney corner well wrapped in bacon, and give him to me for my early breakfast."

Featherflight says, "Yes, father." Then, as before, the giant laid his head down on the floor with his head in Featherflight's lap. She combed his hair, and brushed his head, and he fell fast asleep. Jack goes to bed, his room at the top of the stairs. As soon as the giant is snoring in bed, Featherflight softly calls Jack and says, "I have the keys of the treasure house; come with me." They open the treasure house, take out bags of gold and silver, and loosen the halter of the best horse in the best stall in the best stable. Jack mounts with Featherflight behind, and off they go.

At three o'clock in the morning, not thinking of his order the night before, the giant wakes and calls, "Jack, get up."

"Yes, sir," says the first drop of blood.

At four o'clock the giant wakes, turns over, and says, "Jack, get up."

"Yes, sir," says the second drop of blood.

At five o'clock the giant wakens, turns over, and says, "Jack, get up."

"Yes, sir," says the third drop of blood.

At six o'clock the giant wakens, turns over, and says, "Jack, get up" . . . and there was no answer.

Then with great fury he says, "Featherflight has overslept herself; my breakfast won't be ready." He rushes to Featherflight's room; it is empty. He dashes downstairs to the chimney corner, to see if Jack is hanging there, and finds neither Jack nor Featherflight. Then he suspects they have run away, and rushes back for his seven-leagued boots, but cannot find the key under his pillow. He rushes down, finds the door wide open, catches up his boots and rushes to the stable. There he finds that the best horse from the best stall from the best stable has gone. Jumping into his boots, he flies after them, swifter than the wind. The runaways had been galloping for several hours, when Jack hears a sound behind him, and, turning, sees the giant in the distance." O Featherflight! Featherflight! all is lost!"

But Featherflight says, "Keep steady, Jack. Look in the horse's right ear, and throw behind you over your right shoulder what you find." Jack looks and finds a little stick of wood, throws it over his right shoulder, and then there grows up behind them a forest of hard wood.

"We are saved," says Jack."

"Not so certain," says Lady Featherflight, "but prick up the horse, for we have gained some time." The giant went back for an axe, but soon hacked and hewed his way through the wood, and was on the trail again.

Jack again heard a sound, turned and saw the giant, and said to Lady Featherflight, "All is lost."

"Keep steady, Jack," says Featherflight. "Look in the horse's left ear, and throw over your left shoulder what you find."

Jack looked, found a drop of water, throws it over his left shoulder, and between them and the giant there arises a large lake, and the giant stops on the other side, and shouts across, "How did you get over?"

Featherflight calls, "We drank, and our horses drank, and we drank our way through."

The giant shouts scornfully back, "Surely I am good for what you can do," and he threw himself down, and drank and drank and drank, and then he burst.

Now they go on quietly till they come near to a town. Here they stop, and Jack says, "Climb this tree, and hide in the branches till I come with the parson to marry us. For I must buy me a suit of fine clothes before I am seen with a gay lady like yourself."

So Featherflight climbed the tree with the thickest branches she could find, and waited there, looking between the leaves into a spring below. Now this spring was used by all the wives of the townspeople to draw water for breakfast. No water was so sweet anywhere else; and early in the morning they all came with pitchers and pails for a gossip, and to draw water for the kettle. The first who came was a carpenter's wife, and as she bent over the clear spring, she saw, not herself, but Featherflight's lovely face reflected in the water. She looks at it with astonishment and cries, "What! I, a carpenter's wife, and I so handsome? No, that I won't," and down she threw the pitcher, and off she went.

The next who came was the potter's wife, and as she bent over the clear spring she saw, not herself, but Featherflight's lovely face reflected in the water. She looks at it with astonishment and cries, "What! I, a potter's wife, and I so handsome? No, that I won't," and down she threw the pitcher, and off she went. In the same manner come the wives of the publican, scrivener, lace-maker, etc., etc.

All the men in the town began to want their breakfast, and one after another went out into the market-place to ask if any one by chance had seen his wife. Each came with the same question and all received the same answers. All had seen them going, but none had seen them returning. They all began to fear foul play, and all together walked out toward the spring. When they reached it, they found the broken pitchers all about the grass, and the pails bottom upwards floating on the water. One of them, looking over the edge, saw the face reflected and, knowing that it was not his own, looked up. Seeing Lady Featherflight, he called to his comrades, "Here is the witch, here is the enchantress. She has bewitched our wives. Let us kill her." And they began to drag her out of the tree, in spite of all she could say. Just at this moment Jack comes up, galloping back on his horse, with the parson up behind. You would not know the gaily dressed cavalier to be the poor, ragged boy who passed over the road so short a time before. As he came near he saw the crowd and shouted, "What's the matter? What are you doing to my wife?"

The men shouted, "We are hanging a witch; she has bewitched all our wives, and murdered them, for all we know."

The parson bade them stop, and let the Lady Featherflight tell her own story. When she told them how their wives had mistaken her face for theirs, they were silent a moment, and then one and all cried, "If we have wedded such fools, they are well sped," and turning walked back to the town.

The parson married Jack and Lady Featherflight on the spot, and christened them from the water of the spring, and then went home with them to the great house that Jack had bought as he passed through the town.

There the newly married pair lived happily for many months, until Jack began to wish for more of the giant's treasure, and proposed that they should go back for it. But they could not cross the water. Lady Featherflight said,

"Why not build a bridge?" And the bridge was built. They went over with wagons and horses, and brought back so heavy a load that, as the last wagonful passed over the bridge, it broke, and the gold was lost.

Jack lamented and said, "Now we can have nothing more from the giant's treasure-house."

But Lady Featherflight said, "Why not mend the bridge?"

So the bridge was mended,
And my story's ended.

Newell 1893: 54–62. ATU 313. Mrs. J. B. Warner of Cambridge, Massachusetts, a charter member of the American Folklore Society, communicated this version of The Magic Flight to William Wells Newell, first editor of the society's journal. Mrs. Warner said she learned the story from her aunt, Miss Elizabeth Hoar of Concord. If we unchivalrously assign "a certain age" to either of the women in question, we may then safely suggest that this text provides evidence of the story as told in Massachusetts in the early to mid-nineteenth century. Newell apparently read the story at the Second International Folk-Lore Congress, London, October 1891. Though it had been printed in the proceedings of the Congress, Newell also printed it in the *Journal of American Folklore*, explaining that "the excellence of the version makes it of general interest." Among the interesting things about the text are two social/political notes that are struck as Featherflight takes Jack around the grounds and then prepares for the giant's return. "Lady Featherflight told of the treasure in the strong room, till Jack wondered why he was born without a sixpence. Soon they went back to the house, and Jack helped, and Lady Featherflight prepared supper." Jack wonders about the social discrepancies in a world that makes the giant rich, but leaves him poor. Then he helps Lady Featherflight with work that was clearly, in the eighteenth and nineteenth century, women's work. The lady will in turn help him with his work, and then secure for him more than enough gold to last his lifetime.

The name "Featherflight" reminds us that in many versions the heroine spends a certain amount of her time in bird form. The combination of a hero called Jack and a giant as villain suggests origin of this version in the British Isles, although the incident of hiding in the tree is usually associated with ATU 408, The Three Oranges, a tale practically unknown in the British Isles tradition. The formulaic ending with the bridge has generally passed out of British/American storytelling but lingers on in the Gullah tradition (see chapter 11).

6. Jack and the Animals Seek Their Fortune

Once on a time there was a boy named Jack, who set out to seek his fortune. He had not gone but a little way when he came to a horse. The horse said, "Where are you going, Jack?"

He said, "I'm going to seek my fortune. Won't you go along too?"

"Don't know, guess I will." So they walked along together.

By and by they came to a cow. The cow said, "Where are you going, Jack?"

He said, "I'm going to seek my fortune. Won't you go along too?"

"Don't know, guess I will." So they walked along together.

By and by they came to a ram. The ram said, "Where are you going, Jack?"

He said, "I'm going to seek my fortune. Won't you go along too?"

"Don't know, guess I will." So they walked along together.

By and by they came to a dog. The dog said, "Where are you going, Jack?"

"I am going to seek my fortune. Won't you go too?"

"Don't know, don't care if I do."

So they all walked along together. By and by they came to a cat. The cat said, "Where are you going, Jack?"

Jack said, "I'm going to seek my fortune. Won't you go too?"

"Don't know, guess I will." So they all walked along together.

By and by they came to a rooster. The rooster said, "Where are you going, Jack?"

"I'm going to seek my fortune. Won't you go too?"

"Don't know, don't care if I do." So they all walked along together.

They traveled along until it began to grow dark, and then they were looking for a place to spend the night, when they saw a log cabin in the edge of a woods.

Jack went up to the house and found the door unlocked, and went in. After looking about he found a good bed upstairs and plenty of good food in the cupboard. There was a fire on the hearth. As he could see no one living there, after he had eaten a good supper and fed all the animals, he began to make preparations for the night. First he led the horse out into the stable, and fed him some hay, for he found plenty of good hay on the mow. Then he took all the other animals into the house, and he found the door closed into the locker, so he stationed the dog under the table near the door, so that he might bite any one who might chance to enter the house. The cat lay down on the hearth, and the rooster perched on a large crossbeam, and then he stationed the cow at the foot of the stairs, and the ram at the top of the stairs that led to the loft. Then he covered up the fire, put out the light, and went to bed, and was soon fast asleep.

Now it happened that this valley was the home of two wicked robbers, who had gone out during the day in search of plunder. Late in the night Jack was awakened by a great noise, for the robbers had returned and opened the door, expecting to find things as usual. They were suddenly grabbed by the dog, who bit them furiously, barking all the while.

At last they managed to escape from him, and started to the fireplace, thinking to strike a light. One of the robbers tried to light a match by a coal which he thought he saw shining in the ashes; but this was the cat's eyes and as soon as she was molested she flew on them and scratched their faces dreadfully, till they were glad to escape from the fireplace.

They went from the fireplace toward the stairs, but as they passed under the rooster's perch he dropped very disagreeable material [*these words to be whispered*] upon them.

The robbers groped their way through the dark to the foot of the stairs, meaning to creep up to the bed and rest till morning, but just as they reached the stairs they were suddenly caught on the horns of the cow, and tossed up in the air. The ram called out, "Toss 'em up to me!" Before they lighted he caught them on his horns and tossed them up in the air.

And the cow called out, "Toss 'em down to me!" Before they lighted she caught them on her horns and tossed them up in the air.

Then the ram called out, "Toss 'em up to me!" And before they lighted he caught them on his horns [*etc., to be repeated ad libitum*]. And so they tossed them back and forth until they were all mangled and bloody.

At last they managed to escape from the cow's horns, and thought they would crawl off to the barn and spend the rest of the night. As they passed the dog in going to the door he gave them a parting snip, but they escaped from him and found the way out to the barn. When they tried to creep in at the door the horse began to kick them so dreadfully that they had to give that up, and were only just able to creep off to a fence corner, where they laid down and died.

As soon as Jack found that everything was quiet he went to sleep, and slept soundly till morn. After, he got up and dressed himself. By and by he looked about and found there was a large bag of gold under his bed, which had been stolen from time to time by the robbers.

So Jack kept the gold, was well provided for, and lived happily forever after with his faithful animals.

Newell 1888: 228–30. ATU 130. As told in Mansfield, Ohio, about 1855. Submitted by Fannie D. Bergen, Cambridge, Massachusetts. (See note on "Johnny-cake," in this chapter.) Jack also accompanies the animals in Scottish, Irish, and Appalachian renditions of this story, though the animals are alone in the well-known Grimm version, "The Bremen Town Musicians." Note that the line "Toss him up to me" has been appropriated from the rooster by the two horned animals. I do not know the significance of the detail, "He found the door closed into the locker."

7. The Forgetful Boy

A man had a boy who when he was sent on errands would forget what he was sent for. So one day, when he sent him to the butcher's to get a sheep's pluck, to make him remember he told him to keep a-saying, "Heart, liver, and lights."

So the boy started saying:

> Heart, liver, 'n' lights!
> Heart, liver, 'n' lights!

By and by he came across a man puking. He took him and gave him a whipping, and said, "You want I should puke up my heart, liver, and lights, do you?"

"No," said the boy; "what shall I say?"

And the man told him to say, "I wish they may never come up!"

So the boy went on, saying,

> Wish 'ey may never come up!
> Wish 'ey may never come up!

By and by he came across a man planting beans, and he took and whipped him and said, "You wish my beans should never come up, do you?"

The boy said, "No, what shall I say?"

"Say, 'I wish fifty-fold this year, and a hundred-fold next!'"

So the boy went on, saying:

> Wish fifty-fold this year,
> 'N' a hundred-fold next!
> Wish fifty-fold this year
> 'N' a hundred-fold next!

By and by he came across a funeral, and they took and whipped him, and said, "You wish fifty-fold to die this year and a hundred-fold next, do you?"

The boy said, "No, what shall I say?"

"Say, 'I wish they may never die!'"

So the boy went on, saying:

> Wish 'ey may never die!
> Wish 'ey may never die!

By and by he came across a man who was trying to kill two dogs, and he took and whipped him and said, "You wish the dogs should never die, do you?"

The boy said, "No, what shall I say?"

"Say, 'The dog and the bitch are going to be hanged!'"

So the boy went on, saying:

> The dog 'n' the bitch are go'n ter be hanged!
> The dog 'n' the bitch are go'n ter be hanged!

By and by he came across a wedding party, and they took and whipped him and said, "You call us a dog and a bitch, do you?"

The boy said, "No, what shall I say?"

"Say, 'I wish you may live happily together!'"

So the boy went on, saying:

> Wish y' may live happily together!
> Wish y' may live happily together!

By and by he came across two men who had fallen into a pit, and one of them had got out and was trying to get the other out. And he took and whipped him and said, "You wish we may live happily together in this pit, do you?"

The boy said, "No, what shall I say?"

"Say, 'One's out and I wish the other was out!'"

So the boy went on, saying:

> One's out 'n' I wish t' other w's out!
> One's out 'n' I wish t' other w's out!

By and by he came across a man with only one eye, and he took and whipped him till he killed him.

Kittredge and Hayward 1890: 292–93. ATU 1204/1696. This fairly popular tale is found throughout the South and Midwest. But this version comes from Massachusetts. It was submitted to the editor of the *Journal of American Folklore* with the following letter:

Dear Sir— Inclosed you will find a copy of one of the old stories I used to hear when I was a boy, as near as I can reproduce it by the aid of a cousin who used to hear it with me. My grandmother heard it in childhood at North Bridgewater, now Brockton. You will see that I have tried to give the exact words as they sounded to me, as nearly as I can represent them. I doubt this having any real value in the line of "folk-lore," but you can judge better than I. I don't remember any application that was made of the story then, but in repeating it now it seems to me it was told for a warning to forgetful boys. The exact form of expression in one or two places we cannot now recall, but have given it as nearly as possible. I have never met the story or any semblance of it in print or in conversation. I should be glad to know it survives anywhere, and if so, whether coming from the same source, and with what variations. I have fragments of others, some of which are certainly allied to the celebrated world-wide stories like Cinderella.

Yours very truly,
Silvanus Hayward.

Hayward here presents a tale that his grandmother might well have learned as a child in the late eighteenth century. Her particular version seems English in origin. The version in Joseph Jacobs's *More English Fairy Tales* ends less abruptly. The one-eyed man has the boy say, "The one side gives good light, I wish the other did." The boy next comes to a house, one side of which is on fire. Believing he must have set the fire, bystanders haul him off to prison. In the end a judge condemns him to die.

Grimm 143 is the same tale type, but with very different chants. Several other stories about simpletons can be found in succeeding chapters of this volume.

8. The Three Brothers and the Hag

Once upon a time there were three brothers who lived together. They were very poor. One day one of them said, "I will go and try to make my fortune." He went and travelled about for a long time. Finally he reached a house in which an old woman lived. He asked, "May I stay here over night?"

She said, "Yes, come in." He entered. She showed him to the room in which he was to rest and he soon went to sleep. During the night he heard a noise. He arose and crept softly to a chink, through which he saw a light shining. Then he saw the old crone sitting at a table and counting heaps of money which she kept hidden in her house. He crept back to bed and listened to the clinking of money. Soon he heard the old woman snoring, and when everything was quiet, he ran and searched for the treasure. He found it and carried it away.

While he was running to get far away from the old woman, he came to a meeting-house. The meeting-house said: "Sweep me."

"No," said he, "I cannot stay."

He walked on and soon he came to a field which said: "Weed me."

"No," said he, "I have no time," and went on.

Soon he came to a well which said: "Clean me."

"No," said he, "I cannot stay." He went on. At noon he came to a field in which there was a tree. He sat down under the tree and counted the money.

When the crone awoke and found both the treasure and the young man whom she had allowed to sleep under her roof gone, she went to pursue them. She passed the meeting-house and asked:

> Have you seen a boy
> With a wig, with a wag,
> With a long leather-bag,
> Who stole all the money
> Ever I had?

The meeting-house replied: "You will find him in yonder field under a tree counting his money." She went on and passed the field, which she asked:

> Have you seen a boy
> With a wig, with a wag,
> With a long leather-bag,
> Who stole all the money
> Ever I had?

The field replied: "You will find him in yonder field under a tree counting his money." She went on and came to the well. She asked the well:

> Have you seen a boy
> With a wig, with a wag,
> With a long leather-bag,
> Who stole all the money
> Ever I had?

The well replied: "You will find him in yonder field under a tree counting his money." She went on and finally reached the field. There she found the boy asleep under the tree. She cut off his head, took her treasures and carried them back home.

After some time the second boy said, "I will go and try to make my fortune." He went and travelled about for a long time. Finally he reached the house in which the old woman lived. He asked, "May I stay here over night?"

She said, "Yes, come in." He entered. She showed him to the room in which he was to rest and he soon went to sleep. During the night he too heard a noise. He arose and crept softly to the same chink, through which he saw a light shining. Then he saw the old crone sitting at the table and counting the heaps of money which she kept hidden in her house. He crept back to bed and listened to the clinking of money. Soon he heard the old woman snoring, and when everything was quiet, he ran and searched for the treasure. He found it and carried it away.

While he was running to get far away from the old woman, he came to the meeting-house. The meeting-house said: "Sweep me."

"No," said he, "I cannot stay."

He walked on and soon he came to the field which said: "Weed me."

"No," said he, "I have no time," and went on.

Soon he came to the well which said: "Clean me."

"No," said he, "I cannot stay." He went on. At noon he came to the field in which there was a tree. He sat down under the tree and counted the money.

When the crone awoke and found both the treasure and the young man whom she had allowed to sleep under her roof gone, she went to pursue them. She passed the meeting-house and asked:

> Have you seen a boy
> With a wig, with a wag,
> With a long leather-bag,
> Who stole all the money
> Ever I had?

The meeting-house replied: "You will find him in yonder field under a tree counting his money. She went on and passed the field, which she asked:

> Have you seen a boy
> With a wig, with a wag,
> With a long leather-bag,
> Who stole all the money
> Ever I had?

The field replied: "You will find him in yonder field under a tree counting his money." She went on and came to the well. She asked the well:

> Have you seen a boy
> With a wig, with a wag,
> With a long leather-bag,
> Who stole all the money
> Ever I had?

The well replied: "You will find him in yonder field under a tree counting his money." She went on and finally reached the field. There she found the boy asleep under the tree. She cut off his head, took her treasures and carried them back home.

After some time the third boy said, "I will go and try to make my fortune." He went and travelled about for a long time.

Finally he reached the house in which the old woman lived. He asked, "May I stay here over night?"

She said, "Yes, come in." He entered. She showed him to the room in which he was to rest and he soon went to sleep. During the night he too heard a noise. He arose and crept softly to the chink through which he saw a light shining. Then he saw the old crone sitting at a table and counting heaps of money which she kept hidden in her house. He crept back to bed and listened to the clinking of money. Soon he heard the old woman snoring, and when everything was quiet, he ran and searched for the treasure. He found it and carried it away.

While he was running to get far away from the old woman he came to a meeting-house. The meeting-house said: "Sweep me." It was a large meeting-house, and he knew it would take a long time to sweep it. Nevertheless, he stopped, and swept and cleaned it carefully. Then he went on.

He came to a field which said: "Weed me." It was a large field, and although he knew that it would take him a long time to weed it, he stopped and weeded the whole field.

He went on and came to a well which said: "Clean me." Although he was afraid the old woman would overtake him, he stopped and cleaned it thoroughly. He went on.

At noon he came to a field in which there was a tree. He sat down under the tree and counted his money.

When the crone awoke and found all her treasure and the young man, whom she had allowed to sleep under her roof, gone, she went to pursue him. She passed the meeting-house and asked:

> Have you seen a boy
> With a wig, with a wag,
> With a long leather-bag,
> Who stole all the money
> Ever I had?

The meeting-house did not reply, but threw stones at her and had almost killed her. It was all she could do to get away. She came to the field and asked:

> Have you seen a boy
> With a wig, with a wag,

> With a long leather-bag,
> Who stole all the money
> Ever I had?

But the field made a cloud of dust and stones which drifted into her face and almost blinded her. It was all she could do to get away. She went on and came to the well. She asked:

> Have you seen a boy
> With a wig, with a wag,
> With a long leather-bag,
> Who stole all the money
> Ever I had?

Then the water in the well began to rise and overflow. It took her down into the well, where she was drowned.

The boy went home with his treasure, and lived happily ever after.

Conant 1895: 143–44. ATU 480. Prof. L. Conant of the Worcester Polytechnic Institute heard this rather amoral story from a schoolmate at Littleton, Massachusetts, about 1827. I have expanded the text according to Conant's indications. The story is more commonly told about two girls, as in the Kentucky version in Leonard Roberts's *South from Hell-fer-Sartin* (1955: 65–68). A tale with a chorus to be chanted or sung is called a *cante fable*. Though this genre is generally considered rare, there are a number of *cante fables* in the various U.S. traditions. *Cante fable* versions of ATU 480 that emphasize the pursuit of the girls (or, as here, boys) probably derive from English tradition. There is also a very similar Eastern European tradition, identified as ATU 480A* (the asterisk is part of the number), involving three sisters, not two, but they go to rescue a baby brother who has been captured by a witch. As in the present story, the first two fail because they will not take time to perform services for the objects (apple tree, oven, etc.) that ask their help.

9. The Cat and the Mouse

> The cat and the mouse went into the oven together.
> The cat bit off the mouse's tail,
> and the mouse bit off the cat's thread.
> The mouse said, "Aye, gi' me my own taiiil again."

> "I woont without you go to the cow and get me some milk."

> "Titty mouse hop, and titty mouse run,
> To the cow I come.

Do cow gi' me milk, I give cat milk,
Cat gi' me my own taiiil again."

"I woont without you go to the barn and get me some hay."

"Do titty mouse hop, and titty mouse run,
To the barn I come.
Do barn gi' me hay,
I give cow hay, cow gi' me milk,
I give cat milk, cat gi' me my own taiiil again."

"I woont without you go to the blacksmith and get me a lock and key."

"Titty mouse hop, and titty mouse run,
To the blacksmith I come.
Do blacksmith gi' me lock and key,
I give barn lock and key, barn gi' me hay,
I give cow hay, cow gi' me milk,
I give cat milk, cat gi' me my own taiiil again."

"I woont without you go to the sea and get me some coal."

"Titty mouse hop, and titty mouse run,
To the sea I come.
Do sea gi' me coal,
I give blacksmith coal, blacksmith gi' me lock and key,
I give barn lock and key, barn gi' me hay,
I give cow hay, cow gi' me milk,
I give cat milk, cat gi' me my own taiiil again."

"I woont without you go to the cock and get me a feather."

"Titty mouse hop, and titty mouse run,
To the cock I come.
Do cock gi' me feather,
I give sea feather, sea gi' me coal,
I give blacksmith coal, blacksmith gi' me lock and key,
I give barn lock and key, barn gi' me hay,

I give cow hay, cow gi' me milk,
I give cat milk, cat gi' me my own taiiil again."

"I woont without you go to the miller and get me some corn."

"Titty mouse hop, and titty mouse run,
To the miller I come.
Do miller gi' me corn,
I give cock corn, cock gi' me feather,
I give sea feather, sea gi' me coal,
I give blacksmith coal, blacksmith gi' me lock and key,
I give barn lock and key, barn gi' me hay,
I give cow hay, cow gi' me milk,
I give cat milk, cat gi' me my own taiiil again."

The miller gave him some corn, and he gave it to the cock.
The cock gave him a feather, and he gave it to the sea.
The sea gave him some coal, and he gave it to the blacksmith.
The blacksmith gave him a lock and key, and he gave it to the barn.
The barn gave him some hay, and he gave it to the cow.
The cow gave him some milk, and he gave it to the cat.
And the cat gave him his own taiiil again.
But after all his trouble,
the tail was of no use
to the poor mouse.

Newell 1900: 228–30. ATU 2034. In his headnote to this tale, William Wells Newell says that this "familiar nursery tale was obtained by the editor of this Journal [i.e., Newell himself, almost certainly, though he had completed his stint as editor of the *Journal of American Folklore* by the time this item was published] many years ago from Miss Lydia R. Nichols, of Salem, Mass. (now deceased), and represents the story as current in New England at the time of the earliest memory of the reciter, about 1800." Cumulative tales like this one have proved especially popular with young children. This version probably has British roots. Halpert and Widdowson (926–43), with reference to the tale of The Old Woman and Her Pig (ATU 2030), have much of value to offer concerning cumulative tales. Other cumulative tales will be found in succeeding chapters.

10. Johnny-Cake

Once upon a time, there was an old man, and an old woman, and a little boy. One morning the old woman made a Johnny-cake and put it in the oven to bake. And she said to the little boy, "You watch the Johnny-cake while your father and I go out to work in the garden." So the old man and old woman went out and began to hoe potatoes and left the little boy to tend the oven.

But he didn't watch it all the time, and all of a sudden he heard a noise and he looked up and the oven door popped open, and out of the oven jumped Johnny-cake and went rolling along, end over end, towards the open door of the house. The little boy ran to shut the door, but Johnny-cake was too quick for him and rolled through the door, down the steps, and out into the road, long before the little boy could catch him. The little boy ran after him as fast as he could clip it, crying out to his father and mother, who heard the uproar and threw down their hoes and gave chase too. But Johnny-cake outran all three a long way and soon was out of sight, while they had to sit down, all out of breath, on a bank to rest.

On went Johnny-cake, and by and by he came to two well-diggers, who looked up from their work and called out: "Where ye going, Johnny-cake?"

He said: "I've outrun an old man, and an old woman, and a little boy, and I can outrun you too-o-o!"

"Ye can, can ye? we'll see about that!" said they, and they threw down their picks and ran after him, but they couldn't catch up with him, and soon they had to sit down by the roadside to rest.

On ran Johnny-cake, and by and by he came to two ditch-diggers, who were digging a ditch. "Where ye going, Johnny-cake?" said they.

He said: "I've outrun an old man, and an old woman, and a little boy, and two well-diggers, and I can outrun you too-o-o!"

"Ye can, can ye? we'll see about that!" said they, and they threw down their spades, and ran after him too. But Johnny-cake soon outstripped them also, and seeing they could never catch him they gave up the chase and sat down to rest.

On went Johnny-cake, and by and by he came to a bear. The bear said: "Where ye going, Johnny-cake?"

He said: "I've outrun an old man, and an old woman, and a little boy, and two well-diggers, and two ditch-diggers, and I can outrun you too-o-o!"

"Ye can, can ye?" growled the bear; "we'll see about that!" and trotted as fast as his legs could carry him after Johnny-cake, who never stopped to look behind him. Before long the bear was left so far behind that he saw he might as well give up the hunt first as last, so he stretched himself out by the roadside to rest.

On went Johnny-cake, and by and by he came to a wolf. The wolf said: "Where ye going, Johnny-cake?"

He said: "I've outrun an old man, and an old woman, and a little boy, and two well-diggers, and two ditch-diggers, and a bear and I can outrun you too-o-o!"

"Ye can, can ye?" snarled the wolf; "we'll see about that!" and he set into a gallop after Johnny-cake, who went on and on so fast that the wolf, too, saw there was no hope of catching him and lay down to rest.

On went Johnny-cake, and by and by he came to a fox that lay quietly in a corner of the fence. The fox called out in a sharp voice, but without getting up: "Where ye going, Johnny-cake?"

He said: "I've outrun an old man, and an old woman, and a little boy, and two well-diggers, and two ditch-diggers, and a bear and a wolf, and I can outrun you too-o-o!"

The fox said: "I can't quite hear you, Johnny-cake, won't you come a leetle closer?" turning his head a little to one side.

Johnny-cake stopped his race, for the first time, and went a little closer and called out in a very loud voice: *I've outrun an old man, and an old woman, and a little boy, and two well diggers, and two ditch-diggers, and a bear, and a wolf, and I can outrun you too-o-o!*

"Can't quite hear you; won't you come a *leetle* closer?" said the fox in a feeble voice, and he stretched out his neck towards Johnny-cake and put one paw behind his ear.

Johnny-cake came up close, and leaning toward the fox screamed louder than before: "I'VE OUTRUN AN OLD MAN, AND AN OLD WOMAN, AND A LITTLE BOY, AND TWO WELL-DIGGERS, AND TWO DITCH-DIGGERS, AND A BEAR, AND A WOLF, AND I CAN OUTRUN YOU TOO-O-O!"

"You can, can you?" yelped the fox, and he snapped up Mr. Johnny-cake in his sharp teeth in a twinkling of an eye.

Bergen 1889: 60–63. ATU 2025. Fanny D. Bergen, who submitted this story to the *Journal of American Folklore,* recalled her grandfather and aunts telling it repeatedly in northern Ohio in the 1850s:

> Johnny-cake's answer to the various ones whom he encounters in his wild race was repeated to us in a hoarse chant and, I remember, gave the impression of being loudly and tauntingly called back to the listener, by the rapidly vanishing Johnny-cake.
> The final word, too, of this chorus, was always pronounced very slowly, in a specially loud tone. At the climax, when the sly fox grabs the unsuspecting Johnny-cake, the narrator would make a spring at the rapt listeners to the tale and scream OH! so as to make the children jump . . . . If some child to whom our story was unknown was for the first time present, our attention would be so divided between listening to the story and watching to see our little comrade start, that we were pretty sure to lose guard over ourselves and we too would involuntarily jump and laugh in concert.

Nineteenth-century versions with the fox eating the Johnny-cake on the way across the river are also presented in early volumes of the *Journal of American Folklore.*

Emeline Brightman Russell of Goliad, Texas (see chapter 9), a contemporary of Fannie Bergen's aunts, tells a version of "Johnny-cake" dating from approximately the same era and in some ways remarkably similar to the present version, including the episode in which the wily wolf, in this case, pretending to be deaf, calls Johnny-cake close so he can devour him. Mrs. Russell precedes her [written] narrative with the following description:

> It is necessary in explanation to the little ones of the present generation to say how the johnny-cake was baked in the time when Grandma was a little girl. People would have an oak or hickory board, much like the middle of a barrel head, about six inches across. On this board they would pat out corn-meal dough about an inch thick, and then spread cream all over it with a knife and make it smooth, and put the board down on the hearth before a bed of coals or hot fire and bake the edges first. Then, when the dough was baked about the edges, they would set the board up straight with a flat iron behind it to hold it up. When the lower side was brown, they would turn the upper side down so that the johnny-cake might bake an even brown. When it was browned just right, they would take it up on the table and run a case knife under it to loosen it from the board. Next they turned the board upside down on a clean table; then they slipped the johnny-cake, brown side down, back on the board, after smoothing it again with cream, and set it up again in front of the iron, turning it once and baking it until it was a nice brown. And there never was sweeter bread to eat with butter or milk than this. (Dobie 1927: 31)

11. The Three Little Pigs

Once, an old sow had three little pigs.

The first little pig said, "Mother, may I go out and seek my fortune?"

"No, no, the Old Fox'll eat you ALL up."

"No, he won't if you build me a house of straw."

So she posted off and built him a house of straw.

Then along came the Old Fox, and said,

"Piggy, Piggy, *please* let me in."

But Piggy would not.

"If you don't, I'll go up on top of your house, and blow and blow and knock it down, and eat you ALL up."

Piggy would not.

So he went up on top of the house, and blew and blew and knocked it down, and ate Piggy ALL up.

The second little pig said, "Mother, may I go out and seek my fortune?"

"No, no, the Old Fox'll eat you ALL up, as he did your little brother."

"No, he won't if you build me a house of wood."

So she posted off and built him a house of wood.

Then along came the Old Fox, and said,

"Piggy, Piggy, *please* let me in."

But Piggy would not.

"If you don't, I'll go up on top of your house, and blow and blow and knock it down, and eat you ALL up."

Piggy would not.

Then he went up on top of the house, and blew and blew and knocked it down, and ate poor Piggy ALL up.

Then the third little pig said, "Mother, may I go out and seek my fortune?"

"No, no, the Old Fox'll eat you ALL up as he did your little brothers."

"No, he won't if you build me a house of stone."

So she posted off and built him a house of stone.

Then along came the Old Fox and said,

"Piggy, Piggy, please let me in "

But Piggy would not.

"If you don't, I'll go up on top of your house, and blow and blow and knock it down, and eat you ALL up."

Piggy would not.

So he went up on top of the house, and blew and blew till he blew his whistle off, but he couldn't blow it down, so he came down, and said:

"Piggy, Piggy, don't you want some nice apples?"

Piggy said, "Yes, I do."

"Well! come over to my house in the morning, and I'll give you ALL you can pack home."

So Piggy went over in the morning, before he was up, and stole ALL he had, and took 'em home, and peeled 'em, and threw the peelings out the door, and turned the key just as Old Fox came along.

"Piggy, Piggy, where did you get such nice apples?"

"I went over to your house before you were up, and stole ALL you had."

"Piggy, Piggy, don't you want some nice potatoes?"

Piggy said, "Yes, I do."

"Well! come over to my house in the morning, and I'll give you ALL you can pack home."

So Piggy went over in the morning, before he was up, and stole ALL he had, and took 'em home, and peeled 'em, and threw the peelings out the door, and turned the key just as Old Fox came along.

"Piggy, Piggy, where did you get such nice potatoes?"

"I went over to your house before you were up, and stole ALL you had."

"Piggy, Piggy, don't you want some nice fish?"

Piggy said, "Yes, I do."

"Well! come over to my house in the morning, and I'll give you ALL you can pack home."

So Piggy went over in the morning, before he was up, and stole ALL he had, and took 'em home, and scaled 'em, and threw the scales out the door, and turned the key just as Old Fox came along.

"Piggy, Piggy, where did you get such nice fish?"

"Why, I went down to the river, and held my tail in all night, and when they nibbled, I jerked."

"Do you think I could catch any?"

"Yes, you could."

So he went down to the river, and held his tail in ALL night, and in the morning it was frozen fast, and he couldn't get it out.

By an' by Piggy came down with her tea-kettle to get water to make her coffee, and there he was frozen in, tight and fast.

"Piggy, Piggy, please chop me out."

"No, no, you'd eat me ALL up."

"No, no, Piggy. I wouldn't disturb you anymore."

So at last, she went back to the house, and got her hatchet, and chopped and chopped till she got him out.

"Now-I've-got-you! Now-I'll-eat-you-ALL-up."

But Piggy ran and ran, and banged the door, and put her back against it just as Old Fox came up.

"Piggy, Piggy, please let my nose in, it's so cold," he kept saying.

So, at last, she let his nose in.

"Oh, Piggy! it smells so nice in here, please let my eyes in."

So she let his eyes in.

"Oh, Piggy! it looks so beautiful in here, please let my ears in."

So she let his ears in.

"Oh, Piggy! the kettle sounds so nice, please let my whole head in."

So she let his whole head in.

"Oh, Piggy! my head's so good and warm, please let my fore legs in."

So she let his fore legs in.

"Oh, Piggy! my fore legs are so good and warm, please let my body in."

So she let his body in.

Then he jumped, and his hind legs and tail came in.

"Now-I've-got-you. NOW-I'll-eat-you-ALL-up!" *(Accompanied by a jump.)*

"Oh! what's that I hear coming? A pack of hounds!"

"Oh, Piggy! where'll I hide? Where'll I hide?"

"Just jump into my churn."

So he jumped into her churn, and she took the kettle of boiling water, and poured it over him, and then she churned and she churned till he went ALL to butter.

Owen 1902: 63–65. ATU 124/2. As told to Mary A. Owen "by Mrs. A. C. Ford, an old lady of eighty-two years. She had it from her grandmother, who in turn had it from hers, one of the colony of Scotch-Irish that came to this country, reaching Londonderry, N.H., in 1718. Mrs. Ford says that in her childhood the tale was a favorite with New England children, or, at least, with Maine and New Hampshire children." The formulaic quality of the story, well captured in this rendering, continues to make it a favorite with American children. The Tail-Fisher episode as an independent story (ATU 2) often attaches to the Br'er Rabbit cycle. Either the third piggy has a sex change, or it is his mother who comes to the river for coffee water. All three English versions in Briggs's *Dictionary of British Folk-Tales* end with the villain down the chimney, as in the Disney cartoon. But the ending with boiling water poured on the trapped fox (or wolf) is quite common in field-collected American versions.

Part II

THE IBERIAN FOLKTALE
IN THE UNITED STATES

Amerian folktale traditions that derive from Spanish or more generally from Iberian tradition show great consistency, though each tradition has its own peculiar stamp as well. This is not surprising since all derive ultimately from a common, richly romantic, Iberian tradition. Many of the same tales are found in Puerto Rico, in the Hispanic Southwest, in Louisiana, and among the Cape Verdeans of New England. These include the popular märchen such as Cinderella (ATU 510), The Devil's Daughter (ATU 313), The Two Sisters (ATU 480), and many variations on the theme of Juan del Oso (John the Bear) an Iberian oikotype (particular ethnic or national version) of ATU 301B. Also popular are numbskull stories, formulaic tales, and wisdom tales. The popular Catholicism of the culture often finds expression in the tales, with the Virgin or St. Joseph becoming the magic helper or donor and the devil becoming the villain.

The island of Puerto Rico has been a very rich source of stories, especially the romantic märchen and the Juan Bobo stories. In the mid twentieth century Puerto Ricans came to major east coast cities in large numbers. In New York and elsewhere educators have collected tales from the Puerto Rican community to be adapted as educational materials in schools established for the education of ghettoized children.

Tales from the Spanish Southwest were collected intensively in the early to mid-twentieth century by Aurelio M. Espinosa (e.g., 1914), José Manuel Espinosa (1937), and Juan B. Rael ([1957]), and more recently by Marta Weigel (1980, 1988), Nasario García (1992, 1997), and members of the Texas Folklore Society (e.g., Boatright 1953, 1954; Hiester 1961). Though this tradition is basically Mexican, without as much influence from American Indian, Anglo- or African American sources as one might expect, at least one of our examples draws on Indian and African American elements to produce a startling rendition of the Tar Baby story.

Of the three Hispanic traditions represented in this collection, the Louisiana Spanish, brought there by Canary Islanders (Isleños), is the least well documented, and probably the least robust. The tales here included were collected approximately fifty years ago, and even then the pickings were a little slim.

The Iberian tradition is also a strong component in Cape Verde storytelling. The Portuguese brought to the Cape Verde Islands the same stories that the Spaniards and Canary Islanders brought to Hispanic parts of the New World. The Cape Verdeans, in turn, brought these tales to New England. But sojourn off the African coast has strongly colored the Cape Verde repertoire. Instead of tales about the rascal Pedro Urdemalas or the numbskull Juan Bobo, Cape Verdeans tell tales about the rascal Nho Lob' (Brother Wolf) and his numbskull nephew Tobinh'. A third infusion into the Cape Verdean tradition came from the Arabian Nights Entertainment. Galland's translation into French made these stories popular in the early eighteenth century. Many tales entered oral tradition on the Iberian Peninsula and from there were brought to Cape Verde by the Portuguese, where the tradition may have received reinforcement from Africa and the Near East. In any case, these tales have survived and thrived, and Cape Verdeans now regard them as a characteristic and distinctive part of their communal repertoire.

CHAPTER 2

PUERTO RICO

The Oldest Depository of American Tales

Ponce de Leon established the first Spanish settlement in Puerto Rico at Caparra in 1508, only fifteen years after Columbus returned home from his first voyage, and the present capital, San Juan, was founded in 1521. Americans occupied the island in the Spanish American War of 1898, and the Spanish ceded it outright in the Treaty of Paris that ended that war. Over the next sixty years Puerto Rico was progressively integrated into the fabric of the United States, acquiring home rule, status as a free commonwealth, and U.S. citizenship for its people. And so, though politically one of the newest parts of the United States, in terms of European settlement it is the oldest.

As might be expected of such a Hispanic settlement now nearly five hundred years old, Puerto Rico has a strong and rich folktale tradition. In 1913 the New York Academy of Sciences and the Insular Government of Puerto Rico came together to conduct a total scientific survey of all aspects of Puerto Rico and the Virgin Islands, including the folk culture. The anthropological part of the survey was entrusted to Franz Boas, who commissioned J. Alden Mason, a linguistician at the Field Museum in Chicago, to oversee the collection of folktales and folk poetry and song. Mason spent over a year, 1914–1915, in Puerto Rico.

Mason apparently utilized two principal collecting methods to gather this wide array of folk materials. For his own field collecting he concentrated on the mountain town of Utuado, with its peasant Jíbaro population, and the coastal town of Loíza, with its black population. In these towns adults wrote out material for him, and he recorded mostly adult men on wax cylinders. The bulk of the collection, however, came from schoolchildren all across the island. Working with the Puerto Rican Department of Education, Mason coordinated a massive effort in which teachers in the various municipal districts had their students write out the material. Mason himself oversaw this project, traveling to towns and villages and up mountainsides to talk with teachers and students in schools all over the island and to listen to their riddles, songs, and tales.

The result was a truly monumental collection. Indeed it is impossible to conceive how so much was accomplished in scarcely more than a year. When he returned to the United States Mason immediately began publishing this body of material in the *Journal of American Folklore*, working with Aurelio M. Espinosa, associate editor for Hispanic folklore. The first riddles appeared in 1916, the last folktales in 1929. The folktales alone fill 570 pages.

The present chapter presents six hitherto untranslated tales from the Mason collection illustrating the beauty and breadth of the tradition he documented. It also includes a tale each from two other collectors, Rafael Ramírez De Arellano, who collected even earlier than Mason, and Ralph Boggs, who collected in 1927.

12. The Basil Maiden

Well, sir, once there was a carpenter who had three daughters, all of them pretty. They lived not far from the king's palace, in a little house with a garden. In that garden were all kinds of flowers, and also a beautiful bed of basil.

Now, the carpenter's work took him away from his house much more than he liked, and that's why the three girls were often left by themselves to work at home.

In this city there was a king who was always butting in and asking questions and putting riddles to whoever was around or crossed his path.

One morning the king went out for a walk. He was passing by the little house when he saw Carmen, the oldest daughter watering the bed of basil. When he saw the girl, the king asked her,

> Fair maiden, you water that basil with care:
> Tell me, how many leaves grow there?

The poor girl was so embarrassed she ran behind the house without answering.

The next day he walked past there again, but this time the second daughter, María, was watering the basil, so the king asked her the same question and the girl responded in the same way.

On the following day Pepita, the youngest of the three, was watering the basil. She was also by far the prettiest and nicest. As soon as the king saw her he said,

> Fair maiden, you water that basil with care:
> Tell me, how many leaves grow there?

Immediately Pepita responded to him like this:

> To your kind riddle, sir, I reply:
> How many stars are there in the sky?

Well, the king had thought she would respond the way her sisters had, and he was very embarrassed not to have a come-back for the girl. So he left, promising himself that he would get even.

A few days later the king disguised himself like a candy man and set out to hawk candy in the neighborhood where the three girls lived. Since they all had terrible sweet tooths, as soon as they heard the candy man hawking his wares they went to call him. When the candy man went into the girls' house he said he was selling his candy for kisses, and only for kisses. The two older sisters left the room in a huff, but the youngest one stayed behind, bargaining with the candy man. Finally she agreed to give him a kiss for each of the candies she wanted from his tray.

The king went back to the castle, changed his clothes, and waited till it was time to water the bed of basil.

When watering time came, he walked past the little house and said to Pepita,

> Fair maiden, you water that basil with care:
> Tell me, how many leaves grow there?

And Pepita responded:

> To your kind riddle, sir, I reply:
> How many stars are there in the sky?

The king answered:

> I've got another, and it's a dandy:
> How many kisses for a piece of candy.

Well, Pepita was hurt and embarrassed, and she ran into the house.

Some days passed without the king showing up at the garden again. But Pepita found out that he was sick. Then she decided to get even with him. She disguised herself as Death and went to the palace with a mule. She managed to gain entrance to the king's room, where she told him, "I have come to get you. Your days are numbered."

The king begged her to let him live. He'd do anything, he said, to stay in this world a few years more.

Then Pepita told him that the only way to save himself was to kiss her mule under the tail. Since the king wanted to live a long time, he lifted the tail and began to kiss the mule. He gave it a lot of kisses. Death had said that he would live a year for each kiss.

Pepita went off with the mule, and the king began to get better and got completely well.

Right away he set off down the street to the garden. There he met Pepita watering the bed of basil, and he asked her,

> Maiden, watering the basil with care,
> Say how many leaves are growing there?

And Pepita responded:

> To your kind riddle, sir, I reply:
> How many stars are there in the sky?

The king answered:

> I've got another, and it's a dandy:
> How many kisses for a piece of candy.

And Pepita shot back:

> Let's see if you dare crack this nut:
> How many kisses on my old mule's butt?

The king now realized that Pepita was a very smart girl and that she would suit him very well for a queen, but still he wanted to get even. So he sent for the carpenter to come. And he told him that he would like to marry his daughter, but only on condition that she come to the palace neither naked nor clothed, and neither in a coach, nor on horseback, nor walking. Otherwise, he was going to kill both father and daughter. The poor carpenter went home very sad. But when Pepita found out what had happened she sent to find a fishnet, and she put that on. Then she told her father to tie her to the neck of her mule. And that's how she went to the palace. So the king saw how clever she was and how she'd make a wonderful queen, and he married her. And they lived . . .

> Happy ever after
> In a palace nice
> And had me over
> For pheasant on rice.

Ramírez de Arellano 1926: 49–52. ATU 879 (H875**A). Translated by editor. Ramírez, who began collecting about 1905, does not identify storytellers. The colloquial character of the Spanish suggests that he tried to write down the tales from dictation, just as he heard them.

This novelle is relatively unknown in English-language and Germanic traditions, but very popular in the Iberian tradition of both the old world and new, and in the Mediterranean tradition generally. Sometimes it leads into ATU 875, the story of the wise queen who nevertheless violates her husband's interdiction against meddling with his decisions: banished from the castle, she is allowed to take with her the one thing she prizes most, and takes her husband (see "The Clever Daughter" in chapter 16, below). In his Spanish American tale type index Terrence Leslie Hansen assigns this particular combination of two tales the type number H875**A.

13. Juan Bobo and the Riddling Princess

All this has happened many times before, but this time it happened in that noble and faithful municipality, Rabid City, in the province of Cur, in the kingdom of Going-to-the-Dogs, in the reign of the great king Don Pedro Growl. There was in this kingdom a boy called Juan, a fool like many another, a bobo.

Now the king had a beautiful daughter who was blind in one eye and cross-eyed in the other. The king put out a notice telling the Rabid Citizens that he would give a handsome dowry and the hand of the most beautiful Princess Rabies (which in their language means *Rosebud*) to the man,

whoever he might be,
>> whether deaf in the knees,
>>> or squint-eared,
>>>> or lame-sided:
> he would give his gorgeous daughter as a bride to
>> whoever unriddled the riddle she posed,
>>> and posed in turn a riddle she could not unriddle.

With Her Cleverness herself would he reward the one who entered and won.

"Ay, Madre," said Juan Bobo, "I'm going riddling."

"Where is it you think you're going, you donkey-brain? Are you tired of all the ways you used to worry me, and ready to start tormenting me in some new way? Let's see if you can go to bed!"

But the foolish boy made a bundle with his one nightshirt and headed off for the city where they were promising a princess. As there were no roads, he wandered over mountains and through wilderness until he came to the edge of the sea. There he saw a little fish flopping around on the beach. He picked it up and tossed it in the water.

"Thank you, Juan Bobo," said a husky voice. It was the fish's mother. "God preserve you from wolves and other wild animals."

He went on his way, well pleased with that good wish. Soon he came to the shore of a river, tried to ford it, and couldn't. Then he spotted an old horse standing high on the bank. He realized that it wanted a drink but couldn't get down to the water, so Juan filled his hat and gave it water to drink.

"Thank you, Bobo of all bobos," said the horse—and, by the way, it was all skin and bones. "Help me down to the river, and then get on my back."

Well, Juan, being a bobo, did exactly that, and the horse took off. It was going so fast that it would have trampled on some baby pigeons if that bobo on its back hadn't seen them in time. But Juan did see them and turned the horse aside.

"They've fallen out of their nest," said the horse. "There it is, up in that tree there, the one with its crown up there in the clouds. See, their mother's crying for them. Climb up and take them back to their mother."

So that's what the bobo did, climbing and climbing. He was gone on this difficult ascent for six days, feeding himself on fruit he picked from the tree. When he came down exactly six days later, he found the horse, all skin and bones, still waiting. He got on its back and it took off so fast that in the blink of an eye they came to the city ruled by the king who had promised his daughter in marriage. Juan noticed that inside the great gate of the city there was a wall of human heads. They were the ones who couldn't unriddle the riddles posed by the princess, nor pose a riddle that she couldn't unriddle.

Without a word to anybody, Juan Bobo headed straight for the palace. But before he got far he spotted a huge bonfire, a full league across, burning in front of the royal castle. It was fed with the bodies of those who had tried their hand at riddling.

Juan Bobo stuck his spurs in the bony flank of his horse and—oh, to have seen it—it jumped right across and landed in the courtyard, to the astonishment of everybody there.

"Whoosh, Whoosh," panted the horse.

"Here I am," said Juan, "to riddle and not be unriddled."

"Stranger, as you came through our fair city didn't you wonder about the piles of heads and bodies that you saw?" [someone asked him].

But he gave this guy an order: "I've come to riddle and not be unriddled."

They brought him to the king, who looked up and down in disdain at this bobo wearing a coat made of mattress ticking. Just then the princess came in. She lost no time in posing her riddle:

> Though not from so high as a star,
> Still I fall from on high,
> And I am, for the man who finds me,
> The apple of his eye.
> But you, with your foolish rashness,
> Bold stranger at my door,
> Will surrender your head to my father,
> As wiser men have, before.

"I've got one in my pack," said Juan. "It's a *star apple*, a star apple, by God." And he pulled one of the delicious maroon-colored fruit out of his bag.

So the princess had lost the first round: star apple was indeed the answer to her riddle. And immediately Juan said,

> You can pump me all you want,
> Or go and ask your kin,
> But the answer is so easy
> To miss it is a sin.

They couldn't unriddle it. Juan Bobo, laughing all the while, gave them three days. They consulted the great wise men. They sent emissaries to all the countries, discovered and undiscovered. Nobody knew. They gave up and admitted defeat.

Then Juan Bobo told them: "If you make a mistake and eat a gourd instead, it'll kill you. It's *pumpkin*, by God, a pumpkin."

They all agreed that a pumpkin had to be the right answer. "The bobo is mine," said the princess.

"You're going to have to suck your thumbs a bit longer," said the king. And then to Juan: "The other day, while the princess was taking a walk on the beach, she lost a ring. And the winning riddler has to unriddle where it is and bring it back."

Figuring that he could escape on his horse, Juan said, "Give me a little time."

He went out into the courtyard, hopped on, and galloped away. He spurred the horse and it took off like lightning.

When they came to the ocean the horse stopped dead, planting its hooves on the beach.

"Now is no time to stop. You can't be tired. Giddyap, horse."

But the horse said to him, "Look how you're talking. I'm no more horse than you are. Light down, foolish boy." And he turned into a caballero (the horse, that is: Juan already was one). He pulled out a long, strange-looking whistle and blew a long, ear-splitting blast on it. Suddenly all the fish were there at the edge of the beach.

"Please, Señores," said the horse-caballero, "which of you knows anything about the ring of the Biscay princess?"

"I don't know, I don't know," they all answered.

"We need the grouper," said the juey, the giant crab.

So the horse-caballero blew his whistle again. Immediately the grouper showed up with his huge, bulging stomach. "Do you know anything about the ring of the Biscay princess?"

"I was just about to get it when the porgy snapped it up right under my nose," said the grouper. "So I brought them both, the ring and the porgy. Here they are." And he spit them out on the spot.

Crazy with joy, Juan Bobo ran to the palace and gave the ring to the king.

"There's still one little thing," said the king. "You will have to pick her out from a whole crowd of girls that I will show you." The king had set up a search for all the cross-eyed girls in his kingdom and in all others. He had taken such care in selecting them that they all looked exactly alike.

You can imagine what a tight spot Juan was in. But suddenly three young birds fluttered through the window and landed on one of the girls, settling on her head and on each shoulder. Juan recognized the three birds that he had helped to their nest.

"Oh, wonder of wonders, my darling," cried the king proudly. "Even the birds come to celebrate your beauty."

Nobody could deny that Juan had picked out the princess. There was nothing for the king to do but let Juan and her get married.

When the king died, Juan was chosen king. He ruled and governed his people with wisdom, without being absolutely absolute in his rule. What I am trying to say is, he was a model king. And he didn't forget his mother either. He had her come live in the castle!

Mason and Espinosa 1922–1929: 35: 23–25. ATU 531/554/851. Translated by editor. Mason, who collected the tale about 1914, supplies no information about the teller. This is one of some seventy tales about Juan Bobo, a generally good-hearted but weak-brained lad who regularly stumbles into good luck, that Mason collected. Like many Puerto Rican märchen, the story is a composite, in this case a combination of three classic märchen types—ATU 554, The Grateful Animals and ATU 851, The Princess Who Cannot Solve the Riddle, with the addition of the magic horse from ATU 531, Ferdinand the True and Ferdinand the False. The tales are intricately interwoven. The story starts out like 851, with the hero determined to answer the princess's riddle at any cost. But, as the hero travels, he is kind to animals on three occasions. One of the animals is the magic horse that will be his helper. After arriving at the palace, he must perform the three tasks typical of the Grateful Animals tale type before he can win the princess. The first of these tasks is the riddling contest (ATU 851). He solves the riddle by his own innocent common sense, in a way appropriate to the riddling stories (which are novelle rather than wonder tales). But for the other two tasks he needs the help of the animals that he has befriended. And, as in Ferdinand the True, the horse turns out to be an enchanted human.

The tale is unusual in the amount of verbal play and sheer silliness it includes. There may well be a literary version somewhere behind this version. The riddles are not riddles in the conventional sense, since they do not actually describe the object that is the answer. Rather, they are a form of charade, perhaps, in which the guesser must identify the syllables of the answer buried within the wording of the verse. A literal translation of the princess's riddle would be:

> I fell [*caí*] from a tall tree;
> All men are myths [*mitos*].
> Riddle me how,
> If that head of yours, child of God,
> Is not blind to the answer,
> Foolish and rash as it [your head] is.
> From others smarter than you,
> My father has cut off the heads.

The answer is *caimito*, star apple.
And Juan's:

> Do I want to use a ladder [es-*cala*] to climb
> That on which your power rests [se *basa*]?
> Unriddle that, my princess,
> Worthy daughter of your race.

The answer is *calabaza*, gourd or pumpkin. In the Spanish, Juan's riddle is also a subtle proposal of marriage—would it be a good idea for me to climb up and stand beside you as your husband and so your equal?

The American folklorist Christine Goldberg has done a far-ranging study of European riddle tales, especially AT[U] 851 (1993).

14. Three Tales of Pedro Urdemalas

A. Pedro and the Magic Kettle

One time there was a man who did many awful things.

One day, when he didn't have any money, he thought of a way to get some. He found a kettle and took it out on the mountain. There he built a fire, set the kettle on the fire, and put some beans into it to boil. As soon as they started boiling he went out onto the road with the kettle and set it down right there in the middle of the road.

Pretty soon three caballeros appeared. They asked Pedro what he was doing, and he replied, "I am cooking my dinner."

"How can you cook your dinner in a kettle with no fire under it?"

"This kettle doesn't need fire. If it did, the water wouldn't be boiling now."

The men wanted to get that kettle and they begged Pedro to sell it to them. But he told them he couldn't sell it because it was the best capital that he could possibly have. But finally the men offered him thousands of pesos and Pedro agreed to sell it. They handed the money over to Pedro and went on their way, delighted with their kettle. And Pedro jumped for joy at having done such an awful thing.

After a while the men had to prepare their dinner, so they filled the kettle with water and rice and set it on the road. But the water did not boil. They hurried back to get a refund from the man who had sold it to them, because it didn't work. But they didn't find him.

B. Pedro and Juan the Crafty

One time Pedro de Urdemalas had sworn he was going to kill Juan the Crafty. Well, a day came when Juan the Crafty saw Pedro coming in his direction. He didn't know how to get away, so he put a big rock on his head. When Pedro came up he said, "Oh, Pedro, old buddy, holding this rock up is killing me. But if I let it go, the sky will crash down."

"Well," said Pedro, "pay me my twenty pesetas and the sky won't crash on you."

"O.K. Hold up this rock for me while I go home and find the money for you. But be careful. Don't let it slip."

So Pedro took it on his head and stood there being careful not to let the sky fall in. Hours and hours went by, and Juan didn't come back. Pedro kept getting more and more tired and he could tell his strength was running out. Finally, when it was already dark and he was totally worn out, he said, "Oh, let it fall," and plopped the rock off his head. The sky did not fall down, and Pedro swore vengeance on Juan. He kept after him without letup, and finally Pedro did play a good one on Juan the Crafty.

C. Pedro and the Giant

Now this Pedro was a fellow who was always boasting about how strong and brave he was. Of course he was neither one, but he was clever, clever enough to trick anyone who came his way. One day he went to look for a job with a giant who used to hire anybody strong enough to keep up with him. The giant was taken in by Pedro's bluster, and he went ahead and hired him, telling him that all he had to do was help out with the chores.

On the first day he suggested that Pedro fill two barrels with water. Pedro grabbed a shovel and, doing nothing about the barrels, set to work digging a trench.

"What are you doing, Pedro?" the giant asked.

"Well," said Pedro, "I'm going to bring the river to the house, 'cause I'm not about to haul water every day in these dinky little barrels."

"Oh, Pedro, you are going to drown me in my own house. Forget about the water. You sure knew what would get you out of that job, didn't you, Pedro?"

The next day the two went out to gather firewood. In no time at all the giant had gathered a big bundle of wood, so he sat down to wait for Pedro. He waited and waited, and finally went to see what was keeping him. "What are you doing, Pedro?" he asked.

"I'm cutting this rattan to wrap it around all that brush out there and drag it back with me."

"Well, quit it," said the giant in dismay. "I'm not going to let you bring pests to the house. You aren't gathering any more firewood."

The giant realized that he hadn't come up with anything that Pedro couldn't do. So one day he told him that tomorrow he would have to drill a hole with his finger in a palm tree he had in his courtyard. That night Pedro was thinking about how to pull this one off. He got a drill, drilled a hole all the way through the tree, and plugged it with fish bait. When the moment of trial came he calmly and coolly stuck his finger through the hole in the trunk of the palm tree.

Finally Pedro challenged the giant to an archery competition, claiming he could shoot farther than the giant. The giant took the first shot. Now Pedro knew that his arm was nowhere near as strong as the giant's, but Pedro also remembered hearing the giant say that his grandmother was the oldest woman in France. So he stepped up to the line as if he had every intention of winning, took out an arrow, and said:

> Fly, Fly, Fly,
> As straight as a lance.
> Hit the oldest old woman
> Alive in France.

The giant grabbed his hand and said, "Don't shoot. You're going to kill my old granny that I love so much. Wait right here till I order lunch for you. But don't do anything else to help me."

And that was that. But we know this is the way our famous old Pedro has always managed to get by.

Mason and Espinosa 1922–1929: 35: 36; 43; 49–50. A. ATU 1539 [K112.1]; B. 1530; C. 1049/1085/1063A. Collected by J. Alden Mason in Puerto Rico about 1914. Storyteller(s) not identified. Translated by editor. I have here gathered three of the many Pedro Urdemalas tales that Mason includes in his great collection. The first two are single episode tales (the self-cooking pot, and the trickster who persuades another to hold up a rock). The second of these tales is, according to Bascom, an African tale rather than a European (1992: 114–36, and especially 132). It demonstrates how in the New World the European trickster takes to himself any good plot, stealing even across continents. The third is a multi-episode story framed as a tale of partnership between a boy and a giant. Such tales, categorized by particular ruse, are gathered in the Aarne-Thompson-Uther classification between numbers 1030 and 1059. ATU 1049, involving bringing in the whole well or the whole forest, corresponds to the first two ruses for getting out of work that Pedro tries in this tale. The last two elements of the tale, the two contests, are more commonly found as independent tale types, as indicated above. While these Pedro Urdemalas stories were told at different times and presumably by different storytellers, it is not uncommon to find Pedro Urdemalas stories strung together in this fashion.

In Hispanic tradition the same tales are sometimes told of Pedro Urdemalas and of Juan Bobo. In fact these two characters sometimes appear indistinguishable. But it seems to me that in the Puerto Rican stories, at least, Juan Bobo is entirely goodhearted and loveable, while Pedro, though also much loved, has an unmistakable mean streak.

15. The Flower of Olivar

One time there was a couple that had three sons. The oldest one was called Juan, the middle one Felipe, and the youngest Carlos. After several years the father lost his sight, leaving this poor family with no resources, because he was the one whose work supported the family. Some time went by with the good man unable to see, but one day an old fellow came up to him and said that if he washed his eyes with water in which the flower of Olivar had been boiled, he would see again. But doing that, he said, would be harder than it sounded.

As soon as the oldest son heard what the old fellow had to say, he set out. He was traveling and traveling, trying to find what they wanted. He left behind a little newly-planted tree and he told his two brothers that when they saw that tree wilt it would be because he was in some kind of trouble. Juan was going along, travelling and travelling, when he came to a river. There he saw an old woman doing laundry, and a little baby crying and crying.

"Granny, don't you hear that baby crying?" asked Juan.

"He is crying from hunger," she answered. "Don't you have a bit of bread you could give him?"

Now, Juan had a whole loaf, but he said that he didn't have any. The old woman said she wished him bad roads and worse trouble.

Three weeks went by. Felipe, the middle brother, began to worry that his brother hadn't gotten back, so he went to look at the little tree. He was very sad to find it dead, and decided on the spot to go and look for him.

When he had travelled for many hours he came upon the same old woman and the same little kid, who was drowning himself. When he saw what was happening he said, "Hey, Granny, that kid's drowning."

"Ay!" She said. "Pull him out. It's too deep and I can't."

But Felipe, instead of pulling him out, shoved the kid further in so he would be sure to drown.

The old woman repeated to Felipe the same words she had earlier said to Juan. So Felipe was on the road about a month and didn't find either his brother or the flower.

When he saw that neither of the two came back, the youngest brother decided to go after them. Even though his mother and father both begged him not to go—for he was the one they both loved the best and he was the one who showed most affection for them—still he went.

When he came to the river he saw the old woman, and the baby crying, and he said, "Granny, don't you see the baby crying? Pick him up and see if he will stop." But she said that the child was hungry and she didn't have anything to give him. Carlos pulled a loaf of bread out of his saddlebag and gave half to the little baby.

The old woman said to him, "Because you are so good, and because you have a noble soul, I am going to tell you where your two brothers are and where you can find the flower of Olivar, so that it can restore your father's sight. But be careful. Your two brothers will kill you if they know that you have found this flower. When you get it, plant it under your foot in the bottom of your left boot."

It happened as she said. Unfortunately he found Juan and Felipe, and they suspected that he had the flower they were looking for. After they searched him they pulled off his boots and there they found it. They killed him on the spot and buried him. Then they went home, restored the sight of the blind man, and said that they hadn't seen anything of their brother.

One day the father told Juan to clear a certain piece of land for planting sugarcane. As Juan began cutting he heard a voice say:

> Don't cut me down, dear Brother.
> Don't let me be cut by another.
> You have already killed me, dear Brother,
> For the flower of Olivar.

He took off running to the house and said they would have to send someone else, he couldn't do it. So Felipe went, and immediately he heard a voice that said:

> Don't cut me down, dear Brother.
> Don't let me be cut by another.
> You have already killed me, dear Brother,
> For the flower of Olivar.

He went and told his parents, who went to the same place, where they heard a voice say:

> Don't cut me down, dear Father.
> Don't let me be cut, dear Mother.
> For my brothers have killed their brother
> For the flower of Olivar.

The mother and father began to scratch away the dirt. There they found Carlos, just fine and the way he had always been. They hugged him, they kissed him, and they asked him what punishment he thought his brothers should receive. Forgiveness, he told them. And so it happened, and they all lived happily together.

Mason and Espinosa 1922–1929: 38: 548–50. ATU 551/780. Collected about 1914; storyteller not identified by Mason. Translated by editor. Like many Puerto Rican märchen, this one is hard to classify, as types flow into one another. In the present case the central episode of ATU 551, the securing of the healing remedy, is completely elided over. The return of the brothers provides a segue into ATU 780, the Singing Bone, here singing underbrush. This tale type too takes an unlooked-for twist at the end, almost becoming a variation of ATU 720, The Juniper Tree: The singing brush returns to life and Carlos is "just fine and the way he had always been."

For a Puerto Rican audience the old woman and her baby would immediately suggest the Madonna and her Son. Juan thus violates literally the first law of love, the first corporal work of mercy. As the King says to the goats in Matthew (25:42): "I was hungry and you did not give me to eat." Felipe goes even further: his reaction to the child smacks of blasphemy. But Carlos is rewarded for his good deed.

The old woman tells Carlos that when he obtains the plant, "*póntela en la planta del pie izquierdo.*" The meaning is clear, but the word choice is arresting. I think that we are to see some connection between his carrying the magic flower at the "plant" of his foot, his growing into a plant, and his ultimate resuscitation when dug up. The Puerto Rican listener would also associate his resurrection with the power of the Virgin (V251.1). The ending of the story, in which forgiveness substitutes for revenge, completes the Christian reworking of these old themes.

I have chosen not to translate *Olivar* (literally, "the olive grove"). The old man tells the blind father that getting the flower will not be easy. But there is nothing particularly hard about getting blossoms from an ordinary olive grove. Furthermore, Mason capitalizes *Olivar*. Apparently, then, the word is intended to identify some mysterious place or person. Since the middle of the story is elided over, we can not know where or what this mysterious *Olivar* is, though the name certainly suggests the Garden of Olives where Jesus underwent His agony. In some other versions the youngest brother himself grows into a flowering olive tree.

16. Flor Blanca

Once upon a time there was a father who had a beautiful daughter that he called Flor Blanca or White Flower. But because she was so beautiful he kept her in a glass case so that she wouldn't fall in love.

One day a young man was passing by, saw her, and asked the father of the girl if he could have a place to stay. Well, this young man stayed on, living there. One day the father had to go on a long journey, but the young man stayed behind at the house. Since the girl was in the glass case, he began to court her until she loved him. Then he asked her how she could break out of the glass case.

"All right," she said. "Papa won't be back for another five days. I can break the glass and we can leave here."

And so it happened. He left and she broke the glass case and went with him, and they travelled along and travelled along. They had been travelling for many days when they came to the edge of the sea. There he turned to say something to her, but she was so worn out and tired that she had dropped down, sound asleep. The fog had rolled in at that point. He tried to find her, calling and calling, but she was so deep in sleep that she did not wake up.

Finally he went on without her, and she still asleep on the shore.

When she woke up it had been some two days since he wandered off in the fog. When she realized that he wasn't there she began to cry. "If Papa comes along now, what am I going to do?" she wailed. "He'll kill me." The girl fretted a lot, and cried even more.

Suddenly there was a boy in front of her. "Why are you crying?" he asked.

So she told him what had happened, and he said, "Don't worry, I can take you to the other side."

She was delighted, so they went, and when they were on the other side he left her alone in a town. But since she was so pretty, everybody showed up at the windows and everybody had to talk to her. So when she got to the town the girl made herself as ragged and tattered as she could, and went to find a place to stay. But as chance would have it, the place where she went was the home of the young man who was her beloved. He was very sick, but she did not even know that he lived there. So she asked for shelter there and the woman of the house told her she could stay, but she would have to stay in the kitchen because her son was very sick and he didn't want to see anybody in the house.

Now he, in his delirium, began to call out for the girl, even though he thought she was nowhere near. He kept saying to his mother, "Oh, Mother, help me to find my White Flower."

His mother went and brought him all the flowers that she could find, until she couldn't find any more flowers, but he didn't want any of them. His mother, you see, didn't understand that the flower he was asking for was a woman, so she kept on looking for white flowers, and couldn't figure it out.

One day the girl said to the boy's mother, "Please, Señora, may I go to your son's room and see him?" But the woman told her no. The girl didn't say anything more right then, but after several days she decided to ask again if she could go in there, but the woman again refused, because she said her son was so sick that it would upset him to see her. But she did tell her son about it.

"My boy," she said, "there is a woman here who wants to come into your room."

Then he said, "Let her come in."

That put the mother in a bad temper. Nevertheless, she went to the girl and told her she could go in, but she ought to change that outfit.

Since the girl in fact had many beautiful dresses (and besides, she had figured out by now that the young man who lived there and was so sick was her beloved), she put on one of the most beautiful.

She went into the young man's bedroom and when he saw her he was crazy with joy. "Oh, Mother, this is my White Flower that I begged you to find." Then Flor Blanca told him all that happened after he lost her. They were married immediately, and they are still living there.

Mason and Espinosa 1922–1929: 38: 527–29. ATU 307/510B/709. Collected about 1914; storyteller not identified by Mason. Translated by editor. Mason also collected standard versions of *Flor Blanca* or Snow White. But in the present case a small number of motifs from the Snow White tale (ATU 709)—perhaps under the influence of ATU 307, which has a similar beginning, and also features sealing the wished-for daughter in a shroud (or casket?)—have been imposed upon a story much more like the Catskins variations of the Cinderella story (ATU 510), to create a novelle. We will never know whether this was a conscious act of creativity or the effort of a storyteller (not necessarily the present storyteller; it could have been someone in the lineage of the present tale) to bring up and piece together half-remembered scraps of stories heard long before.

The translation of the cryptic episode where Flor Blanca falls asleep is rather free. Presumably we are to understand that the young man did not desert the girl; rather, he lost her in the fog. But he must pay even for this failure by prolonged sickness, almost to death.

17. The Wolf

Once there was a wolf who was feeling terrible. He got so sick that he couldn't wag his tail or wiggle his paws or eat, and he was sick a long time. And when he got over being sick he went out one day and met a sow with a string of piglets behind her. And the wolf said, "Good morning, Sister Pig. I'd like you to give me one of your sons because my belly is crying out for a little something to eat, in fact, for a big helping of meat.

The sow said, "Brother Wolf, you will have to take him to the river and wash him." And the wolf was washing the piglet in the river when the sow came up, rammed her snout against him, and shoved him in. Then the mother pig turned away, with all her piglets in a line behind her, and left the wolf to drown.

When he got out, he went on his way. A little farther along he spied a mare with a foal, a nice filly. So the wolf said, "Good morning, Sister Mare."

"Good morning, Brother Wolf."

"My belly is crying out for a bite to eat, in fact, for a big helping of meat, and I'd like you to give me your daughter for me to eat."

And the mare said yes, but first he had to read her a lesson from her primer. And the wolf said O.K. But as he began to read the primer, the mare kicked him with her hoof and ran off with her foal.

The wolf went on until he was very tired. He came to a goat fight, and he went up to the goats and said, "Good afternoon, Brothers. I'd like one of you two to come with me so I can eat you, because my belly is crying out for a bite to eat, in fact, for a big helping of meat."

And the two billy goats said back, "Well, Brother Wolf, first you have to come divide our inheritance for us. We've inherited this mud patch and we've been fighting over how to divide it fairly. We'd like you to settle on the midline, and go stand there, and that'll be fine with us." So the wolf went and stood in the middle, to mark the two halves, and the two billy goats came at him and butted him. One butted him from here to yon, and the other butted him from yonder back here again. And they knocked him down in the middle of the mud patch and left him half dead.

Then the wolf got up and went on his way till he came to a house where there were many nanny goats. And the wolf went up to them and said, "Hello. My stomach is crying out for a bite to eat, in fact, for a big helping of meat, and I'd like one of you to come with me so I can eat you."

"O.K., Brother Wolf, but you have to help us say some rosaries that we have promised to say, and if you help us to keep our pledge, one of us will go with you." So the wolf began telling his beads. Then they untied a dog that the farmer had there, and set him on the wolf to kill him.

When the wolf finally got away he was about dead. He slumped down under a gallows and said, "My father never told me that I shouldn't wash babies in the river, that I shouldn't read primers if I wasn't much of a reader, that I shouldn't divide inheritances if I've never been an estate executor, and that I shouldn't start praying rosaries if I've never been much of a hand at prayer. Come on lightning, strike me in two."

Well, a passing woodman did hit him with an ax, and killed him.

Mason and Espinosa 1922–1929: 40: 380–81. ATU 122A. Mason, who collected about 1914, does not provide the name of a storyteller. Translated by editor. In many versions of this tale the piglet needs to be baptized first. Thus the wolf fails as a priest, a teacher, a lawyer, and a simple good Catholic, and ends up dead under the gallows. But the present storyteller seems more taken with the laconic insolence of the wolf than with the latent Christian message.

18. Mousie Perez

One day Martina, the pretty cockroach, found a penny. She'd never had a penny before and she was out of her mind with delight. "What should I spend it on?" she asked herself. "If I spend it on rice, it won't last. If I spend it on coffee, it won't last. If I spend it on bread, it won't last. If I spend it on meat, it won't last. Nothing I spend it on will last. Oh, well, I guess I'll use it to buy some starch to powder my nose."

So she went to buy some starch, and she left Mousie Perez to watch the pot until she got back. Well, as luck would have it, Mousie Perez fell into the pot. When she got home she went looking for the mouse, who was her husband, and she found him in the pot. Martina, the pretty cockroach, began to weep and howl: "Poor Mousie Perez fell into the pot."

But then the pretty cockroach powdered herself all up with the starch and took her seat by the door.

Soon an ox came by. "Martina, you pretty cockroach," he said to her, "will you marry me?"

"Let's see how you sound," she said.

"Moo, moo."

"That's disgusting! I'm not going to marry you."

A horse went by, and the same thing happened. A lion went by, and the same thing happened. A dog went by, and the same thing happened. A cat went by, and the same thing happened. A bunny went by, and the same thing happened. "When am I going to find another like my dear Mousie Perez?" mourned the poor cockroach. "All these other animals are disgusting."

While she was feeling sorry for herself, a mouse went by. "Martina, you pretty cockroach," the mouse said to her, "will you marry me?"

"Let's hear what you sound like," Martina, the pretty cockroach, answered.

"Well," said the mouse, "I go *eek, eek.*"

"Oh yes, how can I not marry you! You sound exactly like my dear Mousie Perez. You even look like him."

So they were married, and the pretty cockroach took up housekeeping with this mouse like she had with the first one. She even started calling him Mousie Perez the Second.

Mason and Espinosa 1922–1929: 40: 338–39. ATU 2023 (cf. ATU 2022). Translated by the editor. Mason, who collected this lively piece about 1914, supplies no information about the narrator. It is hard not to smile at the intense but short-lived passions of the wee, mismatched couple. The reader who wants the whole sad story of their pestiferous love affair may piece it together after consulting the other two versions of the tale found in chapters 3 and 8.

19. The Children and the Ogress

Once there was a man who had two children, but they had lost their mother. Every day when they went to school they had to pass the house of a woman who used to call out to them, "Come here, dear children. You should ask your father to marry me and you will see how well I take care of you." And every day she would give them honey *sopitas*.

The children went back home, ran to where their father was, kissed him, and said, "Daddy, down there lives a great woman and every day when we're coming home from school she calls us in to tell us that you should marry her, that she would give us honey *sopitas* and take good care of us."

"Oh, my poor children," he answered them, "if only you understood that all this woman wants is to marry me. At first she will give you lots of love and honey *sopitas*, but before long she will give you harsh treatment and *sopitas* of gall." But the children kept pestering their father to marry her, until finally he did just that.

At first everything went well. But the day came when she gave Pedro—for that was the boy's name—such a spanking that his poor fanny hurt for days. And she made the girl—María was her name—go for three days without anything to eat. And the children didn't dare complain, because they knew their father wasn't to blame.

One night they heard their stepmother fighting with their father. She was telling him, "Those kids can't stay here. You have to take them out and leave them on the mountain for the wild animals to eat." When the children heard this they were terrified and decided to run away from home.

They decided to wait a week to see how things were going. But finally one evening the stepmother made up her mind to kill them and grabbed a knife to slit their throats. They got scared and fled out onto the mountain. All night they wandered, listening to the wolves all around them. But whenever María would cry, Pedro would say to her, "Don't worry yourself, little sister, all this will pass." They had been wandering a long time when they saw a faint light. They went toward the cottage and saw that it looked like rock candy. They knocked a piece off and tasted it, and it was sweet. They began to pull off bits of the wall, which was of caramel.

Now, inside lived an ogress, and she stuck out her head and saw those two children. They looked so good that she called out to them, "Come here, dear chicks. See what lovely things I have here. The children went in and she locked the door. She gave them sweets and the poor fooled children let her shut them in like in cages.

At the end of four days the ogress came to see if they had gotten fat. And do you know why she wanted them fat? So she could roast them and eat them. The children figured that out, and María told Pedro, "Don't stick out your finger. Let's kill a little lizard and stick its tail out the hole for her to feel, and that way she'll think that we are skinny."

Every day the ogress came and asked them to let her feel a finger, because she knew that when their fingers were nice and fat she could eat them. But they would stick out the lizard tail, and she would say, "Oh dear, how skinny you two are. When will you be stout enough to help me clean the house and put firewood under the dutch oven?" Time went by and the old ogress, because the food she ate was human flesh, couldn't wait any longer to eat them. She went and opened the cage and pulled them out. "Come here, children," she said. "Go out on the mountain and bring a load of firewood so I can heat the oil in the dutch oven."

The children brought in the wood, heated the oil in the dutch oven, and then called the old ogress and said to her, "Granny, show us how we need to fold ourselves up to fit into the dutch oven so you can roast us."

Now that old ogress was so stupid that she got down on all fours on the rim of the dutch oven. The children gave her one good shove and she fell in and began to brown. When the old ogress saw that she was burning she called out, "Oh, dear chicks, pull me out and I'll give you all my treasure."

But the children didn't want to do that, so they just turned their backs on her. That left the children with all that money.

One day Pedro went to make some purchases and María stayed behind to mind the house. A poor man came by, begging alms, and the girl opened the door and said, "Come in, old man. Tell me some of the story of your life."

Well, he told her that once he had two children, and that for the sake of a wicked woman he had been forced to cast them out. María threw her arms around his neck and said, "You are my father and we are your two children. We met up with an old ogress who had this treasure here, and we killed her and got it all, and now this is all ours."

When Pedro came home he recognized his father. The old man stayed with them and they were all very happy.

This tale was a bowl
Of rice pudding to eat.

Can someone now give us
As zesty a treat?

Boggs 1929: 161–62. ATU 327A. Translated by the editor. Told to Ralph S. Boggs, May 29, 1927, by "a peasant girl, 25 years old, from Lajas, a village on the southern coastal plain. She said she had heard it from her mother in early childhood." Boggs asserts that he has transcribed the stories "word for word, exactly as dictated," but using conventional spelling instead of trying to capture the Puerto Rican pronunciation.

Four of the seven stories that Boggs offers in that issue of the *Journal of American Folklore* end with rhymes. The rhyme that ends this story can be translated literally as follows:

The story is finished, rice with honey sweetening.
He who is listening, let him tell me another, salty (i.e., witty) one.

CHAPTER 3

TALES FROM THE
HISPANIC SOUTHWEST

Hispanic settlers were already establishing their traditional culture in Mexico by the early 1500s. These settlers and conquistadores explored extensively in what is now the southwest United States. Santa Fe, New Mexico, was founded in 1610, and soon a strong Spanish-style outpost was established in the upper Rio Grande valley. But conflict with the indigenous population threatened stable settlements in the hinterlands of New Mexico, Arizona, and southern Colorado, and the Pueblo Revolt of 1680 drove the Hispanic population back to Mexico. The present Hispanic population of that region has its roots in the Mexican resettlement after 1692. The ancestors of those later settlers had come to the New World nearly two centuries before, however, and as a consequence the Hispanic folktale tradition of New Mexico, Arizona, and southern Colorado draws from the oldest stream of European folktales in the New World. Already isolated geographically, and further isolated linguistically and politically by events in the nineteenth century, the Hispanic communities in those mountain and valley villages hoarded their stories and other traditions in a conservative regional Spanish.

The case of Texas is somewhat different. It too waited until after 1692 for serious settlement. Since then, however, because of closer proximity and greater ease of travel, the Hispanic population has been renewed more regularly by immigration from Mexico than is the case with the Hispanic population further north. Such continued to be the case after Texas became politically independent of Mexico in 1836, and today continues to be so, with additional immigration from Central America.

Linguists and folktale scholars, most notably Juan B. Raél and Aurelio and José Manuel Espinosa, collected extensively in Colorado, New Mexico, and Arizona, as well as in Texas, in the decades before World War II. Their collections demonstrated that although the Hispanic population tended to be poor in material possessions, their folk tradition was extremely rich, far richer than this single chapter can possibly convey.

This chapter includes only one story from Raél and one from José Manuel Espinosa, supplementing those long romantic tales with tales from other collectors. These latter include another traditional märchen, an episode from the long, sad story of the romance of the cockroach and the mouse (or were they a flea and a louse?), and a southwestern variation on a group of trickster animal themes. Finally, in "La Llorona," a southwestern version of traditional Mexican legendary material presents itself reworked as a märchen.

20. The Bird of Truth, or the Three Treasures

Once upon a time there lived a man who had three daughters. One day he was called away on business and he said to his daughters before leaving, "Listen, children, do not gossip while I am away for you know the king may hear you."

The king had the habit of dressing as a commoner and eavesdropping among his subjects to find out anything that might be of use to him. This was the reason the man warned his daughters against gossiping, for he was afraid they might say something that might offend the king and get them all in trouble.

No sooner had the man left than his daughters started gossiping. "I," said the oldest daughter, "would just love to marry the king's cook so that I could eat wonderful food."

"And I," said the second daughter, "would just love to marry the king's baker so that I could eat wonderful pastries."

"And I," said the youngest daughter, "would love to marry the king himself and I would like to have three children with hair the color of pure gold like their father's."

Now the king, disguised as a commoner, happened to hear every word the sisters said. When the father of the girls returned the king sent for him and his daughters.

"You," said the king, addressing the oldest daughter, "said that you wanted to marry my cook so that you could eat fine foods. Well and good, you shall marry my cook tomorrow.

"You," said the king to the second daughter, "said that you wanted to marry my baker so that you could eat fine pastries. Well and good, you shall marry my baker tomorrow.

"And you," the king said to the youngest, "said that you wanted to marry me. Well and good, we shall be married next month."

Everything happened as the king had said. The youngest daughter and the king had been married one year when the king was challenged to fight a king from another kingdom. While he was away in battle his wife gave birth to a child. The youngest daughter's older sisters, who were very jealous and envious of her because she had married the king, drugged her and took her baby away, putting a puppy in its place beside her.

They took the baby girl, who had hair of pure gold, away and buried her. Now it happened that the king's retired gardener saw everything that had taken place. He rescued the baby girl and took her home to his wife. The wicked sisters wrote to the king and told him that his wife had given birth to a puppy dog. The king answered and told them to take the best care of it until he returned.

Another year passed and again the king was challenged to fight and again while he was away his wife gave birth to a child. This time it was a boy with hair of pure gold. The wicked sisters buried the second child and the gardener rescued him and took him home to his wife. Again the sisters wrote the king that his wife had given birth to a puppy.

At the end of the third year the king was again challenged to fight and while he was away his wife gave birth to a third child—another boy with hair of pure gold. The sisters did exactly as they had with the other two children. The king became angry with his wife and commanded that she be buried from the neck down and that she be given nothing but black bread to eat. Everyone who passed by her was commanded to spit upon her and to insult her.

The gardener's wife made wigs for the king's babies so that no one might recognize them by their beautiful golden hair. Many years passed and the children grew up and built a magnificent house. The boys were always out playing with the wild animals in the forest while their sister kept house.

One day while the sister was alone a nun came to see her. "Your house is magnificent. I have never seen the like. However you lack the three most precious treasures," said the nun.

"What can these treasures be," said the girl, "that my brothers cannot bring to me?"

"These are the treasures," said the nun, "the golden water, the talking bird, and the singing tree."

When her brothers came home she told them everything that had happened. "I'm going to get you those treasures," said the older brother. His sister prepared his lunch and when he was ready to leave he gave her a knife, saying, "Sister, if this knife sheds blood, you will know that something has happened to me."

A week passed and the knife shed blood. The younger brother was worried about the fate of his older brother and resolved to set out in search of him. His sister prepared his lunch and when he was ready to depart he gave a rosary to his sister, saying, "Sister, take this rosary. If a bead breaks, you will know something has happened to me."

At the end of another week a bead from the rosary broke. The girl was very sad and resolved to go in search of her brothers. She dressed as a boy and was soon on her way.

After days of travel she came to a tiny house that stood on the side of a mountain. Here she found a very old man with a long white beard that reached to his toes, and fingernails that were a yard long, and hair that hung to the floor.

"You must be a sister to the two boys who came here," said the old man, "for there is a deep resemblance between you and them."

"You have seen my brothers," said the girl. "Where are they?"

"They refused to obey my commands," answered the old man, "so they were turned into rock."

"Is there any way to save them?" she asked anxiously.

"Yes," replied the old man, "if you will do just as I tell you. At the top of the mountain there is a house. In this house you will find three treasures. Be careful that you do not take the cage of the talking bird. Be sure to cut only one small branch from the singing tree, and take only a little bit of the golden water.

"While you are climbing [back down] the mountain," continued the old man, "pour some reviving water on every rock you see. [And on the way up,] do not turn back, whatever you do. Many voices will call to you, many voices will taunt and insult you. Pay no attention to them. Many have come in search of the three treasures but none has succeeded in getting them because they have not been able to resist the lure of the voices."

In conclusion the old man warned again, "Do not turn back!"

The girl listened carefully to everything the old man told her. Then she asked him for some cotton to put in her ears. She took a pair of scissors, trimmed the old man's beard, hair, and fingernails, and left. How the voices pleaded, taunted, insulted her. She was tempted to answer them, to turn back. It took all her self-control to keep from turning back, but finally she reached the house.

Inside the house she found the three treasures. She was tempted to take the beautiful cage of the talking bird, but she remembered the warning of the old man and did not. She took the talking bird out of his cage, cut only one small branch from the singing tree, took only a little bit of the golden water, and started back down the mountain. As she descended the mountain she poured reviving water on every rock she came to. Immediately the rocks started turning into people. Finally she came to her brothers, who had also been turned into rock. She brought them back to life and they all returned home.

At last, word of these children who possessed the three great treasures reached the king and he invited them to dinner at his palace. They had never been to the city before and when they saw their mother buried near the palace they did not insult her but said good morning pleasantly. The king was very angry because they did not insult her, but when he learned that they did not know of his orders concerning the woman, he forgave them. The children enjoyed dining with the king very much and invited him to dinner the following Sunday.

The day before the king was to come to dine with the children the talking bird called the sister to him and told her to go to a certain dead tree trunk in the forest and look inside. There she would find some precious pearls which she was to stuff inside the chicken. She was also to set the talking bird in the center of the table and when he spoke the children were to remove their wigs.

Now when the king came the next day to dine the sister asked him to carve the chicken. When the king cut the chicken open he was amazed to see the pearls. "Whoever heard the like!" he exclaimed. "Pearl stuffing!"

"Whoever heard the like," repeated the talking bird. "A father surrounded by his own children and not knowing them."

As soon as the talking bird spoke the children removed their wigs and the king recognized them as his children. The talking bird told the king the whole story and the wicked sisters were punished. The poor mother was taken out of her grave and everyone lived happily ever after.

Weigle 1980–1981: 31–33. ATU 707. Told by Mrs. Guadalupe Gallegos, of West Las Vegas, New Mexico, to Bright Lynn, a college student working with the Federal Writers Project, in 1938, and translated by him. I have edited the translation very slightly. Mrs. Gallegos was the only daughter of a wealthy family, brought up with Indian servants and with a black slave woman as her own nurse. She married at the age of twelve to a man who eventually lost all her fortune. An excellent storyteller, she told Lynn more than forty stories, the majority of which are märchen, many featuring strong heroines like the sister in this tale. Versions of "The Bird of Truth" have been widely collected in Iberian-American tradition, including Cape Verde tradition.

21. Jujuyana, or the Mist of No Return

In the City of Yellow Stones there was a man who raised two daughters and a son. The boy was named Juan. When he reached the age of eighteen, he asked his father for his blessing, because he wanted to go seek his fortune.

Bathed in tears, his father said goodbye. Out on the road, the boy met a farmhand who asked him where he was going. Juan explained to him, and the man told him, "Buddy, you're going the wrong way. Anyone that follows this road comes to a place called The Mist of No Return."

"Well, I will return," he told him, and continued on his way.

Just at sunset he began to see the Mists. That day he traveled until he came to a place where there was a spring. Before long he saw a beautiful girl coming. He walked up and greeted her, but she told him that her mother would kill him. He asked her where her mother was. The girl told him that she was out in the fields, but that her father was in the house. So he went with her to the house. When the old man saw the boy coming to the house, he said, "Young man, what are you doing in these parts? Don't you know that around here is called The Mist of No Return?"

Then the young man asked him for a place to stay. The old man told him to wait until his wife returned, because she was the one who made decisions there. Well, they spent the afternoon talking and enjoying themselves. When the old man knew that his wife would be coming home he said, "Good young man, go cut firewood so that my wife finds you busy."

He was cutting firewood when the woman got home. The first word that she said to the old man was, "Old man, I smell human flesh here. If you don't give him to me, I'll skin you alive."

"Woman, no one has come here but a boy who, judging from his conversation, must be a great knight."

"He'll have come for my daughter," she said.

"You know, I don't," the old man told her.

"Bring him to me so I can look at him and find out his intentions."

Jujuyana went out where he was cutting firewood to get him. "Listen," she said, "the old lady wants to see you. She's going to kill you dead. But if you promise to marry me, I'll get you away so that she doesn't kill you."

"That's fine with me," he told her. "I'm willing."

Then she said, "When the old lady finishes chatting with you, tell her that you came here to see if they will give you permission to marry me."

When he came to the old woman, she asked him what he was doing there. He told her that he had come to see if they would allow him to take their daughter as a wife.

"For that," she told him, "you will need to do three tasks for me. Follow me and I will tell you what the first task is."

They went some distance from the house where there were two ponds, one empty and one full to the brim with water.

"If you want to marry my daughter, tomorrow you have to draw all the water out of this pond with a thimble, and dump it into that one for me."

"All right. If that's what you ask, that's what I'll do, if I can."

"Well, if you can't, I will kill you dead."

In the evening Jujuyana got up and came out to Juan.

"When you go to sleep, rest well. In the morning the old lady will offer you three thimbles, two new and one very old. Pick the old one, and don't worry."

The following morning she brought him three thimbles and he took the old thimble and left for the pond. As soon as he got there he began to fill thimbles of water and take them to the dry pond. But when he got to the dry pond he wouldn't have any water. When it came time for the old woman to leave on her usual rounds, Jujuyana headed out where Juan was. He couldn't even walk now, he was crying so much because he couldn't carry a single thimble of water. She told him, "Come sit close to me so I can smooth your hair."

Juan snuggled up to her, she ran her fingers through his hair, and he fell asleep. In the evening she woke him up and told him, "Get up now. You're done. All the water from the full pond is dumped into the pond that was dry. I'm going now," she said. "Here comes the old lady."

When the old lady came in from doing her work she went to see the work Juan had done, and said, "That was done by Jujuyana, or you have more power than I do. Tomorrow you will clear me all this mountain here, plow it, sow wheat, reap it, grind the wheat, and have bread for me for dinner." It made Juan very sad to see how impossible this task was.

Jujuyana came out to ask what was upsetting him and Juan told her about the next task. Jujuyana told him, "In the morning my mother will offer you three axes, two very good ones and one that is just awful. Choose the awful one and set yourself to work. I will come to give you a hand as soon as my mother leaves."

When the old woman showed him the three axes, Juan chose the really awful one. Within minutes of starting to work he was dismayed to find that blood was pouring from his hand, and he was not able to cut a single tree. Jujuyana showed up and told him to lay his head on her lap and rest.

He lay his head on Jujuyana's lap, she put her hand on his head, and instantly he fell asleep. After a time Jujuyana woke Juan up and told him, "Juan, get up. Take the bread. I'm going now."

Juan got up and saw that the whole place had become a wheat field and at his side was a basket with the bread. He took his basket and went to the house. He found the old woman all worn out, and told her, "Ma'am, I've finished the task you gave me."

"Skill or luck, I suspect that there's more of Jujuyana than of you in this. Sleep well. In the morning I will give you the last task."

With this, the old woman went to bed. Then Jujuyana came and told him, "Juan, my mother is going to give you a task that not even the most powerful genies in the world could do. I won't be able to do it with any of my clever tricks. There's nothing we can do but leave tonight. I am going to hurry and get ready for the trip. Don't come into the house again."

Jujuyana went back in the house and took a mirror, a hairbrush, and a comb. Then she opened the grate, filled her mouth with spit, and spit into the ashes.

Not long after they had left, the old woman woke up and said, "You old drunk, you dead rabbit, Jujuyana is gone."

"Where could she go, woman? Jujuyana! Jujuyana!"

"Sir?" answered the spit.

"You see now, silly old woman! Jujuyana is there."

The two old people repeated their shouts twice more. The second time, the spit answered "Ma'am?" instead. But the third time it didn't answer at all. Then the old woman said, "Do you see now that Jujuyana is gone? Bring me my daughter, or I will do with you as I have done with the others!"

The old man got up and set off at a trot. Now when Jujuyana realized that he was catching up to them, she said, "Juan, here they come after us. Look! Do as I tell you and we'll be all right." As she finished speaking she threw down her hairbrush. Immediately a beautiful, beautiful church appeared. Then Jujuyana told him what he had to do when the old man came looking for them. Transformed into an old codger, Juan grabbed the rope and began to ring the bell.

The old man came up. "Sir," he said, "you haven't seen a man and a woman pass by here?"

"I'm finished, sir. It's time to go in to Mass now."

"I'm asking if you haven't seen a man and a woman pass by here."

"It's time to go in to Mass now, sir."

He stuck his head in the door of the church and didn't see anything but a truly beautiful statue of the Virgin on the altar, so he left. He got back to the house and she said to him, "Where is my daughter?"

"Well, I couldn't find her, nor anyone to tell what happened to her. There was only a sacristan calling people to Mass."

"And you looked inside?"

"Yes, there was a very pretty statue of the Virgin."

"That was my daughter. Go get her. It was my daughter."

Now Jujuyana, when the old man had left, as soon as he got far enough away, made everything disappear, and they set off again. They had gone some distance when she told him, "Juan, someone's coming! They are getting closer! This time I'm going to put a cornfield here. No matter what question they ask you, your answer is that this is common corn that everybody uses."

And Jujuyana threw down the comb and a cornfield appeared. In the middle of the cornfield was a blonde stalk that stuck up taller than all the rest. The old man came up and said, "Sir, you haven't seen a woman and a man pass by here?"

"Sir," he said to him, "this is common corn that everybody uses."

"I didn't ask about the corn you have here. I asked about a man and a woman."

"Sir, this is the common cornfield. Everybody uses it."

The old man turned back. Then Jujuyana made everything there disappear, and they took off again.

The old man came to the house and she said, "Where is my daughter?"

"I haven't found her," he told her.

"Well, what did you see along the road?"

"There was a man," he told her, "and a cornfield, and in the middle of the cornfield was a blonde stalk."

"That was my daughter. Go get her."

"Go get her yourself, you troublesome old hag. Don't bother me anymore."

"Well, now you will see how I get her."

She hitched up her petticoats and set off running. When Jujuyana realized that someone was catching up to them, she said, "Juan, the old lady is catching us! I am going to turn us into birds. When I begin a terrible quacking, spit into the water."

When the old woman came near, the girl took the mirror and threw it down and it formed a pool of water with two birds, two ducks swimming in the middle. When the old woman got there she said, "Oh, you deceiver! You won't escape my clutches!"

The old woman bent down to drink the water out of the pond. When the water was getting very low, the first bird paddled over towards the old woman and wouldn't let the other duck pass. When very little water was left, the first bird began a horrible quacking. The second bird spit into the pond, and that made the old woman cough up all the water into the pond again. Then the old woman said, "Look, deceiver, how you have repaid me in this life! But I warn you that the first time someone else hugs Juan, he will forget you!"

The old woman left.

Then Jujuyana and Juan continued on their way. When they came near Juan's father's house, Juan told her, "My bride, wait here while I go to my father's house to tell him that you are coming and to bring some of my sisters' clothes so that you won't be embarrassed to present yourself before them."

"I don't want you to leave me," she said, "because I am afraid that you will forget me."

"Don't worry," he told her, and set off for his father's house. They saw him coming a long way off, and they were wild with joy. When he got close he told them, "Don't hug me, because I don't want to appear ungrateful."

His mother made her way to him with tears in her eyes. She greeted him and gave him a kiss on the cheek. Then his younger sister broke through from behind and hugged him. After that he couldn't tell them anything. All was forgotten. As if nothing had happened to him.

Juan's father told him, "Son, as soon as we have dinner, I want you to go with your sisters to the entertainment for the viceroy's daughter. She's been married seven times, but by bad luck, each time, no sooner has she gotten married than she has ended up as a widow. The king has ordered all the young men and women to go every afternoon from the hour of prayer until evening to entertain this young lady because she is so sad."

They ate dinner right away and left for the viceroy's manor. The viceroy's daughter had been so grieved that she hadn't talked to anyone. But when this girl saw Juan and his sisters enter, she stood up from her seat with a smile and went to talk to the two girls and to Juan.

The viceroy, her father, was filled with joy and said, "My daughter has found contentment?"

"Father, a pleasant and agreeable young man came in."

"You will be ready to take him for a husband."

"If you wish it, yes," she told him.

Immediately the king announced that the following night the marriage of the viceroy's daughter and Juan would be celebrated, and he himself would see the procession off. Juan's parents were very happy when they heard the news and began to make preparations for the wedding.

Now we are going to see what happened to Jujuyana. When that poor girl found herself stuck where Juan had left her, she discovered that she couldn't remember any of the arts she had learned. She passed the night in great sorrow, sobbing and weeping. When day came, she saw smoke from a poor cottage and set off in that direction. When she got there she knocked on the door and an old woman came out. She brought Jujuyana in and made her feel comfortable. Jujuyana told her that she was an orphan and that she was looking for a way to make a living. Then she said to the old woman, "Dear Granny, please do me a favor. Go to the city like someone who doesn't need a thing and find out what news there is to tell me. It will be a big help to me and I will repay you double."

"Very well," she told her, "I'll go now. You stay here."

The old woman left for the city and in a very short time returned. She came home and told her that Juan was going to marry the viceroy's daughter that very evening. Then Jujuyana begged her please to go to the king's house and tell him that a pilgrim was there in her house that wished to entertain the king, his court, and the bride and groom an hour or two before the wedding got underway. The old lady agreed and did the errand. The king told her to bring her pilgrim at noon so that they could begin once the audience was all assembled.

The last time Jujuyana had stroked Juan's head a hair had remained on her hand, and she felt so much love and affection for Juan that she had guarded it like a relic.

Jujuyana took Juan's hair and formed a little pigeon from it, and took a hair from her head and formed another little pigeon, and placed them both in a box. When the old woman returned, they ate, dressed, and left. When they arrived at the king's hall, she saw Juan at once, seated beside the viceroy's daughter. Jujuyana passed near them, and when she went by, Juan's heart gave a leap, but he didn't know what it could be. The king told Jujuyana to begin as soon as possible.

Then Jujuyana took out the box. She opened the box and set the two little pigeons down in the middle of the room. The little pigeon cock puffed up his chest and withdrew to one side of the room, and the little pigeon hen went to the other side. There she turned and said, "Do you remember, little brother bird, when I went for water and you met me and asked me what place that was, and I told you, 'It is The Mist of No Return'?"

"I don't remember, I don't remember. Remember it yourself," the little cock pigeon said.

"Do you remember, little brother bird, when you went to bail out a pond of water with a cracked thimble?"

The cock pigeon didn't remember this either, but in the middle of her asking more questions, he began to remember. The hen pigeon finally asked him, "Do you remember, little brother bird, when you left me by the well, saying that you were going to get me clothes so that you could present me before your father and your mother, and I, with tears in my eyes, begged you not to leave me alone because you would forget me?"

"Yes, yes, I do remember that. And my name is Juan, right?"

"You've got it now."

Juan jumped up and said, "Your Escorial Majesty, forgive me but I must speak to you. You heard what these two birds were talking about? Well, it's just what happened to me. That same thing happened to me. This young woman, this pilgrim, saved my life in return for my solemn promise to marry her. But I went to my house for clothing so that she could present herself properly before my parents and I forgot her and didn't remember until now."

"The man must keep his promises, but my count's daughter must be satisfied also. What do you propose to offer," the king said to Jujuyana, "on behalf of this young lady?"

"Escorial Majesty, if you tell me this young lady's history, I believe that I can be very useful to her and she will be more than satisfied."

"She has had several husbands but as soon as they have married her they have died. Will you be able to fix this?"

"Sir, if this girl gives me Juan, who is truly my husband, with all her heart, I promise before the king's sovereignty that if she marries, her husband will not die in that way. There is a genie that is in love with her, and that is the reason all that you told me about is happening."

The viceroy's daughter and the viceroy agreed. Then the viceroy's daughter, by her father's order, chose a young man for a husband. The man accepted, though he was nervous about dying. But Jujuyana told him, "Don't be afraid. Genies are under my authority and I govern them. As a pledge of what I say I offer myself here to suffer death in your place."

"Bring the priest to celebrate this marriage," the king said. "And when this stranger has given proof of her promise, we'll celebrate Juan's marriage too."

The priest began the wedding ceremony for the viceroy's daughter. As he was finishing a tremor was heard in the house. Jujuyana rose and recited the following words:

> Genie, king of all genies,
> I need your services at once.

Instantly a monstrous and terrible genie sprang up before them. "I am ready to serve you," he said. "Command and it shall be done."

"A genie, the most unworthy of genies, has been in love with this young lady that has just taken a husband and been married. Put him to shame in the middle of the sea with a millstone around his neck so that he doesn't return to do harm to a single human being."

"Your order will be done at once," the genie said.

Then the king, who was frozen stiff from terror, issued an order: "Neither the priest nor any other person here present may withdraw until we see the outcome of this decree." So they waited that night until it was well past the time when each of the previous husbands of the unfortunate bride had died.

Finally the king said, "There is no doubt that this young pilgrim has been as good as her word." So the king ordered that Juan's marriage be celebrated at once and gave orders to invite all the people of the city to eight days of festivities there in that city. He also ordered that both of the recently married couples remain in the palace for those eight days, because he was still worried that at any moment something might come to cut the thread of life of the young man who had just married the viceroy's daughter. And so the eight-day feast began in that city.

At the conclusion of these eight days, the king called all his court together and announced that when his time came to die they were to crown Juan as king in his place; and in the meantime Juan would be chief counselor of his court. The king offered Juan and Jujuyana half of the palace so that they could live there, but Jujuyana refused, asking the king just to give them a place near the palace where they could put their home. The king granted that favor gladly. They said goodbye to the king and took the road to Juan's father's house. As they approached the door, they realized that they had come to a palace ten times more beautiful than the king's, although Juan, his parents, and his sisters had not noticed it before. But Jujuyana, when she had gone to use her secret powers, had asked the genie to build just such a palace. They all settled themselves in the new palace. Even the kind old woman that had helped Jujuyana was moved into the new palace.

Within a few days the king became gravely ill. Seeing he was at the point of death, the king made his court crown Juan. And when the king died, Juan began to rule that kingdom.

Raél [1957] 1: 316–24. ATU 313/507. Epimenio García of Mogote, Colorado, fifty-eight, told this full and rich version of The Devil's Daughter to collector Juan B. Raél, probably in the summer of 1930 (though Raél also collected in 1940). Mary Beth Wesdock made the translation for this volume. The wordplay in the opening lines is like the wordplay in the opening of "Juan Bobo," chapter 2. This way of elaborating *Once, far away* seems characteristic of certain storytellers in the Hispanic tradition. Incorporating elements of the Monster's Bride story (ATU 507) at the end is an unusual touch.

The Spanish of the tale presents some particular problems. Though the girl seems clearly to be the daughter of the old woman she sometimes calls the old woman *mi nana*, which usually means *my granny*. In this context it is probably a less-than-respectful appellation. Accordingly it is translated "the old lady." A second problem is interpreting the words *como a la hora de nona*. The context suggests that the words refer to the late-afternoon liturgical hour of None, not to nine o'clock, and accordingly they have been translated "in the evening." Finally, the king is regularly addressed as *Saccarial Majestá*. Presumably *saccarial* is a corruption of *Escorial*, the name associated with the old Spanish royal residence in Madrid, and has been translated accordingly.

22. Goldenstar

Once upon a time there was a widower who had one daughter. He had a neighbor who was a widow, and she also had one daughter. And every day his daughter would go over to the woman's house, and the widow treated her very well.

Well, one day the little girl told her daddy that he ought to marry their neighbor.

Her father said no, that he didn't want to get married. But the girl kept asking until finally he married her.

Now this man kept a lot of cattle, and he gave one cow to his daughter and one to his stepdaughter.

One day the stepdaughter said that she wanted to slaughter her cow, and she did. Then the stepmother sent her husband's daughter to wash the tripe and gut in the river. As she was washing the innards, one piece of gut floated away, and the girl ran crying after it. Down the river, she met a woman, and that woman was the Virgin Mary. Our Lady asked her why she was crying, and the girl told her how a piece of gut had floated away.

Our Lady then asked her, "Do you see that little house there on the hilltop? Go up there and sweep the house. Inside you will find a little baby crying. Give him a good smack on his bottom. And behind the door you will find a man. Throw garbage in his face."

The girl left and went right up to the house where the old man and the baby were, and they were Saint Joseph and the Holy Child. Now, she swept the house out and all, but she didn't give the baby a smack on the bottom. Instead she changed his diaper. And as for poor old Saint Joseph, she combed out his hair very nicely.

When she was finished she went back to see the Blessed Virgin again. Our Lady gave her the piece of gut that she had lost. Then she touched her right above the eyes, and a star came out on her forehead.

And so the girl went back home feeling very good.

As she was coming back her stepmother came out and saw her. The woman told her own daughter, "Look who's coming with a star on her forehead!" And when the girl got there they grabbed her and hit her until they wore her out. Then they asked her what she had been doing all this time.

The little girl told them everything. So her stepsister said that she wanted to go out and wash gut too, to see if she could have the same thing happen to her.

So her mother sent her down to the river to wash gut. And while she was washing the gut, a piece broke off and fell into the river. She too ran after it and met the Blessed Virgin, and Our Lady again asked what had happened. The girl said she was looking for a piece of gut that had fallen into the river. Our Lady told her the same thing she had told the other girl.

Well, the girl acted pretty foolish. After she swept the house she threw garbage in Saint Joseph's face and smacked the Holy Child and left him crying. Then she ran back to see Our Lady again. Our Lady gave her back the lost piece of gut. Then she touched her, too, just above the eyes, and out of her forehead grew a green horn.

When she got back home her mother came out to see her. What she saw made her so angry she began hitting at the horn with an axe. But the more she struck it, the greener it grew.

After that, whenever company came visiting, Goldenstar got hidden away. But Greenhorn was dressed in beautiful clothes to sit out where everyone might admire her.

One day, when Goldenstar was home alone, the Blessed Virgin came and gave her a magic wand. She told her that the wand could give her anything she asked for. Right then and there Goldenstar asked for clothes and got dressed and went to Mass. When she got there her stepmother and Greenhorn were already there. She went and sat a little behind them.

Greenhorn turned around, then said to her mother, "Look, there's Goldenstar."

"No, that's someone else," the stepmother said. "She's much too pretty, and besides, Goldenstar doesn't have any clothes that pretty."

When they were all coming out of Mass, the Prince came out behind Goldenstar. When she went to climb into the coach in which she had come, she dropped a slipper. The Prince went running and snatched up the slipper. Goldenstar managed to slip away, and he didn't catch her, but he still had the slipper.

Well, when the woman and her daughter got back home, Goldenstar was already there, sitting in a corner, in her usual rags. When they learned that the Prince was going around to see who had dropped the slipper, and was coming there, the woman hid Goldenstar.

So they put the slipper on Greenhorn, but it didn't fit very well. Then a little kitten who was in with Goldenstar began to mew:

> Here, here, Goldenstar's here.
> Here, here, Goldenstar's here.

The Prince heard that, so he went in and found her and made her try on the slipper. On her it fit very well, so he took her to his house and married her.

Espinosa 1937: 10–12. ATU 480/510A. Told in the summer of 1931 by Bonifacio Mestas, about fifty-six years old, from the village of Chamita, in northern New Mexico. Translated for this volume by the editor. In Hispanic tradition ATU 480, The Kind and Unkind Girls, frequently leads into ATU 510A, Cinderella, as in the present story.

This tale reflects Iberian and Iberian-American customs in two especially notable ways. Devotion to the Virgin Mary is strong in this culture and expresses itself in very personal ways, so that Mary is thought of almost as a member of the family or at least of the community. Accordingly, in märchen and legends she frequently plays the role of helper and donor that is played by fairy godmothers or mysterious old women in märchen and legends from other cultures.[1] Similarly, attendance at Sunday Mass occasions an obligatory weekly public appearance, even by young women of good family who might at other times remain behind the walls of their parents' homes. Accordingly, it is very common for the Prince in this märchen tradition to see his Cinderella first at Sunday Mass and so to fall in love with her from a distance, as it were.

23. Sister Fox and Brother Coyote

For weeks 'Mana Zorra had been stealing a chicken each night from a ranch not far from her abode when one night she found a small man standing near the opening she had made in the wire of the chicken house. The man was only a figure of wax put there by the caporal to frighten the thief. 'Mana Zorra, unaware of this, was afraid but, being very hungry, she decided to speak to the little man and ask permission to borrow a chicken.

"Buenas noches," said 'Mana Zorra.

There was no answer.

"He is either too proud to speak or doesn't hear," said the fox to herself. "If he isn't mal criado [*ill-bred*], then he didn't hear. I will speak to him again."

Going nearer the wax man, she said, "Buenas noches, Señor."

---

[1] Though more common in tales from the Iberian tradition, this is not exclusively an Iberian trait. The Grimm collection, for example, includes a märchen titled "Our Lady's Child" (no. 3) and ends with a section of tales with religious figures as characters (no. 201–10).

The little man made no response whatsoever, and the fox, after sizing him up from feet to head, decided that she had been insulted.

"Ay, the things I'm going to tell this hombrecito," said she. "He shall speak to me this time or I will slap his face."

She walked up to the figure and shouted at the top of her voice, "Step aside, please, and let me pass."

The wax man stubbornly stood his ground and refused to speak.

"Ora veras como yo te hago a un la'o [*Now you shall see how I make you move to one side*]," said 'Mana Zorra.

She struck the little man in the face and much to her surprise her foot was caught and held fast.

"Let me go!" shouted 'Mana Zorra, "or I shall hit you again."

The wax man refused to let go and 'Mana Zorra hit him full in the face with a hard right swing. The result was that this foot too, like the other, was caught and held.

"Ay, como eres abuzón," grumbled 'Mana Zorra. "Listen, amigo, either you let me go or I shall give you a kicking you will never forget."

The wax man was not impressed by the threat and refused to let go. 'Mana Zorra made good her word as to the kicking, but the little man didn't seem to mind at all and added insult to injury by holding her hind feet too.

"I'll bite," she threatened; "I'll bite." And quickly she bit the neck of the wax figure only to find herself caught not only by four feet but by her mouth as well.

"You think you have me," she scolded. "All right, how do you like this for a belly buster?" She pushed him so hard with her stomach that both of them fell rolling to the ground.

Just then who should appear on the scene but 'Mano Coyote?

"What are you doing there, 'Mana Zorra?" he asked.

"No, nothing," she answered. "This Christian and I have come to blows over a chicken. I have a contract with the ranchero which provides me a hen a night, but this little fellow can't read and has made up his mind to interfere. Hold him for me, 'Mano Coyote, and I will get a hen for both of us."

The coyote, a gullible fellow, caught the wax man in a clinch and held him while the fox pulled loose, and continued to hold tight until she stole a hen and escaped into the chaparral. Then, much to his chagrin, he found that he had been tricked, and as a result would likely loose his life.

Dawn found 'Mano Coyote struggling with the wax man, and he was there and still fighting when the caporal arrived.

"A' amiguito," said the caporal. "This is what I have been wanting to find out for a long time. So it is you, Señor Coyote? And I had always thought you my friend. If you wanted a hen to eat, why didn't you come to me like a gentleman and ask for her? However, though greatly disappointed in you, I will give you another chance."

The caporal freed the coyote from the wax man and placed him in a little room with one broken window.

"Don't jump through this window till I call you," said the ranch foreman to the coyote. "My dogs will catch and kill you. Wait until I tie them up and get us a snack to eat. Then when I call, you jump through the window and come to the kitchen."

The caporal heated water and poured it into a large pot that he had placed beneath the window. Then he called, "Come out, Señor Coyote; breakfast is ready."

The coyote jumped through the window and fell into the pot of boiling water. It was surely a miracle that saved his life, but the scalding water took the hair from his body and several toenails from his feet.

"Ay, ay," said 'Mano Coyote, as he crept with flinching feet and sore hide through the thicket. "Mana Zorra will pay for this. If I ever see her again I will kill her and eat her up."

Thus went 'Mano Coyote through the brush whining and swearing revenge until he reached a laguna. There, before him, lay the fox gazing at something in the water.

"Now I have you," cried the coyote. "Now you are to pay for your smart trick."

"Don't kill me, 'Mano Coyotito," pleaded the fox. "Look! I was placed here to watch this cheese."

"What cheese?" asked the coyote.

The moon was full and the reflection lay at the bottom of the laguna.

"There," said the fox, pointing at the reflection. "If you will watch it for me I will get us a chicken. However, be on guard lest the cheese slip beneath the bank."

"I'll watch it for you," said the coyote, "but don't be long. I'm dying for a chicken to eat."

'Mano Coyote had waited and watched several hours when he discovered the cheese slipping beneath the western bank of the laguna.

"Hey, Señor Cheese, don't go away," he called. "If you run away, I'll catch you and eat you up."

While 'Mano Coyote talked, the cheese continued to slip away. The coyote, fearing it would escape, sprang into the laguna and was soaked and chilled to the marrow before he reached the bank again.

"'Mana Zorra will pay for this," he howled. "Wherever I find her I shall kill her and eat her up."

The coyote had hunted the fox several days when at last he found her lying on her back in a small cave beneath a cropping of boulders. She was sound asleep.

"A' 'Mana Zorrita," hissed the coyote, "now I shall eat you up."

"Don't eat me, 'Mano Coyotito," begged the fox. "Look! When I went to get a hen, the caporal asked me to lie here and hold the world on my feet to keep it from falling down. He has gone to get more help and will be back soon to fix it. Ay de mi, 'Mano Coyote, I'm hungry. I know where there is a hen, but she will likely be gone when the caporal returns. Ay de mi, 'Mano Coyote, I'm hungry."

"I'm hungry, too," said the coyote. "Look, 'Mana Zorra; move over to one side. I'll hold the world on my feet if you will hurry and fetch us a hen."

"Good," said the fox, "but take care that the world doesn't fall and come to an end."

"I'll hold it," said the coyote, lying on his back and pushing up with all the strength of his four feet. "However, hurry; I'm hungry."

The fox escaped, and the coyote remained beneath the rock for several hours until he was almost paralyzed by the increasing weight of the world.

At last, being unable longer to stand the pain of his cramped position, he said, "If it is going to fall, then let it fall. I'm quitting this job."

He sprang from beneath the ledge and ran into the clearing. The rock didn't fall and the world showed no signs of coming to an end.

"Ay, ay," said he, "'Mana Zorra shall pay for this. If I ever catch her I shall kill her and eat her up."

At last the fox was found beneath a large bush near a gicotera [*rat's nest, sometimes taken over by bees*].

"A' 'Mana Zorra," he cried, "you have played your last trick, for now I'm going to eat you up."

"Don't eat me, 'Mano Coyotito," begged the fox. "Look! I was on my way to get the chicken when a schoolteacher offered to pay me to watch a class of boys."

"Where are the boys?" asked the coyote.

"There, before us in their schoolroom."

"Where is the money?" asked the coyote further.

"In my pocket," said the fox, as she rattled some broken pieces of porcelain.

"Pos, that's good," said the coyote. "What are you going to do with it?"

"I'm going to buy you a pair of trousers and a skirt for myself."

"Your idea is good," observed the coyote. "However, you must leave some money with which to purchase food."

"Certainly," said the fox. "I shall buy us a chicken apiece. But why did you mention food, 'Mano Coyote? Ay, ay de mi, I'm dying of hunger."

"I'm hungry, too," said the coyote.

"Look!" said the fox. "Watch these boys for me and I'll fetch the hen right away."

"¿Como no?" said the coyote. "Only hurry, 'Mana Zorra."

The fox saved her hide again and the coyote was left with the devil to pay, for the schoolroom was a hornets' nest and the boys weren't pupils but a lively lot of hornets.

The coyote sat listening to the hum of pupils reading their lessons when he noticed that the sound had ceased. "They are loafing on me," he said. "I'll shake them up a bit."

He shook them up and this would have been his last adventure had he not found a laguna into which to dive and escape the swarm of hornets.

"Ay, ay," wailed the coyote, "Mana Zorra shall pay for this. Wherever it is that I find her I shall eat her up, hide and hair."

At last 'Mana Zorra was found in a carrizal—a reed swamp.

'Mano Coyote had not forgotten the hornets' sting, the moon cheese, the world trick, and the wax man.

"Now there shall be no more foolishness," said he. "Mana Zorra must die."

"Don't eat me," pleaded the fox. "Don't eat me, 'Mano Coyotito. Look! I was on my way to get the hens when I met a bridegroom. He invited me to be godmother at his wedding. I felt it would look bad to refuse, and now that you are here you and I shall be padrino and madrina. You know how it is at these weddings. There is always plenty to eat and drink, and when it comes to chicken, there is none better in the world than that served at a wedding feast. Ay, ay, I'm hungry, 'Mano Coyotito."

"Pos, si," said the coyote; "I'm hungry, too. But where is the wedding party?"

"They are to pass at any time now," said the fox. "You stay here and I'll see if they are coming. If you hear popping and cracking you will know it is the fireworks shot by the friends of the couple. I shall be back soon."

'Mana Zorra slipped around the canebrake and set fire to it in first one place and then another. 'Mano Coyote heard the popping and cracking and began to dance with joy.

"Taco Talaco," said he, "here they come. Taco Talaco, ay, Taco Talaco, what a hot time there will be."

He discovered his mistake too late. The fire had trapped him completely, and so ended the career of 'Mano Coyote the dupe, shouting "Taco Talaco" and dancing at his own funeral.

Boatright et al 1954: 30–36. ATU 175/34/1530, Motifs K1023.4–5(ATU 49A)/J1812.4.1. Texas Mexican, collected, or possibly retold, by Riley Aiken. (The style is suspiciously literary.) Aiken gives no information about source, other than to call the collection "Mexican," but a footnote suggests that he may have obtained this particular piece from a man named Santiago Garza.

This cycle of adventures pits the American Indian trickster, the coyote, against the European trickster, the fox (here a vixen). Indian storytellers throughout the West like to string episodes together in a similar fashion to create a cycle of adventures of the hapless coyote. In the present instance, however, as one might expect in a story with Hispanic roots, most of the adventures are Indo-European. The story, then, probably owes more to Reynard the Fox cycles of stories from European tradition than to Coyote cycles in Native American tradition. Although in the broader European tradition the dupe is often a wolf (see the example in chapter 17), apparently, the juxtaposition of vixen and coyote is traditional in the Hispanic Southwest. Aurelio M. Espinosa (1914: 134–35) includes a version with three of the episodes above (the cane, the hive, and the rock), collected in New Mexico in the first decade of the century. And José M. Espinosa (1937: 181–83) includes three New Mexico vixen-coyote tales, two of which share episodes with the present tale.

The first adventure, the tar-baby episode, is usually associated in the United States with African American storytelling. But the development of the story is so different here (with the hero tricking the dupe into holding the sticky figure, which is of wax rather than of tar) that the story may be quite independent of American Negro tradition. Aurelio M. Espinosa (1943), in his catalog of the elements of the tar-baby story, does not include waxworks figures as tar-babies, nor the (not altogether clear) method of escape found in this version.

The episode with the rock also raises questions of African American influence. Bascom (1992: 114–16) distinguishes between a trick found in Indo-European tradition in which the trickster persuades the dupe to hold the rock so that the trickster can steal something from the dupe, and the trick illustrated here in which there is no question of theft, but often a question of escape from the dupe. The latter form of the motif, Bascom asserts, is strictly African. If Bascom is right, and he probably is, then with its African as well as European elements this delicious tale is indeed a gumbo.

'Mana and *'Mano* are, of course, dialectical contractions of *Hermana* and *Hermano* [*Sister* and *Brother*], just as *Br'er* is a contraction of *Brother*.

24. Las Bodas de la Tia Cucaracha

Tia Cucaracha was busily sweeping her house one day, singing while she worked but somewhat sad because she was not yet married. As she passed her broom in a far corner of the room, she heard a noise. Looking down, she beheld to her great surprise a shining silver coin. "How wonderful!" thought

Tia Cucaracha. "Now I can buy some beautiful clothes and some powder for my face and catch a husband!"

After she had returned from her shopping tour, she powdered her face, put on her fine clothes, and sat in the window which faced the street.

It was not long before Tio Perro came along. Noticing Tia Cucaracha sitting there in the window looking so attractive, he paused to talk.

"How beautiful you look!" he exclaimed. "Will you marry me?"

"How is your behavior?" questioned Tia Cucaracha.

"Well, at night I bark, 'Guau, guau, guau!'" answered the dog.

"Then I can't marry you. You would make too much noise and keep me awake," she answered.

Next, there passed by la Paloma, who stopped to rest on the window sill and talk to the beautiful Tia Cucaracha.

"My! how chula you look!" exclaimed the dove. "Will you marry me?"

"No," replied Tia Cucaracha. "You fly around everywhere and someone will soon shoot you. I would be left a widow."

Finally, a rat came along the street.

"Tia Cucaracha, how lovely you are! I had never really noticed before. Will you marry me?" he asked.

"What is your behavior?" she demanded.

"Well, I go around at night saying, 'Eeeee!' and in the daytime I usually sleep."

"That is fine," she said, smiling. "I will marry you."

The baits were celebrated with music and feasting, and the couple went to live in the house of Tia Cucaracha. The first Sunday after the wedding, as Tia Cucaracha was muy catolica, she arose early to go to Mass. Waking up the rat, she said, "Watch the arroz con leche which I have put on to cook. When I return, we will have our breakfast."

Tio Raton agreed, but turned over and went back to sleep. Some minutes later, he awoke suddenly, remembering the arroz, and ran quickly to the stove, where the mixture was boiling. Pobrecito de el! He lost his balance and fell head first in the pot. There Tia Cucaracha found him, patas arriba and quite dead, when she returned.

All the animals came to the funeral, and each expressed his regret for the misfortune Tia Cucaracha had suffered. The dog even said he would not bark at night for a while in deference to the departed.

Tia Cucaracha was very sad for a time, but it was not long before she could be seen sitting in the window again, dressed in her fine clothes and looking for another husband.

Hiester 1961: 233–35. ATU 2023. Told in Spanish by José Hernández to Miriam W. Hiester. Hernández, a Texas enlisted man stationed at Brooke Army Hospital, was a student in the Brooke Hospital Center School where Hiester was teaching. He also told her at least four other stories. She says of her collecting that she wrote stories down later from memory and from notes. She published the story in English in 1961, presumably in her own translation. Hiester considered the story "distinctly Mexican" because of its cockroach heroine: "*La cucaracha,* that pestiferous cockroach which grows to nearly the size of a mouse in South Texas and in Mexico, has always been looked upon with humor and almost fondness by the Mexicans. They regard him as something between a pet and a necessary evil, which they accept with . . . stoic resignation" (233).

This story is widely popular in Hispanic tradition, and a version called "Mousie Perez" is given in chapter 2 above. The tale of "The Louse and the Flea" in chapter 8, though assigned a different ATU number, is an alternate development of the same central situation: two animals usually considered pests are married and the husband drowns in the cooking pot while the wife is away. "The Louse and the Flea" corresponds to the portion of the present story in which the animals express their grief and "the dog even said he would not bark at night." The Anglo/American song "Froggie Went A-Courting," concentrating on the wedding itself, may also be a part of this cycle. It corresponds to tale ATU 2019*, which describes the guests at the wedding of two small and pestiferous animals.

25. La Llorona, the Wailing Mother

Once there was a woman who had three little children. The youngest was two years old, the next four, and the eldest six. Her husband had died, and she had taken a lover.

One day the man she loved left her, and she was alone again with her children. The woman grieved so much over the loss of her lover that she took no more interest in her children. She would give them no food, would not take care of their clothes, and stopped showing them the affection of a mother. She would whip and scold them from morning till night, blaming them because her lover had left her.

One morning in a fit of rage she cried out to the three little children:

"I will fix you . . . I don't want you any longer!"

So saying, she seized a large butcher knife and hacked her little children to death. Then she cut them up into many small pieces, took these to the brink of the river and threw them in. As she threw the last piece into the swift current and watched it carried away, she was seized with a terrible fit of weeping. She beat her breasts, pulled her hair, and began shedding tears and tears into the great river, as she hung her head downward, staring at the water.

She tried to lift her head up to cry toward heaven, but she was unable to do so. Her head hanging downward, she went back to the house, wailing and calling to her children. When she saw the house was empty and she was alone, she went outside again, lifted the knife she was still carrying and plunged it into her heart. No sooner had she killed herself than she was changed into a witch.

She then journeyed toward heaven in search of God. When she got before God, she told Him of her terrible crime on earth and begged Him to give her back her children.

"You shall go back to the earth," said He. "You shall search for the bits of your children in all the rivers of the earth and put them back together again piece by piece. If you cannot find them and put them back together again, you shall not be able to see children over six years of age but that you will kill them."

So the witch woman journeyed from river to river, upstream and downstream, searching for the bits of her children, as she wept and wept. Her wailing voice could be heard for miles and miles, echoing from bank to bank and carried by the wind, as she searched in vain. She shed tears and tears, but never could she find again one tiny bit of her children.

Finally she decided to go in search of people. She came to a castle where lived a king and queen who had a boy of five and a girl of four. The witch woman was taken in as a nurse to the two children because she came to the king and queen weeping and begging to take care of them.

Now she was known as La Llorona, or the weeping woman, because tears always streamed from her eyes. She showed a tender affection for the children and cared for them like a mother.

All the castle was getting ready to celebrate the sixth birthday of the little prince. Everyone was very happy and gay, all save La Llorona. She wept and wailed more than ever before.

"La Llorona, why do you weep so?" asked one of the servants.

"I had a boy exactly that age," sobbed La Llorona.

Then she fell to weeping and wailing, so that her cries echoed through the rooms and corridors of the great castle.

On the night of the little prince's sixth birthday, La Llorona went to the boy's bed, killed him with a knife, and took the dead child up into one of the deserted rooms of the attic.

Next day the servants missed the boy. The king and queen ordered everybody to search everywhere. They could never find any trace of the child. Finally the king and queen gave up the little prince for lost and grieved in their great misfortune.

La Llorona now continued to care for the little princess. Also, another boy was born to the king and queen, and this lifted some of their sorrow.

A year or so passed and the castle was preparing to celebrate the sixth birthday of the little princess. The unfortunate death of the prince was almost forgotten.

Now the fate of the little princess was like that of the prince. She was lifted from her little bed by La Llorona, killed, and taken to the attic room. There were such weeping and sorrow throughout the castle the next day, the voices could be heard for miles around. La Llorona's wailing could be heard above all the others. She beat her breasts, pulled her hair, and shed tears and tears.

The old king and queen as the years went by never quite forgot their great sorrow. La Llorona remained at the castle to care for the last little prince.

On the eve of the sixth birthday of the boy, the castle again prepared for a celebration, but the old king this time set guards over him, to watch so that his fate would not be that of the other two children.

One of the guards noticed just at dusk that La Llorona darted into a near-by room and hid something behind some books on a shelf. He went to look there, and discovered a sharp knife. The guard rushed to the king while the birthday celebration was going on and told him about the knife.

"But La Llorona just took the boy to bed because he said he was sleepy," said the old king.

They all rushed to the little prince's bedroom. Just as they entered, in the darkness they saw a figure picking up the child from the bed and hurrying away with him up the stairs. They followed the figure up and up, until they saw La Llorona there with the child; she was weeping and weeping as she held him in her arms.

They all fell upon La Llorona, the witch, snatching the sleeping boy away from her. They saw the remains of the other two children near-by.

As they were killing La Llorona, her wailing and crying could be heard far, far away. Her wailing was finally caught up with the sighing of the winds outside as she died.

Claudel 1943: 118–20. Motifs E323.5/E411.1.1/K764/E547. Written down in San Diego, California, for collector Calvin Claudel by Conrado V. Garcia, a sailor in the U.S. Navy. Garcia heard it in Tolleson, Arizona, near Phoenix. Claudel says that Garcia came of Spanish, Portuguese, and Mexican ancestry, and was "an exceptionally fine storyteller."

The legend of La Llorona is extraordinarily popular in Mexican and Mexican-American tradition. The wailing figure may have pre-Conquest origins, but as the story is now told, the woman, a mother weeping for her children, is usually identified with some local tragedy (cf. Dorson 1964, 436–38).

The present story, however, is an unusual example of legend reworked as a märchen, complete with king, queen, and royal children. It differs from a traditional märchen, nevertheless, in several respects. The initial situation, a widow taking a lover, is not a typical fairy-tale situation. The central figure, once transformed into a witch, never breaks that "enchantment"; she simply moves from the role of suffering heroine to that of villain. No innocent person, particularly not the queen, is accused of the murders, as happens in ATU 652, The Prince Whose Wishes Always Come True, ATU 706, The Maiden Without Hands, or ATU 707, The Three Golden Children ("The Bird of Truth," the first story in this chapter). Nor are the killed children restored to their parents, as happens, for instance, in ATU 710, Our Lady's Child, or ATU 720, The Juniper Tree. Nevertheless, I have included the story as a counter-example to the several examples of märchen reworked as legends that occur in this volume. The first half of the story seems to belong to the legend proper. Generally a legend narrative would end with God's curse upon the woman if she can not find the lost pieces of her children's bodies, or perhaps include a warning to bring children indoors when the cries of La Llorona are heard. But this piece adds on the märchen-like narrative explaining the final working out of the curse.

CHAPTER 4

ISLEÑO TALES FROM ST. BERNARD
PARISH, LOUISIANA

St. Bernard Parish, on the east (or, here, north) bank of the Mississippi River, is one of the two easternmost parishes (i.e., counties) in Louisiana. Like its sister parish, Plaquemines, it is largely wetland, juts out into the Gulf of Mexico, and historically has depended on fishing, hunting, and trapping as a major source of livelihood. Folklorists working in Louisiana before World War II discovered in and near the St. Bernard town of Delacroix, a settled Hispanic community. The people, who called themselves Isleños, had their roots in the Canary Islands, off the Spanish coast, from which they began migrating about the time of the American Revolution. In fact, Isleños had also settled in other parts of southeast Louisiana, but often disappeared into the general population. Ascension and Assumption are the only other two parishes in which Isleños seem to retain their own identity. In these two parishes and in upper St. Bernard Parish Isleños have continued to practice agriculture, as did their Canary Island ancestors. But in lower St. Bernard the Isleños turned to hunting, trapping, and fishing.

St. Bernard Parish was one of the areas hardest hit by Hurricane Katrina in the late summer of 2005. The residents evacuated almost completely, displaced all across the South as well as elsewhere in the United States. Some families have moved back, but the destruction of homes and businesses is nearly complete. At the time of publication it has not been possible to predict how much of the parish's traditional culture will survive, if any.

In 1941 Junor O. Claudel, a teacher in the public school in the Isleño village of Yscloskey and brother to folklorist Calvin Claudel, had students write out tales that he then communicated to his brother (Claudel 1945). Raymond R. MacCurdy did extensive fieldwork in the region in 1947, published a study of the language, *The Spanish Dialect of St. Bernard Parish, Louisiana* (1950), and wrote four articles on the community for *Southern Folklore Quarterly* between 1948 and 1952. Samuel G. Armistead, visiting the community in the 1970s and 1980s, collected other elements of the rich Hispanic folk tradition of this community, as well as some folktale material (1992). The folktale repertoire reflected in the work of these collectors is a classic Hispanic repertoire, with familiar versions of stories such as John the Bear (ATU 301), The Devil's Daughter (ATU 313), and The Three Golden Children (ATU 707) as well as humorous stories and tales of wisdom. Thus did this small community in the marshes of southeast Louisiana find a place in their lives for a significant folktale repertoire.

Typical Hispanic versions of such stories have already been offered in the preceding two chapters of Part 2, allowing this chapter to focus on material that is uniquely Isleño. This material includes stories from Isleño schoolchildren, in two cases available in both Spanish and English versions, and composite stories that draw on several elements of the Hispanic tradition to create new plots. The French names for children in two of these stories reflect the closeness and even intermingling of Isleño and Louisiana French culture in St. Bernard Parish.

26. The Cruel Mother

A: Louis and Louise

Once there was a lady who had two children. One was named Louise and one was named Louis. Louise went to her grandmother's house very often.

One day when her father came from work, he asked for his little daughter. His wife said she was at her grandmother['s]. She said that Louise was always running and she hadn't come back.

The mother had two pots on the fire. She told Louis to go look at one of the pots, but not to look at the other one. Louis looked at both pots. In the one that his mother told him not to look, he found Louise's head boiling.

When the table was set, everyone sat at the table. Louis didn't want to eat. The mother and father ate. After they were eating, they heard a voice from under the house where the head was buried. It said:

> My father and my mother eat,
> But my brother doesn't taste me at all.

This was heard three times. The father asked, "What is that?" He picked up the flooring and found Louise's head. He took his wife and tied each leg to a horse and let one run one way and the other the other way.

B: La Madre Cruel

Once upon a time there was a woman and a man and they had a daughter and a son. The woman didn't like the boy and so she used to send him to play at his grandmother's. And in the evening when the man came home, he would ask for the boy and his little sister would say that he was at their grandmother's. One day he came home and didn't find him in the house. He sent to look for him, but he didn't come.

His mother had killed him during the afternoon and she had his head cooking in a pot and his body hidden under the planks of the floor. And when they sat down to eat they heard a voice saying,

> Little sister, don't eat me
> The way Mother and Daddy eat me.

The father took up the floorboards and found the body of his son. Then he grabbed the woman—he knew that the woman had done it—he went and grabbed the woman and tied a leg to each—tied her legs to two mules and made one mule go in each direction.

A. Claudel 1945: 215; B. MacCurdy 1952: 240. ATU 720. Version A, collected for Calvin Claudel by his brother Junor, was written out in English by Philomène González, in Yscloskey, Louisiana, 1941. Version B, collected in Spanish on phonograph record by Raymond R. MacCurdy Jr. was told by Philomène González, Delacroix, Louisiana, 1947. It was translated from Spanish by the present editor.

Claudel collected two stories from a girl named Philomène González, and McCurdy collected the same two stories also from a girl named Philomène González. Though Claudel states that she was already fifteen in 1941, and McCurdy states that she was only seventeen in 1947, it seems likely that it was the same girl in both cases, and that one or both were mistaken about the age. González wrote out a total of seven lively stories for Junor Claudel in 1941. For McCurdy González told these stories, the two included here, and a two-motif story about a numbskull named Pedro, doubtless the Pedro Urdemalas also found in stories from Mexico and Puerto Rico. If I am correct in my surmise, then these English and Spanish versions of the same stories from the same storyteller provide an interesting example of a bilingual storyteller captured at two stages in her development. Certainly the two versions, despite obvious differences, retain similarities such as the head in a pot on the stove, the evidence under the floorboards, and the mode of death of the mother, that seem to indicate identity of narrators.

The Spanish version uses the imperative mode in the dead child's chant:

> Mi hermanita, no come de mí
> Como padre y madre comen.

The English version, however, uses the indicative:

> My father and my mother eat,
> But my brother doesn't taste me at all.

These versions of the tale pass over many of the motifs usually associated with ATU 720. The dead child does not transform into a bird, nor does the child return to life at the end. Indeed, the tale here seems well on its way to becoming a legend—a brief, horrific, but also ironic narrative that challenges us to accept the possibility of the supernatural intervening in everyday life. A similar process of transformation into legend is observable in one of the Appalachian versions of ATU 720 included in chapter 12 of the present volume.

27. Love Like Salt

A: Loveness of Salt

Once there was a man whose wife had died and he had three daughters. One day he was sitting out on the porch with his three daughters. He asked them if they loved him. The eldest said she liked him as much as he liked bread. Now the man was very fond of bread. So that was o.k. The other one said that she loved [him as much as he loved] coffee. He drank coffee nearly all day, and her love for him was sufficient. The youngest one said she loved him as much as he loved salt.

He was very mad at that and ordered the men to make a glass box, fill it with plenty of food, and engrave her picture on top. He was going to put her into the box and throw her into the river. So finally the day came for her to be thrown into the river. She was put into the box, and the box was floating away.

Now the king's son was to pick his wife, and he invited all the young girls to come to this party so he could pick his wife.

The king and his son was out riding and they saw this box floating. The king picked it up. The girl told the king why she had been thrown into the river.

Now the day came for the party. Everybody was dressed so pretty. The king ordered that the father of the girl was to have a special seat, and to put his dinner without salt. The girl was dressed so pretty her father and sisters didn't know her.

Soon as the man tasted his dinner, he started to complain about salt. The king came up and started to tell him about what he did his daughter. The man burst into tears and wished he had his daughter. The king showed him his daughter.

The king's son married the girl and the father went back to his home. He was very glad he found his daughter and was very sorry he treated her like that.

B: Annie y Marie

Annie and Marie lived with their father. One day their father asked Annie how much she loved him.

"I love you more than all the world," she said.

He asked Marie how much she loved him.

"I love you like salt on my food," she said.

And he thought that Marie didn't love him because he thought that like salt on food wasn't very much. So he made a man take her out on the mountain, and he told him to cut out her eyes afterwards. But the man, instead of killing Marie, killed a dog and cut out its eyes. And he hid Marie on the mountain. And the next day Annie cooked dinner for her father but didn't put any salt in the food. The father couldn't eat it, and so he told her that he knew that Marie had loved him. And so he said to the man, "I would give everything that I have in this world if I could have Marie back with me."

The man said, "Give me everything you have and I will bring you Marie."

So the next day he brought back Marie and the three lived together happily ever after.

A. Claudel 1945: 209–10; B. MacCurdy 1952: 239–40. ATU 923. Version A, collected for Calvin Claudel by his brother Junor, was written out in English by Philomène González, in Yscloskey, Louisiana, 1941. Version B, collected in Spanish on phonograph record by Raymond R. MacCurdy Jr., was told by Philomène González, Delacroix, Louisiana, 1947. It was translated from Spanish by the present editor. For more information on Philomène González and the circumstances of collection of these two versions, see the preceding story.

The two versions of this story are not as close as the two versions of the preceding story. If, as seems likely, the storyteller is the same for both versions, the most obvious explanation for the divergences is that González did not remember the story very well at the time of the second telling. In addition, she seems to feel more comfortable in written English than in oral Spanish. But circumstances of collection may have adversely affected her performance in Spanish. If, for instance, she had already told MacCurdy the stories, she would be likely to provide only a skeleton retelling on phonograph. She may, furthermore, have hurried the story to get it onto one disk (even though MacCurdy also collected some tales that obviously took several disks to record).

The story will remind readers of Shakespeare's *King Lear*. The second version, perhaps because the storyteller is hurrying or is not remembering the story very well, is quite succinct, and omits the discovery by and marriage with a prince. Both versions retain odd echoes of Snow White (ATU 709). In the first version the girl is exposed in a glass coffin, and in the second the compassionate executioner (Motif K512.2.0.2) substitutes a dog's eyes for her eyes, to fool her father into thinking she has been killed.

28. The Fairy with Hair as Fair as Oatstraw

There were three brothers, Tony, Paul, and Jack. And their poor father was sick. And he died on them. And Tony and Paul went right home and divided his goods. And the little that was left, well, they said, "The one who sticks a dagger the deepest into Daddy," they said, "he gets what's left."

Well, Tony grabbed the dagger and stuck it in up to the hilt.

And Paul, because that was the kind of fellow he was, stuck it in even further.

But Jack says, "Not me. You two keep everything, and I'll go get my poor father and do what can be done." He buried his father beneath the stairs, and set out to roam the world.

He met this old man. The man says to him, "My boy, who watches over you and sent you to me?" Said, "This is my lucky day."

Jack says, "Well, sir, since this is your lucky day, come along with me and I'll take care of you."

And so he stayed with the poor old man. But that poor old man was God. And while he was with him, there was this herd of little ponies went by.

And God saw that he liked this one black pony. And he says, "Well," says God, "what are you looking at?"

He said, "I'm looking at those ponies going by. Oh," he said, "how I wish I had enough money to buy that black one. He sure is a beauty."

"Well," said God, "here you are."

Now that black pony was his own father, but he didn't know it.

During this time that he was living with God, and the black pony was taking care of him, and everything was going good, his brothers went to the king.

"You know the Fairy with Hair as Fair as Oatstraw?" they said. "Well, our brother Jack can go get her for you."

So the king sent for Jack.

"Jack," he said, "your brothers tell me that you can bring me the Fairy with Hair as Fair as Oatstraw."

"Mr. King, sir," says Jack, "how am I going to bring you the Fairy with Hair as Fair as Oatstraw," he said, "when there ain't a soul in this world can find the place where she lives? Why," he said, "she lives in a castle in the middle of the ocean."

The king told him, "Your brothers say you can find her," he said, "and you're a-gonna go and find her. I'll give you three days to get ready."

Poor old Jack went back to his place and burst out crying. The black pony came in and said, "What's wrong, Jack old boy?"

Jack says, "Man," says, "what am I going to do, old pony? Those brothers of mine have told the king that I can bring back the Fairy with Hair as Fair as Oatstraw. How am I going to find her?"

The pony says, "Tell him that you are going to go," he says, "and tell him to make you a boat different from any other in the world, and put on board a band of musicians better than any other in the world, and tell him to give you a cannon, a good wax cannon ball, and a cargo of flour."

So Jack went and told the king. He was going to look for the Fairy with Hair as Fair as Oatstraw. And he told him, "Only one at a time can go on this trip," he said.

And so Jack set out. And when the boat pulled up [at the island castle] he said, "This is the place." And he began to knock where the Fairy with Hair as Fair as Oatstraw lived. "Only one at a time on this trip," he said, "not two." And they began to go in. One fellow would go in, and come out. Then the next fellow would go in and come out. And this maid said to Jack, "By damn," she said, "I ought to bring the Fairy with Hair as Fair as Oatstraw down to see this. This is something you don't see every day."

"Yes, ma'am," says Jack. "I have no idea why they're acting that way!"

"No, sir," she said, "it doesn't make any sense. A body couldn't keep from laughing at it. Let's go get her," she said.

So they brought her down. And when they brought her down, the boat took off with her. Well, when the boat took off, the Fairy with Hair as Fair as Oatstraw raised a terrible fog that began to swallow up the boat. But Jack threw flour on the water and exploded the fog with cannon shots.

As they were going along the Fairy with Hair as Fair as Oatstraw said— now, there was a little ring that she had, and she threw it into the very bottom of the ocean, and she said, "Whoever wants to marry me will have to bring that ring back."

When they got back where the king lived, they had had a good trip. Jack said to the King, "Mr. King, here's the Fairy with Hair as Fair as Oatstraw."

Then the Fairy with Hair as Fair as Oatstraw said, "Well, I'm here, but you will have to go and get the ring that I threw into the middle of the ocean if you want to marry me."

The king couldn't do that, but Jack's two brothers said, "Jack will get it."

Well, poor old Jack went back home. In three days the king sent for him and said, "Jack," he said, "I'm giving you three days to make plans." He says, "You have to go and get that ring the Fairy with Hair as Fair as Oatstraw dropped into the middle of the ocean."

Poor Jack went back to his place, and his little pony came in.

"What's wrong, Jack?"

"What's wrong!" says Jack. "Well, they want me to go and get the ring that the Fairy with Hair as Fair as Oatstraw threw into the middle of the ocean." Says, "How am I going to find it?"

"Tell the king you'll go," says the pony. "But if he offers you a boat, don't take it. Go on foot along the shore. Walk along and walk along," he says, "until you see this big old fish. But," he says, "don't be afraid. Grab him."

Well, Jack did it. He told the king, "I'll go get the ring." He started down the shore, and he walked along, and walked along, and walked along, until he saw this big old fish that he was supposed to grab. He grabbed him by the gills, and the fish said, "For the love of God, Jack," he says, "don't kill me. Tell me what you need."

Jack says, "I need you to find me the little ring that the Fairy with Hair as Fair as Oatstraw dropped into the middle of the ocean."

The fish says, "Grab that little whistle I've got behind my gills, and blow on it."

Jack began to blow that whistle, and he blew and he blew. And all the fishes came up, and nobody brought the ring with them until there came a Johnny-come-lately. This one said, "Yes," he said, "I've got the ring right here on the tip of my nose."

Well, Jack grabbed it and brought it to the king and says, "Here it is, Mr. King."

When the king gave it to the Fairy with Hair as Fair as Oatstraw, she said, "Not you. Jack's the one I'm going to marry because he found the ring, not you."

Then she took seed, loads of seed, and filled a room with it. She said, "Whoever wants to marry me will have to sort all that seed."

Jack's two brothers, they said, "Well," they said, "Jack'll do it."

Poor old—The king sent to find poor old Jack. And poor Jack come once more. The king says, "Jack," he says, "they say that you have to pick out all that seed next, and if not, it'll cost you your life."

Poor old Jack went crying back to his place one more time. His little old pony came in and said, "What's wrong, Jack?"

"What's wrong!" says Jack. "They want me to sort out a whole room full of seeds. How am I going to sort them all out?"

He says, "Don't worry, boy." Says, "Go back there and tell the ants, the little ants and the big ants, say, 'According to the will of God who makes you free, sort out this seed.' And it'll get sorted out."

Well, Jack went back and told the king, told him he was going to sort it out.

He said, "Ants, according to the will of God, sort out all this seed for me." And by the next day all the seed was sorted out.

The Fairy with Hair as Fair as Oatstraw said to the king, she said, "Jack, I'm going to marry Jack, not you."

Well, she set up a big tank of boiling oil. Told the king, "Whoever wants to marry me will have to jump into this tank."

Jack's brothers, they said, "Jack'll do it," because they thought that Jack would boil himself to death in it.

The king sent for Jack. Told him, "Jack, they say, your brothers say that you can jump into this tank and come out on the other side."

Jack says, "How am I going to do that? Get boiled to death, or get pickled. Whether I do it or not, it'll cost me my life, it'll cost me my life."

He broke out crying and ran back to his place. In come the little pony and said, "What's wrong, Jack?"

"They say that I have to let myself down into a tank of boiling water [*sic*]," he says, "and come out on the other side, so that the king can marry the Fairy with Hair as Fair as Oatstraw."

The pony says, "No, Jack." He says, "Kill me and soak in my blood till you're well soaked. And when the king asks you what you soaked yourself in, tell him to kill that big old black bull that he keeps by the seashore, and soak in it, and you wait there, and you'll end up with the Fairy with Hair as Fair as Oatstraw."

But Jack didn't want to kill him. He said, "No, Pony."

The pony said, "No, Jack." He said, "Kill me. Look, I'm your father who's undergoing this for you."

Jack did it. He went, dove into the tank, and came out on the other side. Then he turned around, dove in, and came out on the other side again. And he wasn't cooked.

The king says, "But Jack, how did you do that?"

Jack says, "Mr. King, bring me here that big old black bull that you keep by the seashore, and when you kill it, soak in its blood and then throw yourself in."

Well, that's what the king did. And when he threw himself in, he got cooked up. So Jack got the Fairy with Hair as Fair as Oatstraw, and his brothers cleared out.

MacCurdy 1952: 246–50. ATU 505/531/554, Motif H486.2. Recorded on phonograph disk, 1947, from the telling of Willie Alfonso, approximately forty-five years old, of St. Bernard Parish, Louisiana, for collector Raymond R. MacCurdy Jr. Translated by the editor. The Spanish title, *La Diosa Avena*, translates literally as "The Goddess Oats." And Jack, of course, is Juan in Spanish. This tale is embellished with a rich amalgam of motifs and incidents drawn from a variety of stories, including a hint of the magic boat associated with ATU 513B. Not all incidents, however, are crystal clear. What, for instance, is the purpose of the band of musicians on the ship? What precisely are Jack's men doing at the Fairy's castle that is so amusing? How do they get the Fairy on the boat? And how do the flour, the ball of wax, and the cannon save the ship from the fog?

Tales like this one, in which the hero is sent on a quest for a preternaturally beautiful and magical bride for the king but claims her for himself, are widely popular in Hispanic tradition. A tale somewhat similar to the present tale is also found in Carrière's French collection from Old Mines, Missouri (1937). But the Baughman index of British and American tales does not include any examples (1966). Typically Hispanic elements in this particular telling include the utilization of God in the role of helper or donor, the emphasis on filial piety, and the blithely ruthless denouement in which both the horse and the king are sacrificed to make things easier for the hero (though we must not forget that the horse, being a revenant form of the hero's father, is technically dead already). Note, too, that this tale shares some motifs with "Juan Bobo and the Riddling Princess" in chapter 2.

29. John and His Big Club

Once there was a bandit who killed and robbed the people. One day the bandit came to a house where a lady and her little boy lived. He brought the lady and the boy to a big cave. The bandit kept them in the cave until the boy was fifteen years old. Then one day the boy told his mother that he was going to free her. When the bandit came to eat at the cave, he hit the bandit over the head with a piece of wood.

He [the boy] had never seen flowers, trees or grasses before. While they were walking through the town, the king sent for them. When the boy appeared before the king, the king was surprised to see his own son. The king gave him everything he wanted. He stayed for a while with the king and his mother. Then he told the king he wanted a white horse and a big club so he could kill all the bandits he met.

On his way he met a giant. The giant asked him where he was going. He told the giant that he was hunting for bandits. The giant joined him on his hunt for bandits. After a while they met another giant. He also went with them. Then while the three were walking, they met another giant who also went with them.

Then they heard a cry for help. They went in the direction the cry came from. Soon they came to a big hole in the ground. They heard a girl cry for help. The three went down the hole. John went first.

Down there he met the devil. John hit the devil and cut his ear off. Meanwhile the three giants had come down the hole and rescued the girl. John called to the giants to help him up. But the giants had gone off. He bit the ear of the devil. Soon the devil appeared and said not to bite his ear, that he would help him out of the hole.

When he [John] got out, he met the three giants, but the girl had run away. Soon the four of them came to a cabin in the mountain.

One day John and the two giants went looking for food and left giant number one to cook. While they were away, a mouse, which was the devil, came and asked the first giant for some cheese. The giant said no and threw the knife at him. The devil made the giant cut himself bad.

Then the next day they left giant number two to do the cooking. While John and the other two giants were away, the mouse came again. He asked the giant for some soup. But the giant said no and threw a spoon at him. But while he was cooking, some soup got in his eyes and blinded him. The next day giant number three stayed to cook. The same thing happened as to the other two.

Then the next day John stayed home to do the cooking. When the mouse came and asked John for something to eat, John gave it to him. Then the devil came to his original size and asked John to go to his house.

John had stayed a long time at the devil's house. But the devil's daughter told him that they were going to escape. That night the girl told John to get the thinnest horse in the stable. But John got the fattest horse in the stable. When he brought the girl the fat horse, she told him that the horse would not go fast. Then they started to go away.

Just then her father heard them and got on the skinniest horse and soon was catching up to his daughter and John. But the devil's daughter changed the horse into a house and John into a sack of potatoes and herself into an old farmer. Soon after, the devil and his wife stopped and asked the old farmer if he had seen their daughter and John. The old farmer told them that they went to the right fork of the road.

After the devil and his wife had gone, the devil's daughter changed the sack of potatoes back to John and the house to a horse. Then they went to the left fork of the road. They met a man who had seen the devil and his wife, and he told them that they had been killed by an accident. John and the devil's daughter got married and lived happily ever after.

Claudel 1945: 210–12. ATU 301/313. Written out by Earl González, age fifteen, a student at the St. Bernard Parish public school in Yscloskey, Louisiana, 1941, for teacher Junor Claudel, who communicated the story to his brother Calvin. The title is the one Earl González gave to the story, but the big club turns out not to be an important element in the story.

This story combines two of the most popular tale-types in Hispanic and Francophone tradition, John the Bear (ATU 301) and The Devil's Daughter (ATU 313). The incident of the three (here four) companions cooking usually precedes the first visit to the underworld. And the magic flight motif is usually developed at greater length. In another version of ATU 313 from the Isleño community of St. Bernard Parish, the Devil's daughter instructs the hero to take the horse that is thinner and runs as fast as thought, not the one that is fatter and runs as fast as the wind (MacCurdy 1952: 243). Coffin and Cohen include a beautiful version of ATU 313 from the Louisiana Isleño community in *Folklore in America* (1966: 19ff).

30. Two Tales of Quevedo

A. Quevedo Holds His Ground

I know one about Quevedo that goes like this. One time [he said,] "I"—I mean, "The king doesn't trust me. He doesn't want me on his land. You understand? I can't go to Spain because he doesn't want me on his land. But I'm smarter than he is," he says. "I'm going to go to England. I'm going to bring dirt from England, and I'm going to be on my own land."

And he took his little donkey and a—it would be a, be a cart, like we call it. And he filled it up with dirt.

He was going along and going along, and the king—"Heh! Quevedo! What are you doing here? You know I don't want you on my land."

"I'm not on your land. I'm on my own land." That's what he said [*laughing*]. The cart was right there. "So," he says, "I'm on my own land."

That fellow! You can't win with Quevedo. I don't know anyone who . . . No, you can't win at all with Quevedo.

B. Quevedo in the Bag

[The king] says, "Let's send him to the shepherds. You know, the shepherds. They'll destroy him. They'll take him to the river and throw him in," he says. "Because I can't do anything with him."

They put him in a sack, all right. And there was this restaurant, and the shepherds went in to have some beer, they said, because they were supposed to be at the river at this certain time and they still had quite a few minutes to go. They said, "Yeah, good," and they went into the restaurant. And Quevedo was left.

Well, here comes this other shepherd.

"Heh!" He hits the sack and gives it a big kick and says, "What's going on here?"

"Ooooo! They want me to marry the king's daughter. Man, that king's crazy!"

"He wants you to marry? And you don't want to marry the—? Don't you know that the daughter of the king—that guy's a millionaire," he says. "She belongs to the best family in the world," he says. "Where they live is a paradise. What can I say? And you don't want to marry into that family?"

"No!" says Quevedo.

"Well," says the shepherd, "I . . . [*rest of statement unintelligible*]."

He had come with some animals. He was herding sheep and herding elephants and herding, maybe, bulls, and [*laughing*] goats. He says, "I'll make a deal with you. If you will take the elephants and the, all the stock I have here," he says, "and let me get into the sack, I'll marry her. I'll marry the princess. I won't have to keep on herding this herd."

And Quevedo says, "Well, if that's what you want, get in the sack. I'll get out. O.K.?"

Well, when they came back, those who were the guards, we could call them, huh? When they came back he said, "No! I-I-I-I'll marry her. I'll marry the princess."

"You're going to get married, are you? Make room, so we can come with you. You're going to get married! We're throwing him in the middle of the river, more like it." See. And [*laughing*] they took him to the river, and they threw him in the river.

But Quevedo? It wasn't Quevedo. Not Quevedo. He was with the animals. Ohh! Quevedo had a big haul of animals. He said, "Let's see, what should we do now?" He says, "Let's parade before the—I'm going to parade in front of the king's house, to see if he recognizes me." The king's palace! Did you get that?

So he said—the king came out and said, "Huh? Is that Quevedo?"

"Yeah, it's Quevedo."

The king says, "How can that be? They've already thrown him into the river. And here he is back again?" He says, "Quevedo, what happened? I don't understand. They threw you into the river and here you are."

"Oh, yeah. Yeah. They didn't throw it out far enough for me, not far enough. If they'd only thrown me . . . , I'd have been a millionaire. Ooh," he says, "just look at all the animals I brought back. [*Laughing.*] I pulled out elephants. I pulled out those others that they call giraffes. Didn't believe it—all the animals I pulled out," he said. "But I couldn't get really deep. They threw me [too close to the shore (*? inaudible*)]."

And the king, the king said, "This is a fine situation. I don't know what we're going to do. Oh, well," he said, "what's done is done."

Armistead 1992. A: 148; B: 145–47. A: ATU 1590; B: ATU 1535. Both tales collected by Samuel G. Armistead from Joseph (Chelito) Campo at Delacroix, Louisiana, December 19, 1980. Translated by Armistead and the editor.

Campo, perhaps the last teller of Isleño folktales, was over ninety at the time Armistead interviewed him. He proved to possess a wealth of folk traditions, including riddles, proverbs, and other genres, as well as folktales. Armistead calls him:

> a master raconteur, a folk-artist who loves to perform and who reacts with pleasure to enthusiastic interest in his art. Varying intonation and changing voices, punctuating the narratives with exclamations, asides, commentary, and laughter, he constantly dramatizes his stories in a way that makes it easy to imagine how a rich folktale tradition must once have flourished among the *Isleños*, gathered of an evening at a trapping or moss-gathering *campa* somewhere on the *plería* or on some shrimp boat, hove to for the night, far out in the Gulf. (139)

Armistead interviewed and collected from thirty-six Isleños between 1975 and 1982, gathering what is almost surely the last trawl through this bed of folklore.

The Quevedo of these tales is Francisco de Quevedo y Villegas (1580–1645), a classical Spanish author unaccountably transformed into a particularly Spanish trickster-hero. As a true trickster, he has attracted to himself tales told elsewhere about Br'er Rabbit or Eileschpijjel. Laughing at his exploits has been an especially popular pastime in St. Bernard Parish.

CHAPTER 5

CAPE VERDE TALES
FROM NEW ENGLAND

Ever since transatlantic naval commerce began in earnest in the sixteenth century, the geographic situation of the Cape Verde Islands has attracted commercial ships. There, four hundred miles out into the Atlantic, a vessel could stop to rest, renew supplies and water, trade, or fill out a crew. Such commercial vessels brought Cape Verdeans to the United States first as slaves and later as whalemen. And from the mid-nineteenth century till today ships and then airplanes have brought individuals and whole families in such numbers that Cape Verdeans in the United States now outnumber those in Cape Verde itself. Here they have settled in close-knit communities along the New England coast, finding work in the cranberry bogs, the factories, and the ports, and in the kitchens, parlors, and yards of middle- and upper-class New Englanders. At first, boats regularly plied the waters between New England and Cape Verde, and people who hated the cold regularly went back home for the winter, pregnant women went back to bear their children, and old people went back to die. So when Elsie Clews Parsons set out to collect New England Cape Verde folktales in 1916 this community that had been in America for at least three or four generations was composed, paradoxically, largely of people actually born on Fogo, Brava, or other of the Cape Verde Islands (Parsons 1923a: xi). Changes in immigration laws, implemented in 1922, for a time discouraged people from going back on a regular basis, for fear of not being readmitted. Further changes in immigration laws in 1966, however, resulted in new waves of Cape Verde immigrants into New England and New York.

The Cape Verde Islands were a Portuguese colony until 1975. The people use a language, Kriolu, derived from Portuguese as restructured by African linguistic influences. Hence, in New England, these people were often referred to as *Portugese*. But in the closing decades of the twentieth century independence in the homeland and a changed political climate here in the United States have created in these communities an enhanced sense of their identity as Cape Verdeans. These communities have long had newspapers, radio stations, and social clubs. And the language has had a distinct development here in the United States. The enhanced identity now expresses itself in the revitalization of language and traditional community outlets, in political involvement, in festivals, and in a renewed pride in Cape Verde American history, music, craft, and storytelling.

Thus the Cape Verdeans are perhaps unique among American ethnic groups. Living for more than a century and a half with one foot firmly planted in New England and one foot balanced four hundred miles off the African shore of the Atlantic, they share a double identity. From the very beginning they have been thoroughly integrated into the American economy. Their language, whether English or Kriolu, has become distinctly American. And in time they have come to vote in the same elections, send their children to the same schools, and watch the same television as other Americans. At the same time they have not ceased to be Cape Verdeans, contributing to the economy of those islands from their American incomes, traveling freely back and forth, constantly renewing their American community culture from the Cape Verde fount, participating in that nation's political life, and sometimes still, going back to die. They are Cape Verdeans and Americans both, with no need for a hyphen.

The tales in this chapter come from two sources. Elsie Clews Parsons collected stories in Newport and Providence, Rhode Island, and in Fall River and New Bedford, Massachusetts, as well as on Cape Cod and the island of Nantucket, in the summers of 1916 and 1917. The storytellers narrated in Kriolu, translated on the spot for Parsons by a Newport man, Gregorio Teixeira da Silva, who was born like so many in Cape Verde. Silva then took Parsons's English transcriptions and retranslated them into Kriolu. Finally Parsons made an English version based on Silva's Kriolu version. Many of these tales come from the Iberian repertoire that the Portuguese share with the Spanish. No story is more characteristic of that repertoire than the sensational and strongly moral "The Girl without Hands, Breasts, or Eyes." The Cape Verde repertoire is also famous for its Arabian Nights tales. I have included a version of "Ali Baba" that has been superficially localized in the United States. "The Maria Condon," a mermaid tale, reflects the maritime tradition of the Cape Verdeans.

The remaining two tales come from my own interviews with Yvonne Smart, a librarian in Providence, Rhode Island. Ms. Smart, who spoke Kriolu at home before she went to school, has long been active in Cape Verde affairs. She was part of a contingent from New England who participated in the 1995 Smithsonian Festival of American Folklife, of which "The Cape Verde Connection" was a featured part. She shared a unique animal tale featuring the culture's traditional hero Nho Lobu, and a typically Iberian story, "The Girl Who Wanted to Marry a Man with a Gold Tooth." As she narrates, Ms. Smart spices her English with Kriolu phrases to bring out their Cape Verdean character.

Though the stories in this chapter came into the Cape Verde repertoire from Portugal they, like the Louisiana Creole stories and the Gullah stories in other chapters, exhibit strong African influences in structure and motif. And all have been further shaped by generations of retelling in the Cape Verdeans' second home in New England.

31. The Girl without Hands, Breasts, or Eyes

There was a man had a daughter. She made asylums for the poor. Her father did not know about it until her godfather told him. "Soon you will be a poor man," said his compadre, "seeing how your daughter is spending your fortune." Six months of the year the man spent in town with his daughter; the other six, on his estates in the country. He invited his daughter to go with him into the country. He showed her about his estates. In the last was a pinewood. Here he tied the girl to a pine-tree. He cut her hands off at the wrist, he cut off her breasts and put out her eyes. He left her.

This place was near a king's house. The king had a dog, and they began to notice that the dog was falling off. The king asked the keeper if he cut his rations. The keeper answered, "I give him the regular rations; but he runs off with them somewhere, I don't know where." The king set a man to watch the dog. Every day the dog ran through the wood and took food to the girl and licked her wounds. They told the king. He went to the girl, he unbound her, he brought her to the palace. He told his mother he was going to marry this girl.

His mother said, "It is disgraceful to marry a girl without hands or breasts or eyes." The king answered, "This is my wife."

There was a war being waged, and the king had to go to it. After he went, his wife gave birth to twins. The king's mother wrote to him about it. She said that the children were the handsomest in the country. The letter-bearer stopped at a hostelry where they gave him *opeo* to smoke, took out his letter and read it, and changed it to read that the two children were two puppies. The bearer went on his way; he gave the letter to the king. The king wrote back that they were to treat the dogs like children. On his return journey, the bearer stopped at the same hostelry; and again they read the letter, and changed it to read that mother and children should be cast out of the palace, lest the king return and destroy it. When the king's mother received this letter, she felt sad, but she had to obey the king's word.

Her daughter-in-law said, "Make me two baskets to hang on my shoulders, and I will go. It is my destiny." She went out before dawn with the babies in the baskets. As she went, she wondered if she could find water for the babies to drink. She felt the air cooler, then she felt water around her feet. She reached down to it with her left arm. Then she felt her hand grow, and that she could grasp with her finger. She said to herself, "If God is good enough to give me back my left hand, he may give me my right hand." She reached down, out grew her right hand. "Would that I could have milk for my babies!" she said, and she sprinkled water on her chest. Her breasts grew out, and without waiting to restore her eyesight she began to nurse the babies. After she nursed them, she bathed her eyes and she saw.

She went on. She reached the city of her birth. Her father was dead. To his house all strangers coming into the city were sent. The morning after their arrival they were always found dead. The woman and her babies were sent to the house. At midnight she heard a voice asking her for pardon. It was the voice of her father. He had become a demon. It was he who killed the strangers. His daughter said she would pardon him, and that he must let people know her story. With a tongue of fire he burned into the floor the story of what he had done to his daughter. "Now I can go to rest," he said.

In the morning they came to the house as usual, the priest and the town officials, to take out the dead. They were surprised to find her alive. They called together the City Council to read the writing. The city gave her all her father's property. She was his only child. She came into possession of the house at eleven o'clock. At twelve she had given an order that the house was to be an asylum again for the poor and for strangers.

When the king returned home, he asked for his wife. His mother showed him the letter. He set off at once to find his wife. He traveled so long that his clothes wore out, his beard reached to his waist, his hair to his shoulders. Finally he came to the city of his wife. He was so low in his estate that he went to the asylum. In it were twelve inmates. They argued about taking him in. Some said their patroness would object; others, that she was a good woman and would not object. They decided to take him in, each to give him a spoonful out of his plate. She visited the asylum, she saw the newcomer, she ordered that he be fed. It was noticeable that her children, now growing up, took to the newcomer, and followed him about.

One day he said to her that her ways were like those of his wife, but he knew that she could not be his wife, because his wife had no hands or breasts or eyes. Then she knew that he was her husband. All her property in that place she left to the poor. She returned with the king to his country to be queen.

Parsons 1923a, vol. 1: 180–82. ATU 706. Parsons received this tale from Gregorio Teixeira da Silva of Newport, Rhode Island, born on the Cape Verde island of Fogo. Parsons speaks fondly of Teixeira, who acted as guide and interpreter for her collecting excursions into Cape Verde culture. He died in 1919, before the collection *Folk-Lore from the Cape Verde Islands* could be published, and Parsons dedicated the collection to him. He told Parsons at least five other stories, including Nho Lobu and other animal fables and two other märchen-like stories. All six of the stories he told Parsons have fairly strong lessons. One of them, the following (here quoted in full), may well express the storyteller's bemusement with regard to Parsons and her fieldwork:

> You are like that wolf who told his wife to prepare for him something to eat for
> a week, for him to go and work in a place. He went, he did nothing, he ate, he
> lay down. At the end of a week the woman went to see what her husband was
> doing. When Wolf saw his wife coming, he said to her, "Woman, all this is very
> confidential, you can't see it, you can't see it." He covered it with his cloak.

Did the storyteller feel that Parsons the fieldworker seemed to be very busy, but was in fact doing nothing—nothing, at least, of any value?

ATU 706 is widely popular in Iberian tradition, in the New World as well as in the old. This Cape Verde rendition emphasizes the selfless Christian charity of the heroine. Her generosity leads to her initial trials. Her selflessness is vividly expressed at the moment in which she feeds her hungry children from her restored breasts before she restores her own eyes. And when she returns to her father's house and finds that she is now the mistress of his fortune, she resumes the generous hospitality that she had been forced to abandon early in the story. Ultimately this very generosity brings about her reunion with her beloved husband. In later conversation Parsons was told that the changing of the letters was the work of the girl's father, turned demon (181, note).

32. The Seven Robbers

Once there were two brothers. One was rich, the other was poor. The poor brother gave the rich brother one of his three sons to christen. Every day the child went to his godfather's to get bread. Finally the rich brother said that giving the boy bread every day was very expensive. One day, when his godchild came to his house to get bread, the rich brother took the bread, threw it in his face, and said to him, "Do not come to get bread any more."

The poor brother gathered grass for a living. One day he went out early for grass. But since he was too early, he sat down to wait for daybreak. Soon he saw seven robbers come out of a rock. He heard them say where they were going to steal.

One said, "I'm going to Providence."

Another said, "I'm going to Newport."

Another said, "I'm going to San Francisco."

After they left, he went to the rock and said, "Rock, open!"

He went in and found all kinds of money on the ground, like grass. He had only one donkey and no sack. So he took off his trousers, filled them with money, saddled them on his donkey, and went home. Next day he borrowed a donkey, so he had two, and he took with him a sack. When he came home with all this money, he saw he had so much money he would have to measure it. So he sent to borrow a quarta from his rich brother. He measured the money, and buried it under the bed.

Next day he went again with four donkeys. Again he sent to borrow the quarta. Before this he had bought food by the liter, and his brother thought he could afford to buy only by the liter, not by the quarta. So the brother put some tar on the quarta he lent him. The poor brother measured, and when he sent back the quarta, a gold pound stuck to the bottom of the quarta. The rich brother found it and went to ask his brother where he got it. The poor brother said to him that it was a quarta of corn that he bought.

"No," the rich brother answered, "I found a pound sticking to the quarta. If you don't tell me, I'm going to denounce you in the city."

So the poor brother told him how he saw the robbers come out of the rock, as well as how he got the money.

The rich brother said to him, "You must take me there to get some money."

"Yes, I will take you. Yes. Go home, and come back at midnight! We'll go." The man went home; but, as he was in a hurry to get the money, he came back at ten to crow like a rooster. His brother said to him, "Go home! You are not a rooster. When it is time, I will call you." He went. In half an hour he came back. His brother said, "It is still too early, but we'll go."

The rich brother took five donkeys, the other took two. They went to the same place, and they sat down to wait. When it was time, out came the seven robbers. The poor brother counted them.

When all seven had come out and left, he said, "Rock, open!" They went in and collected money, the two of them. There was a bar of gold there and the rich brother said, "I will take it with me."

The poor brother said to him, "No, don't take it. It's the only one here. They will discover it, they will miss it." But the rich brother took it and put it into his sack.

Next day he didn't wait for his brother, he went alone with twenty donkeys. The robbers had not missed the gold bar. He loaded his donkeys and left.

The next day he took forty donkeys. After he got there, six robbers came out. They had left one there to catch the man who came there to steal. He counted, "One, two, three, four, five, six. Six? It can't be six. It's seven." He counted again. "It's six, but I'm going to make it seven. Rock open!"

He went in, and he was filling his sack. The robber who was inside grabbed him. He put irons on his hands and feet and left him until the other robbers came. They took him, skinned him, cut him up joint by joint, and left him there.

A day passed and he didn't come home. His wife went to the house of her brother-in-law and said to him, "If you don't go get your brother, I'll denounce you in the city."

"I'll go for him," he answered, "but I imagine they've already killed him."

He went back to that place. Seven robbers came out, as usual. He said, "Rock open!"

The first thing he saw was his brother lying dismembered in the middle of the floor. He put him into the sack, took it on his back, and went home. He said to his sister-in-law, "I found my brother cut up piece by piece. I'm going to look for a shoemaker to sew him together. I'll put him in bed and we will make out that he died suddenly."

Now the woman had three boys and one girl. "If one of your boys wants to be a doctor or a priest we'll make him one. If the other has wanted to be a governor, we'll educate him for it. The girl we'll teach what she wants to know. What money you want, or what you need, I will give to you to the end of your life."

They put the dead man in bed and the shoemaker came and sewed him up. They gave him a lot of money for his work.

When the seven robbers came, they did not find the dismembered man. They said, "A robber has been in our house again." The next day they left one robber in the house again, but no one came. The captain of the robbers said that he was going into the city to see where they had buried him.

The first house he came to was the house of the shoemaker. The shoe-maker was at work. The captain said to him, "You sew well. Can you not make me a pair of shoes?"

The shoemaker answered, "That is nothing. Yesterday I sewed up a man's body that they cut up joint by joint." (He had agreed with the poor brother not to tell.)

The captain knew that was the place. He said to the shoemaker, "Go with me. Show me the place. I'll pay you twice as much as they paid you." So the shoemaker showed him the place.

The captain went home. He put the six robbers each into a barrel. He rolled the barrels down the road, rolled them to the house of the widow. He asked her if she wanted to buy molasses. The woman said, "No."

The boys went to the house of their uncle and got him to buy the molasses. They told the captain to put the barrels in the house of their uncle. While they were cooking for the captain, the children took the corkscrew to get out the molasses.

They bored a hole in a barrel. The man inside the barrel asked, "Is it time?" The little boy said to him, "No, wait a while."

He told his mother that somebody was inside the barrel. The mother went and bored holes in all the barrels. "Is it time? Is it time?" they asked.

"Wait a while," said the woman, "wait a while."

The woman took a club. She went behind the captain sitting at the table, and she let him have it on the head. She killed him. Then the woman put a big cauldron of water on the fire. She turned up all the barrels. In each she made a big hole. She poured boiling water into the barrels and she killed all the robbers. Then she sent to call two of her kinsmen. They dug a big hole in the yard and they buried the bodies. The poor brother went back to the rock. He took out the rest of the money, brought it home, and divided it with the widow.

The eldest son of the woman became a doctor; the second son, a gover-nor; the third, a priest. The girl became a schoolmistress. The four children and the widow together built a fine house at their place. The road to their house was paved with gold. When the widow died, she left all her wealth to my father. But my father was such a bum, he drank up all that money and didn't leave me a penny.

Parsons 1923a, vol. 1: 1–5; vol. 2: 1–3. ATU 954. Told to Parsons by Jon Santana, born on the island of San Nicolâo. Parsons thus explains the younger brother's profession:

There are no barns on the Islands. Cattle are pastured or tethered near the house. After the grass has dried, people pull it up and bring in bundles of it for the tethered animals. People are free to get grass wherever they find it. As in the tale, a man may be paid for getting it. (Parsons 1923a, Part 1:1, note 3)

I have revised the translation of this tale, softening the relentless parataxis to make it sound more the way a native speaker of English would tell it. The choppy style of the Parsons text seems due in part to the collecting technique she used (see above). The original style of translation is preserved in the preceding and following tales, though with occasionally modified punctuation.

Arabian Nights stories, especially "Ali Baba" (the present tale, ATU 954) and "Aladdin" (ATU 561), are distinctive of the Cape Verde repertoire, and Parsons collected at least five versions of this particular story. Arabian Nights stories probably entered Portuguese tradition from Galland's French versions in the early eighteenth century (1704–1717). Portuguese editions of the tales would have reinforced the tradition on a regular basis. There is, however, some influence from the oral traditional versions of these tales as well. In the present case, for instance, the opening derives from Iberian oral tradition, and the thieves number seven, as is common in oral versions of ATU 954.

33. The Maria Condon

There was a wolf went fishing. He caught a Maria Condon. He saw her very pretty eyes. He wanted to swallow them.

Maria Condon said to him, "Sir Wolf, don't suck out my eyes! I will give you a twist of my hair. Anything you ask it for, it will give you."

Wolf did not trust her. He said to her, "First give me your hair. I want to try it before I let you go." She gave him a twist of hair. He said, "Maria Condon, by the virtue God gives you, fill me this rock with soup, and a bone in the bottom for me to dive to get." As soon as he asked it, the rock filled with soup, with a bone at the bottom. Wolf was satisfied; he let Maria Condon go.

He gathered a bundle of wood. He asked his Maria Condon to mount him on the bundle of wood to take him home. When he got on top of the wood, it carried him towards home.

He passed by the house of the king. The princess was sitting on the verandah. The princess said, "Oh, what a fool to ride on wood!" The princess scorned him.

He said to his Maria Condon, "By the virtue God gives you, in nine months make the princess bear me a son with a gold star on his head, and a gold apple in his hand."

After a while the princess appeared pregnant. The king was highly grieved. He covered the palace with black. Nobody knew how the princess came to be pregnant. After nine months a child was born with a gold star on its head and a gold apple in its hand. The king summoned all the men of the city to come to the palace. He said that he to whom the child gave the apple would be its father. All came, but to none of them did the child give the apple.

The priest said to the king, "There is one man missing, Mr. Wolf."

The king said to him, "Wolf is not a person." The priest asked the king to send for him, at any rate. Then the king sent four officers to get him. But Wolf refused to go with them, because he knew why they had come to get him. He was afraid the king would kill him. Then the king sent twelve officers after him, with orders to bring him or his head. He came.

As soon as he reached the door of the palace, the child reached him the apple. The king was sad, but he had to marry him to his daughter. Then Wolf took the princess with him.

He asked his Maria Condon to make him a shelter so small that they would have to live in it half in, half out. (He wanted to punish the princess.)

When they went into the shelter, the princess said to him, "Why don't you ask your Maria Condon to make you a palace like the king's, or better?"

"No, never! I want to pay you back for what you did to me."

At meal-time he asked his Maria Condon to give him a tub full of soup made out of a single bean, and with one bean at the bottom.

The princess said to him, "Why don't you ask your Maria Condon to make you eat like people, and at the same time to make you into a fine, handsome man?"

He said, "I'd die if I ate [even] a little." But next day he asked Maria Condon to make him into a fine, handsome boy, and to make him eat like people. The princess was pleased.

That night he asked Maria Condon to make him a high house—*sobrad'*—of seven stories, higher than the king's. The next morning the king saw the *sobrad'*. He asked who had the impudence to make a *sobrad'* higher than his. They told him that it was Wolf, his son-in-law. Then he could do nothing to him. (Had it belonged to any other fellow, he would have sent and killed him.)

Wolf wanted to kill the king, to become king in his place. He invited the king and all the citizens to dinner. When they were all seated at the table, he asked his Maria Condon to put a spoon in the king's pocket. They did not see the spoon. The spoon disappeared.

The king said, "Let us search, and let him upon whom the spoon is found be hanged!" They searched all but the king. The king said, "Search me too! I am a man like you all." They searched him; in his pocket they found the spoon. Everybody was troubled, and begged him to save himself. "No," said he, "my word is one." Then they hung him. Wolf became king in his place.

Wolf said it was a shame to have relatives like Nephew. He sent to have all nephews killed. One escaped up a tree in Wolf's yard. Of all the nephews, he alone was not caught. Wolf sent to get a cow to be killed in his yard near the tree. He sat watching it. By this time he had become like a man, except that his greediness was still in him.

Nephew looked down. He said:

> Head, hoofs, tail, hide,
> All are for my Uncle Wolf.

Nephew said again:

> Head, hoofs, tail hide,
> All are for my Uncle Wolf.

Wolf was so pleased, he said, "This voice sounds like my nephew's. I sent and killed all the nephews, but this voice is like his voice."

Nephew said again,

> Head, hoofs, tail hide,
> All are for my Uncle Wolf."

Then Wolf looked up. He saw Nephew. He said, "Nephew, come down! I am going to take you into my house, I am going to take you into my service. You are a good nephew, I am not going to kill you. You remind me of old times."

That's the end.

Parsons 1923a, vol. 1: 103–6; vol. 2: 67–69. ATU 675. Told to Parsons by Pedro Teixeira, a native of Fogo. By *Maria Condon* is understood both the mermaid and the token from the mermaid. According to Parsons, the word itself seems to be a corruption of *varinha de condão*, meaning "little wand of obligation." Parson goes on to say, "A Brava woman in Nantucket who had been over twenty years in America told me with conviction that her grandmother had seen a Maria Condon" (1923a, 1: 103).

ATU 675 is well documented in Iberian and French tradition in North America. In European tradition the hero of this tale is the typical *lazy lad*. In the present version this role is taken by Nho Lobu, the favorite Cape Verde trickster, much as the role is taken by Jack in similar tales in the Appalachian Scots-Irish tradition. The translator usually renders Nho Lobu's name as *Wolf*, but once as *Mr. Wolf* and once as *Sir Wolf*. (For more on the translator, see the chapter introduction; for more on Nho Lobu see the note to the following tale.)

In more usual versions of the story the object found on the king while he is dining with the hero serves to show the king that the appearance of guilt is not the same thing as guilt. The king assumed that his daughter was guilty of sexual misconduct because she was pregnant. But she was in fact innocent. So the king looks guilty of having stolen the spoon from the Wolf's table, but he too is innocent. In the present version the king who has hastily condemned the holder of the stolen spoon recalls Oedipus who similarly condemns himself to exile.

The episode of the rapscallion up the tree who secures a reprieve by his song serves to introduce Wolf's nephew, his constant companion and regular dupe. The episode is only loosely connected to what goes before. It does not seem to be a tale in its own right, however, though it is reminiscent of ATU 1553B*, about a prisoner who wins reprieve by singing, and include the motifs of refuge in a tree (Motif R311) and winning a reward by kindness or good will (Motif Q40).

34. Nho Lob' and the Moon

Nho Lob', e' éra só ku fómi. Nho Lob' was always hungry. In fact, he would go by somebody's house who was cooking just so he could steal a smell. And so, Nho Lob' one day he was up in—again the story's in Brava—up in Fajã d'Água, which is a port way up in the mountains, and he was laying, laying there. And—it's a port, but there's mountains all around it—and he was laying there and he was looking up at the sky and he looked up and he saw the moon. The more he looked at that moon the better it looked. And he kept saying, "*Adja! El parse só un panéla di keju,* looks just like a slab of cheese." He says, "You know if I could get that moon, I could eat for a long time *pamó dja N ten fómi,* because I'm hungry." So he thought about it and he thought of a plan. So he calls his cousin, I mean calls Tubinh': "*Tubinh'. Ben li gó, Tubinh'.* Come here, Tubinh'."

And Tubinh' says, "*Kuzé ki bu kre,* what do you want?"

He said, "*Oji noti N kre pa bu ben Fijon d'Agu pamódi ten un kuza ki N kre mostra-bu,* come to Fajã d'Água because there's something I want to show you."

So Tubinh', that night he went up to Fajã d'Água, and there he found Nho Lob' layin' on the beach, spread out, lookin' up at the moon, and he was lookin' up at the moon. Tubinh' says, "*Kuzé ki bu sta odja,* what the matter with you?"

He says, "No, no. Come lay down, come lay down, come lay down with me. Look up!" And so Tubinh' laid down like his uncle, like Nho Lob', and he looked up. And he says, "*Kuzé ki bu odju,* what do you see?"

And he said, "*N sta odju lua,* I see the moon."

He says, "*Abri odju grandi,* open up you eyes wide and look and see."

He said, "*N sta odja lua xea,* I'm seein' the full moon."

He says, "No. No, you gotta look real good like me."

So, Tubinh' sat there with his hands on his eyes lookin' up at the moon. And still all he could see was the moon. And he said, Nho Lob' said, "Don't you see that moon? *Un panéla di keju, é di keju,* it's a slab of cheese."

And Tubinh' said, "Ohhhh, yeah. It looks just like a slab o' cheese. You're right. I never knew dat."

"*Si N sabe ki mi é sabidu,* I knew that you were slow."

And he says, "Ohhh, okay."

And he said, "You know what? If we get that cheese we can feed this whole island."

And Tubinh' say, "Oh, but what a good heart you have. You're thinkin' of the people, right?"

"Oh, yeah."

"But, Nho Lob', look how far that moon is. You and I are little, on this little island of Brava. How we gonna get that cheese?"

He said, "*Dja bu sabe ki mi é sabidu,* but, you know I'm smart. I've got a plan.

He said, "Yeah?" Now every time Nho Lob' had a plan, it means that he was thinking about it and Tubinh' was going to do all the work. So Tubinh' said, "What is it?"

He said, "Listen. You know last month that boat came from America? *Txeu bidon na el,* there were lots o' barrels. *Tudu djenti na Brava atxa se bidon,* everybody in Brava got they a barrel." He said, "By now they've emptied their barrels, they using them for all different kinds of things. If we gather all of those barrels, and we put one on top o' de other, I can climb up and get that—cheese up there."

And Tubinh' says, "Aha, but that's a lotta work. Besides, *nha Maria ka to da-nu se bidon,* you know Umania is not going to give us her barrel."

He says, "*Algun nu ten ki furta,* well, some we have to steal" *[laugh].* So Nho Lob' said, "I'm gonna be here waitin', and I will—cause we don't have too much time 'cause this moon is full. And we don't have much time to get it while it's nice and big. So tonight you go at everybody from Fudina, Santa Barbara, Fijon d'Agu, to Mato Grande, to all the places in Brava and get all the barrels you can. You can even use my donkey. And bring 'em here and we'll pile 'em up and I'll climb up and get the cheese. You hold them on the bottom."

And so Tubinh' was thinkin', "That's a loootta work!" But he was willing to do it, because after all they're gonna have enough food for all the people on the island. So he set about and gathered all the barrels he could get from every place: some he stole, some he begged, some he borrowed. He brought them all up to Fajâ di. And they started to pile them up right on the beach one on top of the other. And Tubinh' would hand them up and Nho Lob' would pile them up. And Nho Lob' got on top of the barrels and he reached up. And he couldn't reach it, and he said, "*Ai, Tubinh', nu meste más,* gotta get one more."

So Tubinh' went and he looked all around, found another barrel that he hadn't seen. He brought that barrel, he handed it up, and Nho Lob' was up there, [and it was] just out of his reach, couldn't get [it with] that one. And he said, "*Ai, Tubinh'*, just one more, it's within reach." He said, "You know [*sniff*], *Na ta txera*, I got the smell of it." He said, "You know, we're real close."

And Nho Lob' now, he was on top of the barrels, and the barrels were kinda wavering. And he was going back and forth, and he said, "Ohh, I see one, it's way down dere." And Tubinh's sayin', "Where? Where? Where?"

And Nho Lob' was pointin' to de barrel on de bottom. And he said, "Dat one, dat's the one I want."

And Tubinh' says, "Are you sure?"

He says, "Yeah, take that barrel and hand it up to me."

So Tubinh' took the barrel from the bottom and he went . . . and when he did, Nho Lob' fell and all the barrels came down. Well, just at that time, the sun came out. And Nho Lob' and Tubinh', they never got the cheese. That's why the moon is still up there in the sky.

Smart 1996. ATU 1250A/1319*, with echoes of ATU 34. From the telling of Yvonne Smart (concerning whom see the following tale). This is her account of how she learned this story.

> There was a young man named Al Vicente who, umm, was born handicapped. And he liked stories. He didn't speak English very well, but, uhm, right before he went to Cape Verde he said—this is very sad—he said, "Ma'am, I want to tell you a story. And then when I come back I'm gonna sit down and tell you stories. Well, he went to Cape Verde and died. *[She gives a wry, sad laugh.]* So I only got one story from him.

Nho Lobu is the perennial trickster in Cape Verde lore. *Nho* is a contraction similar to the English contraction *Br'er*, and *Nho Lob'* means *Brother (or Br'er) Wolf*. His nephew Tubinhu is his unfailing dupe. *Tubinhu*, means *nephew*, but also functions as the nephew's name. Although Silva translated these appellations for Parsons early in the twentieth century (see previous story), they are usually not translated today by Cape Verde storytellers who narrate in English. The wolf as trickster or would-be trickster is a frequent character in European animal tales.

While each of the individual motifs of the present tale is found in European tradition, there is no exact equivalent in the Aarne-Thompson-Uther classification for the particular complex of motifs that makes up the whole, and the complex itself may be more properly African than European.

35. The Girl Who Wanted to Marry a Man with a Golden Tooth

There was a young girl in Brava who was very pretty. And she knew she was pretty, but times were really tough. And she had several sisters and brothers in the family, and they hardly had anything to eat. So what they had to eat was something they called *totok'* and *totok' sin nada.*

Now *totok'* is like a corn fritter. Okay? And usually you have this corn fritter with potatoes or you have it with meat or something. *Totok' sin nada* is *totok'* with nothing else, that's it. Or they say, *"Totok' ku totok': totok'* with *totok'."*

So this is all her family had. And she said, "Ohhh, when I get married I'm gonna leave this place so I never have to eat *totok'* again." And so she got to that time when men were coming looking for her hand in marriage. And—her father was a reasonable man. He wasn't just gonna marry her off to anybody. So when the man came and asked for her hand he would go to her and say, "So-and-so came and asked to marry you, and what do you think of that?"

And she would always say, *"E' ka pa mi,* he's not for me." She always had an excuse: this one was too short, this one was too tall, this one's feet were flat-footed, or, you know, whatever. So finally her father was getting pretty upset, and he said, "You know, what is this? Every time a young man comes and presents himself to marry you, you don't want him? Now, maybe your standards are a little bit too high."

And she says, "Oh no. *Pa mi só un ómi ku un denti di oru,* for me only a man with a golden tooth. I will only marry a man with a golden tooth."

Now in that time in Brava you couldn't get a golden tooth if you were from Brava. In order to get a golden tooth you had to come from America or Portugal or someplace else. So in fact what she was saying is she wanted to marry a man that was coming from outside, because really she wanted to leave.

So it just so happen that the Devil had heard about this woman, and he had his eye on her. And the Devil, who knows everything, he heard her tell her father that she wanted a man *ku un denti di oru,* with a golden tooth. So he said, "Aha, I've got my way." So he arranged the next time that a ship pulled into Furna Brava, he was on that ship. He had a suit on, a tie, a white shirt, he had brand-new shoes, but most of all he had a golden tooth.

Now what happens in Brava when ships pull in, everybody goes down to the dock to welcome them. Whether you've relatives coming or not. So it happened that her father was down at the dock when the ship came in. Men bring them [the passengers] on their shoulders on to shore. And the first thing he saw was that golden tooth with the sun shining on it. He said, "Aha." So he went over to the Devil, who was disguised as a man, and he said, "A-ah." He started talking to him and said, "And uh, where you from?"

He said, *"A li, a la,* from here and there."

And he said, "What do you do?"

He says, "Oh this and that."

He says, "Oh." He says, "Well, I live in Santa Barbara. Not too far from here. And uh, I would be pleased if you would come, and visit with me and my family."

And he said, "Oh, I, I will. You know, I have some things to do, but I will." He was taking his time.

Meanwhile, the man went back and he told the daughter, "Oh, I got a man. *El é bonitu*, nice looking man. He's got a suit and, best of all, he's got a golden tooth." And so when the daughter heard this, and he'd come by boat, just what she was looking for, she got all dressed up, she combed her hair, she's all set.

In a couple of days he came by. Now, he saw that girl, he had his eye on her, 'cause he thought that was just the one he needed to bring back to him to be his wife. So he was cool. He took his time and, you know, he courted her, you know, with the eyes, and all that stuff. And uh, then he said to the father, "You know, you have a nice daughter, I'd like to marry her."

And the father said, uh, "Will you take care of her?"

He says, "Oh, I will take care of her like nobody else can take care of her."

And he said, "Will you take . . . ?"

"I'll take her to a place where nobody else would ever go."

So he said, "Oh. Sounds pretty good." So he told the daughter about the suitor.

And the daughter said, "Okay, we'll arrange for a wedding." Now this was a hurry up wedding, because the boat was about to leave pretty soon, and the priest wasn't too happy about it, 'cause he wasn't too sure about this stranger. He hadn't talked to him right yet. But, rather than just see the girl go off in disgrace, he married them. He married them, and the night, the wedding night, he said, "No, we have to go to the ship, because we are going to set sail early in the morning." So right after the wedding—they had a big wedding; and all she kept saying, "*Agora N ta kume*—now I'm never gonna have that *totok' sin nada* again."

Okay, and so they got married, went to the ship, and she kept saying to him, "Where are we going?"

He said, "Oh, here and there."

And finally, he took her to hell.

And he sat her down and he said, "You were the one that was so proud. Now, what you gonna have? You're not gonna have *totok' sin nada*. You're gonna have mud." And so, there she is in hell to this day eating mud and thinking, "Oh how good was that *totok' sin nada.*"

Smart 1996. Hansen Type *340C-H, Motif G3033.1.2 (Devil as well-dressed gentleman)/H312.2 (Successful suitor must have gold teeth). Told to the editor by Yvonne Smart, a librarian in the Providence [Rhode Island] Public Library system. Ms. Smart, who is active in Cape Verde community affairs in the Providence area, learned the story at the time of the Smithsonian Folklife Festival in 1995, when New England Cape Verde culture was a featured part of the festival. "This is a story that a woman who went to Washington with us in the last festival—her name is Bia Di Fuma; Bia is nickname for Mary but her real name is Cleophas Perry, and she comes from Brava—and when we came back she told me this story."

An early version of this novelle is found in the *Pentamerone*, first tale of the third day. A variant is also included in Parsons's collection of Cape Verde tales (1923a: tale 37). And tales of girls marrying the devil are also found on the Sea Islands (see chapter 11 and Parsons 1923b: tales 33–34). In the present instance, the novelle has been conflated with a moralizing fable, uncategorized by Aarne Thompson-Uther, about a child who despises bread and is subsequently forced, like the Prodigal Son in the New Testament, to sustain self on something much less appetizing.

English has to some extent supplanted Kriolu among American Cape Verdeans in recent decades. And it is in English that Ms. Smart tells her stories. When I showed her the transcripts of this and the preceding tale, she was at first surprised and distressed to discover such an informal level of English usage in the narratives. A degree-holding librarian, she consistently uses standard English in her professional and everyday life. And yet it seems only natural that as she re-immerses herself in local culture to tell a story, she should unconsciously reach for the language in which she has heard such stories told over the years, the informal Cape Verde English of the home, the factory, the waterfront. The informality of the usage vouches for the authority of the performance.

Part III

FRENCH TRADITION IN THE OLD LOUISIANA TERRITORY

French settlement in the New World began in southeastern Canada in the sixteenth century. Missionaries led the way, followed by trappers and merchants, creating settlements across lower Canada and down into Michigan, Illinois, and Indiana, where surviving French place names still attest to the courage of the early explorers. Rene Robert Cavalier, Sieur de La Salle, suspecting that the Mississippi drained the whole central continent, set out from the junction of the Illinois River in February 1682. Floating down the Mississippi, he arrived at the mouth in April. He claimed the land he had traveled through, the land drained by the Mississippi, for France, and named it Louisiana, after the Sun King. French fur traders poured into the western part of the territory, but stable settlements were slow in coming. New Orleans was not settled till 1717, St. Genevieve, the oldest town in present-day Missouri, in 1735, and St. Louis not until 1764, when the territory had already been ceded to Spain. During this period of Spanish control French continued to be the dominant language of the region. French-speaking Caribbean immigrants and merchants and Creole-speaking black slaves likewise from the Caribbean reinforced but also modified the original language brought by French settlers. The Treaty of Utrecht, which assigned permanent possession of Nova Scotia to England, resulted in yet another French-speaking population coming to the region. Nova Scotia supported a strong colony of French Acadians. In time, the English came to distrust these colonists, who clung to their French language and Catholic religion. Finally, in 1755, the governor, Charles Lawrence, ordered that the Acadians be deported. Refugees dispersed to other English colonies, to England and France, to the West Indies and Falkland Islands, and to Louisiana Territory, bringing with them their distinctive version of French language and culture. In Louisiana Territory they settled not only in the region still called Louisiana but apparently also in present-day Missouri, where there was already a small French population. French culture survived in Missouri up into the twentieth century. But industrialization, urbanization, and two world wars have taken their toll: though the folkways still influence the culture, the language is now moribund. In the state of Louisiana, however, the story is different. There elements of African, Native American, and many European cultures stew in a French gravy or roux, blending to create a delicious gumbo. Southern Louisiana has become a major tourist region, and visitors, whether to New Orleans or to the Acadian Parishes, immediately notice the distinctly French richness of the local culture.

Twentieth-century folktale collecting revealed substantial folktale repertoires in three French-speaking populations from the old Louisiana Territory: the black Creole, the Acadian or Cajun, and the French from around Old Mines, Missouri. The French language and with it the märchen repertoire seems to have died out in Missouri, but both language and tales survive and thrive among Cajuns and black Creoles in rural southern Louisiana. The French repertoire has much in common with the Spanish repertoire, sharing many core märchen. The Bouqui and Lapin stories, however, are closer in spirit to Gullah and southern black Br'er Rabbit stories. And each group, in the manner of societies and cultures in all times and places, has refashioned the märchen, the animal tales, and the numbskull tales in their own image.

The northern French speakers that we in the United States call French Canadians also boast a rich folk heritage. In the twentieth century, folklorists have collected literally thousands of Canadian French tales beyond our northern border in the Maritimes and in the St. Lawrence Valley. But folklorists in the United States have tended to focus on the musical aspects of this heritage, so we do not know how well its stories have survived here. The final tale in this volume, however, provides one rich example of French Canadian storytelling.

CHAPTER 6

LOUISIANA CREOLE TALES

The word *Creole* can be confusing, especially when talking about the complex social and racial hierarchy that developed in Louisiana in the seventeenth through the nineteenth centuries. Most broadly, in Louisiana usage the word denotes someone not considered French "racially," whose native language is nonetheless French. Thus, old French-speaking German families in New Orleans are Creole. In rural southern Louisiana, however, the principal group of French speakers not considered French is black or African American. Thus, in rural Louisiana, the term *Creole* usually refers to black French-speaking people (many of whom, of course, also have considerable French ancestry), while the term *Acadian* or *Cajun* usually applies to the white French-speaking population (some of whom are not predominantly of French ancestry). This rural black Creole group is the one whose traditions are represented in the present chapter.

People of African descent came to Louisiana from the Caribbean along with the earliest French settlers. Because of proximity to the Caribbean, there has been regular reinforcement of Caribbean and African elements in Louisiana black culture. Rural Creole French, developed from Caribbean French and retaining a certain percentage of Africanisms as well, is easily distinguishable from the Cajun French that the Creole's white neighbors brought with them from Nova Scotia. Of course, in the three hundred years that the two groups have shared their lives, there has been a rich exchange both linguistic and cultural. But to this day rural Creole French remains distinctive.

As might be expected, the European tradition most strongly represented in this repertoire is French. Two of the stories in this chapter, for instance,

"The Eggs That Talked" and "Catafo," are versions of stories found in Perrault. But all the stories also demonstrate African elements. Two include African motifs. Two are more free-form and lack the strong märchen structure of European stories, and one of these is tragic as well.

The other tradition strongly represented in the repertoire is the animal story tradition. Most of the same animal stories told by Gullah and plantation southern black people, by Native Americans, and by Hispanics, are also told by Creole storytellers. In the Creole versions, however, the two principal characters are called—even when the stories are told in English—Bouqui and Lapin, the names also used for the principals in many French Caribbean versions of the tales. Lapin is clear enough. That's Rabbit. But who or what is Bouqui (pronounced Bookee, with accent on the second syllable)? The name comes from the word for *hyena* in the Ouloof language of Senegal. But Bouqui does not seem to be a hyena. Calvin Claudel says he is a rabbit like Lapin (1943–1944b: 287). And indeed, he sometimes seems to be a rabbit. But at other times he seems bigger, stronger, and less intelligent. He often plays the fox role in the stories, and just as often the wolf or bear (dupe) role. But he isn't a fox or wolf or bear either. He's just Bouqui.

The tales in this chapter come from two collectors. Alcée Fortier was a professor at Tulane University who did most of his collecting in the last quarter of the nineteenth century. Lafayette Jarreau was a student at Louisiana State University who collected for an M.A. thesis completed in 1931. Unlike the collectors of rural southern black traditions further east at the same time, Fortier, Jarreau, and other Louisiana collectors, because they were interested in exactly how Creole French was spoken, tried to take down tales right from speakers and in their exact words. This means that we now have a remarkable record of the märchen and animal tale traditions of rural Louisiana Creole speakers between the Civil War and World War II. In this chapter the tales have been translated into fairly standard English. But Calvin Claudel, in his translations of the tales that Jarreau collected, has managed to capture an echo of the way English too is spoken by bilingual Creole speakers. Though this chapter offers tales from older collections, recent fieldwork (Ancelet 1994) demonstrates that Creole folktales are by no means extinct.

36. The Talking Eggs

There was once a lady that had two daughters named Rose and Blanche. Rose was mean, and Blanche was good. This mother liked Rose better even though she was mean, because she was the mother's spit and image.

She forced Blanche to do all the work, while Rose sat in the rocking chair and rocked. One day she sent Blanche down to the well to fetch water in a bucket. When Blanche got there she saw an old woman who said to her, "Give me a little water, my child, I beg you; I'm very thirsty."

"Yes, Auntie," said Blanche, "here's your water." She rinsed out her bucket and gave her cool water to drink.

"Thank you, little one, you are a good girl. God almighty is going to bless you."

A few days later, the mother was so hard on Blanche that she ran off to the woods. She was crying, not knowing where to turn, because she was afraid to go home, when she saw the same old woman walking before her.

"Ah, little one, what is making you cry? Who did you something bad?"

"Oh, Auntie, Mama beats me, and I'm afraid to go back to the cabin."

"Well, little one, come with me. I'll give you supper and a place to sleep. But you have to promise me you will do all I tell you, and you won't laugh at anything you see."

She took Blanche's hand. They started walking in the woods. As they advanced, the tall grass started opening before them and closing behind their backs. A little further, and Blanche saw two axes doing battle together. This seemed very funny, but she didn't say a word. They walked on further, and see, there were arms fighting together. A little further yet and it was legs. Finally she saw two heads fighting each other, and they said to Blanche, "Good day, my little one, the good Lord will help you."

At last they got to the old woman's house, and she said to Blanche, "Build a fire, little one, so as to cook supper." Then she sat in the chimney corner and took off her head, put it on her knee, and began to look for lice.

Blanche thought that very funny, but said nothing at all. The old woman put her head back on, and gave Blanche a big bone to put on the fire for their supper. Blanche put the bone into the cookpot, and lo and behold, the pot was soon full of good meat.

She gave Blanche a single grain of rice to crush in the mortar, and suddenly the mortar turned full of rice.

After supper, the old woman said, "Blanche, if you please, my little one, scratch my back." Blanche scratched her back, but her hand was all cut up. This old woman had bottle glass on her back. When she saw Blanche's hand was bleeding, she just blew on it, and the hand grew well again. When Blanche got up the next morning, the old woman said to her, "Now you must go back home, but since you are a good girl, I want to make you a present of some eggs that talk. Run to the henhouse. All the eggs that tell you to take them you must take. All the eggs that say you mustn't take them, these you must not take. When you get on the road, you must throw the eggs behind you, over your head, so that they will break."

As Blanche walked on she broke the eggs, and there were all sorts of pretty things that came out of those eggs: there were diamonds, gold, a fine coach, a beautiful dress.

When she reached her mother's, she had so many pretty things that they filled the house, so that her mother was very glad to see her back. The next day she said to Rose, "You must go to the woods to look for that same old woman. You need a beautiful dress like Blanche's." So Rose went to the woods and met the old woman, who told her to come into her cabin. But when she saw the axes fighting, the legs that were battling, the heads fighting, the old woman who took off her head to scratch her lice, she started to laugh and make fun of all she saw, so that the old woman immediately said to her, "Ah, my child, you are not a good girl; the good Lord will punish you."

But the next morning, she said to her, "I will not send you back with nothing. Go to the henhouse and take the eggs that tell you, 'Take me,' but you mustn't take those that tell you not to take them."

Rose ran to the henhouse, and all the eggs started to say, "Take me," "Don't take me." Rose was so bad that she said, "Oh, yes, you that say 'Don't take me,' you are the very ones I want." So she took all those eggs that said, "Don't take me," and with those, she left. As she walked along, she started throwing and breaking the eggs. Suddenly the road was full of snakes, toads, and frogs galloping after her. There were lots of whips, too, and they started to sting her hard as anything. Rose ran, screaming and screaming. She finally got to her mama's but was too exhausted to say one word. When her mama saw all that vermin and all those whips following her, she grew so angry that she ran her out like a dog and told her to go live in the woods.

Fortier 1888: 142–45. ATU 480. Translated for this volume by George Reinecke. Fortier gives no information about the storyteller. This is a version of the tale of "The Kind and the Unkind Girls," a tale widespread in U.S. and European tradition, and in Africa as well. The present text seems to graft African elements upon the basic European plot, with the girls bearing the names of the girls in a fairy tale by Madame le Prince de Beaumont. The strange events in the tale work together to create a mysterious but also hilarious world. The African motif of talking eggs especially appeals to the imagination. Robert D. San Souci has retold this Creole version of the story in a charming picture book with illustrations by Jerry Pinkney (1989).

37. The Little Boy of the Government

There was once a woman who was very bad, and she had a daughter who was as bad as she was. One day she had a son, but, instead of being glad, she was furious, and wrote to her husband that she was going to send him the boy for him to kill as he had done with the older children. But the boy had received from a man, to whom he had done a favor, a bow and six arrows, which he had hidden, and no one knew he had them.

One day the mother received a letter telling her to send the child. She told him then to prepare to go with his sister and that they would meet a blue lake and a red prairie, but he was to pretend to be blind and was to say nothing, otherwise the bad spirits would catch him. The boy started with his sister, and they arrived at the blue lake. "Oh how pretty it is," said the child, and immediately the lake regained its ordinary color.

"You are a fool," said the sister. "You will see what you will catch."

On leaving the lake and the prairie the boy had heard a voice which said, "Thank you, thank you."

Finally, they arrived at the house of the father who was the Government. He was very tall, and he had only one foot. He tried to catch the boy to kill him, but the latter took his bow and shot an arrow between each one of his father's toes, and one in his heart.

As soon as the man was dead, the little voice which said, "Thank you," found its body in the house of the Government and became a beautiful princess. "Oh! it is you," said she to the boy, "who gave back their natural colors to my lake and my prairie, and who killed the Government who had robbed me of everything I had. I shall marry you, and we shall punish your mother and your sister, who killed your little brothers." The wedding took place and they sent me to relate it to you.

Fortier 1906: 123. ATU 590(?), Motif F531.1.3.3 "Related in the Creole dialect" by Edmée Dorsin of St. Mary Parish, Louisiana, and set down and translated by Alcée Fortier. Fortier provides no more details, though the fact that he submits Dorsin's three tales, without French text, some seventeen years after his last submission to the *Journal of American Folklore,* and eleven years after publishing his collection in monograph form suggests that in 1906 these tales were but newly collected.

This mysterious tale is too confused and too ill-remembered to assign to an ATU number with any confidence, but it has a haunting intensity. The one-footed ogre in it suggests an Irish connection somewhere. That this father/ogre is called the Government suggests allegory, but the tale resists allegorical interpretation. The formulaic ending is widespread in European storytelling, but not so common in the United States.

38. Catafo

Catafo was the eldest of three little brothers. They lived with their mother and father in a little cabin right by the woods. The family was poor and did not have enough to eat.

So one night the old wife told her husband to go lose the children far off into the woods from where they never would return. Catafo heard this and planned to fool his parents and save himself and his two little brothers. He filled his pocket with flour.

So it happened. The following morning the old man called his children early. "Get up, children," called he. "Come walk into the woods with me."

Catafo and his two little brothers followed their father into the woods. He went far, far with them, and Catafo sowed the flour as they walked.

"Wait for me here," finally said the father, when he thought he had gone far enough. "I shall meet you again later. I am going to go a little ways off there."

But the old man never returned. So Catafo took the trail of the flour and told his little brothers to follow him. They followed the trail until they got out of the woods. They reached the house not long after their father.

"Look, the children have come back," declared the old woman, all surprised. "You did not lead them off far enough. That's why they found the path to come back."

After he had gone to bed, Catafo heard his mother tell his father he had to go lose them again in the morning. So he got up softly and filled his pocket with grains of corn this time.

After they were on their way into the woods again the next morning, Catafo sowed the grains of corn all along the way. Finally, their father told them to wait for him in a place where he thought the children were good and lost. And they were well lost, but Catafo intended to follow the trail of his grains of corn.

Catafo waited for the old man a little while, and when he saw he was not going to return, he told his little brothers to follow him, taking the trail of the corn. He followed it for half a mile, but after that, he could not find another grain at all. The little birds had eaten the grain, and the boys were good and lost. Catafo did not know what to do. He decided on a direction to take, and he and the two little brothers left.

Night came upon them, and they were more lost than ever. The youngest began to weep, and this troubled Catafo all the more. He wanted to go on, but the youngest said he was tired and afraid in the dark. They continued a little way farther, and Catafo saw a light far off in the woods. He showed this to his little brothers, and it gave them a little courage. Catafo made up his mind to go spend the night there. He went to knock at the door, and an old woman came out to talk with him. She was surprised to see children there at that hour. She asked them what they wanted.

"I want a place for us to sleep," answered Catafo. "We are lost and are hungry."

"I can do nothing for you all," explained she, "because my husband is a devil and will eat you all when he returns."

Catafo talked her into giving them food and a place to sleep. They slept in the same bed with the children of the Devil. When Devil returned, he smelled fresh meat.

"What's the fresh meat I smell?" Devil asked his wife.

"It's the beef meat you brought here yesterday," explained she.

"Oh no! it smells better than that," replied Devil. "I won't believe that."

He lifted the mosquito-bar of the bed.

"Ah, three children!" exclaimed he. "Now I am going to have some supper! Let me go sharpen my knife to cut off their heads."

Devil went into the kitchen to fetch his butcher knife. Catafo heard this, and he woke up his little brothers.

"Get up!" he cried to them. "We must leave now."

They did not want to get up, but he made them get up anyway. They went into the woods again. When Devil returned to the bedside, he did not notice well what he was doing. He seized his own three little children from there one at a time, cutting off their heads. It was his own children he killed. After he saw his mistake, he was angry to death. He looked for Catafo, but he had already left.

Devil got upon his big mule, Ti-Toup, and he took after them. Catafo was going fast, but Devil was gaining on them. One of the children heard him coming. The mule made six hundred steps at a time. Devil would shout:

"Six hundred steps, Ti-Toup! Six hundred steps, Ti-Toup!"

Catafo saw that they soon would be caught. So he and his two brothers climbed a tree. When Devil got there, he saw them in the tree and stopped.

"Now I will get you all!" called Devil. "I have a big sack under you, and if you look down, you'll fall into it."

"You can wait, if you want," called back Catafo, "but we'll never look down into your sack."

"I am not so sure about that," answered Devil.

Devil sat under the tree holding his sack open, as he looked up. He waited there a good little while. When he saw they would not look down, he got up and began to sing and dance. The youngest looked down and fell into the sack.

"That's one!" cried he, tying up the mouth of the sack.

A little while afterwards the second looked down below and fell down.

"That's two!" shouted Devil. "The third one isn't far off."

"Oh yes, he's far off," called down Catafo. "You can sing and dance all night, but I myself will never look down below."

He never did look down either. Devil was getting tired. He told Catafo he would climb up after him if he did not come down.

"Climb if you will," replied Catafo.

Devil climbed the tree. When he was up there, Catafo jumped to the ground. He opened the sack, telling Devil that when he would look down, he would fall into the sack himself. So it happened. Devil looked down; and as he fell into the sack, Catafo tied its mouth, having let out his little brothers.

They took a stick and beat Devil until they killed him. They turned toward the house again, and Devil's wife was more than surprised to see them alive. Catafo related how they had killed Devil, and she was glad.

"I want you all to come live with me," said she. "I shall be very glad to have you all, because my husband killed my own children." And that is how Catafo and his little brothers found a home to stay, with Devil's wife. They stayed there all their life, well satisfied.

Claudel 1943–1944a: 225–28. ATU 327A/B/330. Told by Anéus Guérin of Pointe Coupée Parish, Louisiana, 1931, to Lafayette Jarreau. Translated by Calvin Claudel. Guérin, a delightful storyteller, is also the source of the following story. The ending with the children up the tree suggests the African ending of "Barney McCabe" and other tales of rescue by dogs. The same ending occurs in some Appalachian versions. Jane Muncy (Roberts 1955: 44; and see chapter 12) has the hungry pursuer say:

> Merrywise, jump down in my puddin-tuddin bag.

But, like Catafo, Merrywise succeeds in turning the tables. For Merrywise the pursuer is a witch, and he weights the bag down with stones and drowns her. For Catafo, as for most heroes of ATU 330, however, the pursuer is the devil, and he beats on the sack till he has beaten the devil to death.

39. Bouqui and Lapin

One day Compère Lapin was working with Compère Bouqui on a farm. They were cropping together that year, and they had arranged to divide the crop equally at the end of the year. It was very hot that day, and Compère Lapin wanted to fool Compère Bouqui in some way or other.

"What do you say if we buy a jug of wine today?" suggested Lapin.

"Fine!" agreed Bouqui. "You will go get it yourself."

Compère Lapin went to fetch the wine. When he returned, he put it in a ditch where there was shade. He went to work again, but did not try to keep up with Bouqui. He took his time, cheating on his compère. Bouqui was working fast to get finished, and Lapin was far behind. Suddenly Lapin exclaimed:

"Ooh!"

"What's the matter?" requested Bouqui.

"There's someone calling me," explained Lapin.

"Go see who it is," suggested Bouqui.

Lapin left, went toward the jug and took a drink. When he returned, Bouqui asked him why he had stayed so long.

"I was called for a christening," explained Lapin.

"Is that so?" questioned Bouqui. "What did you name the baby?"

"I named him First-One," continued Lapin.

They started working, and soon Compère Lapin was called again. He went to take another big drink. When he returned, he told Bouqui it was another christening and he had called the baby Second-One. Next he went to perform a third christening and named this baby Third-One. This time he finished drinking all the wine, turning the jug over before he returned to his work.

"Ah now!" exclaimed Bouqui when it was time to quit, "let's go drink us some wine now."

They went to the jug and saw it was turned over. There was not a drop of wine left in the jug.

"Too bad!" declared Lapin. "Our wine is all lost."

Bouqui was sad, disappointed, and tired. Compère Lapin felt good as he returned to his cabin.

A little while after that Bouqui and Lapin went into the field to see their potatoes. There was a good crop. The potato plants were big and full of flowers. They stayed there a long time, talking and admiring their labor.

"It's almost time to dig our potatoes," said Lapin "How are we going to divide our crop? Do you want to take the roots, and I'll take the plant?"

"Oh no!" replied Bouqui. "Myself, I want the pretty plant."

"As you wish," agreed Lapin.

When they took in the potato crop, Bouqui brought all the pretty plants into his storeroom. He had nothing at all. Lapin took the roots, and he had food for the whole year.

Later on, it was time to harvest the crop of corn. Bouqui made up his mind that Lapin would not fool him on the corn. He said he wanted the roots this time, and Lapin told him to choose as he wanted again. Bouqui took the roots, taking them to his storeroom, and he had nothing. Lapin took the stalks, and he had a lot to eat for the whole year.

During the winter, Bouqui went to ask Lapin for something to eat. Lapin refused him. Bouqui almost died from hunger that year, and he decided not to work on shares with Compère Lapin anymore.

Compère Bouqui was very dissatisfied, but he was to be still more unhappy yet before he would be done with Lapin.

They were courting the same girl, a princess. She was a pretty girl, and she liked Lapin better. Bouqui was jealous, and he wanted to know whether he or Lapin would marry the girl.

"I'll tell you what we'll do," suggested Compère Bouqui to Lapin one day. "We'll have a race. We'll leave here together tomorrow morning. He who gets at the girl's place first will marry her."

"Fine!" agreed Lapin. "We shall run a race."

As they had planned, the following morning they started the race. Compère Lapin beat him by a long distance. When Bouqui got there, he asked Lapin to give him another chance. "What do you want to do this time, Compère Bouqui?" asked Lapin.

"Let's see," thought Bouqui, scratching his head. "Oh yes! Let's boil a big pot of water, and he who jumps over it wins the girl. Do you want to try that?"

"As for me, I'll do whatever you want," replied Lapin.

They boiled some water until it was boiling over. They placed it in the yard by the house, and it was decided that Lapin should jump first. Lapin started running to make his jump but when he got up to the big pot, fear seized him and he did not jump.

"It's high, yes!" exclaimed Lapin.

He tried again. This time he jumped it.

"It's your turn now, Bouqui," said Lapin.

Bouqui started running. When he jumped, he fell into the middle of the pot. The water was so hot, he was cooked before he could count to four.

After that, Bouqui's family had a grudge against Lapin. They blamed Lapin for the death of their son, Bouqui; and they watched for the chance to pay him back in the same way.

Compère Lapin would come to steal water from their well every night. Now old man Bouqui knew it was Lapin who was stealing his water. When Lapin came for water that night, he saw a little tar baby. He could not make out who it was. He walked all around it, looking closely. Finally, he got up enough courage to talk to it.

"Get away from that well!" cried Lapin.

But it did not act as if it heard. Lapin advanced more closely, crying out:

"Go away! Go away, before I hit you a blow with my foot."

But it did not pay any attention at all. Compère Lapin struck a blow with his foot, and his foot stayed stuck.

"Let my foot go!" cried Lapin. "Let me go, or I'll strike you with my other foot."

As he struck, the other foot stayed stuck, too. Lapin struck with his other two, and they stayed stuck, too. Then he struck with his head, his body, all staying stuck on the tar baby. Lapin was well caught.

The following morning old Bouqui found Lapin in his trap.

"Now I have you!" exclaimed he. "I will go kill you, and I think I'll burn you."

"Burn me if you will!" cried Lapin, "but I beg of you not to throw me into the briars behind the fence there. That would be too mean a death."

"I am going to give you the worst death I know," added old man Bouqui, "and it's into the briars you go."

He went off with Lapin, to throw him into the briars. When he got by the fence, he threw him over. Lapin fell into the middle of the briar patch. Old Bouqui looked through a crack to see him die, but Lapin only laughed at him. Bouqui realized his mistake, but too late.

"You threw me exactly into my home here," shouted back Lapin, running quickly toward his place.

"He's a bad fellow, yes, that Lapin!" exclaimed old Bouqui to himself, turning homeward very regretful.

Claudel 1943–1944b: 288–91. ATU 15/1030/30/175/1310A. Told by Anéus Guérin of Pointe Coupée Parish, Louisiana, to Lafayette Jarreau, probably in 1931. Translated by Calvin Claudel. I have restored the title *Compère,* however, which Claudel translated *Comrade.*

Two of the tales that make up Guérin's cycle are among the most popular tales in the U.S. tradition: Farming on Shares and Tarbaby. Tarbaby is almost exclusively an animal trickster tale, and the animal is almost always the rabbit (but see the version in chapter 3). Farming on Shares, however, can be adapted to many different sorts of trickster relationships. Guérin here incorporates into Farming on Shares the very nearly as popular Theft by Playing Godfather, a story that, like Tarbaby, belongs most properly to the rabbit cycle, at least in U.S. tradition. Daniel Crowley has suggested that the story, as told in black American tradition, is more probably of African origin (1977: 43–46). Though the two stories fit together seamlessly as if made for each other, this seems to be a unique instance of combining the two. On Bouqui and Lapin, see the introduction to the present chapter. In these animal stories, differences are often settled by a jumping test or contest, as in Smith's Texas version of Godfather Rabbit in chapter 10.

CHAPTER 7

CAJUN TALES

The Cajuns of southern Louisiana derive their name and much of their distinctive culture from the Acadians, some six thousand of whom settled in Louisiana in the thirty years following their 1755 expulsion from Nova Scotia. These French-speaking Acadians settled not in New Orleans but in the swampy bayou country on either side of the Atchafalaya Basin or on the flat prairies of southwest Louisiana. There they largely absorbed the European peoples that had come before or that came later—Spanish, German, Scotch-Irish, and English, as well as some of the Native Americans—and there they lived side by side with the black Creoles, who spoke a quite different creolized French. Consequently, though white families in the Acadian parishes (counties) of southern and southwestern Louisiana might have English or Spanish surnames, their language and culture was likely to be Cajun French. In time, two somewhat separate subcultures developed. The bayou Cajuns supported themselves trapping, fishing, and gathering Spanish moss, while the prairie Cajuns raised crops and cattle.

The discovery of oil near Jennings in 1901 began a period of crisis for Cajun culture. The Cajun folklorist Barry Jean Ancelet describes it thus:

> Oil was discovered . . . and the trickle of Anglo American immigration became a flood. At about the same time, the rise of American nationalism began to affect the region. Local school board policies reflected the State Department of Education's desire to impose mandatory education exclusively in English, banning French from the schools. The First World War and the Great Depression combined to fuel the melting pot's fire, and ethnic groups across the country

came to understand that they were minorities in the new context of a homo-geneous America. The development of mass media and modern transportation opened previously isolated regions. . . . The French language became the symbol of a cultural stigma. . . . Even the musicians began to perform western swing and country music, singing in English as soon as they had learned enough. By the end of the Second World War, however, Cajuns began to show signs of learning to better negotiate the American mainstream in a way that would allow them to preserve their own cultural identity. Musicians were among the first to announce the change by returning to traditional sounds. (1994: xx–xxii)

Cajun French did not die out. Moreover, a certain orientation toward rural life is still characteristic of the region. And Ancelet has even been able to publish a substantial collection of Cajun and Creole tales all collected in the last quarter of the twentieth century.

From Ancelet's book this chapter includes a märchen told as a saint's legend, that of St. Geneviève. In addition it includes three tales from Leota Claudel, a woman from Avoylles Parish whose stories were collected by her son about 1940. Two of these are regular märchen and one is a Bouqui and Lapin animal tale. Four other tales were collected or discovered by George Reinecke and Ethelyn Orso, folklorists at the University of New Orleans and associates in editing the *Louisiana Folklore Miscellany*. Tales from the *Miscellany* include two unusual märchen and two tales about the Cajun numbskull Jean Sot. All of these stories come with genealogies ("my mother," "my grand-father") that reach back well into the nineteenth century. From these quite old tales, however, it proves but a short jump to cyberspace, where other old tales circulate in a fresh guise as Cajun jokes. Folklore despises no channel of communication, and in the present generation the internet may be the chan-nel through which humorous stories, many of them very old, circulate most freely. Indeed, one of the Cajun jokes included here from an internet source retells a story that Chaucer used in the Canterbury Tales.

40. Golden Hair

There was once a lord who lived in a manor with his wife and son. Because the son had hair the color of gold, he was called Golden Hair. Now, in front of the manor-house was a huge cage in which was kept a large bear. The lord prized the bear above all else he had, even above his wife and Golden Hair, because the bear was able to talk. When Golden Hair was lonesome, he liked to go near the cage and talk with the bear. So one day his father said, "Golden Hair, I forbid you to talk with the bear or go near the cage." Then he said to his wife: "Here, you keep the key to the cage, but if the bear escapes I will kill you." And he added to his son: "Tomorrow, Golden Hair, is your fifteenth birthday; and if you obey me well, I shall bring you a present."

The next day the lord brought his son a golden ball. Then he went out to see and feed the bear. Every day he did this while the bear walked around the cage. It was said that the bear had been a beautiful woman, a former wife of the lord, and by magic he had changed her into a bear.

After his father had gone for the day, Golden Hair went out to play with his new golden ball. He threw it up and down, and it flashed under the blazing sun. At length he threw the ball some distance, and it flew into the great cage. He went to the cage and said to the bear: "Bear, return me my ball, will you please?"

The bear stood still, looked at Golden Hair and answered: "You had forgotten me, Golden Hair. Now that you have a golden ball you don't come to talk to me anymore. I cannot return you your ball unless you let me out."

"That I cannot do," answered Golden Hair. "My father forbade my even coming near the cage. He will probably punish me very much for letting my ball fall into it. Besides I have no key. My mother keeps it at her side on a ring."

"I know how you can get it from your mother," began the bear. "Go to your mother. Tell her that your head itches and that you wish she would look to see if there are lice on it. While she is combing your hair, you can slip the key from the ring hanging at her waist."

Golden Hair hesitated but at length agreed. When he reached his mother, he said, "Mother, my head itches. Will you please pass the comb through my hair to see if I have lice?"

His mother, surprised at this request, took her large silver comb and combed her son's hair into her lap. While she did this, he reached for the key. "Golden Hair," at last said she, "I see nothing in your hair. Perhaps it was only your imagination." He went hurriedly to the bear, holding the key tightly in his hand.

"How shall I return the key without being found out, after I let you out?" asked Golden Hair.

"Do as you did before. Say your head itches very, very much and you wish she would look again for lice," answered the bear.

Golden Hair opened the cage. Out came the bear, giving Golden Hair his golden ball. The bear was free. Again Golden Hair went back to his mother and said: "Dear Mother, I am sure I have lice in my head. It itches me very, very much. Will you please look again for lice?"

"Son, you should go out to play with your golden ball," replied his mother, "and stop worrying about your hair. I think it is your imagination."

Golden Hair then grew worried and became pale for himself and for his mother, because he now wondered what his father would say and do. So he begged his mother again: "Please, Mother dear, pass the comb through my hair once more." Then his mother took her large silver comb and carefully combed his hair again and again. While she did this, he put the key back on the ring, and at last said, "Mother, perhaps it was my imagination. I shall go out to play."

When the lord came home, he went first to the bear's cage and found it gone. He went to his wife in great anger and said: "The bear is gone. What has happened?"

"I don't know," answered the wife in terror. "Here is the key. I have not been to the cage today."

"I will kill you!" exclaimed the lord in wrath. "I warned you not to let the bear escape. It was in your care."

Golden Hair, who had come into the manor-house, heard his father as he began to kill his mother. He then fell to weeping and pleaded, "Father, Father, do not kill Mother. I stole the key from her side, and I let the bear escape, because my golden ball fell into the cage."

Now it happened that the lord had in his stables a very, very wild stallion horse, which one dared to ride. He decided to punish Golden Hair by binding him to the wild horse's back. Into his son's pocket he put a letter describing who he was, in case the boy should be found. The wild horse galloped away madly, with Golden Hair swaying from side to side. After galloping and running, finally the animal halted at the gate of a large strange-looking house, with Golden Hair's senseless body hanging down into the dust. An ugly old giant came outside and took Golden Hair from the horse's back. He read the letter in his pocket, brought him inside, and revived him. After Golden Hair had recovered, the giant said to him: "You shall help me around the place. Take care of it well while I am away and do the work. But there are certain things that you must never, never do: Never feed my horse in the stable, never clean the ashes from the fireplace nor sweep from under my bed the shucks that fall from my shuck mattress; for if you do any of these things, you shall die."

After he had said this, the giant left the house. Golden Hair thought about what the giant had said for a long time but decided to go feed the horse anyhow. Before he did this, he cleaned the ashes from the fireplace and also swept the shucks from under the bed, placing on the outside the shucks and the ashes with the nails in them. When he came to the horse with a sack of corn, the horse, who was able to talk, spoke to Golden Hair: "My master will kill you for disobeying him. You should escape and go away before he returns. In the large back room of the house you will find a saddle, a bridle, and a sword. Bring them quickly and saddle me. We shall escape before it is too late. Also get three sacks. In one place shucks, in another ashes, and in the last put some nails. Bring them along with you."

Golden Hair went to the room and found the saddle with a golden pommel, a bridle with a golden bit, and the sword with a hilt of solid gold. These he took, and filled the sacks hurriedly and brought them out to where he had left the horse, which he saddled immediately. The horse said, "Now tie the sacks on the side, and let us be off."

Golden Hair put his foot into the stirrup, mounted onto the saddle, and was away with the sacks hanging to the side. After they were at a distance, the giant returned, saw he had been disobeyed, and found his horse missing. With a group of horsemen he followed in pursuit.

Golden Hair saw them coming and was greatly worried. Then the horse said: "Empty the sack of ashes." Golden Hair did, and up rose a mountain of ashes, covering and almost smothering the riders with dust. But they got through the ashes and caught up again.

"Throw out the sack of shucks," said the horse.

As Golden Hair shook them out, there arose a mountain of shucks. But the riders went around and soon caught up with them again.

"Now empty your sack of nails," said the horse. Then there rose up a mountain of nails, and the riders became entangled and slid down the side. Golden Hair and the horse escaped. Finally they reached a wooded grove on the side of a mountain from which could be seen a great castle and town nearby. The horse then said to Golden Hair: "Let us stop here, Golden Hair. Build a cabin. Then go to the castle to look for work. Buy yourself a wig in the town so that no one will recognize you."

So Golden Hair unsaddled the horse, built a hut, and left for town. At a shop he bought a cheap, ugly wig with a few coins he had, and then went on to the great castle. He went to the gardener and said, "Sir, I am a stranger. I stay outside the town, and I need work."

Looking at this youth with the ugly hair, the gardener answered: "There is no job for you here. Besides, the king does not engage strangers."

But just as Golden Hair was about to leave in despair, the gardener said: "I need someone to remove caterpillars from the vegetables. If you will do this, I shall give you some food and a few pennies a week."

Golden Hair agreed and began to work immediately. Every evening he returned to his hut, bringing corn for his horse, which he now loved very much and with which he discussed his affairs as wormer of vegetables at the castle garden. At night he slept, his head resting on the saddle.

Now, every day when he had finished worming the vegetables and after he had removed his wig, Golden Hair combed his hair at a fountain in the courtyard nearby. One day while he was wetting and combing his hair, he heard someone come up to him. Quickly putting on his wig, he looked up and saw a very beautiful young girl.

"Who are you and why are you so frightened?" asked she.

Golden Hair looked at the beautiful maiden with admiring eyes and finally said, "I am a stranger here. I help the gardener to worm the vegetables."

Then came the maid servant who called out: "Princess, come away. It is time to go." Golden Hair was left in amazement, because he then realized she was the princess, the beautiful daughter of the king.

It was announced one day that there were to be games of chivalry in the town near the castle. Should someone win the games three times in succession, he would be given the beautiful daughter of the king in marriage. Upon hearing this news, Golden Hair hinted to the gardener that he might like to enter the games also. There was an old wooden horse nearby. So the gardener said jokingly: "Here, boy, you can enter on this nag, if you will."

"Perhaps I shall," replied Golden Hair.

When Golden Hair reached home, he told his horse what had happened. He likewise told him about the games that were to take place. Then his horse said, "Look in the saddle bag. In it are clothes for riding and games."

Golden Hair took off his old clothes and wig, put on his beautiful riding clothes, and rode out to the games on his horse with his golden sword at his side. He appeared in his flowing golden hair. Everybody was filled with admiration for the handsome young man whom they had never seen before. Everyone asked who he was, but could not find out. When the games began, he won every race and contest. As he left the place when the games were over, all the people cheered madly for him.

At the castle everyone talked about the winner. The princess was not to be there, however, until the last games of the third week, when she was to meet the winner and be married to him if he had won three successive times. So the princess was anxious for the handsome golden-haired knight to win, since she had heard about him.

One day Golden Hair was combing his hair again. While he was washing at the fountain before putting on his wig, the princess again came upon him. This time she saw him without his wig. His hair looked very, very beautiful in the sunlight.

"Why do you wear that ugly wig?" asked the princess.

"My father was a cruel lord and banished me from home," answered Golden Hair. "I wear the wig to keep from being recognized and caught."

Taking the letter about him from his pocket, he showed it to the princess and told her how he lived on the outside of town. Every day after that the princess met Golden Hair at the fountain, and they began to fall in love. Golden Hair was now more determined than ever to win the games; so he went to them again the next week. Everybody was greatly surprised and wished to know who the noble-looking stranger was—he with the golden hair. But Golden Hair hastened away to his hiding place, curried and fed his faithful horse, and went to the castle.

The following week Golden Hair said to the gardener, after he had talked to the princess again: "Sir, lend me the wooden horse. I shall vie for the princess in the games tomorrow."

"You are indeed a silly young man," answered the gardener. "If you want to look foolish, take the old wooden horse. Naturally it doesn't move."

The next day at the field some people saw a knight with ugly hair arrive, carrying a lifeless wooden horse. They laughed and said: "Surely you cannot enter with that." Golden Hair had left his faithful horse nearby. He then returned for him, leaving the wooden horse behind. He quickly got into his riding clothes, mounted his horse, and came back, his shining golden hair floating in the breeze. And everyone shouted: "Hurrah for the fair-haired rider!"

The princess had arrived and was sitting next to her father, the king. When she recognized Golden Hair, she was very much surprised and pleased, but said nothing to her father about her having met him in the courtyard and about his helping the gardener by taking worms from the vegetables.

"If the fair-haired knight wins today," said the king, "your hand will be given him in marriage, my daughter."

"I have heard that he is a good rider and knight-at-arms," said the princess as she smiled.

Again Golden Hair won with his big black horse. Everybody was wild with excitement, because no one as yet knew who Golden Hair was. Then all the nobles and lords brought Golden Hair to the princess and king. The king was surprised when the princess was overjoyed to meet Golden Hair. Then Golden Hair told the king and all the nobles who he was, presenting the letter from his pocket.

Golden Hair and the princess were married at a great wedding ceremony in the castle, where all were invited, everyone from the lowest to the highest rank in the land. And Golden Hair and the princess lived happily ever after.

Claudel 1941: 257–63. ATU 314. This and the following story Calvin Claudel collected from his mother, Leota Edwards Claudel. Mrs. Claudel grew up in Avoyelles Parish in the last decades of the nineteenth century, but was living in Chalmette at the time her son published the story. Though principally of British (English and Scottish) extraction, she was raised by a French family after her parents died, and grew up speaking French. In her youth neighbors in the area around Marksville, Mansura, and Goudeau would gather in someone's home for "la vielle," an evening of conversation and entertainment. Stories were an important element of such occasions, and her foster father, Fey Goudeau, was a popular raconteur. From him she heard these tales and many others, and told them in remarkably full versions.

Golden Hair tied to the horse may remind some readers of Byron's Mazeppa.

41. Snow Bella

Once there were two sisters sitting near the fireplace while snow was falling outside. One of the sisters at her sewing, looking up at the snow through the window, suddenly stuck her finger with the needle with which she was sewing. She pressed her finger, hurt by the sting of the needle, and a drop of red, red blood fell on her dress. "You should make a wish," said the other sister, "and it will be granted for having lost your drop of blood."

"Then I wish," began the sister, "that some day I shall have a most beautiful daughter, whose cheeks and lips will be as red as this blood and whose skin will be as white as the snow falling outside."

It turned out just as the sister wished. She married a very handsome young man and had a girl whose lips and cheeks were deep red like the blood that had dropped from her finger and whose skin was as fair and white as the snow. She was so beautiful that she called her Snow Bella.

However, Snow Bella's mother, the sister who had lost the drop of blood while sewing when it snowed, became ill and suddenly died. Her husband was married again to a very cruel and wicked woman, who became Snow Bella's stepmother. Her stepmother vainly thought herself very beautiful, and no sooner was she married than she became violently jealous of Snow Bella's great beauty. So she treated the girl most cruelly, making her do all the house work. She also began plotting and planning a way to get rid of her stepdaughter.

"Snow Bella," began the cruel stepmother, "come with me into the woods today. We shall look around for some herbs and roots for my skin."

So they both walked and walked until they reached a deep, dark place in the woods. "You search over there, and I shall search somewhere else," suggested the stepmother. "After a while we shall meet here again, to return home."

Snow Bella gathered roots until nearly dark and returned to the place, but the stepmother was not there. She waited and waited, but no one came.

Finally Snow Bella began walking. It soon got dark, however, and she was lost. Suddenly she came upon a little hut in the woods, from the window of which shone a wee light. She knocked at the door, and a young man appeared, saying, "Who is there?"

"My name is Snow Bella," said the girl, "and I am lost in the woods. May I come in for the night?"

"Come in," replied the young man. "I live here with two dwarf brothers, who are asleep. We all work in the deep woods. There is a little soup left. Perhaps you are hungry."

"Thank you very much," answered Snow Bella. "It is so kind of you to give me something to eat."

After the young man had warmed the soup in a huge black pot, hanging over the fire of the fireplace, Snow Bella sat at the table and ate.

"Tell me about yourself," spoke the young man.

"I lived with my father and my cruel stepmother," began Snow Bella. "I am afraid she has lost me in the woods and does not want me back home. I really don't know what to do."

"That is too bad," sympathized the young man. "As I said before, I live here with my two brothers, who are dwarfs. Tomorrow I shall talk to them about you, and perhaps we shall be able to help you. You may sleep on my bed here, near the fire. I myself am very tired and must say goodnight."

The young man went off to bed on some straw in the next room, while his two brothers were snoring on their tiny feather beds. After Snow Bella finished her soup and piece of black bread, she went to bed, falling fast asleep.

The next morning she was softly awakened by the young man, while the two little dwarfs with dark skin and wrinkles stood nearby. He said, "These are my two brothers, Snow Bella. You may live with us, if you wish. While we work in the woods, you can keep house for us. Be careful, though, whom you talk to, because you are very beautiful and harm may befall you."

Now the wicked stepmother, thinking that Snow Bella was eaten up by wild animals in the forest, did not worry about her any more. All day long she combed her hair and admired herself before her looking glass. Suddenly she heard someone outside calling out in a sharp voice: "Mirrors to sell, mirrors to sell."

The stepmother went to the window and called out to the vendor, who was a hunched and wrinkled old man, wearing thick glasses over his tiny eyes, "What kind of mirrors have you to sell?"

"Little mirrors, my lady—little mirrors that talk when spoken to. Ask a question and the truth will be answered."

"Give me one," agreed the wicked stepmother, thinking that this would be a good way to find the whereabouts of Snow Bella, if still alive.

The stepmother immediately hung the little mirror on her wall, gazed into it and sang:

> Tiny mirror, tiny mirror,
> Of this town and all the land,
> Tell me, if you can,
> Who is everywhere
> Most beautiful and fair?
> While I look in you,
> Answer true, answer true.

The mirror sang back:

> Lady, lady in the mirror,
> Snow Bella's the name,
> Whose beauty's the fame
> Here and everywhere—
> Most beautiful and fair
> As ever maid be,
> And at the dwarfs' lives she.

"Ah, Snow Bella is at the dwarfs'," cried the jealous stepmother. "I must do away with that girl. To think that she is fairer than I!"

The next day, while the angry stepmother was fretting around for a plan to kill Snow Bella, she heard the sharp voice of the vendor again: "Jewelry to sell, jewelry to sell."

"What kind of jewelry have you?" she asked the wizened old man with impatience.

"Ah, the most cunning sort of trinkets, my lady," replied he. "Here is a necklace wrought with tiny darts in the beads. Whoever wears it will die instantly. Very cunning jewelry, heh, heh. . . ."

"Quick, give me the necklace," bargained the stepmother.

The wicked woman set out for the hut of the dwarfs. When she came to the door, the dwarfs were all away at work in the woods for the day. The stepmother threw a hood over her face not to be seen, and she rapped at the door.

"I have a pretty, pretty necklace to sell," said the jealous woman to Snow Bella, who came to open a tiny crack in the door.

"I have no money," answered Snow Bella, who was nevertheless attracted by the beautiful necklace. "I cannot buy it."

"Beautiful maiden, open the door a tiny bit more, so I can show it to you," enticed the stepmother.

"I am forbidden to open to strangers," replied Snow Bella.

"Only put your pretty neck out, so I can try it on, to show you how beautifully it fits you," coaxed the mean stepmother.

So Snow Bella put her head outside the door, and the stepmother slipped the necklace onto her slender neck. The poor girl instantly fell dead to the floor. The wicked woman went away laughing to herself with joy and rubbing her hands in satisfaction.

Finally the young man, who had become very fond of Snow Bella, and who was as large as an ordinary human being and more handsome than his brothers, came home with the two dwarfs. He saw Snow Bella dead on the floor. With the help of his two brothers he picked her up, brought her to the bed, and began rubbing her hands to try to revive her. Everything was in vain, because the pretty girl was dead, and all the color had left her cheeks. Finally the older dwarf noticed the necklace around her neck, exclaiming, "This necklace around Snow Bella's neck is something new! She did not wear this before today."

Saying this, he snatched away the necklace, breaking it from her neck and throwing it to the floor. Soon Snow Bella's color began returning, and she stirred. The young brother and the dwarfs were overjoyed to have her back alive. They all wept, as she embraced them around the neck.

"Snow Bella," said the older dwarf, "you must be careful, my lovely child. . . . Tell us, who was it? Tell us if you have enemies."

"It was no one," replied Snow Bella, not wishing to worry the dwarfs.

After the wicked stepmother was home several days, thinking now Bella surely dead, she again went to her little mirror on the wall. She decided to try it again, repeating her song:

> Tiny mirror, tiny mirror,
> Of this town and all the land,
> Tell me, if you can,
> Who is everywhere
> Most beautiful and fair?
> While I look in you,
> Answer true, answer true.

The mirror sang back:

> Lady, lady in the mirror,
> Snow Bella's the name,

Whose beauty's the fame
Here and everywhere—
Most beautiful and fair
As ever maid be,
And at the dwarfs' lives she.

"Can it be possible that this wretch of a girl is still alive?" the enraged stepmother questioned herself. "I shall kill her forever this time."

While pacing the floor the next day, she heard the same vendor's voice through the window: "Combs to sell, combs to sell."

"Over here with your combs!" cried the woman in exasperation. "Tell me what kind of combs they are."

"My lady, these are round combs, set with tiny poisoned jewels," explained the vendor. "This circular comb covers the head and kills the wearer on the spot."

"Give me one quickly," said she.

The next day the stepmother disguised herself as an old, old woman and set out for the hut of the dwarfs. She knocked at the door, which was opened to a crack by Snow Bella, who asked, "What do you want?"

"I am a poor old woman," whined the cunning stepmother. "Please buy a comb, buy a comb from me. You are so beautiful; it will deck your pretty black hair."

"Oh, no," replied Snow Bella. "I cannot talk to you."

"It will only cost you a few pennies," said the woman. "Here, put your head out, and I'll try it on you."

"Please do not beg me," continued Snow Bella. "I want to help you, but I don't know you."

"Here, my pretty child, let me slip it into your hair. If you don't like it, you may return it right away."

So again Snow Bella put her head outside the door, and the crafty stepmother pushed the comb into her pretty black tresses. She fell back inside dead, dead.

When the dwarfs and their brother reached home that evening late, there was no fire, no food, and nothing done. Snow Bella lay dead in a heap on the floor. They picked up her lifeless body and placed it on the bed. The younger of the two dwarfs began to rub her hands and cheeks to try to bring her back to life. But the beautiful girl was cold. The youngest brother lighted a lamp. Noticing the evil comb in her hair, he exclaimed, "That comb! Where does it come from?"

He pulled it from Snow Bella's hair and threw it to the floor. They all rubbed her, bathing her face with warm water. Finally she opened her beautiful, large eyes. "Where am I?" asked she.

"You are all right," answered the young man holding her hand.

"You and your brothers have been so wonderful to me. I know not how to express it," said Snow Bella.

"Snow Bella," warned again the oldest of the three, "you must be careful in the future. You are too beautiful. It is the fate of some that their beauty bring them good fortune and happiness but it is your beauty brings you only misfortune and suffering. . . . I fear it is your wicked stepmother. So beware of women at the door in the future."

When the wicked stepmother reached home again, she sang and rejoiced at what she had done to Snow Bella. "How wonderful I feel," said she to herself, "since I am rid of that bad girl. I know now I am the prettiest in all the land. . . . Yet I think I shall try my little mirror again." So she sang while sitting before the mirror:

> Tiny mirror, tiny mirror,
> Of this town and all the land,
> Tell me, if you can,
> Who is everywhere
> Most beautiful and fair?
> While I look in you,
> Answer true, answer true.

The mirror sang back:

> Lady, lady in the mirror,
> Snow Bella's the name,
> Whose beauty's the fame
> Here and everywhere—
> Most beautiful and fair
> As ever maid be,
> And at the dwarfs' lives she.

"This is the limit," gasped the cruel woman in a fit of rage. "Kill her I will. Kill her I will. What shall I do to the wretch?"

The next day while the wicked stepmother was brooding and thinking how to kill Snow Bella, again the vendor called to the window, "Apples to sell, nice red, red apples to sell."

"Bring me your apples, old man," exclaimed the woman. "How are they?"

"Ah, my dear lady," said he, "one bite into the peeling and one is dead—a most malefic poison. Yet they are crimson red and most sweet to smell."

"Give me one quickly," said she. "I shall see whether this wretch will live to be fairer than I and fairest of the land."

This time the stepmother disguised herself as a man and set out again for the hut, carrying the apple neatly covered in a basket. She knocked at the hut door.

"What is it?" asked Snow Bella, peeping through the key hole.

"I have the sweetest and reddest apples on earth," cajoled the stepmother in the voice of a man. "They are very cheap, especially for you, beautiful maiden."

"I cannot let you in for anything on earth," replied Snow Bella, who looked longingly at the crimson fruit.

"Here, my child," coaxed the woman. "Try this one. I shall roll it in under the door."

Snow Bella picked up the poisoned apple, and the wicked stepmother at the key hole watched her bite into it and fall dead to the floor. She went away dancing for joy and sure that Snow Bella was dead forever.

The three brothers soon came home, saw Snow Bella dead upon the floor, picked her up again and put her on the bed. They did everything in vain for three days to revive her, but she remained cold and dead. The apple with the part bitten out of it was lying on the floor. So they knew Snow Bella had been poisoned by it. At length they all built a coffin from the fine wood they worked at in the forest. They set up all night to wake for Snow Bella, their lovely little housekeeper, whom they loved so much. The tears streamed from their eyes. Next day they dug a grave into the greensward nearby and began carrying the coffin to the grave. One of them stumbled and tilted the coffin, shaking up Snow Bella. The jolt shook her so much that the piece of apple she had swallowed came out from her throat into the coffin. Finally, she began stirring in the coffin, and one of the dwarfs saw her and told the others about it.

"She is alive!" cried he. "Beautiful Snow Bella is alive."

They took her from the coffin and wept again for joy, Snow Bella embracing each in turn around the neck, because she had learned to love the dwarfs for their faithful kindness and their warm tenderness. She had also learned to love deeply the handsome young brother, who likewise worshipped Snow Bella.

"This must be the end of the wicked stepmother!" shouted the older dwarf. "Let us go to kill her."

Now the stepmother was home rejoicing and arranging herself before the mirror, which she addressed again:

> Tiny mirror, tiny mirror,
> Of this town and all the land,
> Tell me, if you can,
> Who is everywhere
> Most beautiful and fair?
> While I look in you,
> Answer true, answer true.

The mirror sang back:

> Lady, lady in the mirror,
> Snow Bella's the name,
> Whose beauty's the fame
> Here and everywhere—
> Most beautiful and fair
> As ever maid be,
> And at the dwarfs' lives she.

"Hateful mirror," cried the stepmother, taking the mirror from the wall and dashing it to bits on the floor.

Just then in came the two dwarfs and the youngest brother. With knives and clubs they fell upon the wicked stepmother and killed her on the spot, which was the end of the cruelest and vainest woman on earth. The three returned home, announcing the good news to Snow Bella, who became light as a feather for joy, because this was like a terrible weight of sorrow and trouble lifted from her life.

The youngest brother of the two dwarfs, who was now more tall and handsome than any Prince ever was, declared his love for Snow Bella. The two were married, and they all lived together happily ever after.

Claudel 1942: 154–62. ATU 709. Collected by Calvin Claudel from his mother, Mrs. Leota Edwards Claudel, then about fifty-nine years old. For more on Mrs. Claudel see the preceding story. Joseph M. Carriére, the collector of the Missouri French tales in the next chapter, was the original editor of this tale. He inserted the French text of the mirror verses into the English translation:

> *Tit-miroir, tit-miroir,*
> *Dis-moi laquelle*
> *Est la plus belle?*

Quel est son nom
Dans ce canton
Et ce territoire?
Oui, tit-miroir.

O madame, o madame,
Snow Bella s'appelle,
Celle la plus belle
Dans ce canton,
Snow Bella le nom
D'elle chez les nains,
Plus belle des humains.

Mrs. Claudel's large repertoire included Bouqui and Lapin stories and Jean Sot stories as well as märchen. This version of "Snow White," one of the most popular of fairy tales, shows little influence from the Grimm brothers' version, unless in the opening episode. The name Snow Bella suggests both English and Spanish antecedents. And the last sentence but one may contain an oblique reference to the popular Walt Disney film. Snow Bella, however, is not even a princess. All the characters, in fact, are ordinary people, not nobility or royalty. But they do live in the land of make-believe, where wishes come true, mirrors talk, hair ornaments poison, and there are no sheriffs to arrest wicked people (or, for that matter, those who take the law into their own hands). Moreover, only the handsome brother may court the beautiful Snow Bella.

42. Jean L'Ours

The tale of Jean L'Ours was my grandfather's favorite tale in the old days and he would narrate it with gesticulations at many a French gathering on the lonely Louisiana prairie.

Once upon a time, very long ago, there were three powerful men around whom many tales were woven. These were Jean L'Ours (John the Bear), Tord-Chene (Tree Twister), and Pallet (Anvil Juggler). But at one time Jean L'Ours is said to have met and put both to shame by uprooting a tree with a single twist and juggling anvils with only one hand.

After that feat Jean L'Ours came to a sudden decision. So that night he told his mama, "I am a big, strong man. I will not go to school any more. I am going out and see the world."

His mama replied, "Mais, Jean L'Ours, before you go, you must see the priest and see if it is all right."

Jean L'Ours went, and at the door of the church he was surprised to see God Himself waiting for him.

God offered him the gates of heaven if he would stay at home and be a good boy, or a sack, into which anything he wished for would go. But if he took this sack, he could not enter heaven.

Jean L'Ours answered, "Mais, you can have your pearly gates. I'll take the sack."

The next day he started out and as he crossed the road, he saw a farm with many, many buggies, wagons, and oxen carts all around. He walked over to see what the matter was. They told him there was a dead person. Jean L'Ours had never seen a dead person, so he went in and viewed the body. As he did not find a dead person very interesting, he passed on into the kitchen. On the table there were plenty of fried chickens and bread. He thought, "I wish all that would go into my sack," and as God had predicted, in it went with no help at all from Jean.

"Thank the good Lord!" exclaimed Jean L'Ours and hurriedly carried it out through the back door. And away he went to the roadside, where he sat down and ate until he fell asleep.

The next morning he proceeded on his journey. After a few miles he saw another farm with more buggies, carts, and wagons: "There is another dead person. I will go in and wish me another sackful of food."

Jean L'Ours went up to the gate and asked if there were a dead person there too. They answered that nobody was dead; it was a big wedding. He went in anyway, and looked at the bride and bridegroom, but he was not interested in marriage, and soon passed on into the kitchen. This time the table was laden with wine, pork dressing, and cake.

Jean L'Ours wished it into his sack and went back to the roadside, where he ate every morsel before he fell asleep on Mother Earth.

The following day he started into town. Passing in front of a house, he heard a woman crying. Jean L'Ours had never heard that, so he went to the door and asked the woman what she was crying about.

"The devil is coming to get my husband, Pierre, tonight at twelve o'clock."

"Mais," said Jean L'Ours, "that is nothing to cry about."

"Oh yes. Pierre has gone to Confession and Communion before the devil comes to take him away."

Jean L'Ours continued, "I am Jean L'Ours. And I can take care of the devil if you give me something to eat and let me stay here tonight."

The woman invited Jean L'Ours in and started to make some cush-cush in the fireplace. As Jean L'Ours took the rocking chair, she started a stirring and singing.

Pierre entered. "Marie!" he cried. "What are you singing about? The devil is coming after me at twelve o'clock and here you are singing."

Marie calmly pointed her big spoon at Jean L'Ours sitting in the rocking chair. "He is going to take care of the devil."

And so that night they all went to bed and Jean L'Ours slept in the front room right by the door.

But Pierre did not sleep well that night. And, when the clock struck eleven, he shook Marie: "Marie! I have only one more hour to stay with you."

"Oh, go to sleep, Pierre. Jean L'Ours is going to take care of you."

But at the stroke of twelve, Pierre shook Marie again. "Marie! It is twelve o'clock!" And the old devil knocked on the door.

Jean L'Ours opened it.

"What do you want?"

The old devil answered, "I want Pierre."

"I wish you would get into my sack," replied Jean L'Ours and into the sack went the old devil before he knew what was happening to him.

Jean L'Ours tied up the sack, threw it into the corner, and he and Pierre and Marie slept until broad daylight.

After Jean L'Ours had his breakfast of cornbread and milk, he put the old devil on his back and set out to find a blacksmith shop. He found one, but it only had two blacksmiths. He wanted four. So he went to the next town where they had four. There he had them beat the old devil with iron mallets until he promised to let Pierre alone. After that, he opened the sack, and off ran the old devil to hell.

Proceeding on his journey, Jean L'Ours came alongside of a country butchery. He went around to the different tables and wished for the best red meat to go into his sack. When it was full, he went back to the roadside and sat down on Mother Earth, and ate until he went to sleep. But the next morning the neighbors found Jean L'Ours lying there, very sick.

Jean L'Ours told them, "I am going to die, but be sure to bury my sack with me." And he died and was buried with his sack.

On his way up, he stopped at the pearly gates and knocked.

Saint Peter opened the door and asked, "Who is it?"

"It is me, Jean L'Ours."

"You can't come in here," said Saint Peter. "You have chosen the sack instead of the gates of heaven."

So Jean L'Ours went down to hell.

The old devil opened the door and upon recognizing Jean L'Ours, exclaimed, "You can't come in here after you had me beaten by four blacksmiths." He slammed the door in his face.

So Jean L'Ours decided to go back to heaven. When he got to the gates he knocked and then he threw his sack in before Saint Peter recognized him. After doing that, he just wished himself in his sack and there he was—in heaven.

The next morning when God was walking around looking at his saints, he stumbled over the sack with Jean L'Ours in it.

God asked Saint Peter why he had let Jean L'Ours in. Saint Peter said he hadn't. And Jean L'Ours said, "No, I just threw my sack in before Saint Peter shut the door on me and then wished I was in. And here I am."

"Well," said God to Saint Peter, "we haven't any place for Jean L'Ours among the saints, but maybe we can make him our bookkeeper."

And the last we heard about him, Jean L'Ours has made the best bookkeeper heaven ever had.

Mouton and Orso 1971: 21–24. ATU 330, with elements of ATU 301. Mona Mel Mouton, of Lafayette, Louisiana, wrote down this story that her father had learned from his father toward the end of the nineteenth century. Jean L'Ours means John the Bear, and his proper story, ATU 301, about rescuing three princesses from underground, is very popular in French and Iberian tradition. The other two heroes alluded to in the opening of this tale are traditional companions of Jean L'Ours. See chapter 8 for a Missouri French version in which John has these two companions. Here Jean appears in quite a different tale, ATU 330. Appalachian Jack also jumps from tale to tale in this fashion, appearing, in fact, in full versions of both 301 and 330. Couche-couche, which Mouton spells cush-cush, is a stew (cf. *couscous*).

43. The Three Oranges

There were three sons walking about in an effort to find jobs. As one was walking he met an old witch who gave him three oranges and told him that as he ate each orange, a beautiful naked girl would appear, but that she would stay with him only if he could give her some water. He walked and walked and ate the three oranges to quench his thirst. As foretold by the witch the girl appeared but vanished when he couldn't give her any water.

He told one brother about the experience and told him to go to the witch, warning him not to eat the oranges until he was near water. The witch gave him some oranges, but the same fate befell him; the girl appeared and then vanished. He returned and told the first brother about his experience and said that he just could not help himself.

The third brother met the witch and was given three oranges and told not to make the same mistake as his two other brothers.

As he travelled he was quite thirsty and ate two of the oranges. He managed to wait until he reached a well to eat the last orange. When the girl appeared and asked for water, he complied and she stayed with him.

Because she was naked they went off to find some clothes for her. After walking a great distance, they came to a clearing with a store. He instructed the girl to hide in a certain tree near a well and went off to purchase the clothes.

While he was gone, an ugly girl came to gather water for her mother to use in a gravy. When her mother, who was a witch, called for her to hurry, she said, "Oh mom, I'm too pretty, I cannot bring you any water; you ought to see me in the water."

When her mother came to investigate, she saw that her daughter was looking at the reflection of the beauty in the tree. The witch talked the beauty out of the tree and replaced her with her own ugly daughter and told her that when the third brother asked why she was so ugly, she should say he had taken too long, and the sun had ruined her complexion.

The third brother brought the girl home to his parents but was ashamed because of her ugliness. He became ill, and was visited every day by a little bird. The bird was actually the beautiful girl. The old witch had been combing her hair when a tooth had broken off the comb, causing the girl to be transformed into a bird.

The brother was petting the bird on one of its daily visits when he dislodged the tooth of the comb from the feathers, changing the girl back into human form.

He made the ugly girl disappear, married the beauty, and after that they were happy together.

Ashman 1982: 49–51. ATU 408. Told to Charles Richard Ashman by Mrs. Sweetsay Gislair of Galliano, on Bayou LaFourche in the swampy part of Cajun Louisiana southwest of New Orleans. Apparently Ashman was a student of folklorist Ethelyn Orso at the University of New Orleans at the time he collected this tale. Orso regularly published material gathered by her students in the *Louisiana Folklore Miscellany*.

The Three Oranges is practically unknown in U.S. English-language tradition, but not so rare in the U.S. French and Iberian traditions. The story is often told at great length. Mrs. Gellar's succinct version includes most of the main episodes, although the transformation of the Orange Princess into a bird seems to be accidental rather than intentional in the present version, and a subsequent series of other transformations does not occur. This version also includes some local color: the girl is drawing water to make gravy, a standard part of southern meals, and the boy has gone to a store in a clearing, just such a store as one might once have found along rural roads in the southern woods and swamps.

44. Geneviève

There's the story of Saint Geneviève. That's a beautiful story, but I can't tell it. There was a little girl. From the time she was old enough, she visited her friends. She treated them all well. When she grew old enough she married.

Just when she was married, war was declared and her husband was called to serve. They came to get him. And then, he said that she shouldn't worry, that he would speak to the king to have her protected, to take care of Geneviève. But it happened that the king wanted to take her for himself. And she did not want this, to the point where, when the king saw this, he had her guardian killed and he blamed her. They put her in prison.

Then when she was in prison, the little girl whom she had healed—she had healed a little girl who was considered hopeless. She had worked for her and had healed her. So then, when she was older, she kept her always with her. Geneviève was her name. And she looked upon Geneviève as a mother.

So then, she was treated as the opposite of what she really was, as though she were a criminal, as though she went out with men. And then, her husband, when he read the letter, he thought it was true. He wrote a letter to send to the king telling him to—and she had a child—he said in the letter that he must kill Geneviève and her child because he wanted no memory of her if she had gone wrong.

Then he met one of his friends. He had gone to mail the letter. He met one of his friends. He said, "Where do you come from?" He said, "You look so full of pain."

"Well," he said, and he told him the story.

"I can't believe that you believe this," he said. "You don't believe this could be true? I know that Geneviève was too good to do such things. If I were in your place, I would get that letter back."

So he turned around. He went back to retrieve the letter, but it had left. So it went to the king. So the king—Geneviève was in prison—he brought the case to trial. And he read the letter to everyone, what the husband had written, that she should be killed and everything. And he said that two men should take her at eleven o'clock at night and kill her, put her to death.

But the little girl whom she had cured was grown up now and attended the trial. And when the trial ended, she went to the prison. She tapped at the prison window and Geneviève got up. "Who's there?" she said. And then she said that it was she—she named herself—and said that she had come bearing sad news. She said, "You will be killed tonight, and I wanted to see if you wanted to give me a message, something that I should tell your husband. You know that I know that all this is a lie, but it's the king who wills it."

So, "Good," she said. "Go and get me a tablet, pens, and some ink. I'll write him a letter." So she wrote a letter. You should have seen all that she included in that letter. And when she finished the letter, she wrote, "I forgive you because I know that you were told lies, because my conscience is clear. With all that has happened, my conscience is clear." She said, "It was all the king's doing, but I forgive you. All that I ask is that you help people, especially old widows." She wrote all sorts of things.

Then, that night, they came to take her away, and they took her to the woods to kill her. So she knew that she would be killed, but the fellows who went to get her didn't know that she knew. And when they arrived in the woods, one said, "Well, I want you to give me your child."

"Well," she said, "what do you want to do with him'?"

So he said, "We've been sent by the king to kill you and your child, and we are obliged to do it because if we don't, we will be killed."

"Well," she said, "I want you to let me speak for a while."

So they said, "You can say what you like."

"Fine," she said. "You know that those were all lies that were told. My own conscience is clear. It was all the king's doing." She said, "Do you see the moon?" The moon was full. She said, "Do you see how bright the moon is? Well, every time you look at the moon when it will be full, it will be blood red if you kill me."

Ho! This worried them considerably. And she said, "Do you see the trembling leaves on the white oak? Your faces will tremble that way the rest of your lives."

"Ho!" they said. "Well, we're obliged to kill you anyway, because he said that we were to bring back your eyes."

"Well," she said, "kill that dog that is following you and then take out its eyes to take to the king."

"Oh, but," they said, "he will realize that they are not your eyes."

She said, "Don't worry. The king is very troubled now. He will not want to see those eyes." She said, "I would like for you to leave me here in the woods where I will be able to die a natural death. You wouldn't need to kill me."

"Well," they said, "if you will promise us."

She said, "I promise you that I will never go back."

They said, "If you will promise never to go back, we will leave you." And they left her.

And when they arrived before the king, they presented the eyes, but he said that he did not want to see them, and that he did not want to see the two men ever again, that they should leave the city that very night. He did not want to see them again in the city. So the fellows had to leave the city.

Meanwhile, the war had gone on and on. The next day, which was the day the war ended, snow was falling. She started walking in the forest; it was a big forest. She found the trail of an animal. So she said to herself, "I'll follow this trail. Maybe there's a shelter somewhere."

She set out. She followed the trail. She arrived at a place where there was a cavern, like a rock, and there was a room inside. She went inside. She said, "Well, it would be nice in here, but there is nothing to eat." She was talking to herself, "Well, I'll have to—" She left her child there and she began to wander nearby. There she found water, a spring which was flowing. Then they had water. "Well," she said, "this is fine, but we need more. We can't live just on water." So she returned to the cavern. Well, she was in there, and that night a doe came to the cavern, but when it saw her, it didn't want to come in. She started caressing it until finally it came in. And it had a swollen udder. It had lost its young. She caressed it until she was able to start milking it to have some milk. So this provided milk for her and her child.

So she stayed there. It doesn't seem possible, but they say that she stayed there seven years. And her little boy was growing. They talked all the time.

So one day, she became very ill. So she said, "I'm going to die."

He said, "Die, what is it to die?"

"Well," she said, "dying, when you see that I'm no longer breathing, and I'm no longer talking, and I'm no longer blinking, my lips will turn black, I'll be dead. You will leave and follow the sun. You will walk all day long. This will take you two days. When you see that night is falling, you will sleep there and leave again the next day."

"Ho!" he said. "No, I won't do that. I would prefer to stay here with the wild animals."

"Oh," she said, "no. You can't do that. You must promise me that you will go away."

"But," he said, "when I arrive there, they will do to me what they did to you. They will want to kill me."

She said, "Oh, no! They won't kill you. You will ask for your father. He will take you in and take good care of you."

"Fine, then," he said, "I promise you. I will do this."

But then she didn't die. She got better. So when she was better, she started wandering again. And one day, she said, "Tomorrow morning, I am going to leave very early. I'll walk all day long. When I think it is noon, I'll turn around to come back, trying to find fruit." There was wild fruit, but they had eaten everything nearby. She said, "There is no more fruit here. I want to try to find some more. But you stay near the cavern. Don't come out until I return."

"Oh!" he said. "I'll stay."

So she left in the morning and when it was almost noon, there was a little mountain. She climbed up onto the mountain and she saw a wolf coming with a sheep. It was carrying it. And it came right next to her. She always had a branch, she carried a stick. She hit it with the branch. It rolled down howling. Then it ran away. Then she took the sheep and tried to make it drink some milk—she had brought along some milk, but the sheep died. So she said, "Well, I'll try to skin it, if I can find something to." So she went down the mountain and found something to cut with. She went back up and skinned it and then she put the skin on and left.

Several days before this, she had been sitting, and thinking deeply. She went out. Her son said, "What's the matter, mother? You seem pensive."

"Yes," she said, "you don't notice, but I no longer have any clothes to wear and where will I find something?"

"Ho! Well if God is as good as you say," he said, "He will provide you with clothes." She had to smile.

When she had skinned the sheep, she returned. She arrived late in the evening. Night was falling. When she arrived fairly close, she called out. The child, who was in the cave, came out. He ran away when he saw her. He turned around crying. He didn't recognize her. Then, she called out to him; she made herself known.

"Yes, but," he said, "by God, what is that on your back, what are you wearing? That's why I didn't recognize you."

So she told him about the sheep.

"Oh! well," he said, "I told you that God wouldn't leave you like that." She wanted to make herself a dress with it.

Meanwhile, the knight, when he returned, the little girl searched for him from town to town to give him the letter. Geneviève had sealed the letter and given it to her. And she had said not to give it to anyone until her husband returned and to give it to him in his very hands. So when he returned, she walked far away from her home to give him the letter. And he read the letter. He read all that Geneviève had written there. And he saw that it was true, that . . .

So when they arrived where they were to dismount, the king was there. And he had to take his foot out of the stirrup to get down from his horse. They were all on horseback. And when he went to help him dismount, he said, "Don't touch my foot, criminal that you are." He said this to the king. He said, "After all the lies you told me, causing me to condemn my Geneviève. When we get back to the castle, you will not take the podium. I will take it. I will talk. You will go to the same prison as Geneviève." He said all this to the king.

So when they went inside, the fellow mounted the podium and read the letter that Geneviève had written before all the people. Everything that was in it. They had to listen to all that she had written. Until then, everything had been allowed to slip by. Then afterwards, they gave fine parties and invited him, but he never wanted to go. So one day, he [the knight] said [to those who wanted to invite him places], "If you would like to go out to a certain forest," he said (this is where Geneviève supposedly had been killed, he thought), "then I would go."

"Fine. Well," they said, "we'll go there." So they left with mules and carts and baggage and they went into that forest and they made camp and started hunting.

So one day, he was hunting on horseback, but he always went to the part of the forest where he thought Geneviève might have been killed. So one day, he saw a deer, a doe, in fact. He tried to approach it to shoot it, but it kept getting away. So he tied his horse and he took off the back way and followed it to the cavern where it lived. Then it went inside the cavern, and he went very quietly up to the opening. He wanted to kill the doe. And Geneviève was inside. She came out. She said, "Sir, don't kill my doe. It's the livelihood of my son and me."

Then he recognized her. He said, "Oh, Geneviève! Go away from me. I know it can't be you. It's your spirit talking to me. It can't be you."

Then she recognized him. She said, "Oh, Lord!" His name was Lebouche. She said, "Oh, Lebouche! It is I. Here, touch my hand."

He touched her hand and said, "Well, yes, your hand is icy. There is no life in you at all. It's only your spirit talking."

She said, "Oh, no! I assure you that it is I. Look at my wedding ring, the one you gave me at the altar of the church when we were married." And he still didn't want to admit it was she. She raised her eyes to heaven and asked God that he should recognize her. Then he finally recognized her.

"Well, then," he said, "we'll take the horse and we'll leave." And they left.

When they arrived at the camp, they gathered together and they left, but the doe followed them. So when they arrived home, he prepared a home for the doe to live in, and he took good care of it. Poor Geneviève had been milking it for seven years. It was a good provider of milk. So he took care of it as though it were one of their own children.

Then one day, Geneviève died. And they went to bury her. And the doe followed them. It lay down on the tomb. And then he went to get it. He brought it back home. He offered it all sorts of good things to eat. It didn't want to eat. It would turn around and return to lie down on the tomb. And then, it died on Geneviève's tomb.

There, that's the end of the story, but I only tell half of it.

Ancelet 1994: 43–45. ATU 883A (cf. ATU 706, 712). Told to collector Barry Jean Ancelet by Frank Couppel, of Bayou Sorrel, formerly of Bayou Pigeon. Couppel was quite elderly at the time he told this tale, having been born sometime in the 1890s, he did not know what year. He had supported himself by working for oil-company road and canal crews, and by the local traditional trades of fishing and gathering Spanish moss. He learned the tale from his mother. He seems to start out saying what the tale is about and claiming he does not know it. But soon he shifts into a full performance of the tale. The English translation is Ancelet's, slightly altered.

ATU 883 is a widespread tale. In French, Iberian, and German tradition, as here, it is often associated with the apocryphal St. Geneviève de Brabant. Geneviève in turn has been identified with Marie de Brabant, accused of adultery by her husband Louis II, Duke of Bavaria and Count-Palatine of the Rhine, and executed in 1256. A French Jesuit, René de Cérisier, published a popular account of St. Geneviève in 1638, and her story was frequently dramatized.

45. Lapin and Bouqui's Mule

One day Bouqui went to visit Lapin. While at the dinner table Bouqui noticed what fine vegetables Lapin's wife served—squash, pumpkin and fine celery salad.

"What fine food you have, Lapin!" remarked Bouqui. "I wish I had such wonderful vegetables for my household."

"I raise them on my farm," replied Lapin. "Why don't you start a vegetable farm yourself and farm the way I do?"

"That's a good idea," ventured Bouqui. "But I have no mule or seed to start such a farm." After they had all eaten a while, Lapin said to Bouqui, "I know just the thing for you, Bouqui. A farmer nearby has a mule and a sack of peas. You can probably make a bargain with him to get them. You can use the peas to start a crop."

"But what can I offer him, Lapin?" questioned Bouqui. "I have no money. My wife is all I've got."

"I'll tell you what," proposed Lapin. "Trade your wife for his mule and the peas. I'm sure he'll accept. I'll talk to him and fix it up for you. Tomorrow I'll come to see you."

After Bouqui had returned home, he pondered over Lapin's proposition. Finally he said to his wife, who was indeed very pretty, "My wife, I have been thinking about swapping you for a mule and a sack of peas. We can't live in this poverty. So I really need a mule more than I need you."

Next day Bouqui heard Lapin knock at the door.

"I have brought the mule and sack of peas," explained Lapin. "All you have to do now is get your wife over to the farmer's place. He has agreed to the bargain."

At first Bouqui was reluctant, for he had noticed how his wife was pretty, and he really wanted to keep her. However, his wife came up just then with her clothes all bundled and packed ready to leave and said: "No, Bouqui, I shall go. You were stupid enough to want to trade me for a mule and a sack of peas. So I'm going to leave you now for the farmer. . . . Goodbye."

This settled the bargain. Bouqui's wife left, carrying her bundle. Bouqui kept the mule and the sack of peas, and Lapin went home.

Now it happened that Lapin really wanted the mule for himself. So he began to devise a trick to get the mule away from Bouqui. That night he went to Bouqui's barn, unlocked the door and started to lead the mule to his own place. While on his way home, he clipped off the end of the mule's tail and threw it into a pond nearby, where there was a very deep hole.

Next day Bouqui came to Lapin's house and knocked at the door. "Lapin," began Bouqui, "someone must have stolen my mule. Have you seen him?"

"Why, no," replied Lapin.

Just then Bouqui noticed his mule in Lapin's barn, and he exclaimed, "That looks very much like my mule!"

"Of course not," added Lapin. "That mule has a bobbed tail. Your mule has a long tail."

"That's true enough," answered Bouqui, shaking his head, however, in a puzzled fashion.

"I'll go help you to look for your mule, Bouqui," offered Lapin, feigning sympathy. So the two started off together. Finally Lapin reached the pond and exclaimed: "There! Your mule slipped into the deep hole of the pond. I see his tail sticking out of the water."

Lapin walked out over the water on a fallen tree to the place where the piece of tail was floating. He reached down and pulled and pulled on the tail, making out as if he was trying to pull up the mule on the other end of the tail. Finally he flew backwards out of the water, holding the tail in his hands.

"You see, Bouqui," explained Lapin, "your mule fell in here and drowned. I pulled so hard, his tail came off. It's no use; he is lost under the water."

"Yes, that's too bad," replied Bouqui, as he left with a look of despair.

Claudel 1943–1944: 292–94. ATU 1004. Collected by Claudel from his mother, Mrs. Leota Edwards Claudel, who was sixty-two at the time of telling. For more on Mrs. Claudel see the note on Golden Hair. This popular trickster tale sometimes features pig tails stuck into mud.

46. Two Tales of Jean Sot

A. Jean Sot Kills Flies

Jean Sot's mother was ready to go out to a soirée. She was leaving him with his baby brother. "Now, Jean," she said, "you watch your little brother closely and try to keep the flies away from his face." There were no screens in those days and the flies kept coming in the window and landing on the baby's face. Jean sat for a long time waving the flies away, but they would come right back. Finally, Jean became well angry. "All right, you flies," he shouted, "I will fix you," and he went out and got his father's hammer. Every time a fly landed he would hit it with the hammer. When his mother came home she found the baby dead. "Ma Mere," said Jean proudly, "look how many flies I killed."

B. JEAN SOT HELPS OUT

One day the cow escaped into the fields and his mother said, "Jean Sot, go find the cow and bring her home."

An hour later she looked out to see Jean struggling to carry the cow into the yard. He saw her and shouted, "Ma Mere, I called her and called her, but she didn't want to come to the yard, so I had to carry her."

Mama was sad to see her poor son straining so, and she said, "Oh no, Jean Sot, you should tie a rope around her neck and pull her home!"

Later she sent him to the grocery for a *pain de menage*. He bought the bread and asked the grocer for a piece of rope. The grocer had no rope to give him, but he gave him a long piece of string. Jean tied the bread securely in the middle and started pulling it home, thinking, "Ma Mere will be pleased and proud that I now know how to pull things home." So he happily began playing with the extra long string, trying to make designs by lacing the fingers of both hands through it, as his mama had shown him. Mostly just making knots, he finally succeeded in making a design as he entered his home. "Look, Ma Mere, I made a chicken foot," he shouted joyfully.

But his mother was far from joyful, for she had spied her beautiful round country loaf broken off in spots and full of dust. So she scolded the poor imbecile. Then sadly she explained, "Mon pauvre Jean Sot, when I send you for a bread, and you want your hands free to play, put the bread in the nice round cap I made for you. It will go nicely and you can carry it on your head."

A few days later she sent Jean to the neighbor's for some freshly churned butter. "Now, Jean Sot," she pleaded, "no foolishness! Bring the butter home carefully, for I'm making brioche for your supper and you know how you enjoy brioche with lots of butter."

"Good, Ma Mere," said Jean happily, "I'll be very careful," and he hurried off. When he got the butter, he sat on the neighbor's step and carefully put it in his cap, then put the cap back on his head and started for home. But the path was long and sun hot, so when he arrived home his face was drenched with melted butter. "Look, Ma Mere, I perspire butter," he called proudly.

Furious that he lost the butter, his mother slapped him. Then—sad that he was so stupid—patiently explained, "Mon pauvre Jean Sot, when you get butter, wrap it tightly in straw and hurry to the well and cool it. Then when you get to the brook, cool it in the water again; then it won't have a chance to melt before you get home." Then she kissed him and gave him his dry brioche for supper.

Soon after this last episode, Jean Sot's mother got word that her kind neighbor had a nice, fat kitten for her. "Good, Jean Sot," she said. "We have so many mice on this farm, we really have needed a greedy cat to catch and eat them."

So Jean was sent to fetch the kitten. He was delighted with the soft, purring little animal, so he really regretted wrapping it so tightly in straw. Then he hurried to the well, cooled it and cooled it, and when he got to the brook, he cooled it again. Of course, the kitten was no more by the time he got home and he got a good spanking for all his trouble.

Soileau 1973: 44, 45–46. A. ATU 1586A; B. ATU 1696. These stories come originally from Mrs. J. W. Bassett (née Suzanne Fournet), who grew up in St. Martinville in the last decades of the nineteenth century. Mrs. Bassett recalled that she and her thirteen brothers and sisters used to exchange Jean Sot tales for amusement. Her granddaughter, Jeanne Pitre Soileau, collected the first tale (of killing flies) from her in French and translated it. Mrs. W. W. Pitre, of Lafayette, Mrs. Basset's daughter and Jeanne's mother, wrote down the second tale (of Jean's hapless errands) as she remembered hearing it in her own childhood, writing in English, however, rather than in French. The first tale has circulated among American schoolchildren as a cruelty/dead baby joke. The second is widely popular in African American and Anglo-American traditions as well as in the French.

47. Boudreaux and Thibodeaux

A. Boudreaux and Thibodaux Go Fishing

Boudreaux and Thibodaux left early one morning to go fishing. They rented a boat and fished for hours with little success. Toward the end of the day, however, they got into a whole nest of sac-a-lait [crappie]. They put more than fifty of the big milky-white fish into the boat in less than an hour.

"Mais, Thibodaux, we got to mark this spot, yeah, and come back tomorrow."

So Thibodaux reached into his tackle box and pulled out a big black marker. He reached over the side of the boat and put a big X there.

"Mais, cuyon," Boudreaux said. "How you know we gonna get the same boat tomorrow?"

B. Another Fish Story

Boudreaux and Thibodeaux got up real early one morning to go fishing at the lake near their house. When they get there, still in the dark, they remember that the best fishing spot is across the lake, but they didn't bring their pirogue with them. They are trying to figure out how to get across to the other side, when Boudreaux has a brainstorm. "I tell you what, Thib, I'll shine my flashlight on the water, and you walk across on de beam of light."

Thibodeaux tells him, "Mais, you must tink I'm stoopid, or sumting! I know you before today, yeh. Jus' when I get halfway across, you gonna turn off de light."

C. Chickens

Boudreaux spots Thibodeaux walking down the levee the other day, carrying a sack over his shoulder. Well, of course curiosity got the best of Boudreaux, and he asked Thibodeaux, "Hey, Mon Homme, what you got in dat sack?"

Thibodeaux says, "Mais, I got me some chickens in dat sack."

Boudreaux says, "If I can guess how many chickens you got in dat sack, can I have one of dem?"

Thibodeaux replies, "Mais, my frien', if you can guess how many I got, you can have both of dem!"

D. Boudreaux Finds Marie Cryin'

Boudreaux walks into the house the other day to find Marie crying her eyes out. He asks, "Mais, Chere, what's wrong?"

Marie, through her tears, tells him, "I was takin' some ice cubes from de freezer, an' dropped dem on de floor. So I rinsed dem off in some hot water, an' now I can't finds 'em!"

E. Thibodeaux Pays His Debt

Boudreaux and Thibodeaux, and their wives, Marie and Clotile, decided to get together to play some bourre (a Cajun card game) the other night. After a couple of hours of card playing and beer drinking, Boudreaux had to answer the "call of nature," so he got up to go to the bathroom. About the same time, Clotile went to the kitchen to get them some more beer.

While Thibodeaux and Marie were alone, the beer was making Thibodeaux start to feel a little amorous, and he started talking trash with Marie. He remarked how good looking he thought she was, and of course, one thing led to another, and he finally suggested that they should do "the big nasty" together sometime. Marie reminded him that he and Boudreaux were best friends, and that she didn't think that would be right. Well, of course, Thibodeaux kept trying, finally offering her a hundred bucks for the deed. Well, this was too much for Marie to pass up, so she agreed. They planned to meet the next day while Boudreaux was at work, and take care of business.

Bright and early the next morning, Thibodeaux shows up at Marie and Boudreaux's house, and he and Marie pass them a good time all day long. Later he gives Marie the hundred bucks and leaves.

A couple of hours later, Boudreaux gets home from work and asks Marie if Thibodeaux had been by during the day. Marie, a little surprised, nervously tells him yes. Boudreaux then asks her if Thibodeaux gave her a hundred dollars. Marie, real nervous now, tells him yes. Boudreaux says, "Mais, dat Thibodeaux, I can always count on him, yeh. Yestiday, he borrow a hundred dollars from me, and he promise dat he would pass by and drop it off for me before I got home today."

F. Boudreaux Is Dying

Boudreaux is lying on his deathbed, about to draw his last breath, and is surrounded by his wife and four sons. Three of the sons are tall, good-looking, athletic, and intelligent. The fourth is short, ugly, homely as sin, and dumb as a tree. Boudreaux, mustering all the energy he has left, asks Marie, "Chere, before I goes, dere is one ting I wants to know. My fourth son, is he really mine? If he isn't, I understans, but I gots to know for sure."

Marie interrupts, softly telling him, "Boudreaux, don't you worry 'bout dat. I promise you dat he is your son." Boudreaux then passes away, but he dies happy. Marie turns to the three good-looking sons, and says, "I sure is glad he didn't ask me about y'all!"

A: Ray 1999; B–F: Boudreaux 2000. For types and motifs, see below.

Many very old tales, including numbskull tales, tales of clever or faithless wives and husbands, and trickster tales (ATU 1200–1874), circulate today as Cajun jokes. These jokes are told among friends who are Cajun or have an interest in Cajun tradition. The telling usually involves linguistic conventions designed to suggest the distinctive French-spattered dialect of rural English-speaking Cajuns. Like other kinds of jokes, they are likewise transcribed and posted on internet sites or circulated on internet lists. In fact, the internet is probably the place where humorous tales circulate most rapidly and freely in the United States today. In the current internet versions of these jokes the heroes are usually called Boudreaux and Thibodeaux. In a version of Story 1 that I heard in about 1960, however, one of the heroes was called Telephone, a name that plays on the old-fashioned Cajun name Telesphore.

A. ATU 1278. This joke, submitted by Willis Ray, appeared in the summer of 1999 on Blagues-L, an internet list moderated by Jocelyn "Vent de Laitue" Gagnon that distributes jokes alternately in English and French. The joke was in English.

B. Motif D 1524.1, J 1791. This and the following jokes were gleaned in the summer of 2000 from an internet site, The Boudreaux & Thibodeaux Cajun Banner Page, maintained by Dale J. Boudreaux (who refuses to claim kin with the hero of these tales). This is a fairly widespread ethnic joke in the United States. It is a clever parody of stories about walking on water and about mistaking a reflection on water for the real thing. The Aarne-Thomson-Uther classification, however, does not assign it a number among the numbskull stories.

C. ATU 1346A*. This, like the first joke, is an internationally popular numbskull story.

D. ATU 1272* (cf. ATU 1270). This tale offers a good example of how an older motif, putting snow (or in ATU 1270, candles) on the stove to dry, is adapted to modern circumstances.

E. ATU 1420C. This ancient fabliau serves as the basis of Chaucer's Shipman's Tale and of the first tale of day eight in the Decameron. It is one of many Cajun jokes in which the friends Boudreaux and Thibodeaux make free with each other's wives. Jokes such as this and the following, poking fun at the careless sexual mores of the characters, are typical of ethnic humor in the United States, especially when directed toward rural populations.

F. ATU 1425B*. Cf. Motif P233.4, Natural [i.e., illegitimate] son preferred to legitimate. Though typical in that it pokes fun at careless sexual mores, this is a fairly rare joke.

CHAPTER 8

TALES FROM THE
MISSOURI FRENCH

In the Sainte Genevieve district of Missouri, a triangle of land west of the Mississippi River and southeast of the Meramec, French was widely spoken until sometime in the mid-twentieth century. The inhabitants are descendants of the earliest French settlers in what is now the United States. Enterprising explorers and entrepreneurs moved across Lower Canada and down through what is now Indiana and Illinois, finally establishing their first town west of the Missouri in 1735 and naming it Sainte Genevieve after the apocryphal saint whose story is told in chapter 7. They came to this area to mine lead, staying on to mine bauxite and barite as well and to farm. When the British took control of what is now Indiana and Illinois in the French and Indian War, many of the French from that region crossed the river to Missouri. And after the expulsion of the Acadians from Nova Scotia in 1755 some of those French-speaking people too seem to have migrated to Missouri and the Sainte Genevieve district.

Missouri became part of the United States with the Louisiana Purchase of 1803. As English-speaking settlers and German immigrants moved in around them, the Missouri French at first maintained their separate language, culture, and oral tradition. By the 1930s, however, the last French-speaking communities were concentrated in the Ozark foothills of Washington County, around the village of Old Mines and a few neighboring hamlets. The economy of the region was based on subsistence farming and "tiff" (barite) mining. In July 1934 Joseph Medard Carrière came to the village of Old Mines, in the heart of the Sainte Genevieve district, to gather stories in the local French dialect. A young man named Pete Boyer befriended him and introduced him to storytellers. During the course of three summers Carrière collected a total of seventy-three tales. Eight of these stories came from Frank Bourisaw, an elderly man who spent his whole life in the area. "John the Bear" is one of his stories. Sixty-five stories came from Joseph Ben Coleman, a man about forty years old, who had lived for a little while in St. Louis, and then served in World War I before settling back in his native Old Mines. "Prince Green Serpent" and "The Cootie and the Flea" came from him.

In time Boyer, Carrière's guide, also became a storyteller. Though he grew up speaking French, times had changed, even in the Old Mines area, and he usually told his stories in English. In 1989 he participated in the Smithsonian Institute Festival of American Folklife in Washington, D.C. There folklorist Ray Brassieur first heard him tell the story "The Three Pieces of Gold" (Brassieur 1999: 8).

Ward Allison Dorrance also visited the Old Mines area in the early 1930s and collected a wide variety of traditional materials, including at least six folk tales. "Beau Soleil" is a story he took down from a storyteller nicknamed Gros' Vaisse.

Between 1977 and 1980 Rosemary Hyde Thomas led a project to recover Missouri French from the community around Old Mines and to teach it back to the descendants of the old French families. One part of the project involved gathering a group of elderly French speakers to go over selected stories from Carrière's collection and create English translations therefrom. The result was a volume, *It's Good to Tell You* (1981), containing French and English texts of twenty-one tales as well as analysis of the tales and a history of the community.

As these elderly residents recalled stories and storytelling, they provided Thomas with good descriptions of tale-tellers from the 1930s and themselves served as good examples of the region's traditional style of narrative. Storytelling, at least public storytelling, was largely a man's art. It was taken very seriously and old storytellers were spoken of with awe. Not everyone was a storyteller. The *conteurs* could be identified as such by others in the community. Often, apparently, the whole story was largely set or fixed in the storyteller's mind, so that repeated performances by the same storyteller might be very close in wording, gestures, and even pauses (Dorrance 1935: 104; Carrière 1937: 9). Both work and relaxation could provide occasions for storytelling. The principal source of income in the region before World War II was "tiff" or barite. Men (usually) dug the barite out of ground owned by the mining companies, and the mining companies paid them by the ton. Even if they worked digging barite full time, they probably also practiced subsistence farming. Women and children helped by "scrapping tiff," that is, picking through debris around the small mining shafts, looking for scraps of barite that had been left behind. This tedious work was often accompanied by storytelling. But the introduction of backhoes and power shovels in the 1940s put an end to the old mining techniques, and that venue for storytelling disappeared. Dark, fire-heated rooms on long winter evenings and porches or galleries on long summer evenings were another pair of venues that were gradually abandoned. But in 1980 people remembered the old days and the old storytellers:

> Do you remember Uncle Frank Bourisaw? They called him Boy Bourisaw. He'd go to Mom's house and start telling a story. We'd sit down at seven or eight o'clock and he could tell stories that would go on until five o'clock in the morning. He'd just keep on telling all different ones. (Thomas 1981: 239)

The traditional narrative style still survived in 1980. "Most of the storytellers avoided direct eye contact," says Thomas, "and they looked at the audience only occasionally." She goes on to say that they spoke in a loud but introspective tone of voice until they came to dialogue, which they "acted out with gestures" (1981: 240). Dorrance's description of a 1930s narrator describes the same style of narration. But he provides an additional picture of the audience sitting enrapt, though they might break in with cries of wonder. "Grown men . . . , work-hardened hands relaxed in their laps, sit oblivious to the world, sighing, with tears in their eyes, or slapping their thighs and spitting upon the floor in mirth" (1935: 103). The appeal of these tales lingers even in the English translations.

48. John the Bear

It's good to tell you that once upon a time there were an old man and an old woman. The old man was a miller. One morning, he went out to open the spillway of his mill wheel and found a small box. In the box there was a baby boy. The old man picked up the baby and brought it home to his wife. "We're poor," he said, "but it's better to raise the baby than to let it die in the river."

John the Bear grew quickly. After a while, he began to go to school with his stepbrothers and stepsisters. But one day his stepbrothers and stepsisters began to tease him, saying that he wasn't really their brother. He got mad at one of them and hit him, and he broke his jaw. That evening, the little boy told his father about this. The father scolded John the Bear, who said, "But they're after me all the time, saying that I'm not their brother. They got me mad, and I hit one of them."

"Well," said the miller, "they're right. You're not their brother. You're an orphan. I found you in a box on the river, and we decided to keep you rather than let you die on the river."

John the Bear answered, "Well, if you're not my father, I'll just leave you." He said good-bye to his father and mother, and went to the blacksmith, and had him make an iron cane weighing five hundred pounds. Then he went off traveling.

On his way, he met another man who was twisting walnut trees. "What are you doing, friend?" asked John the Bear.

"I'm just twisting up those little walnut trees to tie my gate shut."

"Leave your gate alone and come with me," answered John the Bear. After they left together, John the Bear asked the man his name and said, "My name is John the Bear."

The other answered, "I am called Oak Twister."

As they were walking along, they met another man who was throwing millstones so they skipped on the surface of the water. John the Bear asked him, "What are you doing, my friend?" The other one answered, "I'm playing with these little stones."

"Leave your little stones there and come with us," answered John the Bear.

"Well, all right," answered the man, "I'll come with you."

"What's your name?" John the Bear asked him.

The man told him, "My name is Stone Thrower."

They traveled until late that evening and came upon a fine house with no one inside. John the Bear said to Oak Twister and Stone Thrower, "We'll spend the night here."

The next morning no one had come yet, and John the Bear said to the two others, "Hey! Two of us will go out hunting. Oak Twister, you stay and make our dinner." When the others had been gone for a while, Oak Twister put some meat on the fire to boil in a kettle. All of a sudden, he heard "vroop" on the threshold. It was the Little Man with the Big Beard.

"What are you doing here, you worm?" he asked Oak Twister. "Who gave you permission to come into my castle?"

Oak Twister answered, "No one did."

"What are you cooking there?"

"I'm cooking meat for dinner," answered Oak Twister.

The Little Man asked, "Would you give me a little piece?"

"You can have all of it if you win it," answered Oak Twister.

"Well, I'm all for winning it," said the Little Man with the Big Beard. So they started to fight. Then, the Little Man took one of the hairs out of his big beard and beat up Oak Twister with it. He said, "If I find you here tomorrow, I'll beat you up again."

When John the Bear and Stone Thrower came back, Oak Twister was sick in bed. John the Bear thought, "Maybe this is a place which is not healthy for us." But they made dinner and after awhile Oak Twister got up and ate a good meal.

The next day, John the Bear and Oak Twister went out hunting. Stone Thrower started to make the dinner for them. The Little Man with the Big Beard came back and said, "What? Didn't I tell you that if I found you here today I'd really beat you up?"

Stone Thrower turned around. "What do you want?" he said.

"What are you cooking?" asked the Little Man.

"I'm cooking some meat."

"Give me just a little piece."

"You can have it if you can win it."

The Little Man said, "That's not hard to do." So they began to fight, and the Little Man made Stone Thrower sick, just as he had done to Oak Twister. The Little Man said that if he found Stone Thrower there the next day, this time he would kill him.

When John the Bear came back, he said, "Oh, I see. Stone Thrower is in bed." So John the Bear and Oak Twister made the supper. Stone Thrower was able to get up and eat a good meal. John the Bear said, "It's my turn to stay here tomorrow. If I get sick, too, we'll have to leave. That will mean that this is an unhealthy place."

The next morning, Oak Twister and Stone Thrower went out hunting. They left John the Bear behind to cook the dinner. After they had gone a little way into the woods, Stone Thrower and Oak Twister looked at each other. "What made you sick? Was it a Little Man with a Big Beard, about that tall? Me too. Today he'll kill John the Bear."

John the Bear, back at the house, began to make dinner. The Little Man came back and said, "Didn't I tell you that if I found you here again today I would kill you?"

"Kill?" asked John the Bear. "You look like you could kill someone, you worm."

"What are you cooking in my kettle this morning?" asked the Little Man.

"I'm cooking some meat."

"Let me have a little piece."

"No."

"If you don't give me a little piece, I'll take the whole thing."

"You'll take the whole thing if you can win it."

"That," answered the Little Man, "is easy to do." So they began to fight. John the Bear got near the place where he had his iron cane. He hit the Little Man over the head with it and cut off his ear. The Little Man picked up his ear and ran away as fast as he could, with John the Bear right after him. He arrived at a place where there was a big rock. He moved the stone and jumped into a hole.

John the Bear came back to the house and finished making dinner. When Oak Twister and Stone Thrower came back from their hunting, the dinner was all ready. John the Bear said, "Well, come and eat." While they were eating, John the Bear told them, "You know the Little Man with the Big Beard who made you both sick? I've been to the place where he lives."

So after they had finished their dinner, they all went to look at the big rock. John the Bear said, "Oak Twister, I found you twisting Oak trees to tie up your gate. Why don't you lift up that rock?" But Oak Twister couldn't budge it. Then he said, "Stone Thrower, you can play at throwing mill stones, why don't you lift that rock over there?" But Stone Thrower couldn't lift up the rock either. Finally, John the Bear said, "Oh, I'll go lift it myself." And he picked it up with just one hand.

There was a big deep hole there, where the Little Man with the Big Beard had gone down. They made a windlass, put it over the hole, and put a rope and a handle on it. "Well," said John the Bear to Oak Twister, "you go down first. Bring this bell with you. If you're afraid after you've gone down partway, then ring the bell, and we'll pull you back out." After awhile, Oak Twister began to think about the Little Man with the Big Beard and rang his bell, and they pulled him back up. So then, John the Bear said to Stone Thrower, "Go ahead. It's your turn now." He said, "If you're afraid, ring the bell, and we'll pull you back up." Stone Thrower went pretty far, but then he began to be afraid of the Little Man, and he rang his bell. They pulled him up out of the hole.

Now John the Bear said to them that he'd go down, but without any bell. "I'm going now. If you don't see me after one year and one day, you can leave me. That will mean that I won't come back." They lowered John the Bear into the hole, and when he got to the bottom, he began to walk.

It was like a whole different world. He saw a big brick house. In the window, a pretty princess was sitting. She made signs to him to tell him to go away and not come any closer. He made signs to tell her that, no, he was coming the whole way. She was guarded by a lion, and when the lion saw him, it charged after him. John the Bear split its head open with his iron cane.

The princess was so happy she invited him to come in. She figured she would marry him. But he said, "Oh, no, Princess. I don't want to get married now. Maybe I'll be able to deliver other princesses too."

"Well, two of my sisters are also under spells farther along. One of them is guarded by a little black dog, and the other is guarded by the Little Man with the Big Beard."

"That's the fellow I'm looking for," answered John the Bear. So the princess gave him her golden ball and her silk handkerchief, which had the name of her father and his army embroidered on it.

The next morning, he set out to deliver the second princess. When he got near to where she was, she made signs to him not to come any closer. But he made signs saying, "No." When he got there, the little black dog came after him, but he cut it in two.

The princess was really happy to be safe. She asked him to come in and said, "We must get married."

"Oh, no," he said. "I may find yet another princess who is under a spell as you were."

"Well, yes, one of my sisters, the youngest, is guarded by the Little Man with the Big Beard."

John the Bear said, "That's who I'm looking for." So, she gave him her golden ball and her silk handkerchief, as the first princess had also done. He put them into his pocket, and the next morning he left early to find the third princess.

The Little Man was walking back and forth on his porch. He went out to meet John the Bear at the gate. As soon as they met, they started fighting right away. John the Bear hit the Little Man on the head with his iron cane and split his brain in two.

The youngest princess was so happy to be free that she came running out. She said, "Sir, look in his back pocket and take out the little can of salve he has in there. He'll grease himself up with that and come back as good as ever." She gave him her golden ball and her silk handkerchief, too, as her sisters had done.

The next morning John the Bear and the youngest princess started back to the hole where Oak Twister and Stone Thrower were waiting.

When he got to the shaft, he tugged on the rope, and they let down a basket. He put the oldest princess into the basket, and they pulled her up. When she got to the top, Oak Twister shouted, "She's mine!" And Stone Thrower answered, "No, she's mine!"

They started to argue and were getting ready to fight over the princess, when she said, "Don't fight over me. There's a prettier princess than me waiting down there to come up." So they let the basket down again, and the second princess got into it. But when she got to the top, Oak Twister and Stone Thrower started to argue again.

The second princess told them, "Don't fight over me. There's still another, more beautiful princess waiting at the bottom to be brought up here." So they let the basket down a third time, and the youngest princess got in. When she reached the top, the two men didn't want to send the basket back down to get John the Bear, but the princesses didn't want to leave without him. So Oak Twister and Stone Thrower winked at each other and lowered the basket again. John the Bear got in, and they pulled him up quite a way. But then they cut the rope, and he fell back to the bottom and broke his leg.

Oak Twister and Stone Thrower brought the princesses to the king. They made the princesses swear that they had been the ones who had rescued them. The old king told the two men that they could each choose one of his two older daughters to marry. But the princesses told their father that they would not marry these two men unless they had three golden balls made like that of their youngest sister. They told the king that the balls would have to be exactly like that of their sister or the two men should lose their lives. So the king told Oak Twister and Stone Thrower that they would have to make three golden balls exactly like the one that the youngest princess had, and that if they weren't able to do it, they would lose their lives. But if they did succeed, they would get a silver chest.

During this time, John the Bear was still stuck at the bottom of the hole with his broken leg. He thought about the little box of salve that he had in his pocket and put it on his leg. It got better right away. As John the Bear was wandering around, he passed a tree where a snake was climbing up to eat some baby eagles, and he killed the snake. One day, later on, he noticed, as he was still wandering around, that a beautiful eagle was flying around over his head, at the top of the hole. He said, "Oh, Beautiful Eagle. If I only had your wings!"

She flew down to him right away and said, "What did you say, John the Bear?"

"I was just saying that if I only had your wings, it would not take me very long to get out of this hole," answered John the Bear.

The Eagle answered, "Oh, I'll do everything I can to get you out of here. Go and kill a lot of animals and cut the meat up into small pieces. Tomorrow I'll come back."

The next morning, she said, "Do you have the meat, John the Bear?"

"Yes, I think I have enough," answered John the Bear.

"Now, put it all on my back, and you climb on, too. Every time I holler *Quack,* you give me a piece of meat." And so she flew up, almost to the top of the hole. But then she hollered, "Quack," and he had run out of meat. Instead of going up, they started falling down. John the Bear opened up his knife and cut a piece out of his leg and gave it to the Eagle. When they got to the top, the beautiful Eagle looked at John the Bear and said, "Why is your leg bleeding?"

"Well," he said, "you were saying, 'Quack, quack,' and I didn't have any more meat, so I cut a piece out of my leg to give to you."

The beautiful Eagle said, "Quack," and the piece of John the Bear's leg reappeared. He took it and stuck it back on where it belonged.

Then he left to go see the king. First, he went to an old Goldsmith, who told him why he didn't want to take on the job of making the three golden balls. "I can do good work, but I'm getting old, and I can't see as well as I used to. I'm afraid they'll hang me."

John the Bear said to him, "Go take the job, and I'll make the golden balls for you." So the old man went to see the king and said to him, "Well, King, I'll take the job of making your golden balls."

The king answered, "You're a true friend. But if you don't make them right, I will have to hang you." The Goldsmith answered, "Well, I'll take that chance."

That evening, John the Bear went to make the golden balls. He went into the room where the old man had his tools. He brought with him a big bunch of pecans, hazelnuts, and peanuts. He began to eat, and after a while the Goldsmith's wife went to see how he was coming along. She peeked through the keyhole and saw John the Bear still eating his pecans and peanuts. At nine o'clock, she went back to look through the keyhole a second time. She came back and said to her husband, "Well, dear, he's still eating. You're going to be hanged! You're going to be hanged!"

"Oh, be quiet!" said her husband. "Maybe he's just a fast worker."

At ten o'clock, the old woman went back to see how John the Bear was doing. He had made one golden ball and had put it on a pretty plate. She came back, clapping her hands. "He has one finished," she said.

"Well, I told you that you didn't need to worry," he said. "I told you he was a fast worker."

At eleven o'clock, the old woman went back and peeked through the keyhole again. This time, John the Bear had finished. He had all three balls together on the plate. She came back and said to her husband, "Well, now, he's finished. We can go to bed and sleep in peace." They had no sooner gotten into bed than the old woman sat up and asked the Goldsmith what he was going to do with his money.

"Oh, go to sleep," he answered. "I'll tell you about that tomorrow."

The next morning, he brought the golden balls to the king. When the old king looked at the balls, he couldn't tell one from the others. The youngest daughter was there in the king's room, and she said, "Didn't you have a man help you do that, old man?"

"Yes, Princess, I did have someone help me," answered the Goldsmith.

The princess then said, "Will you please go and get the man who helped you and bring him back here with you."

When John the Bear got to the king's palace, the youngest princess recognized him. She told her father that this man would be able to tell the golden balls from one another. So John the Bear took the three silk handkerchiefs out of his pocket and put one ball on each of the handkerchiefs.

The old king said, "What? Are you the one who saved my daughters?"

John the Bear answered, "Yes, I'm the one."

Then the king turned to his daughters and asked them, "Why did you tell me that the two other men were the ones who had saved you?"

"They made us swear to tell you that they were the ones who had saved us, or else they would have killed us. To save our lives, we told you what they wanted us to." So the king took Oak Twister and Stone Thrower and had them hanged. Then, he gave John the Bear the privilege of choosing whichever of the three princesses he would like to marry. John the Bear chose the youngest, but the king wasn't too happy about that. It was his rule to marry his oldest daughters first.

"But," he said, "since you freed all three of them, I'll let you marry the youngest." They got married and had a big dinner. But I don't know what happened to John the Bear after that.

Thomas 1981: 21–28. ATU 650A/301. Told in French to Joseph Medard Carrière by Frank Bourisaw, at Old Mines, Missouri, c. 1934. Translated under the direction of Rosemary Hyde Thomas (see above, page 205). Of Bourisaw, Carrière wrote:

Mr. Bourisaw is an old man who bears his age cheerfully. Still very active, although he is seventy, this *conteur* is an excellent type of the older generation. He has spent his life in Old Mines, where his family settled at the beginning of the last century [i.e., c. 1800], and he has had to work hard to bring up nine children. He has always been popular with the French folk of the community, because of his energy and his exuberant gayety, which have not forsaken him even in his old age. He told his stories with spirit and his whole person became animated at the dramatic passages.

He learned his repertory from various sources, some from Mrs. Bourisaw, others from an uncle, and a great many at gatherings at his home, or at friends' or relatives'.

Though Carrière gathered only eight tales from him, Bourisaw apparently had a large repertoire. He was still remembered fondly fifty years later, when Rosemary Hyde Thomas visited the community.

The various versions of ATU 301 in this volume indicate the many ways in which this tale can get underway. In the present version the unusual size of the hero is hinted at, but not much is made of it, so that his great strength comes as something of a surprise to the listener. Nor, though he is called John the Bear, is there any explanation of why. The core episode of the rescue of the three maidens seems central to the story. But the episode involving the duplication of the three golden balls is rather unusual. There is some confusion in this episode. John already has all three balls, but the princesses seem to imply that the youngest princess still has hers. Then the goldsmith is reporting directly to the king, though Oak Twister and Stone Thrower are the ones who need to have golden balls made, and presumably they are the ones who have asked him to do the work for them.

The translation is in places more of a retelling. For instance, in the French John the Bear is eating pistachios, not peanuts. And the man with the millstones is playing *jeu de palets* with millstones, not skipping them, and calls himself *Joueur d'Palets*. *Jeu de palets* is a game played with pucks (*palets*). These pucks are tossed, not shoved or slid shuffleboard style, and scoring is as in bowls or bocce. The translation, however, is presented substantially as given by Thomas, with only slight revisions for the sake of clarity, especially in the episode where the eagle carries the hero up out of the lower world. The punctuation and paragraphing too have been altered to fit the style of the present volume.

49. Prince Green Serpent and La Valeur

It's good to tell you that once upon a time there was an old soldier. He had been one of the king's soldiers for a long time and was getting worn out. One day, he went to ask the king for his discharge. The old king said, "Here, La Valeur, here's twenty-five cents. Go and have a drink." But this solution didn't last long. La Valeur quickly had his drink and then came back to ask the king for his discharge. The king said, "Oh, well. I guess I'll let you have your discharge, La Valeur. But don't forget to say good-bye to me before you leave."

La Valeur went to the tailor's and told him that he was leaving the king's army. The tailor said, "Well, La Valeur, why don't you take my turn at guard duty tonight until eleven o'clock. I'll pay you well for your time. I have more work than I can do in here."

So La Valeur took the tailor's turn on guard duty. But when eleven o'clock came and his turn was up, he fired the cannon. It frightened the Grand Vizier, who came to the king asking, "What was that?"

"Oh," said the king, "that was just La Valeur leaving my service and saying good-bye before he leaves."

So the next morning La Valeur left and went traveling. He stayed on the road until he got tired. He sat down on a log and was complaining to himself that he had no more tobacco, because he would like to have a smoke, when the log began to move. "Ah!" said La Valeur. "Are you moving?"

The log answered, "Yes, I'm moving. Go get a bunch of hickory switches and come back and use them to beat on this log." La Valeur went and got his bunch of switches and began to beat on the log with them until he was exhausted and his forehead was dripping with sweat. Then he lay down and went to sleep.

When he woke up, there was a saucer next to him, with tobacco, a pipe, and matches in it. He lit the pipe and began to look around. He saw a handsome prince walking nearby. The prince said, "Good morning, La Valeur."

"Good morning," answered La Valeur. "I don't know your name."

"My name is Prince Green Serpent," the stranger answered. "You set me free by beating me with your hickory switches."

La Valeur didn't believe this was true. "Maybe," he said.

The stranger said, "La Valeur, come and stay with me. You won't have to do anything except eat. I'll give you all the money you want to spend."

So La Valeur went with the prince. He stayed with him for quite a while. He spent his days just going here and there and going from one tavern to another, drinking.

Finally, he got tired of that little village and wanted to leave. So he said to Prince Green Serpent, "I'm going to leave."

The prince answered, "What? Aren't you happy here?"

"Yes, I'm fine, but I'm tired of this place."

"Well, here, take this shirt," answered Prince Green Serpent. "When you put on this shirt you will be invisible, and no one can see you. And here is a sword that will cut fifty feet around you."

Then La Valeur went out traveling again. He came to another town with another king. He pledged himself to the king to work for him, and the king liked him so much that he made La Valeur his son-in-law. But his daughter didn't like her new husband. She was in love with another king who was her father's enemy. When the other king learned that the girl he loved had been married off to La Valeur, he made war on the girl's father. The morning that he was leaving to go off to battle, La Valeur put on his shirt and asked the king, "Do you see me?"

The king answered, "No, I can't see you at all."

So La Valeur took his sword and left at the head of the army. It took him no time at all to destroy half of the enemy army. He took the enemy king prisoner and brought him in to his father-in-law. La Valeur promised the enemy king that he wouldn't harm him, and he told his father-in-law about this promise he had made. They put the king in prison.

La Valeur's wife went to feed him every day and to talk with him. One day, the enemy king told her, "Ask your husband what kind of power he has that he can destroy so many people at the same time. Be nice to him tonight."

When La Valeur came back that night, his wife went to meet him. She acted as though she loved him. That night when they were in bed, she said to him, "La Valeur, my dear husband, tell me how you manage to destroy so many people at one time and so fast."

"Well," he answered, "you know that little box that you kick around every day on the floor? Well, in there I have a shirt that makes me invisible when I put it on. Then I also have a sword that cuts everything in a circle fifty feet wide around me."

"Ah!" answered his wife, "I guess you can destroy a lot of people with those things, all right."

When they got up the next morning, the old king said to La Valeur, "You're the only one of my children who has ever asked me to show you your property." So the next morning, they saddled up horses and set off to visit one city after another, until late in the afternoon. Then, the old king said, "Now it's time to go back home. Tomorrow I'll bring you in another direction."

While they were gone, La Valeur's wife went and let the other king that she loved out of prison and gave him La Valeur's shirt to put on. They saddled up their horses and left. The sun was going down, and as La Valeur was returning home, he saw two horses coming toward him at top speed. He said, "We're done for. My wife has let the other king out, and he will kill both of us." La Valeur and his father-in-law got near the other two, and he asked, "Are you going to kill us?"

"Yes, I'm going to kill you," answered the enemy king.

La Valeur said, "Well, I would like to ask you just one favor. Cut me in little pieces, put me into my suitcase, and tie the suitcase onto my saddle. Then tie the reins onto my saddle so that the horse can't eat, turn him in the other direction, give him a blow with your sword on the left flank, and let him go."

The king let him go in this way, and then killed the old king too. Then he and La Valeur's widow went back home, and they got married.

One day, Prince Green Serpent's guard said, "I see a horse coming toward us at top speed."

The prince said to him, "Open the gate. That's La Valeur." So the guard opened the gate, and the horse came right up on the porch of the prince's house.

Prince Green Serpent took the suitcase into a bedroom and put La Valeur back together again. He rubbed him all over with a kind of salve that he had. La Valeur came back to life but he stayed asleep for a long time afterward. Then one morning, at about nine o'clock, La Valeur woke up, looked all around, and went out to see where he was. Prince Green Serpent was out in his front yard. He asked La Valeur, "How do you feel this morning?"

"Well," answered La Valeur, "I don't feel too good. I feel all broken up."

"How long have you been sleeping, La Valeur?" asked the prince.

"I don't know," answered La Valeur. "I think I've been asleep since last evening." The prince answered, "Well, you've been sleeping for seven years, La Valeur."

"Well, I don't know," answered La Valeur. "I still don't feel very good." La Valeur stayed with Prince Green Serpent for a long time after that.

One day, as La Valeur was sitting by the fire, he was watching these little ants going by and was catching them on the tip of his lance. When he would turn them over on their backs, they would try to take revenge by biting the lance. La Valeur thought this was funny, and he was laughing. Prince Green Serpent asked him, "Why are you laughing?"

"I'm laughing at those little ants taking their revenge on my lance," answered La Valeur.

"What?" said Prince Green Serpent. "Do you want to take your revenge too?"

La Valeur answered, "Yes, I do. I'm leaving tomorrow morning."

The next morning, the prince gave a bridle to La Valeur and said to him, "When you arrive near the town, put this bridle into your mouth, and you will turn into the most beautiful horse anyone has even seen. Find the poorest man in the town and let him catch you. He's a water carrier."

When he got to the edge of the town, by the spring where the old man got his water, he put on his bridle, and the old man soon came. "What a beautiful horse!" he said. "I must try to catch him." So, he tried to catch the horse gently by calling to him, "Cup, cup cup!" He caught the horse by the bridle and brought him back to his barn and filled the manger full of hay for the horse to eat.

After awhile, he came back to check on his horse and found that it hadn't eaten anything. He said to the horse, "Is it possible that a horse as beautiful as you doesn't eat hay?"

The horse answered, "No, I don't eat hay."

The man was surprised. "Can you talk?" he asked. The horse answered, "Yes, I can talk. I want you to get on my back and ride by the king's house. He will ask you where you got such a beautiful horse. Tell him that you bought me. He's going to try to buy me from you. Sell me for one hundred dollars but be sure to keep the bridle."

When the old man rode by the king's house, the king asked, "Where did you find such a beautiful horse?"

The old man answered, "It's one that I bought."

"Don't you want to sell it?" asked the king.

"I'll sell it," answered the old man, "if I get my price."

The king asked, "What is your price?"

"One hundred dollars," answered the old man.

The king said, "Well, all right, bring him into my stable." But the old man forgot to take off the bridle.

The king went to get the queen to see the beautiful horse he had bought. When she came and looked at him in the stable, she recognized him. She said, "Yes, indeed, he is a beautiful horse, but I demand that he be killed by a blow through his heart between now and sundown."

The king went away angry. "We can't keep anything nice around here," he grumbled.

The little servant girl came out to see the beautiful horse. She asked, "Is it possible that a beautiful horse like you will be killed this evening?"

The horse answered, "Yes, but only you can save my life."

The little girl answered, "Can you talk, beautiful horse?"

"Yes," he answered, "a beautiful horse like me can talk. They're going to come and kill me this evening. Ask them for the first three drops of my blood. Take those three drops of blood and put them on each side of the door. Tomorrow morning you will find the three most beautiful trees you have ever seen."

The next morning she went out to look where she had dropped the three drops of blood and found the beautiful trees. Then she went in and told the king to come right away and see the beautiful trees that had grown up next to his door. The old king and queen came, and they found the trees very pretty. But the queen said, "Yes, they are very pretty. But I demand that they be cut down and burned before sundown."

The little servant said, "Is it possible for beautiful trees like you to be cut down and burned?" And the trees answered, "Yes, and only you can save our life. Ask them for the first three chips of wood, and this evening throw them into the millpond. Tomorrow morning, you will find the three most beautiful golden ducks you have ever seen."

The little servant girl went down to the pond to look the next morning and found her beautiful golden ducks. She went to tell the king to come with his rifle and see the beautiful ducks. The king did bring his rifle, and as he was sighting along it getting ready to shoot, the ducks flew away to the other end of the pond. They kept doing this until the king was all soaked with the dew. He went back to his house, and his wife said, "Why don't you put on your shirt'?"

"Well, I never thought of doing that," he answered. He put on his magic shirt and went back to the pond. He began running from one end of the pond to the other, chasing the ducks, until the shirt was all soaked. He took it off and laid it out on some branches so it would dry out. Then, he went back to the other end of the pond, still chasing the ducks.

When the ducks left the other end, they flew right into the shirt. Then La Valeur went and killed the king, and went back to his house, caught his wife, and burned her. He then married the little servant who had saved his life.

Thomas 1981: 118–22. ATU 318. Told to Joseph Medard Carrière, c. 1934, by Joseph Ben Coleman of Old Mines, Missouri, a man about forty years old. Translated under the direction of Rosemary Hyde Thomas. As with the previous story, I have made changes in paragraphing and punctuation and small revisions in the translation. The ending of the story is abrupt, but we are to understand that when the three ducks fly into La Valeur's magic shirt they are transformed back into La Valeur.

ATU 318 is one of the oldest documented tales. The Egyptian tale of "The Two Brothers," which dates to the thirteenth century BCE is a version of ATU 318, combined with ATU 302B and ATU 870C*. Despite its ancient ancestry, however, the present tale demonstrates little ways in which a narrator can Americanize a story. The first king gives La Valeur a quarter for a beer. La Valeur is put into a suitcase (*valise*), not a common piece of luggage in the middle ages (or in ancient Egypt). Prince Green Serpent's house is not a castle but a nice American house with bedrooms, porch, and front yard. And the king gripes that "We can't keep anything nice around here," the gripe of many an American parent.

50. The Cootie and the Flea

Let me tell you that once upon a time there was a Cootie and a Flea that lived together. One Sunday morning Flea left the house to go to Mass. But before she left she put some mush on the fire, and she told Cootie not to stir the mush, knowing very well that he might fall in. After Flea had gone, Cootie took it into his head to go and stir the mush. Poor old Cootie, he fell into the mush, and he drowned.

When Flea came home she called out to Cootie. "Cootie," she said, "open the door." Cootie didn't open the door. Flea went and found a stone, forced the door, and went in. There she found poor old Cootie drowned.

All in tears, she ran from the house. A dog saw her and said, "What's happened to you? You're crying."

"I have plenty of reason to cry," she said. "Cootie is dead."

"Oh my," said the dog, "I—I'm going to howl." And the little dog took off howling.

Soon he came to a wagon. The wagon said, "What happened to you, my little dog? You're howling."

"Well," he said, "Cootie is dead. Flea is crying, and I—I'm howling."

"Oh my," said the cart, "I can't go on anymore." And the wagon began to roll backwards.

Soon it came to a pile of manure. "Wagon," the manure said, "what happened to you? You're rolling backwards."

"I have plenty of reason to roll backwards," it said. "Cootie is dead. The flea is crying, the little dog is howling, and I—I can't go on any longer."

"Oh my," said the manure, "I can't keep it together any longer." And the manure began to spread.

Soon it came to an oak tree. The oak said to it, "Why are you spreading yourself, manure?"

"Well," it said, "Cootie is dead. Flea is crying, the little dog is howling, the wagon can't go on, and I—I can't keep it together any longer."

"Oh my," said the oak tree, "I'm falling to pieces." And the oak began to lose its leaves.

A little bird came to perch on the oak tree. "Tree," it said, "what happened to you? You're losing your leaves."

"I have plenty of reason to lose my leaves," it said. "Cootie is dead. The flea's crying, the little dog's howling, the wagon can't go on, the manure can't keep it together any longer, and I—I am shedding my leaves."

"Oh my," said the little bird, "I—I'm molting." And the little bird dropped out all of its feathers.

It came to a spring, the little bird did, to get a drink. The spring asked what happened that it dropped out all its feathers.

"I have plenty of reason to drop my feathers," it said. "Cootie is dead. The flea's crying, the dog's howling, the wagon can't go on, the manure can't keep it together any longer, the oak's shedding its leaves, and I—I'm molting."

"Oh my," said the spring, "I'm all choked up." And the spring dried up.

The little old woman came with her pitchers to fill them with water. "Spring," she said, "what happened to you? You're all dried up."

"Yes," said the spring, "I have dried up. Cootie is dead. The flea's crying, the little dog's howling, the wagon can't go on, the manure can't keep it together any longer, the oak is losing its leaves, the bird is molting its feathers, and I—I'm all choked up."

"Oh my," said the little old woman, "I can't hold on any longer." And she couldn't. She dropped both her pitchers, dropped them and smashed them.

Carrière 310. ATU 2022. Told to Carrière, c. 1934, by Joseph Ben Coleman of Old Mines, Missouri, a man about forty years old, and the teller also of the previous tale. Translated by the editor. This story about two fond pests is widely popular in both French and Iberian tradition. The Aarne-Thompson-Uther classification spreads it across two numbers, 2022–23, but both involve drowning in the cooking pot. The present text is a rather free translation of the French, driven by the need to find equivalents or stand-ins for the humor of the original. The words for the couple in French, for instance, *pou* and *pouce*, contain a nice pun on *époux* and *épouse (husband* and *wife)*, words that might well lose their first syllables in informal speech.

The ending is certainly abrupt. In other versions the person at the well may be the maid, who comes back to tell her mistress, who ruins the dough she is kneading. When she explains to her husband, he decides to put an end to that nonsense by locking her up. Alternately, the chain can be reversed. In the present story that would require a slight shift in order and the elimination of the manure: the old woman (or maid) stirs the spring, the spring dampens the bird, the bird pecks the oak, the oak beats the dog, the dog shoves the cart in the right direction, and the cart runs over the poor flea, killing her. Or the reversal may end with the flea eating the mush.

51. Beau Soleil

Well, let me tell you, one time there was a man and a woman, and they had three boys. One of those boys was called Beau Soleil [, or Sunny]. Well, there came a time when the old man had to tell the old woman, "We've got three boys, and they are all good for nothing boys." Now, Beau Soleil overheard what he said. So the next morning he said to his father, "I'm leaving here."

So his father said, "Where are you going?"

"I'm going to seek my fortune," he said.

Soon Beau Soleil was [a soldier] stationed in the city. He didn't have any money. So he went to see his captain and borrowed ten dollars from him. Well, Beau Soleil was a great hand at cards and a drunken lout as well. When his money had played out, he got the idea of trying to fool his father. So he wrote him asking for five hundred dollars. Next he wrote his father that he had been in prison and that he'd spent all the money he had been sent. Then, after a while, he wrote his father again to send him another five hundred dollars because he had bought a big theatre.

When that money was gone, he had nothing left. Beau Soleil went to his captain. He wanted a pass to go home. His captain said yes, he could go. "And look," he said, "here's fifty dollars for you."

And so Beau Soleil set out again. He traveled for four days. On the fifth day he came to a little castle. He called out at the gate and a little old granny came out. She asked him what he wanted and he said that he wanted a place to stay the night.

The next morning Beau Soleil got up and looked out at the town. It was in fact the king's own city. And there was a[n other] castle there that was all clouded in mist. Well, the old granny, she said that nobody could go into that castle and come out alive. So of course Beau Soleil, he said that he could go in there and come back out alive. He was sure he could.

"Well," said the old granny, "every morning at this time I go and tell the king the news."

"Good," said Beau Soleil, "that's all right with me. You can go tell him if you want to." And so the old granny went looking for the king.

"Your Majesty, I have good news to tell you."

"Well," he said, "what is it?"

"I have a young fellow up at the house who can go into the Misty Castle and come out alive."

Well, the king said that whoever he was, he should come see him. And that's how it happened that Beau Soleil went to see the king—Beau Soleil!

"Is it true, young fellow, that you can go into that castle over there and come back out alive?"

"Yes, Sire, that's what I said."

"Well, I'd like you to do it."

So Beau Soleil said to the king, "Take me to the Misty Castle this evening about sunset and bring a candle and a prayer book with you."

And that's what happened. That evening they met at the Misty Castle. The king gave Beau Soleil the key to the castle and Beau Soleil went in. Inside he found a table and a chair. He sat down, lit his candle, and began reading in the prayer book.

Well, before long he saw three people, and then two more, that had come in and lit their candles too.

"Well," Beau Soleil said, "I wasn't expecting company this evening."

Immediately these figures said that Beau Soleil should go with them. "O.K.," said Beau Soleil. "If it's not too far," he said.

Well, Beau Soleil went along and went along with them, a long way. Finally he stopped and said that he was worn out. But they said that they still had two miles to go before they got there.

Well, when they arrived, there was a grand king there who came up to Beau Soleil. The king showed Beau Soleil this big rock there, and asked him to lift it up. There was a fortune in gold under it, and the king told Beau Soleil that the gold was for him.

Then the king wrote a letter and told Beau Soleil to give it to the king who had sent him into the Misty Castle.

Well, all around them were graves, a whole city of graves. So next the king wrote something on a piece of paper and told Beau Soleil to take that paper and lay it at the foot of each of the graves. Immediately a whole crowd of people came out, one from each grave. Everybody buried there came back to life. They tried to grab at Beau Soleil but he told them, "If you put a hand on me I'll put you back where you came from." So they all went back to the Misty Castle to play cards and drink.

The next morning Beau Soleil opened the castle door and everybody left for their old homes. The old king looked out his window and saw this huge crowd, so he said to the old Queen, "Look," he said, "at what Beau Soleil has done."

Pretty soon Beau Soleil came looking for the king. He gave him the letter and the king took it and read it. The great king from the city of graves had written that the old king should spend that night with him. But the old king told Beau Soleil, "I can't go there." But Beau Soleil said that he had to. Then the king said, "If you'll leave me alone," he said, "I'll give you my daughter the princess to marry." Beau Soleil said he'd accept that bargain.

And so Beau Soleil married the king's daughter, the princess.

Well, one day Beau Soleil was moping around outside, looking pretty pitiful. His wife came up to him and asked him, "What are you moping about?"

"I'm a bit blue thinking about my mom and my dad. I wasted all their money, and now here I am rich."

"Well, take some money and go see them."

Well, Beau Soleil dressed up in his prince outfit, and his wife sent a maid along with him. Soon they were on their way. On the road they found a castle. Beau Soleil knocked on the door, then he noticed writing over the door that said it didn't cost anything to spend the night there. So they went in and an old woman came to meet them.

Beau Soleil said, "Is that right, that it doesn't cost anything to spend the night here?"

And she said no, that it didn't cost anything.

After a while, when the supper was ready, she went to pull on a rope, and a bell high overhead rang. Then three men came downstairs.

They all sat down and ate supper. When they finished, one of the men asked Beau Soleil if he ever played cards. Beau Soleil said yes. So they went upstairs and started the card game. One of them set out a bottle of whiskey and they began drinking. They raised all Beau Soleil's bets, and soon they won all his money, and then his outfit, and even his underwear. Then they gave him a towel to wrap around himself and threw him out of the inn.

The maid found him and put him in the buggy. Then she brought him home to his father. His father was really mad when he saw him in such a state. So he took Beau Soleil and sent him to the woods to take care of the pigs.

But what about the maid? She went back and told Beau Soled's wife everything that had happened.

"Well," his wife said, "let's go. We're going back." So she put on a prince's outfit, took some money, and went.

When they got to the castle the maid said that it was the place to stop. When the old woman came in, the wife of Beau Soleil said, "Is that right, that it doesn't cost anything to spend the night here?"

Well, when the supper was ready the old woman pulled on the rope again, and the bell rang overhead. The three men came down, and they had supper. Then they asked the wife of Beau Soleil if she ever played cards. She said yes, that she had played cards. "But," she said, "my servant has to come along too."

So they went upstairs and began the game. And they put out a bottle of whiskey, of course. The princess took her glass, but she poured it down her neck into her underwear. They were playing along, and passing the bottle again and again, but the wife of Beau Soleil poured hers down her neck the same way each time.

So after a while the others got drunk, all three of them, but the princess was still sober. Then she won back all the money she had lost, then she won all Beau Soleil's money, and then the prince outfit that was still there. Then she let the three men go to bed to sleep it off.

Then they went looking for Beau Soleil's father. When they got there they asked the old man if they could spend the night. The old man said that the stranger was much too fancy a prince to spend the night with them. But she said that it didn't make any difference how poor he was.

And so they went into the house, and after a little while the old man asked them to come to supper. They were all sitting around the table, all except Beau Soleil. The princess asked the old man if he had only the two sons.

The old man said that there was another one.

"What's his name?"

"He's called Beau Soleil."

"Well, I think he should come and eat with us."

And so they rang the bell to call Beau Soleil. He came in, washed, combed his hair, and sat down. When supper was over, they passed a pipe. Then the old man said to the prince—he really thought he was a prince—that his room was ready if he wanted to go to bed. So then the princess said that she wanted Beau Soleil to sleep there too. When they were alone in the room she asked him if he knew who she was. And he, he said no. So then she took off her outfit and he said yes, that he recognized her.

"Tomorrow morning, now," the princess said, "we're going to really surprise the rest of them."

And so the next morning, when breakfast was ready, they yelled for Beau Soleil to come eat. Well, when Beau Soleil opened the kitchen door, he had his wife on his arm. He was dressed up as a prince and she as a queen. At first his father had no idea who he was, not until Beau Soleil spoke to him.

When they had finished breakfast Beau Soleil went to get all his money and his fortune in gold, and he gave some of it to his father. In fact, he made his father rich. Then Beau Soleil went back home with his beautiful princess.

Dorrance 1935: 108–12. ATU 935/326A. Told to Ward Allison Dorrance, in 1931, by Gros' Vaisse Portell (Thomas 1981: 233), of Old Mines, Missouri. Translated by the editor. *"Gros' Vaisse* (Big Fart) does not refer particularly to the habits of the gentle old fellow whose *sobriquet* it is," says Dorrance, but is rather an example of the penchant for "grotesque nicknames" among the Missouri French (Dorrance 1935: 45). Dorrance had trouble finding storytellers willing to dictate to him. But of Portell he writes:

> On his gallery at evening, with moths flitting against the lamp, and Old Mines
> Creek singing in the dark, he finally consented to speak so slowly that his tales might
> be set down verbatim. Here it was seen to what extent the folk-tale is regarded as a
> ritual.
> Asked to repeat when he spoke too rapidly, Gros' Vaisse answered, after a
> moment's thought, in the same words and with the same gesture or intonation.
> (103–4)

The beginning of the story seems fragmentary, as if the storyteller were not on a roll yet. Portell, the storyteller, for instance, does not say that Beau Soleil joins the army. But as he moves along, the narrative fleshes out. By the time he finishes he has narrated a fairly complete realization of the tale type.

Though the tale is classified as a novelle, the night in the haunted castle (ATU 326A) includes strong magic elements. This particular version also has two elements with biblical overtones. When the prodigal returns, his father, in a reversal of the Prodigal Son parable in Luke, sends the boy off to live with the pigs. Then when the princess comes, she asks the father, as Samuel asks Jesse in I Samuel 16:11, "Are these all your sons?" The answer, as in I Samuel, is that one is off with the herds. Beau Soleil is called in and clothed as regent, as David is called in and anointed royal successor.

52. François Seeks His Fortune, or the Three Gold Pieces

Once upon a time, long long ago, there was a farmer named François who lived in France with his wife and son. François was really poor. He worked hard every day in the fields. He was at work early every morning, and he stayed late, but he still couldn't earn enough to provide the food and clothes his wife and his little boy needed.

So one day when he was talking to his wife he brought up the idea of going to Paris to find work. If he could find someplace to work, a job in Paris, he would be able to provide food and clothes for his wife and little boy. So they talked it over, he and his wife and his son, and finally he said, "Good, I'll go to seek my fortune. I'll come back when I have found work and when I have made enough money to help you two." So he kissed his wife and son, and then he hollered Good-Bye.

He set out walking early in the morning. He walked and walked, and by evening he reached Paris. The next morning he began looking for work. But there were already loads of people there looking for work. All those others were also looking for something to eat and some work to do. So after a while he got discouraged. Then one day he heard that there was a man who had a whole heap of gold, and he lived in a huge mansion in Paris, and he needed someone to work for him.

So the next morning he went looking, found the place, and knocked on the man's door. Nobody answered. So he pushed on the door and it started to open. Then the old man demanded, "What do you want?"

"I've been looking for a place to work to make enough money to take care of my wife and my little boy. They are back at home."

"Well, I need someone to work around the house here," the old man said. "I'll pay you wages and you can stay here at my house and sleep here. And I'll give you your food and clothes. And I'll keep your money until you're ready to leave me."

"Fine," François said. "I'll work for you."

So he worked for him for a great long time. And François, he worked really hard. Well, after all that time he began to miss his wife and little boy and to think about how he'd left them on their own, all alone, and he didn't know how they were getting along. What had they done all that time? So he said, "Well, I'm ready to go back home," he said. "So you can pay me my money tonight."

So he could hardly sleep that night. The next morning the farmer said to his boss, "Do you want to give me my money this morning? I miss my family and I'm going back home."

The old man said, "Well, I understand. You have worked pretty darn hard, and I hate to lose you. But I'm going to give you three gold pieces."

Ainsi, François thought to himself, "Three gold pieces! That's not much money for all the years I've worked for you, *mais j' peut pas faire quelq' chose,* there's not much I can do about it." He didn't say that out loud, though. What he said to the old man was, "You have treated me very well."

Alors he was ready to leave, and the old man said, "I wish you Godspeed."

François had started to walk off when the old man said to him, "If you'll give me one of those pieces of gold, I'll give you a piece of good advice."

François didn't want to give him the money at first. But he began to think, "How much my wife could do with even two pieces of gold." But what he said to the old man was, "*T' étais joliment bon pour moin,* you have been very good to me. I'll give you one of my gold pieces."

Ainsi, the old man took the gold piece from him and said, *"Rapelle, François,* remember, don't ask about things that are none of your business."

François handed over the payment and the old man said, "Yes, it's good advice I gave you. Thank-you, my farmer friend."

He was hurrying away when the old man said, "If you give me another piece of your gold, I'll give you another piece of good advice."

François was ready to walk right up to him and say, "Hey, I've lived with you and eaten with you and slept in your *maison*—" but the old man had been like a *père* to him, and he didn't know whether he should give him the second gold piece or keep it. But what he said was, "Well, old sir, the advice was good the first time. So I'm ready. Say whatever you want to say."

Then the old man said to him, *"Quand tsu part por faire queque-chose,* never leave the path once you've taken it."

François heard what he said, told him, "That's good advice," and turned to go.

Then the old man said to him, "If you give me the third piece of gold I'd give you the best piece of advice you've ever heard."

François said to himself, *en pensee,* "Oh, I don't know. I promised my wife and my son to bring enough money home to take care of them. If I give you another gold piece I won't have anything to show for ten years of work." But what he said was, "[Advice is better] than money. I'll give you the third gold piece."

"Tout ben," the old man said to him. "This is it: Suppress your evening anger until morning."

So François set out for home with empty pockets. When he got underway he began to think, "What a fool I am. I worked all those years and I have nothing to show for it. I don't know what my wife and my boy are going to say about it.

So he walked along, with his head hung down, thinking. Then he heard voices and looked up into a tree. There was a bunch of dwarfs up there busy laying gold coins on the leaves of the tree. The tree was shining with gold. That was something he had never seen. He was just about to stop when he remembered what the old man had said to him about what was no concern of his.

So he had started on again when the dwarfs called out to him, "Say, for years now we've been putting these gold coins up in this tree, and you are the first person who has ever passed by without stopping to take the gold. How come? Why did you just walk on?"

"Well," said François, "this was no concern of mine. So I went on my way."

"No concern of mine!" the dwarf said. "A good thought. You are an honest fellow, and you deserve something. Come on over here and shake the tree. Take all the gold you need."

François thanked the dwarfs. Then he went up to the tree and shook it. All the gold coins fell off. He gathered up all he could carry, but the dwarfs kept saying to him, "Take more than that. Take more than that. Take all you can. We know you'll make good use of it."

Well, François started off again. Then he looked back where the tree had been, but there was no tree, no dwarfs. "No tree. Let me see!"

[Storyteller shakes his clothes as if to see if there are pieces of gold stuffed in them.] He checked to see if the gold was still there. Then he said, "I am sure that there was a tree there. Where has that tree gone?" But his pockets were full of every kind of gold coin to carry home to his son and wife.

Well, when he was on his way again there was a caravan of mules, and the men were going in the same direction he was. One of the men said to him, "Why don't you mount on one of our mules? We'll let you ride with us." The mules were loaded with rolls of silk and linen and bundles of jewelry. When François had taken his place, they set off again. Along went the caravan till they stopped at a place to eat. François got off, and they said to him, "Come eat with us. Aren't you starved? Would you like to get something to drink?"

François said "Yes," but [then] he remembered that the old man had told him not to stop, so he said, "Well, I won't stop," he said. "No."

But the man who had gotten off his mule said, "Come on, come on, come on in with us," he said. "We're going to order something to eat."

"No," he said, "I'm going on. There's the road. Nothing must stop me."

"All right," said the man, "but will you take care of the mules[, water and feed them]?"

"Of course," François said. "You know I'll stop long enough to take care of the mules."

Then [while the muleteers were in the inn having lunch] an earthquake struck. And the inn collapsed on the others—not a single person was left alive. But François was alive, and he had those mules, and all the merchandise. He couldn't just leave them there all alone. So he tied the animals together and led them the rest of the way home.

When he reached home, the village where his wife lived and raised his son, ohh, he stared at the streets, and he stared good and hard. He had been gone a long, long stretch of time, he had. He was almost crying. But he hurried along till he reached his house. He went up to the door and he knocked. Oh, he was so, so. . . . It was his wife who came to the door and opened it. But his wife didn't recognize him—he'd been gone so long, you understand? So he said [to himself], "You don't know who I am. *Ma dzire demain qui j'ai* I'll tell you tomorrow who I am." Then he said, "*Je m'ai chagrin*—I'm in some difficulty," he said. "Do you have some place where I could sleep tonight, I and my mules?"

His wife said, "No, I can't let you stay here in the house. But there is a barn in that field. You could sleep in the hay. You could feed your mules with it and sleep in it too."

So François headed off for the barn. His wife had not recognized who he was. "But when she recognizes me she's gonna really *goddamer.*" So he fed his mules, then he went out to watch the house. Soon he saw a good-looking young man come to the house. Then he saw him kiss his wife. So he said, "Whoa! There's some other guy living with her. She's forgotten me." He grabbed his pistol. He headed up to the house to kill them. Then he remembered what the old man had said to him: Suppress your evening anger until morning.

He didn't sleep a wink that night, thinking about that young guy with his wife. But he stayed where he was till morning. In the morning he grabbed his pistol and ran up to the house to kill the young guy. When he got to the door the guy was standing there. He kissed François's wife and said, "I'll bring you some little something good to eat from the village, Mom."

François said, "That man is my son, that I haven't seen since he was a kid. He and my wife don't know that I have come back." He said, "If I hadn't listened to what the old man had to say, I would surely have killed my own son." He ran into the house and said to the youth, "You've forgotten me, you've forgotten me." He said, "This here is my boy, that I wanted to kill this morning."

The boy was pleased to learn that this was his father. And François had all the gold he'd gotten from the tree and all the stuff from the mule caravan, and with all that he had plenty enough to live a good life with his wife and his son.

Brassieur 1999: 21–24. ATU 910B. Told to Ray Brassieur, January 15, 1998, by Pete "Pierre" Boyer, born 1910, a storyteller from Potosi, Missouri, just south of Old Mines. Translated by the editor. Boyer, when in his early twenties, served as principal guide to Carrière, who called him "alert and obliging" and praised his "interest in local lore" (viii). Boyer learned the present story when he was about ten or twelve from Bea Portais, his mother's aunt, who used to drop over to help out with the load of work because the Boyer family was so large, and to tell the children stories. Brassieur had heard Boyer tell the story at the Smithsonian Institution Festival of American Folklife, on June 24, 1989. Boyer told the story in his Missouri French dialect, while Brassieur translated for the audience. Though Boyer had grown up speaking French, by his own admission his French was rusty from long disuse. No recording is available of that performance.

In 1998 Brassieur visited Boyer in his home in Potosi, especially to record him telling this tale in French. Boyer felt that his French had eroded even further in the intervening eight and a half years. For his performance he worked from an English version that he had written out a number of years earlier when he was still telling stories in public. Brassieur transcribed this French oral narrative, which is essentially an expanded translation from the English written version. When Brassieur published an article about the story in the *Missouri Folklore Society Journal* he used the written English version in the article, giving the French version in an appendix. Since the French version is fuller and somewhat livelier, I have translated it instead of giving Boyer's written English version. Boyer, perhaps unconsciously, uses English words or slips into English phraseology occasionally as he tells the story. I have tried to suggest that bilingual flavor in the translation. The part of the story where François agrees to hear the third piece of advice has typesetting errors that include some words missing before "*d'argent*" (*of money* or *than money*). "Advice is better than money" is a restoration.

The tale type The Clever Precepts is a composite story. Each element in the story has an independent life as a tale of its own, and these independent elements are found throughout North and South America and Europe, and in Asia as far east as India and Indonesia. The composite, in forms generally like the present version, is also an extremely popular folktale widespread in North and South American Hispanic tradition, in Canadian French tradition, and throughout Europe, especially Western Europe (Pichette 1991: 576 and passim). It is relatively rare, however, in non-Hispanic tradition in the United States. Leonard Roberts (1955: 100–102) presents a closely parallel Appalachian version with Irish roots that he heard from two members of a Kentucky family. But the story is not otherwise well collected in U.S. English language tradition. And this is the only U.S. French version I know of.

This story is rather like the preceding story in basic situation: the hero leaves home, amasses a huge fortune, and goes unrecognized when he shows up back home in all his splendor. It also has overtones of other stories, in this case interesting anti-motifs. The hero, unlike Bluebeard's wife, does not violate the curiosity taboo. Nor, unlike Percival, does he suffer from too literal adherence to good advice—he is willing to care for (i.e., feed and water) the mules before going on. The little people, unlike the leprechaun, are happy to give away their gold. The apparent lover turns out to be the hero's son. And, unlike the parents in "Killing the Returned Soldier" (939A), this father does not kill his as-yet-unrecognized son.

Part IV

THE BRITISH TRADITION
OF THE SOUTH

The southern United States constitutes an ever-changing cultural continuum as one moves across it from north to south, from east to west. Each part of the South has its distinctive flavor, and yet the traditional culture of the region is remarkably uniform in language, foodways, mores, and religious outlook. The foundation for this culture is probably a Scottish and Scotch-Irish adaptation to new climate, economy, and political order. But Europeans from all parts of the British Isles contributed to its formation. In addition Germans poured into the South very early on, marrying with British southerners and lending a hand to shape the emerging culture. In time, German foods such as potatoes and sausage and German technology such as log building techniques helped define the culture. But now, after more than three and a half centuries it is impossible to tease apart the various strands of traditional southern culture and confidently assign each strand to a particular people, British or German, Scotch-Irish or English, Hessian, or Westphalian.

The tale tradition presented in this section is no exception. Its European foundation is an amalgam of British and perhaps German elements, often tempered with elements from French, African, and Native American traditions. The term British is used here, by the way, as an admittedly inadequate blanket term to cover all the peoples of the British Isles including the Irish and Scotch-Irish as well as the English, Scottish, and Welsh (and Cornish, Manx, and Channel Islanders, for that matter).

CHAPTER 9

FROM TIDEWATER TO TEXAS

The Southern Lowland Tradition

The lowland South, from Tidewater Virginia across the lower South, through northern Louisiana, and into Texas is a vast agricultural belt. Here have flourished great plantations, substantial farms—often with tenant farmers working part of the land—naval stores, and timber operations. At the farthest western end of this belt the land gives way to arid cattle and oil country. This largely Protestant region, sometimes known as the Bible Belt, bears everywhere the stamp of the dominant English and Scotch-Irish settlers and of the Africans that they brought in to help them work the land and harvest the natural resources. As I noted in the introduction to part 4, other European settlers, especially from elsewhere in the British Islands, from France, and from Germany, also left their distinctive imprint on the culture, and in particular on the oral narrative part of that culture.

Southerners, including the white southerners who are the subject of this chapter, have long had a reputation as storytellers. The tales in this chapter barely skim the surface of their huge repertoire. White southerners would recognize, for example, many of the stories and types of stories found in other chapters of this book. In particular, these white southerners share with their black cousins the animal trickster stories, and they share with their mountain cousins the numbskull stories (as they share with both the legends, jokes, and tall tales that fall outside the purview of this collection). They do not, however, seem to know as many romantic märchen and novelles in this belt as do storytellers in the mountains to the north or in the French and Hispanic regions of the Gulf Coast and the Southwest. This fact may be attributable to weaker Irish and/or German penetration into the lowland South: the Irish and German folktale repertoires, like the French and Spanish, but unlike the English, have a strong component of märchen and novelles. The reader especially interested in southern storytelling should look at *Storytellers: Folktales and Legends from the South*, edited by John A. Burrison. This strong collection surveys southern storytelling from the earliest record, and gives a good idea of the range of materials that form the southern repertoire.

To see the southern repertoire represented in a single storyteller, however, one can not do better than check out the "Tales and Rhymes of a Texas Household, " edited by Bertha McKee Dobie. This article surveys a manuscript prepared by Emeline Brightman Russell of Helena, Texas, and reprints many of the tales from it. Mrs. Russell was born before 1830 and died in 1910. Her father, George Claver Brightman, a journeyman cabinetmaker, lived in Indiana and Florida before bringing his family in about 1840 to Goliad, Texas, where he operated a ferry across the San Antonio River. Her mother, from whom she apparently learned most of her tales, was Nancy Moore of South Carolina, daughter of one Elizabeth Baker. Dobie suggests that the Moores and/or Bakers must have been in South Carolina for at least two generations, citing a reference in Mrs. Russell's manuscript to an early South Carolina spelling book. In 1847 Emeline married a young veteran, Charles Russell, and they settled in Goliad for a time before moving to Helena. Mrs. Russell used to entertain her children by telling and acting out the large repertoire of tales that she remembered from her mother. At the request of one of her children she wrote out these tales when she was past eighty years old. The resulting manuscript includes versions of The Animals in Night Quarters (ATU 130), Johnny Cake (The Fleeing Pancake, ATU 2025; see the note to that tale in chapter 1), The Mouse Regains Its Tail (ATU 2034), The Man from the Gallows (ATU 366, here called "The Silver Toe"), The Kind and the Unkind Girls (ATU 480), Jack and the Northwest Wind (The Table, the Donkey, and the Stick, ATU 563), The Juniper Tree (ATU 720), Stupid's Cries (What Should I Have Said? ATU 1696), Mr. Fox (Baughman, Type 955c), The Old Woman and Her Pig (ATU 2030), The Kid (Ehod Mi Yodea, ATU 2010; related to the Passover song!), Bluebeard (ATU 312), and three tales called "Simon," "The Monkeys and the Redcaps," and "The Young Lions." Versions of many of these tales can be found in chapter 1 of the present volume (as well as in various other chapters), a further indication that the early English-language repertoire of the Eastern Seaboard and

Old Northwest territory was largely British. Mrs. Russell's rendition of "The Silver Toe" is included in this chapter.

53. Katie and Johnnie

One time there was a little boy and a little girl, brother and sister, who lived on a farm in Georgia. Their names were Katie and Johnnie. Their mother told them to go down in the woods and get some switches to make brooms with and sweep both the back and the front yards. This seemed an awful task to Katie and Johnnie since you know back yards in South Georgia cover at least an acre.

Katie and Johnnie left for the woods and found some gallberry bushes for brooms.

Johnny said, "Let's go down in the swamp a little further," and Katie agreed.

Pretty soon Katie said, "What's that?"

Johnnie looked over and saw two delicious-looking cakes hanging down from two ropes on the limb of a tree.

Katie said to Johnnie, "If you pull one, I'll pull the other."

So they did, and about that time down came a big cage and caught those two disobedient kids who had gone farther into the swamp than they were supposed to.

A big giant came up laughing, "Ho! Ho! I've got you now!" and carried Katie and Johnnie off squealing.

He walked—boom, boom, boom—through the forest to his hangout. He gathered up some wood and got an old iron pot to cook the two children in.

Johnnie said, "I wonder what that ol' giant's going to do." He saw the giant getting lightwood knots and saw him strike two stones together— boom, boom—and start a fire.

He said to Katie, "I believe that old giant is going to cook us and we've got to get away. When he comes to the cage, you run this way and I'll run that, and we'll get out of this cage."

The old giant got the water all hot to boil Katie and Johnnie, and he smacked his lips–smack, smack, smack.

He opened the cage and growled at the children, "Come here, you brats."

Boy, the hair on those kids' heads began to rise, they were so scared. When the giant tried to grab them, though, Katie ran one way and Johnnie the other. Before the giant knew what was happening, they had gotten out of the cage and locked him in it! The giant roared and roared and it shook the whole woods and sounded like thunder. But Katie and Johnnie tilted the cage with long sticks and rolled him down, down, down, boom-de-boom-de-boom-de-boom, into the river, ka-doosh-a-dow!

Katie and Johnnie tore out for home as fast as they could go. They got some black gum switches 'cause they thought their mama would spank them for sure, but she was so glad to see them she just hugged and kissed them and didn't whip them that time.

Reaver 1988: 10–11. ATU 327/1117. Told by Sidney Grovenstein (b. 1926), of West Palm Beach, Florida, in the early 1950s. Grovenstein heard the story from his father.

Type 327 typically involves a visit to an ogre's house. "Katie and Johnnie" recalls the subtype "Hansel and Gretel" (ATU 327A) because of its brother and sister protagonists lured by goodies. The tale also incorporates something of the stupid giant tradition. Anglo-American tradition includes a large number of similar stories of children who find themselves in danger of being eaten by a giant but outwit the big fellow. These stories rather freely exchange motifs and incidents usually associated with ATU 327, ATU 328 (Jack and the Beanstalk), and ATU 1000-1199 (Tales of the Stupid Ogre). The reader interested in comparisons should consult other versions of ATU 327/328 in this volume, especially "Barnie McCabe," chapter 11.

Dirt yards, scrupulously weeded of any growing thing, were once a feature of the rural South. It was common to rake or sweep patterns into the dirt, patterns that had to be regularly renewed. Likewise in the rural South, even in my own childhood, it was common to send a child out to cut the switch with which they were to be punished. The switches in the last paragraph of this story are such switches (not broom switches, for which Katie and Johnnie were sent in the first paragraph). The children fear that their mother will want to spank ("switch") them, but do not want to have to go out again to cut the switches for her to perform this ritual with. Rather, knowing they have been naughty, they come home provided.

54. The Story of Sally

Once upon a time a man was traveling through the country. He came to a house where a mother and her three daughters lived. The oldest daughter was named Sally.

The man said to the mother, "I have been traveling a long way, and I am thirsty. Will you give me some water?"

"Yes, certainly," said the mother. But when she looked in the bucket it was empty. So she said, "Sally, go down to the spring and get some cool water for this man."

So Sally took the bucket, and started to the spring. Everybody waited and waited and waited, but Sally did not come back. Finally the mother said to the second daughter, "Do go down to the spring and see what happened to Sally. This man is thirsty."

So the second daughter went to the spring. When she got there, she saw the empty bucket sitting on the ground, and Sally sitting there beside it, resting her chin in her hands.

"Why, Sally, what is the matter? The man is waiting for his water, and you sit here doing nothing."

"Well," replied Sally, "I'm just sitting here trying to decide whether I ought to go back and marry that man or not."

"Why, I hadn't thought of that. I'll sit down and help you decide."

So she sat down beside Sally. The others waited and waited and waited, but the two girls did not return. At last the mother told her third daughter to go down to the spring and find out what was wrong. The third daughter came to the spring and saw Sally and her sister sitting there side by side, resting their chins in their hands. The bucket stood empty on the ground.

"Why, what on earth is the matter with you two?" she said. "Don't you know the man is waiting for a drink of water?"

The second daughter spoke up and said, "Sally is trying to decide whether to go back and marry that man or not, and I am trying to help her decide."

"Well, I hadn't thought of that. I reckon I'll sit down and help you decide, too."

The mother and the man waited and waited and waited, but the girls did not come back. At last she said to the man, "I don't know what has happened to the girls. I will have to go down to the spring myself and bring you some water."

So she went down to the spring. There sat the three girls, thinking. And the bucket stood empty on the ground. When the mother saw this, she got mad.

"What do you mean by sitting there doing nothing? Don't you know that poor man is waiting for a drink of water?"

"But, Ma," the third daughter explained, "Sally is trying to decide whether to go back and marry that man or not, and we are helping her to decide."

"Oh, I had not thought of that. I'll sit down and help you decide."

The mother sat down by the three daughters. And the man waited and waited and waited, but nobody came back. At last he decided he would go down to the spring himself and find out what was the matter. When he got to the spring, there sat the mother and the three daughters, thinking. The bucket stood empty beside them.

"What is the meaning of this?" the man asked.

"Well," replied the mother, "Sally was trying to decide whether to go back and marry you or not, and we are just trying to help her decide."

"Why, that is the silliest thing I ever hear of!" the man said. "I've not asked Sally to marry me. I never thought of asking her to marry me. But I will promise you this much. If I ever see another person in the world as silly as Sally, I will come back and marry Sally."

So the man went on his way. He traveled for a long time. Then one day, he saw a house with a window open, and a heavy board reached from the window to the ground. A woman was standing there with a wheelbarrow. She would stand on the ground for a few minutes; then she would roll the empty wheelbarrow up to the board and empty it on the floor of her house, just as if it was loaded with something. After that she would roll the empty wheelbarrow back down to the ground and begin all over again. The man watched her for a long time. At last he said, "Good morning, madam. Would you mind telling me what you are doing?"

"Why, I have just scrubbed my floors, and I am rolling in sunshine to dry them."

The man thought to himself, "That is as silly as Sally." Then he remembered his promise. So he went back and married Sally.

After they were married, the man had a fine house built. He had to leave Sally at home and go off to work. Pretty soon Sally started exploring her new home. And she found a mirror. Sally had never seen a mirror before, and thinking there was some other woman in it, she broke it. Then she broke all the mirrors in the house. Then, because she could see her reflection in the silver—the knives and forks and spoons—she threw it down in the well.

About this time a man came with some meat and a note from Sally's husband, saying, "This is to eat up the cabbage." Instead of cooking the meat with the cabbage, she cut it all up in tiny pieces and put one piece on each head of cabbage in the garden.

When Sally's husband came home, he saw that all the mirrors were gone. "What did you do with the mirrors?" he asked.

"There was another woman in them, so I broke all of them," said Sally.

"Where is all the silver?" he asked.

"I threw it in the well," Sally answered.

"Then at least give me something to eat. I sent some meat for you to cook with cabbage. Is it ready?"

"Why, you said the meat was to eat up the cabbage. So I put a piece on each cabbage head so it could eat it up."

"This is too much," said the man. "I can't stand it. I'm leaving."

"Let me go, too," said Sally.

"Oh, all right. Pull the door to."

Sally thought he meant for her to bring the door along; so she took it off the hinges and went on down the road behind her husband, with the door on her back. When night came, they were far from any town or house; so they climbed up in a tree to sleep. After a while some robbers came by and sat down under the tree to count the money they had stolen. They counted for a long time. Then one of them said, "I'm so hungry. I wish I had something to eat."

Just at that moment Sally's husband went to sleep and dropped the lunch box he was carrying.

"That's nice," said the robbers. "Just wish for something to eat, and here is a fine lunch."

They counted money for a while longer. Another robber said, "This is bad. I wish we had a table."

Just at that moment Sally went to sleep and dropped the door.

"This place is haunted!" screamed the robbers. "Every time we want something, it drops out of the sky."

They were so scared they ran away as fast as they could, leaving all the money behind. The next morning Sally and her husband came down out of the tree and got all the money. After this, Sally's husband sent her to college to learn some sense.

Stroup 1937–1938: 207–11. ATU1450/1384/1245/1386/1009/1653 and Motif J1791. Told to Thomas B. Stroup by Mrs. T. W. Willets, "formerly of Vidalia, Georgia, who was told the story by her older sister, who in turn had the story from her mother" (207). Mrs. Willets, born c. 1894, first heard the story, presumably around the turn of the century, in either Telfair or Irwin County, in which counties she was raised.

This is an example of a longer story made by stringing together elements of shorter stories. All the elements of this story, the people forgetting an errand in contemplation of a nonexistent problem, the man seeking a woman stupider than his wife (in this case only a prospective wife), the woman trying to fill a house with sunshine, the woman putting meat on the cabbages, and the couple up a tree who drop a door on a robber, all the elements except the woman mistaking her reflection for reality (a variant of Motif J1791) exist widely and popularly in U.S. and world tradition as separate stories. Stroup points out that three of these elements, the stupid girl, finding someone more stupid, and hauling sunshine, are all found together also in stories collected by Elsie Clews Parsons and by A. H. Fauset. It seems clear, then, that these three, besides existing as separate stories, cohere as a single story in southern tradition. ATU 1009/1653, taking the door and dropping it on the robbers, is commonly found as a separate story.

This story departs from tradition in making the man satisfied with only one person stupider than his prospective wife, instead of the usual three that both the tale type and the economy of fairy tales usually require. But the rule of three shapes the story decisively, once the foolish girl is married: she breaks mirrors, drops silver down a well (both variants on the same motif), and feeds the meat to the cabbage, another and entirely unrelated motif.

Well-developed American versions of two of the sub-tales represented here, the man seeking someone more stupid than his (prospective) wife (ATU 1384), and the couple up a tree dropping a door on robbers (ATU 1009/1653), are so widely popular that no representative anthology of American stories could leave them unrepresented.

55. Corn for the Miller

One time there was a farm boy a-riding to mill, with a grinding of corn in a big old tow-sack. He had the corn in one end of the sack and a rock in the other, so it balanced nice across the saddle.

A smart aleck from town come along, and he says, "Your pony is about done for, and it ain't sensible to load him down with rocks."

The farm boy just grinned. "My pappy always done it this way," says he, "and so did grandpappy before him. What's good enough for them is good enough for me." And then the farm boy rode on, but he kept a-thinking about what the fellow said.

Pretty soon here come another smart aleck, and he says, "You have got that poor animal loaded too heavy. No horse ought to carry a boy and a big rock and a sack of corn besides," says he.

"Maybe you're right," says the farm boy. "But I got to take this here corn to mill, and I need the rock to balance it. The only weight that can be took off the horse is me." So then he got down and walked, a-leading the pony, with the corn hanging down on one side of the saddle and the rock hanging down on the other side.

Pretty soon here come the third smart aleck, and he says, "The pony can't hardly stand up, because all that rock and corn is too much for him. And it's a shame for a big stout boy to be walking along like you ain't got a care in the world!"

"Maybe you're right," says the farm boy. "I will tote the stuff awhile, and let the horse have a rest." So he pulled the sack off the saddle and put it on his back.

It was a hot day, and pretty soon the farm boy began to get tired. "I don't mind packing the weight," says he to himself, "it's this here walking that's destroying me." So then he got back into the saddle, but he was still carrying the corn and the rock on his shoulders.

When the miller seen them a-coming he began to laugh. "What for are you carrying the corn on your back?" says he.

"It's too heavy for the poor horse, so I'm a-helping him out," says the farm boy.

The miller laughed louder than ever when he heard that, but he didn't say nothing more.

The farm boy set down on a pile of cobs while the corn was a-grinding, and he thought about it a long time. Finally he figured out what the miller was a-laughing at. "I believe them three smart alecks has made a fool out of me," says he to himself.

Next time he went to mill the farm boy carried his corn across the saddle with a rock in the other end of the sack, just like his pappy and his grandpappy done before him. Pretty soon one of them smart alecks come along, and he says, "Carrying extra weight is wasteful; it would be more economical to take the rock out, and put half the corn in each end of the sack."

"Yes, I reckon it would be saving," says the farm boy. "But when this rock wears out, all I got to do is pick up another one. There's plenty of 'em in our pasture, and we don't give a damn for expenses." So then he rode on, and left the smart aleck a-standing there with his mouth open.

Randolph 1952a: 173–74. ATU 1215/1242A. Told to Vance Randolph by William Hatton, Columbia, Missouri, July 1929. Mr. Hatton believed the story originated in the Ozark county of Lawrence, so this tale may more properly belong in chapter 12.

Type ATU 1242A seems to be a subtype of ATU 1215, with a single simpleton replacing the father and son, rather than a subtype of ATU 1242. In 1215 and in 1242A the simpletons do foolish things to avoid over-loading a horse or donkey. In 1242, however, the emphasis is just the opposite: the simpleton cheerfully and criminally overloads his poor beast.

Baughman found only two versions of this tale collected in English-language tradition, and I have only this one to add. Nevertheless, it is probably more well known than such skimpy attestation would suggest. It is, indeed, the kind of jest that can be elaborated on to illustrate the foolishness of whoever happens to be the butt of conversation at the time. But conversation of that sort seldom takes place around collectors who are looking for ancient traditional tales. In the present version the simpleton gets the last laugh with his deliberate misunderstanding of the criticism and his retort that wearing out rocks does not concern one with so many rocks back home. The retort is surely traditional, but I have not been able to assign a motif number to it.

In January 2007, the following joke, a version of ATU 1215, appeared in the editor's email. The joke is probably an adaptation of a literary version of the tale. A web search showed about two hundred occurrences on the internet, often on management humor sites, dating back to 2003. Baughman's 1966 index, however, identifies no versions in American oral tradition.

An old man, a boy and a donkey were going to town. The boy rode on the donkey and the old man walked. As they went along, they passed some people who remarked it was a shame the old man was walking and the boy was riding.

The man and boy thought maybe the critics were right, so they changed positions.

Then, later, they passed some people who remarked, "What a shame, he makes that little boy walk."

So they then decided they'd both walk! Soon they passed some more people who thought they were stupid to walk when they had a decent donkey to ride. So, they both rode the donkey.

Now they passed some people who shamed them by saying how awful to put such a load on a poor donkey.

The boy and man figured they were probably right, so they decide to carry the donkey. As they crossed the bridge, they lost their grip on the animal and he fell into the river and drowned.

The moral of the story?

If you try to please everyone, you might as well . . . kiss your a** good-bye.

56. The Silver Toe

Once upon a time there was an old man and old woman working in their garden, digging potatoes. And the old woman found a silver toe. She took it in the house and put it under her pillow at the head of the bed. So that night something came and knocked at the door and said in a gruff, unearthly voice very slowly, "Give-me-my-silver-toe. Give-me-my-silver-toe. Give-me-my-silver-toe."

At last the old woman raised up mad and cross and says, "I've got no silver toe for you."

The coarse voice repeated slowly [*drawled out long*], "Give-me-my-silver-toe."

The old woman again says, "I've got no silver toe for you."

It kept on saying, "Give-me-my-silver-toe. Give-me-my-silver-toe."

The old man says in a whisper, "You had better give him his silver toe."

But the old woman jumped up mad and opened the door a little bit, and there was something the like of which she had never seen in her life. She says. "What's them great long ears for?"

"To hear with."

"What's that great long hair for?"

"To sweep my grandmother's hall."

"What's that great long nose for?"

"To smell with."

"What's them great long nails for?"

"To scratch my grandmother's pots."

"What's them great big eyes for?"

"To see with."

"What's them great big teeth for?"

"To bite you, to bite you, to bite you."

Dobie 1927: 41–42. ATU 366. Written down when she was in her eighties by Emeline Brightman Russell of Goliad, Texas, born sometime before 1830, died 1910. For more on Mrs. Russell, see the chapter introduction, above.

This widely popular tale is the subject of an essay by Mark Twain, "The Golden Arm" (Clemens 1897: 7–15). Most American versions, like this one, involve the chance finding of a body part, which is sometimes used to make stock for a soup and subsequently eaten, so that its return is impossible. They almost invariably end with a child-startling shout: sometimes, as in this version, the monster shouts at the victim, "Got you" or "To bite you," and sometimes, as in "The Golden Arm," the intended victim shouts to the monster, "Take it."

This tale type, popular as it is, seems to have infected other tale types in the American repertoire. The shout at the end of the version of "Johnnie Cake" in chapter 1 is probably transferred from this tale type, as may also be the whiney lines of the song in the version of "Juniper Tree" in chapter 13. In the present case, however, the tale itself seems infected from another equally popular tale type. The final dialogue is reminiscent of "Little Red Riding Hood." This infection is not peculiar to the Russell version, however. Dobie had heard a similar version from Ruth Kennedy of Austin, Texas, who grew up in Harrison, Arkansas: "This version, like Mrs. Russell's, had a 'Red Riding Hood' ending."

57. Peter Simon Suckegg

Peter Simon Suckegg
Traded his wife for a duck egg.

The duck egg was rotten
So he traded for cotton.

The cotton was yellow
So he traded it for tallow.

The tallow was so soft
He traded for a calf.

The calf was so little
He traded for a kettle.

The kettle was so black
He traded for a jack.

The jack wouldn't bray
So he traded for a sleigh.

The sleigh wouldn't scoot
So he traded for a boot.

The boot was too big
So he traded for a pig.

The pig wouldn't squeal
So he traded for a wheel.

The wheel wouldn't turn
So he traded for a churn.

The churn wouldn't flicker
So he traded it for licker.

The licker was stale
So they took him to jail.

Wood 1949: 428–29. ATU 1415/2034C. Original informant unknown. Ray Wood, of Raywood, Texas, submitted this item to the *Journal of American Folklore* with the following note (quoted in part) attached:

> This item came from a reader of my feature, "That Ain't the Way I Heard It," in the Fort Smith, Ark., *Southwest Times-Record.* Unfortunately the name of the reader has been misplaced.
>
> In an effort to trace the item to a point of possible origin, I mentioned it in newspaper articles in Arkansas, Texas, Missouri, Oklahoma, and other states, and sent it to collectors in Pennsylvania, North Carolina, Georgia, Virginia, Indiana, Texas, Mississippi, Tennessee, California, and New York. Not one of the collectors, and some had done rather extensive research, had ever heard the item and I found it known only in Western Arkansas, Eastern Oklahoma, and Southern Missouri, and to one reader in Texas who heard it in Oklahoma.
>
> It may be that the item is widely known, and that I have just not found the localities where it is current, but so far as my small facilities for research have revealed, it originated in the Arkansas-Oklahoma-Missouri sector.

The plot of this piece, such as it is, is the plot of ATU 1415, while the formulaic quality of the piece allies it to 2034C. Although this particular formulation of ATU 1415/2034C may well have developed in the Arkansas-Oklahoma-Missouri region, formulaic stories of wonderful swaps are a staple of Anglo-American folklore, sometimes as tall tales, sometimes as songs such as "When I Was a Bachelor" and "Hush Little Baby," and in the present case, apparently, as a nursery recitation. Sometimes the swapper does well, more often, as here, he does badly. The present piece is unusual, however, in that the swapper's fortunes do not unambiguously deteriorate with each swap. Trading a sleigh for a boot, for example, he gets the worse end of the bargain, but trading the boot for a pig he gets the better.

CHAPTER 10

AFRICAN AMERICAN TALES
OF THE RURAL SOUTH
AND THE URBAN NORTH

In the seventeenth, eighteenth, and early nineteenth centuries many thousands of Africans were transported to what is now the United States to be sold as chattel. They arrived on this shore stripped of clothing and possessions, as naked as newborn babes. But by and large they were not newborns but young people and adults who had come of age in a range of rich cultures. In *The Myth of the Negro Past* (1941; rev. ed., 1958) Melville Herskovits argued that these Africans managed to salvage a surprising amount of the cultural heritage of their African homelands and to pass it on to their descendants, despite the trauma of forced removal to this New World. The decades since Herskovits's publication have witnessed an ever-increasing awareness of the depth of this African heritage. Out of this salvaged material the descendants of the original slaves created a range of distinctive African American cultures and at the same time immensely enriched the Euro-American cultures they were forced to serve. Living in close interaction with Euro-American cultures, these same people obviously absorbed a great deal of European culture as well. In particular, black servants on the plantations and in the cities of the South learned many stories from their white masters. Sometimes they passed these stories on in fairly pure versions, sometimes they embellished them with African motifs, and sometimes they infused them with African values and an

African aesthetic, or even created new stories by fusing African and European elements. They also adopted and adapted Native American elements into their story repertoires. When migration north picked up at the end of the nineteenth century, African Americans brought this rich mixture of tales with them to the cities of the East and Midwest, to New York, Washington, St. Louis, Chicago, Detroit, and Kansas City.

The most famous African American stories are the Br'er Rabbit stories, such as were collected and retold by Joel Chandler Harris. In these stories the trickster rabbit attracts to himself shenanigans elsewhere attributed to the African Anansi, the European Reynard, and the countless European Jacks and Pedros. This chapter, like the following one, includes a sampling of those stories. But the Br'er Rabbit repertoire is extensive and relatively well collected, and it is impossible to give more than a hint of the range of adventures that are attributed to this amoral and immortal trickster. I have tried to limit myself to stories with clear European analogues, but recognize that some of these tales are found in Africa as well, and in some cases may have been transported to the New World from there rather than from Europe. Moreover, the episodes in this chapter about Br'er Rabbit and the Church may be completely New World inventions in the mold of trickster tales from the Old.

One of the rabbit stories, the popular "Br'er Rabbit and the Little Girl," is probably intended for small children. The chapter also includes another story for small children, "The Gunny Wolf." These stories, like the versions of "Tar Baby" and "The Devil's Daughter" here included and the story called "The Singing Goose," feature chant-like songs. Such songs, often using words of apparently African origin, are characteristic of the southern African American tales.

In addition to rabbit stories and wolf stories, this chapter also includes versions of two of the most widespread European *märchen* or fairy tales. "The Devil's Daughter" is a Detroit version of a story, also found in other chapters of the present book, in which the hero wins the help of an ogre's daughter to carry out assigned tasks. "Peazy and Beanzy" is a warning tale about two sisters, one nice and the other mean, and what happens to each of them when they go out into the world. This story too is found in other versions elsewhere in this volume.

In this chapter I have privileged early narratives. These narratives often come to us at one or two removes from the original black narrators. In many cases people brought up by black servants have remembered and refreshed their memories of the stories and then recorded them as best they could— sometimes very well. The founding of the American Folklore Society also inspired collecting among black people of the rural South. The work of

Emma Backus is one example. Looking at these tales eighty or a hundred years later, however, we can not know how closely the transcriptions by these early collectors adhered to the actual words of the storytellers, or how far they were only an attempt to recreate the storytellers' narrative and style.

No one can write about African American folktales today, and in particular about the European element in African American folktales, without acknowledging a debt to Aurelio Espinosa for his work on the Tar Baby tale (1930, 1943), to Melville Herskovits for championing the cause of a retained African cultural heritage in African American culture (1941), to William Bascom for his careful sorting out of what is African and what is European in the case of a number of highly popular African American tales (1992), and to Daniel J. Crowley for a lifetime of publications, including his invaluable symposium *African Folklore in the New World* (1977). But the reader must keep in mind that this chapter, focused as it is on tales with European roots, does not claim to tell the whole story of African American folktales.

58. Peazy and Beanzy

Now all you gather round n' I'll tell you 'bout two li'l childrens which was named Peazy n' Beanzy . . . they was sisters. They had a aunt what lived in the far east and they always wanted to go visit 'er. Now Peazy, who was mean and hateful, decided to go first. So one day she started on her way to visit her aunt.

Pretty soon she came to a brook which was all stopped up with brush and stones. That old brook would just go "Buzzzz" n' groowllll so loud 'cause it couldn't skip along its way. But Peazy wouldn't pay no 'tention. She just stepped over it and went on her way.

On the other side of the brook was a big ole plum tree that was all bent over n' broken down, but would Peazy stop and help it? No. She saw it, but just stepped on its branches as she walked 'round.

Pretty soon she got to her aunt's house, but that aunt didn't wanta keep her long. Peazy was lazy n' wouldn't set the table or dust or nuthin'.

She says, her aunt says, "Peazy, you might as well go home. You don't help out your old seek [sick] aunt. . . . You don't wash no dishes or do the chores," she says.

Now lazy Peazy was glad to leave. She wasn't gonna stay at her rich aunt's if she was gonna hafta work. So she left and on the way home she got ohh so hungry. Pretty soon she came to the sad ole plum tree and there—right down in the middle of it—was a little fire and wood all set up, just like a little oven. And there sat a little cake a-bakin'.

"Ohhhh," she says, "I'd like some of that cake." And so Peazy reached down with her hand to get some and swooooosh! came a big black crow a-flying down and picked the whole thing up in its beak . . . just a-flappin' off with it.

Peazy cried, "Ohh, I'm so hungry. . . ." And on and on she walked. Then she came along to that ole buzzin' brook and there, all built up on the twigs and rocks, was the nicest li'l fire. And right in the middle sat a black fryin' pan. Peazy smelled and smelled something good, then she saw in that skillet some fish a-fryin'. She says, "Ummmm, I think I'll just have a piece of that nice fish . . . it look so good." And just as she reached down, that whole brook came unstopped and the fire n' fryin' pan n' fish all went floating down that big ditch.

"Ohhh, me oh my. . . . I's so hungry I thinks I's gonna die. . . ." N' Peazy begins to cry and goes to rubbin' her tummy.

And finally she gets home, her sides so skinny from hunger that her ribs was a-rubbin' together. An' her mother was so mad at her fer bein' bad to the aunt that she even made her scat up to bed without no supper.

Next day Beanzy says, "Maw, why don' you let me visit Auntie?" So off goes the secon' sister to see that good old aunt.

When she comes to that brook, it's stopped up all over again. Beanzy steps right over it. . . . But then she stops n' turns round and says, "Oh, you poor buzzin' brook . . . you wants to run n' play like the other li'l brooks, don' you?" So Beanzy pulls loose the sticks n' stones that was clutterin' it up; then that brook goes merrily runnin' on.

Then she comes to that poor plum tree all broke over n' she says, "Poor tree, you wants to grow tall n' straight so you can have lotsa nice fruit, don' you?" So she ties up that bent tree with a strip of material she tore right off her dress, n' on she goes to see her aunt.

It was even dark when she got there but she wasn't scared. Beanzy goes right into the kitchen and says, "Auntie, what can I do to help you? Can't I set the table or help with the cookin' or somethin'?"

So all the time Beanzy kept busy helpin' her aunt with the chores. N' she stayed one week, then two, and finally a whole month was up and she says to her auntie, she says, "Auntie, I have to go home now to my mommy 'cause she needs me to help her too. But I'll come back to see you again soon as I can."

"You's been a dear li'l child, Beanzy," she says. "You isn't lazy at all like you sister Peazy; so I'm gonna give you this bag of money for your present. You is to take it home for your mommy and for you, but don't give none of it to Peazy, 'cause she's gonna haf' to learn how to earn it by workin' like you already know how."

So Beanzy thanks her aunt n' starts home. Just like her sister Peazy, she sees a li'l cake baking in the middle of the plum tree, but no big crow takes it from her. She looks up n' sees a tiniest li'l hummingbird that comes down n' sits on her shoulder and sings the prettiest li'l melody while she eats the cake. "Ummm, so good!" she says.

Then just like Peazy she sees some fish a-fryin' when she gets to the brook, and ummmmm, she gets to eat that too.

Then Beanzy got home. She wasn't hungry 'cause she'd had so much to eat on the way home. N' when she showed her mommy that bag full of money they both just danced a jig. And her mommy says, "Now ain't you glad I brought you up to be such a unselfish and helpful chile!"

But mean n' hateful Peazy just lay over in the corner a-cryin' and a-kickin' up her heels.

Bad girl. . . .

Now, don' you chilluns be like her!

Reaver 1988: 13–15. ATU 480. "During the 1950s and 1960s," Reaver writes, "this tale became known to young women who were patients in the Florida State University infirmary. It was told them by an elderly black attendant, who wished to remain anonymous but claimed the story came from Louisiana, where her mother had told it to her." Virginia Spencer, West Palm Beach, one of those young women, here relates the story as she remembers hearing it told.

The variant is unusual in that the wicked girl goes first, as in the related ATU 620, and the mother is good, not cruel, to the younger daughter. Readers interested in pursuing the Louisiana connection may look at the version of ATU 480 in the chapter of Creole tales.

59. The Devil's Daughter

Well, you see in those days, way back, we didn't have shipping points and mens t' hire, like we do now to get a job. [This fellow,] he just have to go out and get this job best way he can. Well, there's a old lady there, she's onto some smugglin', mighty few people know it. She had a eagle to carry her.

And so, he remated to her, says, "I'm lookin' for a job. They tell me over at Mr. Devil's you can get a good job."

She said, "Yep."

"So what they expenses? What's the prices?"

Say, "Well, they cost you four quarters of beef. See, one, two, three—the two hind quarters, and the two forequarters. And now if you can get that up, each time [this eagle,] he hollers, you give him a piece, a quarter of that beef." And say, "Now when he hollers th' last time, it'll be on the fourth one." Said, "He'll land 'fore he holler for another one."

Fellow, he goes out an' he buys up four quarters of a beef. The old lady straps him across the eagle's back, and on his wings. He start on over. He catched him round the neck, you know.

Well, he got going, got about two thousand miles, the old eagle squall out, "A-enh-enh-unh!" He reched back in his sack and he reached him a piece of beef, a quarter of a beef.

A-going on again about the same distance, two thousand miles. "A-enh-enh-unh!" He reached on to the left-hand side. He got to make it balance, you know. Two on one side and one on the other. Hand him another 'un. He goin' on.

Go 'bout the same distance again. Oh, he's making less time than thirty-five minutes too, he's swift as any—swifter 'n any train 'r plane we got now. Anyway, he hollered the next time. He got the next quarter, he handed it over to him.

He's getting there. He say, "I ain't got far to go. I ain't got but one quarter, I won't be long gettin' there." And it's gettin' late in the evening too. He want to get there before night, you know, so he can look around. Didn't know the place.

And so he squalled again.

He reched and got the next quarter.

He go, "A-enh-enh-unh!" Hands it to him. He didn't holler no more. See him commence spreading his wings, crook'd 'em, you know, like a buzzard. (You ever see a buzzard crookel down?) He crooked his wing and said, "Whuhh-hunh-unh-unh." Ever like a storm [?]. So he crookeled, he landed like a plane, you know, and taxi off. He don't go far.

He got off. Say, "I looking for Mr. Devil."

His daughter was there, she was there. Say, "Yeah." Say, "Well, come on in." Say, "What d' you want?"

"Your Papa." Say, "I want a job."

Say, "Oh, I think he'll give you—oh, he'll give you one." Course, she's taken a liking to him—time he got offa there, that, she's taken a liking to him. Say, "He'll give you one. But let me tell you now. That eagle, whenever she put you down, she gone, you see. You can't get away. But when you, ever you get off her back, she gone right back to where she come from. There's no way for you to leave. Then, you can't do the devil's work, then he kill you." Say, "Now listen." Say, "Papa'll be here directly, in a hour or two." Say, "It's too late to go to work, but don't you tell him *No* 'bout nothin' he tell to do, you just say *Yeah*."

So he just says, "Okay." He don't know she loves him and—but she know.

Well, he goes on there awhile, the devil comes in about four-thirty. He says, "Who is that there?"

The daughter, his daughter, says, "Why, it's a gentleman lookin' for work."

"Well, if he can do what I wan' him t'do, he hired. Well, now in the mornin' when you get up I want you to go out yonder, clean up a thousand acres of land, burn all the bresh, pile the logs, burn 'em up by—noon."

He went out there and he's a—next morning he's a-fighting the logs, just couldna' see how to handle a axe. He's out there and he swang, goes WHACK-A, WHACK-A, WHACK-A, WHACK-A, that way, plumb till eleven-thirty.

Out come his daughter, and she says, "Oooh," says, "that's all you got done?"

And he says, "Yeah." Says, "I'm desperate. I know I can't do it."

And she go, "Well there, I'll take care of it." Says, "Jes' hand me y' axe." See, the little bushes, was 'bout like this, she called them a tree. Say,

When I hit one side, I hit 'em all.

She hit that bush. [And every tree around,] don't care how big the tree was, she done cut it, just that deep embedded.

Now I hit the other side, I hit 'em all.
One fall, n' all fall.

And the whole thing fell.

When I trim one limb, I trim 'em all.
When I chase one, the whole thing cleaning.
Pile one, I pile 'em all.
When I set fire to one, I set fire to all.
When one burn up, all burn.

She's setting them small ones over there.

So she went on, and the old devil, he's in for dinner. He didn't never reckon what might happen down there. ("You have to do this 'fore dinner.")

He said, "Well, you get it done?"

Said, "Yeah, look out there, see them, see that?"

"Yeah, good job, good job," and he don't like that—[this man,] he's a little too smart for him, you know. He get so he's gonna give him a hard one.

He says, "Well, in the morning, what I want you to do, go out there, plow that land and break it. Plant it, and have roastin' ears for dinner."

He knows he couldn't do it, but the girl had told him, "Say *Yeah,* don't care what he said." So that day he went out there, and he plowed . . . he plowed . . . he plowed.

Eleven-thirty comes—she come to bring him water everyday. See, the old devil, he gone off somewhere. He, he gonna be back by dinner, but he gone off on another job soon that morning. —So he plowed. And she come out and she say,

> I stick one furrow, I stick 'em all,
> I stick plow in one furrow, I stick 'em in all,

say. And she said,

> When I come up once, I come up all.

Together, all the field plowed up." Say,

> When I harrow one row, I harrow it all.

She harrowed it all. She got it all harrowed. Say,

> When I plant one grain, I plants it all.

She plant one grain and it all planted. She say, "Knee-high, uh, waist, anh, waist—"

> Knee high, waist high, head high,
> Tossle, shoats, roastin' ears.

She say, "Now, pull a row for dinner." She pulled a row, he pulled a row and they went in. They all there.

"Ah, you get done that corn?"

Say, "Yes sir, yes sir, I got it. Have roastin' ears here for dinner."

Devil said—well he didn't know what do. He say, "Well, I'll see you in the morning." He's aimin' to kill him that night, y' see. But his daughter, she always knows his thoughts. So she slips out there, to the shack, you know, when the devil's, devil's all sleeping, around early—late—that night. So he—she come back and she knocked on the door, said, "Listen." Said, "Daddy's aimin' to kill you tonight." Said, "Now, I love you." Said, "Let's get up and escape from here." Say, "He got two fast horses. I got his fastest horse[s].

He's got his fast bull and fast boots. But 'fore he wake up we both can't go in his boots, we both can't go on his bull, so we'll take the fast ones." So they got up and they rid, started riding there early that night.

And so about ten or eleven o'clock in the day, her old man woke up and find out they'd gone. The devil—they'd got wa-a-a-y yonder. And she could look back, she'd see him five or six hundred miles back. Says, "Ohhhh," says, "looky yonder I see Daddy's coming." Says, "He's wearing them boots and," say, "he's bound to overtake us."

The man, he began to get scared. He said, "Lord," said, "what we goin' do?"

She say, "I'll tell you what I'll do." Say, "I'll turn into a lake and be a duck and be swimming over it, and you be a man shootin' at him."

So when he come by, the devil, oh, he's tellin' his boot;

> Step, boot, step,
> five hundred miles.

And every time he step, well there's five hundred miles.

So he sees the duck and he's shooting at it, and the man passed on—the devil passed on by. And after a while he come back. He done wore them boots, boots, out.

> Step, boot, step.

Hundred miles a step.

Now he's got to go plumb back home and get his bull and that was the fastest he got. He, he, it jumps three thousand miles a jump. Well, they lit out. You know, they had a long run, yet he go back and come up. So here he comes, and she looks, she looks back, she seen him 'bout eight thousand miles behind. She says, "Look, yonder come Daddy." Says, "He's riding that bull." Said, "He's bound to overtake us, I know that."

He says, "Lord, what we going—?" Oh, he was scared then, shore enough. And she said, "I'll tell you what to do." Said, "Hand me a thorn." She hand him a thorn. And she says,

> When I plant one thorn, I plants 'em all.

Said,

> Eight feet long, eight feet high,
> hundred feet wide, fifty feet thick.

And so they was up, getting up that quick, now there. She was on the other side and it was growing yonder way across this way for depth and thickness. So he, devil ran up to that, and the bull couldn't jump, and so he had to go back and get a axe blade, you know, to cut the bushes. And so while he's going back, they got away. And so, last I heard of them, they's alive and living happy in his country.

Suggs 1952?. ATU 313. Told to Richard M. Dorson by J. D. Suggs, aged about sixty-five, born in Mississippi but living in Calvin, Michigan, at the time, either 1952 or 1953. Recalling his "husky, melodious voice," Dorson calls Suggs "the best storyteller I ever met." He thus describes their first encounter:

> I drove down to Suggs' house, faced with cheap brick siding, and found him smiling expectantly at the stranger. "I hear you know lots of stories," I said at once. "I know a million of them," he responded with a wide grin and, standing on the grimy floor with his numerous barefoot daughters peering out from the bedroom, we swapped yarns for two hours straight. . . . For whole days, from morning till midnight, he dictated tales to me, or recited them into the tape recorder, faultlessly and with great gusto. "I hear a story once and I never forget it." . . . Eventually he volunteered nearly two hundred narratives and twenty-five songs.

The present text seems to represent a different performance from the one represented by the text that Dorson offers in *American Negro Folktales* (1967) and earlier publications. As well as differing in some details, this text is a bit more circumstantial, perhaps because Suggs was taped. Dorson, when he wrote tales out in longhand as they were told, sometimes missed details. Even the recording is not always easy to understand, as Suggs's voice hurries over a word or phrase or fades a bit. The variation of *say, says,* and *said,* too, is probably not as arbitrary as it looks. The difference is often difficult for the ear to detect. Which one Suggs uses seems to depend on the phonetic context, but I have not tried to reconstruct the controlling rule at work there. Consequently, there are doubtless some faults in the transcription, even beyond the questioned words and phrases. The "faultless" quality of the narrative, however, is notable. There is hardly a stall, only one or two stumbles in the whole performance.

ATU 313 is one of the most widely distributed of the märchen. The Suggs version, however, has some unusual features. There are only two tasks, rather than the usual three, and only two escapes on the magic flight from the devil. That magic flight itself combines elements from the two basic subversions, one in which the characters are transformed and one in which they cast objects behind them that grow into obstacles. Versions of the magic flight vary as to whether the hero and heroine are on a single horse or on a pair of horses. I have transcribed the text as if they were on two horses, but it is not absolutely clear on the tape whether the girl says "his fastest horse" and "the fast one," or "his fastest horses" and "the fastest ones."

The beginning of the tale is particularly unusual, with the hero riding off on an eagle in search of work. This eagle may constitute a relic from or a reinterpretation of an older form of the story in which a wounded eagle is helped by the hero. The African American version of this story in *The People Could Fly,* by Virginia Hamilton (1985), also begins with the eagle flight, as do some other African American versions.

Suggs also uses several unusual words in this narration. By *shoats* he seems to mean the early, undeveloped ears, though perhaps he is thinking of *shucks*. And by *remated* he seems to mean something like *represented,* though perhaps he is thinking of *remitted. Crookel* and *tossle* are self-explanatory. Suggs seems to like noises. For the eagle sound he imitates a siren. For the sound of the eagle landing he imitates the sputtering of an airplane engine. For the axe the sound is loud, but more verbal, as indicated: WHACK-A.

Carl Lindahl has also transcribed this performance in his recent *American Folktales from the Collections of the Library of Congress* (2004: 206–11). Our two transcriptions were completed independently, and readers may find it instructive to compare them. Lindahl's is more free, mine more literal. But it is also clear that we heard and understood some passages slightly differently.

60. Beg Billy and the Bull

The story I'm gonna tell, the title of it is "Beg Billy and the Bull." And Beg Billy is Billy himself, and he named his bull Billy. And so, after, he raised this bull from a little bitty calf. And the bull could talk, and that's the first time he heard of a talking bull. And so Beg Billy went out with the bull, and he grew so fine that everybody was jealous of his bull. And the Queen herself was jealous of the bull. She said she would not rest at all until that bull was dead. And so they told Billy, "We got to kill your bull and make beef out of him."

And he worried about it, and he told Billy, he said, "Billy, my boy," he said, "they gonna kill you and make beef out of you." He said, "The Queen wants you dead."

And so he said, "Well, you tell them to let you to put a rope around my head and let you get on my back, 'cause you want to be on my back when I die. And have the queen herself get out in the clear—out in a field—by herself."

And so the Queen was out and in a big clear. And she put on her scarf, her big shawl had round, called a fascinator. She's all waiting with arms all fold, ready for the heated excitement. So just as the men led the bull out and they got ready to strike the bull, then the bull raised up in the air and came right smack down with his feet and cut the Queen's head off.

And then he kept flying [a long time], and he ran out in a big pasture. And when he got over to the big pasture, he said, "Billy," said, "Now I want you to get up in a tree and hide." Said, "[Another bull is coming.] Now, I'm gonna kill him and I'm gonna drink his blood." Say, "But now, you get outta sight, 'cause if they smell you blood, they kill you too."

So Billy went up the tree and he watched. And they fought the ground hard and they fought it soft, and they fought it hard and they fought it soft.

Just cut it to ribbons. So finally Beg Billy's bull threw this other bull and cut his throat and drank his blood. So he made certain he was real dead. And he said, "All right, Billy, my boy. Come on. We got work to do." So then they went to a little pasture. He flew over there and this bull came out and he start pawing sawing, you know, and they met. And of course they start fighting. They fought the ground hard, they fought it soft. And so finally Beg Billy's bull threw the other bull, cut his throat, and drank his blood.

And so finally . . . he said, "Now, after I've killed two bulls now, next bull gonna kill me and drink my blood." Said, "What I want you to do, I want you now to get in the clear."

And so Billy started crying and he said, "I can't do without you."

He said, "Listen. Reach behind my head and you'll get a stick, and you keep it. And when I'm dead," say, "you take your knife and cut a piece of my hide, and I want you to make a belt. And you wear this belt and put it around your waist. And take this stick and carry it over your head three times. And this will give you the strength of a thousand men beside yourself." Said, "Now, when you get hungry, you gonna want to eat." Said, "Well, you reach into my left ear and you'll find this napkin. And take it by the folding tip and you spread it out and food will be on it. And you eat all you want, and then when you shall have finished eating, take it by the corner and shake it and the food will disappear."

So Beg Billy did this. And finally, after he wandered and wandered in the pasture he cross a—got over a fence. And he even saw an old man out there milking his cows.

[The old man,] he say, "Every day my cows come up here and something has took all the milk. I can't have milk. What am I going to do?"

And Billy say, "Well, I'll mind you cows for you."

He say, "You will? How much you gonna charge?"

"I won't charge anything."

He say, "Well, I'll have to pay you." Said, "What I want you to do is just to mind my cows and see what is drinking all the milk."

So Billy went out in the pasture. I think it was about eleven o'clock, and a great big giant came out and said, "What are you doing over here?"—talking, you know.

He say, "I'm minding my master's cows. Something is drinking their milk."

And so he started to Billy, and told him he was gon' kill him. Billy tightened his belt and raised the stick over his head. And this giant came to him. And so he whupped this giant and he killed him.

And he went home and the man got some milk. And he said, "Oh, this is wonderful. I'm so glad I'm getting milk."

And then after, the next day at the same hour, here come—another giant come out with two heads and four eyes. And he said, "Well, you think you gonna kill me like you did my brother, but you can't do it." So Beg Billy pulled his belt together and waved his stick and so he killed this giant.

And the next day—they come out every day, come out until it was whole five days and these five days he had five; until it was six days, of course he had six. And the last giant he killed had six heads and twelve eyes. And Billy killed every one of them. And then when he got to the cows, they came up and had so much milk he filled all the pots—the wash pots—and pans. And then, out of the yard, the milk just ran from the cows' udders. And they had a milk pool in the yard. And [the old man,] he said, "Lord, had it not been for you, what would I have done? And these giants were taking my milk, and that's how I make my living."

So at that time a crier came and said, "The Queen has lost her ring in the well." And Beg Billy ran across there, and they said, "The one who finds this ring will marry the Queen." And her father said he would give them half of his kingdom, because the Queen want to be happy and he have to have something to make the Queen happy.

So everybody, they drew, they drew water, they drew water, they came up nothing, nothing. So Billy said, "Let me have the bucket."

They said, "Ahh, you too little."

So he said, "Let me have the bucket, please."

So they gave Billy the bucket.

Billy let the bucket down, and he turned the bucket around, and when he picked the bucket up. . . . The others had just dropped the bucket down; Billy turned the bucket upside down and dropped it in the well. And when it hit the bottom—you see, it was a wooden bucket—and when it hit the bottom and turned over, SCRAPE, well, he brought it up. And there was the Queen's ring. And so they was trying to find Billy so that he could marry the Queen. But when Billy found it, when he found the ring, he hid.

And that's the end of the story.

Cook 1972: 4–7. ATU 511. Collected by Lovelace Cook, a University of Virginia student of Charles Perdue, from Cora Lee Knott Ross, born about 1903 in Tishabee Flats, in Greene County, Alabama, the granddaughter of Virginia slaves. Ross taught for fifteen years as principal of a junior high school in Greene County. She subsequently worked as a dietitian, a house director at Alabama State College, and a staff member at the Montgomery Community Action Agency.

It is hard to know whether the Queen who loses her ring in this variant is the very Queen who ordered the death of the bull, her head now miraculously restored to her body. If she is, that would explain why Billy hides with the ring and frustrates her attempts to find a husband. The hero's name, Beg Billy, the magic napkin, and the giants identify this variant as belonging to the Irish tradition of ATU 511. Closely related versions are also found in Appalachia. (A fine Appalachian example can be found in Henry Glassie 1964: 97–102.) In these Irish and Appalachian versions the hero is more commonly called Billy Peg or Billy Beg, a princess rather than a queen is seeking a husband, and eventually that princess finds and marries Billy. But African American storytellers often see no need for such pat happy endings, as Cora Lee demonstrates in her variant of the present tale.

61. The Forty-Mile Jumper

Once upon a time there were two men who were traveling along. And at dusk they came upon a hotel which was far out in the country. Now the men did not know it, but the hotel was kept by an old witch. A heap of people had gone in that hotel but nobody had ever seen anybody come out. The men did not know that though, and they stopped and asked if they might spend the night.

The old witch said certainly, but that they must sleep with her own two daughters. The men did not object to that. They ate supper and went to bed. And the two men and the two girls slept in the same bed.

The old witch told the two girls to be sure to wear their nightcaps, and when they had gone to bed she came into the room and made sure. That made the two men suspect something. So when the girls were asleep, the two men took the nightcaps from the girls' heads and put them on their own heads.

By-and-by, when the old witch thought that the men and the girls were asleep, she crept in, in the dark, and felt around for the nightcaps. Then she cut off the heads of the ones who did not have on nightcaps. But she did not know that she had cut off the heads of her own two daughters. Then the men got up without making any noise, and slipped out of the hotel as quietly as they could, and ran off down the highway as if their shirttails had been afire.

When it was day, the old witch went in to get the men's treasure. And when she found that she had cut off the heads of her own two daughters, she got on her Forty-Mile Jumper and went after the men.

She jumped and she jumped and she jumped; and before long the two men saw the old witch coming on the Forty-Mile Jumper. One of the men went running across the hill, and the other man climbed an exceedingly tall tree.

The man across the hill was calling the dogs:

Bah-manecker, Rody, Kai-an-ger,
Bah-manecker, Rody, Kai-an-ger.

The old witch came to where the man had climbed the tree, and she got off the Forty-Mile Jumper, and she took her ax, and she started to cut down the tree. And every time she hit it a lick she said,

> Willie Willie Willie, come down,

and the chips flew down.

And the man up the tree said,

> Willie Willie Willie, come up,

and the chips flew back up.

And the man across the hill was calling the dogs,

> Bah-manecker, Rody, Kai-an-ger,
> Bah-manecker, Rody, Kai-an-ger.

And the old witch said,

> Willie Willie Willie, come down,

and the chips flew down.

And the man up the tree said,

> Willie Willie Willie, come up,

and the chips flew back up.

And the man across the hill was calling the dogs,

> Bah-manecker, Rody, Kai-an-ger,
> Bah-manecker, Rody, Kai-an-ger.

And pretty soon they heard the dogs coming,

> Ah-ooh ah-ooow!
> Ah-ooh ah-ooow!"

Then the dogs came to where the old witch was chopping the tree, and they jumped on the old witch and ate her up.

Then the two men got on the Forty-Mile Jumper, and they jumped and they jumped and they jumped until they came to the hotel. And when they went into the hotel, they went into the cellar, and they found all kinds of treasures and things.

And that is why a heap of people had gone into that hotel but nobody had ever seen anybody come out.

Parler 1951: 422–23. ATU 327B/315A and Motif B524.1.2. From the telling of Flora Smith, Wedgefield, South Carolina, early in the twentieth century. Mary Parler, who supplies the story, provides the following information about the teller and the presentation:

> Flora Smith, an old Negro woman who lived in the village of Wedgefield in central South Carolina [between Columbia and Sumpter], told my brother and me many stories before the First World War. Mam Flora was what would be called a baby-sitter nowadays. Of all the tales she told us, the one we demanded most often was the story of the "Forty-Mile Jumper." In 1924, when Mam Flora was "way up in ninety," I refreshed my memory by having her tell it to me again. She told the story in the modified Gullah spoken by the Negroes of Wedgefield, but I have translated it into standard English.

We can not know, at this remove in time and space, to what extent the text is an attempt to recapture Flora Smith's way with the tale, and to what extent it is a retelling in Parler's own style. Lindahl (2004: 548–50) includes a different performance of this tale in which Parler tells the rhythmic episode of the chopping and rescue in much the same way, though she exhibits more variation in both wording and detail in the initial episode and in the closing of the story. The formulaic character of the chopping/rescue episode suggests that with regard to that part of the story, at least, what we have is faithful in substance to Flora Smith's own style and words.

This unusual text presents Hansel and Gretel as a traveling salesman story with just a hint of local legend about it. The climactic motif of the story, the chopping of the tree and the rescue by dogs with strange names, is conventionally identified as ATU 315A. Stories climaxing with this motif are popular and widespread in American tradition, both black and white. For a fuller discussion see the note to story 71 in the next chapter.

Mary Parler, who in her later years taught folklore at the University of Arkansas, in time became the wife of Ozark folklorist Vance Randolph.

62. Br'er Rabbit and the Church

A. When Br'er Rabbit Got Br'er Bear Churched

One year Br'er Bear he have a pen of fine hogs just ready for the smoke-house. But just before the Christmas season come on, every morning when Br'er Bear fotch out his corn to feed the hogs, Br'er Bear he done count them, and he find one gone; and the next morning Br'er Bear done count them, and he find one more gone; and so it go twell nigh 'bout the lastest one of Br'er Bear's fine fat hogs done gone.

Now Br'er Bear he 'low he bound to find out who the thief what steal his hogs; so all enduring the Christmas holidays Br'er Bear he visit 'bout among his neighbors constant, and they all say, "What come over Br'er Bear, he getting that sociable?"

But when Br'er Bear visiting, Br'er Bear he be a-looking, and he be a-smelling for them fine hogs.

Well, Br'er Bear he go to visit Br'er Fox, and he don' see nothing and he don' smell nothing; and then Br'er Bear he go visit Sis Coon, but he don' smell nothing and he don' see nothing; then Br'er Bear he call on Br'er Wolf, but he don' see nothing and he don' smell nothing.

Then Br'er Bear he call on Br'er Rabbit. Br'er Bear he knock on the door, and Miss Rabbit she open the door, and invite Br'er Bear in. Br'er Bear he say, "Where Br'er Rabbit?" and Miss Rabbit she say, "Br'er Rabbit gone to quarterly meeting. Being as he one of the stewards of the church," Miss Rabbit say, "Br'er Rabbit just feel bound to 'tend quarterly meeting."

Br'er Bear he say he want a fresh drink, and he go out to the well-house, and he see where they been killing hogs. Now Br'er Bear he know Br'er Rabbit didn't put no hogs up in the pen. Br'er Bear he walk round and round, and he say, "I smell the blood of my land."

And Br'er Bear he fault Miss Rabbit with Br'er Rabbit stealing all his fine hogs, and Br'er Bear say how he going straight up to the quarterly meeting to church Br'er Rabbit, and he a steward of the church, and Br'er Bear he roll his hands and arms in the blood and say he going to take the proof.

Now Miss Rabbit certainly are a faithful wife. When Br'er Bear start off down the big road towards the quarterly meeting, Miss Rabbit she take a short cut through the woods, *lipity clipity*. She get there before Br'er Bear.

Miss Rabbit she go in and take a seat 'longside Br'er Rabbit. She whisper in his ear, "Trouble, trouble, watch out. Br'er Bear he say he smell the blood of his land. Trouble, trouble." Br'er Rabbit he say, "Hush your mouth," and he go on with the meeting. Now Br'er Bear ain't the onliest man what been losing hogs that Christmas. Br'er Wolf he done lose some o' his fine shoats; somebody done take his onliest hog outen Br'er Fox pen. They take it up in meeting and make it subject of inquiry. They put it on old Br'er Rabbit, so the old man don' know which way he going to get to, when Br'er Bear walk in, and his hands and arms covered with the blood, what he take to prove up old Br'er Rabbit before the meeting.

Directly Br'er Bear walk in the door with the blood on his hands, Br'er Rabbit he clap his hands and he shout, "Praise the Lord, brethren! The Lord done deliver me and bring forth this witness!" and the people all that distracted they don' listen to a word poor old Br'er Bear say, but they all talk, and take votes, and they church old Br'er Bear right there; and that why old Br'er Bear ain't no churchman. But Br'er Rabbit he run the church yet, and they say how he never miss quarterly meeting.

B. When Br'er Rabbit Was Presidin' Elder

Now Br'er Rabbit he never get to be no sure 'nough presidin' elder. Br'er Rabbit he always been a meeting-going man, but it all along of his trifling ways that he never get no higher than a steward in the church. Br'er Rabbit he never get to be a preacher, not to say a sure 'nough presidin' elder.

But one year Br'er Rabbit he get powerful ambitious. He see all his neighbors building fine houses, and Br'er Rabbit he say to hisself he going to have a fine house. So Br'er Rabbit he study and he study how he going to get the money for his house, and one day he say to Miss Rabbit, "You bresh up my meeting clo's."

So Miss Rabbit she get out Br'er Rabbit's meeting clo's, and bresh 'em up, and take a few stitches, and make the buttons fast.

One Saturday Br'er Rabbit he put on all his meeting clo's, and his churn hat, and take his bible and hymn-book, and cut hisself a fine walking cane, and Br'er Rabbit he start off.

Br'er Rabbit he take the circuit, and he preach in every church, and Br'er Rabbit say how he be the presiding elder of the district, and how he be taking up a collection to build a new parsonage; and being as Br'er Rabbit am a powerful preacher when he aim to try hisself, and preach in the spirit, the people they give with a free hand.

Br'er Rabbit he know just what he was doing, Br'er Rabbit do, and he ride the circuit just before Christmas, and they tells how nigh 'bout the lastest one enduring the whole circuit done rob his Christmas for Br'er Rabbit's parsonage.

Well, when they see Br'er Rabbit's fine house going up and hear how Br'er Rabbit done used they all's money, well, there was a time, you may be sure, and they church Br'er Rabbit; but Br'er Rabbit he don't trouble hisself, he just go on and build his fine house. But bless you, the last shingle ain't laid before here they come begging Br'er Rabbit to come back in the church, 'cause Br'er Rabbit be a good paying member. So Br'er Rabbit he go back in the church and he live in his fine house and hold his head powerful high, and what the people done say they done say, but you may be sure they don' say a word when Br'er Rabbit listen.

Backus 1900: 19–21. A. ATU 1525(?) and Motif K2155.1; B. ATU 1825(?). The stories are printed with no information about storyteller(s). These are the first two stories in a set of ten (not all animal tales) that Backus collected in Georgia at the end of the nineteenth century. Though the 1900 publication does not identify time or place, it seems likely that these tales were collected in the same part of Georgia as a later set that Backus and Ethel Hatton Leitner published in 1912, also in the *Journal of American Folklore,* and identified as coming from Grovetown in Columbia County (just west of Augusta). Backus apparently supplied the *Journal of American Folklore* editor with some discussion of performance style in both natural and induced contexts. The editor's note at the end of the collection summarizes this information, incorporating a quote from Backus:

> As to manner of recitation, the grown people are usually so diffident that they tell the adventures with little more expression than is shown by the printed text. When, however, a narrator is found who is willing to present the tales in their proper delivery, the presentation is extremely amusing. A man will seldom forget his bashfulness, but a woman will sometimes do so. "I don't know how they do it, but they will say 'lipity clipity, lipity clipity,' so you can almost hear a rabbit coming through the woods. They talk animatedly, especially in the dialogues, and change the voice to represent the different animals, but not in a chanting tone. Before me they do not use many gestures; but when a woman tells a story in this way, she becomes so animated as to be somehow 'going all over.'" (Backus 1900: 32)

The editor goes on to provide further details about repertoire, variation, and provenance, as supplied by Backus:

> Usually, however, after they have declared their ignorance of more stories, no amount of coaxing will induce the reciters to continue, even though they may be willing. It is seldom that more than four or five tales can be obtained from one narrator.

> In some cases the tales have been obtained in a number of different versions, varied in every conceivable way. The divergence lies in the detail, and in the expansion of the narrative, the actions being identical. In reply to the question "Who told you this?" they always answer, usually saying: "My father," or "My grandfather." The collector is of the opinion that the men tell the tales to one another much more than do the women. (Backus 1900: 32)

This sort of attention to details of style and performance is remarkable in a publication of this early date. The implication that telling rabbit stories is more a man's than a woman's art, that it is an art for adult entertainment, and that the stories do not regularly get told across gender lines is certainly suggestive. Backus is also unusual in eschewing bizarre spelling to indicate dialect. Her collection is consequently remarkably readable at the same time that it seems, as far as we can tell from this distance, to capture the idiom, syntax, and sentence structure of the storytellers.

While I have, in accordance with the plan of this book, assigned ATU numbers to the tales, the assigned numbers refer to tale types that are unusually broad and vague. I know of no stories that provide very close parallels to these two adventures of Br'er Rabbit and the church, though the first seems to involve a variation on the motif of smearing a dupe with blood to make him seem guilty (K2155.1). It is impossible, at this date, to know whether these two stories were told together or not, but they are united in subject and in taking place both at Christmas time.

63. Mr. Rabbit in Partners

Once upon a time they was a bear, a fox, a rabbit, and a coon, and a wolf. They all got together one time and they decided to buy 'em a large—buy 'em a big piece of land. So they went ahead and they bought the land. And then after they bought it, then they seed that it needed claring up. Course they couldn't get anybody to clare it up for 'em. They tried and tried to get grubbers to grub it up, but they couldn't get anybody. And so they wanted to get it ready so they could cultivate it, plant it. And so they said one day to each one another, they said, "Well, the only way that we can do this, I reckon—get that land all fixed and ready in time—is for us to do it oursef." So they said, "Well I reckon so, can't get anybody to do it for us."

So they went to work then, bought up a whole lot of groceries and things like that, got 'em over to they homes, and they set the morning when they all would staat to work. And so the morning come when they—They went ahead then before they left the house and made 'em a big fire and put on a great big pot of peas and got 'em staated to cooking in order for the peas to be done at dinner time, so they could all go home then and have they dinner and rest awhile, and then they would come back to they work. And so they did. They got the peas started. They all walked on out then—Mr. Rabbit, Mr. Fox, Mr. Wolf and Mr. Bear, they all came on down to the field, walking and talking. When they got down there they all staated to work grubbing, and cutting, talking and everything, and they worked good for a good while. And 'long after while why Mr. Rabbit hollered, "Hey!"

Someone say, "What's the matter with you, Mr. Rabbit? You gone crazy?"

"No. I jest thought I heard my wife hollering a while ago."

"Oh, man, go on to work, they ain't nobody a-calling you. What you hollering about?"

"Well, all right." And Mr. Rabbit went ahead then and they all worked and worked and worked and worked. D'rectly Mr. Rabbit hollered, "Ho!"

Say, "Now, Mr. Rabbit," say, "what's the matter?"

Says, "Man, my wife called me." Say, "That woman jest worries me to death." Say, "I guess I better run on up and see what is the trouble with her."

So he struck out then, runned very fast, and he got to the house, and why he run right on in to the kitchen whar the peas was a-cooking at. And he seen the peas was a-getting along pretty good and he got him some and staated to eat. So he eat all the peas he wanted. And he got all he wanted, then he come on back then, walking along, and got down there and—.

Said, "Mr. Rabbit, you got back!"

"Oh, yeah, I got back."

"Well, what was wrong? What was matter with your wife?"

"Oh, man, I got prettiest newborn baby up there you've ever seen in your life. My wife jest hollering for me to come up there and name it."

"Did you name it?"

"Oh, yeah, I name it."

"What did you name it?"

"I've-Jest-Begun!"

And he went ahead then and he worked and worked a while, and went ahead, going on with his work, and went, "A-HEY!"

"Mr. Rabbit, now you'se crazy, now what's the matter with you? Why don't you cut that out, go to work?"

"Well, I thought I heard my wife calling me. Well, I ain't going to pay no attention to her this time. Jest let her holler."

And so he went ahead and worked, you know, and worked awhile.

D'rectly, "HEY!" again.

"Mr. Rabbit, is you crazy? What's the matter with you? You ain't heerd nobody calling you?"

"Oh, yes, they is." Says, "My wife called me again." Says, "That woman run me wild. I better go on up there again." Say, "I'm going to go this time, but I sure ain't going no more. I tell you that."

He went on up there and run right in to the pot of peas, staat eating. Got there, you know, and eat and eat. Eat all he wanted, and he turn around, and he come on back. Got back down to the boys, whar they was working.

Say, "Mr. Rabbit, what was the trouble this time?"

"Well, my wife had another pretty little old baby there and she wanted me to name it."

"Well, did you name it?"

"Sure, I named it this time."

"What did you name it this time?"

"Half-Gone."

He went on to work then. He worked and worked a while, and they talked, you know, and laughed and having fun working.

D'rectly Mr. Rabbit hollered out again, "HO!"

"Oh, Mr. Rabbit, what do you keep on acting that-a-way for? Why don't you cut that out and go to work? We don't hear nobody holler."

Say, "My wife, well, I know my wife called me again. Man, she calling and worrying me. I said I wasn't going no more, but I'm going this time. I know I ain't going no more['n] this time." Say, "Next time she call I jest ain't going."

He pulled out then and he went on. Got up there, he went right straight on to the kitchen then. He went to the pot of peas, see how it was getting on. Course peas was getting on further about being cooked done. He staat to eat. He eat and eat and eat—he jest cleaned 'em all up. Jest scraped them all out. Didn't leave any. Got through. When he come on back then, walking very slowly, he was tired and didn't move much. Got down there.

"Oh, my wife had another little old pretty baby over there."

Say, "Mr. Rabbit, how'd you get along this time? What was wrong?"

"She jest can't name none of those babies. She has to have me name every one of them. I don't know why she can't name a baby."

"Well, did you name it?"

"Yes, I named it."

"What did you name it this time?"

"Well, I named it Scrap[e]-Bottom."

So they went ahead then and they worked and worked and worked—dinner time, close to dinner time then—and worked on a while, and so dinner time come. So they begun to get hungry, and they felt like eating something. They talked all the morning about that pot of peas they had and how they was going to eat those peas and they was going to lay off and get the peas and rest a while after they got full from nice peas. So they decided, "Well, we better go on and eat then and come back after a while, after we rest a while." So they pulled out then, and went on up there. Got up there, and they all reshed right on in to the pot of peas, see how the peas was getting along. When they got there, they looked, and all the peas was gone. No peas, no nothing. Everything's gone.

Well, they all looked upon another, say, "Well, what's wrong?"

"What's become of the peas? Why, sombody's been here and eat up all the peas."

Well, it come up on, say, "Why, Mr. Bear, you, what about it, you been here?"

"No, man, you know we've all been down there working."

"Mr. Rabbit, you know anything about this?"

"No, I don't know a thing about this."

"Well, now, you been to the house, two, three times now, and you bound to know."

"No; I don't know a thing about it; I don't know nothing about 'em. I ain't had time to fool with no peas this morning. I had to tend to my wife, name the babies and everything; I ain't even been around the pot."

"Well, now, Mr. Rabbit, somebody knows something about this."

So then they all got together.

"Well, now something's got to be done about—now what we going to do about it—all this?"

Then they all got together and then they decided on what they was going to do. Say, "Well, I tell you, the way we'll do now will be to dig a great big old deep pit and we'll put bresh and logs in the bottom of it and we'll dig it so wide, and each one of us will run and jump it; and the one that falls in it, that's the one that eat the peas up; and them that jumps it clare, course, they all right; they won't have to be responsible for it."

So they dug the pit; spent the rest of the day, I guess, digging the pit jest like they want it. And then when they got it all fixed why then they said, "Well, who's going to be the first one to jump?"

Well, Mr. Rabbit, he decided he want to jump first. So Mr. Rabbit backed off a good ways and come a-taring as hard as he could chase. He made his jump so fur over it, why he jumped 'bout five or six foot further than the width of the ditch was in the clare.

And next to come, Mr. Wolf. He jumped. Next come Mr. Fox, he jumped over. Next come Mr. Coon, he went over. Poor Mr. Bear, he come along jest a-toddling. He went to jump and he got about half way and away he went down in it.

And said, "Oh, yes." Mr. Rabbit said, "I told you I didn't eat those peas. You see Mr. Bear eat those peas up."

So Mr. Bear, he was burned up as a punishment for eating all the peas.

Boatright et al. 1953: 220–24. ATU 15. Told by Richard Smith of La Vernia, Texas, probably in the late 1940s. Smith, who apparently worked in dairies all his life,

> worked on the dairy farm of the Sinclair family for five years. Many years afterwards
> the late John Lang Sinclair, author of 'The Eyes of Texas,' invited his old friend to
> visit him in New York. Recognizing Richard's ability as a storyteller, Mr. Sinclair had
> Richard record a number of his stories on the office Dictaphone. Later Mrs. Sinclair
> (Stella A. Sinclair) transcribed Richard's dictation. (Boatright 1953: 256–57)

This is one of the most popular of the animal tales, but the irresistible food is usually butter or honey rather than peas (field peas, presumably, since they have to be cooked all day). In some versions of ATU 15 the rabbit passes on the guilt by wiping the telltale butter or honey off his own mouth and onto the mouth of a dupe when the dupe is asleep. The wide appeal of the story of Rabbit "playing godfather" reflects the strong psychological truth of the story. The lure of the peas (or butter, or honey) is so strong that Rabbit goes back again and again for just a little bit more. He delights in veiled language that, while opaque to his hearers, conveys just a hint of the secret he is hiding. But when the terrible result of his irresponsible actions becomes known, unlike us he does not hang his head in embarrassment. He tells a whopper and finds a way to make it believable. Though like us in catastrophic weakness of character, he gets away with his knavery, as we know that we can not.

Alan Dundes, in an essay in *African Folklore in the New World*, has argued that at least some versions of "Playing Godfather" are unquestionably of African origin, especially those that end, as this one does, with a test of jumping over a fire or river to discover the guilty party. The tale has European as well as African analogues but is generally not found among white storytellers in North America while it is very popular among black storytellers. This fact would suggest that Africans brought the tale from their own homelands (Dundes 1977: 43–46). So, while Dundes may overstate the case a bit, it is perfectly plausible that this tale, or at least this set of versions of the tale, might have come to the new world from Africa rather than from Europe. In that case it might not properly belong in the present volume. It is, however, an essential part of the Brother Rabbit cycle and can represent the other side of the cycle from such very European tales as that of Br'er Rabbit selling his wife (chapter 11).

The present version is valuable, moreover, for the rich contextual data with which it has come to us. The long paragraph on Smith, quoted above, is unusual for the period in the amount of data it provides about the storyteller and actual collecting event. It also provides, wholly unconsciously, a number of hints about the context of paternalistic racism within which Smith lived his life and told his stories. In the account Sinclair and his wife are given titles of respect, Mr. Sinclair and Mrs. Sinclair, while Smith is referred to by his first name, Richard, and condescendingly identified as the famous songwriter's "old friend."

64. Mr. Rabbit and the Tar Man

Once upon a time there was a water famine, and the runs went dry and the creeks went dry and the rivers went dry, and there wasn't any water to be found anywhere. So all the animals in the forest met together to see what could be done about it. The lion and the bear and the wolf and the fox and the giraffe and the monkey and elephant, and even the rabbit, everybody who lived in the forest was there, and they all tried to think of some plan by which they could get water.

At last they decided to dig a well, and everybody said he would help, all except the rabbit, who always was a lazy little bugger, and he said he wouldn't dig. So the animals all said, "Very well, Mr. Rabbit, if you won't help dig this well, you shan't have one drop of water to drink."

But the rabbit just laughed and said, as smart as you please, "Never mind, you dig the well and I'll get a drink all right."

Now the animals all worked very hard, all except the rabbit, and soon they had the well so deep that they struck water and they all got a drink and went away to their homes in the forest. But the very next morning what should they find but the rabbit's footprints in the mud at the mouth of the well, and they knew he had come in the night and stolen some water. So they all began to think how they could keep that lazy little rabbit from getting a drink, and they all talked and talked and talked, and after a while they decided that someone must watch the well, but no one seemed to want to stay up to do it. Finally, the bear said, "I'll watch the well the first night. You just go to bed, and I'll show old Mr. Rabbit that he won't get any water while I'm around."

So all the animals went away and left him, and the bear sat down by the well. By and by the rabbit came out of the thicket on the hillside and there he saw the old bear guarding the well. At first he didn't know what to do. Then he sat down and began to sing:

> Cha ra ra, will you, will you, can you?
> Cha ra ra, will you, will you, can you?

Presently the old bear lifted up his head and looked around. "Where's all that pretty music coming from?" he said.

The rabbit kept on singing:

> Cha ra ra, will you, will you, can you?
> Cha ra ra, will you, will you, can you?

This time the bear got up on his hind feet. The rabbit kept on singing:

> Cha ra ra, will you, will you, can you?
> Cha ra ra, will you, will you, can you?

Then the bear began to dance, and after a while he danced so far away that the rabbit wasn't afraid of him any longer, and so he climbed down into the well and got a drink and ran away into the thicket.

Now when the animals came the next morning and found the rabbit's footprints in the mud, they made all kinds of fun of old Mr. Bear. They said, "Mr. Bear, you are a fine person to watch a well. Why, even Mr. Rabbit can outwit you."

But the bear said, "The rabbit had nothing to do with it. I was sitting here wide-awake, when suddenly the most beautiful music came right down out of the sky. At least I think it came down out of the sky, for when I went to look for it, I could not find it, and it must have been while I was gone that Mr. Rabbit stole the water."

"Anyway," said the other animals, "we can't trust you any more. Mr. Monkey, you had better watch the well tonight, and mind you, you'd better be pretty careful or old Mr. Rabbit will fool you."

"I'd like to see him do it," said the monkey. "Just let him try." So the animals set the monkey to watch the well.

Presently it grew dark, and all the stars came out; and then the rabbit slipped out of the thicket and peeped over in the direction of the well. There he saw the monkey. Then he sat down on the hillside and began to sing:

> Cha ra ra, will you, will you, can you?
> Cha ra ra, will you, will you, can you?

Then the monkey peered down into the well. "It isn't the water," said he. The rabbit kept on singing:

> Cha ra ra, will you, will you, can you?
> Cha ra ra, will you, will you, can you?

This time the monkey looked into the sky. "It isn't the stars," said he.
The rabbit kept on singing.

This time the monkey looked toward the forest. "It must be the leaves," said he. "Anyway, it's too good music to let go to waste." So he began to dance, and after a while he danced so far away that the rabbit wasn't afraid, so he climbed down into the well and got a drink and ran off into the thicket.

Well, the next morning, when all the animals came down and found the footprints again, you should have heard them talk to that monkey. They said, "Mr. Monkey, you are no better than Mr. Bear. Neither of you is of any account. You can't catch a rabbit."

And the monkey said, "It wasn't old Mr. Rabbit's fault at all that I left the well. He had nothing to do with it. All at once the most beautiful music that you ever heard came out of the woods, and I went to see who was making it." But the animals only laughed at him.

Then they tried to get someone else to watch the well that night. No one would do it. So they thought and thought and thought about what to do next. Finally the fox spoke up. "I'll tell you what let's do," said he. "Let's make a tar man and set him to watch the well."

"Let's do," said all the other animals together. So they worked the whole day long building a tar man and set him to watch the well.

That night the rabbit crept out of the thicket, and there he saw the tar man. So he sat down on the hillside and began to sing:

> Cha ra ra, will you, will you, can you?
> Cha ra ra, will you, will you, can you?

But the man never heard.
The rabbit kept on singing:

> Cha ra ra, will you, will you, can you?
> Cha ra ra, will you, will you, can you?

But the tar man never heard a word.
The rabbit came a little closer:

> Cha ra ra, will you, will you, can you?
> Cha ra ra, will you, will you, can you?

The tar man never spoke.
The rabbit came a little closer yet:

> Cha ra ra, will you, will you, can you?
> Cha ra ra, will you, will you, can you?

The tar man never spoke a word.

The rabbit came up close to the tar man. "Look here," he said, "you get out of my way and let me down into that well."

The tar man never moved.

"If you don't get out of my way, I'll hit you with my fist," said the rabbit.

The tar man never moved a finger.

Then the rabbit raised his fist and struck the tar man as hard as he could, and his right fist stuck tight in the tar.

"Now you let go of my fist or I'll hit you with my other fist," said the rabbit.

The tar man never budged.

Then the rabbit struck him with his left fist, and his left fist stuck tight in the tar.

"Now you let go of my fists or I'll kick you with my foot," said the rabbit.

The tar man never budged an inch.

Then the rabbit kicked him with his right foot, and his right foot stuck tight in the tar.

"Now you let go of my foot or I'll kick you with my other foot," said the rabbit.

The tar man never stirred.

Then the rabbit kicked him with his left foot, and his left foot stuck tight in the tar.

"Now you let me go or I'll butt you with my head," said the rabbit. And he butted him with his head, and there he was; and there the other animals found him the next morning.

Well, you should have heard those animals laugh. "Oh, ho, Mr. Rabbit," they said, "now we'll see whether you steal any more of our water or not. We're going to lay you across a log and cut your head off."

"Oh, please do," said the rabbit. "I've always wanted to have my head cut off. I'd rather die that way than any other way I know."

"Then we won't do it," said the other animals. "We are not going to kill you any way you like. We are going to shoot you."

"That's better," said the rabbit. "If I had just stopped to think, I'd have asked you to do that in the first place. Please shoot me."

"No, we'll not shoot you," said the other animals. And then they had to think and think for a long time.

"I'll tell you what we'll do," said the bear. "We'll put you into a cupboard and let you eat and eat and eat until you are as fat as butter, and then we'll throw you up into the air and let you come down and burst."

"Oh, please don't!" said the rabbit. "I never wanted to die that way. Just do anything else, but please don't burst me."

"Then that's exactly what we'll do," said all the other animals together.

So they put the rabbit into the cupboard and they fed him pie and cake and sugar, everything that was good; and by and by he got just as fat as butter. And then they took him out on the hillside and the lion took a paw, and the fox took a paw, and the bear took a paw, and the monkey took a paw. And then they swung him back and forth, and back and forth, saying: "One for the money, two for the show, three to make ready, and four to go." And up they tossed him into the air.

And he came down and lit on his feet and said:

> Yip, my name's Molly Cotton-tail;
> Catch me if you can.

And off he ran into the thicket.

Cox 1934: 342–47. ATU 175/1310A. This version comes at two removes from black tradition. Dora Lee Newman learned it from her father who learned it from family servants in West Virginia, sometime before 1918. But it merits inclusion because of the chant, the rich detail, and the unique variation on the ATU 1310 ending.

The story of the Tar Baby is widely known in this country, and was much sought by early tale-collectors as the quintessential Br'er Rabbit story. Minton and Evans thus summarize the relevant research on the origin of the story:

> While Aurelio Espinosa's model study (1930, 1943) found this narrative's African-American branch to derive primarily from Indo-European traditions, albeit with

some contribution from African and Euro-African strands, [Melville] Herskovits argued to the contrary that "whatever its place of absolute origin, the tale as found in the New World represents a part of the cultural luggage brought by Africans to this hemisphere" (1958: 272–73; cf. also Crowley 1962: 67–68). Both positions have much to commend them; neither is wholly conclusive. (2001: 23)

In the present text the provocation for constructing the tar man is that the trickster is helping himself to water. This is the more usual African provocation. In the United States, however, stealing peas is at least as usual a provocation, just as the briar patch is the usual (non)punishment. These two elements, pea stealing (or greens stealing) and briar patch hurling, are featured without the tar baby episode in the next story.

65. Br'er Rabbit and the Little Girl

Lil' girl had some greens in her garden. Br'er Rabbit kep' 'ere eatin' up her greens. Lil' girl say, "Br'er Rabbit, don't you eat all dem bigges' greens! Come ober here where I is, and I let cher eat dese here lil' ones."

So Br'er Rabbit he come ober to eat lil' greens, and lil' girl ketch him.

Den Br'er Rabbit th'ows back his head and 'gins to sing:

Lee cum Lee cum Gen-i - ke-buk-o-buk Lee ki.

Lil' girl say, "Sing dat song ergin." But Br'er Rabbit, he won't sing.
Lil' girl say, "I fro you in the ribber!"
Br'er Rabbit say, "*Fro* me in the ribber!"
"I fro you in de creek!"
"*Fro* me in de creek!"
"I fro you in de well!"
"*Fro* me in de well! Des any place you minds to, but in de brier-patch."

So course lil' girl, she fro him brier-patch; and Br'er Rabbit jump up en clap his feet togedder, and say, "Bred and born in de brier-patch, lil' girl, bred and born in de brier-patch!"

Harvey 1919. ATU 1310A. Emily N. Harvey writes: "The following story was collected by me at Fort Mitchell, Ala., from plantation Negroes. The song, both the 'words' and the air, I have verified by having it sung by different members of the family. They tell me that the story as told by their grandfather always included the song." This seems, then, to be a synthetic text based on the telling of various members of the same family.

66. The Gunny Wolf

A man and his little daughter lived alone in a forest and there were wolves in the forest. So the man built a fence round the house and told his little daughter she must on no account go outside the gate while he was away. One morning when he had gone away the little girl was hunting for flowers and thought it would do no harm just to peep through the gate. She did so and saw a little flower so near that she stepped outside to pick it. Then she saw another a little farther off and went for that. Then she saw another and went for that and so she kept getting farther and farther away from home. As she picked the flowers she sang a little song.

Suddenly she heard a noise and looked up and saw a great gunny wolf and he said [*low, gruff voice*], "Sing that sweeten, gooden song again."

She sang,

> Tray-bla, tray-bla, cum-qua, kimo.

Pit-a-pat, pit-a-pat, pit-a-pat, pit-a-pat [*said softly to represent the child's steps*], she goes back. Presently she hears [*coarse deep voice, to represent the wolf's steps*] PIT-A-PAT, PIT-A-PAT, PIT-A-PAT coming behind her. And there was the wolf, an' 'e says [*wolf voice again*], "You move?"

[*Childish voice*] "O no, my dear, what 'casion I move?"

"Sing that sweeten, gooden song again."

She sang,

> Tray-bla, tray-bla, cum-qua, kimo.

Wolf, he gone.

Pit a-pat, pit a-pat, pit-a-pat, she goes back some more. Presently she hears [*deep voice, as before*] PIT-A-PAT, PIT-A-PAT, PIT-A-PAT coming behind her, and there was the wolf, an' 'e says, "You move?"

"O no, my dear, what 'casion I move?"

"Sing that sweeten, gooden song again."

She sang,

> Tray-bla, tray-bla, tray-bla, cum-qua, kimo.

Wolf, he gone.

PIT-A-PAT, PIT-A-PAT, PIT-A-PAT coming behind her and there was the wolf, an' 'e say, "You move?"

"O no my dear, what 'casion I move?"

"Sing that sweeten, gooden song again."

She sang,

> Tray-bla, tray-bla, cum-qua, kimo.

Wolf, he gone.

Pit-a-pat, pit-a-pat, pit-a-pat, she goes back some more. And this time when she hears PIT-A-PAT, PIT-A-PAT, PIT-A-PAT coming behind her, she slips inside the gate and shuts it and wolf, he can't get her.

Whitney and Bullock 1925: 178. ATU 333 and Motif K606. Maryland, before 1925. This story takes an African motif, escape by singing, to develop the basic situation in "Little Red Riding Hood." Plotless though the resulting story may be, it is widely popular in the United States. Apparently very small children relish the formulaic language, the delicious threat posed by the wolf, and the successful evasion executed by the little girl.

67. The Singing Geese

A man went out one day to shoot something for dinner, and as he was going along, he heard a sound in the air above him and looking up saw a great flock of geese, and they were all singing:

> La-lee-lu, come quilla, come quilla,
> Bung, bung, bung, quilla bung.

He up with his gun and shot one of the geese and it sang as it fell,

> La-lee-lu, come quilla, come quilla,
> Bung, bung, bung, quilla bung.

He took it home and told his wife to cook it for dinner and each feather, as she picked it, flew out of the window. She put the goose in the stove, but all the time it was cooking, she could hear in muffled tones from the stove,

> La-lee-lu, come quilla, come quilla,
> Bung, bung, bung, quilla bung.

When the goose was cooked, she set it on the table, but as her husband picked up his knife and fork to carve it, it sang,

La-lee-lu, come quilla, come quilla,
Bung, bung, bung, quilla bung.

When he was about to stick the fork in the goose, there came a tremendous noise, and a whole flock of geese flew through the window singing,

La-lee-lu, come quilla, come quilla,
Bung, bung, bung, quilla bung.

And each one stuck a feather in the goose. Then they picked it up off the dish and all flew out of the window singing,

La-lee-lu, come quilla, come quilla,
Bung, bung, bung, quilla bung.

Whitney and Bullock 1925: 179. Motif E168. Collected in Maryland, before 1925. I have found no exact parallels to this strange little one-motif tale. But I find it irresistible. I am calling it African American on the strength of the goose song and of the position of the story in the volume. The closest European analogs are tales of Irish pigs that revive after being cooked and eaten (Thompson, Motif Index, under this number) and the story of the cattle of the sun in the *Odyssey*. Songs like the goose song appear fairly frequently in African American tales. See, for example, the Tar Baby variant in this chapter.

68. Sleeping Beauty

A. La Dora Was a Pretty Girl

La Dora was a pretty girl,
She lived up in a castle high.
One day there came a wicked witch,
She point her stick right in her eye.
She fell asleep a hundred years.
The princess clucked the hinges down.
The princess picked La Dora up,
    Tra, la, lala, la, la, lala!

B. Here We Go Round the Strawberry Bush

Here we go round the strawberry bush,
    This cold and frosty morning.

Here a young lady sat down to sleep,
    This cold *etc.*

She wants a young gentleman to wake her up.

Write his name and send it by me.

Mr. ———— his name is called.

Arise, arise, upon your feet,
    This cold and frosty morning.

A. Yoffie 1947: 44; B. Newell 1883: 224. ATU 410. The first text comes from St. Louis, 1944, and the second from Galveston, probably about 1875. Herbert Halpert (1947: 422) has identified the St. Louis version as Sleeping Beauty, though it has strayed rather far from the fairytale plot line. Newell himself has so identified the second version, though this identification seems less certain.

Concerning the St. Louis text, version A, Yoffie writes: "A little colored girl in one of the playgrounds sang this and said it was a ring game. But no one else in that playground knew the song, nor could I find any child in any of the playgrounds in my survey who knew it or any song like it" (44). Yoffie indicates that the name may have been Mavora, not La Dora, and suggests the emendation plucked for clucked. Another emendation that suggests itself where the song has "The princess clucked the hinges down," is "The prince, he clucked the hinges down," and similarly for the following line. It is possible that each line of this text in fact represents a stanza:

> La Dora was a pretty girl
> Pretty girl, pretty girl,
> La Dora was a pretty girl,
> Tra, la, lala etc.

Newell comments at the end of the Galveston text, version B, that "Some unintelligible Negro rhymes follow." He also suggests that stanza 5 was repeated with different boys' names until a satisfactory name was found. The tune was probably some variant on "Here We Go Round the Mulberry Bush," a tune that would also work for version A as I have expanded it.

Unlike the game versions of favorite stories that children create spontaneously, the present games are more formal and artificially structured, with the children standing in a ring, singing, and indulging in ritualized kissing. Such singing and kissing game versions of Sleeping Beauty are nevertheless well attested in France and Germany as well as in the United States. A much fuller New Jersey text calls the girl Thorn Rosa, whence, perhaps, the strange name La Dora in version A above. If, as Halpert suggests (1947: 422), version A is German in origin, the black community that played it may have learned it in St. Louis rather than bringing it with them from the South—if, indeed, it was played in St. Louis, and not learned elsewhere by the girl who sang the song.

Newell's final comment on "Here We Go Round the Strawberry Bush" can serve as a reminder of the inherent impossibility of doing justice to the material in the present chapter and indeed in this whole work:

> We infer, therefore, that the game, apparently so natural an invention, originally represented some form of the world-wide story of the "Sleeping Beauty." If this be so, to explain its history would lead us to write of Northern lay and mediaeval legend; we should have to examine the natural symbolism of primitive religions, and the loves of ancient gods. The kissing-romp . . . would be connected with the poetry and romance of half the world.
>
> In any case, this interlinking of the New World with all countries and ages, by the golden net-work of oral tradition, may supply the moral of our collection. (225)

TALES FROM THE COASTAL
GULLAH TRADITION

In the eighteenth century, indigo and rice plantations in coastal Carolina and Georgia imported slave labor from the Bahamas and directly from Africa. This new population brought with it a rich mixture of traditions, African, Iberian, and British. The new mix developed and flourished long after slavery days, especially on the Georgia and Carolina Sea Islands.

The area was relatively isolated up until the 1960s. Access to islands was often by boat only. People farmed or tenant farmed and fished. They formed mutual aid societies, such as the Moving Star Society on John's Island, to provide a financial buffer in times of crisis and at the time of burial. Singing and storytelling at home and ecstatic (but not Pentecostal) religious services several times a week were the principal social outlets. In the 1960s came the Civil Rights movement and, at almost the same time, resort development that provided some jobs, but generally of a more menial sort. Since the 1960s modernization has proceeded apace. The children's television network Nickelodeon has even produced a series, *Gulla Gulla Island*, based on the culture of the Sea Islands.

The Sea Islanders and their coastal neighbors developed the distinctive language called Gullah, a creole based on English but including African loan words and grammatical elements. In this chapter we can see how collectors and editors have wrestled with the issue of how to transcribe this language. The children of the Penn School used standard written English to set down their stories. Other collectors here drawn upon, however, attempt to set the stories down in Gullah. Each collector or group of collectors has devised a different system for doing so. Guy Johnson (1930) and the WPA collectors experimented with spelling to suggest pronunciation while Carawan and Carawan (1989) used standard spelling as far as possible. While it is no longer fashionable to use specialized spelling to indicate dialect, the phonemic differences between standard English and Gullah are not generally familiar to English speakers outside the Coastal region. For this reason it seems not unreasonable to let stand the efforts of collectors to present the language as it is spoken. And so this chapter whenever feasible follows the spelling of the tale as first printed, but avoids collectors whose spelling has been excessively influenced by literary and stage dialect. One of the tales, however, "The Coon in the Barrel," really needed a translation. This latter tale is apparently an American oikotype (special national or regional subtype) of the tale Dr. Know-All (ATU 1641). The version included here is the earliest known printed version. I have presented it as printed, in Gullah; but because the attempt at rendering Gullah is almost impenetrable, I have followed it with a fairly literal English translation.

Readers will detect that the range of Gullah phonemes is narrower than that of English, with fewer vowel and fewer consonant sounds. Among the most distinctive grammatical features in the following stories are these:

(a) The subjective and possessive, singular and plural forms of most nouns and pronouns are the same:

> *He grab he hoe.*
> *De king wife dead.*
> *De dawg take all dem big man.*

(b) The third person singular of verbs in the present indicative active is usually the same as the first and second person singular:

> *She have to do hard work.*
> *She run home.*

(c) Structure words such as prepositions, articles, and the verbs *be* and *do* are sometimes absent where they would be expected in standard written English:

> *We far from home and we very tired.*
> *King had daughter an' dis woman had daughter.*

(d) The same pronouns are used for masculine and feminine (which seems especially confusing to speakers of other forms of English):

So his broder say to him, "Sister Mary, I'll kyarry you" [*her broder . . . to her*].
John's wife chose Mary for his maid [*for her maid*].

If at first the Gullah in a story seems strange, try reading the story out loud, or half out loud, the way children first read.

The Gullah repertoire of the Sea Islands is rich in stories about Brother (Br'er or B'er) Rabbit, in stories in which European and African motifs are inextricably intertwined, and in *cante fables*, that is, stories that include a strong sung element. In each case the repertoire is distinctive. The Br'er Rabbit stories seem especially rich in psychological truth. The Africanized märchen may take a tragic turn at the end. And the *cante fable* melodies are plentiful and haunting. This chapter has tried to sample that richness. And so . . .

Step on de tin!
Tinny wouldn't ben!
Dat de way
My story en!

69. The Coon in the Barrel

One time er rich Buckra hab er senserble ole man serbant wuh come from Afreka. Dis ole nigger bin know ebryting bout ebryting. Nobody could tun um wid questun. Eh Mossa try um heap er time, an eh ebber did mek right answer. Eh fren try um too, an dem nebber ketch um duh miss. De Buckra brag heaby on de ole man, an berry offne eh win bet topper um. One day de Buckra man gen er big dinner, an eh eenwite heaper fren ter him house. Eh lay er wager say nobody kin ax eh ole serbant er questun wuh him couldnt answer, an eh gie eh fren lief fuh try de ole man any fashion dem want. De money pit up, an de fren call one boy, wuh bin er wuk bout de lot, an dem sen um der wood fuh ketch one coon. De boy gone wid eh dog. Wen dinner done ober, and de gentlemans duh set een de piazza duh talk, de boy come back wid er roccoon. Dem call fuh er barrel, an dem tek de coon an pit um een an head um up complete, so nobody kin see wuh day eenside.

Den dem sen fuh de ole Afreka nigger. Eh bin er hoe cotton der fiel, and nobody bin tell um wuh mek dem sen fuh um. Eh come; and den eh Mossa say: "Ole man, we sen fuh you fuh tell we wuh day een dis barrel." De ole man look at um, an walk roun um, an notus um close, an listen fuh see ef eh could yeddy anyting duh mobe. All de gentlemans duh watch um. Wen de ole man mek up eh mine eh couldnt fine out wuh day een de barrel, eh stop, eh study, eh cratch eh head, an den eh mek answer: "Mossa, hoona done head de ole coon dis time."

Eh no bin know say him bin er speak er true wud bout wuh bin een de barrel. Eh bin er talk about ehself wen eh say dem bin head de ole coon dis time, but eh Mossa an de tarruh gentlemans no know, and dem all gie de old man big praise. Eh Mossa win de bet, an eh share de silber money wid de ole man.

TRANSLATION

One time a rich buckra [*white man*] had a sensible old manservant that came from Africa. This old negro knew everything about everything. Nobody could stump him with questions. His master tried a heap of times, and every time this man made the right answer. His friends tried him too, and they never caught him in a miss. The buckra bragged hard about the old man, and pretty often he won bets on account of him.

One day the buckra man gave a big dinner, and he invited every one of his friends to his house. He laid a wager, saying that nobody could ask his old servant a question that he couldn't answer. And he gave his friends leave to try the old man in any fashion they wanted.

The money was put up, and the friends called a boy who was working about the lot, and they sent him to the woods to fetch a coon. The boy set off with his dog.

When dinner was over and the gentlemen were sitting on the piazza [*porch*] to talk, the boy came back with a raccoon. They called for a barrel and they took the coon and put him in and hid him completely, so nobody could see what was there inside.

Then they sent for the old African negro. He had been hoeing cotton in the field, and nobody told him what made them send for him. He came, and then his master said, "Old Man, we sent for you to tell us what there is in this barrel."

The old man looked at it, and walked around it, and noted it closely, and listened to see if he could hear anything moving. All the gentlemen there watched him.

When the old man made up his mind that he couldn't find out what was there in the barrel he stopped, he studied, he scratched his head, and then he made answer: "Master, you got the better of the old coon this time."

He didn't know that he had just said a true word about what was in the barrel. He was talking about himself when he said they had bested the old coon this time, but his master and the other gentlemen didn't know that, and they all gave the old man big praise. His master won the bet, and he shared the silver money with the old man.

Jones 1888: 89–90. ATU 1641 (Minton-Evans subtype B5). Jones provides no information about where he learned this tale, though he asserts that tales such as this were "often repeated before the war," meaning the war of 1861-1865; in the time when he was publishing, however, they were "seldom heard save during the gayer moods of the old plantation darkies" (v). Elsewhere in his volume, and especially in the last pieces, he provides details, albeit much romanticized, about individuals and about the way of life of those who worked on the rice plantations. Jones probably wrote the story out from memory, somewhat the way Joel Chandler Harris wrote out the Uncle Remus stories, after hearing just such an elderly former slave tell it. One of the factors motivating him to publish his collection was to demonstrate the difference between Coastal Gullah and the language of middle Georgia as presented by Harris (v).

John Minton and David Evans have examined the story of the coon in the box (2001). They contend that it is a distinctly American variant of the European story often called Dr. Know-All. In British and Irish versions of that tale the captured creature is a fox. The know-it-all, when caught out, says, "Well I guess you caught this old fox at last," thus unwittingly identifying the captured animal. In the United States, they contend, the raccoon became just as well known for slyness as the fox, and people who were clever or sly were commonly called coons. Consequently the story might feature a captured raccoon instead of a fox. The logical next step was making the story one about a clever or sly black man, and incorporating it into the cycle of John and the Master stories about how the black servant outwits the old master.[1] Minton and Evans believe that the story was already being told with a black hero even before the word *coon* became a colloquial term for a black man. But when the word *coon* acquired a racial connotation, some time after the Civil War, the final line took on a double irony.

There is no record of The Coon in the Box (or Barrel) earlier than the present text, and the work of combining and transforming this European tale was apparently done in the post–Civil War era. The Coon in the Box then is a distinctly American märchen created by incorporating the British form of a European folktale into an African American story cycle and submitting it to the accidents of development in colloquial language so that the catch line became doubly ironic. In its early African American form the story served to celebrate the cleverness and luck of the servant. That continued to be the case even after the word *coon* acquired its second not-quite-complimentary meaning—for the hero, by appropriating the credulous Master's diction, gets the best of the Master or, in this version, of his doubting friends (see Minton and Evans 2001: 59–64, 101, and passim).

[1] These John and the Master versions might still focus on a fox rather than a raccoon, as in a version collected in Virginia by Daryl Cumber Dance (Minton and Evans 2001: 59).

70. The Mermaid

De King wife dead an' King marry 'nodder woman. King had daughter an' dis woman had daughter, an' dey treat her daughter good, but not treat de King daughter good. She have to do hard work, an' de odder gal do nuttin'. So de po' gal go down to de water an' cry. Mermaid rise up an' say, "What you cry for, li'l gal?"

"My mudder die an' my fadder marry agin an' my step-mudder have daughter. Dey treat me bad an' won' give me 'nough t' eat."

De mermaid say, "Come down wid me." She take her down under de water to de purties' place. Give her all kin' o' good t'ing t' eat. Den she bring her back up. Dat night, de gal not want a bite t' eat after de odders done eat, but she feel so glad. Nex' day she go back to de water an' sing:

Dee, dee, dad-dy. Take me down, pret-ty Joe.

> Dee, dee, daddy,
> Take me down, pretty Joe.

An' de mermaid rise up an' take her down an' give her plenty good t'ings t' eat, den bring her back up. So dat night, dey keep wonderin' why she not eat. Fin'ly de step-mudder daughter say she gwine fin' out.

Nex' day she follow de gal to de river an' hear her sing:

> Dee, dee, daddy,
> Take me down, pretty Joe,

an' she see de mermaid rise up an' take de gal down. She run home an' tell her mudder an' de King what she see. So nex' day dey all t'ree went down to de river widout de King daughter knowin' it. De King sing:

> Dee, dee, daddy,
> Take me down, pretty Joe.

But no mermaid. Den de step-daughter try it:

> Dee, dee, daddy,
> Take me down, pretty Joe.

An' up rise de mermaid. King shot de mermaid daid.

When de King daughter come down to de river, she sing like she always sing, but no mermaid. She step down in de water an' sing again:

> Dee, dee daddy,
> Take me down, pretty Joe.

But no mermaid. She went on deeper an' deeper, singin' dat song all de time, till she drown. Dat's end o' my story.

Johnson 1930: 148–51. ATU 480/511. Collected by Guy Johnson from a student at the Edding's Point School, St. Helena Island, South Carolina. Though this clearly seems to be a combination of ATU 480, The Kind and the Unkind Girls, and ATU 511, One-Eye, Two-Eyes, Three-Eyes, the tragic twist at the end is most unusual. Parsons collected a very similar version from Ada Bryan at Edding's Point School in February 1919 (1923b: 137–38).

Many of Johnson's fine texts come from schoolchildren on the island. He offers the following description of these student storytellers and their art:

> The older people rarely tell the stories to white people, it is true, but the children tell them naïvely and with plenty of skill. On the way to school, at recess time, at parties, at home around the fireside, or at work, the young folk tell stories and riddles. They may deviate from the traditional version of a tale, but they are good at supplying new incidents and at combining several stories to make a new one. If part of a story is supposed to be sung, they sing it rather than recite as many adults would do. If Br'er Rabbit is supposed to make a funny noise as he runs down the road, this is supplied with an ingenuity which attempts to outdo the other fellow. (136)

71. Barney McCabe

We learn some these stories from my uncle, Harry Williams. He was kind of rough, but he really could tell some stories.

Once upon a time it was a twin sister and brother. The sister name was Mary and the brother name was Jack. One day they decided to go on a long traveling. But Jack was a wise child and he told Mary to go in the house and ask mother could we go.

Her mother say, "Yes, you could go, but take care."

So Jack say, "Wait a minute, Sister," and went to the barn and get four grain of corn.

And Mary said to Jack, "What you gonna do with that corn?"

Jack said, "In a long while, you will see." So he put the corn in his pocket.

Then before he leave home Jack told his mother, say, "Mama, I got three dogs, Barney McCabe, Doodle-le-doo, and Soo-Boy. I going to leave a glass of milk on the table. If you see that glass of milk turn to blood, I want you to turn my dogs loose." So they went on traveling and all the time wondering what the end was going to be. Pretty soon it come dark and they begin to get weary. They knocked at an old lady house. The old lady run to the door, say, "Who is it?"

Jack say, "Me, Mama. Could we spend the night here? 'Cause we far from home and we very tired."

Old lady say, "Oh yes, come on in."

All that time she was a witch-craft and the children didn't know it. She fed them and put them to bed. She had a knife she call "Tommy Hawk." After she put the children to bed she began to sharpen it up:

Penny, get your knife,
Penny, get your knife,
Penny, get your knife, go shock 'em, shock 'em.

Hump back a Josie back a see Antony,
Mama and your daddy tell me so,
See so, I think it so
Tam-a ram-a ram.

Children say, "Grandma, what's all that noise? We can't sleep."

She say, "That ain't nothing but your grandma frock-tail switchin' to get your supper hot. You all go back to sleep."

So Jack begin to wonder how they can get out of there. Then he remember the old lady have a room full of pumpkin. Jack takes two pumpkin and put 'em in the bed and cover 'em over, pretend it was he and his sister. Then Jack throw one grain of corn to the window, and it turn into a ladder. Jack and Mary climbed the ladder down and they start traveling for home.

The old lady sharpen her knife faster:

> Penny, get your knife,
> Penny, get your knife,
> Penny, get your knife, go shock 'em, shock 'em.

> Hump back a Josie back a see Antony,
> Mama and your daddy tell me so,
> See so, I think it so
> Tam-a ram-a ram.

She didn't hear no noise, so she sneak in the room and chop up the pumpkins in the bed. Then she ran in the kitchen and got a dishpan, and pull back the cover. And when she think she putting the meat in the pan for cook for breakfast, she drop the pumpkin in the pan. And Jack and Mary was long gone.

She get mad, grab Tommy Hawk and flew down on those children. The children drop another grain of corn and it turn a tall pine tree. And Jack and Mary flew up in that tree. The old lady start cut on the tree, say:

> A chip on the old block, a chip on the new block,
> A chip on the old block, a chip on the new block.

Then Jack drop a grain of corn down from the pine tree, and back home that glass of milk turn to blood. Them dogs begin to holler. Jack's mother ran in the yard and turned the dogs loose.

Jack say:

Barney McCabe, and Doodle-le-doo, and Soo-Boy,
Your maussa calling you.

Dogs say:

Maussa, Maussa, coming all the time,
Maussa, Maussa, coming all the time.

Old witch say:

A chip on the old block, a chip on the new block,
A chip on the old block, a chip on the new block.

Every time she chip, the tree lean and lean. Jack call:

Barney McCabe, and Doodle-le-doo, and Soo-Boy,
Your Maussa almost gone.

Dogs say:

Maussa, Maussa, coming all the time,
Maussa, Maussa, coming all the time.

Jack drop another corn, the last corn, and it turn a bridge. And then
when the old witch pull the ax up for take the last chop and chop Jack and
Mary in the head, the dogs ran up. Barney McCabe cut her throat, Doodle-
le-doo suck her blood, and Soo-Boy

... drag her on the bridge,
the bridge bend,
and that's the way
that story end.

Carawan and Carawan, 1989: 103–5. ATU 327–28/315, Motif B524.1.2. From Mrs. Janie Hunter of
John's Island, South Carolina, c. 1960. Mrs. Hunter was one of the leaders of the Johns Island

Moving Star Hall Singers. The mother of thirteen children, she thus describes storytelling in her own childhood:

> When we was small, we didn't 'low to go no place, but we have all we fun at home.
> On weekend when we do all work what told to us and after we finish work at night,
> we sit down and we all sing different old song, and parents teach us different game
> and riddles. We go and cut the wood and wrap up the house with green oak and
> muckle wood, then we all stays by the fire chimbley and listen to stories. (Carawan
> and Carawan 1989: 96)

The Carawan and Carawan volume contains many photographs of Mrs. Hunter, her fellow islanders, and their island.

The present *cante fable*, usually with only one or two choruses, is extraordinarily popular in both English and French and among both black and white storytellers across the South and beyond. Mrs. Hunter's beautifully realized version, with four distinct choruses, has been widely performed by professional and revival storytellers. The distinctive climax of this story, rescue by the dogs of the master who has taken refuge in a tree, is very strong, perhaps dominant. This element is conventionally but probably mistakenly identified as part of ATU 315. William R. Bascom has argued for the African origin of this element and discusses over one hundred versions from Africa, Latin America, and the United States (1992: 155-200). In an article answering Bascom, Christine Goldberg has suggested that the element or motif came to America "not only from Africa but also from southern Europe" (1998: 43). Whether or not of African origin, the element is common in tales told by white Americans as well as by black Americans. In the present case the story of the dogs and the tree is incorporated into a tale representing the Hansel and Gretel/Escape from a hungry ogre group, ATU 327–28. The resulting complex, which we might dub Hansel and Gretel Escape by Calling the Wonderful Dogs, is extremely popular in the Sea Islands. In the following story and in stories in other chapters we see the dogs with splendid names incorporated in other ways and into other tale types.

72. The Deserted Children

An ol' man an' his wife had eight chil'run. An' dey come a famine, couldn' get anyt'in' to eat, time was so hyard. An' in dat countree were wil' people. He took fo' o' de chil'run—two boy, two girl—an' t'row um out in de fores', an' keep fo' home.

Dese fo' chil'run been out in de woods fo' night an' fo' day. De two oldes' fumble away an' fumble away until dey finally fin' deir way back home.

So John an' Mary dey couldn' fin' de way back home. So dey staid in de woods, an' John fin' a holler. Him an' his sister staid in dat holler. An' ev'y day John would go out hunt fo' food, wil' berries, shakeapen [*chinkapin*], an' diffun' food for him an' his sister. So one day more'n all John went out to hunt food. He fumble an' fumble until he get on de aidge of de wood, an' he saw a buil'in'. He t'ought he'd go up an' see what it was. An' when he wen' up, dere was a shop, big shop.

He saw dese cake an' t'ings in at de winder. He didn' see no one. He stepped in, an' he reach his han' an' get fo' o' dese cake. Whils' he comin' out de do', he heard, "Squizz . . . z!" He look 'roun', an' he saw a woman in de corner was blin'. Dis woman take him fo' a kyat, yer know.

So he wen' into de woods wid de cake, an' he give his sister one an' a ha'f, an' he eat one an' a ha'f.

His sister say to him, "O Broder Johnnie! whey you get home-made grub?" He tell his sister dere is a house out dere he fin'. So his sister says to him, "O Broder Johnnie! kyarry me, an' le' me go wid you an' le' me get some mo'!"

So his [*her*] broder said to him [*her*], "Sister Mary, I'll kyarry you; but dere is an old woman dere blin', an' when she say 'Squizz . . . z!' you [*will*] run an' laugh, an' he [*she*] ketch us."

He [*she*] say no, 'e wouldn' laugh. So he 'blige his sister, 'e kyarry him [*her*] dere de nex' day.

When Johnnie step into de shop, he step a w'ong boa'd, an' de boa'd crack. An' de ol' lady say, "Squizz . . . z!" An' he [*she, Mary*] run off from de do', an' say [laughing:], "ke, ke, ke, ke . . . e!" An' de wil' man was bakin' out on de side, run out an' ketch bof of dem. Dey was people eat people. So he had a big kyage to fatten 'em in right in f'ont of de do'.

So he put John an' Mary bof in de kyage. An' 'bout twelve o'clock he take Mary out de kyage an' put Mary in de house wid his wife to wait on his wife till dey ready to eat him [*her*].

Dat evenin' dey was to kill John. Was near de swamp. A big rat run t'rough de kyage. Whils' de rat was goin', John ketch de rat an' cut off his tail. De ol' man come to de kyage to see wheder John fat o' not. John poke de rat-tail to him. You know he had no sense, he t'ought dat was John finger. So he wen' back to de house, tol' his wife he can't kill dat feller, ain't fat yet.

So nex' mornin' Mary wen' to de kyage, play wid de rat-tail, lose de rat-tail. De ol' man come to de kyage an ax' John show him his finger. John had no rat-tail den, had to show him his finger, all 'ca'se of his sister. John poke his finger t'rough de kyage. Ol' man says, "Fat, fat, fat!" Unlock de do', take John out, kyarry him to de choppin'-block.

When he get John to de choppin'-block, start to put John head on de choppin'-block, John make a groan, says, "I'm a man f'om my fader."

Ol' man was sca'd den to kill John, so he tu'n John loose. He said, "Boy, I will sen' you out on my farm to min' my cattle."

John said, "All right, sah!"

So he sen' John out, an' he give John a gun an' two dawg. An' John name dese dawg Cut-de-T'roat, Suck-de-Blood.

Now, de ol' man said to his wife in de house, whey Mary wus now, "When dat boy come home to-day, I'll put pize [*poison*] in his victual, an' I'll kill um."

Man step out de do'. Mary sing,—

Eh! Broder Johnnie!
Olee man say
When you comin' home,
He sure to put pizen in your victuals,
An' he sure ter kill yer dead.

An' John understan' his sister. He sing,—

Eh! Sistuh Maree!
An' I un'erstan' you.

John come home, wouldn' eat. Nex' day, no, ol' man conclude to shoot him. "Ol' Lady," say, "I get dat boy. I'm goin' up to de gate wid er deer-skin on. I sure shoot him dead when he come home." Mary sing,—

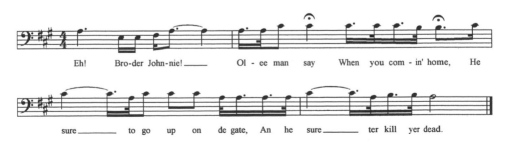

Eh! Broder Johnnie!
Olee man say
When you comin' home, he sure to go up on de gate,
An' he sure ter kill yer dead.

John walk to some road, an' when he comin' home, he missed de ol' man. De ol' man up on de gate in his deer-skin. John come up underneat' de bush an' shot de ol' man in de deer-skin dead. Say, "Sister Mary, I got him. I kill him. He's right in de road dere."

An' de ol' man wife fell suspicious den.

An' jus' befo' he [*she*] dead, he [*she*] call John an' Mary: "John an' Mary, come here!" Dey bof wen' to him. He [*her. She*] said, "See did prupe'ty? All dis prupe'ty belongs to yourn. But see dat well dere? If you sweep di't into dat well, a might beas' arise an' 'stroy you all."

So John min' de cows as usual, an' he leaves de homestud fo' his sister. 'E [*She*] take ca'. One day Mary 'member what de ol' lady say: "If you sweep di't into dat well, a mighty beas' arise an' 'stroy you all." "I goin' to sweep di't in de well." Go an' get de broom. John been in de fiel' den mindin' de cow.

So soon as Mary sweep de di't into de well, de beas' come up to Mary. Say, "Ain't you de sister of John?"

He [*She*] say, "Yes."

Say, "John have got two dawg; an' you adwise John to keep dem dawg home to-morrer, I won' do anyt'in' wid you."

John was a witch. He knowed right off dat his sister been done an' sweep di't in de well. He come home, an' he didn' said anyt'in' to his sister. So dat night his sister said to him, "John, when you gone in de mornin', mus' left Cut-de-T'roat an' Suck-de-Blood home wid me, 'cause me 'fraid to stay here." So John said to um [*her*], "Sister Mary, dis is de firs' trouble you eber bring me into. I don' wan' you to bring me into no mo' trouble; but, anyhow, I lef' de dawg home wid you."

So John take his gun an' his bow arrow, an' wen' an' min' his cow jus' de same. When John get out in de fiel' he fin' dat de lan' was a distan' off f'om his house. John saw de beas' come up to him. John say to de beas', "Ah, you a wise man!"

De beas' say to John, "You still wiser."

John say to de beas', "Beas', if you 'low me to go up on dis tree an' shoot my bow five time, an' if my dawg ain't come, I'm yer man."

So de beas' so sure he got John, he tol' John, "You can go up an' shoot 'em a hundred time."

But John never have but five arrow, you see, so he couldn' shoot a hund'ed time. Den John shoot de firs' time. Dis was John cry,—

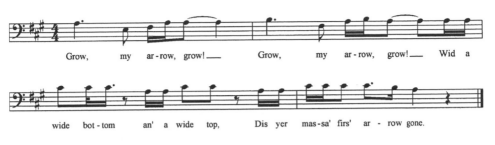

Grow, my a-row, grow!
Grow, my ar-row, grow!
Wid a wide bottom an' a wide top,
Dis yer massa's firs' ar-row gone.

Dat time Mary got de axe home, drivin' de stake down deeper an' deeper [*to fasten the dogs*]. Cut-de-T'roat jumpin'. John cry again:

Eh! Come, Cut-de-T'roat!
Eh! Come, Suck-de-Blood!
Wid a wide bottom an' a wide top,
Dis yer mass's secon' ar-row gone.

He had to sing to give 'em time.

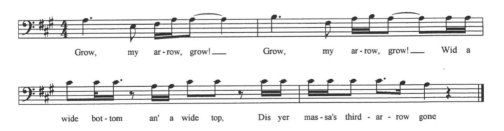

Grow, my ar-row, grow!
Grow, my ar-row, grow!
Wid a wide bottom an' a wide top,
Dis yer massah third arrow gone.

Cut-de-T'roat got loose, cut off Suck-de-Blood chain. One t'ousan' mile to go. Soon as his mossah got down to put his foot in de beas' mout', dey been dat distance to save de mossah life.

He said, "Cut his t'roat!" Nex' word, "Suck his blood!" Den John come off de tree, an' take his two dawg an' gone on home.

Said when he got home, "Sister Mary, dis is de secon' trouble you got me into. I leaf you. Take all de t'ings." Take his dawg an' gone.

Walk twenty mile. Meet up wid a sign: "Any man dat enter de city an' kill de mighty beas' would marry de king daughter." So de direction was on dat sign whey de king house was. De beas' had been done kill ten or twelve mans cou'tin' de king daughter. So John an' his dawg enter into de city an' make right fo' de king house.

An' when John get up on de step, put his firs' step, de beas' caught his laig. John cry, "Cut-his-T'roat, cut his throat!" De dawg cut his throat. John say, "Suck-his-Blood, suck his blood!" De dawg suck his blood.

John wen' into de house. Saw all de mans in de house. Had no pertection, glad when John come an' kill de beas'. John didn' know de king daughter; but de king daughter walk right to John, hug him an' kiss him, said, "Dis my husban'." Said, "Now, befo' we married, you got a sister, go get yer sister. Tell my fader hitch up de fas'es' horse he got in his stable."

An' so dey did, go de twenty mile, get back dat night. When John get back to de do' dat night, de weddin' was goin' on. Dese big man couldn' kill de beas', but dey could have de weddin'.

John get mad 'bout dat. John didn' go into de house. John sent his dawg into de house to clear way de house fo' him. De dawg take all dem big man an' t'row dem outdoors. Den he an' Mary went in. Den after dey married, John wife chose Mary for his [*her*] maid. She made up all dat bed, weddin' bed an' all dat. An' one of dose big men gib' Mary t'ousan' dollars to put somet'in' on his [*her*] broder's head. Nex' mornin' John was dead.

In dose days, not like to-day—dead to-day, an' wouldn' bury until to-morrow—bury de same day. Fam'ly all set up on de box [*coffin*], Mary an' king daughter. Oder people walk. To-day dey go in kyarridge.

John dawg wen' on; an' dey 'mos' get to de potter fiel', an' Cut-his-T'roat, he brave dawg, break de box open. When he bruk de box open, John rise an' stan' 'mongst de congregation, an' said to his sister, "Ah, Sister Mary! dis is de t'ird trouble you brought me to. Now I'm goin' leave you forever." John an' his two dawg fly away to heaven. Mary an' de king daughter an' all dem big man dey went to hell.

Parsons 1923b: 83–88. ATU 327–28/315/300, Motif B524.1.2. Told to Elsie Clews Parsons by Jack Brown of Beaufort, North Carolina, February 1919. Apparently Mr. Jack, as he was called, told the tale to Parsons, at least the first time, during a tale session that lasted from midnight till dawn as Parsons was getting a ride on an oyster boat to Savannah. This tale makes a neat contrast with the preceding tale, also about John and Mary and the dogs. Wonderful dogs are likewise a feature of ATU 300. Here they serve to splice that tale, about the hero rescuing the princess from a monster, onto the popular Sea Island tale complex ATU 327–28/315 (which I have dubbed Hansel and Gretel Escape by Calling the Wonderful Dogs; see tale 72, above).

This story is easier to understand if the reader reads it out loud. Even then, however, it is not clear what John means when he says he is "a man f'om" his father, nor why the wild man is frightened by this claim.

73. Rabbit Pretends He Sold His Wife

One time, you know, Br'er Rabbit had done something to the king. The king decide that he would kill Br'er Rabbit when he goes to bed. Br'er Rabbit had an idea the king would do something to him, so he studied what to do. He decided to put his wife in front of the bed, and he would sleep in the back room. When the king came that night, he hit Br'er Rabbit wife with an iron and killed her dead, and he went back home. Old Br'er Rabbit, so schemy, dressed his wife, put her into the buggy and went to town. He entered a store and bought a bottle of dope and send it to his wife by a white boy. The little boy took dope to the woman, but she didn't take it. The little boy hit the woman with the bottle because she didn't take it.

"Oh! You killed my wife! Give me a thousand dollars for my wife." The store keeper gave Br'er Rabbit the money, and Br'er Rabbit went back home. The king said to Br'er Rabbit, "Thought I killed you last night!" Br'er Rabbit said, "You killed my wife and I got a thousand dollars for her." The king went back home and killed his wife and went to the store to sell meat. The people found out that it was his wife, so they caught the king and sewed him up in a bag and threw him overboard. That was the last of the king.

Anonymous 1925: 220. ATU 1535, Motif K2152. This tale from St. Helena, South Carolina, was written down by a pupil at Penn School. The editor, presumably Ruth Benedict, who was editing the *Journal of American Folklore* at the time, or Elsie Clews Parsons, who wrote the next article in that issue of the *Journal*, and who published other school collections in the *Journal* and produced a collection of Sea Island tales, gives no further information about the storyteller. The bottle of dope is a bottled soft drink such as Royal Crown Cola or Nehi Orange.

This story is an interesting example of the way that the Br'er Rabbit cycle attracts to itself stories of European tricksters and clever lads. ATU 1535 is quite popular in U.S. tradition. Killing the dupe's wife occurs regularly in fuller variants of the tale, such as "Little Horny and Big Horny," in the next chapter. And the fuller tale, like the present tale, usually ends with the dupe being sewed in a sack and drowned.

74. B'er Rabbit, B'er Partridge, and the Cow

De rabbit an' partridge was goin' out stealin'. Come by a cow-lot. De rabbit said to de partridge, "Brother Partridge, here is our Christmas right hyere."

Partridge say, "What is it, B'er Rabbit?"

"Man, don't you see all dis fresh meat standin' in dis lot?" Said, "Le's kill one of this cows!"

So dey killed a cow, an' it come on sundown befo' dey got trough cleanin'. An' de rabbit see de sunset fixin' to go down' an' he said to de partridge, "B'er Partridge, le's get a piece of dat fire on!" He said, "Dat's my wife ower der, bu'nin' brush."

B'er Partridge say, "I think dat's de sun goin' down, B'er Rabbit."

He said, "No man, dat ain't no sun. Dat's my wife bu'nin' off my new groun'."

An' so Partridge he flew out fo' de settin' of de sun. An' whiles he was gone, B'er Rabbit give all de cow away to his sweetheart.

Partridge got tired flying fo' de sun, an' tu'ned around an' comin' back to B'er Rabbit. B'er Rabbit heard him comin'; an' B'er Rabbit say, "Fly up, B'er Partridge, in a hurry! De cow goin' in de groun'." He had stuck de cow's tail down in de groun'.

He said, "Hol' back on dis tail, B'er Partridge, 'fo' de cow get away!" An' Partridge pull back on de tail, as Buddy Rabbit tol' him. An' he pulled de tail out de groun.' B'er Rabbit said, "Dere, now, you done broke de tail off."

An' Partridge say, "What will we do, B'er Rabbit?"

Say, "I don know. You sure let all de cow get away."

Then B'er Partridge say, "Well, we'll diwide de tail up."

He said, "No, you can have de tail, B'er Partridge."

Said, "If you don' want none, B'er Rabbit, I'll be glad to get it."

An' he say, I sure don' want none, cause I got plenty meat what I get day befo' yesterday."

"I t'ank ye, t'ank ye, B'er Rabbit. T'ank ye, 'cause you ce'tainly done me a favor givin' me dis whole tail by myself."

Parsons 1923b: 32–33. ATU 100 and Motif J1806. Told to Else Clews Parsons, in February 1919, by John Crawford, about thirty, born in Lancaster, South Carolina, and at the time of the telling a cook for a soldiers' club in Beaufort, South Carolina.

Parsons mentions the obstacles she, as white and female, met while collecting in the Sea Islands.

James Murray, in whose cabin on Hilton Head I had been enjoying a very good and fruitful time, told me that, had I staid on in the house of the white man where

I first suggested story-telling, he would have told me no tales "fo' no money, not fo' a week." And he added . . . "We wouldn' tell riddle befo' dem, not even if we was a servan' in deir house." (xiv)

As for obscene tales, Jack Brown told her, "Oh, you want dem kin' o' tales too! I could tell you a heap o' dem tales, but I blush fo' you" (xx). Nevertheless, he did agree to tell two rather mild tales, each about a husband finding and chasing away the lover (or lovers) his wife is hiding in the house. But "James Murray said that he knew twenty-five or thirty 'men's tales'; 'but,' he added, and too firmly for challenge, 'I wouldn' go t'rough wid 'em'" (xx). The greatest problem of all, she says, was that storytellers felt that they should narrate in standard English, sacrificing the "vigorous and expressive" Gullah in which they customarily told the tales: "The temptation to try to use school-taught language in telling tales to a white is strong" (xx).

Finally, of the difficulties of transferring a tale to print, Parsons writes:

The characteristic emphasis of Negro tales, the drawl, and the tricks of speeding up, are difficult to indicate on paper. Italics and exclamation-points are but feeble indicators; and how can one express by printers' signs the significance of what is *not* said—a significance conveyed by manner or by quietness of intonation, of which a good story-teller is past master. It is almost as difficult to convey the values of the curt conclusion which is also characteristic of artistic Negro narration—unless the reader can be counted on. (xx–xxi)

CHAPTER 12

THE SOUTHERN MOUNTAINS I

From the Blue Ridge to the Ozarks

The amount of story material from the southern mountains is staggering. Archives in the South and throughout the country—for collectors come in and then carry material back to home institutions—overflow with tapes of wonderful tales and taletellers. In the early 1930s Ralph Steele Boggs, then at the University of North Carolina, collected North Carolina tales. At the same time Vance Randolph was collecting in the Ozarks. Then the WPA brought Richard Chase, who published *The Jack Tales* (1943) and *Grandfather Tales* (1948) (see chapter 13). The stream has continued unabated. In the 1950s Vance Randolph's Ozark books began to appear. Marie Campbell published *Tales from Cloud Walking Country* (1958) at about the same time. Leonard Roberts published *South from Hell-fer-Sartin* (1955), a representative collection of Kentucky tales, and, somewhat later, *Sang Branch Settlers* (1974), a monumental collection of stories and songs from the Couch family. And more recently came Charles Perdue's *Outwitting the Devil* (1987) and my own anthology *Jack in Two Worlds* (1994). Meanwhile collections of tales from Donald Davis (1992) and from Jackie Torrence (1998) have also appeared. And the National Storytelling Center in Jonesborough, Tennessee, has been publishing anthologies with a generous sampling of southern mountain tales (e.g., Smith 1988).

The southern mountains include not only the Blue Ridge, the Cumberland plateau, and adjacent areas of the southern Appalachians, but also the

Ozarks of Arkansas and Missouri (and Illinois), largely settled by outmigrants from Appalachia. In all these regions a somewhat homogeneous population of Scotch-Irish and Germans, with an admixture of English and French, practiced subsistence farming, established small towns, moonshined and bootlegged, argued Calvinist, Arminian, and Holiness theology, and worked for the outside lumbering and mining interests that also brought in pockets of southern- and eastern-European immigrants.

Though the outside world and its products was more accessible to southern mountain communities than we tend to realize, the inhabitants often preferred to remain generation after generation in the same place, creating a sense of stability and a foundation for rich traditional culture. Before the coming of electricity in the 1930s, 1940s, 1950s, and even the 1960s, visiting one another or gathering in stores or outside church was the most generally available form of recreation. And telling stories was the favorite form of conversation. The old, old stories could fill long hours of work or winter evenings, or soothe wakeful children. Transformed into legends or jokes, they passed from person to person in the store, outside the church, or at the crossroad.

Obviously it is hard to choose a sampling from such a rich tradition. The present chapter includes stories from the southeastern Appalachian states of Kentucky and North Carolina, from West Virginia, and from the Ozarks. All are stories widely popular in the region, though some of the particular versions are distinctive.

75. Rawhead and Bloodybones

Once upon a time there was a woman and she'd married a man that had a daughter, and she had a daughter. Her daughter was real ugly, hateful, and everything that she shouldn't have been. And his daughter was real beautiful, sweet, kind and nice, and everyone loved her. But everyone hated the other woman's daughter and she was jealous. So she went to a witch, a friend witch of hers, and asked her what to do to get rid of this real pretty girl.

So she said, "I have an idea." Said, "You tell your daughter to get in the bed and tell the other girl that your daughter won't live unless that she goes after a bottle of water for her."

So she said, "Well, then what shall I do?"

She said, "Then just give her some little old food and I'll take care of the rest of it."

But the woman said, "I'm not pleased." Says, "I wanna know what you're going to do."

She says, "Well," said, "I'm going to have a gang of horses run over her." And says, "If she gets by that some way, I will have a gate that every time it pinches, its poisonous fangs will kill her."

She said, "Well," said, "all right."

So she went back home and she told her daughter that when her step-daughter came in from working, out getting water, for her to lay down in the bed and to pretend like she was sick. So she did, and she laid down and begin to groan.

She says, "Oh, I don't think I'll live."

So the other daughter came in and says, "What's the matter?"

And she says, "Nothing can help me except that you go to the end of the world to get me a bottle of water."

She said, "Well then, I'll do that." 'Cause she was kind and good and she wanted to help everybody.

So she got a bottle and got some cornbread and some water and started out. She sit down to eat her lunch and they's an old grey-bearded man came up. He had real long beard 'n was real short and looked like a elf—almost.

And she says, "What do you want, sir?"

And he said, "I'd like to eat dinner with you."

And she said, "All right." So she divided her food with him.

He said, "Thank you for your kindness, and for being so good to me I'll give you this stick." And said, "When you go a little piece longer," said, "you'll meet a gang of horses. And you shake this stick at 'em and say, 'Down, horses, down,' and they won't bother you."

She said, "All right." So she came a little ways longer and she saw a gang of horses and they were coming at her. She shook the stick and she said, "Down, horses, down," and they disappeared. She sit down to eat her supper—it was dark—and this old grey-bearded man came up again. She said, "Well, what, you want some dinner this time?"

And he said, "Yes." So she gave him some. And he says, "Now," says, "use that same stick you've got to the gate." Says, "You'll come to a gate by the well at the end of the world. And," said, "when you do, you shake your stick at the gate and say, 'Don't pinch me,' and it won't pinch you."

So she went on. And she came to this gate, and she says, "Don't pinch me, gate," and it didn't pinch her. She went on through and she let her bucket—the open-mouthed bottle, more like—let it down into the well and she drew up something and it looked like a skull. And it was bloody and it had bones on it. It was the Rawhead and Bloodybones. And she said, "What do you want?"

And it said, "Want you to wash me and dry me and lay me down easy."

So she washed it and dried it and laid it down easy. Then she drew up another one, and another one and another one, and a fourth one, and they all wanted her to wash them and dry them and lay them down easy. And not only did she do that, but she laid them down in the sun where they could take a sun-bath. So then she got her water and started home. And after she got out the gate the first Rawhead and Bloodybones says, "She's pretty," and said, "I wish that she'd be twice as pretty when she got home."

Another one said, "Well, she smelt good and I wish she'd smell twice as good when she got home."

And another one said, "Well," said, "she was kind and good and sweet and everybody loved her, and I wish everybody'd love her twice as much when she got home."

And the other one said, "Well," said, "I wish when she got home that first time she combed her hair that a whole lot of gold would fall out."

And so when she came to the streets in her home town everybody smelled something so good, and they thought that a florist shop must be moving in or something, because everything was smelling so good. And they looked out the window and there she came down the street and they couldn't hardly look at her she was so pretty. And the kindness just glowed out all over her. When she got home her stepmother was surprised to see her—very much surprised—and she said, "What are you doing home?"

And she said, "Well, I brought this water," and she brought the water and gave it to the girl, and she drank it and got up and started running around. And she said, "I'm glad I made you well, little sister."

And she said, "Oh, go off and shut up."

And then her mother says, "I'm surprised to see you back." Said, "I wished you hadn't come back. You just bring hatefulness into this house every time you come."

And she said, "Well, my head feels like it's itching." Said, "Will you please let me comb it in your lap?"

She said, "No, I wouldn't let you comb your head in my lap. What do you think I am, a garbage pail or something?"

And she said, "Well then, I'll comb it in my own lap." And she went off in the corner and begin to comb her hair, and when she combed it gold fell out.

And her stepmother said, "Oh, honey, come here. I'll let you comb your head in my lap."

And she said, "No," said, "I don't want you to now. I can comb it by myself." So she combed all the gold out.

And the stepmother was real angry at the witch. She thought that her own daughter could go just as soon as her stepdaughter could. So she sent her daughter off with a big fine meal and everything. And she came to this tree where this other girl set down and ate her lunch. And this man poked his head around the tree and said, "May I eat lunch with you?"

And she said, "No, I don't want your old dirty beard dragging in my good food." Said, "You just go off and hush up. I ain't gonna let you eat with me."

He said, "Well, all right."

So she came to these horses and these horses tromped on her—she was tough, and didn't hurt her much. But they weren't gonna hit her as hard as they were this other girl, though. So she went on by and she came to this gate and it pinched her, and hurt her—it wasn't poison then, though. And she came on in and saw Rawhead and Bloodybones. I mean, she drew them up, and the first one she drew up, it said, "Wash me and dry me and lay me down easy."

And she said, "What do you think I am, your maidservant? I ain't gonna do nothing to you. I don't want to put my hands on you. Get out of my water bucket."

And it said, "All right," and it crawled off in the sun and she drew up another and she said, "I told you to get out of my water bucket and hush. I don't like you. Go off like the other one did."

And so it did. And another one, and another one, and she talked sassy talk to them and was mean to them. And she got her water and started home. And after she got through the gate the first Rawhead and Bloodybones says, "She was ugly, and I wish when she got home she'd be twice as ugly."

And the other said, "Well, she smelt bad, and I wish when she got home she'd smell twice as bad."

And the other one said, "Well, she was mean and hateful, and you could tell she didn't get along good in this world. I hope she gets along twice as bad."

And the other one said, "Well, I hope when she gets home that snakes and frogs fall out of her hair."

And so she got on home. She was going through the streets with a bottle of water and everybody smelled something terrible, and they opened their windows, and there was that—ooh—a horrible looking monster walking through the street and just had meanness glowing out all over her. And she looked like, uh, something from somewhere else that wasn't in this world. She got home and her mother said, "Gee!" says, "You've changed a lot since I saw you last." Said, "You look prettier than you were." She said, "Come here and let me comb your hair."

She started combing her hair and all the snakes and frogs and everything that was in the country started coming out of her hair. And they all came out and it ran her and her daughter off. And her stepdaughter lived happy ever after, there with her money.

Muncy 1949. ATU 480D; c.f. ATU 551. The storyteller, Jane Muncy, was only eleven years old when Leonard Roberts visited the Hayden School in Leslie County, Kentucky, in 1949. A lively storyteller with a fine choice of words and images, she told Roberts at least five stories. She learned stories from her grandmother, with whom she lived, and from other relatives. We have transcribed the tale anew from the original recording, so the reader can compare this transcription with Roberts's own excellent transcription printed in *South from Hell-fer-Sartin* (1955: 54–58).

In the year 2000, more than fifty years after Muncy told this story, folklorist Carl Lindahl succeeded in locating her and her husband, Bob Fugate. They had moved from eastern Kentucky and lived in Melbourne, Florida. Jane Muncy Fugate told Lindahl about the strong woman, her grandmother, who took over raising her when her divorced father enlisted in the army in World War II. She explained how important the stories were to her, and confided that she believed they were central to her healing when the traumatic breakup of her parents' marriage, followed by her father's enlistment in the army, left her essentially an orphan. Mrs. Fugate went on to become a social worker and to rely on the tales as an important resource in working with psychologically wounded children and adults. Lindahl collected a number of tales from Mrs. Fugate and from one of her aunts, Glen Muncy Anderson. Discussion of Jane Muncy Fugate and her family as storytellers is one of the centerpieces of Lindahl's book *Perspectives on the Jack Tale and Other North American Märchen* (2001). There he includes versions of "Rawhead and Bloody Bones" told by the adult Mrs. Fugate and by her Aunt Glen. In his collection *American Folktales from the Collections of the Library of Congress* he devotes a whole chapter to her stories. He also includes one of her aunt's stories in a chapter of stories told for children. Lindahl and Fugate's account of the significance of tales in one child's life is one of the most detailed (and most moving) discussions in American folklore studies of folktale function and context (Lindahl 2004: 279–86).

The story as here told seems to be Scottish in origin, somewhat reminiscent of the version in Robert Chambers's *Popular Rhymes of Scotland* (1870: 105 ff). A very similar version occurs in the manuscript of Emeline Brightman Russell, discussed in chapter 9, but each of the inhabitants of the well is identified only as "a little thing" (Dobie 1927: 42–45). I found no reference in either Thompson's Motif Index or in the Aarne-Thompson-Uther classification to versions involving a search for water and kindness to disembodied heads. The quest for the water may be borrowed from ATU 551, The Water of Life. And Katherine Briggs says that the motif of heads in a well "occurs both in English and Celtic folk-tales" (Part A, vol. 1: 520).

76. Three Drops of Blood

One time there was a young man and a young woman who lived in the mountains and they fell in love and they got married. And they built a log house and they lived way back in the mountains. And they had a daughter, and then they had another daughter, and then they had another daughter, so they had three daughters. And they loved the daughters. The daddy especially, though, loved the youngest one—actually better than he loved the rest of them.

And the whole story starts when one day in the springtime he decides he's gonna go to town. And it's one of the first times in the springtime that he's gone to town. The gardens are planted and the crops are kinda started and as he leaves to go to town he goes to his oldest daughter and says, "Do you want me to bring you anything?"

And she says, "Well, I do. I want you to bring me a dress that's green."

He says, "What color green?"

She said, "I want it to be the color of every tree in the forest once the frost stops coming in the springtime."

So he said, "Okay, okay."

Then he goes to the next-to-the-oldest daughter, the middle daughter and he says, "Do you want me to bring you anything?"

She says, "Yes, I want you to bring me a dress, too."

"Well, what color do you want?"

"Well, I want it to be the color of every tree in the forest after the frost starts coming in the fall."

So he says, "Okay, okay."

So he goes to the youngest daughter—she's the one he really loves the most. So he says, "Well, do you want me to bring you anything?"

And she says, "Oh no. I don't want you to bring me anything. I just want you to come home safely. But," she says, "you know how I like flowers."

So he takes off and he goes to town. Well, he goes to town, he does all his business and he does all his shopping around. And he finds the dresses, he actually finds one that's the color of all the trees after the frost stops coming in the spring and he finds another one the color of all the trees after the frost starts coming in the fall. And on his way home he's riding his horse and as he goes through a clearing he sees this big rose bush that's covered with white roses. And so he thinks about his youngest daughter whom he didn't get anything for, and her saying how she liked flowers. So he decides he'll go over and he'll pick her a big armload of white roses—they're big, long stem, beautiful white roses. So he goes over to the bush and he starts to break off a rose and he hears a voice come out of the woods behind him. And the voice says, "You break that and I'll break you."

And he looks all around and he can't see anything. And he turns around and he starts to break it again. And he hears this voice that says, "You break that and I'll break you."

And he looks all around, and he calls and says, "Is anybody there?"

And this voice comes back—he can't see anybody, he can't tell if they're hiding behind a tree, if hiding in some bushes or what—but a voice comes back and says, "That's mine, don't break it."

And he says, "Well, I just wanted to take some home to my daughter. She likes flowers."

And the voice says, "You can take some, but you have to pay me the first thing that comes out to meet you when you go home."

Well, the man thought about it a little bit and he thought, "Okay. I have this old dog up at my house and every time I go home, it comes running out barking, out to the road, barking out to the gate. I don't care about that ole dog anymore." And so he says, "Okay, that's a deal. If I can have all the roses I want, you can have the first thing that comes out to meet me when I go home."

So he breaks a big arm of roses. And he goes home on his horse. As he gets up there his dog is asleep under the porch, and his youngest daughter is looking for him, to see if he gets home safe. And so here she comes running out to the gate. And he starts saying, "Go back." And he starts whistling for the dog, and she keeps coming.

And all of a sudden she says, "Well, why did you want me to go back?"

And he said, "Oh, never mind, never mind. Don't worry about, don't worry about it."

So they go in the house. He gives the dress to the oldest daughter. He gives the other dress to the middle daughter. And he gives all the roses to the youngest daughter, but he doesn't seem very happy.

Well, that night after supper he hears a big noise out by the gate, it's just an awful noise. And he goes out there to see what it is and from behind some hedge bushes he hears a voice saying, "Time to get paid."

And he says, "Go away. Go away. Go away. Get out of here. I'm gonna send the dog out on you."

Well, he opens the gate and he sends the dog out and the dog goes, "Rowl, rowl, rowl, rowl." And never comes back.

"Time to get paid."

Well, he goes back in the house and he tells them what happened, that night. And the two oldest daughters say, "Oh, we're not scared of anything, we're gonna go out there and see what it is and run it off."

So they go out to the gate, they open the gate and they come screaming back. They didn't even see it, but it started making such an awful noise they come screaming back.

So the youngest daughter says, "Well, you made a deal. You made a promise. You promised and you have to keep it. I'll have to go." So she walks out of the house. Goes down and she goes out the front gate. And when she disappears behind the hedge, she's gone.

Well, as it turns out when she got behind that hedge, she saw the biggest white bear she had ever seen before. And she started to run from it, but it said, "Don't run, get on my back."

She was scared to death, but it kept saying, "Get on my back." And she went over and she got on the white bear's back. Well, as soon as she did, it started walking through the woods, just carrying her away. Taking her away from her parents' house that she would never, ever see again. And she went through the woods. They went on and on and on and on. And in a little while they were passing through a clearing. And in that clearing there was a big wide rose bush covered with roses. And as the bear passed that rose bush, she reached out to try to pick off one last rose and the thorn caught her finger. And her finger bled three drops of blood that landed on the white bear's back.

Well, the white bear took her on through the woods, till he came to a house. And took her right up, and in the front door of the house. And as soon as they got inside the house, he turned around and stood up. And just then the sun went down, and as the bear stood up on his back legs, he turned into a man. She said, "Who are you?"

And he said, "My name is White Bear Whittington. I've had a terrible curse put on me. And I have to be a bear."

She says, "You mean you have to be bear in the day time?"

He says, "Well, not necessarily the day time. I have to be a bear half the time. I can either be a bear at night and I can be a man in the day time or I can be a man at night and I can be a bear in the day time. Now you decide which you'd rather have, because you're gonna live here with me and you're gonna be my wife." He said, "You'll probably want me to be a man day time. That way I can go with you places, and we can go everywhere, and we can do things, and we can visit back at your house, and we can—and everybody can see us. And then at night you can go to bed and I can turn into a bear and I'll curl up and sleep on the floor. Or if you would want me to be, I could be a bear in the day time and then at night I could be a man and I could sleep with you."

And she looks at him one time, and she says, "I'd rather have you be a bear in the day time and a man at night."

So that makes him kinda happy. So they live at that house and they become, I guess like husband and wife, though I never heard any story about 'em getting married or anything like that, but they lived there. He's a bear in the day. He's a man at night. And as time passes they have one baby. They have another baby. They have another baby. And she's getting homesick for her mother and daddy. Not really homesick for them, but she wants them to know that she's okay because, as far as they know, she's just dead.

So she starts saying to White Bear Whittington, "I want to go home and see my mother and daddy, so they'll know I'm alive. I want to see my sisters and see if they've grown up."

He says, "You can't go. You can't go. Cause if you go I'll have a curse put on me that's worse than ever."

"Oh, please let me go. Please let me."

"You can't go."

Finally he says, "Okay, we can go there, but they can't see me. And you can't tell them about me. About being a bear and a man. And you can't tell them my name. You can tell them everything else, but you can't tell them any of that."

So she fixes the babies up and so that she can carry all of 'em. And she gets on his back, and he carries her all the way up to the gate and the house where she remembered living when she was growing up. He waits outside behind the hedge.

She goes walking now with three babies. And there her mother and daddy and her sisters, and they have a big ole fit and jump around. And they say, "Tell us everything. Tell us everything. Oh, we're glad you're back."

She says, "I'm just here for a visit for like a little while, and I can't tell you very much."

"Well, tell us where did you go?"

"I can't tell you really where I went."

"Well, tell us where these babies . . ."

"Well, see, I . . . I have a husband now."

"What's his name? What's his name?"

"I can't tell you his name."

"What do you mean? You're married to somebody and you have three babies and you don't know his name?"

"I know his name, but I can't tell you. I can't tell you any . . ."

The questions just went on and on and on and on and on. And she looked at her daddy and he looked so sad. And finally she decided, "Well, I really can't tell them where I live or how to get there or anything, but I, I think I just have to just whisper my husband's name to my daddy."

So she leans over and she says, "Don't tell anybody, but I'll tell you his name. His name is White Bear Whittington." And when she says, "White Bear Whittington," she's looking past her father out the window of the house, and she sees White Bear Whittington, who is now a man. And he's walking over the top of the hill away from the house where she is, and sees three drops of blood on his white shirt on his back.

Well, she leaves her babies there and she says, "I've gotta go. I've gotta go. You have to keep the babies. Something terrible's happened."

And she tears out of the door and she starts running after him. When she gets to the top of that hill, she sees him just disappearing across the next hill. And she runs as fast as she can, as hard as she can. When she gets to the top of that hill, he's just disappearing into the woods on the mountain side. When she disappears into the woods, she sees him just going across the top. She follows him for days. She can never get any closer. Every time she almost loses the way, there's some kind of little sign to show her which way to go. There may be a fork in the trail and she looks and looks and looks. And down one fork there may be a drop of blood on the ground. Or she looks and looks and looks and there's something that's broken off a limb, or a track. But she can't catch him, and she goes on until she is totally, totally exhausted.

Well, about that time she came to a little house. And she decided that maybe these people have seen White Bear, and they know what happened to him. And she goes up and knocks on the door. And this ole lady comes to the door who looks like she's about two hundred years old. Her nose is about three feet long. And she takes her inside because she looks real pitiful, and she tells her whole story to that ole lady.

And the ole lady says, "Well, you better stay here and rest up."

"No. He'll get away."

"No. He won't get away. He won't get away. I promise he won't get away. Stay here and rest up. He won't get any farther away than he is now."

So she stays there and she works for that ole lady. And she works there for several days. Well, finally she starts saying, "Well, I better go on and try to find my husband. I better go try to find White Bear."

And the ole lady says, "Well, I need to give you something that will help take care of y', and to do that you have to stay here and work just three more days."

She says, "Okay. I'll stay and work three more days. Tell me what to do and how to help you."

Well, all day long one day, they shear sheep. They were shearing sheep the whole day long. And they bring all the wool in that night. And they get ready. The next day they're gonna card and start spinning it. And at the end of that night that ole lady gave her one little gold nut, about the size of an acorn. And she said, "Now keep this, this will help you out."

Well, the next day they started working again, and they worked all day carding the wool and then spinning it. They'd card the wool and spin, they'd card and spin all day long. And at the end of that night when they got ready to go to bed she gives her one more little gold nut. It's about as big as a hickory nut. And she says, "Keep that, it's the second one: it might help you out if you need it."

Well, the next day they started weaving cloth and they weave cloth all day long. And that night when they got ready to go to bed, the ole lady give her a gold nut. It's about as big as a walnut. She says, "Now take these with you, use them very carefully. Use them one at a time. You can trade them, you can do all kinds of things with them, you can sell them. But keep them till you're really sure you really, really need them. And they'll help you out."

Well, she starts off again with the three gold nuts. And almost as soon as she leaves, going across the top of the next hill she sees the back of White Bear Whittington with those drops of blood on his shirt. And she follows faster and faster and faster.

In about three days, she's coming over the top of a hill and down below there's a river where women are washing clothes. And out in that river standing up to his waist in the water, is White Bear Whittington. And he's pulling off his shirt. She goes running down there and he's talking to all the women who are washing their clothes. And he says, "I've lost my wife, I've lost my wife and I can't remember what she looks like, but if she would wash my shirt the blood would come out."

Well, all the women look at him and he's a real nice looking guy. And they come up and they think, "Oh, I could wash the blood out and then he'll think I'm his wife. Oh, boy, this'll be pretty good." So they're lined up in a row and they're all taking turns trying to wash his shirt. And they beat on it and they hit it on the rock and they rub sand on it, but the drops of blood just get a little bigger, little bigger, little bigger.

Finally, she gets down there in line. She's gonna take her turn because she knows it'll work and everything will be okay. She's waiting in line, she's waiting line, and she smells something awful. And she looks around and it's the bad breath of this big ole ugly woman, who's waiting in line behind her. And she thinks, "I'm glad I'm in front of her, cause if she got up there she might run off with White Bear Whittington, and I might not never see him again.

Well, she got up there, and that ole woman kept punching her, a-saying, "You can't wash anything. You can't wash his shirt. You wait till I get a hold of him. I'll do it right and I'll take him and he'll be my husband."

Well, they got closer and closer and finally it's her turn. She takes White Bear Whittington's shirt, and she just rinses it through the water.

It comes out of the water completely clean.

But that ole bad breath woman sees it coming out clean. And she grabs it out of her hands and holds it up and waves it around and says, "Look, I did it. I did it. I got it clean. I got it clean."

And right then White Bear Whittington goes off. She's so big and so strong she picks him up and carries him just like he's a baby. And she carries him off up the hill, and they disappear in a house together.

Well, they go up there and she lives with White Bear Whittington, the ole woman, the ugly one with the bad breath and everything lives with him. Her daddy lives, too. And he's kinda glad somebody else is around cause she's kinda un—, unpleasant to be around with.

And, so his real wife goes up there and meets her. And she says, "I know that man you have in there is really nice looking. Ah, I'd really like to spend the night with him."

Well, the ole woman says, "Well, how much could you pay me?" Like she'd just let anybody spend the night with him, if she'd pay her enough.

She said, "Well, I don't have any money."

And she says, "Well, you must have something."

"Oh." Then she remembers she has the gold nuts. And she reaches in her pocket and she pulls out the first gold nut. And she says, "I will give you this, if you will let me spend one night with your man."

The ole lady says, "Ha, whadda I want that for?" She kinda smacks it out of her hand and when that gold nut that's like a acorn hits the floor on the front porch, it pops open and gold thread comes out. Thread, wool-looking thread, that's real gold. And she starts pulling the thread out. And more comes out. And more comes out. And no matter how much she pulls out, it keeps coming. And the ole woman says, "I got to have that."

So she says, "Okay. You can keep it, if I can spend the night with your man."

Well, on the way to the night, that ugly ole woman mixed up White Bear Whittington this sleepy drink. So she gave him a terrible, terrible sleepy drink. And she went in there that night. The real wife did. And he's so asleep, she can't wake him up, no matter what she tries. She tries everything. She can't wake him up. And she keeps singing;

> Three drops of blood I've shed for thee.
> Three little babes I've borne for thee.
> Mountains I've crossed to come for thee.
> The oceans I've swam to come find thee.
> White Bear Whittington, turn to me.

And he stays asleep all night long.

Well, the next day she doesn't know what to do. Doesn't know what to do. So she goes back up there and she talks to the ole woman again. And she says, "I need to spend one more night with your man."

The ole woman says, "Well, what've you got to give me?"

She reaches in and she pulls out the next gold nut that's about as big as a hickory nut. She says, "I can give you this."

The ole woman says, "I've already got all the gold I want. What would I want with that?" And she smacks it out of her hand and when that gold nut hits the porch floor, it pops open and out pops a gold spinning wheel. And it's spinning and as it does all on it's own it starts to pick up the gold thread that come out of the other gold nut, the gold wool, and it start spinning it into real gold thread. And the ole woman says, "Oh, I gotta have that."

So she says, "Okay, you can have it, if I can spend one night with your man."

Well, she goes in there later on, and he's been given another sleepy drink. And all night long she says,

> White Bear Whittington,
> White Bear Whittington, turn to me.
> Three drops of blood I've shed for thee.
> Three little babes I've borne for thee.
> Oceans I've swam to come to thee.
> Mountains I've climbed in search of thee.
> White Bear Whittington, turn to me.

All night long he stays asleep. But all that night she shakes him so much, and she beats him around so much that when he wakes up the next morning he kinda feels like he hadn't had much sleep. And his clothes are kinda half off and covers half off the bed and his bed's all messed up and he feels real sore. And he thinks, "Well, something's been going on in the night around here. I been sleeping really well, I been missing all of it. I'm gonna have to try to stay awake tonight. See what I'm missing."

Well, that day she goes to see the ole woman and she says, "I need to spend the night with your man. I really need to spend the night with him one more time."

And the ole lady says, "Well, what, what have you got to give me?"

"Oh, I've got something else." She reaches in and she pulls the gold walnut out of her pocket. She says, "I've got this. This is the last thing I have."

And the ole woman says, "Why would I want that?" She smacks it out of her hand. And the gold walnut hits the floor, and it pops open, and out pops a whole loom that's golden. And it picks up the thread that the golden spinning wheel was spinning out of the golden wool that came out of the first nut. And all on its own, it starts weaving golden cloth. And the ole woman says, "Oh, I gotta have that."

She says, "Okay, you can have it, if I can really spend one more night with your man."

Well, that afternoon she fixed White Bear Whittington, the ole ugly woman fixed up White Bear Whittington this sleepy drink. And she gave it to him. And he thought, "Now I been sleeping really well and I think I been missing something cause I kinda wake up kinda sore and with my clothes all messed up and all the cover off the bed." So, she turned her back, he poured that sleepy drink down through a knot hole in the floor.

That night when it's time to go to sleep he acted like he's asleep. Well, his real wife came up there and she went in. She got over to him and she says,

> Ohhhh, Ohhhh three drops of blood I've shed for thee.
> Three little babes I've borne for thee.
> Mountains I've crossed to come to thee.
> Oceans I've swam in search of thee.
> White Bear—

As soon as she says his name he wakes up. And he recognizes her. And they spend the rest of the night in there together.

Well, the next morning the ole lady comes back up and tries to get in, but when she does the door is locked. And they don't come out of there for a loooong time. Well, while they're in there, 'member I said her daddy lives up there. Well, he hadn't been in there. She goes in there and she got her daddy. And she said, "They got me locked out, my man's in there and they got me locked out. I want him back. I want him back."

So the daddy says, "Well, let me go up there and see what's going on." So the daddy goes up to the door and he knocks on the door. White Bear Whittington looks out and he sees the ole man. He says, "Whadda you want?"

The ole man says, "You gotta come out. You gotta come out. My daughter's your wife or actually she's your ole woman. And you gotta come out again."

He says, "I'm not gonna come out. I'm not gonna . . ."

"You gotta come out. You gotta come outta here."

Says, "I'm not gonna come out."

Says, "Why?"

He says, "Well, I can't. Well, let me tell you a story. Let me tell you a story. Once upon a time there was a man who had a golden chest that had in it everything that was valuable to him in all the world. And he loved it very much, but one day he lost the key. And he searched and searched and searched and he found another key. It was made out of iron, and it worked, but it didn't work as well at all. But later he found the real golden key again. Now which key do you think he should keep?"

The ugly ole woman's father said, "He should keep the golden key. You keep her. This ole woman that you've been with in here is my daughter, and she's bad enough for me to be around. I hate for you to be around her. I'll go get her busy and y'all sneak outta here and run away."

So he went back down there. While he was talking to ugly woman, who was his daughter, the real wife of White Bear Whittington slipped out the door. She got on his back. They ran all the way. And you know what? They got home that night. He'd been a man all day. And he stayed a man at night. And he's a man again the next morning. And he's a man again the next night. And so, since he was a man all the time now, it was safe to go back up there to visit at her house. And they went back up where she grew up and they got the three little babies back and they took 'em home. And she and White Bear Whittington lived there happily as far as I know from then right down until now.

Davis 1996. ATU 425A. Recorded by Davis for the editor, May 29, 1996. Apparently Davis was alone, speaking into the tape recorder. Davis's family always called this story "Three Drops of Blood," though in the southern mountains variants like the present one are more commonly called "White Bear Whittington." There are also other versions in which the enchanted prince is a dog, a toad-frog, or a cat. At the end of the recording Davis indicates that his family tradition allowed unusual room for alternate motifs when telling this story:

> That's all I can remember about the story of White Bear Whittington. I'm trying to remember if there's anything that came back to me in the process of telling it. I know that sometimes the way the gold nuts would work would be a little different. Um, sometimes instead of the gold wool coming out of the first nut, a hairbrush or comb would pop out of it. And if you picked the comb up and combed your own hair with it, you would comb strands of golden hair out of your own hair, I remember that sometimes. I don't think that was all the time, but sometimes being in that. Sometimes the dress colors that the first girls ask for would be different. One of them might ask for a dress a color of all the fish in the sea. Um, then the other one would do one better, she would ask for a dress the color of all the flowers that bloom in the fields. So any way that the dress colors could be made up differently was sometimes different about the story. The thing that I never really thought about, hearing as a child, was that woman never had a name, in the whole story. The only person that had a name in the whole story was White Bear Whittington. It was clearly the story about him. And the thing that I could never quite follow, listening to it as a little child, was all the business at the end about how it ends up with the golden trunk and the key and all that stuff. Later I figured all that part out. But, um, um as a child it never seemed to me like it quite ended. It was not a very child-like ending on the end. It was more an adult kind of ending. But everything came out fine, and, uh, I just loved the mystery of it, the drops of blood, uh, the bear that turned back and forth. So, uh, that's White Bear Whittington, um, all of it, and about as well as I can remember it.

In an earlier conversation Davis told me that yet another family variation required the heroine to weave dresses (or fabric?) in wonderful colors to bribe her way into her sleeping husband's room. But she must weave on an invisible loom that she can see only by looking into a mirror. The colors of the dresses at the beginning of the story and in this alternate version recall Jane Gentry's version of "Catskin" in which the heroine shows up at the ball on three nights wearing, successively, dresses the color of all the clouds in the sky, the color of all the birds in the air, and the color of all the fish in the sea. (On Jane Gentry, see next chapter.)

77. Little Horny and Big Horny

Well, there was two men, one was named Little Horny, and Big Horny. Well, Little Horny, he had an ole pore horse: hit just looked like it couldn't make it atall. Well, Big Horny, he had a big fine team and, uh, Little Horny, he went over and borrowed Big Horny's fine team to plow with.

Well, Big Horny, he come down the road and Little Horny's saying, "Git up, all three of my big fine hosses. Git up, all three of my big fine hosses."

Big Horny said, "Now, Little Horny," said, "looky here." Said, "If you're saying that as I come back up the road," said, "I'll kill your horse," says.

Well, he went on.

Well, he come back and Little Horny seed him a-coming and said, "Git up, all three of my big fine hosses. Git up, all three of my big fine hosses."

Well, Big Horny said, "I told you, didn't I?"

Well, he just hauled down and he killed Little Horny's hoss. He didn't have none at all.

Well, Little Horny, he skinned him out and dried his hide and took it uptown to sell. And he went into a woman's house and he said, "Uh, lady," said, "can I stay all night here at night?" Said, "I've got an ole news-teller here and," said, "I can't hardly make it with it and," said, "could I stay overnight?"

And she said, "Yes," said, "you may stay all night. You just take your news-teller and go on upstairs."

Well, he took it and went on upstairs and, well, her man come in. Little Horny, he's a-laying watching through a knothole everthing she done.

So when her man come in she said to him, said, "Uh, honey," said, "they's a man upstairs." Said, "He's got a news-teller for sale." Said, "Make him come down and let's hear it talk some."

Well, he said to him, said, "Come on down and make that thing talk." Said, "We—we wanna hear it talk some." Said, "We may buy it."

"No," he said, "I feel tard and bad. I don't feel like it."

"Oh," he said, "come on down." Said, "We wanna hear it."

Well, he brought it down, he shuk it and shuk it and held it up t'year and said, "What'd say?"

Said, "They's a baked pig in the stove."

Old woman said, "That's a lie, that's a confernal lie." Said, "They's no pi— baked pig in the stove."

"All right," he said, "you go see."

Went and seed and thar was the baked pig.

Well, said, "Make it talk some more," said, "and see what it says this time."

Well, he shook it and shook it and had 't up to his ear. "What'd it say that time?"

Said, "It—they's a man under the bed."

"Oh," the old woman said, "I know that's a lie, that's a black lie!" Said, "That's a confernal lie!"

Said, "Go see."

Well, the old man, he went and seed there was a man under there. Well, he took after him and he run him all over that place and never did catch him, and he come back and he, "All right, feller," he said, "what will you take for that thing?"

He said, "Uh, half a bushel of gold."

"All right." He set down and he borrowed Big Horny's half bushel. Well, it was wet and some of the gold stuck to it and he met Big Horny coming up.

"All right, Little Horny," [he] said, "Where'd you get s'much gold?"

"You killed my hoss and I dried the hide and took it uptown to sell it," and said, "I got this gold for it."

"Well, if that's the way, I'll go back and kill both my hosses." He went back and killed both his hosses and dried their hide and put them on a wheelbarrow and took them uptown. "Dry hides for sale! Dry hides for sale!"

They said, "You git outta here." Said, "We'll kill you just as quick as we can get something on—in our hands to do it with." Said, "You get them things outta here."

Well, he went back. He said, "Little Horny," he said, "I mean to kill you this time."

Said, "What fer?"

Said, "You've caused me to kill my hosses." Well, he throwed a pop bottle at his—at Little Horny—and killed Little Horny's mother.

"All right," Little Horny said, "you've killed my mother." Said, "I'll take her uptown and sell her." Well, he loaded her on a hill—wheelbarrow and started uptown and, uh, he got up in town and he's a-hollering, "Corpse for sale!" . . . No, he's saying, uh, he met a drunk man—that's the way it was.

And [the drunk man,] he said, "What you got there?"

"Ay," he said, "this is my grandma."

And he said, "You want a drink of liquor?"

"No," Little Horny said, "don't believe I want any."

"Yeah," he said, "take a drink."

Well, Little Horny took a drink, and he said to Little Horny's grandma, he said, "Uh, here, old lady," said, "you want a drink?"

She didn't speak. He said, "If you don't speak to me," said, "I'll knock you off that wheelbarrow." She didn't speak. So he hauled down and he just knocked her off the wheelbarrow.

"Now," Little Horny said, "you've killed my grandma," said, "you're gonna pay for it."

"Well," said, "I'll tell you what you do now." Said, "You take this ole lady out here and I'll help you, and" said, "we'll bury her and never say no more about it, and," said, "I'll give you a half a bushel of gold."

Little Horny said, "Let's go."

Well, they took her and buried her. Well, he set down again atter Big Horny's half a bushel, and it was wet and some of the gold stuck to it.

Well, he met Big Horny a-coming again. "Little Horny, where in the world did you get s'much gold?"

"You killed my grandma and I took her uptown and sold her."

"Well, if that's the way of it I'll go back and kill my grandma." Well, he went back and he killed his grandma. He put her on a wheelbarrow and took her uptown. "Corpse for sale! Corpse for sale!"

"Why," they said, "you get outta here, or," said, "we'll kill you with everything we can get our hands on!" Said, "You get up—go now!" say.

Well, he went back, said, "Little Horny," said, "I mean to drown y'. This is one time," said, "I mean to drown y'."

Little Horny said, "What fer?"

Said, "You caused me kill my grandma." Well, he made him a big ole box, you know, and he put Little Horny in it. And he roll—rolled him 'till he got him to the seashore.

"And now," Little Horny said, "you better got off and hunt a pole to roll me in with." Said, "If you start pushing me in with your hands," said, "you'll go in all over."

Well, while he's gone to hunt a pole to roll him in with a man come along with a big gang of cattle and he pecked on the box. He said, "What are you a-doing in there?"

"Ay," said, "Big Horny's a-fixing to send me up to heaven."

"Well," said, "If that's the way of it," said, "You get out of that box and take this drove of cattle and go on with it, and let him send me up to heaven."

"Alrighty," said, "I'll do that." Well, the man let him out of the box and he nailed, uh, this man up in the box and he took the cattle and went on.

Well, Big Horny come back, and with his pole into the ocean he went. "Well, now," he said, "that's the last of Little Horny." Said, "He'll—I'll not see him no more."

Well, in a week or two, why he met Little Horny. "Why," said, "Little Horny, I thought I drowned you." Said, "Where'd you get so many cattle?"

Said, "You sent me up to heaven, and I got me a drove of cattle and come back."

"Well, if that's the way of it," said, "let's send me up to heaven."

Well, he put him in a big box and rolled him into the ocean and that was the last of Big Horny.

Burton and Manning, Audio Tape BM26. ATU 1535. Told by Ethel Birchfield to Thomas Burton, perhaps around 1975, and transcribed from a tape of the performance. Birchfield was a lively storyteller with a wide repertoire of jokes and humorous stories, as well as songs. In her stories characters quite regularly exclaim, "By faith and my cross," much as characters in the Hicks-Harmon stories in the next chapter exclaim, "Bedads," but the expletive is unaccountably missing from this story.

This tale is widely popular in the southern Appalachians and beyond. It is, for example, a staple in the repertoire of the Hicks-Harmon family, but told as a Jack tale with the two brothers Will and Tom as the antagonists who kill Jack's little heifer (see chapter 13). For an extended discussion of the tale in southern Appalachian tradition, see McCarthy, Oxford, and Sobol 1994, chapters 4 and 5. Henry Glassie has suggested that the name Horn reflects the syncretism of German and Scotch-Irish culture in the region and indicates that at some point the story was brought over from the German, for the name "can be nothing but a very slight corruption of 'Hans,' the German name for Jack" (Glassie 1964: 90).

78. Polly, Nancy, and Muncimeg

Once upon a time there was an old widder-woman, and she had three daughters. One was named Polly, one was named Nancy, and one was named Muncimeg. The old lady taken sick and she divided up her inheritance. She give Polly her house and garden, she give Nancy the rest of her land, and she give Muncimeg her old pocket penknife and gold ring. Muncimeg thought she was cheated and she said, "Law me, Mommy, you just give me this old pocket penknife and gold ring."

The mother said, "You keep 'em and they'll come in handy when you are in trouble.' And she died.

Well, they made it up to go on a journey to seek their fortune, Polly and Nancy did. And Polly said, "Well, what shall we do with Muncimeg?"

Nancy said, "We'll lock her up in the house."

They locked her up in the house and started out on their journey. After they got down the road apiece, Muncimeg started to worrying and taking on about her fortune. She said, "Law me, my mommy's old pocket penknife and gold ring." The door flew open and she had nothing to do but take out after 'em.

Polly looked back and said, "Law me, sister Nancy, I see sister Muncimeg a-coming." Said, "What will we do with her?"

Nancy said, "Le's kill her!"

"No," said Polly, "le's take her with us."

"No, le's not," said Nancy. "Le's stop her up here in this old holler log."

They put her in the old holler log, stopped her up good and went on. Muncimeg was crying and taking on.

She didn't let them get far along till she said, "Law me, my mommy's old pocket penknife and gold ring." The stopping come out of that old log. Out she come and after 'em she went again.

Polly heared her coming and stopped and said, "Law me, sister Nancy, I see sister Muncimeg a-coming again." Said, "What will we do with her this time?"

"Le's kill her."

"No, le's let her go with us."

"No, le's stop her here in this old holler tree."

Well, they stopped her up in the old holler tree and went on. Muncimeg let 'em get gone and she said, "Law me, mommy's old pocket penknife and gold ring." Out come the stopping and out she come and away she went after 'em.

Nancy heared her behind 'em and said, "Law me, sister Polly, I see sister Muncimeg a-coming. What will we do with her!"

"Le's kill her."

"No, le's let her go with us."

Well they agreed to let her go along with them. They went along till they come to an old giant's house and stopped to stay all night. The old giant had three girls and they put these three girls in a room to sleep with his three girls. The old giant was up 'way in the night whetting his knife. And Muncimeg, who had stayed awake, raised up and asked him, says, "What are you whetting that knife for?"

"Aah, go to sleep. Cut meat in the morning."

He whetted right on his knife and then went to his old lady and asked her, "How can I tell our three girls from them three girls?"

The giant's old lady said, "Why, our three girls wears nightcaps."

Well, old Muncimeg heard 'em talking and she eased up and slipped the nightcaps off the giant's girls' heads and put 'em on her head and her two sisters' heads. The old giant come in and he cut his three girls' heads off in place of the others'. Old Muncimeg knowed all about it, of course, and early next morning she waked Polly and Nancy and helped 'em escape before the giant and his wife waked up.

They wandered along the road that day and come to the king's house. He put 'em up for the night, and while they's a-talking the old king told them about the old giant living across the way a piece. He told them he had three sons and said, "I'll give you my oldest son for the oldest girl if one of you will go to the old giant's house and drownd his old lady."

Well next morning they talked around and bagged Muncimeg into taking him up on it. She went to the old giant's house and laywayed the well. When the old lady come out to draw water she headed her in the well—drownded her—and the old giant heared the racket and come running out there. Saw who it was and took after Muncimeg just a-roaring, "I'm going to pay you for this, Muncimeg. You caused me to kill my three girls and now you've drownded my old woman. I'm going to pay you for this!"

Muncimeg come to the river and couldn't make it across. She said, "Law me, my mommy's old pocket penknife and gold ring." And she leaped the river and went back to the king's house. The king give his oldest son to her oldest sister Polly.

"Well," he said, "I'll give you my next oldest son for your other sister if you'll steal his horse, and the horse the giant has is covered with gold bells."

Muncimeg agreed to go back again and steal his horse. She got him out of the barn and she started riding him, and them bells started rattling. The old giant woke and jumped out of bed and run out there after it.

Muncimeg saw him a-coming and said, "Law me, my mommy's old pocket penknife and gold ring." And she become small and jumped in the horse's year [ear] and hid. Well, the giant tuck the horse and put him back in the barn, went back to sleep. She comes outten his year and started riding him off again. The bells started rattling. The old giant heared 'em and he jumped out to see about his horse.

Muncimeg heared him and she said, "Law me, my mommy's old pocket penknife and gold ring." And she became small and jumped under his mane and hid. Giant tuck him and put him back in the barn and went back and got in bed and went to sleep. Muncimeg come out from under his mane and started off. The giant took after her but she was too far gone. He called out, "Hey, Muncimeg, I'll pay you for this. You caused me to kill my three girls, you drownded my old woman, and now you've stole my horse. I told you I'd pay you for this!"

Muncimeg come to the river with the old giant right in behind her. She said, "Law me, my mommy's old pocket penknife and gold ring." And the horse jumped the river with her and she rode in to the king's house.

The king was glad to see her come in with it and give her his next oldest son for her older sister Nancy. He said, "Now I'll give you my youngest son for yourself if you'll steal his gold. He sleeps with it under his head."

Muncimeg went back over there, found the gold sack under the old giant's head, and while he was asleep she slipped it out and started to run away from there. She slipped and fell and the old giant come up from there and caught her. He took her in the house and tied her up in a sack and hung her up to the joist. He said, "I told you, Muncimeg, I'd pay you for this. You caused me to kill my three girls, you drownded my old woman, you stold my horse, and now you're trying to steal my gold. I told you I'd pay you for it. I'm going to make you mew like a cat, bew like a dog, and I'm going to make your old bones ring like teacups and saucers, knives and forks."

He went out to get him a frail to frail her with. She said, "Law me, my mommy's old pocket penknife and gold ring," and down come the sack and out she come. She caught his old dog and cat and put 'em in the sack and rounded up all his knives and forks, teacups and saucers. Put 'em all in the sack and hung it back up to the joist. She got out beside the house and listened for him. The old giant come back with a frail, and the first lick he warped the sack, "Mew" went his cat. The next lick he warped, "Bew" went his old dog. The next lick he warped he broke up his dishes and teacups and saucers. "I told you, Muncimeg, I'd pay you for it!"

When he tuck the sack down he poured out his old cat and his old dog and all of his broke-up dishes. And he looked out and saw Muncimeg making it for the river. He tuck after her calling, "I told you, Muncimeg, I'd pay you for this. You caused me to kill my three girls, you drownded my old woman, stold my horse, stold my gold, you caused me to kill my dog and cat and caused me to break all my dishes. I told you I'd pay you for this."

He was gaining on her by the time she got to the river. She said, "Law me, my mommy's old pocket penknife and gold ring." And over the river she went, safe from the old giant. She took the gold back to the old king's house. She got the king's youngest son for a husband, and they all went back home and lived happy.

Roberts 1974: 228–32. ATU 328. Told to Leonard Roberts by Jim Couch, in Putney, Kentucky, in 1952. In *Sang Branch Settlers* Roberts presents some hundred songs and sixty tales from the Couch family, principally of Harlan and Leslie Counties in Kentucky. Most of the tales came from Jim, and most of the songs from his brother Dave. They had learned them from their mother. But other family members also knew these tales and songs, or others. The family had a rich folk culture that it shared with its community, and it earned a widespread reputation for good songs and tales.

"Polly, Nancy, and Muncimeg" is one of countless variations on the theme of young children who inadvertently spend the night with an ogre and eventually outwit him or her (ATU 327–28). When there are three children they are most often boys, but Muncimeg has a firm place in Appalachian versions of this tale, and indeed, girls figure in this tale complex in Scotland, Ireland, and elsewhere in northeast Europe as well as in Appalachia. Muncimeg's name seems Scottish. The Scots word *munsie* means "a person deserving contempt or ridicule; an odd-looking or ridiculously-dressed person" (Robinson 1987: 430). Just the sort of thing a mean older sister might call her little sister. In Edinburgh castle there is a huge cannon, big enough for a person to slide into the barrel, called Muncy Meg.

79. The Old Man and the Witch

You wanna hear the one about the little old man and the Bimbo dogs? Well, sir, he had—I like this pretty well, this story. This old man, he had an old cow. He lived in the mountains. Well, you know you have to grab the cows to milk. When the evening comes you have to milk. (Your grandpa has cows up there, don't he? And he has to go out to his cows at night to milk 'em. And he has to bring 'em to the barn at night.)

And this man, his old cow was gone that night. She just traveled everywhere to get grass to eat. And she'd gone a long ways down in the valley on the other side of the mountain. And this old man, he took his cane and started after his old cow. And he didn't take his Bimbo dogs with him. (He had three Bimbo dogs.) And he just started out after her—it was a nice evening, and he just started out a walking after his old cow. And away he started; and he went up the mountain. And he kept going and going up the mountain and looking after his old cow and he couldn't find her. And he went clean to the top, and he looked down in the valley, and he saw that old cow down there in the valley. And he started down after the old cow, and went a-walking slow, but he got down there where the old cow was.

And when he got down there, this old witch was down there in that valley, a-waiting for him. And the old witch saw him. And that old witch she thought she had it made, that she would get the old cow and get him both, and blow him into the ground outta sight with her horn. And they ride a broomstick—you saw old witches though: they're hard critters, they are. And this old, this old man he kept ahead walking, and walking down till he got down to where the old cow was. And he's just getting ready to walk around behind her to drive her home and that old witch attacked him then, right there. She was going ta drive him in the ground outta sight. Well, this old man, he was a pretty fierce little feller. He's old, but he could fight. And he had his cane, and he commenced to fighting the old witch. Around and around they fought, two or three rounds.

And pretty soon he couldn't do it. And he hollered:

Hee-hi-ho, where's my Bimbo dog?

And the Bimbo dog heard it. He had three of them, and they was a-laying in the yard. And the little one, he was a fierce little feller, he just comes right now. He was the first one got to his master, the little Bimbo dog was. He went up, up to the top of the mountain, and he looked, and he smelled, and he saw the little old man, his master, down there a-fighting that old witch. Well, that little old Bimbo dog, he just went like a streak of lightn'. And he went faster than ever, for he wanted down, to help his master, cause his master always fed him and took care of him. And he went down, and that there old little Bimbo dog took after that witch and he knocked her down the first time. But he wasn't hardly big enough. And he knocked the horn out of her hands. She held her broomstick. She held to that broomstick, and they fought and fought. And he fought her good, but pretty soon that witch was a fighting hard. And the little Bimbo dog raised up and stood on the grass, and she took him a whack along the side of his head and knocked that little dog down. And the little dog couldn't get up. And she grabbed her horn and she went [*makes noise of horn blowing*] and blew that little dog in the ground out of sight.

And that just set the old man to fright, and he didn't know what to do. He'd got up on his stick he had, for the old witch had knocked him down once. But the old witch didn't get him clean down hardly, and he was a-fighting the old witch. And he commenced to hollering,

Hee-hi-ho, where's my Bimbo dog?

That was the second-sized dog; he was bigger than the little dog. And he just went as hard as he could go. He's just like the little dog. He went just like a streak of lightning. And he got up on top of the mountain and went up this side, and he looked down the valley. And down there they was a-fighting, the old witch and this little old man, his master. They was a-fighting it up and down. And just as that dog got down there, the old witch had done knocked the little old man, his master, down. But she didn't kill him, or hurt him too bad. And that old Bimbo dog, 'course that made him mad. He was the second-sized dog, and he was big. Well sir, he, he knocked the horn out of her mouth—she had grabbed the horn: she was gonna blow him clean outta sight—and he grabbed the horn, he did, the old big dog, and did just give her a shake and tore her dress. And, oh, he worked hard on her, he worked hard on her, he—and the little old man, he thought he had it made. And just about the time that he thought he had it made, that old witch got the drop on him some way or other, and she got ahold of her horn. And, first thing you know, she hit that other dog along the side of his, side of the head. She hit him left handed and she hit the other dog right handed. And she got both dogs.

And this little old man, got to feeling, sir, that he['d] be a goner. He commenced to crying. He was a-cryin', and hollering for mercy that old little old man was. And this great big Bimbo dog—he hollered,

Hee-hi-ho, where's my big Bimbo dog?

And sure, that old Bimbo dog, he was a little lazy, but man, he was wicked! He just took up that mountain and down that side of the valley, just a-going up. And he knowed right where the old cow was. He knowed where they liked the hay, up over the side of the hill. And he got there, and she had that old man down on the ground and she was a-reaching for her horn. She was a-gonna blow him in the ground outta sight. Well sir, that big old Bimbo dog saw it. And he got in save—just in time to save him. And he got that old witch. The first thing he done, he throwed her down, and he choked her and got her horn away from her, and he took to her. He was vicious. He was big—them old big mountain dogs, they got big. And he just got her right now and he killed that old witch. He killed that old witch.

And the old man, he got up, scrambled up out of the, out of the grass, and off the ground, and went to his big Bimbo dog and said, "We done it, didn't we?" He said, "We done it!" [*Storyteller laughs here.*] Well, that big old dog knowed that the old man, he didn't do so much. But he['d] helped the old big dog a whole lot, for the old man, he'd been a-fighting with that cane. Yes, sir, they'd killed that old witch. And the old man, he took the horn, and he blowed his little Bimbo dog outta the ground, and he blowed his other dog outta the ground. And they all went home, and they drove the old cow ahead of 'em. And they got home, and they took the old cow down and put her in the barn. And he milked the old cow, and went home happy. And that was that story. That was that story. It was pretty good, I thought.

Anonymous 1978. ATU 315 and Motif B524.1.2/G275.2. Told in the 1970s by a Ripley, West Virginia, man in his late seventies to his son, son's wife, and three grandchildren, so that the son could tape record it. The son had made a recording in 1970, but that tape had been erased. The recording was made after dinner in the son's house in Portsmouth, Ohio. It was transcribed by the son's eldest child, a daughter, who was fourteen at the time of telling, eighteen when she took a class at Ohio State University taught by Bill Lightfoot. Daughter/transcriber has requested that names be withheld. The storytelling grandfather, the third generation of West Virginia English and German stock, learned the stories from his own maternal grandfather who was not able to "work brittle" (Anonymous 1978: 19), but could entertain the children with stories. The maternal grandfather apparently had quite a full repertoire of stories that he repeated often.

The storyteller spent his working life as a carpenter. In retirement he made dollhouse furniture to sell as well as practicing woodworking and carving to create things for his family. He first heard his grandfather's stories when he was very young. He declares that there were many Bimbo dog stories and it could take his grandfather half a day to tell them all. He heard the stories many times, perhaps ten times a year in his childhood. Well into his seventies the storyteller told the stories regularly to his own grandchildren, whenever he visited. He believed that he was the only one of the nine brothers and sisters who told the stories to his children and then grandchildren. The stories, he said, "beared on his mind" (19).

The student's collection includes two other stories, both of which the storyteller learned from the same maternal grandfather. One tells of a courageous "wild mother hog" [*sic*] who fought a bear and so saved one of her piglets, and the other tells of a "great big ol' Bimbo dog," a stray that shows up and saves a family from starvation. Like the present story (if one accepts the actuality of witches in the workaday world), both of the other stories are essentially realistic in style and presentation: the mother hog is not a talking pig, the dog does not have magical powers. According to the granddaughter/transcriber, the storyteller's manner of narrating was usually without much expression. He would sit in a chair with his grandchildren on the floor around him. Usually he began, "Well, sir, . . ." but there were no other formulaic phrases of opening or closing. He used indirect discourse instead of quoted dialogue. In the closing pages of her collection, the granddaughter comments on the values of respect for animals, family cohesion, and self-reliance that inform the stories. She also says that "since the stories have never been outside of our family they become a shared 'secret' of sorts," and so help reinforce family solidarity. The present text removes most of her specialized spellings and adjusts some of the punctuation, but retains the capitalization of the mysterious epithet *Bimbo* that is applied to the dogs.

This story seems to be built around the same motif, B524.1.2, featured in the stories about helpful dogs in chapters 10 and 11. In the present version the tree has disappeared, the chant has become a call, and the three dogs come in succession, with only the third able to effect the rescue. G275.2 is a slightly broader motif: Witch overcome by helpful dogs of hero.

80. Old Bear

Once upon a time there was a little boy who was very hungry. He went to his mother and asked her for something to eat. She gave him a bowl of beans and a bowl of kraut. He took them outside and sat down on a bench to eat. All at once he saw a great, big, black bear. It was coming out of the woods.

The little boy ran and hid. The big old bear ate the little boy's bowl of beans and kraut and went on down the road.

The bear came to an old man working in the fields. The old man said,

> Old bear, old bear, what makes you so stout?

The bear said,

> Eat a bowl of beans, eat a bowl of kraut,
> Eat you too, if you don't watch out.

Then the old bear ate the old man, swallowed him whole, shoes and all. Then he went on down the road.

The big black bear came to an old woman hanging out wash. The old woman said,

> Old bear, old bear, what makes you so stout?

The bear said,

> Eat a bowl of beans, eat a bowl of kraut,
> Eat you too, if you don't watch out.

And he did. He swallowed her whole, bonnet and all.

The old bear went on 'til he came to a little boy fishing. The little boy looked at the bear and said,

> Old bear, old bear, what makes you so stout?

The great big bear said,

> Eat a bowl of beans, eat a bowl of kraut,
> Eat you too, if you don't watch out.

And the old bear ate the little boy, fishing pole and all.

The old bear went on 'til he met a little girl playing with her doll. The little girl said,

> Old bear, old bear, what makes you so stout?

The great, big bear said,

> Eat a bowl of beans, eat a bowl of kraut,
> Eat you too, if you don't watch out.

And the old bear ate the little girl, swallowed her whole, doll and all.
The old bear went on his way. Suddenly he heard a voice cry,

> Old bear, old bear,
> I want back my beans, I want back my kraut.

The old bear turned around and there was the first little boy with his daddy.
The little boy's daddy hit the old bear with his ax and killed him dead. Then
he split open the great, big, black bear's stomach.

Out jumped the old man, shoes and all. "I'm out," said the old man.

Out jumped the old woman, bonnet and all. "I'm out," said the old
woman.

Out jumped the little boy, fishing pole and all. "I'm out," said the little
boy.

Out jumped the little girl, doll and all. "I'm out," said the little girl.

"And I'm all out of beans and kraut," said the first little boy, "and I'm still
hungry." He started to cry.

"Hush," said his daddy, "and mommy will cook old bear for you to eat."
And she did.

Vanover 1980. ATU 2028. Told by Viola Wright, June 21, 1980, to Johnny Vanover, who was taking editor's folklore class, taught for Morehead State University at Pikeville College, Pikeville,
Kentucky. Versions of 2028 are widely dispersed in the South.

This is one of my favorite tales to tell. I was astonished, however, when I went back to
read the original transcript that I had not looked at in more than fifteen years. In my telling,
the tale has grown in length, complexity, and detail, quite without my realizing it. For example,
I send the hero to visit his grandmother, who gives him the beans and kraut to take home to
his mother. The bear eats the food while the boy is climbing a fence on the way home. The
devoured old woman smokes a pipe and the devoured boy plays with a yo-yo. And the hero's
daddy shoots the bear, among other changes and developments. But no one says "I'm out." One
peculiarity—perhaps even structural weakness—that I have become aware of as I tell the story is
that there is no connection in this version between the four victims and the boy and his family.
In the Beech Mountain tradition the various victims, all of one family, are devoured as they successively return from the store where they have gone for soda and salt to make biscuits. A squirrel finally tempts the bear out onto a limb, he falls and splits open, and all including the squirrel
go back to make biscuits for supper.

The storyteller, Mrs. Wright, was a fifty-year-old teacher at Dorton High School, where
Vanover also taught. She was reputed to be able to tell the future through dreams. She learned

many stories from her father, Frank Sloan. She told Vanover a variety of stories, including another fairy tale "The Wicked Stepmother" (ATU 720: The Juniper Tree; see below), a neck riddle story, ghost legends, and humorous, supposedly true anecdotes, as well as family stories (though she was not willing to let him tape these last).

81. Old Kitty Rollins

Once upon a time a traveler was a-riding down the road, and he seen a house that was chuck full of cats. There was cats running all over the place, and setting on the gallery, and some had even got up on the roof. One great big tomcat walked over to the traveler and says, "When you get to the next house, stop and tell 'em that old Kitty Rollins is dead." He could talk just like a human, with a big loud coarse voice at that.

So the traveler rode on, and the next house he come to looked like it was plumb deserted. But the traveler got down and went in anyhow, and there was just one old bedraggled-looking cat a-setting in the corner by the fireplace. "I come to tell you that old Kitty Rollins is dead," says the traveler. The old bedraggled-looking cat jumped up and says, "By God, I'll be king yet!" and out of the door he run.

Randolph 1950: 80–81. ATU 113A. Collected by Vance Randolph from J. H. McGee, Joplin, Missouri, July 1934. Mr. McGhee said he had heard it from some children at Sparta, Missouri, around 1900. This story is widely popular in the British Isles, and fairly well known in the United States as well. Sometimes told as a legend, the story is reminiscent of "Sop Doll" (chapter 13) and other stories about witches in the form of cats.

82. Three Versions of the Juniper Tree

A. The Wicked Stepmother

Once upon a time there was a little boy and a little girl who lived with their father and a wicked stepmother. When the father was at home, the stepmother pretended to be good to the children, but when he was gone, she was very mean to them.

One day the father was gone from home. The wicked stepmother said to the little boy, "Go upstairs in the trunk and get me some apples." The little boy went upstairs and opened the trunk to get the apples. The trunk was big and the little boy had to stand on tip-toe to reach the apples. As he was getting the apples out of the trunk, the wicked stepmother slipped up behind him, slammed down the trunk lid, and cut off the little boy's head.

The wicked stepmother dared his little sister to tell what she had done. If she told, her head would be cut off too.

The wicked stepmother cooked the little boy for supper. At supper the little girl wouldn't eat, but just sat there crying. The stepmother told the father that the little girl was crying because her brother had run away that day.

After supper, the little girl had to wash the dishes. She gathered up the bones of her brother, wrapped them in a dish rag, and buried them in the garden.

Soon after this, the father was gone again for the day. The stepmother called the little girl and told her to go upstairs and get her an apple. The little girl went upstairs and opened the trunk. As she leaned in to get an apple, the wicked stepmother started to slam down the trunk lid. The little girl was too quick for her. She jumped back, ran down the stairs to the outside, and hid.

The stepmother searched and searched for the little girl, but couldn't find her. When the father came home, she told him that the little girl had run away to find her brother. The father was broken-hearted at losing his two children. He went out in the garden and sat down under a tree. All at once a little yellow bird on the branch over his head started singing. At first the father paid no attention to the bird. Then he listened and the little bird was singing:

> Wicked is your woman's way
> And she has a debt to pay.
> Your little son is dead,
> With the trunk lid.
> With the trunk lid
> She cut off his head.
> In the garden his body lies.
> To get back your children the witch must die.

The father got up from under the tree and went into the house. He told his wife that he was hungry for some apples, and to go upstairs and get him some. She went upstairs and opened the trunk. As she leaned over to get the apples, he slammed the trunk lid down on her neck and cut off her head.

Suddenly he heard the sound of laughing children. He looked out the window and saw his two children in the garden. He ran out and hugged his children, and they lived happily ever after.

B. Pennywinkle! Pennywinkle!

Once upon a time there was a woman who got mad at her husband about something, so she killed their baby with the fire-shovel. Then she skinned the baby just like a rabbit, and cut it up just like a rabbit, and cooked it just like a rabbit. When her man come home that night she set the meat on the table. Him and her was not speaking, so he didn't ask nobody what kind of meat it was. He set down and et every scrap of the meat, and the woman sent her daughter to put the bones under the marble stone down by the spring-house.

Nobody said a word all evening, so pretty soon they went to bed, but they could not get no sleep. It seemed like something was a-crawling around in the house, and crying. After 'while, the man, he says: "Who's there? What do you want?"

And then the little ghost hollered back:

> Pennywinkle! Pennywinkle!
> My Maw killed me, my Paw et me,
> My sister buried my bones
> Under a marble stone!
> I want my liver and lights
> And wi-i-i-ney pipes!
> Pennywinkle! Pennywinkle!

And when the fellow heard this, he got to thinking about what it meant. So after 'while he got out of bed and went down to the spring-house and found the baby's bones under a marble stone.

Well, the fellow set there a while, and whetted up his knife. Then he went back to the house and cut his wife's head off. The step-daughter, she run away through the woods, and nobody ever did find out what become of her. The folks took the baby's head and skin and bones out from under the marble stone and put them in a regular little coffin and buried them in the graveyard. And that is the end of the "Pennywinkle" story.

C. Mother, Mother, Don't Step on Me

Once a man went away to look for work, and left his wife and children at home. One day the wife was very hungry, and there was nothing to eat in the house. So she killed her youngest child, and cut the body to pieces, and boiled them in a kettle on the stove. She ate the meat and buried the bones under the doorstep. Whenever she would go out the door, she would hear a voice saying,

> Mother, mother, don't step on me.

The old man came home, and one day he went out the door and heard a voice saying,

> Father, father, don't step on me.

He suspected his wife, and asked her about it. Finally she confessed and he killed her.

A: Vanover 1980: 7–8; B: Randolph 1950: 83; C: Boggs 1934: 297–98. ATU 720. Tale A was told by Viola Wright, a teacher at Dorton High School, Pike County, Kentucky, June 5, 1980 (see "Old Bear," this chapter). Tale B, told by Lon Kelley, Pineville, Missouri, July 1930, was learned from Kelley's parents, who were pioneer settlers in McDonald County, Missouri, and collected by Vance Randolph. Tale C, told by Ulyss Daughtridge, age twenty, of Edgecombe County, North Carolina, a student of Ralph Steele Boggs at the University of North Carolina, was collected by Boggs some time before 1934. (This version more properly belongs in chapter 9, as Daughtridge's family lived on an old plantation near Rocky Mount, on the North Carolina coastal plain, but is included here for convenience of comparison.)

These three versions, separated by fifty years or so, attest to the popularity of this grim tale. (Baughman cites about twenty versions.) I suspect that a part of the appeal is the tale's plausibility. Indeed, the third version is really more of a legend than a märchen. In Grimm no. 47, which may well be the prototype of all of these versions, the mother, crazed by jealousy, kills the stepson in order to favor the girl, who is her daughter and the boy's half-sister. Version A above, though much simplified, is quite close to Grimm, especially with regard to the apples in the chest. Oddly enough, however, the bird's song is quite different. Version B, generally speaking, is further removed from Grimm, but the song is much closer to that in Grimm, with a remembered echo of "Tailypo" (ATU 366: "Tailypo, Tailypo; all I want's my Tailypo" [*said in a whiney voice*]; story in Cox 1934: 341–42). Version C, as I have said, turns the tale into a legend. It may well have been told to Ulyss as true, though he in his turn seems to report it to his professor as just a story. None of the three stories agree among themselves as to the motivation for the murder, nor does any of the stories preserve the motivation that is found in Grimm.

83. Mr. Fox

Riddle:

> Riddle to my left, riddle to my right,
> Where did I stay last Friday night?
> The wind did blow, my heart did ache
> To see the hole in the ground that Fox did make.

Solution:

A girl promises to meet her lover in the woods. She arrives before him and climbs a tree. The lover and another man arrive and begin to dig a grave, remarking about robbing and murder. The girl keeps silent until they are gone. She later traps the robbers with the riddle.

Roberts 1955: 243. Baughman Type 955C. Leonard Roberts presents this riddle version of the Bluebeard tale Mr. Fox, which he declares is common in the southern mountains, as he knows it, not as collected from anyone else. The very brief text from Jane Gentry of North Carolina may represent the same riddle tradition (Carter 1925: 372; see next chapter). In fully narrative versions of this story the denouement is usually like that of "The Pea Story" in chapter 17. At a party the heroine, surrounded by kinsmen and neighbors, entraps the would-be entrapper by proposing as a riddle some variation on the above stanza. Her kinsmen and/or neighbors then kill Mr. Fox.

CHAPTER 13

THE SOUTHERN MOUNTAINS II

The Hicks–Harmon Beech Mountain Tradition

In 1943 Richard Chase, who had begun folktale collecting in North Carolina with the WPA, brought out the most successful collection of American folktales in publishing history, *The Jack Tales*, a book that has remained in print for more than six decades. Chase based his collection almost exclusively on tales gathered from a single family of storytellers, the complexly interrelated Hickses, Gentrys, Wards, Proffitts, and Presnells of Beech Mountain and Hot Springs, North Carolina. Chase was not the first, however, to visit with members of this family and collect from them. Isabel Gordon Carter had already published, in a 1925 *Journal of American Folklore* article, a number of tales collected from Jane Gentry (1863–1925), who had also sung for Cecil Sharp. This group of tradition-bearers, of storytellers and singers, is descended from David Hicks, who emigrated from London around 1760 and died in 1792/3, his son Big Sammy Hicks, who died in 1835, and his grandson Council Harmon, who died in 1896. Other folklorists and historians have followed Carter and Chase, identifying, interviewing, and gathering the lore of the descendants of David Hicks and Council Harmon. Collectors Mellinger Henry (1938) and Herbert Halpert (Chase 1943: 186) even found cousins with the old family name of Harmon in Cades Cove on the Tennessee side of the Smoky Mountains. By now, the songs and tales collected from this family, in all their versions and variants, would fill many a box. The books and dissertations alone would load down a couple of shelves.

The Hicks-Harmon family tradition is important not only because it includes so many excellent storytellers and singers, but even more so because it is a single-family tradition that has been documented now for over seventy-five years. It provides an unprecedented opportunity to see how stories move through oral tradition and adapt to the styles of different taletellers. At the same time, a note of caution is in order. Though mountaineers born and bred, family members are not stereotyped illiterates. Education was cherished even by the earliest members of the family to be interviewed. Jane Gentry, who told stories to Carter and sang for Sharp, moved her family to Hot Springs so her children could more easily attend school at the Dorland Institute. And Marshall Ward, who first put Richard Chase in contact with his family, was an elementary school teacher. The family knows Chase's books. If fact, almost as soon as *The Jack Tales* was published, this book began to exert an influence back on the tradition, as one can see when comparing Maude Gentry Long's post-Chase versions of stories with the pre-Chase versions of her mother Jane Gentry. But Chase did not collect and publish the full family repertoire, and many other tales circulate in the family apparently uninfluenced by print.

This Beech Mountain family repertoire is huge. By my count, approximately fifty stories are widespread in the family, while some family members apparently know or knew many more. Though the stories are clearly European, it is not easy to identify a single point of origin. David Hicks was English, and the English part of the repertoire includes stories such as "Catskins," "Whitebear Whittington," and "Little Dicky Wigbun." Not all the ancestors, however, were English. Council Harmon, for instance, the ancestor most frequently cited as the source of the stories, reportedly had a German or "Dutch" father. Many of the stories, including such core stories as "The Heifer Hide" and "Old Fire Dragon," may well be German. It is unlikely, however, that all the stories were inherited. More likely, this family with a penchant for storytelling drew stories to it the way honey draws bees, so that in time the family repertoire incorporated material from English, Irish, Scots-Irish, German, and perhaps even Huguenot neighbors. A Scots-Irish influence, for example, could explain the fondness for Jack tales.

This chapter gathers stories from four storytellers representing four generations of the Hicks-Harmon family. Two tales come from Jane Gentry, the earliest witness to the tradition. To one of these, a cante fable, I have added the tune as collected a few years later from a Tennessee cousin, Samuel Harmon. Two tales come from Marshall Ward (1906–1981), who practiced his craft weekly in his fifth-grade classroom. One comes from Ray Hicks (1922–2003), at one time the uncrowned king of American storytellers. And one comes from Orville Hicks (1951–), who has devoted himself to carrying on the family tradition, especially through performance in schools. I have arranged the stories in order of the birth dates of the narrators. The Ward and Ray Hicks stories are expansive, running to many pages and filled with detail. The Gentry stories are unabashedly earthy, while the Orville Hicks story, told for a contemporary juvenile audience, tailors a potentially obscene plotline accordingly. Four are stories widely shared in the family. Many versions by family members can be found in folktale archives around the country, and all four are included among Chase's recensions in *The Jack Tales*. One story, however, "The Three Pigs," at least as here told, may be Marshall Ward's own personal take on that popular tale.

84. Old Stiff Dick

They uz a little old boy long time ago, didn't have no mammy or poppy, jest growed up in the hog weeds, and he didn't even know his name, but everybody called him Jack. And he jest stayed here and yonder, wherever he could drop in at night.

So one day he was a walkin' the road and he had him a belt around his waist and he had him a little old knife and he was a whittlin' and makin' him a paddle. So he come along past a mud hole and there was a lot of little old blue butterflies over hit. So he struck down with his paddle and he killed seven of the butterflies. So he goes on a little piece further and he comes to a blacksmith shop, and he gets the blacksmith to cut letters in his belt:

> Stiff Dick
> Killed seven at a lick.

So he goes on a piece further and he passes the king's house. King runs out and says, "I see you're a very brave man; I see where you've killed seven at a lick."

"Yes, bedads, I'm a mighty brave man."

So the king says, "Stranger, I want to hire a brave man to kill some animals we have here in the woods. We have a wild municorn here killin' so many people, soon we'll all be kilt. If you'll kill that municorn, we'll pay you one thousand dollars, five hundred down, and five hundred when you bring the municorn in."

So Dick says, "All right."

So the king paid him five hundred dollars. Stiff Dick stuck that in his pocket and said to hisself, "Bedads, if they ever see me around here again." And he tuk out. When he got way up in the mountains the municorn smelled him and here it come,

> Whippity cut,
> Whippity cut,
> Whippity cut.

Stiff Dick tuk to runnin' and the municorn after him. The municorn was jest clippin' Stiff Dick. They run up the mountains and down the ridges.

So, long late in the evening, they started down a long ridge, the municorn jest a runnin' after Stiff Dick. An' away down at the end of the ridge Stiff Dick saw a big oak and he made a beeline to see if he cud clumb hit. So the municorn was jest gettin' so close that agin they got there the municorn was jest behin' him. Jack jest slipped around the oak right quick and the municorn stove his horn into hit and he just rared and plunged.

As soon as Stiff Dick saw he was fastened for all time to come, he went on to the king's house. King says, "Did you get the municorn?"

Dick says, "Municorn? Laws an' massy, never was nothin' but little old bull calf come tearin' out there after me. I jest picked it up by one ear and tail and stove it agin a tree and if you all wants hit, you'll have to go up thar and git hit." So the king got him a great army and went up and killed the municorn, come back and paid Jack five hundred dollars more.

King says, "Now, Stiff Dick, there's one more wild animal living up here, a wild bull-boar. I'll give five hundred dollars now and five hundred more when you ketch hit."

Jack tuk the five hundred dollars and say to hisself, "You'll never see me anymore." But after he'd gone a little ways here come the wild boar after him,

> Whippity cut,
> Whippity cut,
> Whippity cut.

All day long around the mountains, across the mountains and down the ridges, all the day just a runnin'.

So, along late in the evenin', away down in the holler he saw an old house and when he got down there the door was open. So he run right in the door and up the wall and the wild boar run right after him and laid down under him. Boar was tired and soon fell asleep. So Dick eased up the wall and over and down the outside and shut the wild boar up in there.

So he went down to the king's house. King says, "Did ye git the wild boar?"

Stiff Dick says, "Wild boar? Laws a massy, I never saw nothing but a little old boar pig come bristlin' up after me. I jest picked hit up by the tail and throwed hit in an old waste house. And if you all wanst hit, you'll have to go up thar and git hit." So king got up an army of men and went up and killed the wild boar and went back down and paid Stiff Dick his other five hundred dollars.

King says, "Now, Stiff Dick, there's one more wild animal we want to git killed. That's a big brown bear." So he give Dick another five hundred dollars. Stiff Dick says to hisself, "If I can jest get out of here, no brown bear 'ul never see me." So he got way up on the mountain; old brown bear smelled him and here he come,

Whippity cut,
Whippity cut,
Whippity cut.

Across the hills, up the ridges, every way to dodge the bear. The bear uz right after him.

So, late in the evenin', way down at the end of a ridge he saw old pine tree that had been all burned over and was right black. Jack made a beeline fur that tree. The bear was jest a little ways behind when Jack run up the tree. Bear was down at the root of the tree and he was so mad he tried to gnaw the tree down. Hit gnawed and gnawed. Jack keep a easin' down on another old snag and another old snag and directly he got on a snag jest above the old bear and the old snag broke and Jack fell just a-straddle the old bear and they jest burnt the wind.

Stiff Dick was so tickled, and so scared too, that he was jest a hollerin' and screamin' and directly he run the bear right thru the town and the soldier boys heard him a screamin' and they run out and shot hit. Stiff Dick got off it when it fell, and he was jest a swearin' and a rarin'. He was swearin' he was breakin' hit for the king a riddy horse. And king come out and heard Stiff Dick a swearin' he was a breakin' the bear for the king a riddy horse and he got mad and made the soldier boys pay Dick five hundred dollars. And when I left there, Stiff Dick was rich.

Carter 1925: 355–57. ATU 1640. Jane Gentry apparently told this tale without a blush to Isabel Gordon Carter. According to Herbert Halpert's note in *The Jack Tales*, Sam Harmon of Cades Cove, Tennessee, Gentry's cousin who knew Little Dicky Wigbun, also knew this story, as did the Beech Mountain Wards. All vouch for the inscription on the hero's belt (Chase 1943: 192).

The blue butterflies, however, are suspect. Blue is not a common butterfly color, and killing butterflies seems wanton and unmotivated. Though Chase also identifies the insects as such (Chase 1943–1959), I wonder if, somewhere along the line of transmission, they were blue bottle flies and somebody misheard.

Gentry calls her hero both Dick and Jack. It is not clear whether she intends to identify her hero as Jack, the hero of so many tales from this family tradition. Calling him Jack in the opening sentence may be a case of confusion or inadvertence on her part, as it clearly is in the next tale. She starts calling him Jack again, however, in the middle of the story. And at the end the name occurs four times in succession. So ultimately, it is not completely clear whether his name is Dick or whether he is Jack and Stiff Dick is just a moniker he assumes. For a unique take on the identity of Jack, see "Sop Doll," later in this chapter.

85. Little Dicky Wigbun

Little Dicky Wigbun, he was a little bit of a man and his wife didn't like him nary a bit. She loved the old passenger. (I don't know what the old passenger was. They 'as men use to travel about and they called 'em the old passenger.) So she was all the time playin' off like she was sick and sending Little Dicky Wigbun to the Clear Apsul Springs to get Clear Apsul Rum fer her. (I don't know what Clear Apsul Rum were, it's just in the story; they didn't really have anything like hit.) She was hopin' the wild varmints 'd get him and eat him and she c'd have the old passenger.

So one day he 'as going down to the spring and he met the peddler. Peddler says, "Dicky, where you started?"

"I've started down to Clear Apsul Springs to git my wife some Clear Apsul Rum."

Peddler says, "Dicky, I'm jest as sorry fer you as I can be. Your wife don't care nothing fer you."

"You think she don't?"

"No, she's just sendin' you off down here to see if you won't get killed by the wild animals. You jest get in this knapsack of mine and let me carry you back to your house and let you see what's going on."

"Well, I believe I will," says Dicky. So Dicky got in the haversack.

Got to Dicky's house and the peddler says, "Kin I stay all night?"

"Yes, I guess ye can, but my husband's not here."

So he went in and says, "Mrs. Wigbun, kin I bring my haversack in? I dropped hit in a mud hole down the road a piece and I'm feared I'll get my rations wet."

"Yes, I guess ye kin."

So the peddler went out and cut a couple of holes so's Jack [*sic*] c'd see out and just picked him up and carried him into the house.

So the peddler says, "Let's all sing some little ditties."

"All right," the passenger says.

"Well now, Mrs. Wigbun," says the peddler, "you sing the first one, then Mr. Passenger, you sing the next one, and then I'll sing one."

So Mrs. Wigbun sings:

> Oh, Little Dicky Wigbun, to London he's gone
> To buy me a bottle of Clear Apsul Rum.
> God send him a long journey never to return,
> Through the green wood and below.

"Well now, Mrs. Wigbun, that's a pretty song. Sing hit agin."

> Oh, Little Dicky Wigbun, to London he's gone
> To buy me a bottle of Clear Apsul Rum.
> God send him a long journey never to return,
> Through the green wood and below.

"Well now, Mr. Passenger, you sing your'n."

> Oh, little Dicky Wigbun thinks
> Who eats of his sweets and drinks of his drinks.
> And if God spares my life, I will sleep with his wife,
> Through the green woods and below.

"That's pretty. Sing hit agin."

> Oh, little Dicky Wigbun thinks
> Who eats of his sweets and drinks of his drinks.
> And if God spares my life, I will sleep with his wife,
> Through the green woods and below.

"Now, Mr. Peddler, you sing your'n," says Mis' Wigbun.

> Oh, Little Dicky Wigbun, he's not very fur,
> And out of my knapsack I'll have him to appear.
> And if friends he don't like, I stand to his back,
> Through the green fields and below.

So

> . . . they hung the old passenger all right away
> And they burnt Dicky's wife the very next day,
> Through the green fields and below.

Carter 1925: 366–68. ATU 1360C. Jane Gentry of Hot Springs, North Carolina, told this tale to Isabel Gordon Carter in the summer of 1923. Surprisingly, the Grimm collection includes a rather explicit version (No. 95), in which the adulterous suitor is the village priest or pastor. The standard for appropriate kinder-reading has changed in the last two hundred years. Phillips Barry, in the *Bulletin of the Folksong Society of the Northeast* (1960: no. 3, p. 6) reports that the magic drink in the oldest known English version is called the water of Absalom.

In this story and in another story, "Lazy Jack and His Calf Skin" (ATU 1535), Gentry calls the adulterous suitor *passenger*. Apparently, when she (or perhaps someone earlier in the chain of transmission) first heard these stories as a child, the suitor was called a pastor but the word *pastor* was not part of her vocabulary, and so she had to interpret what she was hearing as best she could. Telling the story as an adult, Gentry is clearly puzzled by the word *passenger*, but convinced that it is the word she first heard in these stories.

Carter, who was more interested in stories than in song, did not give a tune for the ditties included in this cante fable. Fortunately, however, Mellinger Edward Henry and Mrs. Henry, who were more interested in song than in stories, collected the tune and words of the ditty a few years later from a cousin of Jane Gentry, Samuel Harmon of Cades Cove, Tennessee. Mrs. Henry first collected the piece on August 13, 1930; then they returned in 1931 and got a slightly more complete version that Henry published in *Folk-Songs from the Southern Highlands* (1938: 153–54). The closeness of the words of the ditty in the two renditions suggests that Gentry and Harmon both had learned essentially the same family version of Little Dicky's story, and that both would have used approximately the same tune. Here, with the accompanying tune, is Little Dicky's tale as Harmon gave it to the Henrys:

> In London there was a spring noted for its healing qualities. The wife pretends she
> is sick and sends Dicky for a bottle of the water. She sings the first stanza as a signal
> that Dicky has gone and that the pastor can come from his hiding place.

Lady sings:

> Little Dicky Whigburn to London is gone
> To bring me a bottle of clear applesom;
> The Lord send him a long journey never to return,
> Through the green woods and the willows.

Pastor sings:

> Oh, little does Dicky know, or little does he think
> Who eats of his eats or drinks of his drinks;
> And God spare me my life, this night I'll stay with his wife,
> Through the green woods and the willows.

A pedlar comes along, who has just met Dicky on his way to the spring. When he sees the pastor and hears the wife singing he understands what is up, hurries back to catch Dicky, and persuades him to get in the hopsack and allow himself to be taken back home. As they reach the house, the pedlar sings out stanza 3.

Pedlar sings:

> Oh, Dicky Whigburn he's not fur
> And out of my hopsack I'll have him appear;
> And if a friend he does lack, I'll stand at his back,
> Through the green woods and the willows.

Dicky gets out of the hopsack:

> Good morning, fair gentleman all in a row;
> The chief of your secret I very well know."
> They beat the old pastor and right straight away;
> They whipped Dicky's wife the very next way [day?]
> And Dicky and the pedlar together did stay.

Both Carter and Henry divide the third line of the lovers' and the peddler's ditties, printing it as two [half-]lines, but musically the lines go to a single phrase of the four-phrase tune. Presumably for the final stanza that phrase (the third phrase, beginning at the end of measure four) was sung twice, for in Harmon's version the final stanza has five full-length lines, and the fourth line echoes the third in sentence structure. Herbert Halpert recorded the full tale from Sam Harmon on April 2, 1939 (Lindahl 2004: 36–39). The ditty shows considerably more divergence from the Gentry version, suggesting changes over time. But details of plot are close, including the ploy to get the knapsack close to the fire and the pedlar's compliments that get the wife and preacher to sing their songs twice. The last stanza in Harmon's earlier performance, as given by Henry, however, becomes two full stanzas in the later version, as given by Halpert, suggesting that Harmon, at the time of the Henry recording, had a lapse of memory.

86. Sop Doll

Well, this Jack—now I've been a telling y' about a lot of Jacks, y' know: this is different generations. One Jack'd come on, and Jack number one, two, three, four, five, six, seven, eight, nine, ten, right on up to twenty Jacks. Y' know, they named Jack after Jack because he was lucky. Well, this was about the fifteenth Jack and he lived with his dad and mother for a long time, and he got grown and got tired of stayin' around, y' know. All young people like to get out and see what they can do, and we call it going out and trying they fortune.

So Jack 'cided he get out and try his fortune. He cleaned up and dressed up and put on his best clothes, told his daddy and mother good-bye and left 'em, and tuck off and walked and traveled for about a year and he come into another kingdom. His clothes was getting ragged, and his money give out, and he hadn't much to eat, and he come to an ol' farmer's house. He said, "Mister," he said, "I'm just about broke, got not much to eat. I'm a-looking for a job." Said, "Would you have any work a man could do?"

"Well," he said, "I'll tell y' how it is with me," he said. "My wife's sick and I don't have no one to help me and," he said, "I've got one of the finest mills in all this country. And," says, "you can grind a hundred bushel a day—corn, wheat, rye, oats, and barley, and buckwheat—but nobody'll tend that mill." Says, "I hire people to start that mill and about one day is all they get done. I go back the next morning and there they are dead, and we don't know what's killing 'em. And find 'em dead." Said, "There's been three men in the last three years that's died at this mill. Now, if you want to take this job, I'll be glad to have y' and this job will pay y' well." Said, "I'll give you half the toll you make and I'll take half for the mill. And," said, "people will pay good toll because they want their stuff ground and they have to go for hundreds of miles to get it ground." Said, "I'll get on my horse and ride around today and tell 'em I've got a miller. And," said, "people'll be here in less than an hour if you want to tend the mill."

"Well," Jack said, "Mister, that sound like a good proposition."

"You forgetting one thing. People just work one day there and die."

"Well," Jack said, "I b'lieve I'll just take my chances on it and see what happens."

"All right," said the ol' farmer. "If you'll do it we'll get the word out right now." Said, "I've got about ten bushel down there of corn that I want you to grind into meal right now while I'm getting the word out."

And he took Jack down to the mill and showed 'm how to operate the mill and how it worked, and it run, you know, by water power. Well, he turned the water on and the ol' mill begin to skreak and pop and crack and it began to go, and Jack he ground a bushel for the ol' farmer to clean the mill up, and said, "We'll just make feed out of this 'n and get the mill cleaned up. It's been a-setting there a long time." Got it cleaned up and everything started.

The ol' farmer jumped on his horse, went out and said, "Now we got a miller." Said, "He may not last no longer than a day. If you want your mill—corn—ground, your wheat, your oats, your rye, your barley, your buckwheat," said, "bring 'er in."

And so he started off, everbody did, by coming in with wagon loads. Why, they was about ten wagon loads just setting in line a-waiting. Jack, he begin to ground. He ground and ground and ground and my guess is he ground a hundred, over a hundred, over a hundred bushels that day. And, you know, Jack done purty good that day. If he ground a hundred bushels, he got a tenth. He got ten bushels for grinding that day and the ol' farmer got half of it and he got half the ten, so that give 'm five bushels for grinding that day. So, Jack was well pleased with that 'mount. So Jack was real, real, tired that evening. He didn't even get any meals after he eat that evening. He just went to bed about ten o'clock and went to sleep. And he slept 'til plumb day light. He got up the next morning, 'cided he would get his breakfast. And he looked around and he found a li'l cold meat there and he fried his meat, 'cided he make 'm some gravy and he tuck and fried out some o' the grease and stirred it up with some water and he went to stir up the flour in his gravy. And—there was a big, eight windows cut out, just eight holes, no glass in it, nothing, up way high on top o' the room. And it was a good big room where he stayed.

And so all at once it got dark.

Something got in the window.

And up there set great big black cats.

And one come down and jumped out o' the window and jumped on the table, stuck his paw in his gravy and said, "Sop doll in your gravy, Mister?"

And Jack said he just watched at 'em. Them the biggest cats, big fat cats he'd ever seen in all his life. They must been big as dogs almost.

Another 'n jumped down and said, "Sop doll in your gravy, Mister?"

And Jack said, "You'd better quit sopping you doll in my gravy. 'Bout the next cat that sops his doll in my gravy, I'm going to cut his paw off with this here knife!" Jack had a great big cleaver there, like you chop up meat with.

Down come one. Said, "Sop doll in your gravy, Mister?" And Jack whacked hit's paw off with that cleaver, and the ol' cats all jumped out the window and went, "Meow, whow, whow." And that one, he whacked his paw off, fell in the bowl.

And Jack, he reached down in the bowl to get the paw out and when he got it—the paw—out, it come out a woman's hand, and hit happened to be her left hand and hit had a wedding ring on it. Well, Jack just stuck that in back o' his pocket. He said, "I'm gonna save this gravy," said, "y' know, with those people dying down here. And I want to see what's them cats a putting in this gravy." So Jack just poured that out in a fruit jar a sitting there, and then he washed out his bowl, fried out 'm some more grease, made 'm some more gravy. He eat his meat and bread and gravy. That morning, hit tasted extra good. He was real hungry. Had the ol' mill going 'bout day light.

And 'bout day light, the ol' farmer come down. "Well, Jack," said, "how'd it go last night?"

"O purty good," said, "last night, not a thing bothered me last night. But this morning I had a kind of funny and strange experience." He said, "This morning I was getting my breakfast and," said, "I had everything ready. The bread was baking, the meat a frying. Start to make my gravy and," said, "I was getting my gravy ready and I set a bowl of gravy, just stirred up the—all at once the room got dark and up there in them eight windows set eight big black cats." Said, "I never seen nothing like it in all my life. And," said, "one jumped down and said 'Sop doll in your gravy, Mister?'" Said, "Another one jumped down and sopped his paw in my gravy and said, 'Sop doll in your gravy, Mister?'" Said, "I told the next cat that sopped his doll in my gravy, I was gonna cut hit's paw off. I grabbed a great big cleaver there that you hack up meat with. And," said, "that next one jumped and said, 'Sop doll in your gravy, Mister?'" said, "I sopped his paw off, and," said, "they all went 'Meow, whow, whow,' and out they went and away they went. I went to take that cat's paw out of my gravy and look-a-here what it turned into." He pulled out that hand and showed it to the ol' man.

He said, "Lord have mercy," said the ol' man. "That hand," says, "I know," he said. "That's my wife's hand." Said, "It's got my wedding ring on it, my diamond ring on it," he says. "I'd know that hand anywhar."

"Well," Jack said, "there must be witches around here."

"Yes," said the ol' farmer, "must be."

He said, "I saved that gravy." Said, "How clost is it to the clostest doctor around here? I'd like to have it analyzed." Said, "I b'lieve that's why people's been a dying: they've been a poisonin'm."

"Oh," the farmer says, "yeah." Said, "You just grind away, and," says, "I'll run to town and have it analyzed." So he run to town and he was gone about three or four hours and come back. He said, "Jack, the doctor said they was enough o' poison arsenic in that there gravy to kill the whole town."

"Well, now y' know why people's been a dying at your mill."

"Well," he says, "we gonna have to do something about this." Said, "We gonna have to find out about this."

"All right," said Jack, "now, what can we do?"

[Farmer] said, "We'll go to the house and we'll check this hand and see if I'm right."

"All right," said Jack. They cut the mill down and got caught up, and most o' the people had quit coming anyway, and Jack, he ground most of the meal now and maybe hit be an hour or two 'fore anybody come in. So, they rode over to the ol' farmer's house, and his wife was in there sick.

"Oh," she said, "I ain't able to get up this morning." Said, "I'm feeling awful bad." Said, "You'll have to get your own breakfast."

"Well," said the ol' man, "I can do that all right, Honey," said, "but I would, 'fore I get the breakfast," said, " I would like to see your left hand."

"Oh," she said, "I'm feeling so bad, I don't wanta stick my hands out from under the cover."

"Yes," said, "stick out your hand, Honey." Said, "I want a see that purty diamond ring I bought y'." Said, "That makes me feel good to, to know you're wearing it."

"Well," she said, "I might've pulled it off. I don't know if I'm wearing it or not." She worked around and stuck out her right hand.

"Oh, Honey," he said, "you never wear your ring on your right hand." Said, "I want a see your left hand." And she wouldn't stick hit out, and the ol' farmer just reached over and grabbed her left hand and jerked hit over and sure 'nough her hand was gone. And she had hit kindly tied up where it had been cut off, to keep it from bleeding. "Well," the ol' farmer says, "well, you see Jack, we're right," he says.

She's got seven friends. She says, "I'm sick this morning. Will you please send out and get all o' my seven friends?" And said, "Left 'm come in. I want a talk to 'm."

"All right," said the ol' farmer. He sent out and told all her seven friends to come in. They came in an', boy, they was talking up a storm. They was talking so big about what they gonna have to do. They were gonna have to kill everbody in that country. If didn't, they'd be killed. And while they was doing that, Jack and the ol' farmer nailed the door and nailed up the windows, and they didn't even know they was in it. More than that, they poured a barrel of kerosene on it and set it on fire, and the first thing you know, he'd burned up everone of them witches. Everone, the house, and everthing went up into blaze, and he got all the witches in that country. Now, the ol' farmer had no house to live in and he said, "Jack, we'll just live together in the mill and," said, "we'll just work together in the mill, and," said, "we'll just go halfers." Well Jack and the ol' farmer, as far as I know, still yet tending the mill and getting 'long just fine.

Ward c. 1970: side A. ATU 326, Motif D702.1.1. Marshall Ward, of Banner Elk, North Carolina, told this tale to Ambrose Manning of the English department over the mountain at the East Tennessee State University. Like Ray Hicks, Ward has a very strong southern mountain accent. He pronounces *tired* and *fire* much more like *tarred* and *farr*. And he softens consonant endings, especially *-d* and *-ing*. The transcription ignores these regular nonstandard pronunciations, but sometimes indicates elisions that the reader would otherwise not be aware of.

Sop Doll is an example of a märchenized legend, in this case a very widespread legend fitted into the frame of the popular märchen ATU 326, in which the hero must prove himself by spending the night in a haunted structure. That bit of piecing was done long ago, for Jane Gentry, more than forty years senior and only second cousin to Ward, knew the same story and told it in 1925 as she had heard it from her father. Halpert's notes on the tale (Chase 1943: 192) are useful.

87. Three Little Pigs

One time there was 'n ol' sow and three pigs lived away back in the woods and they was getting along just fine. The pigs was growing great big. The pigs was name' Tom, Will, and Jack. Well, they growed, get bigger n' bigger, and after awhile they got up to be great big pigs, shoats, 'r almost hogs. The ol' mother said to 'em one day, "Well, boys," said, "I believe you ought to go out in the world and try your fortune. You ought to go out and build you a home of your own. Build it strong and stout so the ol' wolf or the ol' fox can't get in and eat you, a bear or nothing can break into your home. Build it strong and stout, build it big and large—big enough till I can come and see you and all your brothers can come and see you and all can get in the house at one time.

Well, the little pigs, they said the way it'd be, they'd go if Mother went ahead and fixed ever one a basket of food that would last 'em at least a week. She got all the food fixed up and then she gave each one a sled and a little bag to tie on the sled to haul the vittles. And they got the vittles on. She give 'em each one a bed, n' a axe, n' a saw, and things to work with. Well, she went on out and bid them good-bye, they all took off. Tom went east, Will went west, and Jack went south.

So they kep' on traveling and traveling. After while, Tom, he met a great big wolf, and the ol' wolf said, "Where you going, Tom?"

"Oh," he said, "I'm going out in this world to try my fortune."

"Well," said, "what are you going to do?"

"Oh," said, "I'm going to build me a house and live by myself, work, and make a living."

"Well," the ol' wolf said, "now, let's see here. What are you going to build your house out of?"

"Well, something stout and strong. Brick and mud, maybe rock."

"Oh," said the ol' wolf, "you don't want to lift the ol' big heavy rock. You don't want to make up mortar and put the rock together. You don't want to have to buy brick and carry it in. Why don't you jest buil' your house out of something that you can find? Why," he said, "right down the road here is a great, big, fine cornfield, plenty of stalks and shucks and straw, and stuff like that." Said, "You can build a warm bed out of it, warm house. Oh," said, "you could have the best house in the world." Said, "That's what you have ought to build. Well?" said the ol' wolf.

"I don't know," said Tom. "I'll think of something." So anyway, he began to work and work and work and work, and after awhile he 'cided he'd do what the ol' wolf said. He went down in the big cornfield. He shucked and pulled corn stalks and picked grass. He built a great big house, and it was really warm. Oh, he was real proud of it: plenty of corn to eat, wouldn't have to work hard.

Well, after awhile, uh, Will, he's going on down and great ol' big fox met Will going down the road. "Ho," he says, "Will, where are you going?"

"Oh," he says, "I'm a-gonna try my fortunes. I'm gonna build me a house and," he said, "I'm gonna make it big and large so all my brothers come and see me, and my mother."

"What you think you're gonna build it out of?" said the ol' fox.

"Well," he said, "I'll tell you. I'm gonna build it out of something strong like rock and brick and mortar—mix—and so on."

"Oh," said the ol' wolf [fox], "That would never do." Said, "It'd break your back—be hard work. Why," said, "down here."—the ol' fox said, "Down here is a great, big, wheat field. Boy," he said, "why don't you go down there in the middle of that wheat field and build you a big fine house out of straw and hay and sods and things like that, and," said, "be a lot easier to do and it won't break your back a-doing it and," said, "Lord, you'll be right in the middle of a big, fine, wheat field where you can jest eat all the wheat you want, and won't have to work for it."

"Well now," he said, "that sounds pretty good. I'll look it over," said Will. So Will went down the wheat field and, boy, it was good, juicy wheat and looked fine to him. Well, he 'cided he'd do it, yes. So he went on in there and got him hay and straw and—wheatstraw—and sods and built him a fine house, big house, out of it and it was good.

Well, so he went on—uh, Jack had gone on down the road wa—his way—and on his way, he met a great, big, black bear. And the ol' bear said, "Jack, where you going?"

"Oh," Jack said, "I'm a-going out in the world, to try my fortune. I'm going out here somewhere and build me a house and I'm gonna build me a big house."

"All right," said the ol' bear, "build you a big house. Said, "Break your back," said, "carrying big rock, carrying mortar, carrying water to stir it up with, and the time that it'd built, you'd be an ol' hog ready to die."

"Well," said Jack, "maybe not. I'll go on and see what I can do."

So he went way out in the woods—he found a whole lot of big acorn trees and them trees was filled with acorns, wouldn't be long till be falling. And there was a lot of stone—found a good mortar pool—hole—and he stirred up a lot of mortar. He began to roll them big rock in. He made him a great big rock house, put him some windows in, made him a big chimbley, big fireplace. And it took him 'bout a month to get his house built, while Tom built his house in a week, Will built his house in a week.

Well, time went on. One night Tom was snoring away and something peck, peck on the door. Tom jumped up. "Who's 'ere? Who's 'ere? Who's 'ere?"

"Ohh, it's the big ol' wolf." Said, "I come over, thought I'd spend the night with you and have some fun."

And Tom said, "I'm 'fraid of you, Mr. Wolf. I'm afraid you'll eat me up 'f I let you in."

"Oh no, I wouldn't eat you up," said the ol' wolf. "I want to be your friend."

"Well," Tom said, "I don't know about that."

"If you don't let me in," the ol' wolf said, "I'll blow and I'll blow and I'll blow and I'll huff and I'll puff and I'll—by the hair of my chinney chin, I'll blow your house in and eat you up anyway."

Well anyway, the ol' wolf was a-beginning to huff and puff and blow, and finally at last he blowed the top Tom's house off. It scared Tom so, he run and run and run, and the ol' wolf right behind him. And he come to Will's house and said, "Oh, Will, Will, Will, let me in quick." Said, "The big wolf's after me." And Will let him in. And shut the door. And barred the door. And then the ol' wolf got to Will's house and says, "OK! Will," said, "let me in." Said, "If you don't," says, "I'll huff and puff and by the hair of my chinney chin," says, "I'll blow your house in." And so, uh, Will and Tom was scared to death and he huffed and he puffed—

And about that time here come the ol' fox and said, "What are you doing?" Mr. Fox said. "That's my pig." Said, "I got him to build a house out of straw and him to build in this wheat field," and said, "so I could eat him up."

And they 'gan to huff and puff, both of 'em did, and they 'gan to blow, and they blowed the top of the house off and jest as they blowed the top of the house off, Tom and Will jumped out. They runned, they runned, they runned, they runned, and they kep' on run—running, running, and they run and they run and they run and after while they come to Jack's house and they said, "Oh, Jack, Jack," said, "let us in." Said, "'S an ol' big wolf and an ol' big fox, red fox, is after us." Said, "Please let us in." And, uh, Jack jerked the door open and they ran in, they shut the door and barred it and locked it.

That time the great, ole, big bear come in. "You two, what you doing on my territory, you wolf and fox!" Said, "I told Jack to build out here where these big acorn trees was. And," said, "looks like he's done a good job."

"Well," say, "we were going to get in." So the ol' wolf, he huffed and puffed and huffed and he puffed and he said, "By the hair of my chinney chin, piggies, I'm a-coming in." And the piggies, they sit back and listened. The ol' bear, he huffed and puffed. The fox, he huffed and puffed. And they couldn't puff it down. It 'as built out of stone and mortar and it 'as real strong. And they puffed and puffed. They huffed and puffed and blowed and blowed till they blowed the blower out. And they was out there, jest dead. And the ol' fox, he began to think how he 'as gonna get in the house. The ol' wolf, he began to plan. And after a while the ol' bear, he began to plan. Well, after awhile they went up on top of the house and looked at the chimbley. Chimbley was too small for the ol' bear to go down. The ol' wolf said he might get down the chimbley and the fox said he might also. But they was afraid to try it down the chimbley—had a big, hot fire in the chimbley. And the little pigs put on a great big brass pot and had a great big lid to flock on it. And the ol' wolf said to the fox, said, "You the smallest." Said, "You try it first, and I'll come behind you." Said, "If you get down, I can." So the ol' fox, he went down the chimbley, banged into that hot water. And at that time the ol' wolf come down in the hot water, and the little pig slammed the lids on, and he cooked and boiled the ol' fox and the ol' wolf,

and they was poppin'
and crackin'
and fryin'.

And the ol' bear couldn't get in.

So the ol' bear, he went up and said, "Little pigs, little pigs, I'm a-getting cold out here by myself. You wouldn't please let me in?"

The pigs said, "We afraid of you, ol' bear. We afraid you eat us up."

"No," said the ol' bear. He said, "I wouldn't, I'd be your friend." Said, "Jest let me get my little tip end of my nose in, to smell that good fire and what's a-cooking in there."

And they said, "O.K., We'll let you stick the tip end of your nose in, but," said, "you can't come no farther." So they opened the door and the ol' bear, he stuck his nose in, and the little pigs began to push the door together, and mashed the ol' bear's nose.

"Oh," he said, "little pigs, little pigs, don't be such cowards." Said, "I wouldn't hurt you." Said, "I jest want to get in and warm myself. Let me," said, "stick my tail in." So they let him stick his tail in. And then they shut the door on his tail and mashed it a little, he took it out. "Now, little pigs," said, "I'm real cold." Said, "My paws are cold. Let me stick my paws in." Little pig opened the door, let him stick his paws in. And he warmed a little while, and the little pigs thought it 'as kind of fun there.

"Oh, pigs," said, "my back part jest a-freezing up." Said, "Let me stick my back parts in."

"All right," said little pigs, and he eased his back parts in.

"Now, little pigs," said, "that feels so good, let me ease in jest a little more." They let him ease in a little more, and he kep' on easing and easing, got half in. "Now, little pigs," said, "jest let me come on in all the way and warm up," he said. "I wouldn't hurt you little pigs." And so the ol' bear, he got in, laid down before the big frying fire cracking and a-popping, and, and in that kettle was the ol' fox and the ole, and the ol' wolf, jest a-popping and a-cracking and a-frying. And the ol' bear, he laid there, and he began to snore. He went to sleep and began talk in his sleep. He said, "Hmumm, I can eat one pig tonight, and in the morning I can eat one pig, and at dinner time I can eat the other pig. Won't they make a good morsel of meat for me to eat?"

And, and the little pigs said, "Know what he's going to do?" Said, "He's talking in his sleep. He said that he's gonna eat us up." Said, "What we gonna do?"

About that time, Jack, he run out and left 'em to holler. Said, "Whoo-eee. Sic 'em, sic 'em, sic 'em, sic 'em."

And the ol' fox—the ol' bear—jumped up, said, "What's a matter, what's a matter?"

He said, "The king's men and all his dogs coming."

Says, uh, he said, "Where can I hide, where can I hide?"

And, uh, he said, "Right here is a great big, uh, churn." Said, "You jump in this big churn." He said, "I shut the lid up and, and, uh they won't know you here." And so the ol' bear, he squeezed down in the churn—it was real tight. They put a big lid on it and they grabbed some nails and nailed it up. Real tight. The ol' bear down there thinking that they coming.

And that kettle was plumb full of boiling water. They pulled that kettle off and they'd already killed the ol' wolf and the ol' fox. They 'as ready to eat, they was real cooked, stewed up good. And, you know, the little pigs, they jus' took bucket-fulls that hot water and began to pour down in that churn. And the ol' bear begin to cry: "A-urr-a! That's hot! That's hot, little pigs, don't pour that stuff there, pour something cold—something jest a little colder." They kep' pouring that hot, boiling water down in there. And after a while, it cooked the ol' bear and killed him.

So the little pigs lived in Jack's house, they eat the ol' bear and they eat the ol' fox and eat the ol' wolf as long as they last. And then they stayed and eat acorns and they go back to the cornfields and get corn and go to the wheat field and get wheat, so they growed great big hogs. Went and got their mother. Lived happy ever after.

Ward c. 1970b: side A. ATU 124. Marshall Ward told this story to Tom Burton or Ambrose Manning. Ward is at his expansive best in this tale. He develops each episode with a good deal of dialogue. He uses a special voice for the bear. He holds out words such as *big, strong,* and *now.* He uses some words in an unusual way, notably *flock,* which seems to mean "to put on or cover." The *sled* here mentioned is a common piece of Appalachian farm equipment used to drag heavy loads across the ground, not necessarily (or usually) over snow or ice. His pronunciation too is distinctive. *Fire* sounds more like *farr, where* like *whurr.* Begin and *begun* are hard to distinguish. While this transcription generally avoids specialized spellings, some are used to suggest elision in places where standard spelling seems to obscure the rhythm.

This is a favorite nursery tale of American children. The ending in which the villain (more commonly a fox) hides because he fears the threat of dogs and is subsequently killed with boiling water—and perhaps churned into butter—is common in Appalachian versions, though the triple villain is not. While the idea of calling the three pigs Tom, Will, and Jack may have occurred independently to Ward, he is not alone in using these names. Roberts includes a version in *Sang Branch Settlers* (1974: 269–71) that also uses these names. Hamish Henderson once collected a Scots version in which they were called Dennis, Biddy, and Rex (Briggs 1970: vol. 2: 572–74).

88. Jack and Old Fire Dragon

This here story I'm gonna tell, uh, my grandfather Benjamin, Ben for short, teach me this tale when I was a little boy. And the name of it is "Jack and Ol' Fire Dragon."

So now, in the winter time, in the fall of the year, say along now in this time of year, they would hafta start clearin' ground to make food, or vittles they called 'em, vittles, for another year of—vittles is the way they called the food. So, Will and Tom and Jack is the three boys. So they was around the log cabin, like boys is, come up prickin' around. And their dad, their father, come out and said, "All right now, boys," said, "this ain't gonna do." Said, "We be needin' some ground cleared," said, "over by that little track of land that I hunt."

So they fixed up a wagonload of the vittles, the tools, the broad axe (the axe is to build 'em a little log cabin with). Well they took the wagon, a yoke of ox. Went all over in to that little track of land. So they worked there a week or somethin' to get 'em a log cabin built; they built 'em a mud-rock chimney to it, and a porch. So when they got it done, they sent Tom and Jack, went t' clear ground. And Will was to stay at the house and cook dinner. And then when he's done, he was to go back over and help clear that ground. So, he fixed a mess of fresh beans, cleaned 'em, put 'em on a old cash cooker to cook 'em by the mud fireplace. Put in a couple or somethin' of ash cakes apiece, put it in the ash and cover it up with coals.

So he—they fixed two boards hewed out with the broad axe to hit to let them know when to come, when dinner was ready. Like a bell, come on out of that, ring a dinner bell. Where I worked at the farm, there was a dinner bell, but that was their dinner bell: they hit two boards together. So Will went out and hit the boards, step back in, looked out through the door, the front door, and there come a man with a big blue beard down t' here, and was spittin' balls of fire, bouncin' over the yard and some'd hit the porch and scorched the place, the boards, before they'd hewed 'em out. And Will's eyes, they popped out, and he run behind the door and hid. So, ol' Fire, he'd scooped up a mess of beans they had up on the table, y' see, ol' Fire Dragon come in, eat all that dish, eat the dish of beans up. Then went in and checked the pot, and eat the whole pot of beans as well, he did. Reached down and got his pipe out and put a great big coal of fire in his pipe, held a great big— woulda held a peck. So he lit the pipe up and fetch 'er for a few draw, and gosh, when that pipe got started, it got dark in there was smokin'. And he went out through the yard with smoke a bellowin' out his pipe. And then he spit out a lump of fire-ball, that way, and draw his pipe again.

And so, well, Tom and Jack got in. Will come out behind the door and Tom says, "Will, where's the dinner?"

He said, "Oh my gosh," he said, "if you'd a-seen what I seen you wouldn't want no dinner." He said, "When I beat them boards together, they call a giant man through the yard, had a big blue beard," he said; "he spit balls of fire, they bounced and burned." Said, "If one hit yuh, yuh'd burn a-blazin'." Said, "I hid behind the door. Had a dish of beans scooped up," said; "he come in and eat that whole dish up and went in and emptied the pot." But he said, "He found and dug in and found my ash cakes and eat them up." See them was cookin' down in the ashes.

They begin to laugh. Tom, he jus' said, "Ha, ha! Ha, ha!" He said, "We won't get ground cleared with brothers like you." Said, "When a man come in or whatever, let him eat our lunch, eat our dinner, vittles up." Said, "We'll starve to death here clearin' ground." Said, "We thought you could beat that, Will."

"Well," he said, "don't brag, Tom, you and Jack," he said. "Tom, tomorrow will be your turn."

So Will and Jack went back and cleared next day. Tom stayed to get them somethin' to eat. Fixed up a mess o' beans, put 'em on to cook. When it came time, he put the ash cakes in. When it got ready, he beat the boards, scooped out a mess o' beans, set 'em on the table. He looked out and there come what Will had said. His eyes, he run in there and hid.

And so ol' Fire Dragon spit them balls o' fire around. He come in, he took the dish of beans up, and went in and emptied the pot and eat the ash cakes up again. Well all, with his pipe a drawin', that stunk, oh gosh, he stuck it down in that tobacco. And he acted like it was tastin' good, too, after he eat all that food up, I bet, while smokin' his tobacco.

So Jack and Will got in to eat. Will said, "What's wrong, Tom?" Says, "You give it t' me yesterday." Said, "What's wrong?" Said, "Where's the dinner?"

He said, "Jack," he said, "Will's right." He said, "If you see what me and brother Will see, you won't want no dinner."

So Jack, he jus', oh he said, "I got two older brothers"; said, "now we ain't gonna clear ground," said, "if I can't do no better than you. You'ns 's older than I am," said, "and let a feller come in here and eatin' up all the time." Said, "That isn't gonna work." Said, "Somethin's gonna hafta change around this place."

"Well," he said, "don't brag, Jack." Said, "Tomorrow your turn."

So Will and Tom went to cleared. Jack stayed and he fixed the beans, and biscuits. Put 'em on to cook, and he got to doin'. He scooped out a mess and went out and beat the boards t'gether. Will and Tom come, started to come down. Here come that man. He was spittin' balls of fire, and Jack jus' stood there on the porch. Said, "Hello there, Dad!" Said, "Jus' in time for dinner, Dad." Said, "Jus' wait a minute or somethin' and my brothers will be here and we'll eat t'gether."

"No, no, don't wanna bite." 'Cause y' asked him, he didn't want none. He wanted to take it to make it taste gooder. So he said, "All wanted to do was to stop by and light my pipe." So he went in, put the tobacco in and got out a great big chunk o' fire and lit the pipe. Got it a drawin', and that smoke it was a bellowin'. And jus' as he went out through the yard to where he live a piece, Jack took out behind him to see where he went at.

And so Will and Tom got in and said, "Oh my gosh." Said, "He's eaten Jack today and left the dinner." Said, "Oh, poor Jack. He's eat him up." They mambered around a while, said, "Well, Jack's gone. He's eat up, and with a man like that," he said, "he's eat him and didn't make an even meal, small as he was." Said, "Maybe make him a bite. We jus's well set down and eat and get back to clearin' ground."

While they was a-eatin', Jack had followed him down there and he went way down the canyon of the mountain and he went in a hole in the ground, down in a thicket.

And so Jack come in jus' before they'd finished eatin' and come in on them. And said, "Oh," said, "you'ns eatin' the dinner up ain't y'?" Said, "Couldn't y' wait?"

"Oh," he said, "we thought Fire Dragon had eat you up for his dinner t'day," said, "bein' it was left."

He said, "No," said, "I asked him to eat, and went out on the porch and he said he didn't want none. Said jus' stopped by to light his pipe. And," said, "when he got his pipe lit and all that smoke a-goin'," he said, "I let him get a little piece and I followed him." He said, "He went down yonder in a hole in the ground."

So that changed all the ground clearin'. That changed 'cause the ground clearin' wasn't on their minds. They went there and looked at that hole, where Jack took'em to it. And they went with a froe and the other piece that yuh strip, with the splits that were around 'em, to make a basket. So they went to work a-makin' a big wood, big split, round split basket. And to make a split rope to let one another down in there in. And so they worked there a-carvin' out that white oak, to make that basket. They worked around three days gettin' that basket fixed to let one another down in that hole to see what was down in there. And so they got 'er done, went down to the hole.

And Will was the oldest. They said, "Now, Will, you the oldest. Let's let the oldest go first." So they put Will in the basket and let him down. And he jus' jerked the split rope when he wanted to be pulled back out. And so, directly the rope shook and jerked, so they pulled Will back out. Said, "What'd you see?"

Said, "I seed a house down in there."

So they put Tom in, let him down. He let it go down a little bit, and stayed a little while longer. And he jerked the rope and they pulled him out. Jack and Will said, "Tom, what did you see?"

He said, "I seed a house and porch."

Well they put Jack in, he let it go down, down, down, down. The basket caught on the gable of the house, the eave, the gable there, it slid on down, on the porch roof. And the basket slid off the porch roof, and set down in the yard. And Jack got out.

And so ol' Fire Dragon had taken two [*sic*] girls, back when they was just small. And he raised 'em down under the ground. They didn't know nowhere else. And one's name was Martha, the oldest. They was sisters. And the middle one was Myrtle. And the third one was Marie, beautiful.

And so Jack went around to the left where the door was at, and he hit on the door. A second or two there the door skreaked a little open there. And he wasn't expectin' to see what he seed.

There was a beautiful girl, her hair. He begin to talk lightly, a little bit. He wanted to get around her, yuh know, for a date.

She said, "Lawd's me," said, "man, whoever you are, if you think I am beautiful." Said, "My name is Martha." Said, "The second room you get in, my middle sister Myrtle really is beautiful, you think I'm beautiful." Said, "Jus' wait 'til you get on in there."

Jack got on in there, and boy, he seed her. And he was startin' to get around her a little bit. And she said, "Oh gosh, don't do that." Said, "My sister Marie is the youngest one in the next room, and you think that we beautiful," said, "wait 'til you get in there."

So Jack got on in there. He got started around Marie. And directly it hit her that she wanted him to be her husband. And she said, "Now, young man," said, "what's your name?"

He said, "My name's Jack."

"Well," she said, "now if the Fire Dragon comes, catches you here," she said, "he'll kill everyone of y's, burn you up with a fire ball in this house." And said, "He's got a silver sword," said, "but it's heavy to your side." Said, "But you get it and do a little trainin'." Said, "See if you can get us outta here." And so she made a ribbon, a bow, took a bow, and let Jack pin it in her hair, so when he got her out, that'd mean she was his wife. And so she put a wishin' ring on Jack's finger.

And so Jack trained with that there silver sword and ol' Fire Dragon come in and he found Jack in there. And he was a burnin' Jack up, tryin' to, with fire balls. Jack was dodgin', brushin' 'em off. Directly he got in a way with that sword and slashed Fire Dragon's head off. It bounced on the floor.

She said, "You did it! You did it! You did it!"

And so he put Martha in the basket. And Will and Tom was up there thinkin' it was Jack, been gone that long and shook it. And so Jack shook the rope and put Martha in. And they was expectin' Jack to be in the basket. And out shot that beautiful girl and Will said, "Gosh," he said, "Tom, it's a daughter." And said, "This is mine! This is mine!"

Tom said, "No, gosh, you can't have her." Said, "Now that ain't gonna do."

Will said, "Now maybe I need her."

She said, "Oh don't do that." Said, "Don't do this," said, "the middle one, the second one's that's a comin' is a' beautiful than I am."

So they just forgot all about it and shoved the basket back down in. And Jack put Myrtle in. Brought her out, and Will said, "All right, Tom, you can have that first one."

Tom said, "No, you can have her." Said, "I'll take this second one."

She said, "Don't argue about me." Said, "Boys, the third one that's a comin' is the youngest one, Marie." Said, "She's beautiful."

So they really put it back down in there, and Jack put his'n in. Shook it and it come out with her. So Will said, "All right, Tom," said, "you can have the first two. I'll jus' take this one." Said, "I'll give you two sisters."

Tom said, "No, I'll give you two sisters."

And so Marie says, "Don't argue about me." Said, "You see this ribbon he pinned in my hair, the bow?" Said, "That was fixed so if he got me outta here and the other two, that I belong to Jack."

"Well," they said, "if that's the deal, let him stay down in there," and threw the basket, rope and all.

Poor ol' Jack. Now we've got to get him out. He's in there, down in that hole, where his brothers throwed the basket and all. And said, "We'll have all three of the daughters." But the bow is on there.

And so, Jack, he stayed around in there several days. Eat up all the vittles that the Fire Dragon had in there, food, the vittles. And all he could find. And one day, he was a sittin' a lookin', and happened to be rubbin' his hands to see how cold he was gettin', with nothin' to eat. And he happened to see that wishin' ring. And he seed it, and he said, "I wish that I was at home in the ol' chimney corner at home where I was raised." And there he was.

His mama come in and said, "Jack," said, "I thought you was supposed to be over helpin' Will and Tom clear that new ground."

He said, "That's where I'm started right now."

And so he got over there. And Will and Tom took good care of the three daughters. And so they talked on it and agreed. And Will took Martha, and Tom got Myrtle, the middle one, and Jack got his, with the bow in her hair yet. And they went and got a preacher and got married. And the last time I was down through that settlement, they was shanties all over them hills. So that's the end of the Fire Dragon.

Ray Hicks 1985. ATU 301. From a performance by Ray Hicks of Beech Mountain, North Carolina, videotaped in the 1980s for Dr. Thomas Burton, then teaching at and now retired from East Tennessee State University. This seems to be one of Hicks's favorite tales to tell, as there are a number of performances of it in archives. Hicks is perhaps the most expansive of the Beech Mountain storytellers. He was invited to perform at the first National Storytelling Festival in Jonesborough, Tennessee, in 1973, and became a fixture of the festival thereafter. A National Heritage Fellow, he has performed widely and influenced many other storytellers, including nephews Frank Proffitt Jr. and Orville Hicks.

The story of the underground journey and the three princesses is fairly widespread in English-speaking American tradition. But it is ubiquitous in the Hispanic tradition where, as Juan Orso, Jack the Bear (or Jack the Bear's Son), the hero is unusually strong and, rather than clearing land with his brothers, journeys in the company of marvelous companions such as those found in the stories of Six Who Travel through the World and The Land and Water Ship (ATU 513A, B). Versions that represent this tradition are included above in chapters 8 and 4.

The unusual use of the verb *prick* that appears in the second paragraph of the tale may shed light on the use of the verb in the opening line of Canto I of the first book of Spenser's *Faerie Queene*:

A Gentle Knight was pricking on the plaine.

89. Fill, Bowl, Fill

Okay, this old man lived way back in the mountains—him and his wife—and he had two girls. And, said, them girls was just beautiful. And the boys around 'ere got to come courting them girls, from miles around. That old man was kinda rich and them boys around 'ere he didn't think was good enough to come see his girls 'cause 'ey was poor. And so he said, "I'm gonna have to put a stop to it." And he made a rule. He went outside and he put a ring up in his yard. He said any boy come to court his girls had to bring a rabbit and put it in that ring. If the rabbit stayed in the ring ten minutes, they could marry either girl he wanted. But if the rabbit didn't stay in the ring he'd cut their heads off.

So the girls was real beautiful, like I said. The boys, few of 'em, kept a coming anyway. Said 'ey wanted one of them girls. They'd bring 'em a rabbit and they would turn it loose in that ring. The rabbit would make one circle and run out and take off through the woods. The old man go cut their heads off. It wasn't long, what few boys was left around 'ere got too scared to come see the girls. But one day Jack decided he'd go get him one of them girls. He was kinda fond of the youngest girl. He told his momma, said, "I'm going up 'ere." And, "said, "I'm gonna see if I can win that youngest girl."

Momma said, "Jacks, don't go." Said, "Every boy went up 'ere got their head cut off." Said, "He'd cut your head off."

Jack said, bedad, that he'd just have to cut it off. Said, "I'm kinda in love with that youngest girl. I gonna go after her."

So she fixed Jack up a li'l ol' poke of ash cake there, and give him a bottle of water. Jack headed out and his momma begged him not to go, but he headed out anyway. It come late up in the evening and he come to a li'l ol' clearing out there and a big ol' log setting there, and he set down to eat his supper. When he set down to eat, this ol' man popped up out of nowhere—great long beard, white hairs—and said, "Can you spare me a bite to eat?" Said, "I'm hungry."

Jack said, "Yeah, Daddy, set down and eat with me." Said, "Glad to."

The ol' man sat down, and Jack reched in his poke there to get his ash cake out. When he pulled it out, said, the cake turned into big ol' spice cake. Him and that man eat more—they'd eat, more cake'd come in it's place. He reched down to get his bottle of water and when he opened it up to drink it, said, it was the best wine he'd ever drunk in his life. Him and the ol' man sat there and drunk that wine and that ol' man said, "Jack," said, "I know where you headed." Said, "You been good to me. Gimme your dinner and e'rything." Said, "You're headed up 'ere ta see 'at ol' man, 'at got them girls." Said, "You going get your head cut off."

Jack said, "Bedad, I might get it cut off. But," said, "I'm going up 'ere."

That ol' man said, "Like I said Jack, you been good t' me and," said, "I'm gonna help you. But," said, "have you got any faith?"

Jack said, "Don't know." Said, "Ain't never tried my faith out."

He said, "Here, you take this stick." Give Jack a long stick. Said, "You go out there behind that rock, where that spring's at. And," said, "you stir in 'at water till it turn into wine."

Jack took the stick and went out there behind the rock and come t' that spring, and he went in t' stirring. He stirred and stirred and stirred 'ere for a long time and—'bout to give up. But he stirred a li'l more and the water got to turning red. It give Jack more faith and he stirred that much more and 'rectly the whole spring turned into red wine.

Jack took that bottle-full back out there and that man drunk it and said it was the best wine he'd ever tasted. He said, "Jack," said, "you got a lotta faith. And," said, "while you 'as gone" he'd hewed Jack out a wooden drill 'bout twelve inches long. Out of wood. And he said, "You take this drill, up there t' ol' man. And," said, "you put it in the middle o' that ring, that drill. And," said, "as long as that drill's in that ring when you turn your rabbit loose in there," said, "that rabbit'll stay in that ring—long as that drill's in there."

So Jack caught him up a big rabbit and put it in a sack, and got the wooden drill, and went up to the man's house.

Ole man come out and said, "Can I help you, son?"

Jack said, "Yeah, I come see if I can win your youngest daughter."

That ol' man said, "You know the rules here." Said, "You put a rabbit in that ring yar, if it stays ten minutes, you can have her, but if it don't I cut your head off." Said, "I'm even makin' a new rule." Said, "If you make that rabbit stay in that ring ten minutes, you can cut my head off and have all my money and my youngest daughter, too."

So Jack walked out there in the middle of that ring and put that drill, wooden drill that man made, right in the middle of that ring. And he got his big rabbit out of the sack, and put it in the ring. Rabbit looked up and seen that wooden drill, it was sumpin' magic about it, and he took in to running. Running around and around and around. That man kept watching it, and he looked down at his watch: about five minutes was up. He begin to sweat. He went in the house and he told his oldest girl, said, "You go out there and see if you can buy that drill." Said, "That's what keeping that rabbit in that ring."

Oldest girl went out there and said, "Jack, give y' a thousand dollars for that drill."

"No, bedad," said, "you come back in ten minutes," said, "and I'll give it to y'."

She went back in the house and said, "Daddy, I cain't buy that drill."

And he looked down, seven minutes was up, and he told his youngest girl. Said, "You go out there and see if you can buy that drill."

And she went out there and said, "Jack," said, "I give you two thousand dollars for that drill."

Jack said, "No." Said, "You come back in ten minutes and I give it to y'."

She went back in the house and said, "I cain't buy that drill, neither."

About eight minutes was up, and that ol' man was sweat just pouring off o' there. He told his old woman, said, "You go out there and buy that drill." Said, "Ole Jack's gonna kill me in 'bout two more minutes."

And she went out there and said, "Jack," said, "we'll give you anything you want for that drill."

Jack said, "No." Said, "You come back, the ten minutes, and," said, "I'll let you have it."

She went back in the house and told her ol' man, said, "I cain't buy that drill."

He looked down at his watch: nine minutes was up. He said, "Well, look like Jack's gonna get to kill me." And he started outside but he had a big old wooden bowl there on the table. He picked the bowl up and went out there and said, "Jack," said, "nearly—ten minutes is nearly up." Said, "Looks like you're gonna get to kill me. But," said, "'fore you kill me will you sing this bowl full of lies for me?"

Jack said, "Bedad, I'll try." And he hand the bowl out and Jack looked at it and said,

> Well, the oldest girl she come out
> All fired to buy my drill.
> I fooled around and I kissed 'er well.
> Fill, bowl, fill.

Jack says, "It full of lies yet?"
"No, bedad, ain't but one drop in it." Said, "Sing some more."
Jack said,

> Well, the youngest girl she come out
> All fired to buy my drill.
> I fooled around and I kissed 'er well.
> Fill, bowl, fill.

He says, "It full yet, ol' man?"
"No Jack, ain't but half full." Said, "Sing some more."
Jack said,

> Well the oldest—well the old woman she came out
> All fired to buy my drill.
> I fooled around and I kissed 'er —

He said, "Hold it, Jack, hold it." Said, "It's full of lies, running over."
Said, "Go ahead and cut my head off."

And Jack cut his head off. Got all of his money, and his youngest girl.
And they got married and her and Jack rode off, and, said, lived happy ever
after.

Hicks 1990: side A. ATU 570. Told by Orville Hicks of Boone, North Carolina, a cousin of Ray
Hicks, on a tape designed for commercial distribution. He recorded the tale at the Appalshop
studio, Whitesburg, Kentucky, in February 1990. Orville Hicks's mother was a granddaughter
of the legendary storyteller Council Harmon, and he grew up listening to her tell stories. He
now performs tales professionally, especially in schools. When not performing he supervises a
recycling center in Boone, where his tiny office has become a hangout for swapping yarns and
sharing good talk.

Hicks's version of this tale reflects the influence of Richard Chase's book *The Jack Tales* on
the Beech Mountain tradition. Chase, in a note to the tale in his book, says, "The point of singing
the bowl full of lies seems to have been lost in the Ward-Harmon tradition. Doctor Stith
Thompson cleared up this point for the present editor who restored it here." Chase goes on to

say that Marshall Ward, from whom Chase learned the tale, "said simply, 'sing the bowl full'" (Chase 1943: 193). The tune that Orville Hicks uses, however, is not the tune from Virginia that Chase splices into the version in *The Jack Tales* (1943: 95). Perhaps it is the Ward-Hicks-Harmon family tune.

In other versions of this *cante fable* the hero's ditty is in fact true. He has to herd rabbits without losing any. The women of the household offer to trade kisses or sexual favors for one of the rabbits and Jack manages to accept without actually losing the rabbit. When Jack sings his ditty at the end of the story, each woman in turn announces that it is lies and so the bowl or sack is full. On the last stanza the old man or king himself stops the hero from revealing the shame to which he has submitted his wife (or in some versions, to which he himself has submitted). When Vance Randolph published an Ozark version of the tale in 1952 he said that the story-teller he learned the story from had "two versions, one for mixed company and another for male audiences" (Randolph 1952: 185–86). The tale is also found in American Iberian traditions (e.g., Rael [1957]: vol. 1, 23–32). For an article-length discussion of American versions of this tale, see McCarthy 1993.

Part V

OTHER PEOPLE, OTHER TALES

Longer folktales cannot survive if a culture does not provide room for storytelling. Unfortunately many immigrants did not find that room for storytelling—except, perhaps, by the children's bedside—in the American culture to which they came or which they helped create. Consequently, when folklorists began collecting tales in the United States they sometimes found out that people did not know märchen and other long tales. At other times, they failed to find out that people did in fact know tales but were embarrassed to tell them because they were "for children." Sometimes, too, as almost happened in Appalachia, some more showy part of the tradition, such as music, foodways, or Christmas traditions, so attracted the folklorists that they failed to ask about stories. So whether overlooked, dropped, or relegated to the children's bedside, the folktale traditions of many European-American groups have never been collected.

Nevertheless, industrious scholars have found a remarkable number of storytelling communities in the United States, far more than could be encompassed in one volume. Part 5 presents some representative examples. The Pennsylvania Germans (chapter 14) are a group whose material culture and foodways have tended to overshadow their oral traditions in popular perception, but a substantial number of tales have been documented in this group. The Yankee Irish, chapter 15, are so much a part of the larger American picture that collectors have almost overlooked them—almost, but not quite: Stories and storytellers have attracted collectors here and there. Chapter 16, the third chapter in this section, seeks to indicate the range of other sub-cultures represented in U.S. storytelling, and the process by which European tales become Americanized. Chapter 17 illustrates the Americanization process as the stories pass into Native American repertoires. The chapter emphasizes Indian repertoires, but offers one example each of Yup'ik and Hawaiian Polynesian tales. And finally, chapter 18 is a case study of a particular tale, offering a more detailed presentation of one storyteller, her family, her ethnic background, and her story, complete with photographs of her as she tells it.

CHAPTER 14

GERMAN TRADITIONS
IN PENNSYLVANIA

German and German-speaking Protestants, especially Anabaptists, flooded into Pennsylvania in the eighteenth century, settling much of the eastern third of the state, moving from the Susquehanna valley into the Poconos. In the early nineteenth century German Catholics followed, some eventually settling beyond the Alleghenies in agricultural communities such as the sister towns of Fryburg and Lucinda in Clarion County. By the mid-nineteenth century still more German settlers were coming to work in the mines, the forests, and the mills all across the state. These people brought their stories with them and told them to the youngsters around them.

The "Pennsylvania Dutch," as the descendants of the earliest settlers are called, have been particularly assiduous in preserving their traditions. Barns, furniture, illuminated calligraphy (fraktur), and foodways have attracted the most attention. But the Reverend Thomas R. Brendle and William Troxell turned their attention to collecting and translating tales from the local dialect, publishing their rich collection through the Pennsylvania German Society in 1944. This chapter includes a generous sampling of the Brendle/Troxell material. The two tales of Mrs. Kate Moyer are especially interesting, demonstrating great freedom in refashioning märchen material into a new märchen in one case and into a fabliau in the other. The chapter concludes with a märchen from the Western Pennsylvania Catholic tradition.

90. The Enchanted Sisters

Long ago, there was a woman who always wept as she rocked her little son to sleep. One day he asked her why she wept. She, with tears and sobs, answered, "You have three sisters and they are all enchanted."

"When I am grown, I will free them," said the boy.

"You cannot free them, and do not try," answered the mother.

"I can, and I will," said the boy.

Now, the names of the three sisters were Hilldegadd, Gaddelheid, and Beaddrees.

When the boy was grown, he took a tomahawk and a horse, and rode away into the black forest. The forest was thickly grown with underbrush, and often the boy had to cut a way through with the tomahawk. When he could no longer cut a path for his horse, he tied him to a tree, and then forced his way through the undergrowth until he came to a very tall hollow tree.

He called, "Hilldegadd, Hilldegadd." There was no answer. He called again, "Hilldegadd, Hilldegadd." Then came a voice, "What do you want?"

He answered, "I am your brother, and I am come to set you free."

"Go away! Go away!" said his sister. "Here lives an eagle, and the other day he bored the eyes out of a little boy. Go away, before he returns home."

The boy would not leave, so his sister let down a silken ladder, and the boy climbed up into the hollow tree, where she hid him away.

"My husband," said his sister, "is an eagle for one whole week, and then a man for the next week, and when he is an eagle, he is very cruel and merciless."

The eagle came flying home. He sensed that something was not as it should be, and restlessly peered around in the hollow tree. His wife, however, quieted him and got him to lie down and sleep. When he awoke, he was a man. Then the boy came out of his hiding place and was received with great kindness. He spent a very happy time with his sister and her husband. When the week was almost over, the man told him to depart, saying, "I shall soon become an eagle, and then I will harm you."

But before the brother left, he gave him three eagle feathers, saying, "When you are in danger rub these feathers in your hands, until they are warm, and then you will receive help."

The boy left the hollow tree and traveled on until he came to a huge cliff, in which there was a bear cave. He called, "Gaddelheid, Gaddelheid."

She answered, "Go away! Go away! Here lives a fierce bear. The other day he came home with his nose covered with blood."

The boy pleaded with her, and finally she took him into the cave and hid him. "My husband," said his sister, "is a bear for two weeks, and then a man for two weeks. At this time he is a bear, and very, very fierce."

After a little while the bear returned, sniffed the air, and growled, "I smell human flesh."

"No! No! You do not. Lie down and sleep," said his wife. He did so, and upon waking was a man.

The boy came out of his hiding place and was kindly received. There he stayed two weeks, and they were happy ones, even happier than the week he spent with Hilldegadd and her husband. When the two weeks were almost up, the man came to the boy and said, "I shall soon become a bear, and then I will harm you. Go away."

But before the boy left, he gave him three bear hairs and told him, "When you are in danger rub these hairs in your hands until they are warm, and then you will receive help."

The boy journeyed on until he came to a large body of water. Far out in the water he saw a smoking chimney. He swam out, looked down the chimney, and saw a glass house. He called, "Beaddrees, Beaddrees." No answer. He called again.

"What do you want?" came the answer.

"I am your brother, and I have come to free you," said the brother.

"Go away! Go away! The whale will soon come home and kill you," cried his sister. He, however, went down the chimney into the house.

The whale returned and saw that his wife was ill at ease and troubled, and though he spoke to her, she would not answer. So he went out and swam around the house, lashing the water in his rage until it became murky. Then he came in. His wife, feeling that the murky water concealed the presence of her brother, spoke to the whale and told him to lie down and sleep. When he awoke, he was a man. For three weeks he was a whale and for three weeks a man.

The boy spent a happy time with them in the glass house under the water, even happier than with the other two sisters. Towards the end of three weeks the man told him that he was to go away. "Soon," said he, "I shall again become a whale and then I will harm you."

He gave him three fish scales, telling him, when in danger, to rub them in his hands until warm and help would appear.

The boy left and went back through the forest until he came to the tree where he had tied his horse. He found the horse torn to pieces. This had been done by the bear.

So he went on through the forest until he came to a beautiful piece of ground in the midst of which stood a beautiful small house. He saw nothing living about the place except a large bull that was grazing on the green grass before the house.

The boy bravely walked toward the house, but he had not gotten very near before the bull rushed on him. The boy quickly rubbed the three bear hairs, and immediately the bear appeared and tore the bull into pieces.

Then out of the body of the bull a goose arose and flew away. Seeing this, the boy rubbed the eagle feathers, and the eagle came swiftly through the air and killed the goose.

A golden egg fell from the body of the goose down through the sky into the water; and the boy rubbed the fish scales, and the whale came and brought the golden egg.

The boy took the golden egg, broke it open and found a golden key. Immediately the enchantment was broken, and his three sisters and their husbands appeared at his side.

Together they went to the beautiful house, which they found locked. The boy took the golden key and unlocked the door. Within they found a beautiful girl who had been enchanted. She had been asleep, but when the door was unlocked, the enchantment was broken and she became free from all her bonds.

The boy took the girl for his wife, and together they all went home to the mother who cried for joy when she beheld them.

Brendle and Troxell 1944: 11–14. ATU 552 and Motif D791.4. Told by Kate Moyer of Egypt, Pennsylvania. Mrs. Moyer told at least five stories. Brendle and Troxell translated these from Pennsylvania German to English for inclusion in their collection. The editors included very little, however, about when or how they collected the tales.

This perfect little tale is composed of elements each associated separately with another tale. The girls are apparently carried off (or married off) as in ATU 425, to husbands that are animal and human by turn, but violent when in animal shape, a reversal of ATU 425. Their brother goes seeking them in a reversal of the pattern of ATU 451, which usually features a sister seeking long-lost brothers. Having visited each of his sisters, he rescues a captive princess, as in ATU 302, who is sleeping, as in ATU 410. In the final plot resolution the three sisters, the three animal husbands, and the sleeping princess are all disenchanted when the hero discovers in an egg the magic key to an enchanted dwelling, a quite rare motif. (D791.4: Thompson cites only one occurrence of this motif, a Lithuanian tale.) More typically, the egg contains the life of the ogre or demon who has enchanted all those characters, and the hero breaks the enchantment by smashing the egg itself, as in ATU 302.

91. The Three Brothers

Once upon a time, there were three brothers who set out from home to travel into other parts of the world. On their journey they came to a large forest.

They travelled on and on through the forest without seeing a house or meeting a human being.

Finally they came to a hut where an ugly old woman dwelt. Out in the yard a kettle with food was hanging over a fire.

The brothers were very hungry and they straightaway went to the kettle to get food. But before they were able to touch the food, the old woman cried shrilly, "Don't taste that food. Come into the house and I shall give you food."

They went into the house and the old woman gave them food to eat. She used a burning sliver for a light—though, when she opened her mouth, she showed such long ugly teeth that they would have been better faggots than the sliver.

After they had eaten, she besought them to stay for the night. To this they consented, but because there was no room for all of them in the hut only one, the eldest, slept there and the other two slept outside.

The next morning the brothers were surprised to see that the old woman had become ten years younger.

She made breakfast for them and asked them to stay there during the day and over night. That night the second brother slept in the hut and the other two outside, and in the morning when the woman made breakfast for them they saw that she had become another ten years younger.

They remained there for another day and at night the youngest brother slept inside and the other two out in the yard, and in the morning when she made breakfast for them they saw that she had become another ten years younger, and was a young and beautiful woman.

After breakfast, she gave them presents to take along on their travels. To one she gave a cent, to the second, a tablecloth, and to the third a thumbstall.

They continued on through the forest, but the way was long and lonely with no houses and no people. They became tired and hungry, and sat down by the road to rest.

As they sat there, the one who had received the tablecloth, said, "I have a tablecloth but nothing to put on it."

While he thus spoke, he idly spread the cloth out on the ground and said, "I wish we had something to eat," and straightaway, to the utter amazement of the brothers, the very food for which he wished appeared on the tablecloth.

They feasted heartily, and when they had their fill, the brother to whom the tablecloth belonged pulled at the edge of the cloth and all the remaining food disappeared.

They went on and he who had received the penny, becoming disgusted with its value compared to the tablecloth, took it, and saying, "Of what benefit is it to me?" threw it to the ground; but one of the other two went and picked it up, and found to his surprise that under the cent lay another cent.

They continued their journey and the one who had received the thumbstall said, as he put the thumbstall down over his thumb, "What use have I for this?"

However, when he had pulled the thumbstall down over his thumb, he became invisible.

They came to an inn, where they stayed for some days. When they were hungry, the tablecloth was spread; when they wanted money, the cent was cast to the ground; and when the third desired to make a clandestine visit to the innkeeper's wife, he put on the thumbstall!

Brendle and Troxell 1944: 28–30. Related to ATU 327/328 and ATU 563/566. Another tale from Mrs. Kate Moyer. The tale draws upon märchen elements to create a narrative that seems to have no exact cognates. As in several versions of ATU 327/328 in this volume, three brothers, of whom the youngest is the most enterprising, stay with a witch, but their stay turns out very satisfactorily for all concerned. As in ATU 563 and 566, they leave with magic gifts, and as in 563, go to an inn. There, for all intents and purposes, the story ends, a fabliau (a tale told for the sake of its earthy humor) rather than a märchen. A thumbstall is a thimble or thimble-like tool or covering, sometimes of leather, worn on the thumb, especially by shoemakers and sailmakers, but also by cannoneers and bishops.

92. The Best of Three

A young man told his mother that he would like to marry but feared that he might not choose a good wife, and he would like to have his mother's counsel.

His mother said to him, "Saddle your horse and ride to the home of the girl that you have in mind. When close to her home, dismount and tie your horse to a tree. Then, go toward the house, and when the girl appears, as she will, say to her, 'My horse has been suddenly taken with colic. Would you kindly give me a handful of the scrapings of the kneading trough for him.'"

The son did as directed. He rode until he came close to the home of a girl whom he knew fairly well. Then he dismounted, tied his horse to a tree, and walked towards the house. The girl came out on the porch, and he asked her for a handful of scrapings of the kneading trough.

She answered, "That I shall gladly give you."

She went into the house, and came back with two heaping handfuls saying, "If this isn't enough, I can get more."

The young man thanked her and left. He returned to his mother and recounted to her his experience. She shook her head, and said, "Try again."

On the following day, the son rode forth again. To his request, the second girl replied, "When we are through baking, we clean our kneading trough, and there are no scrapings to be gotten."

When his mother heard his account, she shook her head, and said, "Try again."

He rode forth the third day, and went towards the home of a girl of whom he had heard but whom he had never met. To his request, she answered that she didn't know whether she could get any scrapings for him but she would try.

After a while, she came out with a small handful and said, almost apologetically, as she gave them to him, "This is all I could get out of the corners of the trough. I am sorry that I cannot give you more."

He thanked her and rode back to his mother, who smiled when she heard his story. "That," she said, "is the one for you. Seek no further."

Brendle and Troxell 1944: 94–95. ATU 1452. From Lebanon County, Pennsylvania. This is Grimm No. 155 "Choosing a Bride." Baughman (1966: under Motif H381.2.2, "Bride test: thrifty scraping of bread tray,") reports versions from North Carolina and Missouri. Brendle and Troxell explain that this story rests on the proverb *Mittelmas, di beschde Schtras:* Between the extremes lies the best course."

93. Stone Soup

A peddler during a rainy period stayed several days at the home of Mrs. A———. In his conversation he now and then referred to a wonderful stone soup that he had lately eaten. The curiosity of Mrs. A——— was aroused and she asked him, "How is this wonderful stone soup made?"

"If you make it for me, I'll tell you," answered the peddler.

"I'll make it," answered the woman.

The peddler went out into a field and picked up a round cobble stone. He washed it thoroughly and took it to Mrs. A———, saying, "Cook this well for one hour."

This she did. Then he told her to add corn, cabbage, string beans, tomatoes, onions, and potatoes, also parsley and seasoning; and finally a chunk of beef cut up into small pieces.

The soup proved to be most delicious and afterwards Mrs. A——— told her neighbors of the wonderful stone soup that she made at the direction of the peddler, and of all its ingredients.

"I suppose that would have been a good soup without the stone," commented one of her neighbors.

Brendle and Troxell 1944: 205–6. ATU 1548. From Oscar Laub, Egypt, Pennsylvania. An American child is likely to know this story from the enduringly popular picture book by Marcia Brown. But the story has also circulated widely in oral tradition in both the new and the old world. According to Brendle and Troxell, "The term '*Schteesubb*' [stone soup] is used facetiously in the [Pennsylvania Dutch] dialect. For example . . . , '*Was gebts fa Middâg?*' '*Ich wees net, ich denk Schteesubb.*' ['What did you have for noon dinner?' 'Nothing. I drank stone soup']" (206). Here the märchen has become a legend, an ironic, possibly true tale about a real person, identified only as Mrs. A———.

94. Eileschpijjel

A. Farming on Shares

The devil and Eileschpijjel farmed on shares. The first year they agreed that the devil should have that part of the crop which grew above ground, and Eileschpijjel that part of the crop that grew under the ground. Turnips were planted and when the division of the crops was made, Eileschpijjel got the roots and the devil the foliage.

The second year, the devil said that he wanted what grew under the ground and Eileschpijjel should have what grew above the ground. Wheat was planted and the devil got the roots and Eileschpijjel the grain.

The third year, the devil, hoping to get the better of Eileschpijjel, said that he wanted both the tops and the roots of the crop, and Eileschpijjel should have the middle parts. Corn was planted, and Eileschpijjel got the ears.

B. Logic Is Logic

Eileschpijjel went with a two-horse team for wood. As he threw piece after piece on the wagon, he said, "If the horses can pull this piece they can pull the next one."

Reasoning thus, he kept on loading until the wagon was completely filled. Then he found that the horses were unable to pull the load.

He proceeded to unload, saying as he threw piece after piece off, "If they can't pull this piece, they can't pull the next one."

Reasoning thus, he kept on unloading until the wagon was empty. Then he drove home with an empty wagon.

Brendle and Troxell 1944: 160–61; 172–73. A. ATU 1030. B. ATU 1242. The first tale is from an unnamed storyteller in Lehigh County, the second from Robert Ohlinger of Wescosville, Pennsylvania. Eileschpijjel is the beloved Pennsylvania incarnation of the German trickster Tyl

Eulenspiegel. To Pennsylvania Germans of an earlier generation, however, he often seemed to be a real person. Brendle and Troxell recall being told that he "often came to my grandfather's house," or he "was still living when my father was a little boy," or even, "My father knew Eileschpijjel well" (153). The present two stories show how in the Pennsylvania German tradition he combines the qualities of trickster and numbskull. He may be busy tricking his greedy or stupid neighbors and associates—or the devil himself. But he is just as likely to be busy failing hopelessly at some task. Indeed, the above tale about hauling wood recounts one of the most popular of his exploits. A number of the Pennsylvania Eileschpijjel stories appear further south with Br'er Rabbit or Jack as heroes. And both of the Quevedo stories in chapter 4 are also told of Eileschpijjel.

95. Counting Noses

Do you know why the Swabians before they decide a matter say, "Let us count noses?" It was this way.

Thirteen Swabians were traveling through the country, in a group. One day they got the notion that one of their number was missing. To find out whether all were there they took to counting. The first one counting, "I am I, you are one, you are two," and so on until the last who was twelve.

"There are only twelve of us," said the one who counted.

"You are wrong," said another. "Let me count."

So he counted: "I am I, you are one, you are two," and so on to the last who was twelve.

A third counted, with the same results.

They could not agree whether one was missing or not; but to settle the matter they decided to stick their noses in the mud, and then count the marks. This they did, and found that all thirteen were present.

Commented one, "I sort of thought that all were here."

Brendle and Troxell 1944: 110. ATU 1287. In many traditions, a particular regional or ethnic group will be singled out for supposed stupidity and made to figure in numbskull stories. In Indiana and Ohio such stories are told about Kentuckians, in Kentucky about Irishmen, in Ireland about Kerrymen. And at one time in Germany and among Pennsylvania Germans the stories were told about Swabians. Even Grimm includes a story of Seven Swabians (no. 119). The present story is immensely popular with young children, who can remember making the same mistake as these Swabian heroes. It is widespread in the United States, perhaps especially in the South. Roberts, in *South from Hell-fer-Sartin'*, gives a version in which nine Irishmen stick their noses "in a big cowpile laying there," and then count the holes (1955: 118).

96. The Miller's Daughter

Well, long, long, long ago, I don't know what, in what country it was any more, but it was among the mountains, there was a miller that lived with four beautiful daughters. They had beautiful long hair, and [were] really beautiful. This miller had a nice wife, but she died with what they called quick consumption. You know what that was. That was an old saying of—for—for a disease, wasn't it? She died and left these four girls. Some were sixteen, some were .... I think sixteen was the oldest. Then there was just, like two years apart . . . down. And they had such gorgeous hair. So the miller had this here mill. And each week one girl would come in, and done all the floors. Ri—oh, uh—sweeping them, the grain that he would spill, er. They had to keep the mill real clean them days because they were narrow boards, 'n it was. You could almost eat on—off the floors, when the grain fell. So he . . . one day, now he has these four girls, 'n he's—he's putting them through school, but one at a time had to come to the mill to help him. They were to fill the sacks with grain, they could sweep, they done a lot of nice things for their Daddy.

And so, one day, as she was sweeping, or putting the—putting the grain into a—hoppers to grind, a nice looking man came in. With a—he was dressed in a dark suit and a bib, black-rimmed hat, with a tie on. And they looked out the window, and he had two beautiful, black horses. And she said, "Dad! You're getting somebody that's something!"

So when he came in, he said, uh . . . I don't know what this miller's name was, anymore. That I cannot tell you. She—he called him something. And she said—he said, "My! But you have a nice mill here. And they say you make the best mill of the—flour."

So he said, "Yes, I've kept busy." He said, "My wife died, and, uh, I ... One week, one girl comes in and does the chores for me, and the next one, another one does. But they are—I'm trying to get them a good education."

So he said, "I have a lot of grain out there, and I'll give you a good price for—give you a good price for the grain, but could I have one of your daughters? I live way up the mountain side," and he said, "I would—I just have to have a daughter. My wife died too."

So he said, "Oh, I don't know if I could let any of my chi-children go. They're pretty young. The oldest one here is helping me, and the next one is only sixteen years old."

"Oh," he said, "I bet she can cook and clean. And there's nothing to do. I have horses, and cows, and pigs, and chickens. I have a whole mountain side. Some days, I'm gone for two days before I get back, and there's nobody. Everything, there's a piano there, and musical instruments, and anything you want to cook for yourself, or for me."

So he said, "How much will you give her?"

He said, "I'll give her ten dollars a week."

"Why," he said, "before I ask her, she—she can go." Because ten dollars in them days was big wages, see? So she went, packed up her little suitcase, and away she went. And he went up, way up on the mountain, 'round and 'round the mountain side. Beautiful place, a great big house. He had a lot of horses to ride. He had cows, and chickens, and pigs, and sheep, anything. And he told the girl, "All you need to do is cook just ordinary meals for me. I like ordinary meals." She said, "That's—I can. I can bake bread out of our flour, and I can bake pies, and I can bake cookies." She was thrilled when she'd seen the house, how beautiful it was. So he said, "I'll take you. There is a room upstairs, at the top of the stairs, for you." And he said, "In the morning, I'll show you every room." So she was tired from the ride. So he took her suitcase up, and left her. He said, "Take care of yourself, and in the morning, I'll see you at breakfast." So she went to bed. And then she got up about five o'clock, and started to get dressed, and get ready for downstairs. And he she—he asked her how she had slept. She said, "Oh, like a log. I think I will live here a long time." She said, "I'd love it." He said, "Boy, that's nice words, coming from a little girl—lady like you." He said, "When we're done eating, I'm gonna show you the whole house."

So they did. He took her through the house. Big living room, piano, big organ . . . uh, no, no, no, uh, radio, television in them days, you see, just this musical stuff. She said, "Oh, I like to play the piano, but we're so busy down home, we never could play anything." He said, "You can play all—all the time, because it's only my meals. This house don't get dirty. It's up here in the mountains." Well, she was—she was really tickled.

He said, "There's only one drawback. You can go in every room in the house, but there's one little room near the rest—the toilet (called the bathroom the toilet in them days). Don't go in that room. I keep it locked, up there is the key. I tell everyone where the key is, but never go in there."

"Oh," she said, "I won't."

He said, "Come out here, I'll show you something. Now here's your little blue egg. You put that in your pocket, in your apron pocket. Wherever you go in this house, never take it out, only when you go in the bathroom. You let it in your apron when you take—you get your bath, and let it in your apron."

So she says, "Oh, that's all right."

"The little blue egg will follow you around wherever you are all day. And if you do something wrong, that blue egg will tell me."

So she says, [*chuckles*], "Well, I [*unintelligible*] . . . I'll do it."

So he said, "Whenever," she told—he told her—the father, "I will bring your daughter home in four weeks, if she could stand it up there."

So the girl—oh, she loved it, though, what with that little blue egg. If she—if she took her apron off, she put it in another apron, see. And she liked this so well. So four weeks went. He says, "Oh, I think I'll take our yellow team of horses and go down—take you down to see your dad."

"Well," he said when he got her down there . . . He—he had a yellow team of horses and the father was so pleased how nice that girl looked. She got lots to eat, and she loved it so. And the man just adored the girl. So he said—she said—Dad said, "Are you gonna stay?"

"Oh, no, Dad. I'm going back with—" (whatever his name was. I—I don't remember his name, but I know he was a tall man. He always wore a big hat—black, or brown, or straw.) So she went back with him. So this went on, oh, a little bit. She thought, "Isn't this fun! Such a beautiful home, he goes away at times for three days, and I'm here all alone. What's that darn little blue egg to do to me?" So she thought, "I'm gonna get that key down, and I'm gonna unlock that little door there near there, and I'm gonna look in!"

So she opened the door, and looked in. And there were three barrels in there. And she got a little scared when she went over near them. And she thought it was hair she'd seen, but she wasn't sure what she'd seen. The little blue egg jumped out of her—just jumped out of her apron pocket and said, "Drink Blood! Drink Blood! Your head will be cut off tomorrow!"

(See, this is just a story. [*Followed by a round of laughter*])

So, boy! He came home and they were eating breakfast, and he says, "And where's your little blue egg this morning?"

"Oh," she said, "I don't know! I was up there cleaning, and it jumped out of my pocket and broke all up. I cleaned it up."

He just took her upstairs, cut her head off—I don't know what with her body—and stuck it in the barrel. So then he gets out—gets a pair of brown horses and puts the brown suit on, and down the hill he went. He wasn't—he fixed himself like a different man. And he went down to the miller. And the miller was glad to see him because the miller said, "I have another daughter up on the mountain side. Did you ever come across her?"

He said, "That's why I'm here! My—some man told me that the miller got one of your daughters, but I haven't been over."

So, that's all right. He talked to him awhile, 'n he said, "Could I see one of your girls?"

"Oh, yes, I've got two more over in the—one is sweeping, and two more over in the house."

So pretty soon, the—one of the girls come over. They started talking nice together, 'n they said, "Are you up in the mountain where my sister is?"

He said, "I don't know if it's near or not, but we heard that this little girl working up there, somewhere."

So the miller said, "Well, I can get—give you her." And he gave him a big sum of money for—if the girl would stay a month.

The miller was so happy to think what these girls were bringing in to him. So off he went with the second girl, but the miller didn't know him from the other man, see. He thought it was a different man. So he got up, and she was baking a pie one day. And her little blue egg—he made her go with the blue egg in her apron, and never take it out, "Because bad luck will come to you." So she never took it out, she kept it in there all the time.

And so, one day, she decided when he was away, she was gonna go up and look at what is in that building [*sic*], that little building [*sic*]. So she went up. The egg jumped out of her pocket, and said, "Drink blood! Drink blood! Tomorrow your head will be cut off!"

So she was scared when she heard them words! So she cleaned up the old mess, but she didn't look at the barrels, there were three there. She got out of there and locked the door, put the key up. And when he came home that night, he'd been gone a couple of days, she says, "Oh, I've got something to tell you. I'm so—very sorry. My blue egg jumped out of my apron when I was stooping over, and it cracked. I could show you how bad it is cracked."

He says, "You don't need to show me."

So he took her in that room, and he cut off her head, and stuck it in the barrel, and goes down again to get another girl. This is the third one—third girl. So he had white horses this time when he went down, and the miller didn't know him. So the—this girl, uh, the miller had to get—he offered two hundred dollars a month, if he could have her. And the miller said, "Oh, my! That would help me. I have lots of work to do, and get somebody to help." So he took her home.

Now, this girl liked this man very much, and she got along real good. And he was taking her up the mountain to—away—at night—once in a while, at night. She was enjoying it, playing the piano. She was having a good time. "But, it seems funny, I've never come across—my other sisters haven't come home. And where are they, up here on the mountains?"

So she asked this man if the houses were close up in the mountains. He said, "No, no. Maybe fifty miles apart. If your sisters are, they're about fifty miles from here."

So she said, "Oh, that's too far!"

"Maybe someday, I'll take you in my carriage, or my buggy, and we'll go hunt them."

Everything sounded good, see. So she—one day, he went away, and he said, "I won't be back for three or four days, now. You just enjoy yourself."

So she got her work done, and she thought, "Well, this is a good day. Now three or four days, he ain't going."

He told her about that place in the wall, and that she shouldn't ever take her little blue egg out, keep in her apron.

So he's gone. She watched his carriage going up over the mountain. Then she thought, "This is a good day for me! I'll take my apron off, and I'll lay it on the bed. And I'm gonna take the key down, and I'm gonna see what's in them barrels!"

So she si—she went in and she almost fainted!

Here was—in the—her two sisters' heads was bubbling up in the barrels! They were dead! He cut their heads off!

Well. She got one of the horses and went home, and told her dad what she'd found. And her dad couldn't believe it. So she said, "Dad, got that—gotta get this man. He's crazy! He's lost his mind. He's the—something's wrong, he's killing people, and I'll be the next one!"

So he said, "What could we do?"

And she said, "Well, Dad, he didn't bring me down. I came down. I don't want him to know that I was down. So, I tell ye—you make some popcorn, big bag of popcorn. And I will drive the horse back. And I will drop popcorn—"

Nobody knew where his place was, see, nobody did. Whenever the old man down at the mill would ask, "Where's this beautiful house?" or "Where's this man?" What his name was, nobody knew.

So the girl says, "Dad, the popcorn, I'll set it on the back of the buckboard, and I'll drop popcorn along the road, up." And she said, "You go to the cops. Get the police, and I'll go home and be just the same with that man when he comes home."

So when he come home, he was so tickled that she was there, and everything was fine.

"Where's your little blue egg?"

"It's in my pocket."

So, he says to her, "Did you play the piano?"

"Oh," she said, "I played and sang, the birds sang with me. I went out and got chickens, 'n I—a lot of peep-peeps right now."

They talked together so nice. So in the meantime, the man that, uh, home, her father got a hold of the policemen. And, now the police—the policemen couldn't ride very long on the road, because where these—where this big house was, he could see anybody ever was driving on that road, coming up, see? So, anyway, he—he got the cops, and he—the man walked and hunted—hunted for the popcorn. And the popcorn road is how the man got up to the place. And the cops come in on him—I think he was out in the barn—and they got him. They tied him up, and took him—I guess someplace where they—he—he was crazy! He had lost his mind over his wife, this here man on the hill. So, I don't know.

Isn't that 'bout the end of it? They, uh, the little girls got a big reward for finding this man that was doing this. He had done other terrible things. But it was the little blue egg they have to watch out for! That's it. (*Everyone laughs.*)

Neuland 1994. ATU 311. From the performance of Emma Neuland, Lucinda, Pennsylvania, 1994. This Bluebeard story is fairly closely related to Grimm tale no. 46, "Fitcher's Bird." Mrs. Neuland first told it to me in July 1993. Mary Alice Shmader, another Lucinda woman, had taken me to Mrs. Neuland's house specifically to hear the story. I took my three children back to visit Mrs. Neuland the following summer so that they could hear the story. Mrs. Neuland learned this story as a child from an elderly woman who sometimes came to her house. "That's the only story she'd tell. And I used to tell it to my sisters and brothers, and they loved that story. . . . Yeah, my mom said I should never tell it to little children, but a whole line of them Shmader kids just loved that story." Mrs. Neuland's family was poor. When quite young she herself took service in the home of a wealthy widower, and in time married him.

Though Mrs. Neuland has been telling the story for many years now, the story has not ossified. The two tellings I recorded differ in such details as the life before the mother died and the total number of daughters. In the earlier telling, the third girl has come down with the villain when she plans with her father how she is to be rescued. She drops the popcorn from the villain's carriage. Note that the märchen is told in the style of a legend, with emphasis at the end on how grief had driven the man crazy. In fact, so involved in the verisimilitude of the story was the narrator in her 1993 performance that she became momentarily embarrassed when she reached the one frankly magical element, the talking egg.

CHAPTER 15

THE IRISH-AMERICAN
TALE TRADITION

According to legend, St. Brendan crossed the western ocean in the sixth century. But if he came to the New World, he did not stay. The first substantial Irish immigration into what is now the United States began in the 1630s, a time of civil unrest in Ireland. Periodically thereafter, in times of unrest or hardship and especially in the mid nineteenth century at the time of the Potato Famine, the Irish have come in such numbers that today approximately one in six Americans claims some Irish ancestry. Ireland has one of the richest storytelling repertoires in Europe. And Irish Americans have a reputation as storytellers. But in the United States Irish storytellers have favored the anecdote and joke, not the longer tales, and I found very few full-length märchen collected from Irish-Americans. And some of those, such as "Jamie and the Wee Ones" and "How Death Came to Ireland," below, seem to be summaries of plot rather than full-fledged performances. Story 60, "Beg Billy and the Bull," in chapter 10, is also at least partly an Irish story, though told by an African American.

This chapter begins with a tale from Sara Cleveland, a rare master storyteller from Brant Lake, New York. Her tales were gathered by the great American folklorist Kenneth Goldstein. The next two tales represent the interface of legend and märchen. The fourth tale is a composite märchen, a phenomenon very common in Irish tradition, that has been Americanized in an interesting way. The chapter closes with a numbskull story to demonstrate that the Irish are quite capable of laughing at themselves.

97. Little Red Nightcap

There was a man who lived in Ireland and he had three sons. His wife died and he married another woman who was an old biddy. She hated the three boys and did everything she could to make life miserable for them. And she was always trying to get the old man to chase them away from home but he wouldn't agree to that. But one night she got him real drunk. She kept feeding him drinks until he was so drunk he finally agreed he'd do anything to shut her up.

So in the meantime the youngest son happened to be going by the window, and he heard them talking, and listened. So he went out to the little shack in back where they stayed and he told the brothers that the woman wanted to get rid of them. She had told the old man that when the boys got to sleep they would burn the shack down and that time they'd get rid of them once and for all. So the boys decided they'd go out in the woods and watch. They didn't think the old man would agree to something like that, but they thought they'd be on the safe side and stay in the woods.

So they took what little food they had and they went out in the woods. And pretty soon out came the old woman. The old man he'd got so drunk he passed out. So she had to do the dirty work herself. She set fire to the building and stood there watching it burn and was very happy jumping up and down.

The boys felt pretty bad to think their father would do something like that to them and they decided they'd better go somewhere else. So they took off down the road.

They hadn't gone down the road too far when they saw an old beggar along beside the road and he asked them for some food. Well the two older ones told him they didn't have only enough food for themselves, and they couldn't give him any. But the youngest son, he felt sorry for the old beggar, so he gave him a part of what he had. And he told his brothers, "He's older than I am and he needs it a lot worse than I do."

Well, the two older brothers didn't agree. They told him he was foolish to give away his food. They didn't have hardly any anyway. But when he got hungry he could go without, if he was fool enough to give his food away.

But—Sean was the youngest boy's name—and he gave him the food anyway. And the two brothers went down the road. So the old beggar gave Sean a blackthorn stick and he told him it was a magic stick, that any time he got in trouble to say to the stick, "Arragowan," and the stick would get up and fight for him.

So Sean took the stick and thanked him and started down the road after his brothers. They looked back and they saw him coming and one said to the other, "There, look at the poor fool. He's so weak now he can't stand up. He has to get a stick to help him walk and yet he'll give away his food." So they kept talking to him and making fun of him when he got up with 'em but he never told them the black stick was supposed to be magic. And they kept on going.

So pretty soon they came to a town where everybody was weeping and crying and carrying on. And when they asked what was wrong, the people told them that the king's daughter had been stolen by Little Red Nightcap, and if anyone could get her back, the king would give him a big bunch of gold and the daughter for a bride. Well, the two older boys thought the gold sounded pretty good. But Sean he thought, well, he wouldn't mind having a wife. So they decided they would go down looking for the girl.

So the king gave them some food and he gave them a man to show them where Little Red Nightcap lived. So they went down the road and by the time they got to where this cave was with a big hole that went down in the ground, the man pointed out the cave to them and then he left. He didn't want no part of Little Red Nightcap.

Well, they go up to the cave and the oldest brother, Pat, said that he was the oldest; he would go down the hole first. So they took the food out of the basket and put a rope on the basket and they lowered him down this hole into the bottom of the cave. So he hadn't any more than got down there and he decided he'd eat. So he got his food all ready to eat and he'd just about sat down to eat when out popped a little man with a red cap on his head and he said he wanted something to eat. Well, Pat told him he only had food enough for himself. So, thereupon, the little man grabbed a club and started beating him up. And he beat him until Pat ran over to where the basket was and he tugged on the rope and the other brothers hauled him up. And he told them he'd enough of that. He wasn't going down again.

So the next time it was the second son's turn. His name was Dennis. So Dennis got in the basket and they lowered him down the hole with his food. So, he got the food ready to eat and while he was starting to eat out popped the little man with the red cap on his head again. So he said he wanted some food. Well, he told him he only had enough to eat for himself. He didn't have any to give away. So Little Red Nightcap picked up the club again and he started beating him up. So Dennis ran over to the basket and climbed in and tugged on the rope and they pulled him up out of the hole. And he wouldn't go back.

So the third time it was Sean's turn. So Sean got in the basket with his food and they lowered him down the hole. So he hadn't any more than got ready to eat than in popped Little Red Nightcap again. And he said he wanted some food.

So Sean said, "Well, there it is. Help yourself."

And he said, "No, I want you to wait on me."

And Sean said, "If you're hungry enough, you'll help yourself."

So Little Red Nightcap grabbed a stick and started for Sean.

But Sean had taken his blackthorn stick with him down the hole. So he said to the stick, "Arragowan."

So the stick up and started beating Little Red Nightcap. And it beat him so hard that Little Red Nightcap finally told him if he'd make the stick stop whipping him—beating him up like he was—he'd give him the king's daughter and all his gold and jewels also.

So Sean finally let the stick give him a few more whacks, and then he told him to stop. So he got the king's daughter and he got all the jewels and all the gold and then Little Red Nightcap took off.

So Sean went over to where the basket was and he put all the gold and the jewels in the basket and tugged on the rope and the two brothers hauled it up. So they sent the basket down again and then Sean put the girl in it and tugged on the rope and sent her up. So that time before the basket came down it took a little longer and Sean thought that was kinda funny. So when the basket came down that time instead of getting into the basket himself he took a big rock and put it in the basket and tugged on the rope and they pulled the basket back up. So they got it up just about halfway and they cut the rope and down come basket, rock, and all.

So Sean said to himself, "Well that's nice. That's a nice thing to do. Now how am I supposed to get out of here? What'll I do down here?" And he paces around and he's doing a lot of thinking. In the meantime, while he's doing all the worrying, down this big hole comes a great big bird. And Sean said to the bird, "If you will fly me out of here on your back, I will give you all the food I have." Well the bird was pretty weak, but Sean gave him some food and he got stronger and Sean climbed on his back with the basket of food. And they started up the hole. Well, they got up quite a ways, and Sean kept reaching around putting a piece of meat into the bird's mouth. And they almost got out, but just before they got to the end of it, they ran out of food. And the bird was getting weaker. So Sean took his knife and reached back and cut a slice off his backside and reached around and stuck it in the bird's face. So that way they got out of the hole.

So Sean took his blackthorn stick and he started back towards the king's town, where he lived. And the more he walked, the madder he got. And he kept thinking all he'd do to those two brothers if he ever did catch up with them. So he finally came into the town and he was pretty mad by that time, too.

The two brothers were there strutting around and telling everyone how brave they were and of all the wonderful things they'd done, and how they had got rid of old Red Nightcap, and how they rescued the girl. And the girl, all she'd do is cry and she wouldn't say she'd marry either one of them. She wouldn't pick between the two of them.

So all at once, in the midst of their bragging, they look up and there's their brother Sean. So they said to him, "How did you get out?"

And Sean said, "I flew out, and you two had better start flying right now." So he said to the stick, "Arragowan," and the stick took right off after them.

So the girl came over to Sean and said to her father, "This is the man that saved me, and I won't marry anyone else." So the king gave the girl to Sean and they were married.

And then Sean got thinking about how his father was. So he decided he'd better go home and see how the father was making out. So he went home, and the old man was feeling terribly bad to think that he had did such a thing. And the old woman had died in the meantime. So Sean took the father and the girl and went back to the king's palace and the last I knew they were still there. And as for the brothers, I don't know whether they ever did get away from that stick. The last I heard they were still running.

Goldstein and Ben-Amos, 1970: 45–51. ATU 301. Sara Cleveland (1905–1973) of Hudson's Falls and Brant Lake, New York, told this story to Kenneth Goldstein and William Ivey in July 1968. Cleveland had a large repertoire of tales and songs. She learned this story from her mother, Sara Wiggins, whose parents, according to Goldstein, came to the United States from Ireland in 1840 (156). Cleveland was also a prodigious singer of traditional songs, and she would sometimes perform stories and ballads in Goldstein's classes. Much of the material collected from her by Goldstein is now at the University of Mississippi and the Library of Congress. Lindahl includes all the Library of Congress tales, including the present tale, in his collection (2004).

This version of ATU 301 is quite different from other versions printed in this volume, especially in the order of events. The magic beating stick in the story suggests ATU 563–64, in which a beating stick forces a thief to return stolen property. The tale also has strong echos of ATU 592, in which a poor boy gives all he has to a beggar and in return receives a magic fiddle that forces people to dance. By playing this fiddle until people plead with him to stop, he obtains his ends.

The name Little Red Nightcap suggests a redcap, a type of evil fairy found in British folklore, though Irish fairies too are frequently described as wearing red caps. The flying bird motif, frequently associated with this tale, also occurs in Sugg's version of "The Devil's Daughter," chapter 12.

98. The Fairy Birth

There was a woman in the neighborhood who attended births; most of the people couldn't afford a doctor, and would rather have had the woman even if they could have had the doctor. The woman's name was Brigit. She had great skill in her calling, so that her fame had spread about the country. It was no strange thing for a person to come from miles away in search of her, and she was always willing to make the call. Nor had she ever come to any harm.

One night, when the town was asleep, she was wakened by a knocking. It was not usual for her to be called in the dead of night; and, further, she knew of no event impending in the neighborhood. But she put up a light anyhow, and went to see who was there.

A tall, dark man stood at the door. She had never seen him. He was well dressed, but he had a strange air about him. Though he spoke quietly and with grace when he told her what he wanted her for, he didn't somehow make himself clear enough. Or else it was that Brigit hadn't fully awaked.

His people were in the hills, he said, and one of the women was taken suddenly, and they had no one with them that had Brigit's skill, from what he'd heard tell of it. Would she go with him to attend the birth?

Brigit didn't particularly want to go, because of the stranger's air; and still she did want to go, because of the woman in pain. "All right," she said, "I'll go with you, with the grace of God. And now won't you sit in by the fire until I bring out my horse?" But the stranger declined to enter the house, and said he must keep an eye on his own horse—it was a spirited animal, dark and black-maned as its master.

The two of them, Brigit and the stranger, set off quietly enough toward the hills, all in the light of the full moon. Brigit said little, waiting for the stranger to speak; and he said nothing at all. They had not gone very far when they came to a turn in the path and Brigit suddenly found herself in a part of the country she had never seen before. It was completely strange to her, although she knew every bit of country for miles around. "This is strange country," she said. "Where are your people, anyhow?"

"It's not far to do," said the man, "we'll be there shortly now."

"Indeed, will we?" said Brigit. "I'm of mind to turn back here unless I know where I'm going."

"We are almost there," said the man. He looked at her oddly and then said, "I wasn't going to tell you this—indeed, I'm not supposed to—but I can see you're a good woman. Now, when we come on my people, be just as well spoken to them as they to you; but by no means take food of them when they offer it to you."

Brigit didn't like the sound of this, though she lost some of her fear of the man himself. She had little time to think further, however, for they came now in sight of his people's encampment. "Remember what I told you," the man said. She had no chance to ask why because the people flocked to them and made them both very welcome. She herself was treated with great courtliness, and was aided promptly in every way as she went about making her preparations. Yet there seemed something strange about the whole thing, because here it was the dead of night and all were as wide awake as if it were midday and some of the people continued to dance about in a ring and make merry as if nothing at all were going to happen.

Anyhow, she assisted the young woman in question, and brought a boy into the world for her. There was much rejoicing at this, and Brigit felt well pleased. It wouldn't do for the people, though, but that she must sit down to eat a little something with them. They asked her and asked her, and practically begged her to stay awhile to eat; but Brigit remembered what the dark man had warned her against, and she remained firm. At last, the people that asked her to stay were almost in tears. Still she refused. Oddly, all the time she felt there was a good deal of laughing going on about her; yet she couldn't tell who was doing it.

Finally, Brigit took horse and went off with the tall stranger by the way she came. As they rode along, she decided to ask him why he had told her to refuse all food. He looked at her for a moment after she asked him and said, "'Tis lucky for you, and unlucky for us, that you ate nothing; for, if you had eaten but one mouthful, you would never return to your own world again. As it is, we have lost you; and you'll go back none the worse."

Then it dawned on Brigit that she had attended a fairy birth, and that she was still in the world of fay. She was about to make the sign of the cross when they came to a turn in the path. Her guide smiled gravely on her, and she suddenly found herself back again where she had entered the land of fay, in plain sight of the town. The man himself had vanished completely, and his horse.

"It was only the grace of God that saved me," she would say in later years.

Travis 1941: 200–201. ATU 476** and Motif F372.1/C211.1. James Travis, who submitted this story to the *Journal of American Folklore*, heard it from his father, who learned it in turn from his mother, a woman born and raised in Ireland. This is a legend version of a tale widespread in Irish tradition, but also known in English and Welsh tradition. (It is Tale XL in Joseph Jacobs's *English Fairy Tales*, 1898.) Sean O'Sullivan (Seán Ó Súilleabháin) provides a fuller version and annotation (Tale 26) in *Folktales of Ireland*. And a version in Vance Randolph's *Who Blowed Up the Church House?* collected in 1950, comes from the Arkansas storyteller's grandfather, who told it at the end of the nineteenth century (1952: 123–24, 213–14). In fuller versions, the woman may do something at the beginning of the story that attracts fairy attention and leads to being taken among the fairies as a midwife. In the version in O'Sullivan, for instance, she expresses pity for an unusually large pregnant toad. Usually, as in the present version, the fairy man who acts as her guide pities her and protects her from actions that would harm her. But in many versions, though not in ours, the woman while in the fairy world acquires magical sight in one eye that enables her to continue to see the fairies. When her fairy guide discovers this fact some time after their return, he blinds the offending eye.

99. Jamie and the Wee Ones

In times gone by, a boy named Jamie lived in a little cottage with his mother, who was a widow. He was her sole support. The neighbors thought him the best son ever heard of.

His other neighbors, the ones he couldn't see (i.e., the fairies), thought him ignorant. An old ruined castle about a quarter of a mile from the cottage was the abode of the "wee folk." Sometimes the castle lighted up, and little forms could be seen dancing and flitting about and the sound of music could be heard. Jamie often wondered about them, and one night picked up his cap and started to the castle to find out. Although his mother warned him not to go, he went anyhow.

In a grove at the side of the ruin he stopped for a little while and listed to the fairy revelry. Some of the fairies were dancing, others playing, some drinking and feasting. When Jamie entered the castle, they all welcomed him and told him that they were going to Dublin to steal a lady. Jamie decided to go too. A troop of horses appeared at the door of the castle. The little folk and Jamie mounted, and their steeds rose into the air. Over houses, over mountains, over towns and cottages they went. Suddenly the fairy riders shouted, "Dublin! Dublin!" They were going to visit one of the finest houses.

They all dismounted near a window, and, inside, Jamie saw the beautiful face of a lady, who was lying asleep in a splendid bed. He saw her lifted and carried away. A stick dropped in the bed took the lady's form. All the fairies took turns carrying her. Finally Jamie asked for his turn. He dropped her down at his home, and the angry fairies turned her into all kinds of shapes but Jamie kept her. The little women told Jamie that he should have no good of her, and made her deaf and dumb.

He told his mother that he had brought a beautiful woman for company. The mother could think of nothing to say, but wondered how such a fine lady could live with them. Then she gave the lady her best clothes. The latter cried very much at first, but finally adapted herself to her new life and helped by knitting and by feeding the pigs.

About a year later, Jamie said he was going away to seek his fortune. As he was passing the ruined castle, he heard the "wee ones" talking among themselves about the bad tricks they had played upon the lady and Jamie. One tiny woman said that Jamie would be surprised if he knew that three drops from the glass she held in her hand would make the lady hear and speak again. Jamie rushed into the castle, snatched the glass, and ran home with it. He gave the lady three drops of the liquid it contained, and immediately she was able to speak. They talked around the fire until late at night.

Next day she sent a message to her father, telling him where she was. No answer came. Jamie and the lady then went to Dublin, travelling on foot. No one recognized her, and she was told that her father's daughter had died seven years before. Not even her father recognized her. He called her an impostor, and when she showed him a ring, demanded to know how she had obtained it. Then she asked him to call her mother to come and look at a mole on her neck. The mother knew her by the mole, but sadly said that her daughter was shut up in a coffin. Jamie then told them what had happened, and finally succeeded in convincing them that the lady was really their daughter. The latter refused to allow Jamie to return home, and sent for his mother to come to them. She came, and Jamie and the lady were married. They lived in Dublin, and after the death of the lady's father, inherited all his wealth.

Brewster 1939: 306–8. ATU 612(?) and Motif D1500.1.11. Told by Jeanne Rhodes of St. Louis, Missouri, October 23, 1938. Learned from her grandmother, Ella Bridget English Smith, also of St. Louis, who immigrated from Limerick, and who knew several old tales, including a version of The Devil's Daughter (ATU 313). This and the preceding story are recognizably märchen, but have been refashioned into something much closer to legend in overall effect. And indeed Irish-American culture seems to make more room for legends than for märchen.

100. How Death Came to Ireland

An Irishman told this story about a king of France. He said the King of France, he wanted to git married, but he couldn't find no one that suited him. So he went traveling through the country hunting a wife. He come to a wilderness where an old hermit monk lived. The king, he stayed there awhile with the old monk, and they'd go hunting. One day they was out a-hunting and they saw three white swans. The king, he wanted to kill them, but the old monk, he said, "No, don't kill them." The king asked him why, and the old monk he said, "They ain't swans. They're the girls who come to the lake every day to swim." The old monk had lived a thousand years, and he knew all about them things.

The king, he wanted to catch the three girls. But the old man said that the only way they could catch them was to git their clothes, and that would be hard to do, for the three women swam so fast that he couldn't git the clothes. But the king kept on insisting about catching the three girls, so the old monk give him a pair of ten-mile boots to put on. The king, he put on the ten-mile boots and slipped up the bank of the lake and stole the three girls' clothes before they knowed it.

Then the girls swam to the shore, where they saw what the king had done, and they begged for their clothes. But the king wouldn't give them back without they'd take him along with them. The three women, they agreed to. The oldest girl took the king first, and she flew away with him, and her sister followed. She carried the king a long way till she came to a mountain, and then she dropped him. The second sister, she caught him and carried him across the mountain and on a long way till she got tired. Then she dropped him. The youngest sister, she caught the king and carried him the rest of the way. She was the one the king was going to marry.

When they got to the home of the three sisters though, the king, he couldn't tell them apart. But the youngest, she give him a sign: she held her knees close together, and the other two, they held their knees apart. And they were married and lived very happy. But the king wanted to go back to France. His wife told him that he couldn't, for he'd die if he did. He kept on insisting on going back. His wife, she fixed up a flying ship to take him back, but she told him that he'd die if he got out. The king promised not to git out of the ship, but come right straight back.

When the king got to France, he forgot all about what he'd promised his wife. He stepped out on the ground and Death was right there, and he nabbed him.

"Don't take me, Death," the king said. "Take these old men around here. I'm young."

"I want you," said Death, holding on tight to the king.

The king saw that Death was going to take him anyhow. So he said, all right, he'd go if Death would get in that box he had along also. Death got into the box, and the king slammed the lid shut and fastened it tight so he couldn't git out. Then the king got in his machine and flew back to his wife.

When the king got back to his wife, he told her what had happened, and he started to open the box Death was in. His wife stopped him and said, "Don't open that box here. If you do, we'll all die."

They didn't know what to do with Death. But a big storm come up over the ocean, and they took the box with Death in it and dropped it into the ocean. The box floated a long time in the ocean until it came to Ireland and was washed on shore. Men got the box up on the shore and began to wonder what was in it. Two big Irishmen got sledge-hammers and broke the box open. Death flew out and killed every man of them. And he started to killing people all over Ireland. That was why the Irishmen left Ireland and come to America.

Neely 1938: 121–23. ATU 400/313/413/465 and Motif Z111.1.1. Collected by Charles Neely from Frank Schumaker, Grand Tower, Illinois. Neely believed that Schumaker learned it first or second hand from an Irish immigrant working in the iron foundry in Grand Tower. Many Irish had settled in the Ozark foothills of southern Illinois, in the region known as Egypt. This fascinating parable of the Potato Famine reflects memories of a number of tales. The basic structure is closest to ATU 400, but has echoes of ATU 313. The initial situation is precisely that of ATU 413, in which a holy man in the wood teaches the hero how to win the maiden by grabbing her clothes and running. Bringing Death back in a box is reminiscent of the task of bringing God back, associated with ATU 465, a tale that may also feature the swan-maiden opening. The hero, moreover, in ATU 465 is usually a king, as he is in this tale. The story of capturing Death circulates widely as a separate tale, though the ATU classification does not give it a tale number (but cf. ATU 330). Usually, however, Death is captured in a knapsack: stupid giants are captured in boxes (G514.1, K714.2).

Composite tales are very common in Irish tradition, and ATU 400 frequently combines with ATU 313. But Seán Ó Súilleabháin and Reidar Th. Christiansen, in *The Types of the Irish Folktale* (1963), describe nothing that looks like this particular combination. I was also unable to find anything there that looks like the preceding tale. This fact may, perhaps, indicate how creative Irish storytellers can be.

101. The Mare's Egg

Once there was an Irishman going along a road. He met a man with a load of pumpkins. Never having seen any before, the Irishman asked what they were. The man told him that they were mares' eggs. So the Irishman bought one, intending to raise himself a colt. As he was going up a hill the pumpkin fell off his shoulder, rolled down the hill, and, hitting a stump, burst open. A rabbit behind the stump jumped up and went running across the field. The Irishman, thinking that this was the colt, started in hot pursuit, yelling, "Hee haw, Colty, here's your mammy."

Brewster 1939: 298. ATU 1319. Told by Mrs. Dora A. Ward, of Princeton, Indiana, on July 20, 1938. Mrs. Ward learned her tales from an Irish aunt, Mrs. Carrie McMurtry, who at one time lived in Lynnville, Indiana.

"Irishman" jokes were extremely popular in the United States up through the World War II era. As this example shows, the Irish themselves relished them and shared them among themselves. This particular tale is a ubiquitous numbskull story, well Americanized in that the giant fruit is a pumpkin and the dupe is a Greenhorn. Leonard Roberts includes an Irishman version in *South from Hell-fer-Sartin* (1955: 121), but the dupe may be any handy numbskull. In American tradition this tale is so popular that this anthology would be incomplete without it.

CHAPTER 16

TALES FROM OTHER
COMMUNITIES, ETHNIC,
REGIONAL, OCCUPATIONAL,
AND FAMILIAL

The United States has never had a nationwide, organized, and concerted folklore collection program such as that, for example, of the Irish Folklore Commission. The WPA state Writers' Projects of the 1930s were perhaps the closest thing we have had, and yet the focus of those Writers' Projects varied from state to state. Consequently, folktale collecting has had to depend on opportunity and enthusiasm. As earlier chapters in this volume show, some American groups, such as the southern mountaineers, have been extremely well studied by a number of collectors. Others, such as the Missouri French, by a small number of collectors, sometimes by only one. In addition, many excellent collectors have focused on the immigrant generation (see introduction) or on customs or music instead of tales. And some groups and communities have been unaccountably overlooked. Moreover, other sorts of groups, such as occupational or social groups, also generate folklore. This chapter will look at a few additional groups, social or occupational as well as ethnic or regional, most of them not widely collected from, in order to suggest the true but hidden range of the European folktale repertoire in the United States.

One of the earliest systematic projects to collect regional folklore in the United States was that by Emelyn Gardner in the Schoharie Hills of

New York, north of the Catskills and west of Albany, in the first decade or so of the twentieth century. For her M.A. thesis, Gardner returned to the region where she had taught high school for five years. There she collected many sorts of folk material, published some of it in the *Journal of American Folklore* (1914), wrote her M.A. thesis, and finally, in 1937, published her collection in book form. The first two stories in this chapter are regional stories from Gardner's Schoharie field collection. Like the southern stories of Part 4, however, they represent a strong British strain of storytelling, perhaps enriched with a German admixture.

Other tales in this chapter range well beyond the Iberian, French, and British/German traditions. The Polish, an ethnic group found in large numbers in many regions of the United States, are represented by "The Black Kitty" and "The Bewitched Princess." The Scandinavians, among whom, apparently very little currently survives in the way of märchen, are represented by a märchenized legend, "The Powder Snake." Other stories in the chapter come from the fringes of the European folktale world. "The Clever Daughter," a story that the narrator remembered from her girlhood, is an Eastern European Jewish version of a novelle widespread in Europe. "Sam Patra and His Brothers" is a young Gypsy boy's version of a favorite Indo-European märchen. The Armenian Hodja Nasreddin tales are trickster and numbskull tales in eastern Mediterranean dress. "The Two Dreams" is a novelle with a long-documented European history.

School, work, and social programs such as Scouting and summer camp often provide environments where Americans come into contact with people of different ethnic, religious, regional, or social backgrounds. These social settings may also develop their own traditions and oral heritage. Storytelling in particular has proved a staple feature of camp and Scout life, and has often found a place as well in the school and the workplace. One of the storytellers in this chapter, Joe Woods, achieved local fame as a storyteller in the workplace. An immigrant from Poland, he worked in the lumber camps of the Michigan Upper Peninsula. What makes his stories "American" is the unique North Woods lumber-camp setting in which he told them. Woods, who also told stories when he worked in the mines, tells how, in an adaptation of American Indian custom, the other men in the lumber camp would give him tobacco and cigarettes to keep him narrating (Dorson 1949: 28).

The school and library are other places where storytelling has found a home. This chapter does not include school or library stories because they are already well represented in other chapters. Marshall Ward of the Beech Mountain Hicks/Harmon family told many a tale as he taught fifth grade in Watauga County, North Carolina. Ward's cousin Jane Gentry worked for

Dorland School, where she was often called upon to tell stories to the assembled scholars. Her daughter Maud Long became in time a noted teacher and storyteller. One of Long's tales is included in *Jack in Two Worlds,* along with tales from Bonnie Kyofski and Leonard Roberts, two other important American storytellers who taught at both the school and college level. On days of bad weather Betty Carriveau Sherman (chapter 18) liked to tell her Wisconsin fourth-graders the long märchen she had learned from her father. Cape Verdean Yvonne Smart tells stories in her position as librarian for a Providence Public Library branch in a Cape Verdean neighborhood. Many librarians and teachers draw upon printed sources for storytelling, but Smart, Kyofski, Ward, Gentry, and the other teacher and librarian storytellers here mentioned are able to draw upon their own family and community stock of tales to carry on the oral tradition.

In the contemporary United States it is not always easy to attribute a single ethnicity to a family. People marry across ethnic and regional lines and incorporate into family culture items gleaned from across the spectrum of general American culture. What can be said for the family culture as a whole can also be said for the family's tales, for of course families do tell tales, especially at the family dinner table and in the family car. This chapter includes two short, humorous tales collected from members of the same extended family. Each of these two stories also has connections with summer camp. One was brought home from a Girl Scout camp and the other is frequently heard at Scout camps. Camp, in fact, is often the first place beyond the family circle where children get a taste of storytelling. The public audience of the campfire and the private audience of the cabin provide rich contrasting opportunities for honing narrative skills.

As in other chapters, the emphasis in the present chapter is on the repertoire from Europe and adjacent Asia Minor as it has become assimilated and acclimated. Consequently, most of the examples come not from recent immigrants but from members of communities long established in the United States. An exception was made for the tales of Joe Woods, tales that became American in being adapted to the American lumber-camp environment. The chapter concludes with two more exceptions, both from the Armenian community in California. Armenians are an Indo-European people originally from Asia Minor but long dispersed throughout the Eastern Mediterranean world from Egypt to Greece and the Balkans, and east to Iran. The first of these two exceptions is the set of Middle-Eastern Hodja Nasreddin stories. These stories come from Christian Assyrians and Armenians who have come to California from Syria, Lebanon, Iran, and Iraq. There in California the stories are told in English among a people who share a common cultural background but not always a common language. The stories serve to create community bonds in the new American environment. Hence, I submit, they have become American stories. The other example of immigrant folktale is the last story in the chapter, "The Two Dreams." For this story, we are fortunate to have two performances, one by an immigrant mother and one by her daughter. This double narrative gives us an unusual chance to catch the assimilation process in action. The mother's version already shows evidence of an American context: the hero is a bookkeeper, the "king" is the businessman who is his boss, and at the end the couple goes off on a shipboard honeymoon. Furthermore, no detail in the story is inconsistent with an American context. The daughter's version is even more clearly American, with the man inviting his boss home for dinner, planning a typical American wedding, and finally leaving on a cruise ship.

102. The Pea Story

When Ellen was a little girl, her mother died. So Ellen grew up with no one to take care of her except her father, and he didn't know much about raisin' little girls. One day, when Ellen had growed to be a young lady with many beaux, she looked out of the window of the farmhouse where she lived with her father and saw a handsome stranger in a high hat ride past on a splendid black horse. Ellen thought that she had never seen such a fine young man.

The next day while Ellen was working among her flowers, the young man again come riding down the road, this time on a beautiful white horse. As he come opposite Ellen, he stopped his horse and said, "What beautiful flowers you have."

Ellen said, "Yes, would you like some?"

He said he would; so Ellen picked him some, and he thanked her and then rode away. After this, every day the stranger would appear, every time on a different horse. And every time he would stop and have a chat with Ellen, who looked forward to his visits with great pleasure. One Sunday afternoon as he started off, he said to Ellen, "My house is only a mile through these woods just beyond your house. Will you come to my house some day? I'll sow these peas that I brought with me, and when the peas blossom, you come. Will you?"

Ellen said if she could get her father asleep, she would.

Every day after that Ellen would walk to the edge of the woods to watch and wait for the peas to blossom. At last one day when she came to the edge of the woods, she saw the long line of peas in blossom. So the next day she got her father to take a nap, and started out to follow where the peas led.

After she walked a long ways through the deep woods, she come to a little footbridge. Something told her she hadn't better go any further, but she remembered her promise to the young man and went on. Pretty soon she saw in front of her a great big house with a front door all black. When she got near enough to see, she read on the door:

Don't be too bold;
Your heart's blood will soon run cold.

Ellen almost fainted away from fright, but just as she was on the point of turning back, she heard the sound of a horseman coming. She listened, and heard it again, this time nearer. She remembered the words on the door, and thought she might be able to hide somewhere inside the house until the horseman had gone by. So she opened the door and went in.

She looked around the room but could see nothing but men's clothes hanging along the walls and on hooks from the ceiling. The clothes were all wonderfully rich and costly, trimmed with beautiful lace and buttons. She didn't see a good place to hide in this room, so she hurried on to the next. That was full of clothes, too, only it was ladies' clothes. Silk, satins, and velvets lined the walls and hung from the ceiling. She wondered what might be in the next room, and she went in. To her horror, she saw nothing but the bodies of young ladies without any heads or legs or arms. She would have fainted away if she hadn't heard voices outside the house. She looked out and saw her lover getting off from his horse, on which were also two dazzling young ladies. He was having a fine time laughing and talking as he helped them off.

Ellen looked about for a place to hide and discovered three hogsheads. She looked into the one nearest to her and found it was full of legs and feet; she hurried to close it, and looked into the next which she found was almost full of ladies' heads. More horrified than ever, she opened the last one. It was almost full of ladies' hands and arms. But she heard her lover coming with his ladies, and jumped into the hogshead among the dead hands and arms. She pulled some of them over her head and fitted the cover of the hogshead on as well as she could. Then she waited. She heard her lover come in with the ladies; heard them laugh and talk; heard him pay them fine compliments; and then heard him command them to dance for him. The first one said that her parents had never let her dance, so she did not know how. Then Ellen, who was peeking out through a hole in the hogshead, saw him cut off one of the young lady's legs, then the other, and drop them into the first hogshead. Then he cut off her head, and dropped it into the second. Then with her hands and her arms he come to the hogshead where Ellen was. But Ellen was so well covered up that he did not see her, and just dropped in the hands and arms, and begun with the second young lady. He treated her the same way he had the first. Then he hung up the bodies and took the clothes out. And a few minutes later Ellen heard him ride away.

Ellen took a beautiful ring from one of the young ladies' hands and put it on her own finger. From the wrist of the other she took a bracelet, all jeweled, and put it on her own arm. Then she prayed to the good Lord to save her life, and she clumb out of the hogshead and run from the house toward her own home. Just as she was coming to the little footbridge she heard voices, and she knew they was those of her lover and her dearest friend who was being led off to her destruction. Ellen hurried to hide herself under the bridge, and waited for the two to go by.

Then Ellen run on home, where she found her father asleep just as she had left him. She waked him up and then fainted away. Her father thought she must be sick, and he laid her on a couch and waited for her to come to. When she did, she was afraid to talk for fear she would be overheard, so she called for pen and paper and wrote out an account of everything that had happened to her.

Her father read it, and said, "The young man will most likely come again, as it is Sunday night and your birthday. We must plan to trap him. We'll invite all the neighbors—the highest and biggest—to your birthday party in three days. And we'll invite the young man, too."

When the three days come around, and it was time for the party, there was a barrel driven full of spikes placed outside Ellen's house. Inside the house there was all the finest young men and women of the country round. Last of all there come into the room where the company was Ellen herself, pale as death, dressed in heavy mourning—the bracelet she had taken from one murdered young woman on one hand, and the ring of the other on the other hand. I said "last"—but the strange young man hadn't come yet. When he finally appeared, he asked Ellen to speak to him outside. She told him she would after he had seen the others. So he went in and was immediately swept into a chair which had been placed for him in the center of the room. The rest all set down close around him. When the young man saw no means of getting away, he waited for what might come.

Everybody there done for the party what he could. Some sung songs, some give riddles, some told dreams, and others, stories. They asked the young man for a story, but he said he didn't know any to tell. He was told he must do his part, so he finally said that he would whistle. And with that he whistled right out a robber tune. The folks looked at each other, but held their peace, for they knew Ellen's part was to come.

When the young man had finished, the company asked Ellen what she was going to do. "I can't sing," she said. "Mother never let me tell a story, but I had a peculiar dream the other night which I will tell if you would like to hear it."

They all said that they would like to hear it, and drew their chairs up till the circle was small and close. Then Ellen put up the hand with the ring on in such a way that the young man couldn't help but see it. After the folks had a chance to see how the sight of the ring would affect him, Ellen begun: "The other night I dreamed that I was sixteen years old and lived alone with my father. One day I looked out of the window and saw a fine young man in a high silk hat go riding by on a beautiful black horse. The next day, when I was out among my flowers, he come again; this time he stopped and asked me for some flowers. I gave him some, and he put them in his buttonhole, and rode away into the woods near our house."

At this, the young man got nervous and said, "I'm not feeling well; I must have some air." But the folks wouldn't let him out till they had heard the rest of the story. So Ellen went on: "The next day the young man come again, and every day for many days until I come to love him more dearly than I can tell. I had no mother to care for me and to teach me to beware of false young men. So one day when the young man asked me to go to his home in the woods when the peas that he said he would sow blossomed, I didn't know any better than to go. Every day I went to the woods to see if the peas had come up, and when they did, I watched to see when they blossomed. At last, one day, when I come to the edge of the woods, I saw the long line of peas in bloom. So the next day I got my father to take a nap, and started out to follow where the peas led.

"After I walked a long ways through the deep woods, I come to a little footbridge. Something told me I hadn't better go any further, but I remembered my promise to the young man and went on. Pretty soon I saw in front of me a great big house with a front door all black. When I got near enough to see, I read the door:

> Don't be too bold;
> Your heart's blood will soon run cold.

"I almost fainted away from fright, but just as I was on the point of turning back, I heard the sound of a horseman coming. I listened, and heard it again, this time nearer. I remembered the words on the door, and thought I might be able to hide somewhere inside the house until the horseman had gone by. So I opened the door and went in.

"I looked around the room but could see nothing but men's clothes hanging along the walls and on hooks from the ceiling. The clothes were all wonderfully rich and costly, trimmed with beautiful lace and buttons. I didn't see a good place to hide in this room, so I hurried on to the next. That was full of clothes, too, only it was ladies' clothes. Silks, satins, and velvets lined the walls and hung from the ceiling. I wondered what might be in the next room, and I went in. To my horror, I saw nothing but the bodies of young ladies without any heads or legs or arms. I would have fainted away if I hadn't heard voices outside the house. I looked out and saw my lover getting off from his horse, on which were also two dazzling young ladies. He was having a fine time laughing and talking as he helped them off.

"I looked about for a place to hide and discovered three hogsheads. I looked into the one nearest to me and found it was full of legs and feet; I hurried to close it, and looked into the next, which I found was almost full of ladies' heads. More horrified than ever, I opened the last one. It was almost full of ladies' hands and arms. But I heard my lover coming with his ladies, and jumped into the hogshead among the dead hands and arms. I pulled some of them over my head, and fitted the cover of the hogshead on as well as I could. Then I waited. I heard my lover come in with the ladies; heard them laugh and talk; heard him pay them fine complements; and then heard him command them to dance for him. The first one said that her parents had never let her dance, so she did not know how. Then, as I was peeking out through a hole in the hogshead, I saw him cut off one of the young lady's legs, then the other, and drop them into the first hogshead. Then he cut off her head, and dropped it into the second. Then with her hands and arms he come to the hogshead where I was. But I was so well covered up that he did not see me, and just dropped in the hands and arms and begun with the second young lady. He treated her the same way he had the first. Then he hung up the bodies and took the clothes out. And a few minutes later I heard him ride away.

"I took a beautiful ring from one of the young ladies' hands, and put it on my own finger. From the wrist of the other I took a bracelet, all jeweled, and put it on my own arm. Then I prayed to the good Lord to save my life, and I clumb out of the hogshead and run from the house toward my own home. Just as I was coming to the little footbridge, I heard voices, and I knew they was those of my lover and my dearest friend, who was being led off to her destruction. I hurried to hide myself under the bridge, and waited for the two to go by.

"Then I run on home, where I found my father asleep just as I had left him. I waked him up, and then fainted away. My father thought I must be sick, and he laid me on a couch and waited for me to come to. When I did, I was afraid to talk for fear I would be overheard, so I called for pen and paper and wrote out an account of everything that had happened to me.

"My father read it and said, 'The young man will most likely come again, as it is Sunday night and your birthday. We must plan to trap him. We'll invite all the neighbors—the highest and biggest—to your birthday party in three days. And we'll invite the young man, too.'"

When Ellen had finished the story of her dream, she stopped and said she would have to rest. As she ended, the young man got very pale and put his hands in his pockets as though he expected to find something there. But the company didn't wait to see what it was. They rushed forward, clinched him, and drug him out to the barrel outside of the house. They put him in the barrel; then they nailed it up and drug it to the top of a hill near by. Then the company divided; half stayed at the top of the hill, and the other half stationed themselves at the bottom of the hill. When the folks at the top rolled the barrel to the folks at the bottom, these pulled out a spike, and rolled the barrel up to them at the top; these pulled out another spike. And so they went on until every spike had been pulled, and the body of the young man was all bloody and torn.

Without waiting to bury him, the men followed Ellen to the house in the woods and found that it was the home of a band of noted robbers. The men hid themselves, and as the robbers come in, one by one, with their victims, they were hung among the bodies of those they had murdered. Much of the stolen property was give back to the proper owners. And the people of that part of the country, for the first time in many years, could enjoy life, free from the fear of robbers.

Gardner 1937: 146–51. ATU 955. Told to Emelyn E. Gardner by Mrs. William (Aunt Jane) Buell of Conesville, in the Schoharie Hills of New York, August 1914. Mrs. Buell "said that she would tell of something which had happened on their farm in olden times as it had been related to her" (Gardner 1937: 151). Of this story, Gardner says:

> Certain stories were considered to be the property of individuals who told them particularly well, and no one else could be induced to tell them. Such was "The Pea Story" of the present collection. As Aunt Jane Buell related this tale . . . she would rise from her chair to point out the wood in which the robber had lived. She would graphically indicate the well-worn path down which he had ridden his various steeds from the wood to what had since become her own well where, she had been told, he had stopped to ask for a drink of cold water from the charming girl whose parents had lived in Aunt Jane's house. So vivid did the informant make the events of the tale that it was difficult to realize that they had not taken place in Conesville. (99)

Gardner wrote out stories from memory and "copious notes," rather than from dictation, a fact that may explain the too perfect repetition in this text (Gardner 100). For more on Mrs. Buell, see the note to the next story.

This Bluebeard tale, of the Robber Bridegroom type, should be compared with Mrs. Emma Neuland's tale, of the Three Sisters type (ATU 311), in chapter 15 (and with the Mr. Fox riddle in chapter 12). Both Buell and Neuland tell the story as if it were a local legend. Moreover, a number of cognate motifs, including barrels, repeated visits by the handsome stranger, and seeds or grain dropped to mark the way to the Bluebeard's hideout, connect the two versions.

103. Lazy Maria

Once upon a time, there lived a man with three daughters, who, as he thought, were old enough to look out for themselves. So he called them to him, and said, "It is time to go out in the world and seek your fortune. I'll start the oldest first. Go and see what luck you have in the world!"

So the oldest girl took her bundle of clothes tied up in a big kerchief, and away she went. After a while, just as she was beginning to feel hungry, she saw standing right near her a cow. The cow said,

> Milk me, milk me, or my bag will bust!
> Milk me, milk me, or my bag will bust!

No sooner had the cow said this, and the girl was wishing for something to milk the cow into, than she espied right near the cow an oven. From it came a voice, which said,

> Take me out or I'll burn up!
> Take me out or I'll burn up!

The girl looked inside the oven to see what was talking, and there was a fine loaf of bread. She took it out, dug the centre out of it, and filled the hollow with milk from the cow, then had a meal of bread and milk. She said, "The old man sent me out, and I must be doing well."

After she had eaten all the bread and milk she wanted, she went on her way. Pretty soon she came to an apple-tree full of apples.

> Shake me, shake me, or my limbs will break!
> Shake me, shake me, or my limbs will break!

said the apple-tree.

So the girl shook the tree until her lap was full of apples. When she had eaten all the apples she wanted, she put some in her kerchief and went on her way. Towards dusk, she came to a fine-looking mansion, and she thought she would inquire if they wanted anybody to work for them. Seeing a man standing in front of the house, she called out, "Halloo!"

"Halloo!" answered the man, who liked the girl's looks.

"Do you want a girl to work for you?" asked the girl.

"I think we do need one," answered the man; "but my master isn't home to-night, so you had better stay all night. Which door would you like to enter? One is a gold door: if you go in through it, you will be covered from head to foot with gold. The other is a tar door: if you go in through it, you will be covered with tar."

"Oh, I don't mind!" replied the girl. "I had just as soon be covered with tar as with gold."

"You are so humble, you deserve to go through the golden door."

"I don't care," repeated the girl.

Thereupon the man led her through the golden door; and the gold clung to her nose, her fingers, her ears, to every part of her, until she was completely covered with gold. When she was well inside the house, the man said, "We have two places where we put those who come here. Will you sleep under the ladder with the cats and dogs, or will you sleep in the high bed with all your gold and glitter?"

"I'd just as soon crawl under the ladder with the cats and dogs as to sleep in the high bed."

"Being as you are so humble, I'll put you in the high bed with all your gold and glitter."

When she reached the room where the high bed was, she saw that everything was of gold. The gold from everything she touched stuck to her, even the golden sheets; and in the morning, with the golden sheets clinging fast to her, she thought she was rich enough to go home. So home she went. When the family saw her coming, her father said, "What! Is that lazy whelp coming back? I'll get the horse-whip and whip her to death!"

The girl, however, as soon as she came near enough to make herself heard, cried out, "O Father! I'm rich, rich!"

And sure enough, the father had never seen so much gold in his life as he now saw on his daughter. As soon as he touched her, the gold fell off from her to the ground. The father ordered the girl to tell where she had been. When he heard the story, he decided to send the second daughter to try her luck in the same way.

The second daughter had precisely the same experiences as her sister, and she too returned home "rich, rich!" Then the father said, "Now for Lazy Maria! She's never been good for anything yet. Let's see what she can do!" To her he said, "Even if you are our baby, you must go."

So Lazy Maria took her bundle on her shoulder and started. Soon she came to the cow, which said,

> Milk me, milk me, or my bag will bust!
> Milk me, milk me, or my bag will bust!

"Go along, you old bitch! I don't care if it does," replied the girl. Then the voice from within the oven cried out,

> Take me out or I'll burn up!
> Take me out or I'll burn up!

"Burn up, then! I won't touch you. I won't work when I'm all tired out," complained the girl, and went on her way. When she came to the apple-tree, it cried,

> Shake me, shake me, or my limbs will break!
> Shake me, shake me, or my limbs will break!

"Let your limbs break, then! I shan't shake you," said the girl, and went on. When she came to the mansion, the man on guard told her of the two doors, and asked her through which she wanted to enter. "I want to go through the golden door," said the girl.

"All right!" and the man pushed her through the tar door. The tar stuck to her hair, filled her eyes, and covered her from head to foot.

"Oh, my father will kill me!" she cried.

"Where will you sleep,—under the ladder with the cats, or in the high bed?" asked the man.

"In the high bed, tar and all," at once decided the girl.

"All right! Creep under the ladder." And the man pushed her among the cats and dogs. "You must be more humble," said he, "if you would get on in the world."

The next morning the poor girl, all covered with tar as she was, started for home. When the family saw her coming, they rushed out to see the gold; but when they discovered that she was covered with tar instead of gold, they cried, "Let's whip her!"

"Oh, no!" said her father. "Let's scrub the tar off!" but, scrub as they would, they couldn't get it off, because, you see, it had been put on by a witch. They scraped and scraped until they scraped the hair off her head, and the skin off her fingers and toes. At last, they scraped off one of her warts, and there lay the witch. At that, all the tar fell off, and Lazy Maria was free once more. But while her two sisters were rich and could go and come as they liked, Lazy Maria always had to stay at home, poor.

Gardner 1914: 307–10. ATU 480. Told to Emelyn E. Gardner by Mrs. William (Aunt Jane) Buell, in August 1913. "Other members of the same family spell the name Bull. Mrs. Buell is related to the Brink family, of which many members have been great story-tellers, fortune-tellers, witch doctors, and, as Mrs. B. says, unusual people. Mrs. B. learned these stories from hearing her mother tell them; and, as she has a most retentive memory, I doubt not that they are very nearly as she heard them. She thinks that her mother was German" (307, note 1). Mrs. Buell was living in the Schoharie Hills of New York State when Emelyn Gardner visited her.

This is a widely popular tale in American as well as in European tradition. It is unusual to find three sisters instead of two in tales of this type (except in Italian and Finnish versions), and rarer still to find a tale in which märchen values are so inverted: the two older sisters are the generous and kind ones (though at the end they apparently endorse beating poor Lazy Maria, who sounds a bit simple as well as lazy), while the poor youngest child, whom everyone despises, turns out to be just as worthless as everyone thought.

104. The Black Kitty

Pat had three sons. Two supposed to be smart, and one a little bit dummy. He was lazy, quiet, never get mad, never cry. So they call him Crazy Joe, the two brothers. Well, when they grow old now, the old Pat told them: "My dear son, you two got to go into the world, and learn something how life going round. That be good for you and for me. And Joe, because he little bit weak, he got to stay home with me." (You know that crazy little Joe couldn't go away.)

So the two brothers packed the satchels with supplies, tell the father farewell, and started round the world. But little Joe, he think too, but in a different way. "My brother think they would smart me, 'cause I'm crazy." So he stole one loaf of bread [*Mrs. Woods:* "He took it—he didn't stole it"], and he started on his way, take a short cut. He was there before they come. When two brothers come to the crossroads, they find Joe sitting there, crying. So the two brothers was awful surprised. They asked him, "What the dickens you doing here, Joe?"

So Joe say: "I wanta see the world too. You left me home with the father. I don't wanta stay home" [*crying*].

But the brother told him, "You gotta go back, that's all."

But Joe said, "No, I can't go home, 'cause I don't know which way."

So one brother calls the other brother on one side and whisper to him: [*softly*] "Joe—let him go. If he get lost we don't have to divide the father's gold with him. Let him go, let him get lost."

So they come back and say, "All right, Joe, you can go. We give you some supplies from our satchel."

There was a crossroad there. So each brother take different road. Each brother go three different way. "And year from now we gotta come back on this crossroads. And each brother gotta bring present for father, to show they was in the world"—didn't matter what kind. (I know, I was there—Joe was me.)

So they went. One brother went south, another went north, and Joe went east. And Joe was walking all day. And at night he come to the big woods. He eat his dry bread, and drink water from the springs, take off his coat, spread it on ground, put a stone under his head and fall asleep.

When he was sleeping, something whisper in his ear: "Get up, get up. Go farther." He get up, look around, can't see nobody. Then something whisper him again. So he take his coat, put on, and start to walk. When he walk about half hour, he come to big black castle—magnificent black castle. It was a big bronze door with a big knob. He turn the knob, and door open easily like feather. He step inside, and—oh, heaven—a table was there, and on the table was silver and gold dishes and fruit—cherries, bananas—and everything, like in a king's castle.

He opened the door and started walking on the cloister. Then he find a niche in the wall. There was black kitty chained to the wall. And he went on his knee, put a hand on the kitty head, and started to pet her. And he say, "My pretty kitty, my pretty kitty."

[*Mrs. Woods:* "My pretty *black* kitty."]

And the kitty, "Say that again."

Now the kitty say, "Now you see that table there. Go and eat and drink as much you want. Then go upstairs and go to bed. But don't oversleep. Wake up before twelve and come to me again. You save my life."

[*Mrs. Woods:* "How kitty can talk?"]

But he had it on his mind; he can't sleep. So before twelve he coming there. And she says, "Take me on your lap, and pet me, and tell me always, `My kitty, my kitty, my black kitty.' And remember, don't scare what's going happen. Just say, `My kitty, my black kitty.' Makes no difference how you scare."

Before twelve o'clock, big storm come, thunder, lightning, and hailing. And big voice ask him: "What you doing here? Get out from here, you gonna get killed." But he didn't say nothing but "My kitty, my black kitty." And all once everything get quiet; show was over.

Then kitty say to him: "Thank you, my dear friend. God bless you."

Then kitty's four legs get white. She told him to go back, eat and drink and sleep, and come back to him next night, same thing.

Second night when he come and take kitty on his lap, the kitty told him: "Be brave, my boy. Don't say nothing, just 'My kitty, my black kitty.'"

Then, at once everything gonna get black, storm and thunder again, and big devil twelve feet tall come with a big fork, putting in his breast, and say, "I gonna kill you."

But he didn't say nothing, just "My kitty, my black kitty."

Then, when the devil disappear, beautiful lady come in, with a purse full of silver and gold money. "Here, my boy, I give you all my money, so you can get out from here and you be rich man—you can buy nice present for your father." But he just say, "My kitty, my black kitty"; he never get scare.

So that's over, and the kitty turn half white. And the kitty told him, "Be happy, sleep, and on the third night come again."

But the third night was worse for all them two. It was look like all world was going fall on him. Big dragon run to him to swallow him. Big soldiers, all in iron, run on him with a big lance, going to stick it in him. The big boa constrictor come, going twist him round his head. But he didn't say nothing but "My kitty, my black kitty."

At last his two brother come. [*Mrs. Woods:* "He think it was his two brother."] They ask him what he doing there. It's time he coming home with them. They try to trick him, to ask a question. But he didn't say nothing but "My kitty, my black kitty."

Well, the time is over. Kitty all white. And kitty say, "My friend, take the chains off from me." And from kitty she turn to the beautiful princess, with a golden dress and diamond crowns on the head. Then she says, "My friend, come with me now." She take him upstairs; they walk on thirty marble steps, to the armor hall—swords hung up, king's throne was there. When they come there, there was beautiful old gray lady sitting in the throne chair, and the old gray man sitting in the throne chair, asleep.

And she says, "That's my father and mother." Then she take them down under the ground, to the dungeon, and show him thousands and thousands of soldiers, servants, consuls, senators, all kinds of dignitaries, ladies and gentlemen, animals, dogs and cats. So she said, "That's all my people."

Now so they went back into the dining room. And they had a lunch, and they had a good sleep. So the princess told him: "You gotta one year time to wait for your brother, to meet them on the crossroads. So on that time we gonna live like common man and wife. I be your wife, you be my husband."

[*Mrs. Woods:* "There was nobody to marry them."

Joe: "I should have marry them, but I wasn't priest."]

When the time come to go back to the crossroads to meet brother (they was only half a day's walk), she give him a gold belt with a diamond, rubies, sapphires, looking like rainbow, with the word "Fortune." And she told him, "Remember, *under no condition,* don't show that to your brother." And to show present for his father to his brother, she giving him common table knife.

Then she told him: "Remember, Joe, if you want to save me, my father and my people, so we come home, you gotta go to your father home, you gotta destroy something every day, the next day double, the third day double again. And should be whole year like that. And that precious belt, you give it father when you come home, but don't show it brother."

And they kiss each other for good-bye, and they start walk to the crossroad. And there his two brothers was waiting for him. And they were sure surprised, they were thinking he was lost. But he was there, and fat like vegetable.

When they shake hands, they ask him what kind present he got for father. So Joe showed them knife. Other brothers showing. One had big smoking pipe, from Germany. "Father will be awful glad." And the other brother had a pocketknife with a nail file and a screw driver and a cutting blade and cork puller.

Well, they come home together. And giva the father present. Oh, the father was glad, and kiss each son—one was in the Germany, the other was in the French.

And Joe say, "Oh, I have a nice house, and a nice girl, Katie, and I marry her too. And father, she send you nice present—not knife like I show you brother." So brother whisper to brother, "He's crazy."

But when he pull it from under his coat, that diamond belt, the father can't talk even, so surprise. And they make big eyes on him. The father hug him.

So they settle down, and Joe starts destroying. The first day he step on a chicken and kill him. So he destroy what father had on the farm—horse and cattle and wagons—even the fences. And brothers was awful mad at him. But father take the belt to the city to the jeweler, and ask him what is the worth for it. And jeweler just like turn into stone. He says, "Man, where you get that? That's worth kingdom. Not enough money in the whole country to pay for that—to buy that."

So when he come home, he told the two brothers, "Don't bother Joe. If he destroy all the property, I still be rich yet."

Well, when there is nothing left on the farm, for he destroyed everything—the bush, everything what grows—then he set fire on the building. Then when the building burn out to the foundation, he scrub a hole, put a few potatoes in it for breakfast, and tell the brother, "Come on, have one."

But the brothers was ready to kill him, they was so mad at him. But the father says, "Let the Joe alone."

Then when he was eating potatoes, and the father and brother standing by the cold ashes, they heard a heavenly lurid music. And when they turn head, on the east, they see the parade of gold people, band was playing music, and on front was the king and queen on the throne, and behind was beautiful princess, sitting with baby on the arm.

When they come close to Joe, he was still baking potatoes. So the king and queen climb down out the throne, and come to the Joe. And the king say, "My son, my son, in the name of my people I thank you thousand times for saving our people, for bringing them to life."

Then princess come, with the baby on arm, and say, "Here, Joe, here's your wife and son." And Joe get up and kiss the wife and boy baby. And then he turns to his father and brother, and he says, "That's my wife, Katie, and my baby." And his father was crying like baby himself, big fat tears was running his cheek.

Then the king and the queen and the princess take the father and him—the brother didn't want to go—and take them back to the castle. Then the old king resigned, because he was too old and tired, and maka Joe king.

His father only lived there one year and didn't like it with the rich people, so he went back to the farm. And Joe raised a big family—lived very happy.

That's the end of the story.

(There was a curse on those people there.)

Dorson 1949: 33–37. ATU 402/326. Told by Joe Woods of Crystal Falls, in the Upper Peninsula of Michigan, to Richard M. Dorson, at Woods's home, September 3, 1947. Woods learned his tales in his native Poland, but told them in the iron mines and lumber camps of the Upper Peninsula, as well as in the family circle.

> When I was night shift at Balkan mine at Alpha, I used to tell stories to the trammer
> boss—easy job. When I got tired working in the mines, I went in the lumber camps
> and told stories there. Wouldn't finish one night, so next night the boys would put
> cigarettes, tobacco in my mouth, ask me to finish. I told them in Polish and Slavish.
> (Dorson 1949: 28)

Woods's grandfather "was a big farmer, had thirty acres." His father was a road commissioner who also had a military record. Woods said he learned many of his tales from a beggar named Andrew Bakus, who would spend the night at his father's house. "I wasn't supposed to listen, but I opened the door crack and listen. And I always remember" (Dorson 1947: 19, 58.).

Dorson says of Woods's stories:

> What impressed me most about Joe Woods's folk tales was their power to entertain,
> a point always sidetracked in academic discussions of origin and distribution. They

brim with life and movement, humor and graphic detail. The plots in their full dress possess an interest-provoking symmetry and suspense. Joe's everyday language and snappy dialogue salt the narratives that turn so flat and stilted in the printed collections and translations, no matter how vociferous their claims to fidelity. His interspersions . . . clarify the peasant point of view. (Dorson 1949: 28)

In his transcription, Dorson has tried to be faithful to Woods's exact wording, but has not, he says, tried to indicate Woods's pronunciation, of which he identifies the following distinctive features. (1) Woods does not pronounce *th: dem, fadder, t'ink, eart'*; (2) he substitutes *v* for *w: vat, vorl, sveet, vun;* (3) he substitutes *f* or *w* for *v: giff, leafe, willage, adwice;* (4) he lengthens *i* and *u: heem, keesing, droogstore, bankroopt;* (5) he shifts accents: *mineester, pendoolum, castull.*

The original transcriptions that Dorson made from Joe Woods's dictation are preserved in the Lilly Library of Indiana University. Here is an early section of this story as Dorson took it down in his neat longhand on that September day.

So de two brudders packed de satchels wid de supplies, tell de fadder Furwell, and started round de world. But little Joe, he tink too, but in a different way. "My brudder tink dey would smart me, cause I'm crazy." So he stole one loaf of bread (Mrs: he took it—he didn't stole it), and he started on his vay, take a short-cut. He was dere before dey come. Ven two brudders come to de crossroads, dey find Joe sitting dere, crying. So de two brudders vas awful surprised. Dey asked him, "Vat de dickens you doing here, Joe?"

So Joe say, "I vanta see de worl' too. You left me home wid de father. I don't vanta stay home." (*crying*)

But de brudder tol' him, "You gotta go back, dat's all."

But Joe said, "No, I can't go home, cause I don't know vich vay."

So one brudder calls to odder brudder on one side and visper to him, "Joe let him go. If he get lost, ve don't have to divide de fodder's gold vid him. Let him go, let him get lost." (*soft*) So dey come back and say, "All right, Joe, you can go. Ve give you some supplies from our satchel." (Dorson 1947: 20, 1–2)

This transcription reveals a sixth feature of Woods's pronunciation, the frequent omission of final *s: take, brudder.*

105. The Bewitched Princess

A long time ago, the princess was born to the king. All peoples was asked to the party, except one fairy. So she put oath on her, so that when she come to sixteen year old, she die and turn black. Should be buried in a glass casket, put on a pedestal in a little church. When any body can stay with her over three nights, then she come back to the life and her position.

So the king father puts the soldier overnight to guard his daughter. But when he come in the morning, they find only bones from the soldier, and rats.

So, when king lose so many soldiers, people start to get mad, to complain. So the king order, "Put the convict there, the lifer." They lost good many lifer. Then come turn one boy who was a convict for life, but he never was guilty, no crime—only circumstantial evidence put him in the crime house, the prison.

So when they take him out the prison they give him everything, eat, drink, so he could be happy, 'cause it was his last day. So he run away from that party, went by a little creek, see old gray-whiskered man (must be God—people believe that in the old country). And the old man ask him, "My boy, can you give me some water? I'm so weak I can't get down to drink myself."

So the boy cupped his hand and gave him drink from his cup hand.

Then old man asked him: "My boy, can you tell me what's your trouble? I can see from your face that something bothering you."

So the boy's tell him whole story—how he got into the prison, and how he got to guard the princess now.

Therefore, for some time the boy and the old man was whispering between themselves. So the boy's went back and they take him with music and a parade to the church, and they lock him in the church with the dead princess.

That old man must be tell him, "Under no circumstances show him to the dead princess overnight."

So the first night he hide himself in the cloister, behind the organ. There was two minutes to twelve, the top of the casket started to raise up, and princess jump out of the casket. And started hollering: "Oh, where are you, I'm hungry. Oh, where are you?"

And when the time come, after one minute, she has to go back to the casket.

So when he come down and look on her, her head to the breast is turned white. And in the morning when they come open the church, boy was still shaky about life. So they take him on the shoulders and they carry him on the parade ground, right to the king. The king kiss him on the forehead, says: "My son, you are lucky. You don't have to go another night—it is against the law—but I wish you would try one more."

So they give it him lots to eat and drink and put him in that church again, for second night. The second night, he laid on a pedestal. When she open up the casket, the top cover him up. (He lay along side her, you see.) And then she come up at one minute to twelve and was hungry, 'cause she didn't eat last night you know, and she look all over but she didn't find him nowhere. So when she cover up herself, he see she white to the hip.

So in the morning they take him again, they give him best things what they had in the town. And the third night they take him back into the church. So, from time when he come there to time when he hide himself, he was praying, for himself and for the princess.

And the time come to hide himself, he went on his knee at the head of the casket. At one minute to twelve, when she open the casket and jump out, started looking for him, he jumped inside the casket and cover up himself.

When her time come, to come back to the casket, and she tried to open the casket and can't, she fell down on the floor with a dead faint. And he get out the casket, run on knee by the princess, put hand on her heart, and heart started whispering. And her cheeks started get pink. And she was all white. And he sit on a pedestal, and sit her on his knee, and bended down his head and put his lips on her lips (you can understand that, can't you?) and he kiss her.

And she open it eyes, put hand down his neck and says, "Oh, my angel." And she come to the life all white.

And in the morning when they come, and they sees the boy and the princess standing there holding each other's hand, and the peoples was looking like crazy, staring, didn't know what happened. And they take boy and princess to the king's house, put each on one side by the throne, and the king say, "My son, by my will my daughter is your wife." And he gives him blessings and they were married. And after the king dead he become the king.

They had big wedding and I was there. I fell asleep on a manure pile, and they had big cannon they wanted to fire. So they took some manure to put in the cannon (to tamp it), and they put me in. So it made a big bang, and blew me across the ocean to tell you this story.

Dorson 1949: 37–39. ATU 307/410. Told by Joe Woods of Crystal Falls, in the Upper Peninsula of Michigan, to Richard M. Dorson, September 3, 1947. See preceding tale.

As might be expected, this horrifying märchen is relatively rare. Its theme of ghoulish cannibalism, while rendering it unsuitable, perhaps, for nursery entertainment, would nevertheless win it rapt attention in the mine or lumber camp. Woods's tales often feature scatological or sexual elements as well, as in the preceding tale. The present tale also includes a three-night test much like the hero's test in the preceding tale.

106. The Powder Snake

Once there was a low marshy place near a little town. Everyone was afraid to go near this slough, because there was a monster snake that lived there. People always avoided the place, going around it whenever they had to pass that way. This deadly poisonous reptile was known as the powder snake because it sprayed its victims with a powder, blinding and killing them instantly.

Now there was a mother and her son who lived not far away from this slough. They were very poor; and although the boy was only a lad of five, he had to do chores and help take care of his mother. Every morning he drove their cow out to pasture, taking a machete knife along with him, to find choice bits of grass for the cow after he had staked her out. Every day he went farther and farther looking for grass because the cow had already eaten all the grass in the pasture, and he had cut all the juicy weeds and grass that lay in patches near by.

"Son," said his mother one evening after she had milked the cow, "the cow doesn't give any more milk. You will have to find more grass for her to eat, or we are going to starve."

"All right, mother," replied the son.

So the next morning the lad arose very early, took his knife and drove the cow to the pasture. But there was not enough grass left in the pasture for the cow. She was very hungry and began sniffing the tiny bits of grass left and tearing at them with her long tongue and pulling them into her mouth.

The lad started walking and walking, in search of some grass and weeds to cut and bring to the hungry cow. It was already late autumn, and the frost had begun to kill all the plants. The boy found an occasional stray wisp of grass, cutting it and carrying it away with him. After he had cut a handful, he would lay it into a little pile upon the ground, intending to pick it up on his way back.

As the lad went farther and farther, he did not realize he was getting near the slough. As he got nearer, there were more weeds and grass; this led him on closer and closer. Suddenly, he reached the edge of the marsh. He was seized with terror, standing still for a moment and holding a large armful of grass.

On the bank of the slough he saw a huge snake sleeping. He knew that was the terrible powder snake. He dropped his grass and turned to run away. He looked back again at the snake, which was still sound asleep. The boy was no longer afraid and felt as if drawn by some power toward the creature. He advanced closer and closer, holding up the machete in his hand. When he was right upon the monster, he dealt a machete blow over its head with all his might, then ran away as fast as he could. The powder snake whipped about in a fury, spraying deadly powder in every direction.

The boy forgot his grass and the cow, running back to town as fast as he could. As he passed people on the road, he would cry out, "I got him! I got him!"

"What did you get?" asked one of the villagers.

"I killed the powder snake!" cried the little boy.

"That's impossible," laughed one of the fellows. "If you had been near the snake, you'd be dead now and wouldn't be here to tell the tale."

"I tell you, I got him!" shouted the boy. "I cut his head off with my machete."

Then the lad held up the machete, and sure enough, there was blood on it.

"Maybe the boy is right," said an elderly man. "Let's walk down there and get a look from a distance."

All of them agreed to go; but as they approached the slough, some of them began to drop back, until only the boy and the old man were leading the way.

"I must go back home," one of the fellows excused himself. "I have work to do."

"I have a sore foot and can't walk," explained another.

Soon the boy and the old man had reached the bank of the slough, and sure enough, the monster was lying dead. All the trees and grass were burned away and dead from the spray of the deadly powder. So the lad and the old man walked up to the snake.

As soon as all the people saw the two unhurt and right upon the reptile, they all ran up, shouting and screaming, "Kill it! Kill it!" They came up with rakes, hoes, and knives and fell to hacking away at the dead monster. A vile, stinking, greenish fluid poured from the sides of the snake. "We have killed it!" shouted everybody.

"Be quiet, all of you!" ordered the old man. "This lad here killed the powder snake. We owe everything to him."

Finally, everyone agreed that the boy had killed the snake. The folk carried him back to town on their shoulders, proclaiming him a great hero.

All the townsfolk made him and his mother a present of something— food for them to eat and hay and grain for the hungry cow. So the brave lad and his mother lived happily ever after.

Claudel 1943: 113–15. Cf. ATU 300. Calvin Claudel learned this tale from Edmond Esping, a sailor hospitalized in San Diego early in World War II. Esping, from Minnesota, Minnesota, was born in 1920. His mother came from Christiana, in Norway, and his paternal grandfather immigrated from near Bergen. Apparently Esping retained his fascination with snakes all his life: when I called him at his home in Minneota, June 3, 1998, he told me a personal experience story about killing a puff adder.

The somewhat romantic level of diction raises questions about how the story was collected and set down. Esping may have written the story out. Unfortunately, when I spoke with him he no longer remembered meeting Claudel and communicating the story to him. Esping also contributed a second story, "The Snake That Suckled," remarkably similar in structure, about a cow being sucked dry each day while in the pasture. The boy hero lies in wait and discovers that a huge rattlesnake with fifty bell-like rattles comes to feed from the cow. When the cow hears the rattles, she is transfixed and suffers the snake to drain her dugs. The boy too, hearing the rattles, is "conjured" and cannot move. But when the snake has finished, the boy is able to follow it. The snake has drunk so much that it becomes stuck halfway into its hole, and the boy shoots it with the gun he has brought along. "The boy returned to fetch the cow home, told his mother about the monster rattlesnake. She kissed him for joy. They never missed their milk again, and lived happily ever after." While it is possible, in the case of these two tales, that märchen have absorbed snake superstitions (e.g., that snakes can puff out a deadly powder; that they can milk cows, motif B765.4; that they have hypnotic powers, B765.14), it seems far more likely that common snake lore and legends have been transformed into märchen. Both tales begin with an initial situation common in northern European tales: a poor widow and her son have been reduced to dependence on a single cow. "The Powder Snake" develops as a very truncated version of "The Dragon Slayer," with echoes also of the New Testament parable of the guests who make excuses not to attend the wedding feast. "The Snake That Suckled" includes elements of stories such as ATU 530 and ATU 550 in which some mysterious devouring force threatens the family and the hero must keep watch to solve the mystery.

Though the Scandinavian märchen tradition is very rich, and Scandinavian immigrants to the United States were very numerous, I have been unsuccessful in finding any other Scandinavian-American märchen material. If, however, Esping himself was the one who developed this story in its present form, and I suspect he was, his story demonstrates that märchen must have been known in his community. Otherwise, that young man could not have used the märchen formula so successfully to recast a snake legend.

107. 'Twas a Dark and Stormy Night

> 'Twas a dark and stormy night
> And the rain in torrents fell.
> Said the pirates to Antonio,
> "Antonio, tell us a tale."

And thus the tale began:

> "'Twas a dark and stormy night
> And the rain in torrents fell . . ."

Hickey 2002. ATU 2013/ Motif Z17. James Hickey, the editor's brother-in-law, recited this version, at the editor's request, while driving to a family celebration in July 2002. Hickey, from Hazlet, New Jersey, grew up on Long Island. In his early seventies at the time of the recitation, he remembered the piece from his childhood, when it was recited by "my Uncle Harry Cusak, a soldier of fortune and lighthouse keeper." Apparently, Cusak did indeed live a vagabond life before he finally married Hickey's aunt and settled down to operate a lighthouse on the Connecticut coast. Hickey's children now recite the piece, and the editor first heard it from Hickey's older son.

William L. Alderson, who was teaching at Reed College at the time, sent the following version, current in his family, to *Western Folklore*, where it was printed in 1952. Alderson says that the recitation was current in his family.

'Twas a dark, stormy night on the Susquehanna river, when a band of robbers were gathered together. The chief struck up a story and it went like this: "'Twas a dark, stormy night . . ." (88)

And so it goes. William Bucksot, of Hammond, Indiana, told Herbert Halpert:

I think it's a bed-time story [my uncle] used, to quiet [us] two boys down. We'd be bothering Mother, and he'd tell it to us mainly to quiet us down . . . "The boys were sitting around the campfire and Big John said to Little John, 'Tell us a story.' And this is the story he told: 'The boys were sitting around the campfire . . .'" That just keeps on going like that till you go to sleep. (Halpert 1942: 88. Punctuation modified.)

The story may also feature cowboys, Indians, or especially Boy Scouts, who know that campfires are for sitting up late and telling long stories. Indeed, the editor has heard his son's Scoutmaster tell the boys his version.

108. Knives and Forks

About a hundred years ago or so, these three German fellows immigrated to the United States. They settled down in Cincinnati and each of them got a job. One got a job in an opera house, one in a factory that made cutlery, and one in a candy factory.

Now, these three fellows spent most of their time with each other, and they never did learn much English. In fact, the fellow working at the opera house only learned to say [*singing*]: "Me-me-me, me-me." The fellow that worked in the cutlery factory learned to say [*chanting*]: "Knives and forks, knives and forks." And the fellow that worked in the candy factory learned to say: "Goody, goody, gumdrops."

Now, these three fellows would meet every Sunday and spend the day walking along by the river, even though the area down by the river was a pretty seedy neighborhood. Well, one Sunday they had just started walking and they came to a place where an alley came right down to a pier. And there in the mouth of the alley was a dead body. Somebody who'd been shot in a brawl the night before. They just stood around it, asking each other, "What should we do, what should we do?"—talking in German, of course.

While they were still there, trying to figure out what to do, a police van pulls up and two policemen jump out with their guns drawn.

"All right," the first policeman says, "who did this?"

The first fellow, who didn't understand what they are asking, of course, replied with the only English he knew: "Me-me-me, me-me."

"What did you kill him with?" asked the second policeman.

"Knives and forks, knives and forks," said the second fellow.

The policemen looked at each other, and then one of them said, "Ok, we're going to have to take you all to jail."

To which the third German fellow said, "Oh! Goody, goody, gumdrops."

McCarthy 2006. ATU 1697. My daughter, then aged ten, heard this tale at a Girl Scout camp in western Pennsylvania, about 1996. For a while it was a favorite joke for her and for her younger sister. I too started telling it, and this is the way I tell it, setting it in Cincinnati. Much of the enjoyment of the story comes from the way the first two phrases are performed. The opera house phrase is sung like a soprano practicing: "Mi, mi, mi, etc." The cutlery phrase is chanted with a rising inflection on "knives" and a falling inflection on "forks." My daughters regularly reversed the last two exchanges, I think because they found the chanted phrase "Knives and forks" irresistibly funny, and felt it made the better ending to the story. That may also be how my older daughter first heard the story. Their compulsive father insists on putting the questions in more logical order, but the daughters may be right about the better way to tell the story.

This is a popular American story, perhaps most often told of a Mexican arrested in the United States or (with Spanish phrases: *Si, señor, Por favor, Muchas gracias*) of a Gringo in Mexico. So told, it reflects long-standing ethnic tensions in the United States. I do not know where the Girl Scout who first told it to my daughter heard it with German heroes. But the outlandish phrases in her version give the tale an air not of ethnic tension but of inspired silliness.

109. The Amazing Old Men

An eighty-year-old man went to the doctor for a checkup and the doctor was amazed at what good shape the guy was in. The doctor asked, "To what do you attribute your good health?"

The old timer said, "I'm a turkey hunter and that's why I'm in such good shape. I'm up well before daylight and out chasing turkeys up and down the mountains."

The doctor said, "Well, I'm sure that helps, but there's got to be more to it. How old was your dad when he died?"

The old timer said, "Who said my dad's dead?"

The doctor said, "You mean you're eighty years old and your dad's still alive? How old is he?"

The old timer said, "He's one hundred years old and, in fact, he hunted turkey with me this morning, and that's why he's still alive . . . he's a turkey hunter."

The doctor said, "Well, that's great, but I'm sure there's more to it. How about your dad's dad? How old was he when he died?"

The old timer said, "Who said my grandpa's dead?"

The doctor said, "You mean you're eighty years old and your grandfather's still living! How old is he?"

The old timer said, "He's one hundred eighteen yrs old."

The doctor was getting frustrated at this point and said, "I guess he went turkey hunting with you this morning too?"

The old timer said, "No . . . Grandpa couldn't go this morning because he got married."

The Doctor said in amazement, "Got married!! Why would a one-hundred-eighteen-year-old guy want to get married?"

The old timer said, "Who said he wanted to?"

Smith 2003. ATU 726. This is another tale that now circulates as a joke. It was submitted to the Internet joke site *Blagues-L* by E. W. Smith. A number of versions of this joke can be found on the Internet, word-for-word nearly identical. But the reason for vigor and longevity varies from version to version—turkey hunting, as here, or golf, or being Italian or Polish. Apparently, storytellers today plug in whatever health secret accords with their wishful thinking.

110. The Clever Daughter

Once a noble landowner sent for his three leaseholders. One leased his woods, one his mill, and the third, the poorest, his inn. The nobleman asked them three questions.

"First, what is the fastest thing in the world?

"Second, what is the fattest thing in the world?

"And third, what is the dearest thing in the world?

"He who answers my riddles correctly will have to pay me no rent for ten years. But he who answers wrongly will be driven from my lands."

The leaseholder of the woods and the leaseholder of the mill thought they knew the answers right away. Surely the fastest thing in the world was the nobleman's horse, the fattest thing in the world was his pig, and the dearest thing in the world must be the woman he would someday marry.

The innkeeper went home in despair, because he knew that surely the answers must be more complex than that, yet he had no idea what they might be. His daughter, who was as clever as she was beautiful, asked him what was wrong. But when she heard the riddles, she only laughed and told him:

"Thought is the fastest thing in the world, the earth is the fattest, and sleep is the dearest."

So the innkeeper returned to the nobleman. Sure enough, the leaseholder of the woods and the leaseholder of the mill had guessed the wrong answers to the riddles and were sent away. But when he heard the innkeeper's answers, he frowned.

"You are correct. But these solutions never came from your own mind. Tell me who told you what to say?"

The innkeeper confessed it had been his daughter.

"If you have such a clever daughter," the nobleman said, "I wish to see her. Let her come to my mansion neither walking nor riding, neither dressed nor naked. And let her bring me a gift that is not a gift."

The innkeeper returned home more worried than before. But his daughter only laughed. "Don't be afraid, Father. There's nothing to worry about. Only buy me a fisherman's net, a goat, two doves, and a good chunk of raw meat."

Puzzled, he obeyed. The girl took off her clothes and wrapped herself in the net, so she was neither dressed nor naked. She sat astride the goat, her feet dragging on the ground, and so went along neither walking nor riding. When she had reached the nobleman's mansion, the dogs were set upon her, but she threw them the meat and went safely on her way right into the mansion. Going up to the nobleman, she told him, "I have brought you a gift that is not a gift," and released the doves, which flew out an open window.

The nobleman was delighted. "I wish to marry you, clever one," he told her. "But you must first agree never to meddle in the decisions I make at my law court."

She agreed, and so they were married and lived quite happily for a time. Then one day the girl saw a weeping peasant under her window and asked him for his story. He told her:

"My neighbor and I own a stable. I have a mare, he has a wagon. Now, my mare gave birth to her foal under the wagon, and my neighbor claims the foal is his. And when we brought the case to the nobleman, he agreed with my neighbor. That is why I weep."

"No need for tears. Go get a fishing rod and line and pretend to fish in the sand right under the nobleman's window. When he asks how you can possibly catch a fish in dry sand, you must answer, 'If a wagon can give birth to a foal, I can catch fish in dry sand.'"

The peasant did just as she told him and won his case. But the nobleman realized his clever wife must be behind his answer and told her:

"You failed to keep our agreement. Take the finest and dearest thing you can find in my mansion and return to your father's home."

She never begged, she never cried. "All right," she said calmly. "But first we must have one last meal together."

He agreed. She made sure he ate and drank enough to put him soundly to sleep, then had servants place him in his carriage. Together, she awake, he asleep, they drove to her father's inn. There, the nobleman awoke and asked in astonishment, "How did I get here?"

"Why, you told me to take the finest and dearest thing I could find in your mansion and return to my father's home. I could take no finer, dearer thing to me than you."

"I see," said the nobleman, pleased and embarrassed. "In that case, let us make up and go back home."

And so they did and grew old together in peace and happiness.

Sherman and Chwast 1992: 104–6. ATU 875. This is Sherman's own version of the story, which she and Jacqueline Chwast published. She says she probably heard it in her childhood from her Russian-Jewish grandmother. Though the story does not seem especially popular in U.S. traditions, it includes many popular and widespread motifs: difficult riddles (H630 ff. et al.), paradoxical tasks such as coming neither riding nor walking and neither naked nor clothed (H1050 ff.), unfair and unreasonable judgments (J1191), and claiming by wife of dearest possession (J1545.4). Hispanic versions of ATU 879 The Basil Maiden, for instance, often incorporate the story of the foolish judgment and the choice of dearest possession, thus emphasizing once again the cleverness and wisdom of the young heroine (see chapter 2).

III. Sam Patra and His Brothers

Once upon a time, there were an old man and an old woman. The old man was a king, and the old woman was a queen. She was about forty-five years old but had never had any babies. But one night she dreamed—and the first dream she had that night was that if she tasted a fish, she would have some babies. So she got up from beside the king and called for her waiting woman: "Woman, woman, go get me a fish."

"What fish?" asked the waiting woman, and to herself she said, "That old queen is crazy."

The queen said, "You know the pond . . . that pond has one big fish . . . that one big fish, I want to taste of him . . . I just now dreamed about that fish."

The woman said, "What about that fish?"

The old queen answered, "I just dreamed about that fish. If I taste it, I will have a son whose name will be Sam Patra."

"Then," said the woman, "I know what I'll do. If you want the fish, I will put the old fisherman to catch him, and he will surely catch him."

So the waiting woman went and told the old fisherman. And when she had finished telling him, he said, "I cannot catch any fish in that pond. It is too deep and you cannot see the fish and you need too long a line to reach." But the fisherman tried to reach the fish. Soon he came back and said to the waiting woman, "I tried my best to catch him, but I cannot."

When the woman heard that, she looked sorry and went back to the queen.

The queen asked, "Why are you sorry, woman?"

The woman's answer was, "Why should I not be sorry? The fisherman tried his best to catch the fish, but he couldn't."

As soon as the old queen heard that, she was sorry too, and cried herself back to sleep. This time she dreamed that if she did not eat of the fish, she would die. She woke up frightened and called to the sorry waiting woman, who had remained by her bed: "Woman, woman, wake up, and go get all the fishermen in town."

The waiting woman ran out and woke up all the fishermen in the town. They brought all their nets to the pond and soon had the one big fish. They gave it to the waiting woman, and the woman gave it to the queen, and the queen got up and gave it to the cook, saying, "Cook, you had better not taste this fish or I will kill you."

The cook said, "All right, I'll cook the fish and I won't taste it." Then she dropped it in the boiling kettle and cooked it.

The waiting woman came into the kitchen and asked the cook, "Did you put any salt on the fish?"

"No," said the cook. "The queen told me not to taste it, and I cannot season it without tasting."

So the waiting woman, who knew how the queen liked her food, went and tasted the fish. Right away she grew sick, and she whispered to the cook. But the cook did not understand, and she too tasted the fish and grew sick.

Then the queen shouted from her bedroom, "Why don't you bring me the fish to eat?" The waiting woman put some in a silver dish and took it to the queen. As soon as she tasted the fish, she also grew sick.

And the queen had a baby, and the waiting woman and the cook each had a baby at the same time.

The queen's baby was Sam Patra, the cook's son was Sylvius, and the waiting woman's son was Lazillia. But when they grew older, the three children called themselves brothers because they looked so much alike.

When the three boys had grown into men, one of them said one day, "Oh, brother Lazillia, let us go for a little hunt."

"And with what will we shoot big animals?" asked Sam Patra.

Lazillia said, "I shall take my bow and arrow," and Sylvius said, "All I shall take is my sword," and Sam Patra said, "Well, then I shall take my gun with me. Are you ready, brothers, to go?" They took their horses and went, and left a note for the king to read where they had gone.

When they reached the bridge over the river, they slept for the night, because they were afraid to sleep anywhere else.

Soon it was about one o'clock at night and the giant on horseback, who rode about in the woods, came to the bridge, but the horse shied and did not want to pass. The giant cursed and said, "What is the matter, my horse? You never were scared here before." The horse seemed to answer, "Giant, you might get killed by Sam Patra." But the giant cursed again and muttered to himself, "I'll show Sam Patra what I can do with him."

But Sam Patra knew by the steps of the horse that the giant was coming. And as soon as the giant said that, Sam Patra jumped up and said, "Here I am, giant. What kind of fight do you want?"

The giant called back from the darkness, "Do you want to fight with me?"

"Yes, I want to fight. How do you want to fight? Swords are no good, swords are dirty. Hammers are dirty, axes are dirty, everything is dirty, but God left only wrestling."

Then the giant answered, "Are you ready to fight by wrestling?"

"Yes," said Sam Patra, "I want to fight."

They threw off their wraps and started to wrestle and the giant grew angry because Sam Petra was so strong. He shouted loud and grabbed Sam Patra by the toe of his foot and threw him into the mud. Sam Patra got hold of the giant's legs and threw him into the mud, in the same place along the river bank. Then the giant threw Sam Patra by the hips, but he jumped up and threw the giant from beneath the armpits. The giant arose and threw Sam Patra by the shoulders. Next Sam Patra got the giant by the neck and held his head in the mud while he reached for the sword. Then he killed him.

Now the giant's horse belonged to Sam Patra so he tied it to the bridge and went again to sleep.

In the morning when Lazillia and Sylvius awoke, they cried out, "O brother, we had a terrible dream. We dreamed we would meet a double-headed giant." Then they saw the strange horse tied to the bridge, and asked, "Whose horse is that?"

"That," said Sam Patra, "was the giant's horse—but now it is mine." But they did not believe it and asked the horse, "Did Sam Patra kill a giant?" The horse just shook its head. So Sam Patra had to show them the head of the giant where it was lying in the mud.

Then they were frightened and said, "Now I know we shall get killed by the double-headed giant."

Lazillia said, "Let us go back home to the good old king and queen before we get killed."

They all went back home and told the old king, "We have killed a one-headed giant and dreamed that a two-headed giant will follow us. We are afraid to go out of the castle."

But the king laughed and said, "I'll put soldiers out to catch the giant and get him into a cage and then we shall kill him."

But when the two-headed giant heard what had happened to the one-headed giant at the hands of Sam Patra, he got a great sledgehammer and set out to smash in the walls of the castle.

He walked right over the king's soldiers and with one blow made a little hole in the wall of the castle so that he could get in. He made for the king, but Sam Patra snatched his sword and kept him off. The giant grabbed back the sword and swung at Sam Patra and just touched the skin of his neck. Lazillia shot from behind the one head with the arrow, and when the giant turned the other head to see what had happened, Sylvius with his sword cut off the other head. They all got back in the corner and watched the giant die; and when he was still, Sam Patra said, "Father King, now each of us has killed a giant. We are exactly alike."

"I am not sure," said Lazillia, "for I want to get married." When Lazillia told them that, they all wondered who could be the girl. When no one was looking, Sam Patra and Sylvius went out the door and over the fields to an old king who they knew had two daughters. The oldest one was named Auska. The second one was Mattillia, and Mattillia liked Sylvius and Auska liked Sam Patra. They both got married the same day and got back to the castle with their wives on the same day that Lazillia got back with his wife. And they found that the three wives were sisters and that the wife of Lazillia had been stolen from her home when she was a baby.

After thirteen years, the old king and queen died and the three brothers ruled the country.

After thirteen more years, Sylvius, in a terrible fever, also died. The two brothers who were left looked at one another and Lazillia said, "Now, our brother is dead, what shall we do? Let us kill ourselves."

Sam Patra said, "Why should I kill myself? I am a little bit different from my brothers."

But Lazillia answered, "I am going to kill myself after my brother."

Then Lazillia went and shot himself.

Sam Patra felt sad. He said to himself, "My two brothers, born when I was born, and who looked like me and did as I did, are dead. The poor old king and queen are dead. What shall I do now? I am not very different from my brothers."

That night he gave the kingdom to Auska. Then he took the bow and arrow of his brother Sylvius and shot the arrow straight up into the air. "I shall see if it is to be," he said. For three days and nights the arrow did not come down and he did not move. On the fourth day he saw it coming and he gave a kiss to Auska and said, "Good-bye, wife. And good-bye, wives of my brothers." The arrow struck him right on the top of the head and pinned him to the ground.

Demitro 1927: 19, 58–59. ATU 303/1070(?) and Motif G512/G361.1.1/T69.1.1/F831/F836. Told in the 1920s by Steve Demitro, of whom Diane Tong (1989:173) writes:

> The October 1, 1927, issue of *The Survey,* a magazine by and for the socially conscious—Jane Addams was a contributing editor—was devoted to the Gypsies. Included were four tales by a fourteen-year-old Gypsy named Steve Demitro, translated from the Romani. Although a photograph of the storyteller is reproduced, there is no information about him except that he was an American Coppersmith (Kalderash) Gypsy. This engaging tale is one of the few published Gypsy stories told by children.

It is also one of the few published stories told by American gypsies of any age. Wherever this text says *waiting woman* or simply *woman,* the tale as published says *waiter.* I have assumed that the Romani word translated *waiter* actually refers to the Queen's waiting woman, not to a waiter, and have changed the English text accordingly.

More commonly in this tale there are two "brothers," rather than three. Often horses and hounds consume scraps from the fish and consequently a like number of magical colts and magical pups are born. And the adult adventures of the "brothers" are rather different from those here recounted. The second half of the story as here told may well be an improvisation based on standard folktale elements.

112. Hodja Nasreddin

A. The Pot

Did you hear what he DID? One day he went to his neighbor to borrow a very big pot to cook in, and the next day he took it back with a little pot inside. The neighbor said, "What is that little pot doing there?"

And Hodja said, "The pot was pregnant, and it gave birth." The neighbor liked that, and kept both pots.

A few days later, Hodja went back to the neighbor's house to borrow the big pot, but this time he didn't bring it back. After a few days, the neighbor came over and said, "Where's the pot you borrowed?"

And Hodja said, "Oh, it died."
And the neighbor said, "How can a pot die?"
Then Hodja said, "If a pot can give birth, it can die."

B. Donkey Eggs

Nasreddin was at the market one day, and a man sold him some watermelons, telling him that they were donkey eggs. He paid too much for them, but he wanted to have a new little donkey. On the way home, he was going down a hill and stumbled, and the watermelon fell on a rock and broke open. Underneath the rock there was a rabbit sleeping, and when the watermelon fell on him, he ran away. Mullah Nasreddin ran home and told his wife, "I bought a donkey egg, I bought a donkey egg!" When she wanted to see it, he said, "The egg broke, and the baby donkey ran away."

C. Guard the Door

One day Nasreddin's wife told him that she was going to a wedding, and that he should stay at home and guard the door—that means to protect the house. Well, he didn't like to stay at home because he wanted to go to the wedding too, and have some fun. So he decided to go. He took the door off and put it on his back, and started walking down the road. Someone saw him, and said, "Nasreddin, where are you going with that door?"

And he said, "My wife asked me to guard the door, so I am doing that."

D. The Prophecy

One day Nasreddin was sitting on the limb of a tree, sawing between himself and the tree, and a man came along and said, "Hodja, if you saw off that limb while you're sitting on it, you'll fall." Hodja kept on sawing, and then he and the limb fell.

He told the man, "You must be a holy man to be able to predict that! Tell me when I am going to die."

The other man thought he would have some fun with Hodja, so he said, "When your donkey farts three times, you are going to die," and the man went off.

Nasreddin started walking behind his donkey, and the donkey farted once. Then in a little while, again. And then after a while, again. Then Nasreddin lay down by the side of the road.

A friend of his came along and said, "Mullah Nasreddin, what are you doing there, lying by the side of the road?"

Nasreddin said, "Can't you see? I am dead."

The friend said, "But you are chewing gum. Dead men don't chew gum."

And Nasreddin said, "I guess you're right—I'm not dead after all." And he got up and walked off.

E. The Lost Ring

One day Mullah Nasreddin was out in the garden, on his hands and knees, digging in the dirt. His neighbor looked over the wall and saw him and said, "Mullah Nasreddin, what are you doing?"

He said, "I'm looking for my wife's gold ring."

So the neighbor told him he would help him look for it, and they very carefully dug and scraped the entire garden, but didn't find it. The neighbor asked Mullah Nasreddin, "Are you sure your wife lost the ring in the garden?"

And Mullah Nasreddin said, "Oh, no; she lost it in the house."

The neighbor said, "Well, then why have we been looking in the garden?"

And Nasreddin answered, "Because the light's better out here."

F. Who Do You Believe?

One day Nasreddin's neighbor came to borrow his donkey, and Nasreddin didn't want to lend it, so he told the neighbor, "The donkey is not at home."

Just then, the donkey started to cry very loud. The neighbor said, "Hey, I thought you said he wasn't home, and now I hear him!"

Mullah Nasreddin said, "What kind of person are you to take a donkey's word over a man's word?"

G. The Big Barn

Nasreddin had a brother that he hadn't seen for a long time because they moved to different places. One time they met in another city and started talking about what had happened since they saw each other. Mullah Nasreddin's brother started bragging about what he owned, and said, "I have a barn that's so big, before a cow can walk from one end to another, she gets pregnant and has a calf—it takes so long."

Nasreddin said, "That's nothing! I have a cow that's so big, her head reaches up to the stars, and when her tail is in one country, her head is in another."

The brother said, "Oh, yeah? Where do you keep a cow like that?"

And Mullah Nasreddin said, "In your barn!"

Bynum 1989: 371–74. For types and motifs, see below. Told to Bynum by "Assyrians and Armenians from Iran, Syria, Iraq and Lebanon," in California in the twenty years preceding 1989. Though the historical Hodja Nasreddin was probably a Turkish Muslim, both Muslims and Christians tell and love these stories. Seven stories are included here because, according to Bynum, "if someone tells a Hodja story," the telling of stories "cannot end until seven tales are told" (371). International trickster and numbskull motifs and tales mingle in these stories with American jokes adapted to the Hodja Nasreddin character. Thus, the series demonstrates how once a trickster or numbskull secures a place in a narrative tradition that character attracts available stories to himself. Jack and Br'er Rabbit are other clear examples of this narrative phenomenon. And the "Polack" was the subject of innumerable numbskull jokes in the United States at the very time these Hodja Nasreddin stories were collected.

The Mullah Nasreddin is a popular and versatile trickster/numbskull in Greece, the Balkans, and throughout the Near and Middle East. Albert Wesselski published a two-volume collection of Nasreddin tales in 1911. But Nasreddin did not on that account quit fitting himself into new situations and jokes. Whatever the crisis, he rises to it, appearing in (in)appropriate jokes. So pointed can these jokes become that publication of them can prove dangerous. In August 2000, the political satirist Ibrahim Nabavi was jailed without trial in Iran, just four months after he had published a collection of Mullah Nasreddin stories that became a top seller. Though Hodja Nasreddin is a Near-Eastern trickster/numbskull figure, the present tales (but obviously not all Hodja Nasreddin tales) have European analogs and seem adapted from European tale types. Moreover, in these particular tales we see the Mullah fitting into American immigrant jokes and situations.

A. ATU 1592B. Told by a Syrian Armenian mechanic, who burst out with the story "as if it just happened yesterday" (Bynum 371), and repeated the story spontaneously three times more within a few weeks. The storyteller's first sentence indicates how real this character is to him. Bynum calls this one of the favorite Hodja stories. It is related to the motif of the colt born from a wagon in the story "The Clever Daughter" in this chapter.

B. ATU 1319. Told by an Assyrian woman. A popular tale among many groups in the United States. An Irish-American version is included in chapter 14.

C. ATU 1009. An Assyrian man "laughed, and told this one, which may have expressed his own frustration at having to stay at home and care for his elderly parents" (Bynum 373).

D. ATU 1313A. Told by a middle-aged Assyrian man. After "But you are chewing gum," the storyteller apparently interjected, as an aside, "We call the gum *data.*" Bynum describes this story as "difficult for Americans to understand, but . . . quite amusing and very popular among Middle Easterners" (Bynum 372).

E. Motif J1920. A joke widely popular in America. Storyteller not identified. J1920 is the general number for absurd searches. One senses that the particular motif of searching where the light is better must be a widespread numbskull motif, but the ATU Classification does not so identify it.

F. Motif J1552.1.1. Another joke popular in America, but also included in the Wesselski Nasreddin collection mentioned above. Told by an Assyrian woman.

G. ATU 1960E/1920. Often told as a Texas put-down joke. Told by "an Assyrian young man, age 18, who enjoys portraying himself as quite clever and worldly" (Bynum 373), the present story seems particularly suited to a community of newcomers. Lying contest stories are so various that the ATU Classification does not attempt to categorize all possibilities. The exact dynamic of the present lying contest is best represented in ATU 1920D*. Though the subject matter is different, in that tale as in the present joke the final lie builds on what has gone before: When the final liar is questioned about his claim that he snuffed out a cigarette on the moon, he says it is possible because of conditions described in the previous lies—he climbed into the sky on the piece of string described by the first liar, and climbed back down on the plant described by the second liar.

113. The Two Dreams

A. The Mother's Version

So, I don't know, heard this when I was a little girl. And there was this guy which was called Des Cartes. And he was dreaming always about a, in his dreams, about a girl, very beautiful, you know. And that happened many, many times, so he got upset and he said, "Gosh, I have to," you know, "look around and see where I can find this girl."

So he decided, you know, he looked in his town, and he didn't see anybody resembling to the person. So he decided to take a trip, you know, go from town to town, or cities, or whatever, and see if he can find the girl. And he took lots of weeks until he got into a town. And passing by on a street, he saw a little window, you know, at a nice beautiful building. And a head that was exactly the face of that girl he dreamed about.

So now he went to a guy around the place and asked, "Whose is this building, this beautiful house?"

And he said, "Well, it's a well-to-do businessman," you know, "and that's his wife." So now he didn't know how to get in touch with the woman, you know, how to see her. And he decided that it would be wise to go and find a job in this businessman's place, you know.

So he went there and said, you know, "I'm a bookkeeper, and I'm coming from another town. And I need money. And can you hire me, I mean, do you need a hand with something?"

And he said, "Sure, let's give it a try and see if it works," you know. So he hired the guy.

And after a while he said, "I wish to meet your wife."

And the businessman said, "No, she's sick, she's not feeling well. She cannot entertain." You know, he always found something to say so he wouldn't see her. But always when he was passing by and looking at that window, he was seeing her, and she was seeing him.

So many times he was doing a great job at his place, you know, and the boss was very happy about his work and he starts getting a lot of confidence on his work and what he's doing. And he said, "One of these days I want to see you married."

And the guy said, "Well, I will," you know, "as soon as I get more money and I'll be able to take care of my wife."

"And, you know what? I wish to build you a house, close to mine, almost as nice as mine," you know.

And he said "Okay." And they started building a nice house close to the businessman's house. And when the building was almost finished, Des Cartes told the workers and said, "Listen, I want to make a tunnel from this house to that house across the street," or near the street. I don't know now how it was, but it was real close. So after they'd finished the tunnel, he killed the man so nobody would know about it.

And the first time when the tunnel was finished he went over to his boss's house, and he opened the place and said, "You know something? For many years I'm dreaming about you, and I want to meet you and I want to talk to you."

And she said, "My name is Shastade, and I had the same dream for many years. You know, I dreamed about you, but I didn't know who you are and where you are. So I got married and I have a very severe husband who doesn't take me out," because she was really beautiful and he was very jealous. So she says, "I don't go out. Even the windows, as you see, are so small so I can't," you know, "people can't see me."

And this way they start seeing each other, you know, once in a while. Whenever he knew that the boss wasn't home, you know. He was going over, especially when he was taking trips, you know, with his business when he was going here and there. So in the evenings he was coming over and talking to Shastade and saying that he really wished her to be his wife. She says, "Well, look what's happened. I'm married and, not that I'm happy, but that happened and I have to live with him."

And he said, "No. I'll think of something. I'll arrange something."

And one of the nights that she was talking to him, he see a nice ring on her hand, you know. He said, "Oh, that's pretty. It's interesting." And she took it off and put it in his hand. And the next day when he went to work, he forgot to take it off. So the boss see the ring and he said, "Gosh, when did you have that ring?"

He said, "Well, I bought it."

"Where did you buy it? You know, my wife has that same ring." And he started worrying and thinking. So next thing, he goes home to check on his wife and make sure that she has the ring. So at the same time, the guy goes underneath the tunnel, you know, and gives her the ring, and says, "Look what happened," you know. "I forgot to take it off, and he noticed it." So she puts it back and so when her husband comes in he sees the ring, so nothing happens. He goes back to work.

And another day he says, you know, "I want to marry. I found a girl and I want to marry."

And he says, "Gladly. I'm very happy for you. I can even be your best man if you wish."

He says, "You are going to bring your wife, aren't you?"

He says, "No," you know, "I don't take her out. She doesn't feel good and usually I don't take her out." But he was asking to make sure she didn't come, you know.

So he said, "Okay," and tells her a date. And she gets dressed up like a bride, and they go up to church, you know. And after that, they celebrate a big party. The guy, he tells to his boss that soon as they make the celebration, he's going to take her on a honeymoon, take her on a ship and go away, you know. For honeymoon. So she gets dressed and everything, they go to church, and from church they go to a big place where they celebrate.

And he turns and says, "You know, it's very strange, but this girl looks exactly like my wife."

And he says, "Well, you know how it is. People look like each other. Like the rings; they're alike. And the same with persons." To make sure, you know, he goes home to check on his wife. And meantime, the girl undresses and goes back to her house, and when he comes in, everything was all right. She was, you know, working on needlepoint or something.

And she says, "Oh, where were you? Why aren't you home?" and this and that, you know. And she gets sort of upset that he's not home early and this and that.

So he comes back to the wedding and he sees the girl dancing. And then he says, "Okay, I'll take you to the port," you know, "and take you to your ship and go."

And they all go together and say, "Bye and thank you. You were a real father to me, you know, you gave me a job and build me a house. And I'm very indebted to you."

So he says "Bye-bye," and the businessman comes home, and his house is empty, you know. He starts pulling his hair and curse. "What did I do? I marry my wife with the guy!" He got crazy looking around for how it happened. And he sees the tunnel door and goes in and it leads to beside his house. "I gave away my wife with my own hands," you know.

And that's the way the story ends. And the kids lived ever after, many years and have fun. That's it.

B. The Daughter's Version

There was an accountant, and he had these dreams every night. And he dreamed about this woman. And these dreams kept recurring and this woman's face was so vivid that he really wanted to meet her. And he knew that if he met her that she would be the only love in his life.

And so he decided that he would leave his job and roam around the towns until he found love, the woman that was in his dreams. So he set off and was roaming around, and after a while it was hopeless. He had run out of money and he ended up in this town.

He found out there was a man who needed an accountant, so he decided he might as well just go get that job, get some more money, and then set off again looking for this woman.

So he went to this businessman and said, "I am an accountant, and I want this job."

And he said, "Sure," you know, and the businessman gave him a job. And he liked the young man so well, that, and his work, also, he liked his work, that he said, "Listen, I'll make a home for you right next to my house. And you live there and that way you'll be near me and we won't have to run back and forth with the papers and the work."

And he said, "Sure, fine."

One day as he was walking home, the young accountant happened to look through the window of the businessman's house and he saw the face that was in his dream. And lo and behold, there was the woman. And he ran home and he couldn't stop thinking about her. So he was talking to the businessman the next day, so he said, "Why don't you and your wife come over for dinner?"

And he said, "No, I don't let my wife out, she stays at home."

So he says, "Well, why don't you come over for dinner?" So he brought the guy over for dinner, and they had a nice dinner. And he found out that the wife was so beautiful that the man couldn't let her out of the house.

He was determined to have that woman. So every day—he got some workers, and every day they worked on a tunnel to the businessman's house. Finally the tunnel was completed: he went to the woman.

And he saw her, and surprisingly enough, she had been dreaming about him. So they fell in love at first sight. And they planned to meet through the tunnel when the husband was out. It was easy because the accountant always knew when the businessman was at work, and when he wasn't. So every time he was at work, he would rush home and see the woman.

The businessman, who was the husband, gave this beautiful woman a really pretty emerald ring. And she gave it to the young accountant and said that she wanted to give him something so she gave him that ring.

And that same day, the young accountant and her decided that they were going to get married and run away together. But they didn't know how to do it. So, they were pondering over it and the guy had a great idea. So they decided to go through with it.

The young accountant went to the businessman and said, "I've met this beautiful girl, and I want to marry her. And I want you to be my best man."

And the businessman is thrilled. He says, "Sure, I'll be your best man."

And the young accountant said, "And of course I want your wife to be the maid of honor."

And he says, "No, no, I don't let my wife out, but I will gladly be the best man."

So the day of the wedding rolls along, and naturally the bride was going to be the businessman's wife. And she got a wedding dress together and they went under the tunnel and they went to the wedding. Now when the businessman saw her, he was flabbergasted

Before that, the ring, the young man was wearing the ring and the businessman saw the ring. And he said, "My god, where did you get that ring?"

And he said, "Well, I've had this ring for a while."

He said, "That's funny," he says, "excuse me." He left and he went rushing home. In the meantime, the young accountant went rushing to the businessman's house, went through the tunnel and gave the ring back to the woman, and went back home.

And by the time the businessman got home, the woman had her ring on. He went rushing upstairs to her room, and he said, "Let me see your hand." She showed him her hand and he said, "Oh."

And she said, "What's wrong?"

And he said, "Oh, nothing, nothing."

She said, "You know, you never trust me and you come running home all the time. And first you've locked me up in here and asides from that, you don't even trust me now that I'm locked up. You never let me go out," *etc., etc.*

He says, "Well, I'm sorry, Dear," blah, blah, blah.

Okay, so then the thing about the wedding came up. And he, the businessman, was asked to be best man and what not. So the day of the wedding rolls around, and his wife was the bride. So he went to the wedding and he notices the bride, and he says, "My god. My wife looks just like that. Who is she?"

He says, "Don't be silly. It can't be your wife. Remember our rings looked alike."

And he says, "Yes."

So he says, "Well then, why can't people look alike?"

So the guy says, "I can't believe this." So he says, "Look, excuse me for a minute." So he went rushing off again to his house; naturally, they rushed the woman back through the tunnel. She changed, she sat down. The husband came running back and he went straight to see her.

And she said, "Well, I've had enough! You know, you always run home to see if I'm here. You don't trust me," *etc., etc.* They had a big to-do.

He said, "No, I'm sorry, Honey," you know; "from now on I'll be more trustworthy, but I've got to go now." So he leaves again, goes back to the wedding. She naturally gets dressed again and goes back through the tunnel.

So they're back at the wedding, and the guy says, the young accountant says to the businessman, "You know I've decided to go on a cruise, and we're going to go to some far-off land." I don't know where. And that's where they're going to go on their honeymoon.

So the man says, "Okay, that sounds terrific," and he gave them some money, you know, to spend or whatnot. Like a bonus, whatever. And he sent them off on the cruise and they left.

The businessman comes home. He goes upstairs, and he's decided to be good to his wife. He goes upstairs; there's nobody there. And then it dawns on him that this is what was going on. He runs around the house, he's trying to figure out how it all happened. He finally comes upon a panel and he realizes that there is a secret doorway. And the tunnel and he notices there's a tunnel. He goes through the tunnel and notices it leads to the guy's house. And he says, "I've been such a fool!"

And naturally, the moral of this story is that if you have something that you think is valuable, it's not to your benefit and not to its benefit, or her or his benefit, to keep them locked up or save it. It's only valuable if other people know its value. You've got to share things, that, something that is beautiful or something that is valuable or important to you, with others. Or else you're going to lose it because you don't know how to care for it properly. So, that was the moral of that story.

Burger 1978. ATU 1419E. Collected by Erna Burger, a student of Linda Dégh at the University of California, Berkeley, in 1978. The narrators are a mother and her nineteen-year-old daughter, Marcrid and Aghavni Arakelian, Armenians whose family had fled from Turkey in the nineteenth century. The Arakelians immigrated to the United States from Romania when Aghavni was six, and in 1978 lived in the Armenian community in Los Angeles. Marcrid Arakelian was a lively narrator who usually told stories in Armenian. This English-language performance was unusual, and perhaps a bit stilted. Aghavni, the second storyteller, was at first reluctant to tell the story herself, but agreed to after she had assured herself that she "remembered correctly." Though Aghavni learned the story from her mother, the first storyteller, the collector noted that she used fewer gestures and fewer formulaic expressions than her mother, and explained or rationalized her story as she went along.

This novelle belongs to the family of the tales that Clouston, in *Popular Tales and Fictions,* calls "The Elopement" (1887, II: 212–28). Widely documented in medieval manuscript tradition, it forms one of the standard tales in the story cycle *The Seven Sages of Rome,* where it serves to demonstrate how untrustworthy are wives and how foolish are husbands who try to prevent their infidelity. The tale also occurs in one manuscript of the *Arabian Nights* and in other near-eastern collections. The motif of an underground passage to facilitate adultery figures in a number of Italian works, including Boiardo's *Orlando Inamorato.* Despite the ancient pedigree of the tale, however, it has here been Americanized rather thoroughly. The knight has become a bookkeeper, the husband a businessman, and the knight's ship a honeymoon cruise ship. There are further differences between the mother's and daughter's versions that indicate how the daughter has carried the Americanization process still further. The mother calls the hero a bookkeeper, while the daughter uses the more contemporary term accountant. The daughter suppresses the killing of the mason who constructs the tunnel, a very old element in the story, but one that is suppressed even in some medieval versions. And in the daughter's version the hero obtains employment without ever having seen the woman of his dreams. It is only later that he finds out that his employer's wife matches his dream, whereas in the mother's version the hero seeks employment precisely because the woman of his dreams is married to the man in question. Finally, the daughter adds a moral to the story, a moral very much in line with American democratic and communitarian values, and much at odds with the moral attached to the story in medieval times.

CHAPTER 17

EUROPEAN TALES IN NATIVE
AMERICAN TRADITIONS

We tend to think of contact between Europeans and Native Americans as universally hostile. But the first centuries of European settlement on the North American continent also offered many occasions of extended friendly contact. Judging from the evidence, contacts were often marked by storytelling, for the native peoples learned many European stories. These European stories, as gathered from Native American peoples, tend to reflect the same pattern of influence we have already seen in this collection: Although other traditions also infiltrated Native American repertoires, the dominant traditions are the French, the Hispanic, and the British. In the sixteenth and seventeenth centuries the *voyageurs* and *coureurs des bois*, French-Canadian traders and trappers, dealt with and wintered among native peoples in the Northeast, and westward as far as the Rocky Mountains, on both sides of the present Canadian border. Many tales with a French flavor have shown up in collections made in that belt of North America. The Pueblo people of the Southwest were settled and agricultural, and lived, sometimes amicably, alongside Hispanic farmers. There the Amerindian repertoires show a strong Hispanic influence. Similarly agricultural peoples in the Southeast often lived amicably with British neighbors, intermarrying with them and with African Americans as well. There European animal tales found a welcome in the native repertoire. Scholars long speculated that one significant result of this particular cultural exchange may have been the transfer of the rabbit, the native trickster, to a starring role in

African American animal tales: Br'er Rabbit as Native American. This speculation was based on the fact that in West Africa the spider played the trickster role, and trickster tales in the Caribbean and South America often feature the spider. But we now know that in central Africa, from which African tribal peoples were also brought to the United States, the hare is a major trickster, figuring in some tales cognate with U.S. African American Br'er Rabbit or Bouqui and Lapin tales (cf. Bascom 1992: 86). Consequently, Br'er Rabbit's claim to Native American ancestry now seems more tenuous.

Other European/Native American contacts also helped spread tales. The mountain men in the Rockies repeated the French pattern of wintering with native peoples, and left stories there, as did the trappers and fur traders, many of them Russians, living among the Yup'ik (Eskimos) of Alaska. In Hawaii, missionaries shared tales with the native Polynesians, and Hawaiian translations of Grimm stories appeared in newspapers.

We must be careful, however, not to cry Aarne-Thompson-Uther at every Native American tale we see. European and Native American repertoires share broadly circumpolar themes and themes that are nearly worldwide. Certainly not every tale of marriage to an animal is "Beauty and the Beast" or "East of the Sun, West of the Moon." Not every clever coyote is Reynard in disguise. And not every poor girl who marries a powerful chieftain's son is Cinderella.

The term "Native American" is often used as a synonym for Amerindian, but there are in fact at least three racially and linguistically distinct native peoples in what is now the United States, namely the Amerindian, the Yup'ik (Alaskan Eskimo), and the Polynesian (Native Hawaiian). All of these people have rich narrative traditions that welcomed European plots and motifs and adapted them to the native style. The stories I have selected for this chapter, though barely skimming the surface of this rich set of repertoires, illustrate some of the range of ways native peoples have adapted European tales to fit them into native culture. "The Cock and the Fox" seems little altered from European fables. The Zuni ant tale is a cumulative tale likewise not notably different from Hispanic versions of the same story. The series of Miami tales about the grey fox, though they demonstrate native imagination in the details, seem to retain the over-all structure of a European Reynard cycle. The Idaho coyote stories seem more thoroughly assimilated into native tradition, though the tale of the three pigs with which the cycle ends still includes all the episodes traditional in English tellings of that tale. The tale of "The Steer and the Lion's Den" and the tale of "The Toad Prince" are long European märchen, the second more thoroughly assimilated than the first. In the Hawaiian tale the union with native themes is so thorough that it would be very difficult to identify the story as European if the telltale dog did not betray it.

Finally, the Yup'ik story of the "Muskrat Husband" may well not be European at all. I have included it as an example of a story that tempts us because of its familiar themes. These themes, however, are broadly circumpolar, and may well have been familiar elements of Yup'ik storytelling long before European contact. Though very similar stories appear in European—especially northern European—tradition and though Eskimo people do know European stories, we can not be sure whether this particular story is native or imported.

114. The Grey Fox and the Wolves

The grey fox took his leave, indulging reflections on the nature of red foxes and hunting treaties, till the night overtook him, hungry and exhausted. He was then on the margin of a lake, where he observed men's tracks in the snow; these conducted him to a hole in the ice, where the neighbouring inhabitants had set a fishing net. Curiosity led him to examine what success these people were likely to have, and having drawn up the net, secured the contents, replaced it, and loaded himself with as many fish as he could carry, after having devoured as many as he could eat, he returned by the same way, taking care in his return, as he had done in descending, to march in the men's tracks, and make no fox-impressions in the soft snow.

After depositing his stock, preparing to go to rest, he was accosted by a wolf, who led by the scent, asked him how he came by his fish, as he had all the indications of having made a wonderful great fish-meal. "Brother wolf," says the fox, who was afraid of his hoard, "come along with me, and I will shew you how you may do as I have done. You have only to go to the hole in the ice, to which these tracks will conduct you; sit down on the hole; you are provided with a much finer tail than mine; thrust it deep into the water, and continue there motionless for some space of time; the fish will at length begin to take hold; and as soon as you find by the weight that you have a sufficient number attached, suddenly draw up your load, and you will have a rich repast; by this method I took almost as many as I could eat in a single haul; your success must be much greater."

The hungry wolf listened with avidity, thanked his benefactor, and in a few moments placed himself in a fishing position, with his tail in the water; where, notwithstanding the intense cold, he remained without motion for a considerable time; expecting to find by the encreasing weight, the promised indications of his success.

At length, supposing that his feeling was destroyed by the extreme cold, he resolved to see what he had caught: when to his great surprise, he found the hole entirely frozen over, and his tail so firmly enclosed in the ice that all his efforts to disengage it proved abortive. Every moment the effect of cold and hunger was decreasing his force and adding strength to his fetters, and the jests of the fox still added to his tortures. In the morning the countrymen arrived, who, seeing the bones and scales of the fish, which had been scattered by the fox, and catching the wolf as it were in the fact, dispatched him with their hatchets, and after unprofitably drawing and resetting their nets, dragged the carcase of the wolf to the shore.

The fox with the flesh of the wolf and his stock of fish, lived luxuriously for several days, but the vigilance of the countrymen, now awakened, prevented his catching any more fish. He had, however, other resources; he had already picked up some straggling geese and outards, and had more than once visited a roost. But fearing the noise might alarm, he made a safer attack upon the store-hut, where the provisions for the winter were preserved in a frozen state; and continued to live plentifully till, approaching one night with his usual caution, he observed a man on the watch.

The next day he invited a cousin of his friend, the deceased wolf, to partake of the fare he had left, and having excited rather than satisfied his appetite, told him how he came by his dainties, and as soon as the watch was set the next night, having offered his services as a conductor, led the wolf to the opening of the hut, and retired. The alarm was quickly given, the opening was closed, and the howls of the wolf soon satisfied his conductor that his credulous friend was no more. Conceiving they had dispatched the marauder who had so long trespassed upon them, the good people relaxed their vigilance, and the fox found means to renew his depredations. He continued them till the diminution made in several heaps of provisions told him that new suspicions must arise to provoke new vigilance.

Abandoning this scene therefore, after picking the bones of the wolf, he pursued his journey without any adventure till he overtook on a beaten road a machine as large as a common wigwam, drawn by a number of horses, and conducted by two men. So soon as he observed the men advance before, he took the opportunity of slipping behind and leaping into the waggon. There he lay perdu, the remainder of the day, feasting, and when the night closed in, collecting those articles which were most to his taste, dropped them down gently one by one upon the road. Satisfied with his selection he finally leaped from the waggon himself, collected his scattered booty, and retired to a place of safety. He repeated this practice so often that the men who conducted the teams, ignorant of the thief but resolved to be on their guard, closed up their waggon in such a manner that it was impossible to gain admittance.

He then bethought himself of the following stratagem; he advanced by a bye way to a considerable distance before the team, and having rolled himself in the snow, filled his mouth, ears, and nostrils, with blood, which he drew from a fresh wound in one of his legs. He laid himself down in the track where the waggon was to pass, retaining his breath, closing his eyes, lolling out his tongue, and exhibiting every other symptom of death. "A lucky chance," cries one of the countrymen, as the waggon approached the place. "A grey fox dead; we will fling him into the waggon, and take off his skin when we stop to feed." The grey fox played his part so well that he created no suspicions, and in a few moments found himself deposited agreeably to his wishes. As he knew this was the last time he could possibly gain admittance, he made a most provident use of the occasion, and effected his escape just before the waggoners stopped to bait. Finding the dead fox gone and their provisions plundered, they were filled with astonishment, and after many wild conjectures, concluded this to be one of Machi-Manitoo's frolicks.

The store the fox had got enabled him to live well for a whole moon. He then told his story to one of his friends, the wolves, and finding his resources nearly exhausted, encouraged the wolf to adopt the same expedient. The wolf was easily persuaded. He lay down personating death in hopes of a rich recompence, when the waggoners forewarned, observing him almost in the same spot where they had been imposed upon by the fox, severed his head from his body, as a just punishment for his intended fraud, and as his skin was of no value, drove their team over him and left him. The fox waited till the road was clear, and then drawing the body aside as his perquisite, resorted to it from time to time to supply his necessities.

Smith 1939: 202–4. ATU 2/41/1. According to G. Hubert Smith, John Dunne recorded the group of tales from which this selection comes from Mahican-Miami Chief Little Turtle (Tchikanakoa). The text is as Smith gives it, except for paragraphing. Dunne included the tales in his "Notices Relative to Some of the Native Tribes of North America," in the *Transactions of the Royal Irish Academy* (IX: 107–24, Dublin, 1803). Accordingly, these are probably the first texts of European folktales ever collected from the very mouths of storytellers in the United States— and collected, ironically, not from Europeans but from Native Americans. Folklorists may be interested to know that the editor of the *Transactions* at that time was one of the founders of the Royal Irish Academy, Thomas Percy, Bishop of Dromore, famous as the editor of *Reliques of Ancient English Poetry* (1765).

In the text John Dunne published in the *Transactions*, the tales are strung together in a cycle somewhat like the Native American Coyote cycles, but perhaps more like the European Reynard cycle. The three episodes selected come from the middle of the cycle. They are preceded by a series of episodes in which the grey fox enters into partnership with a red fox, fares badly in their joint ventures, and finds himself deserted by his partner. The grey fox's next three adventures are the ones here given. After these adventures he goes on to dupe a hedgehog and a bear (ATU 49) and a panther (mountain lion) (ATU 47A). In the end he meets up again with the red fox and proudly offers to share with him his meal of panther meat. "The red fox complied, reserving some better food which he had brought with him, for a time when there would be no invitations, still preserving his advantage over his ancient ally, well knowing that whatever pretensions to superiority his friend might have among the other tribes, he could never rank high in the nation of foxes." The partnership thus forms a frame for the cycle, with the two foxes allied unevenly again at the close, as they were when they began their adventures.

115. Coyote and Fox, Bear, Wolf, and Little Pig

1. HOW SPOKANE FALLS WERE MADE

Coyote and Fox were travelling together and they were coming up from below. When they got to where Spokane Falls now is, Coyote said to Fox, "I believe I'll get married. I'll take one of the Pend d'Oreille women for my wife."

So he went to see the chief of the Pend d'Oreilles about getting one of the women for a wife. The chief was not willing to let his women intermarry with other tribes, so he told Coyote he could not have any of the Pend d'Oreille women for a wife.

Coyote said, "Now I'll put falls right here in the river, so the Salmon cannot get past them." That is how Spokane Falls were made.

5. COYOTE AND THE CRYING BABY

Coyote went on to a place called Sleeping Child. As he was going through the woods, he saw a child in its cradle-board leaned up against a pine-tree. The baby was crying and crying just as hard as it could cry. Coyote called for the baby's mother, but he could get no answer. He called again and again for the mother to come and take her baby. But the mother didn't come.

Then he took the baby to quiet it, and he said, "I know how I'll stop your crying." He put his finger in the baby's mouth for it to suck. The baby sucked a while, and when Coyote took his finger out of the baby's mouth there was nothing left but the bones.

He put in another finger and another, until there was nothing left of all his fingers but the bones. Then his hand, then the arm, the other hand, the other arm, his feet, his legs, all of him, and then there was nothing of Coyote but the bones.

In a few weeks Fox came along that way, and he saw the bones of Coyote lying on the ground. He jumped over them, and Coyote came to life again.

Coyote said, "I have slept a long time."

Fox said, "You were not asleep. You were dead. What for did you go near that baby? It is one of the Killing People. That is the way it kills every one that goes through these woods."

Coyote said, "It kept on crying so hard that I put my finger in its mouth. It felt pretty good, so I put in another and another until it was all of me. Give me a knife and I will go back and kill that baby." So Coyote went back and killed the baby.

9. COYOTE IN BUFFALO COUNTRY

Coyote travelled on from there. After a while he had nothing to eat. He was pretty nearly starved. He went into a tepee about noon and lay down to rest. He was very weak because he had had nothing to eat for a long time.

He heard some one holloa, but he couldn't see any one. Then some one called again, and after he had looked carefully for some time he saw Eagle a long ways off. Eagle told him that far away from there was a very rich country where there were plenty of Buffalo all the time. "I am going there," said Eagle, "but you can't go, you're too poor."

Then Coyote got mad. He said, "I can go any place I want to. I am going to go there." Coyote started out, and in fifteen days he got there. The place is on the Missouri River, not far from Great Falls. There was a big camp of people at this place. Bear was their chief. The people did not like Bear at all. When they killed lots of Buffalo, Chief Bear would always take the best pieces for himself, all the good meat, and the nice chunks of fat.

Coyote wanted to be chief himself, so he went out and killed a big Buffalo and stripped off all the fat. Then he cut the meat in strips and hung it up to dry. After that he built a big fire and heated some stones red hot.

Chief Bear found out that Coyote had killed a Buffalo, and he came to look at the meat. "This is nice meat," said Bear, "I'll take this."

Coyote said, "I saved some fat for you." Then Coyote took one of the red hot stones, and put plenty of fat around it. Then he shoved it into Bear's mouth. This killed Bear, and then they made Coyote chief.

Bear had been a great Medicine Man, and whenever he wished for anything it always came to pass. It was Bear who had caused the Buffalo to stay around in that country all the time, so when Coyote became chief all the

Buffalo went away. In ten days the people were starving. Every one said, "Coyote is no good of a chief."

Coyote went out to hunt for Buffalo. He was all alone, and he hunted for five days, but he couldn't find any Buffalo at all. He was ashamed to go back to the people without anything, and so he kept right on.

In a little while Coyote met Wolf.

"Where are you going?" said Wolf.

"I am going to travel all over the world," answered Coyote.

Wolf went on ahead, and pretty soon Coyote heard a wagon coming after him. He looked around and saw that the wagon was full of meat. Coyote lay down by the side of the road, and pretended he was dead. The driver stopped his horses. "This is pretty good fur," said he. So he threw Coyote into the wagon and went on.

Coyote ate and ate all the meat he could hold. Then he jumped off the wagon, and ran away. Pretty soon he met Wolf again.

"Well," said Wolf, "you look fat. Where did you get the meat?"

Coyote told him that he had played dead and lay on the roadside. The driver picked him up, threw him into the wagon, and drove on. "Now," said Coyote, "he picked me up for my fur, and your fur is much finer than mine; he'll take you quicker than he did me."

Wolf lay down on the road, and pretended he was dead. Pretty soon the wagon came along. The driver stopped his horses and jumped out. "Ha, ha," he said, "Wolf looks as if he were dead, but I'll see this time." So he took a big club and hit Wolf on the head, and then right away he hit him another lick.

Wolf was pretty nearly killed. He jumped and ran away as fast as he could. He was awfully mad at Coyote. He said, "I know Coyote did this on purpose. I'll kill Coyote, that's what I'll do."

Wolf ran, and Coyote ran. After a while, Wolf overtook Coyote. "I'm going to kill you," said Wolf, "that's what I'm going to do to you. What for did you play that trick on me? I am going to kill you right now."

Coyote said, "Wait, I have something to say to you. Wait till I have said it. Then you can kill me after that."

"All right," said Wolf, "what is it?"

"Well," said Coyote, "there are only two of us. It isn't fair for us to fight alone. Let us get others to fight with us. Then it will be like one tribe fighting another. Let us get some other fellows to fight with us, and let us fight fair."

"All right," said Wolf.

Wolf went in one direction, and Coyote in another. Wolf saw a Bear, and he said to Bear, "Come with me and fight against Coyote."

"I will," said Bear. So Wolf and Bear went on together. In a little while they met Boar. Wolf said to Boar, "Come with us and fight against Coyote." "All right," said Boar. So they took Boar along. Then there were three in this party, Wolf, Bear, and Boar.

Coyote had gone the other way, and he had Cat and Dog in his party. Coyote and Wolf had agreed to meet at Butte. Coyote had said, "If you get there first, wait for me, and if I get there first I'll wait for you."

Wolf and his party got there first, and they waited for Coyote and his party to come up. Pretty soon Bear looked out and said, "I see Coyote and his party coming. He has Cat and Dog." "Yes," said Boar, "and Coyote is a brave man, but we'll do the best we can."

Coyote was all dressed up—nice beaded moccasins and everything very fine. Coyote was a great chief. Then Coyote and his party came up, and the two crowds fought. Coyote killed all of his enemies. Then he went on alone.

10. Coyote and Fox Separate

Coyote kept on alone till he met Fox, his partner. They went on together till they came to the White Man's camp. They had had nothing to eat for a long time, and they were both very hungry.

Fox said to Coyote, "You play dead and I'll take you to the White Man and sell you for a sack of sugar. Then, when the White Man cuts the strings that tie your feet, you must jump up and run away."

Coyote agreed to this plan. Fox took him and sold him to the White Man for a sack of sugar. He took the sack of sugar and went away. The White Man took his knife and began to skin Coyote's legs. Coyote yelled and tore, and finally he broke the strings that held his feet together, and ran away. He was awfully mad at Fox, and he said, "If I find my partner I will kill him sure."

After a while he met Fox and he said, "Where is the sugar? I want my share of the sugar."

Fox said, "Why didn't you come right away? I was so hungry I ate it all up."

Fox said, "I am going back now. I am not going any farther."

Coyote said, "I am going to keep right on."

So they parted there. Fox went back and Coyote went on alone.

11. Coyote and Little Pig

Coyote kept on alone for a while. When he was tired of travelling he built himself a little house and stayed in it for a while. Then he started out again.

When he had been travelling for some time, he came to a place where the road divides.

The Three Pigs had come there before Coyote, and each had taken a different road. They went out to find homes for themselves. When they parted, they said they would come back every month and see each other.

They found nice homes, but Coyote came after them. He killed the oldest brother, then the next oldest, and then he was looking for the youngest brother, Little Pig. Little Pig was the smartest of them all.

After a while, Coyote came to where Little Pig lived, and he said, "Hello! Little Pig."

Little Pig said, "Hello!" But he kept the door of his house closed tight. He had a very nice place.

"Let me in," said Coyote.

"Who is it?"

"It's me," said Coyote.

"Well, who is me?" said Little Pig.

"It's Coyote, and I want to come in."

"You go away, Coyote," said Little Pig. "I don't want you here."

Little Pig was pretty smart. Coyote thought, "He's pretty smart, but I'll fool him, I'll kill him yet." Then he said, "Little Pig, don't you know there is a nice garden about half a mile from here—cabbage and potatoes and everything in it?"

Coyote wished for the garden, and it was there. The next morning Little Pig got up early, and went to the garden and helped himself to everything.

The next morning, when Coyote got to the garden, he looked at all the things. He saw that Little Pig had been there and helped himself to everything and then gone away. He looked around and saw Little Pig down the road about half a mile. He ran and Little Pig ran. Little Pig got into the house first and locked the door and wouldn't let Coyote in.

Coyote knocked at the door, and said, "Little Pig, let me in. I have tobacco and kin-i-kin-ic. We will smoke together."

"No," said Little Pig, "I don't smoke. I don't want your tobacco and kin-i-kin-ic. I won't let you in. You want to kill me."

Then Coyote went away. That night he came back and knocked at the door. "Let me in," said Coyote.

"Who's there?" said Little Pig.

"It's me," said Coyote, "I don't want to hurt you. I want to help you. Let me in."

"Who are you?" asked Little Pig.

"I am Coyote."

"Go away, Coyote. I don't want you here."

"I want to tell you something," said Coyote.

"Well, what is it?" said Little Pig.

"About half a mile from here is a nice big orchard, and all kinds of fruit in it."

"All right," said Little Pig. "To-morrow morning I will go there and get me what I want."

Coyote wished for an orchard to be there, and it was there. Early the next morning he got up and went to the orchard. When Coyote got there, Little Pig was up in a tree gathering apples. He was pretty badly scared when he saw Coyote.

Coyote said, "What have you got there? Some nice big apples?"

"Yes," said Little Pig. "I have some nice big apples. Don't you want me to throw you one?"

"Yes," said Coyote. "Throw me a nice big apple."

Little Pig took a big apple and threw it just as hard as he could. Coyote tried to catch it, but he couldn't. It hit him in the eye and knocked him down. Little Pig jumped down from the apple-tree and ran as fast as he could. Coyote jumped up and ran after him, but Little Pig got in the house first, and locked the door on Coyote.

Coyote knocked and knocked, but Little Pig wouldn't let him in. Coyote said, "I'll come down the chimney."

"All right, come down the chimney, if you think you can," said Little Pig.

Little Pig began to build a fire. Coyote came down the chimney, and fell into the fire, and was burned to death. Fox was not there to step over him, and so he never came to life again, and that was the end of Coyote.

McDermott 1901: 247–51. ATU 1/124. This selection includes five episodes from an Idaho Flathead Coyote cycle submitted to the *Journal of American Folklore* by Louisa McDermott of Fort Lewis, Colorado, presumably collected at the end of the nineteenth century. No further information is supplied in the *Journal.* (Kin-i-kin-ic is a smoking preparation made of bark and dried leaves, sometimes including tobacco.)

Coyote cycles, and the present example is no exception, describe the journeys of the arch-trickster coyote, often along the course of a river, and his adventures along the way. His various mishaps lead to permanent alterations of the landscape, so that the route of his journey remains well marked even until today. He is thus the final shaper of the world in which the storyteller lives. In the present series of tales, for instance, he creates Spokane Falls and also wishes for a garden and an orchard and they are there. Two of the episodes integrate popular European animal tales into the Native American cycle. Both of the European stories here, the story of fooling the driver of a load of food by playing dead and the story of the three pigs (incorporating The Wolf Surprises the Pig in an Apple Tree, ATU 136), are extremely popular in U.S. tradition. There is a sad irony in the fact that the final episode telling of the death of Coyote is a European story.

116. The Rooster and the Fox

The rooster was feeding under a tree when a fox came along. The rooster flew up in the tree to escape.

"Come on down, don't be scared of me; I won't hurt you. Don't you know peace has been declared between the birds of the air and animals of the ground?" said the fox.

"No," said the rooster, "I didn't know of it."

"Well it has. The news has gone around and everybody has heard of it, so come on down," said the fox.

From up in the tree where the rooster was sitting, he could see some dogs coming over the hill, following the fox's trail.

Said the rooster: "Well if that's true, I'll be down directly; I see some dogs coming over the hill to join us."

Before he finished talking, the fox ran off.

Speck and Carr 1947: 81. ATU 62. From Chief Sam Blue. Taken down by L. G. Carr. Sam Blue was, with his sister Sally Gordon, the last of the conversational speakers of South Carolina Catawban, the only Siouxan language in the Southeast. Born in 1873, he combined respect for traditions learned from his mother (b. 1837) with a position as Mormon elder. In the 1940s he began dictating lively tales, in Catawban, to visiting folklorist/anthropologists "in quiet hours of winter evenings or during strolls through fields or scrub woods of the land where the Catawba have lived and struggled to exist for many centuries." (The present text, however, was apparently dictated in English). Though European motifs and plots reflect at least a century and a half of acculturation, his stories likewise reflect "thought . . . framed to harmonize with natural phenomena." (Speck and Carr 1947: 79, 80)

Animal stories are a traditional feature of Amerindian culture in the Southeast. The period from the seventeenth to the early nineteenth century was marked by particularly widespread cultural exchange and intermarriage between Amerindians of the region and Euro- and African Americans, and by free exchange of tales. Consequently many European animal tales show up in the Amerindian collections, as Amerindian plots and motifs show up in African American and attendant southern repertoires. The present tale is known to storytellers red, white, and black.

117. Who Is the Strongest?

Once upon a time it was raining, and the first little red ant came out in [the Zuni town of] Halona. There was still snow, and he froze his foot. He said, "Snow, you are stronger than I am. Are you the strongest thing there is?" The Snow answered, "No. I am not the strongest thing there is. The Sun is stronger than I am, for when the Sun shines, I melt."

The little red ant went to the Sun. He said, "Sun, you are stronger than the Snow. Are you the strongest thing there is?" The Sun said, "No, I am not the strongest thing there is. The Wind is stronger than I am, for when I am shining the Wind blows clouds across my face."

The little red ant went to the Wind. He said, "Wind, you are stronger than the Sun. Are you the strongest thing there is?" The Wind answered, "No, I am not the strongest thing there is. A house is stronger than I am, for I run against a house, and it kills me."

The little red ant went to House. He said, "House, you are stronger than Wind. Are you the strongest thing there is?" The House answered, "No, I am not the strongest thing there is. Mouse is stronger than I am. He makes holes in my body and kills me."

The little red ant went to Mouse. He said, "Mouse, you are stronger than House. Are you the strongest thing there is?" Mouse answered, "No, I am not the strongest thing there is. Cat is stronger than I am. Cat can overtake me and kill me."

The little red ant went to Cat. He said, "Cat, you are stronger than Mouse. Are you the strongest thing there is?" Cat answered, "No, I am not the strongest thing there is. Stick is stronger than I am. If you hit me with Stick, it kills me."

The little red ant went to Stick. He said, "Stick, you are stronger than Cat. Are you the strongest thing there is?" Stick answered, "No, I am not the strongest thing there is. Fire is stronger than I am. If you throw me in the fire, it kills me."

The little red ant went to Fire. He said, "Fire, you are stronger than Stick. Are you the strongest thing there is?" Fire answered, "No, I am not the strongest thing there is. Water is stronger than I am. If you pour water on me, it kills me."

The little red ant went to Water. He said, "Water, you are stronger than Fire. Are you the strongest thing there is?" Water answered, "No, I am not the strongest thing there is. Cow is stronger than I am. When cow drinks me, it kills me."

The little red ant went to Cow. He said, "Cow, you are stronger than Water. Are you the strongest thing there is?" Cow answered, "No, I am not the strongest thing there is. Stone Knife is stronger than I am. When Stone Knife cuts me in the heart, it kills me."

The little red ant went to Stone Knife. He said, "Stone Knife, you are stronger than Cow. Are you the strongest thing there is?" Stone Knife answered, "No, I am not the strongest thing there is. Big Stone is stronger than I am. When I am thrown down upon Big Stone, it kills me."

This is what happened long ago, and that is why we are afraid of the rock.

Benedict 1935, vol. 2: 225–26. ATU 2031. This story is at least as old as the Panchatantra, recorded in Sanskrit before A.D. 500. With an ant as hero, as here, the story is quite popular in Hispanic tradition, appearing in all three Hispanic regions represented in this volume. The Zuni have a long history of contact with Hispanic culture and much of their traditional life syncretizes Native American and Hispanic elements, as does this tale. The ending, "And that is why . . . ," is characteristic of Zuni tales. In a footnote Benedict points out that Zuni children say when they are frightened, "Oh, I am afraid! I shall be killed like the stone knife."

118. The Steer and the Ill-Treated Stepson

A child was much abused (by his stepmother), who would not give him any food, hoping that he might thus die of starvation.

The cattle were under his care, and he had to drive the milking-cows (back to the settlement) at night. Although food was for a long time refused to him by his stepmother, he would come back home every night; and it was truly strange (to see) how he could thus live without being fed. The woman appointed some one to follow the child and watch him wherever he went.

At mid-day, when the boy had gone quite a long way off, he stopped and sat down. Then two men, it seems, came out of the head of a Steer, and gave some food to the child. The spy reported to the woman what he had seen; and she replied, "So it is! If the boy is now alive, it is because he is fed by the Steer which he owns."

The old woman soon managed to get sick, and (her husband) hired many medicine men to doctor her. Her health, however, could not possibly be restored. Now, then, she pretended that while asleep she had received instructions in a dream. She said, "I must give a feast. This is the only means for me to recover; and the Steer owned by the boy must be slaughtered (for the occasion)." The father therefore gave advice to his son, saying, "Would you not spare (the Steer), and (allow) him to be killed? I shall give you a similar one, if you are willing to give him up." By no means! The boy would not spare his own domestic animal; for (there was no doubt that) his step-mother's hatred for him was the only reason why she wanted to do away with the helpful animal.

The child wept, and the Steer came along. "Don't cry!" said he, "for you must consent, and say, 'I shall be willing only if she herself kills the Steer which I own.'" And (the woman) replied, "Yes, I am able to kill (the animal) provided you tie him."

Then the boy proceeded towards a big stump, and he stood on it. The Steer, in fact, had advised him to do so, adding, "We must take to flight; and when I pass by (the stump), I shall put you on my back."

No sooner had the people bound the Steer than (the woman) came up with a sharp knife with which to kill him. But the Steer ran his horns through (her body), thus destroying her instead; and, breaking his bonds to shreds, he escaped and went to the place where the boy was standing on the stump. As the Steer passed by, the child mounted upon his back.

They took their flight to a remote place; and when they came to a large river, the Steer simply swam across it. They had no longer anything to fear, for nobody would now slay the domestic animal, who, in his usual manner, fed the child every day.

After some time they again travelled together, and found another river, which the Steer crossed with the boy sitting on his back. The Ox said the next day, "So it is! We are now to encounter bad luck. Starvation is walking this way, and we shall have to fight her (this) afternoon. After that, I may (be able to) feed you but once more, at noon. For fear, however, that I may be overpowered, I will now tell you what is to be done after our fight with Starvation. While my body is still warm, you must skin me (and remove) a narrow strip of my hide all along the spine, from the nose to the tail, which you must leave attached. That is what you have to do."

Noon was no sooner past than the Steer entered in a great fury, and began to walk back and forth. The boy climbed a tree near by, and watched the struggle that was going on, although he could not see at all (the being) against whom his domestic animal was fighting.

The Steer was defeated in the end and destroyed by Starvation. The child then remembered what he had been advised to do. So he skinned the animal, and, when it was done, he went away. He did not really know whither he was going. That is why the (being) whose hide (he had kept as a charm) conversed with him several times, indicating the way. The boy did not stop until he had reached a place where people were living; and, at the first house he came across, an old woman abiding thereat inquired, "Where do you come from?"

He replied, "I wish to stay here and work."

"What are you able to do?" asked she.

And he said, "I look after cattle: this is what I can do."

And she said, "You are the very sort of servant I have long been looking for."

The boy therefore stayed (with her); and the old woman became "his mother." As he had now to pasture her domestic animals, she gave him a warning. "You must not take my cattle yonder," said she, "for (my land) extends only that far; and you should not go beyond, for my wicked neighbor who lives there is armed with a spear."

The cattle had soon grazed all the grass on the old woman's land, so the boy led them (into the fields) beyond. Again the next day he trespassed on the land of the dreaded neighbor, who then noticed it. "Away with you!" said he. "This is my land, and I do not want you to bring your cattle here."

The boy replied, "It could not be so, for all the grass over there has been grazed." He added, "I have now chosen to fight with you."

The neighbor retorted, "Very well! To-morrow at noon we shall fight together."

The boy wore his strip of hide as a belt when they both met at noon on the next day. Unfastening it from around his body, he at once slashed the other fellow's legs off with it. Now the neighbor lamented, and said, "Oh, do not kill me! Have mercy, and I shall give you all my land!"

The boy, in fact, spared him, and accepted his offer. When her (adopted) son came back home with her cattle, the old woman asked him, "Is it really so? Have you not pastured the cattle on our wicked neighbor's land, although I had urged you not to do so?"

The young fellow answered, "It is so, indeed, and we have fought (over it); but I have compelled him to abandon all his land." And from that time on he allowed the cattle to roam about free.

When the autumn came, the old woman said, "Be off, and sell (one of) our domestic animals! You should not bargain with (the trader) who lives in the village near by, for he is always quite unfair (to the country folks). Try the other one who lives far from the village, instead, as he may give you a larger price. With this sum we shall purchase warm clothes for the winter."

Now then, the boy started for the village with the domestic animal; and, as he had barely covered half of the distance, he met some one who asked, "Where are you taking it to?"

He replied, "I am going to sell it, so that we may get some warm clothes for the winter."

"Let us barter together!" said the other.

The boy inquired, "What will you give me?"

And the (stranger spoke to his dog), saying, "O my domestic! Here you must defecate." Then he pulled out a box containing (two) "tumbling-bugs," and laid the round insects (on the ground). They at once began to roll the (dog's) feces. The man next put down (several) mice and drew out a musical bow (or violin). No sooner has he rubbed the strings than the mice danced.

Now the boy was willing to barter his ox (with the stranger); and when it was done, he came back to his adopted mother's home.

She inquired, "Have you really sold it?"

He said, "Yes!"

"What did you get in exchange?" asked she.

And he replied, "Here it is, the dog, for one thing;" and (speaking to the dog) he said, "O my domestic! Defecate here!" Upon being laid down, the beetles began to tumble the feces about.

The boy next put the mice on the ground and began to rub the stringed bow. The mice, in truth, danced; and the old woman exclaimed, "Wu! This is real fun, and I am much amused."

The next morning she said, "You shall once more go there; and this time you must not fail in trading this ox, so that we may get warm clothes for the winter."

So the boy again started off with an ox, which he was going to sell. There at a distance he saw the same fellow coming along. When they met, the other asked, "Where are you going with the ox?"

"This one," replied the boy, "I am going to trade in order to get warm clothes for next winter."

"Here I am! Let us barter together!" was the answer.

"What will you give me?" asked the boy.

"This is the very thing (for you)," said the man, thereupon pulling out a veil, a very small thing, indeed.

The young fellow inquired, "But what is it good for?"

The other explained, "Look here! You see the large tree standing there?" And he pitched the veil at the tree. It was done at once: (the tree) had been reduced into chopped wood, arranged into several piles.

The boy gave his consent, and exchanged the ox (for the veil). And the stranger added, "Over there lives a wealthy man who may be useful to you, for he always employs a wood-cutter; go there, and he will surely hire you, and you will thus get a great deal with which to purchase your winter clothes."

The young man went back home; and the old woman asked him, "Have you sold it?"

He replied, "Yes!"

"What did he give you?" was her next question.

And, as he said, "Here it is, a veil," she laughed, and exclaimed, "This thing must indeed be warm (for the winter), a veil!"

But he explained, "With this thing I shall indeed realize great benefits." Thereupon he went to the place where stood a number of large trees, pitched the veil, and many cords of chopped wood replaced them. So he said, "Certainly! (By means of) this our bodies shall keep warm."

The next morning he started for the rich man's place, and stood at the door (for a while). The people (in the house) saw him, and reported, "A hireling is standing there."

The chief came around and asked, "What is it for?"

The (young man) replied, "I am looking for work."

The important personage inquired, "What can you do?"

"This I can do, cut wood."

And (the man) said, "You are the very one I was looking for. (You see) that island yonder? It is a big island, and you must chop all the wood (on it)." He added, "At noon you may come back here to eat." And (speaking to another servant) he ordered, "You go there and show him the place where he is to chop wood."

Now they took him along to the large island, and said, "This is (the place)." As they were still there, walking about, the boy made a request. "Pray," said he, "turn around and be off! For it is truly impossible for me to do any work when someone is looking at me." So they went away.

Now, then, he began and pitched the veil at the trees that stood there in great numbers. Long before noon, in truth, the work was done; and all (the wood was arranged) in very many cords. After a while, growing tired of walking about, he thought, "I had better go back to the house now." When he was again seen by the wealthy man's servants, they repeated, "Here he is!" and their chief came. "Why is it so?" asked he; "you are already walking here, although I had advised you to come in only at noon."

The boy retorted, "But it is all done; it is a fact!"

His master said, "Mind you! A lie is a grave matter," and he gave a command (to his servants). "Go there!" said he, "and investigate what truth there is in his statement, 'Now I have done it.'" They made their investigation, only to find that it was really so, and that there was nothing but chopped wood there. Their report was, "It is so, he has done it;" upon which the wealthy man said, "Come in! Quite soon I think they will be through with cooking, and after our meal I will pay you." He asked the boy, moreover, "How did you really do it, for you are not quite grown up as yet?"

"I have chopped (the wood), though," replied the other. "It is quite true"—which he had, of course, done with the help of the veil. When the meal was over, the boy received such a large amount of goods in payment, that he was barely able to carry it to his home. As he reached his mother's house, he exclaimed, "Now, behold! It is your turn to go to the village for the purchase of clothing."

The next morning, in fact, she hired some one to take her to the village, where she bought a large quantity of warm clothes for herself and her son.

Another day the (young man) started for the place where a man of importance resided; and when he arrived there, he was again hired (for chopping
down the trees covering) a very large patch of ground. After a while the work
was all over; and, as the wood now stood in numerous piles, the price which
he received this time still surpassed (what he had received for his first work).

This good fortune, moreover, was all due to the Steer which he used
to own.

Again he went back to the place where his mother lived with the large
quantity of valuables which he had received in payment. "It is really wonderful," said he, "what benefit we derive from the veil."

And the old woman exclaimed, "Never before have I known such pros-
perity. Blessed am I for having adopted you!"

It happened once that he made friends with another young man, who
informed him, "I have been invited to a feast given by the chief's daughter;
and the point is that the fellow who is clever enough to make her laugh (will
get married to her), whoever he may be." So they both started for the feast,
the young man taking with him the mice, the tumbling-bugs, and the dog,
and wearing his every day clothes.

A large crowd of people were assembled there when the feast began;
and (the young men) in turn tried in every possible way to make the chief's
daughter laugh, but without avail. When it was over, they said, (pointing at
the old woman's son,) "Now be it so! Let this one have his turn. He may be
able to make her laugh. To be sure, he will not have to exert himself, as he
looks most comical with his ragged clothes."

The chief said, "By all means! It is now your turn."

So the young man answered, "Just a moment! I will bring along the dog,
my domestic." (Speaking to his dog) he said, "O my domestic! Here you
must defecate;" and upon being laid down, the tumbling-bugs began to roll
the feces about. Then he put the mice on the ground and rubbed the stringed
instrument, and the mice danced.

The girl, indeed, could not help laughing. All those who were standing
around, moreover, burst with laughter. The rich man (her father) said, "This
one is my son-in-law. Now you must all go back to your homes, for it is so!
He has now become my son-in-law." He (spoke to his servants,) saying, "Now
dress him up with the very best clothes that can be found." And so they did.

(After a while the young man) felt lonesome and went out. He met an
Indian who was walking about. "If you are willing to receive a great deal in
payment from me," said (the stranger), "let me first sleep with your wife." The
other replied, "It is agreed!" But (the Indian) now hired (a warrior) armed
with a spear, and commanded him, "Cast this fellow into the lion's den;" and

he dropped the (chief's son-in-law) amongst the fierce brutes, who at once made for him. But the young man simply took his veil and pitched it at the lions, who were all subdued without being killed. He did not remove the veil, and they tried in vain to tear it to pieces. For a number of days, in fact, it was impossible for them to eat when their guardians came to feed them.

Then one of the Lion's begged him, "Pray, have pity on us! Remove the veil!"

"Not yet," replied the young man, "for you were just about to devour me; and if I were to remove it, you would again do the same thing."

The Lion said, "No! We shall only help you, and let the people discover that you are (a captive) here." Now the Lion roared, and some one came to see what was the matter.

When the people found the man there, they reported the matter to his father-in-law. "He is sitting there amongst the Lions, your son-in-law."

The chief said, "Why is it so? Bring him along!" So they did; and he was then able to go to the place where his wife was staying.

The next day he looked for the "spear-man;" and when he found him, he said, "Were you going to kill me? Look here! It is my turn now!" So he drew the veil out and threw it at the (warrior's) house, just to crush it at once into a heap of small bits. His enemy now being slain, the young man went back to his wife's house. He said, "Now I must be off, for no doubt my mother must be worrying."

But the young woman replied, "Not yet! You should not leave until we go there together to bring back your mother with us." So they started together, and arrived at the old woman's house.

She was, indeed, far more pleased than ever, for her son had brought back a young woman (his wife) with him. He said, "We have both come to fetch you."

"Very well," replied she; "but I must first sell all that I own."

He said, "No! We must look for some one who is as poor as we used to be, and give it all away." They found out, in fact, that their neighbor also had long been a widow, living all by herself. So she gave her all she had. Then they took their mother along with them, and went to live at the wealthy man's place. Soon the young man replaced his father-in-law, and became the chief in his stead.

It is quite likely that they are still living there now.

Barbeau 1915: 87–94. ATU 511(AT 511A)/559. From the telling of Mrs. Catherine Johnson, of Wyandotte, Oklahoma, as interpreted (translated) by Allen Johnson, and written down in July 1912 by C. Marius Barbeau, a Canadian folklorist at that time working for the Geological Survey in Ottawa. The passages in parentheses, "not explicitly included in the text" (Barbeau, 83), were added by Barbeau, or in one case by the interpreter.

Barbeau contributed a number of Canadian Amerindian tales to the *Journal of American Folklore*. Apparently, he came to Oklahoma in search of tales from this historically Canadian tribe. According to the 1910–1911 *Encyclopaedia Britannica* the Wyandots (Hurons) in Oklahoma numbered about four hundred in 1905, with another four hundred in Quebec. The story of how Hurons came to be in Oklahoma is an epic story in itself. The collector of this story, Barbeau (1883–1969), went on to become the father of folklore studies in Canada. From Native Americans or First People his interest spread to the French, whose stories pervade much Native American folklore. He collected some four hundred Canadian French tales and seven thousand songs, plus numerous folk artifacts, and published approximately one thousand books and articles (Canadian Museum of Civilization Corp., 2006).

This composite tale includes elements found in a number of tales. According to Stith Thompson, the form of Type 511 that features a boy and a pet ox (AT 511A) sometimes combines with Type 590, a tale that often includes helpful lions (Aarne, Thompson, 1981: 178). This association may explain its present combination with ATU 559, the lions in ATU 590 calling up the lions' den from ATU 559. The trading of cows for magical items seems to be adapted from Jack and the Beanstalk, ATU 328, though such trades also occur in other tales. The superhuman woodcutting recalls the tasks in ATU 313, The Devil's Daughter. Readers will also want to compare the first part of this tale with the African American/Irish version in chapter 10.

119. The Toad Prince

There was a great big camp or community, near[ly] a village. There was a very pretty young girl and the best-looking boy they picked out to be married, and be chief or mayor. The people looked up to them as the most prominent in the village.

When the time came for a family arrival, the community thought it would be best for the medicine man to pick out the maid to be [*or* for?] the mother. So he picked out the best girl. And after that he set a date for the baby to arrive. And he picked out some young men to guard the lodge. Then [they] went out hunting to have a big feast. One got a buffalo, one got an antelope—fowls, grouse, prairie chickens. When they asked the mother what day she was expecting, she said two or three days. Wednesday the child was going to arrive, she told the father.

In this village they have what is called the announcer. In these days the Indians live in a great big round circle—I've seen it myself—it takes maybe five days to go around [to all the camps]. So he got on his horse and went around announcing that the baby is going to be born on Wednesday, that every member of the community should gather around the lodge to help celebrate the arrival. So next day everybody went over, waited around all day, baby didn't arrive, everybody quite disappointed. So they decided to postpone the celebration, went home, waited, village quiet, all listened for a sound. Well they all got up early the next morning, watered their stock, tied them up different places, announcer went around again. Two, three thousand people gathered around waiting for the arrival. But another disappointment, baby still didn't arrive. So they all went home disappointed.

Meanwhile the to-be-mother went out for a little walk, maybe that would help. Walked along a little river, sandy beach, accompanied by her husband, maids. She saw something bubbling up out of the ground. [*Chief Welsh gestures.*] Told her husband.

"Oh, that's nothing, a spring."

"Oh no, it's some animal, I can see his eyes coming out of the ground." She was a little scared. So they went over, and it was a big toad [*gesture*], coming out to sun himself. So they took her home, the maids; she felt weak and scared. So next day the baby arrived, but it was a toad. They were a little bit disappointed. The medicine man tried to perform a ceremony to change him back, had his rattle, and his braves dancing. (He worshiped the Great Spirit, Wahtankheh.) But the only fortunate thing was that it was able to talk. But it had short legs in front, long in back. "Nevertheless," the medicine man says, "we have a baby: we're going to have a feast."

They made a place for him [on a chain] in the corner, and he kept growing bigger. So years went by, and he grew up, as a child you might say, but the others were afraid of him—different type, you know. So he told his mother and father he wanted to get married, but no girl would have him. So they told the chief and also the medicine man and the braves. So they looked around and looked around and finally one girl consented, [the toad boy's family] being the prominent family in the village, you know. She said she'd marry the toad. So the day was set for the wedding, and they all gathered around for the feast. And the man that prays—what do you call him? Wacekiye Wicasa, prayer man—married them, tied the knot. Oh, people were disappointed because the nice-looking girl had to marry the toad. Outside they were happy at the celebration, but inside they were disappointed, felt there was no justice [*laughs*]. So this family had created an in-law, and she moved over to the King's palace, to the lodge.

So days went on, and one morning she wouldn't respond. The maids went in with the mother-in-law and tried to wake her up and found her dead. The toad was lying in a corner tied up, nicest child could be. So they got the best braves for the funeral, the announcer announced that the royal family's daughter-in-law had died, they built a scaffold. The medicine man told the braves to go way out to the baddest lands they could find. And there they took the four sticks and weaved them with bands so they could have a scaffold. And that was where they would bury the young lady. Then they had the funeral procession, and everybody was there except the young toad. They wouldn't let him go. And they all went over to look at him, to see how disappointed he looked. And the medicine man sung a song. (Can't remember [it]). So they all went to the hill, but nobody could get up except the braves: they knew a secret path. And she was wrapped up in buffalo robes and tied with rawhide, and the prayer man gave the prayer, and everybody went home very sad.

Well, by and by the toad wanted to get married again. The father said, "Well, we've lost a good girl, and if anything should happen we'd probably get ostracized from the tribe."

The mother said, "No, he's my child, and if he wants to get married he will." So they had quite an argument over it, and finally the father gave in and went over to the medicine man and the chief. So they looked around and located another beautiful girl. Her father didn't want her to marry him, but the mother said, "He's the royal [family], and he has my consent." So they had another big celebration, and maids of honor and all. So the royals inherited another daughter-in-law.

Things went along nicely, and this one lasted a little longer. But the mother-in-law suspected something and said, "You stay with me tonight."

"Oh no, that's all right, he doesn't bother me."

The next morning she didn't get up, and the mother-in-law rushed in and found her dead. So the maids got her, and they had another funeral, same place.

By this time the community was suspecting something. So they said, "Next time we'll have guards all night to see what happens." They suspected maybe the royal family was jealous because they wouldn't associate with the toad—their son, supposed to be, you know.

Well, the toad wanted to get married again, and they had a big argument, and the mother won out, and they went to see the officials. Same thing happened. And the toad wanted to get married a fourth time. So the tribe had a meeting and decided they'd have a bodyguard. Maybe the mother and father, the royals, were jealous of their son and killed the girl in the night.

So they selected some braves, changed them around, some watch during the day, some during the night. Meanwhile the medicine man was cooperating with the spirits, shaking his medicine rattle, singing, had that performance all night, to drive the bad spirits away. Nothing happened, guards there. Next morning she got up, did the washing, did her business.

But one night she decided to stay awake all night. She heard the old toad jingling, jingling his chains, heard a slap, slap, the old toad coming, gets on her bed. She lay there to see what he would do, ready to give the alarm. He touched her face, kissed her. She lay there, kinda half asleep, pretended she didn't know nothing. Then he kisses her on the neck, loves her up—three or four times. Then he crawls back, falls off the bed, gets killed! Didn't hear nothing after that.

Then [she] hears a man whistling in the next room, opening doors, shutting closets, talking to the guards—and he was the best looking man she ever saw. That was her husband. And she got up in the morning, very happy. And her parents saw this good-looking young man, and didn't see the toad. So they gave her golden slippers, and a golden dress, [a veil] around her head and all down, and had a big wedding, and gave them a palace—but they called them lodges there.

But one day something happened. She got mad at him. He was good-looking, attractive, good singer, everybody stopped and talked with him—the girls. They invited him to a conference, and it kept a little longer, and she put the food back in, and brought it out. So finally she went over there and spoke to him in a harsh tone and said, "You let them have their meeting; you come home and have your dinner." He didn't like that: no way to talk to a prominent man. So he went home, excused himself. And when he was going back she said, "If you stay longer, you cook your own dinner." All the time, you see, she thought he was associating with someone else [, another woman]. But it wasn't true, he was just minding his own business. Come home, no dinner. So this happened once or twice. And he decided to pack up and leave.

"She's not treating me like a husband."

So he packed up and took her golden slippers and went to another village. And nobody knew where he went. The guards, watchmen, said, "Yes, he left after the meeting." Mother, father, wife, all wondered where he went. Wife uncomfortable all night, thinking maybe he was with a girl friend [*laughs*].

Next morning mother and father inquired from her.

"No."

Some party saw him after the meeting, "We saw him going into a house." That was the last they saw of him. They thought, they'll search for him, see. They sent out a searching party, went into every house in the community. Couldn't find him. So they thought they'd wait a few days. No report came along so they'd know where he was at. Finally they decided to inquire at the next village. So they sent some selected braves over, but they came back and reported to the officials that he wasn't there. So they had another meeting, and decided to have another hunting party and send it out to another village. But they were unsuccessful again. And they did likewise a third time. Another searching party, another village. But no strangers there at all.

In the meantime this young lad thought to himself, "I'll marry the girl who can wear these golden slippers." He fleed to a village about four or five villages down the line. He was a total stranger there. So he told the chief, the neighbors at a council, that he was a young man there and wished to get acquainted. And any young lady could wear the golden slippers would be his next bride. So they had a great big circus tent, and gathered all the girls from the suburbs, as you might say, and the girl who could wear the golden slippers would marry this young man. He was so good-looking everybody fell in love with him. So when they saw the golden slippers they went to work massaging their feet, trying to get their feet in the golden slippers. But they were too small or too large to fit the slippers. Those young ladies of that village just went for him. (I read in the paper where a girl took a bunch of flowers to Sinatra on the stage at Chicago, and then fainted. It was the same order.)

By that time the scouts that were out looking for him, traveling from village to village, heard the news about the golden slippers, and carried it back, that anyone who fit the slippers would be his wife and have the slippers and all the jewelry he inherited from the royals. Pretty soon his wife heard about this, and grabbed her shawl, her robe I should say, and took some rations, and went to the next village, and the next, and the next. She was about giving up hopes—it was a false report—when the news came along that this young man was down the line. By gosh, she stayed in this village a few days and pretty soon a young man came along, and she asked him and he said, "Yes, he was here, but he's gone to that other village over there. All the girls try them on but some is too [small], and they slip off, and others is too [big] and can't get in."

So she says, "If that's him, that's my husband." So very next [day] she set out and traveled and traveled and couldn't find the village, but after two days she found it.

"Yes, there's some doings here." And [she] saw some girls walking around there with bloody feet, and asked why they were doing that.

And an old lady said, "There was a nice young man around here with golden slippers, valuable jewelry, [that said that any girl who fit the slippers would be his wife and have all the jewelry he inherited from the royals]. The girls cut their feet with flints." But no one knew the man, and he'd gone on. That was all the information she could get. She didn't say she was his wife. So she gathered up her belongings and set out for another long journey.

And she came to another great village, and saw some girls walking around crying with bloody feet. And they told about the good-looking young man with the jewelry and gowns, [and how any girl who fit the slippers would be his wife and have all that]. "He just left, just went down this road."

"Well, how far is it to the next village?"

"Oh, about a day."

Just before end of the day she caught up with him at the next village, but she didn't tell him who she was. Asked a family there if they'd put her up for a few days. Then the young man told the chief [that any young lady could wear the golden slippers would be his next bride]. So the girls all gathered around. He disguised himself by putting paint on, black here, white there (but when he went through the village, before, he didn't put no war paint on). So in the council ring the chief told them there was a gentleman there from another distant town, and anyone who could fit the slipper to perfect could have the valuable jewelry and gown he'd inherited from the royal family. So they tried to fit the slipper, carved up their hoofs.

This went on for two days. Then she disguised herself, put on some red paint, white paint, her shawl. On the third day she said, "Well, I'll try this time; I'll get in the row." So all these girls sitting on this bench kept trying on the slipper till the last one. Finally she said, "Oh, those are my slippers. I've been looking for them for two days." And she put them on and stood up. She kept her paint on but he took his off.

So he was surprised and said, "All right, here's a girl come from a far distance, fit the slippers, so we'll have a ceremony." And they got the chief and the medicine man and the prayer man and had a big ceremony. And the chief gave them a lodge to stay in. And she took off her paint, and he saw that it was his wife who had followed him all that distance.

And they went back to their place where they originated from, and all the people was very glad and had a big celebration.

And then he said, "I'm going back to my place where I came from, and when I come back you won't be here. So dig a big hole in the ground, and make it solid, with braces, in two days, because there's going to be a big storm coming, and that's when I'm going." Some didn't believe him, but the chief did because this was a strange man. So they built the hole solid, and the storm come, and he said, "Now I'm going over to that land over there, and leave you here on earth, and when I get over there I'll disappear. You'll see houses and people and trees flying in the air—that's a sign of destruction—but don't mind about me." And he told his mother and father and wife to get in the hole. And he sat down like a toad. And a big storm came up, and all the houses flew around, and the people on the hill that didn't believe him. And when the storm was over, he was gone where he came from.

And as a result of that, after a storm the toad comes up out of the ground. I've seen that, out in the Dakotas, after a certain kind of rain and sun, the toads come up. People think they fall with the rain, but they don't.

You know how those big drops of rain splash. My father and mother told me, "After the rain you'll see the toads." And I did.

Dorson 1946: 14–26. ATU 425/433B (cf. ATU 510A). Transcribed from Lilly Library Dorson Manuscript by editor. Herbert Welsh, said to be a grandson of Sitting Bull, told this tale to Richard M. Dorson, September 5, 1946, on a field trip to the Michigan Upper Peninsula. While Chief Welsh told the story, Dorson wrote it out in longhand. He then printed his revised transcription of the tale in *Bloodstoppers and Bearwalkers* (1952: 59–65), where the curious reader can compare it to the present transcription. The method of transcription, in longhand from oral narrative, may explain the somewhat telegraphic style of many of the sentences. The original manuscript contains slips of the tongue (or pen?), which I have corrected in brackets. I have also added an occasional word in brackets for clarity. Finally, in three places Dorson writes "*etc.*" instead of repeating each time the details of the young man's offer to wed any girl who can fit into the golden shoes. I have expanded those *et ceteras*, likewise in brackets.

In Dorson's transcript the beginning of the tale is a bit confusing. It may be that Chief Welsh starts out by describing the ways things were done (selecting the best looking couple to be chief, deciding when children are to be born, hunting to support the couple at the time of birth), and imperceptibly slides into telling that they were done that way in the case of the family in the story.

At the end of the story Chief Welsh continues with further explanation of the deaths of the girls, as follows: "And the women who were choked, they quarreled with their husband and the toad killed them (except for the one who loved him). They buried those people on the scaffold, like the Crucifixion, above the ground, so they'd go to the Spirits. If they were buried below the ground they'd go to hell." Apparently we are to understand that the toad boy is kept tied or chained up all the time, as I have indicated with an addition to the description of him as a child in his corner. When the first girl dies, he is tied up, and when the heroine (the significant fourth bride, as is to be expected in an Amerindian tale) accepts him in her bed she hears his chains.

The tale exhibits prominent features of ATU 425, the Search for a Lost Husband (Cupid and Psyche): the birth of an aquatic or semi-aquatic creature instead of a child, the violation of the marriage by the bride, and the abandonment by the husband, who in many versions is cursed so that he cannot even remember his marriage, the long search, the test, and the final reconciliation. The desire to marry, however, and the successive marriages are more characteristic of ATU 433B. They are also reminiscent of certain versions of Bluebeard (ATU 311-312) in which the monster is cursed to kill women until the right one comes along and releases him from the spell so that they are able to marry successfully. The quest for a bride who fits the golden slippers is, of course, similar to the resolution of Cinderella stories. The tale concludes with a characteristically American Indian ending that tells what happens after the lovers are finally reunited. The etiological coda ("that's why toads come out after a storm") is likewise an Amerindian touch. Welsh is Sioux, and the animals hunted at the beginning of the story are animals a Sioux might hunt out on the Great Plains, not animals native to the Michigan Upper Peninsula, where Welsh was living at the time he told the story. The details of burial are likewise Siouxan.

120. Ka-Ma-Nu and the Mo-o

Ka-ma-nu was a strong handsome man who lived with his parents, sisters and brothers not far from a river where a mo-o wa-hi-ne or "lizard woman" had her cavern. Daily he went to and from this river to fetch water or to get a few shrimps and fresh water fish for supper. One morning while engaged in fishing, he felt himself grasped by a pair of arms, then he was carried under to a cavern at the bottom of the stream. Here he was released.

"Aloha!" said his captor.

Ka-ma-nu turned to look. He saw a slim brown-haired woman, and terror seized him as he remembered the tales his mother had told him about the e-hu mo-o women. He looked about for means of escape, but found none.

"Don't be afraid," she said; "you will be my husband and I will see to it that your family is supplied with shrimp and fish." Ka-ma-nu readily consented and the woman cared for him well, giving him only the best of food. In the meantime his parents looked for his body, believing that he was dead. Not finding it, they supposed it had been carried by the stream to the beach where it had been devoured by sharks.

After a year Ka-ma-nu grew homesick and ceased to relish his food. "Alas! What grieves my husband?" asked his wife.

"Love for my parents," he replied.

"Then tomorrow I will take you to the surface. Go, visit your parents and come back to the river; there I will wait. Remember to kiss no one until you have kissed your father; if you kiss another first you will see me no more."

Ka-ma-nu went home the next day with a happy heart. Just as he stooped to enter his father's doorway, Ma-ka-ni, his dog, ran out to greet him. Ka-ma-nu patted his head. With a howl of delight Ma-ka-ni leaped up and licked his face. The family were overjoyed to see Ka-ma-nu again. He told them of his wife and their pleasant home at the river bottom. Toward evening he went back to the river and saw his wife weeping for him.

"Goodbye, my husband, you will not see me again," she said, and dived into the water.

Day by day Ka-ma-nu came to the bank and called her, but she came no more. He grieved so much that in a few months he died. His father buried him in a cave overlooking the river where he once lived happily with his bride.

Green 1926: 113–14; see also Pukui and Green 1995, 50–51. ATU 313. The volume from which this tale is taken has a headnote saying that most of the tales therein were collected from the tradition of one family in the Kau [Ka'u] district on the island of Hawaii. The family in question was that of Mary Kawena Pukui, neé Wiggin. Mary Pukui learned this tale from her mother, Mary Pa'ahana Kanaka'ole Wiggin, whose own mother had been a dancer in the court of Hawaiian Queen Emma. Her father, Henry Wiggin, from Massachusetts, also spoke Hawaiian fluently, and Mary grew up in a bilingual and bicultural family. A neighbor, Laura Green, was cousin to folklorist Martha Warren Beckwith. Pukui told her family's stories to Green and worked with her to craft English translations. Green sent them to Beckwith, who edited them in three slim volumes, including the one from which this tale came. Pukui went on to become an important scholar of Hawaiian language and culture (Duckworth 1995: ix–xii).

Though the tale is reminiscent of Beauty and the Beast, with the roles reversed, the motif of the dog that licks his master, thus violating the tabu on kissing, suggests that it is rather a variant of ATU 313, here transformed into a tragic legend. In a footnote, Beckwith called the story "a modern European fairy-mistress folk-tale with a Polynesian coloring, but interesting because it shows how the thing is done" (113). I have retained the older system for spelling Hawaiian found in the story as first published.

121. The Muskrat Husband

There was once a village
that lay
on the bank of a river.

This village
had a great hunter
and the great hunter
had a daughter.

Although many young men
asked to marry his daughter,
the great hunter did not permit her
to accept a husband.

There was one young man whom she wanted for a husband,
one of the young men of the village.
And this young man
tried to get her for his wife.
But though he asked to marry her, her father
would not let him,
this man
whom his daughter wanted for a husband.

So it was, and the girl decided in anger never to marry.
. . .
As time passed, even her father
tried to persuade her to accept a husband,
but she did not want to:

she still was angry that the man she wanted to marry
had been rejected by her father.

Well, life went on that way,
in that village there,
on the bank of the river.
. . .
One day,
the great hunter's daughter
went outside;
behind the village some boys were playing
at the bank of an oxbow lake,
noisily chasing something.
She went up to see what they were chasing,
and when she got there,
she saw it was a muskrat!

By that time
the muskrat was faltering,
and though it dove,
it never stayed underwater long;
it looked like it soon would die.

But then
she saved the muskrat by dispersing
the boys who were chasing it.
By the time she made them stop
the muskrat was exhausted; it was practically dead.
. . .
They [the boys] went home,
and she too went home
behind them.
And life went on as usual
for a few weeks.
. . .
Then one day,
while she was doing her chores,
the woman
saw
a man,
and his parka was made of muskrat!

He said to her
that out of gratitude he was coming to ask her to be his wife,
out of gratitude that she had saved him
as she did.

And the woman
accepted him,
because she was still without a husband.

Now, this man was a stranger,
an odd-looking sort of stranger.

Well, he married her, and they lived as husband and wife.

He always caught lots of game when he hunted;
he even caught lots of bearded seal.
. . .
But this man
warned his wife repeatedly,
never ever to take his clothes,
even when they were wet,
and put them by the fire pit
to dry in the heat.

And this was how it was to be,
even if he came home all wet.
. . .
Well, on one occasion
he was all wet when he came home,
and later on she dried his grass bootliners.

When the fireplace
was lit,
she dried them
in its heat.

Her husband was gone while she was doing this,
somewhere outside.
. . .
After a while he came back

Well, when he got inside,
he saw his bootliners,
which had been dried in the heat.
"Ungh!" he sighed,
and he turned around quickly and ran out.

His wife
went out after him.

She saw as she followed him,
that he was running to the lake behind the village.

And she
chased him, running right behind him, because she still wanted him as
    her husband.

Now the lake they were going to
was where the boys had been chasing the muskrat,
and when her husband reached it, right away
he dove in.

When the woman
reached the lake herself, then
she too dove right in.

Both of them went underwater, and then came up together,
as muskrats!
. . .
So, even though he had warned her,
she dried his bootliners in the heat.
By doing this, she made him turn back into a muskrat.

And this woman
also became a muskrat,
right there in the oxbow lake.

And now it is the end.

Imgalrea *et al.* 1984: 59–63. ATU 425A(?) (cf. ATU 552) and Motif B360/D315(327)/B651/C36/ D117(127). Told in Yup'ik to Anthony Woodbury by Thomas Moses, aged about seventy-three, November 9, 1978, in Chevak, Alaska. Translated by Woodbury and Leo Moses, Thomas's son, and arranged in verse lines by Woodbury to indicate the quasi-poetic structure of this particular style of storytelling.

The Yup'ik Eskimo, with a native-speaking population of 14,000 in 1980, out of a total population of 17,000, constitute "one of the largest Native American linguistic communities in the United States today" (Imgalrea et al. 1984: 12). Chevak is a Yup'ik village thirteen miles inland from Hooper Bay on the Bering Sea. Woodbury found that the nearly 500 inhabitants maintained the native language, a rich oral and material culture, and a remarkably traditional subsistence economy of fishing, hunting, and gathering. One of the important functions of storytelling in this community has been to organize and transmit experience, culture, and values. To that end storytelling is practiced by all sorts of people, from little girls to old men, in a variety of contexts, both informal and ceremonial. Narrative style changes with context and performer. Listeners often lean back "with eyes half-closed, responding with satisfied murmurs and comments at appropriate points" (Imgalrea *et al.* 1984: 16). The culture recognizes two principal genres of stories, *qanemciq*, about knowable persons' experiences, and *qulirat*, passed down from ancient ancestors. In *qulirat*, "The Muskrat Husband," for example, the characters are often types (a father, a girl) to whom the storyteller does not assign names.

Woodbury provides a good description of Moses's tape-recorded performance on a "blustery morning" in November:

His daughter-in-law, his two-year-old grandson, and I were present. Born at Qussunaq [the site from which the village moved in the 1940s] perhaps around 1905 or earlier, Mr. Moses spoke with great humor, taking clear pleasure in the enterprise. His style was marked by rapid cadence, but he created an impression of great slowness in scene-setting passages and great speed at moments of action by increasing and decreasing the length of his pauses between lines. While Mr. Moses did not make much use of direct quotation, his narrative voice used a broad range of expressive intonational contours. (Imgalrea *et al.* 1984: 17)

To present the story on the printed page, Woodbury has adapted typographical features from the systems developed by Dennis Tedlock and by Dell Hymes, respectively. The line breaks correspond to pauses. The stanza-like units represent groups of lines ending on a rising inflection, concluding with a line or lines ending on a falling inflection, each succeeding line also being on a lower pitch. These groups exhibit other defining linguistic and auditory features as well. The larger sections, separated by three dots, divide the story rhetorically into major logical units of action.

This well-structured tale demonstrates the difficulty of sorting out European and non-European influences in Native American and African American tales. The core situation, involving marriage to a strange husband and a tabu that must not be broken, is very like the core situation in stories of the ATU 425A, The Animal as Bridegroom type. Stories even more similar to this one, about marriage to seals, are told in Ireland and Scotland. But the motif of marriage to a furbearing animal husband is widespread in circumpolar tradition well beyond Europe. The tragic or semi-tragic resolution is what now distinguishes it most clearly from European märchen, even if the plot should eventually prove to be märchen derived.

Part VI

A CASE STUDY

CHAPTER 18

BETTY CARRIVEAU SHERMAN
AND HER FATHER'S TALES*

Thus far, our collection has focused on the tales themselves, and the ethnic, regional, or other groups they came from, with such information about the particular storytellers as we could offer within the limits of knowledge and space. In an ideal collection, however, each tale would be accompanied by a detailed history of its telling within the storyteller's family, by photographs or videotapes of the performance, and by full analysis of what the story meant to the storyteller. Obviously, such information is not available for storytellers long dead. And even if it were, inclusion of so much other information would limit the collection to eight or ten stories. In this final chapter, however, we present one tale and its teller the way—in a more perfect world—we would have liked to present all of these American tales. The storyteller is of French-Canadian descent, and so this tale completes the survey of American French tradition begun in Part 3.

French-Canadians from Quebec settled rural northeastern Wisconsin in the late nineteenth century to work in the woods and sawmills, to fish commercially, and to farm. They brought with them an array of folk traditions, including woodcarving and needlework, fiddle music and dancing, and the telling of stories like Betty Carriveau Sherman's "Angel Gabriel."

*James P. Leary interviewed Betty Carriveau Sherman, recorded and transcribed the tale, noted the biographical and contextual details, and provided the analysis in this chapter.

According to genealogical records and family tradition, Etienne Carriveau came from France to Quebec in 1668, bringing with him "the kings and castles stories." Thereafter the Carriveau men, who had little schooling, farmed and worked in lumber camps where they heard more tales. Etienne's great-great-great-grandson, John Baptiste Carriveau, brought his family of eleven children to a Wisconsin farm between Stiles and Oconto Falls in the 1890s. His middle son, Joseph (1878–1939), was not only a carpenter, a mason, a building contractor, a farmer, and a lumberjack, but also a fine raconteur. Of the Carriveau men, Joe's daughter Betty recalls her great-uncle Antoine, her uncle Theodore, and her father. "They were all storytellers, all the way down the line, and my father was a great one."

Born in 1908 at Oconto Falls, Betty Carriveau Sherman has fond memories of her father. A handsome man, Joe Carriveau cultivated a big moustache in the manner of French-Canadian men of status: "Mom couldn't stand him without his moustache." As the anthropologist Horace Miner observed in *St. Denis: A French-Canadian Parish:* "For a man the most definite mark of having attained social recognition is the growing of a moustache" (1939: 217). Respected within the community of adults, Joe Carriveau was loved by his seven children. He carved whistles for them, sang French songs, taught them to waltz, organized hayrides and camping excursions to pick berries, and treated them with tangerines. Most of all, he told stories.

Joe Carriveau's narrative repertoire included short "nonsense" stories about lumber-camp characters like Joe Mouffreau, but it was dominated by lengthy tales of contests between some impoverished trickster and a foolish giant or a crafty noble. His brother Theodore was willing to tell similar stories "after sundown," but Joe confined his performances to snowbound winters. Like his moustache, Joe Carriveau's seasonal preference stemmed from a winter-time French-Canadian tradition sustained in northeastern Wisconsin's lumber camps and rural neighborhoods: the veillée or evening social gathering where musicians, singers, and dancers entertained (Miner 1939: 161–62).

As a young girl, Betty recalled: "I actually prayed for blizzards. If we had one blizzard during the winter, we got one story. But if we had three blizzards, that meant three stories." If the children were at school when the blizzard began, Joe Carriveau would hitch a team to a sleigh to collect them. Sometimes the snow was already too high, and Joe broke a trail on foot for his children. Back home, "Mother [Tillie Waymel Carriveau] would be waiting with warm clothes and hot drinks." Joe Carriveau would milk the family's four cows, then "that was story time."

The youngest of the seven Carriveau children might be put to bed, but the others "sat around the old buck stove in the dining room." Joe Carriveau emerged from his daughter's reminiscences as an accomplished storyteller with a penchant for dramatic performance. Seated comfortably, Joe Carriveau assumed the voices of his characters, made faces suggesting their emotions, and mimicked their movements: "He would act out all the parts. . . . My dad would just illustrate everything." In a story Betty called "Jack the Robber," the king invites people to a ball, then scatters coins on the floor to trap an unknown robber. Jack puts wax on the bottoms of his shoes to pick up coins without giving himself away by stooping. At that moment in the story Joe Carriveau would bound from his chair and dance a coin-capturing jig.

Although hard-working Joe Carriveau reserved his stories for wintry veillées when, practically speaking, little else might be done, he savored his tellings, embroidering them with fine details, appreciating each plot's convolutions and repetitions, and teasing his audience.

> That rascal, when he'd get to an interesting part of the story, he'd always have his pipe. And his pipe would always go out while he was telling the story. So then he'd take the pipe out, fill it very carefully, and there we sat waiting, of course. Finally he'd light the pipe. Then he'd put it down again to tell the story. . . . He kept us in suspense.

Many of Joe Carriveau's stories, like "Angel Gabriel," took roughly an hour to tell. And when he was finished, his audience always wanted more. Yet no matter how the children might beg, "he wasn't about to tell another one." No wonder Betty prayed for blizzards.

Although their father might tell stories only a few times a year, Betty and her siblings remembered them well and had their favorites, including "Angel Gabriel" and one they called "Hairy Jack." Joe Carriveau had no names for his stories and, when Betty was young, he told them entirely in French. Later on, she recollected, he told the stories partly in English: "They were fascinating, however they were told." When Betty was still in grade school she began writing down her father's stories in a lined composition book. Often stories disappear when the family language changes. But Joe

The composition book in which Betty Carriveau Sherman wrote out her father's stories.

and his daughter Betty took their family stories in hand and helped them over the language hurdle and into American English.

In 1925, after graduating from high school, Betty began a lengthy teaching career. Sometime after 1949, when she commenced a twenty-three-year stint in the Oconto school system, she introduced some of her father's stories to students. Much like her father, she reserved the stories for days when bad weather kept the children from going outside for recess.

> There was no gym, and they got tired of playing little games. So I thought, "Now why wouldn't they enjoy one of papa's stories?" I started telling stories fifteen minutes in the morning, half an hour at noon, fifteen minutes in the afternoon. Then I would steal ten minutes at the end of the day to finish.

After retiring from teaching in 1973, Betty Carriveau Sherman continued to tell her father's stories for an array of regional audiences: Scout troops, civic organizations, historical societies, and college classes. She also began to write reminiscent articles for family members and for nostalgic magazines like *Good Old Days.* Eventually she drew upon her childhood composition book to recast the stories inherited from her father. The result was *Stories Papa Told,* published in 1981.

Generally faithful to the details of Joe Carriveau's plots and to his oral style, Betty Carriveau Sherman nonetheless made certain changes when offering her father's stories for regional audiences and, eventually, for publication. She named his otherwise untitled stories. And although Betty retained her father's invariable "once upon a time" opening formula, she altered his characteristic conclusion: "And they gave me a good kick in the rear and sent me here to tell you all about it." Considering such language too vulgar for her fourth graders, but also wishing, like her father, to personalize the stories' endings, she opted for: "They told me to come here and tell you all about it, because I was the hired girl." The kids wondered if this were true.

Some stories, like "Angel Gabriel," were shorn of scatology—a common element in the oral tales of French peasants and Franco-American *habitants.* Where her father spoke of "*merde*" [*shit*], Betty spoke of "mud."

> He told that story the way it should be told. The king's boots and stovepipe hat were filled with *merde,* even the two jars of jam were filled with *merde* by Ramiel. I changed it for my school children, but our family heard it as *merde.* (Sherman: personal communication)

And we, the readers, each time we see "mud" we are to know that Betty is thinking "*merde.*" Betty likewise fretted about whether or not the portrayal of roguish or foolish priests was blasphemous, as is evident from an extended aside in her performance of "Angel Gabriel." On the advice of a wise priest, she kept the characters as they were.

122. Angel Gabriel

Once upon a time there were three young men—Bill, Pete, and Ramiel—who lived with their mother in the country. And they were very poor. The young men worked in the fields all day. By fall the crops were in from the fields, the woodshed was full of wood for the winter, the garden was in. And the men came in from the fields.

Their mother put a big kettle of soup on the table and she said, "Boys, you're going to have to go out and seek your fortunes. We've got all the work done. And," she said, "if you go out into the world you might find a job, and you might be able to earn a change of clothes. But if you don't have good luck in finding a job, you're welcome to come back."

So the three boys decided that they would do that. So the next morning they got up early and they packed their turkeys. You know what a turkey is? [A bag] on the end of a stick. They had a good breakfast of bread and milk. And then their mother packed them each a lunch, in a paper sack, of bread and sausage. And they started out.

They walked and walked until they came to a fork in the road. A fork in the road means that one road goes to the right, another to the left, and another straight ahead. So the three boys decided, "We'll stop here." They opened their sacks and had lunch. When they were ready to leave, they said, "Shall we all follow the same trail, or shall we separate here?" They decided to separate.

So Pete took the road to the left. Of course, they shook hands and said goodbye. But they decided that in a year and a day they would meet at the fork in the road and go back home to see their dear old mother. So Pete took the road to the left, and he walked until he came to a sawmill. At the sawmill he noticed that there were a lot of little chips and small items on the ground. And he thought, "Well, this will be a good place to start a match factory." So he started the match factory. And everything went fine because old men sat and smoked their pipes in the evening, they lit their lanterns and lamps and fires, so they used a lot of matches. But in the summer, the men didn't have time to sit and smoke, they didn't have to have heat in their stove, they didn't need lamps and lanterns much. So he just about broke even.

Well then, the other fellow, Bill, had taken the road to the right. And he came to a place and he thought, "Oh, I think I'll start a blacksmith shop here." So he had the blacksmith shop and everything went well during the winter because the runners on sleds always needed fixing, and the horses had to be shod, and everything went fine all winter. But then in the summertime, the horses didn't have to be shod, there wasn't much work. So he just about broke even.

But then Ramiel went straight ahead. He went through a big forest. And when he got to the other side of the forest, he sat down and had the rest of his lunch. As he was having his lunch, he looked around. And he saw in the distance a tall fence. And inside that fence, on the other side of that fence, were tall trees. And he could see that there was a huge house among those trees. He wondered about that place. So after his lunch he took a walk. He came to that place and he threw a pebble up in the window.

A woman opened the window. "Oh, run, young man, run," she said. "This place belongs to a giant. And if he sees you, he'll snuff you up like a grain of salt."

The young man didn't have a chance to get away because at that moment the earth began to tremble. The giant was on his way home. In a few strides he was there. So the woman reached down and picked him up, the little man, and she hid him under a washtub in the corner of the kitchen. He stayed there. The giant came in, of course, and he said [*in a deep gruff voice*], "Woman, I smell the blood of an Englishman."

[*In a high soft voice*] "Oh no, husband, you don't smell any blood. You've been hunting rabbits all morning, and that's the blood you smell." But he wasn't satisfied. He looked in the corners, under the beds, he looked in the closets, all over. But he couldn't find the little Ramiel. So finally his wife said, "My husband," she said, "raise your hand and swear that you won't touch a hair on his head. And if you swear that you won't, then I'll show you the nicest little thing that you ever saw."

So the giant raised his hand and he swore that he wouldn't touch a hair on his head. She went to the corner, lifted the washtub, and out came Ramiel. And Ramiel, that rascal, marched right up to the giant and he kicked him in the leg.

"Oho," the giant said, "you're brave! Why did you kick me?"

"Well," Ramiel said, "I am not afraid of you, Mr. Giant." The giant had promised. And of course Ramiel had heard all this bargaining between the wife and the giant. So he knew he was safe.

The giant couldn't hurt him. So he said, "We'll talk after supper."

So they had supper. It was a big meal the giant's wife had made. Oh, she had a huge platter of beef, another huge platter of pork, another one of turkey. And, of course, all the vegetables that went with it. And they did have a good, good meal.

So after supper, the giant said, "Well, young man, you're a pretty clever young man. I'd like to hire you to work for me."

"Well," the young man said, "I'm looking for work. I'd like to work for you, but it depends on the work you have for me to do."

"Well," the giant said, "there's a king that lives half a mile down the road. And that king has stolen money from everyone in the kingdom. Everyone. And," he said, "he rides past the forest across the road, past my place, and he has a huge chest on his buggy. It's two feet high, two feet wide, and it's four feet long. And that is full of the money that the king has stolen from the people in the

"What you have to do, Ramiel, is get that chest away from the king, and then everything will be even between us."

kingdom. What you have to do, Ramiel, is to get that chest away from the king, and then everything will be even between us."

"Well," Ramiel said, "that's quite an assignment, but I think I would like to work for you. I like to outsmart people anyway. But," he said, "it will take me awhile to think of a plan to get that money away from him."

The giant said, "Take all the time you need, but you do that someday."

So the boy in the meantime brought in the wood, he brought in water, he took care of old Topsy, the old horse in the stable, he took care of the one and only cow. And all the while, he was thinking of a plan. Finally, in the spring of the year, he thought of a plan. So at breakfast time he told the giant, "You know, I have thought of a plan, but I need twenty-five dollars to go to the village to get some things."

"Oh well," said the giant, "you don't spend your money foolishly. Here's fifty dollars. Spend it the way you like."

He had a string on each of the soldiers' arms so that, when he pulled the string from a hollow tree, the guns went up.

So the young man took the fifty dollars. He went to the village. And he bought many, many yards of red flannel. He bought a little jack-knife. And he bought needles and threads and whatever he needed for sewing. And he came back home again. He went out into the wood-shed and he whittled little soldiers, about fifty, seventy-five soldiers, with guns and all. And after they were all whittled out of the wood, he dressed them in red flannel uniforms. When they were all dressed up and had their guns in their hands, Ramiel took them across the road to the big forest there. And he stood those little fellows in the forest, all facing the road. He had a string on each of the soldiers' arms so that, when he pulled the string from a hollow tree, the guns went up.

So at ten o'clock in the morning the king came along. Clip-clop, clip-clop went the old horse. When he got near the tree, Ramiel called out, "HALT."

The man didn't pay any attention to that command. "Giddyup, giddyup."

"HALT!" came the voice again.

The king didn't pay attention again.

"HALT OR WE SHOOT!" he said. And at that moment, he pulled on all the strings. All the guns went up, aimed right at the king's head.

Then the king looked around. "Oh, don't shoot, don't shoot. What do you want?"

"Drop that money you have in your buggy, or we'll shoot." So he gave that box a kick and down it went onto the road. And he gave that horse a good slap with the reins, and away he went.

Now Ramiel had the gold in his possession. He went back to the giant's house to get a water pail, because he couldn't possibly carry that big chest of gold. So he went and got the water pail.

The giant said, "Well, I'll help you." And, of course, it was no task for the giant to lift that box. And they took it home. The giant said to Ramiel, "This gold doesn't belong to us. It didn't belong to the king either. It belongs to the good people of the kingdom. And tomorrow morning we'll get up early and we'll go to each house in the kingdom, and we'll return the money that belongs to those people."

Well that was fine. So the next morning they started out bright and early, and they went from house to house. But some of the people had died, some of the people who lost their wealth had died. And they couldn't return that money. Others had moved away. And they couldn't return that money either. So by the end of the day the chest was almost half full of gold. So the giant put the chest in the kitchen and left it there. They weren't going to spend it. It didn't belong to them.

Not long after that—in a story, time goes fast—it was time for the three young men to meet at the fork in the road. So one morning the young man told the giant, "I'm going home today. I promised my brothers that we'd meet at the fork in the road, and we'd go home to see our dear old mother."

The giant said, "Well good, you hitch up old Topsy in the barn," he said, "and you take the old buggy. It's a long walk to your home, so," he says, "you may as well ride. And you're welcome to come back here as long as you live. You can stay right here and work for me."

The young man was happy to hear that. He went out and hitched up Topsy. (The name Topsy you remember [*to her cousin, Gloria Wernecke, who is listening to the tale*] because her [*Gloria's*] grandfather had a horse by the name of Topsy. It was a red horse with a long mane and a long tail.) Well, when Topsy was hitched to the buggy and was ready to go, he shook hands with the wife, the giant's wife. But the giant said, "Just a minute, young man. You know that gold that you took from the king not long ago? Well, I have no use for it," he said, "and I understand that your mother needs money very badly. Why don't you take that money home to your mother?"

"Oh! Okay, that'll be fine."

So the giant went in, and he got the chest and put it on the back of the buggy. And the young man started out. He got to the fork in the road before his brothers got there. Poor old Topsy was old and she was tired from that long trip. So he drove her to the side of the road, behind the bushes. There was some nice clover there. She was eating clover there. Then Ramiel went back and sat on a stone near the road.

First thing you know, Pete came along. They shook hands and, well, "How was your year?"

"Oh," Pete said, "I didn't do so badly. I had a match factory and I did pretty well the first six months, but then the last six months I didn't do too well. But I do have a few dollars in my pocket."

Well, then the other one came along. It was the same thing again. "What did you do, how was your year?" And all that.

"Well, I did pretty well with my blacksmith shop. And I've got a few dollars in my pocket. How about you, Ramiel?"

"Well," he said, and he turned his pockets inside out. He said, "As you can see, I don't have any money in my pockets, but I'll show you what I do have." And he went behind the bushes and he got old Topsy and the buggy and came out on the road. And he said, "This is what I earned during my year away from home."

The boys didn't think much of old Topsy, because she was ready to fall over. She was so old and tired.

Pete emptied his pocket, put his money on the table. He had forty dollars.

But Ramiel said, "Now you boys go ahead and tell our mother that I'll be along. But you go ahead. Then she'll have time to fix a little lunch for us."

So they went ahead. And when they got home, of course, Pete emptied his pocket, put his money on the table. He had forty dollars. Then Bill put his money on the table. He had thirty-eight dollars. And, of course, they each had a change of clothes. They told their mother, "We didn't do too well during our year, but we've got a change of clothes, and we've got

And Ramiel said, "Put it in that corner." So they did.

a few dollars. But our brother, Ramiel, he didn't do too well at all. Poor man. You should see the old buggy he's got, and the old horse that's ready to fall over dead any minute."

"Oh well," she said, "you two were successful. But it's all right, I'll be glad to see him anyway."

So by the time Ramiel got home, the soup was ready to put on the table. They all had a good reunion, a good supper. But then after supper Ramiel told his brothers, "You know," he said, "I have something in the buggy that I'd like moved down in the basement, down in the cellar. I have to have help."

"Oh yes." They were big strong fellows. They'd be glad to help. So they went out and got the box, brought it down in the cellar.

And Ramiel said, "Put it in that corner." So they did. And then he opened up the lid and needed help to tip the thing over. And there all the money fell out in the corner.

Gold was all piled in the corner.

"Gold! Where did you get that gold?"

"Well," he said, "I earned it."

"But how could you earn that much gold in only one year?"

"Well, I did. And I earned the horse and the buggy too." He wouldn't tell them how he got that gold. But Ramiel told his mother, "I wonder how much gold we have. I would like to know." Now this was another kingdom that they lived in.

"But how could you earn that much gold in only one year?"

So he said, "You go to the king, half a mile down the road in the village, and ask for a bushel basket—some kind of a basket to measure the gold."

"Oh, but what'll I say? What'll I tell them?"

Of course, the real story was that he wanted to measure the cooties that he had gathered. [*Leary:* Like the lice from the lumber camps?] Yes. Oh, but she couldn't tell the king that!

So she went down the road, and she got to the king's castle and rapped on the door. The hired girl answered. She asked for a bushel basket. Well, the king didn't have a bushel basket, but he had a half bushel. "Would that work?"

"Oh yes, that'll be fine." So she took the basket home with her. And, of course, she had told the king that it was cooties. (That isn't in the book, though. [*Laughs.*]) So she went home. They measured and there were almost four bushels of gold coins that had been in that box.

So then she had to bring that basket back. And the hired girl told the king. She said, "The old lady is here. Where should she put that basket?"

"Oh," the king said, "tell her to drop it on the path there outside the house, because you're going to go out there and burn the garbage anyway. And you'll burn it too. We don't want that old basket."

"All right," she told the old lady, "you put that basket on the path and the king'll take care of it."

"It wasn't cooties that they measured after all," she said, "it's gold."

"It's gold. Look at this."

So the old lady went home. But she wasn't home very long when the hired girl went out and picked up that basket to put on the garbage pile to burn. But, as she picked up that basket, a piece of gold fell out. "Oh!" She picked up the gold and she ran inside and showed it to the king. "It wasn't cooties that they measured after all," she said, "it's gold. Look at this."

So the king went out, and he shook the basket. Sure enough, there were several more pieces of gold that fell out. "Aha." So then he said to the hired girl, "You go and get that old woman. I want to talk to her."

So the poor old lady had to come back to see the king. She cried all the way in her apron. They wore long dresses, of course, in those days—and a long apron. She cried all the way. She said, "Oh, don't punish my boy. I know you found out that he has gold, but he didn't steal it. I know he didn't steal it."

"Well," the king said, "if he didn't steal it, where did he get it?"

"We can't get him to talk. He won't tell us where he got it."

"Well," the king said, "your son is either a thief or he's mighty clever. I've got to find out which he is. I'll tell you, tonight all the women in the village will be baking bread at the village oven. And," he said, "his job is to steal the bread out of that oven while all the women of the kingdom are watching."

Oh, the poor old lady cried all the way home. She told her son what he had to do.

"Oh," he said, "don't worry, Ma. That's no big job." He spent the rest of the afternoon upstairs in the attic. And he looked at the rug that his grandmother had made him years ago, and he looked at every thing. Finally it was supper time. The old lady called him down for supper, but he didn't have time to come down. So she brought a plate up to him. And then she went down again and he stayed up there.

He took the spectacles and he put them at the end of his nose.

But by midnight he had found an old trunk, and in that trunk were his grandmother's clothes. A bonnet, a long black dress, a long apron, a shawl. And he put all that on. He dressed like a grandma. He put on her high shoes, button shoes these were. He was all dressed up. And he even found her spectacles. He took the spectacles and he put them at the end of his nose. And he took her cane. Then he walked downstairs, and he hobbled down the road all the way to the village oven. When he got to the village oven, he looked around with the spectacles at the end of his nose. [*In a high-pitched rasp*]

And he took her cane. Then he walked downstairs, and he hobbled down the road all the way to the village oven.

"Well, well my good ladies, what do you think you're doing here?"

"Well, haven't you heard, Grandma? Haven't you heard? There's a robber in town and he's supposed to come and steal the bread out of the village oven."

"Oh, my good ladies, how can he do that with all you nice ladies watching? He can never do that."

"Oh no. Why don't you join us, Grandma? Why don't you join us? Maybe your sharp old eyes will see him."

"Oh, I'd like to stay, but you know I have a bad habit. Every night at midnight I have to have a drink of peppermint, because that helps me sleep. So if all you nice ladies will have a drink of peppermint with me, I'll stay."

"Oh yes, yes." They'd be glad to. This wasn't a drink, this was a box of snuff. Would they all have a little bit of snuff? "Okay." They decided to have snuff with him.

"You and you and you and you." Everybody had a pinch of snuff. But that rascal had mixed the snuff with sleeping powder. So after they had had their snuff and they had sneezed a couple of times, they fell asleep.

So while they were asleep he took the bread out of the oven. He thought, "Well, there's too much bread for me to carry home." But the king had been to the village that day, and he had bought a brand new wheelbarrow. So he loaded the bread into the wheelbarrow, and he decided, "Now I'm ready to go home with the wheelbarrow."

But on his way, he passed the pump. And he decided, "Oh that old king, he deserves to have a trick played on him." So he mixed some mud [*laughs*]. And he filled the first three [*baking*] tins full of mud.

Early next morning the king got up, and he said, "Well, ladies, did you see the robber last night?"

"No, no robber came past this way all night."

"Oh good." So he opened the door of the village oven, and he reached in. "Mud!" [*Laughs*] "Oh!" And he reached in again. "Mud!" More mud. "Oh dear." Now he knew he had been tricked.

Is it all right if I said mud? [*Leary*: Sure.] I've said it all my life. [*More laughter.*]

So the young man went home with the wheelbarrow full of bread and gave the bread to his mother.

So then, of course, the king was pretty angry about this trick that had been played. So he told the hired girl, "You get that old woman to come here again."

So he opened the door of the village oven and he reached in. "Mud! Oh!" And he reached in again. "Mud!" More mud.

So the old lady came. Crying in her apron again. When she got there, the king told her, "I think your son is a real robber. Either that, or he's mighty clever. He played a dirty trick on me last night. And," he said, "tonight it won't be the women of the village that'll be watching, it'll be the men. Ramiel has to steal my riding horse out of the stable. And the men will be watching."

The old lady went home crying in her apron again and told her son what he had to do. "Oh, don't worry, Ma. Men are almost as easy to fool nowadays as women."

So again he went up in the attic and he stayed all afternoon. Then in the evening she brought him his plate of supper. He stayed up there until midnight. Finally he came down, dressed in a stovepipe hat, a swallowtail coat, with a white shirt with stiff collar, and he had found a beard up there. So he put a beard on his face. The old cane, of course, his grandfather's cane, and also his grandfather's spectacles. And at midnight he came down the stairs and hobbled up the road to the king's castle, to the royal stable.

So he put a beard on his face.

And when he got there, he looked around, and he said, [*in a low-pitched quaver*] "Well my goodness, my good men, what are you doing here?"

"Well, haven't you heard, Grandpa, haven't you heard? There's a robber in town."

"A robber! What's he doing in town?"

"Well, he's supposed to steal the king's nice riding horse out of the stable."

"Oh, how can he do that with all you nice men watching? He can't do that."

"Well, stay, Grandpa, stay. Maybe your sharp old eyes will spot the robber when he comes."

"Well, yes, I would stay, but I've got a bad habit." And this time it was the bottle of peppermint. Well, yes, they were happy to have a drink of peppermint. So each man had a drink. "You and you and you and you." But of course he had put some sleeping powder in the bottle, and they all fell asleep. One after another.

Even inside the stable. The door had been locked. And the doorman unlocked the door so [*the old man*] could go in and treat the fellows inside. And those fellows inside: one had a hold of the horse's tail, the other one had the head—holding the mane. And nobody was going to steal that horse. But of course they took a drink of that peppermint too. And first thing you know, they were all asleep.

Well, Ramiel found an old carpenter's horse. A wooden horse that carpenters and painters use. He took the horse out, hitched it to the buggy with the fringe on top, and let it stand there. Then he went back and put the wooden horse in place of the real horse and put a buffalo robe over it. So when the men woke up, they stood up. And one hung onto the tail end, the other one the mane. They didn't know the difference.

Well, early in the morning the king got up and he went out to the stable and asked if the men had seen the robber. "No, no robber came this way all night."

"Good," he said. So he went inside the stable, and he gave the horse a slap on the rump and said, "Get over, Prince." Of course the wooden horse fell. Now he was tricked again and he was quite angry. So he told the hired girl, "You tell the old lady I've got to see her again."

So the hired girl told the old lady. The old lady cried again. "Now," she asked, "what does he want this time?"

She went to see the king, and the king told her. "Tonight it will be not the ladies watching, not the men of the village, but it'll be me and my queen. We'll be watching. And his job is to steal the bottom sheet out of our bed while we're in it."

"Oh!" The old lady went home crying and told her son what he had to do.

"Oh, don't worry, Ma," he said. "Just think, I'll get that sheet. You've never had such nice satin sheets, and now you'll have a nice satin sheet to put in your bed." But in the afternoon, he thought, "Well, maybe I won't be able to pull this one off." So he told his mother, "You know," he said, "I've been home for a few days and I haven't seen any of my friends in town. So," he said, "I think I'll take a walk to the village and see my friends."

And while he was in the village he went to the butcher shops. He asked at all the butcher shops if they would please keep all the innards, all the intestines, the hearts, and everything from inside all the animals they butchered that day. And he said, "I'll pay you for them, and I'll pick them up tonight at six o'clock."

"Oh well, we throw those things away, we don't take pay for such things."

So at six o'clock he came, picked up all the innards, took that all home with him. He had tubs of them. And when he got home he spent his time whittling a man out of wood. A dummy. He made a dummy. And inside that dummy he put all those innards, blood and everything. And then he dressed him up. Put a nice little red cap on his head. And dressed him up in a suit. And carried him to the king's castle. And he knew where the king's bedroom was.

So he took the dummy, and he raised him up in the bedroom window so that the dummy's head and shoulders showed. The king had fallen asleep, but the queen hadn't. And when she saw that head and shoulders come up in the window, she nudged the king and said, "Oh, King, oh, King, the robber's at the window."

"Oh, oh. Where, where, where?" he asked.

"There."

And, of course, Ramiel had dropped the dummy. But up it came again. And the king was watching this time. He took his revolver from under his pillow, and he was waiting. When he saw the head come up: BANG, BANG went the revolver. Shot the poor man, the dummy. Blood flew all over. On the windowsill, on the dresser, on the floor, all over. And of course the dummy fell.

So after this was done, the king said to his wife, "You know, even though I'm the king, I can't shoot a man in cold blood. I'm not any better than anybody else.

So he took the dummy, and he raised him up in the bedroom window so that the dummy's head and shoulders showed.

When he saw the head come up: BANG, BANG went the revolver.

I'd better take that man and take him to the cemetery and bury him. I've got time. It's only two o'clock in the morning."

"Okay."

So he left.

And Ramiel waited until he saw the king pick up the dummy, pick up his shovel, and he carried the dummy—down the road he went to the cemetery. But after the king was gone, Ramiel went back to the house and he stood in the dining room outside the bedroom. He changed his voice so he sounded like the king. He said, "Oh, old woman," he said, "you know that man will be hard to carry. I'd better have a lunch before I leave. Get up and make me a lunch."

"Oh," she said, "well, you know where the blackberry jam is on the cupboard, you know where the bread is. Help yourself. I'm tired."

So he went out in the kitchen and he cut some bread and spread it with blackberry jam and had a good lunch. And when he was finished, he decided, well, he'd play a good trick on the king again. This time he went out and mixed some more mud. [*Laughs.*] Blackberries, you know, they work fast. [*Laughs.*] And he filled the jars with mud. Then before leaving, he filled the king's boots full of mud. The boots were sitting by the kitchen door. And the king's stovepipe hat was sitting on the chair by the kitchen door. So he filled the hat half full of mud, the boots were half full of mud, and the jars of jam on the table were full of mud. Then he went home.

But before he left, he went back to the dining room, and he told the queen, "You know that dead man is going to be hard to carry. Would you have an old quilt or something to wrap him in? It will be much easier to carry him."

"Oh yes," she said, "if he's dead he's not going to take the bottom sheet. You may as well take the sheet that he was supposed to steal." And so she took the sheet off the bed and she threw it out the bedroom door. He caught it and, of course, then he went on home.

Well it wasn't long after that when the old king came back home. Oh, he was hot and sweaty and tired. When he came in, he said, "Oh, I had an awful time. Old woman, get up and make me a lunch."

"What's the matter with you tonight?" she said. "Here you left to bury the man, but before you left you wanted to have a lunch and I told you to help yourself. Then before you left you came to the door and you wanted something, a blanket, to carry him in, and I gave you that sheet. And now here you're complaining that you're tired."

"Well," he said, "I went to the cemetery and I did bury him. And I'm still tired and I'm still hungry."

"Well," she said, "go in the kitchen and help yourself. You know where the bread is, you know where to find the jam."

So he went out in the kitchen and he cut some bread. And then he spread it with jam and took a bite. "Oogh! Mud! Awwk! This jam must be spoiled," he thought. So he went to the cupboard and got another jar of jam and spread another slice of bread. He tasted that and it was the same thing. Then he realized that he had been tricked once more.

So now he thought, "I'm going to go to that old woman's house and I'm going to talk to that young man." So he went to the corner of the kitchen, put on his boots. Splash!

And then he spread it with jam and took a bite. "Oogh! Mud! Awwk!"

They were full of mud. Then he put his stovepipe hat on. Mud! All over his face, his shoulders and all over. He couldn't go anyplace like that, so he called the old queen. "Old queen," he said, "come and clean me up. I'm full of mud."

So the old queen got up, and she cleaned him up. By the time he was all cleaned up he wasn't quite as mad as he had been before. So this time, instead of going to see Ramiel, he told the hired girl, "I've got to see that old woman again."

So the old lady came, crying in her apron as usual. And the king said, "Now your son is either very clever, or he is a real thief. But I have one more job for him."

"Oh," the old woman reminded him that he had promised that he'd only have three jobs.

Then he put his stovepipe hat on. Mud!

"But," the king said, "I have a brother who's a priest. And that priest, every time he hears of one of those tricks that your son has played on me, he's laughing—his mouth is open that wide laughing." He said, "I want that young man to play a trick on my brother, to shut him up."

"Oh." So the old woman went home crying again. And she told him, "You know, this is a man of the cloth that you have to play a trick on. And

Mud! All over his face, his shoulders, and all over.

you could be punished for that." She didn't believe in playing a trick on a priest.

(And of course, in the story, if you're Catholic you have to say priest. If you're not Catholic, you have to say minister. I wasn't sure about this story, the ending of it. And I wondered if I could put a merchant in place of a priest. But my kids said, "No, it wouldn't be the same." So then I went to Father Fox. Well, I happened to be in the hospital and Father Fox came there. He was new in the parish, so I said, "Oh Father, I'm so glad to see you. I have a problem."

(Poor Father closed the curtains around my bed, and he pulled up a chair. "Now what's your problem?" So then I told him about this story in the book. "Oh," he laughed. He thought it was all right to leave it the way it was.

(But then I wasn't satisfied. I went home from the hospital and I was still undecided about that story, the ending of it. So I called Father. I said, "You know, maybe you would like to read the story. Then you could give an honest opinion." So okay, he had time that afternoon. So I went over there with my story. And he read it. He'd laugh every once in awhile. "Where are you now, Father." And he'd tell me: "He's stealing the bread," or "He's doing this or that."

(Finally Father finished the story. And he said, "Oh, I wouldn't change a bit of that story." He said, "Those fellows, priests or ministers, they all deserve a good trick now and then. So you just leave it the way it is. But if you like," he said, "instead of priest or minister, you could put vicar or pastor." Well I figured fourth graders wouldn't know what a vicar was, so I put pastor in my story.)

So. He was supposed to play a trick on the priest. But he told his mother, "You go back to the king and you tell him I haven't had a wink of sleep for three nights, and I haven't slept in the daytime either. And," he said, "I'm tired and I'm going to need a little time to think of a plan."

So the old lady went back to the king and told him that her son needed a little time. He was tired. So the king said that he "can take all the time he needs, but he's got to be sure to play a trick on that brother of mine."

So, okay, three nights later the young man went to the village, and he went to the butcher shops again. And he asked for the feathers of all the fowl, all the chickens and the ducks and the geese that they killed that day. And he said, "I'll pick them up at six o'clock tonight and I'll pay you for them."

"Oh well, we don't need pay for that. We throw such things away."

So he went back to the butcher shops and gathered up all the feathers and went back home. He had a big black butchering kettle full of tar. There was a fire under it and the tar was warm. At midnight he took that tar and he rubbed himself all over with the tar. Then he rolled himself in the feathers. And then he rubbed some more tar on himself, all over, and rolled in the feathers again. Then he rubbed more tar under his arms until he looked like an angel.

Then at midnight that night he walked down the road, went to the church, went inside, rang the bell: DING DONG, DING DONG.

And the janitor heard the bells toll, so he ran to the church and he genuflected. He heard, up above [*in a pompous, ethereal quaver*], "I am the Angel Gabriel." DING DONG, DING DONG. "I have come to get your good pastor. He's done a lot of good on this earth and now it is time for him to go to heaven."

So the janitor bowed out of the church. He was glad the angel wasn't after him. And he went to the pastor's house and said, "Hurry up, hurry up, you have to get dressed. Angel Gabriel is at church waiting for you."

And all the while, the angel was ringing the bell. DING DONG.

So the priest finally got ready. And he stepped inside the church and genuflected and went up to the angel. And the angel had a big gunnysack. And he said, "You've been a good man my good pastor. You've done a lot of good on this earth. Now I will take you to heaven. Jump in this sack."

So the pastor jumped in the sack and Ramiel tied the mouth of the bag securely and he dragged him up the choir steps and rolled him down. Dragged him up the choir steps again, gave him a push, down he went. Bumpety, bumpety, bump, all the way down. Three times he did that.

So the pastor jumped in the sack and Ramiel tied the mouth of the bag securely.

Then he went up to the altar. There were only a couple of steps there. So he dragged the pastor up those steps, rolled him down again. Three times. Then he went outside. There were some more steps. Gave him a kick and down he went.

Then he took the bag by the mouth and he dragged it. Through thistles. Through rain puddles. And in those days priests and ministers, everybody, had chicken coops. So he dragged this sack to the chicken coop, over boards with nails.

He [*the pastor*] kept complaining. "Ouch, ouch."

And the angel reminded him, "It's a long rough road to heaven, my good man, be patient, be patient."

So finally the angel dropped him in the middle of the chicken coop floor. And, of course, the angel left. Well, the chickens get up early. Geese and ducks do too. As daylight came along the chickens gathered around that sack. They'd look first with one eye, then with another eye. They couldn't make out what was in that sack. The geese were curious. They had their long bills and they'd pinch at the sack with their beaks.

The fellow inside, the pastor, kept saying, "Go to the mouth of the bag, go to the mouth of the bag." But, of course, those birds didn't understand what he was saying. At seven o'clock the hired girl came to feed the chickens. She looked at that big sack in the middle of the room and she heard, "Go to the mouth of the sack."

So she went to the mouth of the sack and she undid it. And out came the priest or the minister and stood there. "Oh," he said, "isn't it beautiful in heaven!"

"In heaven?" said the hired girl, "what do you mean in heaven? Look around. You're in your own chicken coop."

So he looked around and, sure enough, he saw the geese and the chickens. Then he realized he had had a terrible trick played on him. So he told his brother about it.

And, of course, this is the end of the story.

They told me to come here and tell you all about it, because I was the hired girl.

Sherman 1993. ATU 402/328/1525A/1737. Told to James P. Leary by Betty Carriveau Sherman at the storyteller's home in Oconto Falls, Wisconsin, July 12, 1993. Leary transcribed the tape-recorded tale and also wrote the introduction to this chapter and the following notes.

Joe Carriveau's "Angel Gabriel," as rendered by his daughter, combines several distinct international tale types, as well as motifs and other plot fragments common to many tales. Elements of The Master Thief, ATU 1525A, form the tale's core: the theft of a horse, the manikin disguise, and the purloined sheet. Among the most commonly told international folktales,

The Master Thief is sometimes combined, as in the Carriveau version, with Type 1737, The Parson in the Sack to Heaven, involving a trickster in the guise of Angel Gabriel.

The opening episode—involving three poor brothers seeking their fortune, their separation when the road forks, and the acquisition of great wealth by the youngest—is typical of ATU 402, The Animal Bride. These elements, combined with reunion at the mother's home and the mother's borrowing of scales from the king, are likewise found in renderings of The Master Thief from the Franco-American tradition, as for example, "Fin Voleur" (Ancelet 1994: 51–59). Typically, however, the youngest brother acquires his wealth after an apprenticeship to thieves. The Carriveau version instead draws upon plot elements common to ATU Type 328, The Boy Steals the Giant's Treasure (popularly known as Jack and the Beanstalk), including assistance from the giant's wife, the giant's nose for blood, and robbery through the mock threat of an overwhelming army. (The last element is cited by Thompson in the 1961 edition, but not by Uther in the 2004 edition.) In this regard, the giant's sniffing of an Englishman's blood in an otherwise French story bespeaks some familiarity with printed versions of Jack and the Beanstalk. The Carriveau tale, however, transforms the giant from a miserly cannibal into a generous friend who co-conspires with Ramiel to dupe a king.

It is fairly easy to identify the broad tale types combined in this narrative. But because folklorists, collectors, and storytellers have often been squeamish about the public revelation of scatological oral traditions, we do not know much about the diffusion of *merde* motifs. In the *Analytical Survey of Anglo-American Traditional Erotica* (1973), however, Frank Hoffman offers motif X716. 2, Tricks involving excrement and defecation, and cites three instances from Alexander Afanasiev's *Russian Secret Tales* in which a low-status trickster shits in some better's hat (254).

A remarkable amalgam of international folktale elements, the Carriveau rendering of "Angel Gabriel" is likewise highly localized to late-nineteenth- and early-twentieth-century northeastern Wisconsin where small farms, lumber camps, sawmills, and horsepower prevailed. Ramiel and his brothers eat the era's typical fare, tote packsacks known in woods talk as "turkeys," and know all about the lice or "cooties" rife in squalid lumber camps. The attic inventory of disguises comes from Betty's own familiarity with family heirlooms. In fact she has occasionally dressed in clothing akin to Ramiel's grandmother garb when performing tales in public.

For this telling, however, she wore everyday clothes and sat at the dining-room table of her Oconto Falls apartment. She was being interviewed regarding the Carriveau taletelling tradition in connection with a survey of folk artists within Wisconsin's Ethnic Settlement Trail (See Teske 1994: especially p. 18). Although not planning to follow the interview with a performance, Betty was gracious enough not only to comply, but to allow photographs as she told the story. This artificial atmosphere was greatly improved by the presence of Betty's cousin, Gloria Wernecke, who had enjoyed the Carriveau legacy since hearing tales as a child from her uncles Joe and Theodore.

APPENDIX

Studying American Folktales

In this volume I have focused on the tales in their immediate ethnic and regional context. I have not duplicated scholarship, especially comparative scholarship, available elsewhere. This note is intended to guide the reader to other comparative scholarship.

Central to folktale scholarship is the concept of tale type. The basic guide to tale types is *The Types of International Folktales: A Classification and Bibliography* (2004) edited by Hans-Jörg Uther, revising earlier work by Antti Aarne and Stith Thompson, and referred to as ATU from the initials of these three scholars. Generally speaking, a tale type is a basic format for a tale, a format that is varied and developed differently by each storyteller, and yet remains recognizable, as versions of Cinderella (ATU 510), for instance, remain recognizable across time and space. Sometimes a tale type has subtypes that seem related and yet have a life of their own, such as the versions of ATU 510 that involve the heroine running away and hiding out in animal skins, working in the home of the hero, and healing him when he is sick. These subtypes are assigned a letter. So the version of Cinderella we are most familiar with, featuring the cruel stepsisters and the midnight slipper, is called ATU 510A, while the version with the heroine in animal skins is ATU 510B. Sometimes a tale type identifies tales that are almost certainly related. But sometimes a tale type is more general, and features certain themes that might occur in otherwise unrelated tales. For example, the many tales about a lost or animal husband under ATU 425 are probably not all related. Beauty and the Beast is not necessarily related to Cupid and Psyche, for example. Indeed, the subtypes of Cinderella may also be unrelated. Sometimes, too, a storyteller or storytelling tradition combines two or more types, as in a number of tales in this volume. This combined tale can also have a life of its own and persist across time and space, showing up in different countries and different decades or centuries.

People who study folktales are often concerned with identifying and commenting on the variation and distribution of tale types. So a reader can turn to the tale type index of a scholarly folktale collection to find what variant or variants of a particular tale are included and what the editor, in the notes, has to say about the variant or variants. To find out more broad information about the tale, however, the reader may need to go further. For American tales the following books are particularly helpful.

Ernest W. Baughman's *Type and Motif Index of the Folktales of England and North America* (1966) is forty years old, but it has not been supplanted. Although many more versions of the various tale types identified by Baughman have surfaced in the last forty years, very few new tale types have come to light in the American tradition. Baughman, then, provides a trustworthy guide to what tale types are likely to occur in American storytelling, and to older sources for versions of those tales.

Herbert Halpert and J. D. A. Widdowson, in *Folktales of Newfoundland* (1996), and Carl Lindahl, in *American Folktales from the Collections of the Library of Congress* (2004), provide versions of almost every tale type also represented in the present collection. Their works are especially helpful because of the excellent comparative notes these editors provide for the stories they include. The reader who wishes to know more about how widespread a tale type such as ATU 313 is in America, or how it varies from region to region, ethnic group to ethnic group, can turn to these two collections. The tale type index in each book will identify which tales in the book belong to the tale type in question and guide the reader to the notes, just as the tale type index in this volume can guide a reader to particular tales and their notes. Halpert and Widdowson include all of North and South America, and beyond, in their surveys, while Lindahl generally confines himself to the United States.

If the reader wishes more extensive guidance on a particular folktale as it appears anywhere in the world, the place to look is *The Types of International Folktales: A Classification and Bibliography* (ATU; see above). In this newest edition, ATU has become a succinct handbook on world folktale scholarship. At the end of the description of each tale, under the heading "Literature/

Variants," ATU lists first any important articles or monographs about the tale. Then, under the same heading, ATU indicates, country by country, collections that include variants of the tale in question. For those who read German there is also a wonderful folktale encyclopedia, *Enzyklopädie des Märchens* (1977–, still ongoing), with articles about many individual tales.

References

Aarne, Antti, and Stith Thompson. 1961. *The Types of the Folktale: A Classification and Bibliography.* Second Revision. FF Communications 184. Helsinki: Academia Scientiarum Fennica.

———. See Uther 2004.

Afanas'ev, Aleksandr. 1973. *Russian Fairy Tales.* Norbert Guterman, transl. Ed. 2. New York: Pantheon Books.

Aiken, Riley. 1954. In Boatright et al, eds. 1954, 24–39.

Alderson, William L. 1952. "Two Circular Formula Tales." *Western Folklore* 11:288.

Ancelet, Barry Jean. 1994. *Cajun and Creole Folktales: The French Oral Tradition of South Louisiana.* New York: Garland Publishing, Inc.

Anderson, Walter. 1923. *Kaiser und Abt: Die Geschichte eines Schwanks.* FF Communications 42. Helsinki: Academia Scientiarum Fennica.

Anonymous. 1925. "Folklore from St. Helena, South Carolina." *Journal of American Folklore* 38:217–38.

———. 1978. "'The Big Bimbo Dog' and Other Stories Told within My Family." Paper submitted to William E. Lightfoot for English 270, Ohio State University, Autumn Quarter. Author's name withheld by request. Folklore Archive, Ohio State University, Columbus.

Armistead, Samuel G. 1992. *The Spanish Tradition in Louisiana, I: Isleño Folkliterature.* Edited by Israel J. Katz. Newark, DE: Juan de la Cuesta.

Asbjørnsen, Peter Christen, and Jørgen Moe. See Dasent 1970.

Ashman, Charles Richard. 1982. "Folklore of Galliano." *Louisiana Folklore Miscellany* 5:48–55.

Backus, Emma M. 1900. "Folktales from Georgia." *Journal of American Folklore* 13:19–32.

Barbeau, C. Marius. 1915. "Wyandot Tales." *Journal of American Folklore* 28:83–95.

Barry, Phillips, ed. 1960. *Bulletin of The Folksong Society of the Northeast.* Publications of the American Folklore Society, Bibliographical and Special Series, vol. 11. Philadelphia: American Folklore Society.

Bascom, William. 1992. *African Folktales in the New World.* Bloomington: Indiana University Press.

Baughman, Ernest W. 1966. *Type and Motif Index of the Folktales of England and North America.* Indiana University Folklore Series, no. 20. The Hague: Mouton and Co.

Bausinger, Herman. *See Enzyklopädie des Märchens.* 1977–.

Benedict, Ruth. 1935. *Zuni Mythology.* 2 vols. Columbia University Contributions to Anthropology, vol. 21. New York: Columbia University Press.

Bergen, Fanny D. 1889. "English Folktales in America." *Journal of American Folklore* 2:60–63.

Boatright, Mody C., Wilson M. Hudson, and Allen Maxwell, eds. 1953. *Folk Travelers: Ballads, Tales, and Talk.* Publication of the Texas Folklore Society, no. 25. Dallas: Southern Methodist University Press.

———, eds. 1954. *Texas Folk and Folklore.* Publications of the Texas Folklore Society, no. 26. Dallas: Southern Methodist University Press.

Boggs, Ralph S. 1929. "Seven Folktales from Porto Rico." *Journal of American Folklore* 42:157–66.

———. 1934. "North Carolina White Folktales and Riddles." *Journal of American Folklore* 47:289–328.

Boudreaux, Dale J. *The Boudreaux and Thibodeaux Cajun Humor Page 2000.* Accessed September 11, 2000, at http://members.nbci.com/cajunguy/index.com.

Brassieur, C. Ray. 1999. "Thereby Hangs a Tale. An Old French Story Survives in Brittany and Missouri: An Unexpected Rendezvous." *Missouri Folklore Society Journal* 21:1–24.

Brendle, Rev. Thomas R., and William S. Troxell, eds. 1944. *Pennsylvania German Folk-Tales, Legends, Once-Upon-a-Time Stories, Maxims, and Sayings.* Pennsylvania German Society Proceedings and Addresses, vol. 50. Norristown, PA: Pennsylvania German Society.

Brewster, Mason J., ed. 1968. *American Negro Folklore.* Chicago: Quadrangle Books.

Brewster, Paul G. 1939. "Folk-Tales from Indiana and Missouri." *Folk-Lore* 50:294–310.

Briggs, Katharine M., ed. 1970. *A Dictionary of British Folk-Tales.* 4 vols. Bloomington: Indiana University Press.

Brunvand, Jan Harold. 1998. *The Study of American Folklore.* Ed. 4. New York: W. W. Norton and Company.

Burger, Erna. 1978. "The Two Dreams." Collected tales submitted to Linda Dégh for course, The European Folktale, University of California, Berkeley, and in her possession.

Burrison, John A., ed. 1991. *Storytellers: Folktales and Legends from the South.* Athens: University of Georgia Press.

Burton, Tom, and Ambrose Manning. Burton-Manning Collection. Johnson City: Archives of Appalachia, East Tennessee State University.

Bynum, Joyce. 1989. "Tales of Hodja Nasreddin—the Immortal Trickster." *ETC: A Review of General Semantics* 46 (4): 370–74.

Calvino, Italo. 1980. *Italian Folktales Selected and Retold by.* George Martin, transl. New York: Pantheon Books.

Campbell, Marie. 1958. *Tales from the Cloud Walking Country.* Bloomington: Indiana University Press.

Canadian Museum of Civilization Corp. 2006. "Civilization CA: Civilization Clicks: Marius Barbeau." Accessed June 3, 2006, at http://www.civilization.ca/tresors/barbeau/index_e.html.

Carawan, Guy, and Candie Carawan, eds. 1989. *Ain't You Got a Right to the Tree of Life?* Athens: University of Georgia Press.

Carrière, Joseph M. 1937. *Tales from the French Folk-Lore of Missouri.* Northwestern University Studies in the Humanities, no. 1. Evanston and Chicago: Northwestern University Press.

Carter, Isabel Gordon. 1925. "Mountain White Folk-Lore: Tales from the Southern Blue Ridge." *Journal of American Folklore* 38:340–74.

Chambers, Robert. 1870. *Popular Rhymes of Scotland.* New ed. London: W. and R. Chambers.

Chase, Richard. 1943. *The Jack Tales.* Boston: Houghton Mifflin.

———. 1948. *Grandfather Tales.* Boston: Houghton Mifflin.

Christiansen, Reidar Th., and Sean O'Sullivan. *See* Ó Súilleabháin, Seán and Reidar Th. Christiansen.

Claudel, Calvin. 1941. "Golden Hair." *Southern Folklore Quarterly* 5:257–63.

———. 1942. "Snow Bella: A Tale from the French Folklore of Louisiana." *Southern Folklore Quarterly* 6:154–62.

———. 1943. "Tales from San Diego." *California Folklore Quarterly* 2:113–20.

———. 1943–1944a. "A Study of Two French Tales from Louisiana." *Southern Folklore Quarterly* 7–8:223–31.

———. 1943–1944b. "Louisiana Tales of Jean Sot and Bouqui and Lapin." *Southern Folklore Quarterly* 7–8:287–99.

———. 1945. "Spanish Folktales from Delacroix, Louisiana." *Journal of American Folklore* 58:208–24.

Clemens, Samuel Langhorn. 1897. *How to Tell a Story: and Other Essays.* New York: Harper and Brothers.

Clouston, W. A. 1887. *Popular Tales and Fictions: Their Migrations and Transformations.* 2 vol. Edinburgh: William Blackwood and Sons.

Coffin, Tristram Potter, and Hennig Cohen. 1966. *Folklore in America: Tales, Songs, Superstitions, Proverbs, Riddles, Games, Folk Drama and Folk Festivals.* Garden City, NY: Doubleday.

Conant, L. 1895. "English Folk-Tales in America: The Three Brothers and the Hag." *Journal of American Folklore* 8:143–44.

Cook, Lovelace. 1972. "Carrie and Cora Lee: 'Talking That Talk.'" Paper submitted to Charles A. Perdue, University of Virginia. Kevin Barry Perdue Archive of Traditional Culture, University of Virginia, Charlottesville.

Cox, John Harrington. 1934. "Negro Tales from West Virginia." *Journal of American Folklore* 47:341–57.

Crowley, Daniel J. 1962. "Negro Folklore: An Africanist's View." *Texas Quarterly* 5:65–71.

———, ed. 1977. *African Folklore in the New World.* Austin: University of Texas Press.

Dasent, George Webbe. 1970. *East o' the Sun and West o' the Moon: Fifty-nine Norwegian Folk Tales from the Collection of Peter Christen Asbjørnsen and Jørgen Moe.* New York: Dover Publications, Inc.

Davis, Donald. 1992. *Jack Always Seeks His Fortune.* Little Rock, AR: August House.

———. 1996. "White Bear Whittington, or Three Drops of Blood." Audio recording made for and in possession of editor.

Dégh, Linda, ed. 1995. *Hungarian Folktales: The Art of Zsuzsanna Palkó.* World Folktale Library, vol. 2. Garland Reference Library of the Humanities, vol. 1736. New York: Garland Publishing, Inc.

Demitro, Steve. 1927. "Folk Tales Told by Steve Demitro." *The Survey* 59:19, 58–59.

Dobie, Bertha McKee. 1927. "Tales and Rhymes of a Texas Household." In *Texas and Southwestern Lore,* edited by J. F. Dobie. Publications of the Texas Folklore Society, no. 6. Austin: Texas Folk-Lore Society.

Dorrance, Ward Allison. 1935. *The Survival of French in the Old District of Sainte Genevieve.* The University of Missouri Studies 10, no. 2.

Dorson, Richard M. 1946. Herbert Welsh. La Anse. Sept. 5. Dorson Mss. box 55, folder 1, Notebook 41. Bloomington: Lilly Library, Indiana University.

————. 1947. Joe Woods. Dorson Mss box 55, folder 1, Notebooks 19–20. Bloomington: Lilly Library, Indiana University.

————. 1949. "Polish Wonder Tales of Joe Woods." *Western Folklore* 8:25–52.

————. 1952. *Bloodstoppers and Bearwalkers: Folk Traditions of the Upper Peninsula.* Cambridge: Harvard University Press.

————. 1964. *Buying the Wind: Regional Folklore in the United States.* Chicago: University of Chicago Press.

————. 1967. *American Negro Folktales.* Greenwich, CT: Fawcett Publications, Inc.

————. 1986. "Folktale Performance." *Handbook of American Folklore,* 287–300. Richard M. Dorson, ed. Midland Book Edition. Bloomington: Indiana University Press.

Duckworth, W. Donald. 1995. "Introduction." In Pukui and Green.

Dundas, Alan. 1977. "African and Afro-American Tales." In Crowley, ed., 35–53.

Dunne, John. *See* Smith, G. Hubert. 1939.

Enzyklopädie des Märchens: Handwörterbuch zur historischen und vergleichenden Erzählforschung. 1977–. Berlin: de Gruyter.

Erdoes, Richard. 1991. *Tales from the American Frontier.* New York: Pantheon Books.

Espinosa, Aurelio M. 1914. "New Mexican Spanish Folk-Lore." *Journal of American Folklore* 27:105–47.

————. 1930. "Notes on the Origin and History of the Tar-Baby Story." *Journal of American Folklore* 43:129–209.

————. 1943. "A New Classification of the Fundamental Elements of the Tar-Baby Story on the Basis of Two Hundred and Sixty-seven Versions." *Journal of American Folklore* 56:31–37.

————, and Mason, J. Alden. *See* Mason, J. Alden, and Aurelio Espinosa, ed. 1922–1929.

————, and José Manuel Espinosa. 1985. *The Folklore of Spain in the American South-West: Traditional Spanish Folk Literature in Northern New Mexico and Southern Colorado.* Norman: University of Oklahoma Press.

Espinosa, José Manuel, ed. 1937. *Spanish Folk-Tales from New Mexico.* Memoirs of the American Folklore Society XXX. New York: American Folklore Society.

————, and Aurelio M. Espinosa. *See* Espinosa, Aurelio M., and José Manuel Espinosa.

Evans, Charles. 1941–1959. *American bibliography: a chronological dictionary of all books, pamphlets, and periodical publications printed in the United States of America from the genesis of printing in 1639 down to and including the year 1820.* 14 vols. Worcester: American Antiquarian Society.

Fauset, A. H. 1927. "Negro Folk Tales from the South." *Journal of American Folklore* 40:213–303.

Fortier, Alcée. 1888. "Louisiana Nursery-Tales." *Journal of American Folklore* 1:140–45.

————. 1906. "Four Louisiana Folk-Tales." *Journal of American Folklore* 11:123–26.

Galland, Antoine. 1704–1717. *Mille et une nuits.* Paris. (*Contes des Mille et une Nuits.* Antoine Galland, transl. Paris: Hachette, 1986.)

Garcia, Nasario. 1992. *Abuelitos: Stories of the Río Puerco Valley.* Albuquerque: University of New Mexico Press, in cooperation with the Historical Society of New Mexico.

————. 1997. *Commadres: Hispanic Women of the Río Puerco Valley.* Albuquerque: University of New Mexico Press.

Gardner, Emelyn Elizabeth. 1914. "Folk-Lore from Schoharie County, New York." *Journal of American Folklore* 27:304–25.

————. 1937. *Folklore from the Schoharie Hills, New York.* Ann Arbor: University of Michigan Press.

Glassie, Henry. 1964. "Three Southern Mountain Jack Tales." *Tennessee Folklore Society Bulletin* 30:88–102.

Goldberg, Christine. 1993. *Turandot's Sisters: A Study of the Folktale AT 851.* Garland Folklore Library, vol. 7. Garland Reference Library of the Humanities, vol. 1697. New York: Garland Publishing, Inc.

———. 1998. "'Dogs Rescue Master from Tree Refuge,' an African Folktale with World-wide Analogs." *Western Folklore* 57: 41–61.

Goldstein, Kenneth S., and Dan Ben-Amos, eds. 1970. *Thrice Told Tales.* Lock Haven, PA: Hammermill Paper Company.

Green, Laura S., coll. and transl. 1926. *Folk-Tales from Hawaii.* Second Series. Edited by E. M. W. Beckwith. Vassar College Field-Work in Folk-Lore. Publications of the Folk-Lore Foundation, no. 7. Poughkeepsie, New York: Vassar College.

Grimm, Jacob, and Wilhelm Grimm. 1812, 1815. *Die Kinder- und Hausmärchen.* 2 vol.

———. 1987. *The Complete Fairy Tales of the Brothers Grimm.* Jack Zipes, transl. New York: Bantam Books.

Halpert, Herbert. 1942. "Big John and Little John." *Hoosier Folklore Bulletin* 1:88.

———. 1947. "Singing Game Variants of 'The Sleeping Beauty.'" *Journal of American Folklore* 60:121–23.

———, and J. D. A. Widdowson. 1996. *Folktales of Newfoundland: The Resilience of the Oral Tradition.* World Folktale Library, vol. 3. Garland Reference Library of the Humanities, vol. 1856. Publications of the American Folklore Society, New Series. New York: Garland Publishing, Inc.

Hamilton, Virginia. 1985. *The People Could Fly: American Black Folktales.* New York: Alfred A. Knopf.

Hansen, Terrence Leslie. 1957. *The Types of the Folktale in Cuba, Puerto Rico, the Dominican Republic, and Spanish America.* Folklore Studies 8. Berkeley: University of California Press.

Harris, Joel Chandler. 1880. *Uncle Remus, His Songs and His Sayings.* New York: D. Appleton and Co.

Harvey, Emily N. 1919. "A Br'er Rabbit Story." *Journal of American Folklore* 32:443 44.

Henry, Mellinger Edward. 1938. *Folk-songs from the Southern Highlands.* New York: J. J. Augustin.

Herskovits, Melville J. 1958. *The Myth of the Negro Past.* Rev. ed. Boston: Beacon Press.

Hickey, James F. 2002. "Twas a Dark and Stormy Night." Collected by editor and in his possession.

Hicks, Orville. 1990. *Carryin' On: Jack Tales for Children.* Whitesburg, KY: June Appal Recordings. Cassette recording.

Hicks, Ray C. 1985. *Ray Hicks Performing Old Fire Dragonman.* Tape 314. Thomas G. Burton Collection. Johnson City: Archives of Appalachia, East Tennessee State University.

Hiester, Miriam W. 1961. "Tales of the Paisanos." In *Singers and Storytellers,* edited by M. C. Boatright, W. M. Hudson, and A. Maxwell, eds. Publications of the Texas Folklore Society, no. 30. Dallas: Southern Methodist University Press, 226–43.

Hoffman, Frank. 1973. *Analytical Survey of Anglo-American Traditional Erotica.* Bowling Green, Ohio: Bowling Green University Popular Press.

Hoogasian-Villa, Susie, ed. 1966. *100 Armenian Tales and Their Folkloristic Relevance.* Detroit: Wayne State University Press.

Hurston, Zora Neale. 1935. *Mules and Men.* Philadelphia: J. B. Lippincott Company.

Hymes, Dell. 2003. *Now I Know Only So Far: Essays in Ethnopoetics.* Lincoln: University of Nebraska Press.

Imgalrea, Tom, Leo Moses, and Anthony C. Woodbury. 1984. *Cevármiut Qanemciit Qulirait-llu: Eskimo Narratives and Tales from Chevak, Alaska.* Fairbanks: Alaska Native Language Center, University of Alaska.

Jacobs, Joseph. 1894. *More English Fairy Tales.* London: David Nutt.

———— 1898. *English Fairy Tales.* Ed. 3. London: David Nutt.

Jarreau, Lafayette. *See* Claudel 1943–1944a, 1943–1944b.

Johnson, Guy Benton. 1930. *Folk Culture on St. Helena Island, South Carolina.* University of North Carolina Social Study Series. Chapel Hill: University of North Carolina Press.

Jones, Charles C. 1888. *Negro Myths from the Georgia Coast: Told in the Vernacular.* Boston: Houghton, Mifflin and Company.

Kittredge, George Lyman, and Hayward Silvanus. 1890. "English Folk-Tales in America." *Journal of American Folklore* 3:291–95.

Lindahl, Carl, ed. 2001. *Perspectives on the Jack Tales and Other North American Märchen.* Special Publications of the Folklore Institute, No. 6. Bloomington: Folklore Institute, Indiana University.

————, ed. 2004. *American Folktales from the Collections of the Library of Congress.* Armonk, NY: M. E. Sharpe, in association with the Library of Congress, Washington, D.C.

————, Maida Owens, and C. Renée Harvison, eds. 1997. *Swapping Stories: Folktales from Louisiana.* Jackson: University Press of Mississippi, in association with Louisiana Division of the Arts, Baton Rouge.

Lüthi, Max. 1970. *Once Upon a Time: On the Nature of Fairy Tales.* New York: F. Ungar Publishing Company.

MacCurdy, Raymond R., Jr. 1950. *The Spanish Dialect of St. Bernard Parish, Louisiana.* Albuquerque: University of New Mexico Press.

————. 1952. "Spanish Folklore from St. Bernard Parish, Louisiana: Part III, Folktales." *Southern Folklore Quarterly* 16:227–50.

MacDonald, Margaret Read. 1999. *Traditional Storytelling Today: An International Sourcebook.* Chicago: Fitzroy Dearborn Publishers.

Mason, J. Alden, and Aurelio Espinosa, ed. 1922–1929. "Porto-Rican Folk-lore: Folk-tales." *Journal of American Folklore* 35:1–61; 38:507–618; 40:313–414; 42:85–156.

Mathias, Elizabeth. 1985. *Italian Folktales in America: The Verbal Art of an Immigrant Woman.* Detroit: Wayne State University Press.

McCarthy, William Bernard. 1993. "Sexual Symbol and Innuendo in 'The Rabbit Herd' (AT 570)." *Southern Folklore Quarterly* 50:143–54.

————. 2006. "Knives and Forks." Ms. in editor's possession.

————, Cheryl Oxford, and Joseph Daniel Sobol, eds. 1994. *Jack in Two Worlds: Contemporary North American Tales and Their Tellers.* Publications of the American Folklore Society, New Series. Chapel Hill: University of North Carolina Press.

McDermott, Louisa. 1901. "Folk-Lore of the Flathead Indians of Idaho." *Journal of American Folklore* 14:240–51.

Miner, Horace Mitchell. 1939. *St. Denis, a French-Canadian Parish.* Chicago: University of Chicago Press.

Minton, John, and David Evans. 2001. *"The Coon in the Box": A Global Folktale in African-American Context.* FF Communications 277. Helsinki: Academia Scientiarum Fennica.

Mouton, Mona Mel, and Ethelyn Orso. 1971. "Jean L'Ours: An Acadian Folktale." *Louisiana Folklore Miscellany* 3:21–26.

Muncy, Jane. 1949. Tales collected by Leonard Roberts. Audio Tape 060-054-F. Bloomington: Indiana University Archives of Traditional Music.

Neely, Charles. 1938. *Tales and Songs of Southern Illinois*. Menasha, WI: George Banta Publishing Company.

Neuland, Emma. 1994. "The Miller's Daughter." Tale told to William McCarthy, 1994, at Lucinda, Pennsylvania, in editor's possession.

Newell, William Wells. 1883. *Games and Songs of American Children*. New York: Harper and Brothers, Publishers.

———. 1888. "Old English Folk-Tales in America." *Journal of American Folklore* 1:227–34.

———. 1893. "Lady Featherflight." *Journal of American Folklore* 6:54–62.

. 1900. "An Old English Nursery Tale." *Journal of American Folklore* 13:228–29.

Nicolaisen, W. F. H. 1994. "The Teller and the Tale: Storytelling on Beech Mountain." In McCarthy et al., 123–49.

Ó Súilleabháin, Seán (O'Sullivan, Sean). 1966. *Folktales of Ireland*. Folktales of the World. Chicago: University of Chicago Press.

———, and Reidar Th. Christiansen. 1963. *The Types of the Irish Folktale*. FF Communications 188. Helsinki: Academia Scientiarum Fennica.

Owen, Mary A. 1902. "Coyote and Little Pig." *Journal of American Folklore* 15:63–65.

Parler, Mary Celestia. 1951. "Forty-Mile Jumper." *Journal of American Folklore* 64:422–23.

Parsons, Elsie Clews. 1921. "Folklore from Aiken, South Carolina." *Journal of American Folklore* 34:1–39.

———. 1923a. *Folk-Lore of the Cape Verde Islands*. 2 vols. Memoirs of the American Folk-lore Society XV. Cambridge and New York: American Folklore Society.

———. 1923b. *Folk-Lore of the Sea Islands, South Carolina*. Memoirs of the American Folk-lore Society XVI. Cambridge and New York: American Folklore Society.

Perdue, Charles L. 1987. *Outwitting the Devil: Jack Tales from Wise County, Virginia*. Santa Fe: Ancient City Press.

Pukui, Mary Kawena, with Laura C. S. Green. 1995. *Folktales of Hawai'i: He Mau Ka'ao Hawai'i*. Bishop Museum Special Publication 87. Honolulu: Bishop Museum Press, 1995.

Raél, Juan Bautista. [1957]. *Cuentos españoles de Colorado y Nuevo Méjico: Spanish tales from Colorado and New Mexico*. 2 vols. Stanford, CA: Stanford University Press.

Ramírez de Arellano, Rafael. 1926. *Folklore portorriqueño: cuentos y adivinanzas recogidos de la tradición oral*. Archivo de tradiciones populares, vol. 2. Junta para ampliación de estudios e investigaciones científicas. Madrid: Centro de Estudios Históricos.

Randolph, Vance. 1950. "Tales from South Missouri." *Southern Folklore Quarterly* 16:79–86.

———. 1952a. "Ozark Mountain Tales." *Southern Folklore Quarterly* 16:165–76.

———. 1952b. *Who Blowed up the Church House? and Other Ozark Folk Tales*. New York: Columbia University Press.

Ranke, Kurt. See *Enzyklopädie des Märchens*. 1977–.

Ray, Willis. 1999. Vent de Laitue: BLAGUES-L: Archives: 1999: Cajun Jokes. Accessed November 13, 2006, at http://www.ventdelaitue.org/blagues-l/archives/1999/Cajun-jokes.html.

Reaver, J. Russell. 1988. *Florida Folktales*. Gainesville: University Presses of Florida.

Roberts, Leonard W. 1955. *South from Hell-fer-Sartin: Kentucky Mountain Folk Tales*. Lexington: University of Kentucky Press.

————. 1974. *Sang Branch Settlers: Folksongs and Tales of a Kentucky Mountain Family.* Publications of the American Folklore Society, Memoir Series 61. Austin: University of Texas Press for the American Folklore Society.

Roberts, Warren Everett. 1944. *The Tale of the Kind and the Unkind Girls: AA-Th 480 and Related Tales.* Detroit: Wayne State University Press.

Robinson, Mairi, ed.-in-chief. 1987. *The Concise Scots Dictionary.* Aberdeen: Aberdeen University Press.

Sandburg, Carl. 1922. *Rootabaga Stories.* New York: Harcourt, Brace and Company.

San Souci, Robert D., and Jerry Pinkney. 1989. *The Talking Eggs: A Folktale from the American South.* New York: E. P. Dutton.

Sherman, Betty Carriveau. 1981. *Stories Papa Told.* New York: Vantage Press.

————. 1993. "Angel Gabriel." Tale collected by James P. Leary, in editor's possession.

Sherman, Josepha, and Jacqueline Chwast. 1992. *A Sampler of Jewish-American Folklore.* American Folklore Series. Little Rock, AR: August House.

Smart, Yvonne. 1996. Interview by William B. McCarthy, at Providence, Rhode Island, in possession of the editor.

Smith, E. W. 2003. Vent de Laitue: BLAGUES-L: Archives: 2003: Old men in good shape. Accessed on November 13, 2006, at http://www.ventdelaitue.org/blagues-l/archives/2003/Old-men-in-good-shape.html.

Smith, G. Hubert. 1939. "Three Miami Tales." *Journal of American Folklore* 52:194–208.

Smith, Jimmy Neil. 1988. *Homespun: Tales from America's Favorite Storytellers.* New York: Crown.

Smith, Richard. 1953. "Mr. Rabbit in Partners." In Boatright et al.

Sobol, Joseph Daniel. 1999. *The Storytellers' Journey: An American Revival.* Urbana: University of Illinois Press.

Soileau, Jeanne Pitre. 1973. "Jean Sot in St. Martinville." *Louisiana Folklore Miscellany* 3:43–47.

Speck, F. G., and L. B. Carr. 1947. "Catawba Folk Tales from Chief Sam Blue." *Journal of American Folklore* 60:79–84.

Stitt, J. Michael, and Robert K. Dodge. 1991. *A Tale Type and Motif Index of Early U.S. Almanacs.* New York: Greenwood Press.

Stroup, Thomas B. 1937. "Two Folk Tales from South Central Georgia." *Southern Folklore Quarterly* 2:207–12.

Suggs, James Douglas. c. 1952. "The Devil's Daughter." Collected by Richard M. Dorson. Audio Tape 060-030b-F. Bloomington: Indiana University Archives of Traditional Music.

Tedlock, Dennis. 1983. *The Spoken Word and the Work of Interpretation.* Philadelphia: University of Pennsylvania Press.

Teske, Robert T. 1994. *Passed to the Present: Folk Arts along Wisconsin's Ethnic Settlement Trail.* Cederburg, WI: Cederburg Cultural Center.

Thomas, Rosemary Hyde. 1981. *It is Good to Tell You: French Folktales from Missouri.* Columbia: University of Missouri Press.

Thompson, Stith. 1946. *The Folktale.* New York: Holt, Rinehart and Winston.

————. 1955–1958. *Motif-index of Folk-literature: A Classification of Narrative Elements in Folktales, Ballads, Myths, Fables, Mediaeval Romances, Exempla, Fabliaux, Jest-books, and Local Legends.* Rev. and enl. ed. 6 vols. Bloomington: Indiana University Press.

————, and Aarne. *See* Aarne and Thompson 1961.

————, Aarne and Uther. *See* Uther 2004.

Tong, Diane. 1989. *Gypsy Folktales.* San Diego: Harcourt Brace Jovanovich.

Torrence, Jackie. 1998. *Jackie Tales.* New York: Avon Books.

Travis, James. 1941. "Three Irish Folk Tales." *Journal of American Folklore* 54:199–203.

Uther, Hans-Jörg. 2004. *The Types of International Folktales: A Classification and Bibliography Based on the System of Antti Aarne and Stith Thompson*. 3 vol. FF Communications 284–86. Helsinki: Academia Scientiarum Fennica.

Utley, Francis Lee. 1974. "The Migration of Folktales: Four Channels to the Americas." *Current Anthropology* 15:5–27.

Vanover, Johnny. 1980. "A Major Collection." Annotated collection for folklore class taught by editor at Pikeville College, Pikeville, Kentucky, for Morehead State University; in possession of editor.

Ward, Marshall. c. 1970a. Recording BM 59. See Burton and Manning.

———. c. 1970b. Recording BM 65. See Burton and Manning.

Webb, Mary. 1797–1799. Papers. Durham: Rare Book, Manuscript, and Special Collections Library, Duke University.

Weigle, Marta. 1980. "Guadalupe Baca de Gallegos' 'Los Tres Preciosidas (The Three Treasures)': Notes on the Tale, Its Narrator and Collector." *New Mexico Folklore Record* 15:31–35.

———, and Peter White. 1988. *The Lore of New Mexico*. Publications of the American Folklore Society, New Series. Albuquerque: University of New Mexico Press.

Wesselski, Albert. 1911. *Der Hodscha Nasreddin: Türkische, arabische, berberische, maltesische, sizilianische, kalabrische, kroatische, serbische und griechische Märlein und Schwänke*. 2 vol. Weimar.

Whitney, Annie Weston, and Caroline Canfield Bullock. 1925. *Folk-lore from Maryland*. Memoirs of the American Folklore Society XVIII. New York: American Folk-Lore Society, G. E. Stechert and Co., Agents.

Wood, Ray. 1949. "Peter Simon Suckegg." *Journal of American Folklore* 62:428–29.

"Wyandot." 1910–1911. *Encyclopaedia Britannica*. Ed. 11.

Yoffie, Leah Rachel Clara. 1947. "Three Generations of Children's Singing Games." *Journal of American Folklore* 60:1–51.

Zipes, Jack. 1994. *Fairy Tale as Myth / Myth as Fairy Tale*. Lexington: University Press of Kentucky.

———. See Grimm 1987.

LIST OF CREDITS

"Catskins" from "The Catskins Garland" in a commonplace book found in the Mary Webb Papers, 1797–1799, courtesy of Rare Book, Manuscript, and Special Collections Library, Duke University. Reprinted by permission.

"Juan Bobo and the Riddling Princess" from "Juan Bobo and the Riddling Princess: A Puerto Rican Folktale" by William Bernard McCarthy. *Marvels and Tales: Journal of Fairy-Tale Studies* 19:2. Copyright © 2005. Reprinted by permission of William Bernard McCarthy.

"Sister Fox and Brother Coyote" from "A Pack Load of Mexican Tales" by Riley Aiken in *Texas Folk and Folklore,* Mody C. Boatright, Wilson M. Hudson, and Allen Maxwell, eds. Publications of the Texas Folklore Society, no. 26. Dallas: Southern Methodist University Press, 1954. 30–36. Reprinted by permission of Texas Folklore Society.

"Las Bodas de La Tia Cucaracha" from "Tales of the Paisanos" by Miriam W. Hiester in *Singers and Storytellers*, M. C. Boatright, W. M. Hudson, and A. Maxwell, eds. Publications of the Texas Folklore Society, no. 30. Dallas: Southern Methodist University Press, 1961. 233–35. Reprinted by permission of Texas Folklore Society.

"La Llorona, the Wailing Mother" from "Tales from San Diego" by Calvin Claudel. 1943. *California Folklore Quarterly* 2:113–20. Reprinted by permission of Western States Folklore Society.

"Two Tales of Quevedo" from *The Spanish Tradition in Louisiana I: Isleño Folkliterature* by Samuel G. Armistead. 1992.Reprinted by permission of Thomas Lathrop for Juan de la Cuesta.

"Jean L'Ours" from "Jean L'Ours: An Acadian Folktale" by Mona Mel Mouton and Ethelyn Orso. 1971. *Louisiana Folklore Miscellany* 3:21–26. By permission of *Louisiana Folklore Miscellany*.

"The Three Oranges" from "Folklore of Galliano" by Charles Richard Ashman. 1982. *Louisiana Folklore Miscellany* 5:48–55. Reprinted by permission of *Louisiana Folklore Miscellany*.

"Genevieve" from *Cajun and Creole Folktales: The French Oral Tradition of South Louisiana* by Barry Jean Ancelet. 1994. Reprinted by permission of University Press of Mississippi.

"Two Tales of Jean Sot" from "Jean Sot in St. Martinville" by Jeanne Pitre Soileau. 1973. *Louisiana Folklore Miscellany* 3:43–47. Reprinted by permission of *Louisiana Folklore Miscellany*.

"Boudreaux and Thibodeaux, Tale A: Boudreaux and Thibodaux Go Fishing" from Vent de Laitue: BLAGUES-L: Archives: 1999: Cajun Jokes. Courtesy of Jocelyn "Vent de Laitue" Gagnon.

"Boudreaux and Thibodeaux": Tales B-F from *The Boudreaux and Thibodeaux Cajun Humor Page* 2000. Courtesy of Dale J. Boudreaux.

"John the Bear" and "Prince Green Serpent and La Valeur." Reprinted from *It's Good to Tell You: French Folktales from Missouri* by Rosemary Hyde Thomas, by permission of the University of Missouri Press. Copyright © 1981.

"Francois Seeks His Fortune, or the Three Gold Pieces" from "Thereby Hangs a Tale. An Old French Story Survives in Brittany and Missouri: An Unexpected Rendezvous" by C. Ray Brassieur. 1999. *Missouri Folklore Society Journal* 21. Reprinted by permission of C. Ray Brassieur.

"Katie and Johnnie" from *Florida Folktales* by Russell J. Reaver. 1988. Reprinted by permission of the University Press of Florida.

"The Silver Toe" from "Tales and Rhymes of a Texas Household" by Bertha McKee Dobie in *Texas and Southwestern Lore*, J. F. Dobie, ed. Publications of the Texas Folklore Society, no. 6. Austin: Texas Folk-Lore Society, 1927. 41–42. Reprinted by permission of Texas Folklore Society.

"Peazy and Beanzy" from *Florida Folktales* by Russell J. Reaver. 1988. Reprinted by permission of the University Press of Florida.

"Mr. Rabbit in Partners" from "Richard's Tales" by Richard Smith in *Folk Travelers: Ballads, Tales, and Talk*, Mody C. Boatright, Wilson M. Hudson, and Allen Maxwell, eds. Publications of the Texas Folklore Society, no. 25. Dallas: Southern Methodist University Press, 1953. 220–24. Reprinted by permission of Texas Folklore Society.

"The Devil's Daughter," courtesy the Archives of Traditional Music, Indiana University, Bloomington, Indiana, and of Gloria (Mrs. Richard M.) Dorson.

"Beg Billy and the Bull" from "Carrie and Cora Lee: Talking that Talk" by Lovelace Cook, Paper 1972-1, Kevin Barry Perdue Archive of Traditional Culture, 303 Brooks Hall, University of Virginia, Charlottesville, Virginia 22903. Reprinted by permission.

"Barney McCabe," as collected from Mrs. Jamie Hunter in *Ain't You Got a Right to the Tree of Life?*, Guy and Candie Carawan, eds. 1989. Athens: The University of Georgia Press. Reprinted by permission of Guy and Candie Carawan.

"Rawhead and Bloodybones," courtesy the Archives of Traditional Music, Indiana University, Bloomington, Indiana, and of Edith R. (Mrs. Leonard W.) Roberts.

"Little Horny and Big Horny," courtesy the Burton-Manning Collection, Archives of Appalachia, East Tennessee State University.

"Polly, Nancy, and Muncimeg" from *Sang Branch Settlers: Folksongs and Tales of a Kentucky Mountain Family* by Leonard W. Roberts. 1974. Publications of the American Folklore Society, Memoir Series 61. Austin: The University of Texas Press for the American Folklore Society. 228–32. Reprinted by permission of the American Folklore Society (www.afsnet.org).

"The Old Man and the Witch" from "The Big Bimbo Dog and Other Stories Told within My Family." 1978. Courtesy of the Center for Folklore Studies Archives at the Ohio State University.

"Mr. Fox" from *South from Hell-fer-Sartin: Kentucky Mountain Folk Tales* by Leonard W. Roberts. 1955. Courtesy of Edith R. (Mrs. Leonard W.) Roberts.

"Sop Doll" and "Three Little Pigs," courtesy the Burton-Manning Collection, Archives of Appalachia, East Tennessee State University.

"Jack and the Old Fire Dragon," courtesy the Thomas G. Burton Collection, Archives of Appalachia, East Tennessee State University.

"Fill, Bowl, Fill," transcribed from the June Appal Recording: Orville Hicks, *Carryin' On* (JA0062). 1990. June Appal is a part of Appalshop Inc., Whitesburg, KY 41858. Reprinted by permission of Appalshop Inc. and of Orville Hicks.

"The Enchanted Sisters," "The Three Brothers," "The Best of Three," "Stone Soup," "Eileschpijjel," and "Counting Noses" from *Pennsylvania German Folk Tales, Legends, Once-Upon-a-Time Stories, Maxims, and Sayings*, Thomas R. Brendle and William S. Troxell, eds. The Pennsylvania German Society Proceedings and Addresses, vol. 50. 1944. Reprinted by permission of the Pennsylvania German Society.

"Little Red Nightcap" from *Thrice Told Tales: Folktales from Three Continents*, Kenneth S. Goldstein and Dan Ben-Amos, eds. 1970. Hammermill Paper Company. Courtesy International Paper Company.

"The Black Kitty" and "The Bewitched Princess" from "Polish Wonder Tales of Joe Woods" by Richard M. Dorson. 1949. *Western Folklore* 8:25–52. Reprinted by permission of the Western States Folklore Society.

"The Powder Snake" from "Tales from San Diego" by Calvin Claudel. 1943. *California Folklore Quarterly* 2:113–20. Reprinted by permission of the Western States Folklore Society.

"The Amazing Old Men" from Vent de Laitue: BLAGUES-L: Archives: 2003: Old men in good shape. Courtesy of Jocelyn "Vent de Laitue" Gagnon.

"The Clever Daughter" from *A Sampler of Jewish-American Folklore* by Josepha Sherman and Jacqueline Chwast. Copyright © 1992. By permission of Marian Reiner on behalf of August House, Inc.

"Hodja Nasreddin" from "Tales of Hodja Nasreddin—The Immortal Trickster" by Joyce Bynum in *ETC: A Review of General Semantics* 46. 1989. Reprinted by permission of the Institute of General Semantics, publishers of *ETC: A Review of General Semantics*, Fort Worth, Texas.

"The Toad Prince" from the Richard M. Dorson Papers, courtesy of the Lilly Library, Indiana University, Bloomington, Indiana, and of Gloria (Mrs. Richard M.) Dorson.

"The Muskrat Husband" from *Cevármiut Qanemciit Qulirait-llu: Eskimo Narratives and Tales from Chevak, Alaska* by Tom Imgalrea, Leo Moses, and Anthony C. Woodbury. 1984. Courtesy of Alaska Native Language Center.

Tale Type Index

Nearly all of these tales correspond to tale types identified in *The Types of the International Folktale* (ATU: see Appendix). Three tales, entered in appropriate order, correspond to tale types from the Hansen or Baughman indexes (see References). These indexes have been created to supplement the ATU index with respect to Hispanic and English-language tales, respectively, and add some tale types that seem to be confined to the tradition in question. Numbers refer to tale in this volume, not page.

MOTIF INDEX

Identifying all the motifs in a collection of tales is an endless endeavor. Some traditional tales, however, are built around a single motif, and may not have a separate tale type number (e.g., J1552.1.1, The ass is not at home, tale 112F in this volume). Some tales, too, may not correspond to a clear tale type number but are congeries of traditional elements (e.g., tale 23 in this volume). And some tales, especially composite tales, may correspond, by and large, to a clear tale type or tale types, but still include as significant structural element a motif not usually associated with the tale type(s) in question (e.g. tale 90 in this volume, which corresponds to tale type ATU 552, but resolves via the non-standard motif D791.4, Disenchantment by finding key to enchanted castle). These are the sorts of motifs here indexed. When one of these motifs also figures in a story of which it is a regular part (e.g. B651), that reference is not included in this index. Numbers refer to tales, not pages.

Motif vol.		*Tale in this vol.*
B360	Animals grateful for rescue from peril of death	121
B524.1.2	Dog breaks bands and kills master's attacker (cf. G275.2)	61, 71, 72, 79
B651	Marriage to beast in human form	121
C36	Tabu: offending animal husband	121
C211.1	Tabu: eating in fairyland	98
D117(127)	Transformation: man to rodent (man to sea animal)	121
D315(327)	Transformation: rodent to person (sea animal to person)	121
D702.1.1	Cat's paw cut off: woman's hand missing	86
D791.4	Disenchantment by finding key to enchanted castle	90

Index of Collectors

Includes names of professors to whom particular collections were submitted. Number refers to tale number, not page.

Index of Storytellers

Includes source of particular stories, when named. Name also listed under collector when the story is self-collected. Numbers refer to story, not page.